I0831566

REINA DEL CÁRTEL

COMPLETE SERIES
OMNIBUS

INTERNATIONAL BESTSELLING AUTHOR

SANTANA KNOX

COVER: TRC designs by Cat

AUTHOR NOTE & SERIES CONTENT

This is a Why-Choose Dark Romance trilogy. Due to the nature of this book, the story will progressively become darker and more violent. Please be advised, you are reading the product of my unhinged mind, this is not a safe space.

I feel I must also advise, this book was the first written creation from my brain. It was a product of purging my own immigration trauma as well as processing the feelings of *never belonging* that come with being "from neither here nor there." It is important that you, the reader understand that our heroine's insecurities are not something that every immigrant or person of Latin American identity feel or experience.

These are *my* wounds that I bare to you.

Contents to consider: (Spoilers possible)

Human trafficking, arson, immigration, drive-by shooting, branding, dubious consent, claustrophobic situations, suicidal ideology, non-consensual drug use, overdose, use of Narcan, mentions of rape, violence, torture, breath play, misogyny, gun play, knife play, explicit language, dubious consent, racism, sexual assault to the FMC (not done by the love interests), torture, mutilation, decapitation, teeth removal, burning, cutting, guns, reckless behavior, child abuse rape/incest (not happening to any main characters)

Gun play, knife play, impact play, erotic asphyxiation & more...

To the immigrant children:
home is a place inside you.

To the women with teeth:
Bite hard.

PROLOGUE

CELIA FLORES - 8 YEARS OLD

It's all gone.

I watch a woman who looks to be nearly my mother's age walking through the family villa as it burns to the ground, her long, raven hair somehow unscorched by the blistering flames as she steps out into the courtyard, not fazed by the surrounding destruction.

"Wake up, Celia!" My mother hissed out through the smoke.

I was in the middle of a dream.

The kind I could never remember after waking, but would still waste the day chasing the feeling. By morning, the plot would be just a distant memory, but I'll miss it regardless. I could beg my mind to bring it back again, but once consciousness hits it's never the same, it'll become so far out of reach that I won't even recall its purpose anymore and once a dream is lost, it's gone forever.

Only the promise of another sleep could reunite us.

The heat of the fire urged me to wake, but the smoke invaded my lungs, promising to lull me back to unconsciousness while the blaze of the flames engulfed my second-story bedroom.

All four walls were surrendering to the embers dancing up them.

"I don't know what to do, Rafa! Cézar! Help me!" My mother's frantic panic was a lead pipe, beating me awake.

With an urgent breath, I choked on the heady smoke that devoured the room. Reaching in the bed next to me, I padded around for my little sister, Carolina, but felt nothing.

"Cézar and I will hold them while we jump, the floor will give out any second now." My father reassured her.

I felt the bed shift under me and suddenly I was being rolled into the blankets.

"Papá! Please, I can't breathe!" I shouted under the layers of fabric.

Carolina's screaming was sharp, piercing through the blankets when suddenly, the mattress below me was gone and all I could feel was the air being pulled from my insides when my body hit the ground. The impact is hard, my lungs falter for one, two, three too many seconds.

Was I outside?

I tried to roll but I was tangled and wrapped in this ball of cushioning that I couldn't force myself out of. Everything was caving in, and I couldn't breathe. The stale smoke and the darkness of the makeshift cocoon were setting my heart off a million miles an hour, "I CAN'T BREATHE!" I screamed again.

Carolina's cry was a comforting sound, she was close, I could hear her. She couldn't have been far from me, she was only six. She was too little to understand what was happening.

I didn't understand what was happening.

"Breathe deep, mija." My papá's voice reached me, the pressure of his hands gripping the blankets surrounding me.

I labor through a long, painful wheeze, my lungs burning as oxygen and stale smoke push their way out of me in a stuttered exhale. The sob pours out of me with no control.

"What is happening, Papá?"

"We must leave México, right now. Our family is in grave danger."

The sound of Carolina's cries would ring louder every hour and soften again as she ran out of strength to weep. I wanted to cry too, but every time the tears pooled in my eyes, I would clench my fists and turn the sadness into anger like my father taught me.

Most eight-year-olds had the luxury of crying, but I was the daughter of the leader of the Cártel. Heiress to the most dangerous criminal enterprise in México. My papá reminded me daily that everything I did, or said was a display of how much power our family held. He said that they wanted to see me crumble and break simply because I was born a woman.

I couldn't cry.

No, I squeezed my fists until my nails dug into my hands.

It was all gone.

We traveled for hours, mostly in silence. Every minute was a rushed blur of madness as we did our best to make it to the border. Cézar's snoring helped me fall asleep after our third or fourth stop for gas. I didn't wake up again until I saw the flashlights of patrol officers at our window.

Cézar wasn't *really* my brother, but he'd been around for as long as all my other memories. He was ten years older but never once acted like his age made him too cool to be around me. His dark hair was kept short, and his copper skin had the same warmth as mine.

If you saw us side by side, you'd probably think we were actually siblings.

"My children are asleep. Please turn that off," My mother spoke to an officer outside of the car.

"We need to make sure they match the photos on the passports," I heard another voice on the other side of her window.

"What time is it?" Carolina asked, her head on my lap taking most of the backseat.

"Still bedtime, go back to sleep," my mother reassured her with a hush.

"Here, is ten thousand enough? It's all the cash we have," my father threw the wad from the glovebox at the cop standing at his window.

"Not bad, but I thought this was the Cártel we were helping? I thought you had fatter wallets than this?" Another man's voice rang out from the darkness.

"Maybe we should turn you back around so we can collect a bigger fee," the woman spoke again.

Cézar struggled to feign asleep, a low growl sounding from deep within his chest in response to the obvious threat.

"Please, we have nothing left. We can pay you more once we are through," My father said to them, in a reasoning tone.

"That's what they all say. Lucky for you I'm feeling generous. I'll let your family through for a discount *if* your pretty wife here does a little favor for me, you know?"

There had not been many times in my life I'd seen my father lose his cool. He was calm, collected, and calculating. That was how he bested his enemy. It was the quality I most admired and hoped to inherit when I got older. The closest I had ever seen him lose his composure was when my Uncle Ignacio's son called me a whore in the middle of a Cártel business dinner.

The dinner itself was a significant event, the remaining three heads of the organization and their families were invited to dine and drink at our home. My father displayed his power, his strength, and everyone could let their guards down to drink without the fear of a knife in their back or poison in their pies. Meals were sacred to our family, it was practically neutral ground.

I had barely caught the insult before I heard the knife swish by from across the table when suddenly blood was pouring out of my cousin Carlito's mouth. Cézar's laugh was that of a maniac when he pulled the blade from his cheek, the blood pouring down my primo's newly deformed face.

My uncle's bitterness was so tangible you could taste it around the room.

That day my father told Carlito he was now as ugly on the outside as he was on the inside. In front of everyone, Papá reminded him and my uncle that they would never hold a position of power in this family and would be lucky to get grunt work once I was seated as queen of the command.

"Look, friend, my wife here is not for sale. However, I can promise you that whether or not my family makes it across this border, will be what dictates how *you* get home tonight. You see, my men are not confined to the walls you and your little government set. They are waiting for me in Ocean Valley, so you can imagine that if I don't make it there in time...Well, they will be waiting for you, in your homes. Mija, what was that address again?" My father said calmly gesturing to me in the backseat.

"1355 Rainwater Court, Chula Vista, California," the words came out of my mouth on autopilot from the hundreds of times we rehearsed this in the car on our way here and I hoped to God that it was the correct one.

"Yes, 1355 Rainwater, they'll be waiting with guns, knives, and bags to put you and your little parts in. Those bags will then be delivered to your mother's house—what was that other address?"

"229 West Main Street, Duncanville, Pennsylvania," I recited the next address from the back of my mind the way we practiced.

The man's eyes widened, quickly turning his flashlight away from my window. I could feel the pride beaming from my papá and a quick check at the half-smile on his face in the rearview mirror let me know I did well.

"Keep the money. Please sir, go on," the man nervously mumbled as he placed the wad of cash back into the car as he signaled Rafael Flores, the king of the Cártel, to move through the gate.

"Now, America," my mother exhaled.

I wasn't sure if it was relief or dread that coated her tongue.

It wasn't anything new to me. We came up here a few times a year for either my papá's work or for holidays to see my mamá's sister, Tía Larissa. But this wasn't a visit, and there was nothing to celebrate. Our whole world just turned upside down, and aside from the blanket I was still half cocooned in, there was nothing I carried with me to remember my home, my country and the remnants of my life.

We spent the next few hours on the road until we finally made it to the outskirts of Ocean Valley. Your typical coastal city, but positioned perfectly so that it extended into the outskirts of a deep forest as well. My aunt Larissa waited outside her large home in her fancy gated community as we turned onto her street. She had the same big smile on her face that she wore every time we drove in, but it didn't reach her eyes this time. She opened my mother's door, quickly pulling her sister in for an embrace, the world dissolving around them as they cried together.

My aunt reprimanded my mother in quiet whispers through their grief, "Yo Sabía!" and words of "This is why Diego is gone," but my mother shushed her sister, both eyes darting to the boy next to me.

Her eyes searched for Cézar who stared in the opposite direction out the window with nothing but apathy. She opened Carolina's door next, but my sister was fast asleep.

"I've got her," My father tried to intervene, but my tía slapped his hand away, rejecting his offer.

"Nonsense Rafael, you've been driving for nearly a day. I'd be surprised if your legs even work anymore. Go rest, tomorrow we focus, and we begin to look for your brother and gut him like the pig he is."

My father eyes softened, "Thank you, Larissa, I don't know who I can count on anymore, I'm glad we can still count on you."

"Tsk, it's *your* family burning houses down, not mine. You'd do well to remember that. I told my sister not to fall in love with a snake, but she couldn't tell a dog from a cantil and now *your* cártel is at my door anyway *just* like I warned her would happen. I love my family Rafa, but there aren't many of us left, so that unfortunately means you too, now come inside." She kissed my father's cheek and tapped his chest with her palm.

Before she could get to Carolina, Cézar had already hoisted my sister into his arms and shuffled his way into my aunt's home, carrying her as if she weighed nothing.

I stepped into the large, two-story stucco, European-style house and marveled at the golden chandelier with thousands of shards of crystals hanging from it. I inhaled the overwhelming scent of cleaner, it was fresh enough I would have bet that she had one of her cleaners come out here hours before our arrival.

My aunt had money, a lot of it, apparently whoever my grandfather was on my mother's side left both of them a lot of money. Money, she never needed because my father had plenty of it to boot.

My mother never really talked about her inheritance because it meant talking about her father, and we didn't do much of that either. All I knew about Jamila Gomes' side of the family was that she lost her older brother, Diego, when I was just a baby.

Soon after, my abuelo died too, leaving her and my tía with the remainder of his fortune. I never met my grandfather on my dad's side either. It was rare for any man to rise to power while his predecessors still had a beating heart.

Being without grandparents was just a side effect of growing up in this kind of life.

"Look how big you are Celia! Come here!" My aunt sang from the balcony.

I walked up to her, trailing my hands on the gold of the staircase railing as my feet tapped loudly on the pristine white marble floor. Tía Larissa was a tall woman, taller than my mother - which likely meant she was taller than I'd ever grow up to be. She had short black hair in the style of a bob that went down to her chin and her forehead was a little too shiny, but she was always smiling, and I was thankful for that today.

"Larissa, are you sure this is okay?" My mother asked as she came out of Carolina's new room, turning the light off behind her.

Her long black hair was fashioned into a braid behind her back, and her coal-black eyes matched mine.

No, mine were somehow darker.

They were my father's eyes.

"Jamila, my sister, this house belongs to the both of us, we've all been through enough now. There are four of you and one of me. The guest house is plenty! Make yourselves at home please. My chef Luís will have breakfast ready in the main dining room by eight-thirty," she turned to look at me before she continued, "If your sister is still asleep, I'll have them put some away for her so that she can eat when she wakes up. Let me know when you are ready to go shopping, you'll be starting school this week and you'll need more clothes than what you've been wearing in the car all day."

"Tía Larissa?" it was a question, but I didn't know what I was asking, I couldn't help but wonder why she was being so good to us.

I mean, I knew she was family, but family was what got us here in the first place.

Family couldn't be trusted right now.

I clutched the blanket in my hand and felt the roughness where the fabric had gotten charred before I was thrown through the second-story window.

"This is what family is *really* for, mija, I know it feels a little confusing right now. I promise you this, you have people that will *always* go to war for you," Tía Larissa said, almost reading my mind as she knelt down to my level and placed a kiss on my head.

For a brief moment the crushing weight of everything lifted from my tiny shoulders as we walked down a busy mall street to shop for new clothes. I thought about school the next day and what it would feel like to start all over. I thought about my English getting better and learning to live like an American kid, like in the movies.

It was small things to cling to as the realization set in that I deviated from the path that had been set out for me since the moment I was born.

We spent hours trying on outfit after outfit, and my mamá gushed every single time Caro came out of the dressing room. It was always followed by my tía swiping her card effortlessly without looking twice at the cost. My mamá looked happier around her sister, as if the pain of what we'd been through was already a distant memory to her. I knew she had been missing her a lot, she talked about it daily, ever since she left México for California.

I understood the bond they had because it was the same for me and Caro. Unlike my mamá and her sister though, Carolina and I had never been apart. Even in our large villa in Guadalajara, we had our own separate bedrooms, but often chose to sleep together. Caro was scared of the dark, and I... was scared of being alone.

There was a comfort to being close in vast spaces, and we learned early on to rely on each other. Where most little girls had a stuffed toy or a doll, they kept with them at all times; I had Carolina, the best little sister in the entire world.

When morning came, the doorbell rang, and excitement rushed through me as I made my way down the large spiral double staircase to head to school. I opened the door to find a short, pale woman with blonde hair and a blonde boy about a head taller than me standing there.

"Cecilia?" The woman asked.

"Um, yes?" I answered with uncertainty as I recognized the new name I was told to go by.

"I am Nina, your aunt's driver. I'll be taking you and your sister to school from now on."

I turned back to my mamá, "I thought Cézar would be taking me?"

"He'll be returning to work with your papá in México tomorrow," she stated vaguely, as to avoid explaining *what type of work* in front of strangers.

"Oh," I mumbled in disappointment, something like anger nipping away at my heels from the thought of being left behind.

"This is my son Ronan, he'll be riding with you to school, I hope that's okay," she chirped almost like she could sense my sadness and was trying to make up for it.

"Hi," the boy waved awkwardly.

He was tall and definitely a couple of years older. His hair was a sandy blonde that fell over his eyes, the forrest green peeking out through wavy strands.

My heart fluttered, pumping a few beats faster than needed.

1

CECILIA

15 YEARS OLD

Ronan traced his fingers down my ribcage, turning the motion upward when I failed to respond to his question. Resting his hand just below my breast, he thumbed the scar on my rib, a flash of heat and an old memory burning at the flesh. I pulled my tank top back down to cover the rest of me, clearing my throat to distract him..

"Stop! That tickles," I pushed his hands away playfully.

He raised a single eyebrow, caging me in on the floor with his arms on either side of my head."Well then, answer my question. Are you finally gonna tell your old man we're more than just friends?"

I tisk, turning my cheek to the side. "You know, traditionally the guy usually does the talking to the fathers in relationships."

"Traditionally, most girlfriends' fathers are around to talk to, and their brothers won't kick my ass. Your dad is like a ghost, man, and your brother? He comes around like once a year and just stares at me while he stabs at his fingernails with his knives."

I laughed, "Just say you're scared, then."

"Why deny it? They scare the shit out of me. But asking a man for permission when he's not even around to stop me from doing it anyway?" He shook his head, "Maybe I'd rather ask for forgiveness instead. At the end of the day his place at the dinner table is still empty." He ran his hands through his hair, unsure if he'd crossed that line yet.

He knew he was teetering it. That boundary I'd drawn between us, where normally I would withdraw at the first mention of my father, our history, or his career. I didn't blame him, in almost eight years of being around me he had never seen Rafael Flores.

Ever since my tío Ignacio burned our family villa to try to steal the cártel from under his nose, he'd been extra cautious. Papá bounced all over México to evade his brother and his men. Moving constantly was the only way to evade assassination attempts and keep my tío from compromising any cártel jobs.

Sometimes he would stay in Guadalajara, for months at a time, and when he would come home for a few days, we all would shut ourselves in from the outside world for protection.

That's why we ended up staying with my tía Larissa permanently. My mamá refused to live alone and my papá was so shattered from the hurt his brother caused us that he couldn't take this one request away from her.

Family was everything.

And I... loved Ronan. There was absolutely no doubt about that. We'd grown up together, from awkward kids fumbling through a friendship that grew into much more as we began to get older. My tía and my mamá always encouraged it because they saw how carefree and *normal* being around Ronan kept me.

I'm sure they figured we would break up as life would naturally drive us apart so there was no concern for them to interject. But puppy love and years of friendship soon became the foundation to a feeling of security I hadn't felt for as long as I could remember, if ever at all.

I now dreaded how fast the future could come knocking at my door, and steal it all away from me.

The thing about being the daughter of one of the most powerful men in the world is that if you didn't already know that about me, then you'd likely only find out when you were taking your last breaths. This secret I held all to myself; I couldn't tell the most important person in my life. It gnawed and gnashed at me from the inside out.

It would be our end someday.

Ronan didn't know that I spent all of my days outside of school or being with him learning about the family business and preparing to take over my papá's place. He didn't know that my weekend trips once a month to go shopping in Tijuana were actually spent sitting at my papá's side being mentored or in a dungeon learning lessons.

"Maybe he *isn't* real," I teased, kissing him softly.

He pressed his lips back into me, forcing mine to part as he pried his tongue into my mouth.

Ronan groaned in frustration, pressing his bulge against me. "You drive me crazy. You're gonna be the death of me," he put his forehead to mine.

My smile faded, "Don't say that," I shook my head. "Look, my papá will be back tonight for a few days, I'll talk to him about having dinner where he can get to know you as my...boyfriend?" The last bit came out as more of a high-pitched squeak as I questioned a word that had never came out of my mouth before this very moment.

The strangeness of it all surfaced and suddenly I was lightheaded and anxious and full of butterflies at the idea of being rejected by him.

We were best friends, two neighbor kids who had been each other's everything from the moment we first met. It didn't feel strange when playing together started to become romantic, or shoulder punches were followed by tender kisses. Even Carolina knew from a single look when it was time to evacuate the room and leave us alone.

We just made sense, from the very beginning.

"Yeah, I'm your boyfriend Cecilia Gomes. I'm your...all of it. Your first date, your first-hand holding, your first kiss, your first, *first*," he whispered, forcing my cheeks to flush with heat.

"You say that like I wasn't yours either, payaso, now let me go pretend like I am the innocent little flower my papá knows me to be, okay?" I waited with raised eyebrows but Ronan lifted me off the ground to kiss me instead.

"Alright, *little flower*, text me a time?"

I nod, "Wear something nice," I tug at his pants pocket, "Not jeans."

"You know I'm not trying to fuck your father, right? Just you." He gives me that devilish smirk that makes my insides feel like hot molten goo before he licks his lips to clarify, "Again."

I shove at his shoulder, "My papá is always in a suit. He says men who want to be respected, dress like it." I explained with a shrug.

He pulled me in again for one final kiss, his words low and hushed in my ear before he lets me go. "I'll wear whatever you want, be whoever you want. Just tell me when and where."

I fought the squeal from manifesting, turning on my heels and sprinting out of his house as fast as possible.

Ronan's mother, Nina, lived only four houses down from my tía, where we had made our permanent home. By the time I got home, my papá was there along with the extra security car and his armed men. I shouted a greeting up to Cézar, who looked down at me from the second floor balcony, resting his elbows on the railing. He was my papá's Sergeant in arms now, an achievement at just the age of twenty five. His hair was kept shaved so that all you could see was the shadow of growth around his head and face. Tattoos crawled up his neck and peaked through the fine suit he wore. A crooked smile curved perfectly onto his face, the glimmer of diamonds on his teeth easily spotted from a distance.

It didn't bother me that he was often mistaken for my papá's protegé, because in the end, the throne wasn't meant for him. And the thing about Cézar, was he valued loyalty above all. Which is why my papá trusted him to seat me in his place and to carry out my orders when he was gone.

"Are you getting shorter, princesita?" He asked teasingly.

I sent him a middle finger in response, the roar of laughter obnoxious as it fell from his mouth.

"Is that Celia?" I heard my papá calling from the billiard room, which he frequently used as his office on the few occasions he brought work home.

I ran into the room and didn't bother looking around before jumping into my papá's arms for a hug. I didn't care that these men could see me as weak for hugging my papá, if they questioned my integrity once I was old enough to take control, I would fire or kill them for it as I was taught.

He accepted my embrace and picked me up like when I was still a little girl, "How have you been mija?" he asked with a tenderness reserved only for me.

"Fifteen, filled with angst and hormones. Now fill me in on what actually matters, please," I said with a pleading tone.

His smile was prideful, but only lasted as long as his silence. "Ignacio burned down two of our warehouses in Tijuana. Over two hundred and fifty million in product," he pulled out photos of the warehouses, completely charred, nothing but frames left of the structures.

"How many died?" I asked.

My papá frowned at my show of concern to our soldiers and their families. "I've already made it right mija, don't worry yourself over that," his lips pressed into a flat line which let me know I disappointed him.

I quickly tried to move past my mistake, hoping I'd be able to bounce back from it, "What else?"

"The good news is he was sloppy, probably sent Carlito to do his dirty work, you know that pendejo is good for nothing. They left plenty of traces, I think we should be able to find them in the next couple of weeks," he told me with a glimmer of hope breaking through his hard exterior.

"I can almost smell him mija, he is so close. He will burn twice as hard for what he put us through," a fearsome glint twinkled in his eye that was all rage and revenge. It *almost* made me forget that this was his brother.

I couldn't put myself in his shoes because I could never imagine feeling this way about Carolina.

Power changes everyone, he enforced into my brain.

"Ronan wants to have dinner with you tonight, Papá, with all of us."

"Who?" He asked as if he had never heard the name in his life, a dismissal that was obviously some way to feel superior to a teenage boy.

I rolled my eyes, "Ay Papá! You know the names of every useless pendejo whose hand you shake, but you pretend you can't remember his name when he's been around for almost half my life now! Be kind please, this is important to him," I slapped his shoulder.

"Important just to him?"

I knew exactly what he was asking. With a heavy sigh, I gave him the response he expected. "I know where my duty lies, Papá, and I will never forget it."

"You must never! The cártel will always want to undermine you because you are a woman. You cannot rise into power with a man at your side because the man is all they will see. You will be judged for his weaknesses as if they were your own, they will look past your legacy. I did not spend your whole life preparing you for this to let some *man* dictate how you are received. Especially some gringo. When the time comes, marriage will find you when the alliance is right mija, and this will open many more doors for us all."

Hope died in my heart right then, "I know Papá, you tell me this often, I understand."

"Good," he cupped my cheek in his hand and kissed the top of my head. "Then I will eat with the boy who has stolen you from me," he winked at me before breaking away with a laugh.

I spent the rest of the day anxiously waiting for dinner time and pestering my tía in the kitchen after she refused my mamá's proposal that we let one of her chefs cook this.

My tía thought dinners like this were too important to be left to the help and that we needed a meal we could taste the love from. I honestly wasn't sure how that would work since I had never seen either one of those two in the kitchen before in the entire time I had been living here, but I wasn't going to deny her an opportunity to do something that she considered to be a gesture of kindness.

"How old are you Ronan?" My papá asked without lifting his eyes from his plate, as if the food in front of him was far more important than this conversation could ever be.

"I just turned seventeen, sir." A fire in his eyes as he lifted his chin up bravely.

"Almost a man then. So, you will be a senior next year, yes? Hopefully moving on to a good school after that. What are your interests?" My papá interrogated him, finally shifting his eyes toward his prey.

"I'll be trying to stay as close to home as possible so I can stay near Cecilia, she is really my only interest, so maybe if I get lucky, UCLA will take me. I don't know what I plan on doing there yet though." He scratched the back of his head nervously and looked down at his plate, then back at me for comfort.

I squeezed his free hand from my place next to him and smiled at him to assure him that he was doing okay.

My papá lifted his eyebrow, my gut churning at the reaction and my grip on Ronan's hand loosening. The correct answer was the one that got him as far away from me as possible, by his own choice.

Papá sucked some imaginary food from his teeth and said in his thick accent, "I will entertain this little romance the two of you have fostered, for now. But there will be a time when my daughter will break your heart because duty binds her to do so. You will not cry, you will not pout, you will not moan. You will not come groveling at this door, you will simply accept this like a man and move on. Do you understand me?"

No sounds of silverware clinking could be heard anymore. My tía and mamá went silent, making eyes at each other from across the table. Ronan's eyes burned through me, my heart physically breaking at that very moment, though I couldn't meet his gaze for reassurance if my life depended on it.

His voice was quiet. "Sir, why?"

"Simply because you are not good enough for my daughter. No single man on this earth ever will be. More importantly though, because she has shoes to fill, and her destiny unlike yours is already mapped out ahead of her. I would not make plans for the future if I was you, son. I would do what is best for you, and only you so that when the time comes you can move on with your life instead of hopelessly questioning why this happened or why no one ever warned you. You are being warned *now*. You are not destined for my daughter. But I will allow you to keep company with her until the time comes where she is needed where she belongs, in México." He dropped his napkin on the plate.

All four women at the table stood as he rose from his chair taking their places seated once again after he cleared from the room.

"Well, that could have been much worse, if you ask me." Tía Larissa nervously chirped, and my mamá clicked her tongue to signal my tía in one of their psychic communication moments.

They both got up together and walked toward the pool house.

"Let's go," Mamá called back when she noticed Caro still seated across from me.

She looked between us with so many questions in her eyes that I couldn't begin to answer. I knew she was hurting for Ronan. He'd been like a big brother to her and the idea that we wouldn't be together wasn't something she probably had ever fathomed. Still, she stood and followed mamá out the door, and it was only when the click of it shutting signaled their exit that Ronan spoke again.

"Are you gonna look at me?" Ronan's voice was already a deep bravado, though I swore it was only a summer or two ago that I teased him for how it cracked.

I couldn't seem to lift my head up to meet his gaze, the weight of my guilt too heavy to hold. Pulling back the tears that fought to escape, I faked a smile, "They're right you know? That's about as well as it could have gone," I managed to say.

"This is bullshit Cecilia. What is he talking about? Why is he putting an expiration date on us? What aren't you telling me?" Ronan forced my chin up to look at him with his fingers.

"I can't tell you more than what you've been told. My papá does important work, and when I get older, he wants me to take over...it." I fumbled awkwardly through the sentence. "There are certain expectations of me when I am to take power, and one of those expectations is to use my relationship status as a way to secure the interests of... the company." I said as quietly as possible, almost hoping he couldn't hear me.

"What the Fuck are you talking about? What are any of you talking about? It sounds like your father is selling you to the highest bidder, so please explain to me Cecilia." He slammed his fist on the table, the tableware clattering from the force of his rage.

"That's not what's happening," I shook my head looking down, unable to believe that he'd think something like that.

He was so angry, but how could I blame him?

For almost eight years I'd been wrapping myself around him and entangling into every part of his life just so he could be told one day he'd have to watch me walk away.

I wasn't guiltless, I did know better, but selfishly wanted to have him anyway. I wanted to keep this charade of normalcy to myself and pretend like one day we'd be the high-school sweethearts who would get married. But he was right, we had an expiration date.

"I think I need to go; I need to clear my head... or something," he said, each word becoming harder to make out as he mumbled through them defeated.

Squeezing his hand until I couldn't feel my own anymore, I whispered, "Please don't leave me,"

"I could never leave you Cecilia, but I need to go home and sit with the fact that you will someday," he unwrapped his fingers from my hand, leaving my heart shattered in my chest.

I squeezed my hands until my fingernails drew blood in my palms like I learned to when I was little, and instead of dropping a tear I grew another shell of ice over my heart.

My papá's visit came and went almost as quickly as ever this time. The difference was the feeling of finality that came with the promise of my tío's head. Once he was eliminated, we were free to live our lives the way we always were meant to.

Maybe I could be Celia Flores again, even though I wasn't actually quite sure who she was anymore anyway.

Ronan was still brushing off the mess that had been the dinner he so eagerly asked for.

My papá wasn't a kind man when it came to his daughters, and he made it well known to anyone who wanted to divert me from the path he had chosen – even Mamá. But Papá had set off a ticking time bomb into my relationship and expected Ronan to act like a man about it.

The truth was, he had broken my heart too that night, but as his daughter, I was expected to understand that it was all for my good.

Ronan questioned years before why my papá always came with multiple cars and a plethora of armed men at his side, or why we holed ourselves inside of my tía's fortress until he was gone. It was pretty easy to dismiss it all as government work and that my papá was high up in the chain as well, and it hadn't been a complete lie.

He *was* the chain.

There was a fine line between gang life and government life and when it was all you grew up knowing that fine line faded quite easily. The number of times my papá had lunch with the president of México every year was more annoying than I could count. My papá definitely made more money than him too.

Cézar was packing up the cars and loading my papá's belongings into the Mercedes Benz the two of them would be taking on their trip back. The rest of his men loaded their bags and weapons into the obscenity that was the armored Land Rover.

Cézar headed back into the house for the rest of the bags as we began to say our goodbyes to Papá, this time it could be a few months until we would meet again. He was so sure he was too close to catch Ignacio and couldn't risk anything bringing him back to us and compromising our safety again.

Tía Larissa stood at the top of the driveway as mamá, Carolina, and I created a perfect queue on papá's side of the car to say our farewells. Mamá was already dramatically crying that she couldn't keep doing this even though at this point it was all we knew. As cold as she was to me, my heart still hurt for her.

I thought about the weekends when I was forced to be away from Ronan for my training, and how hard it was to focus on anything else. My admiration for my mamá grew a bit as I was reminded, she continued on all of this time without my papá near her. Her love, her trust, and her belief in him never wavered, and this allowed her to continue to care for her daughters on her own.

The fifteen-foot-tall glass double door slammed on his foot as Cézar dropped a bag, "Carajo!" He cursed at no one but himself, and I ran to the door to keep it open for him so he could get by with the bags.

"Gracias, Princesita," he thanked me, placing a kiss on my forehead. Before he made it out of the door the loud backfiring of a hundred cars rang out.

Cézar threw me inside and crushed me under his weight. He was screaming something I couldn't make out, but the familiar feeling of not being able to breathe had me instantly spinning out of control.

Cézar was still on top of me but I could hear his gun going off as he shouted to someone, but I didn't know who. He pushed me further into the house and carried me into the coat closet then shut the door.

"Are you hit, Princesa?" he shouted from outside of the closet, but I didn't know what he meant.

I was sure I was screaming but I couldn't be certain that any of the noise was actually coming out of me. I could hear the scraping of something large across my tía's marble floors and the heavy slam of it against the closet door let me know I was barricaded inside.

"Tell me what's happening Cézar!" I pounded on the door with all my might, "Please!" I sobbed as the darkness closed in around me, taking me back to the nightmare I dreaded.

Except there was no heat or smoke this time, only the deafening ringing in my ears.

"I have to go check on Rafa. Princesa, don't move!" I heard his fist on the wall.

I wrapped my arms around my knees and tucked my head in to make myself small.

There was a sharp pain coming from my shoulder where Cézar took me down, but I ignored it and hoped that we would all make it out of this one together again. I knew it was that cobarde hijo de la chingada, Ignacio and his son Carlito, I just didn't know what it was they had done yet.

I could hear Cézar's shouting and cursing and guns firing but I couldn't hear any other voices. Not knowing was the worst, terror began closing in around me again as the closet walls got closer and closer until I could feel them practically crushing me.

I heard the sound of the Benz starting up, and a heavy quiet, draped over me as I slipped into the darkness. I was vaguely aware of someone picking me up and getting placed into the small trunk compartment before the void embraced me completely.

It was the antagonizing sound of the hospital machinery next to me beeping like a perfect metronome that woke me up. The pounding in my head and the soreness throughout the rest of my body reminded me that I had just recently been tackled by a six foot-two brick wall. I could hear my heart rate spike as I slowly came out of the fog and I was reminded of the attack in our driveway.

"¿Qué chingados?" I groaned, my throat raspy and desperately in need of water.

"Finally, you're awake. Stay calm Cecilia, I have a lot to tell you." Each word came out more gently and quietly than I thought possible from Cézar.

I tried to turn toward him in the corner of the hospital room, but my shoulder burned, and I screamed at the pain.

"Don't move too much, you just had surgery to remove the bullet in your shoulder. You got pretty lucky there princesa," he muttered, "I did too."

"How did he hit us?" I asked, my voice void of any emotion as I tried to calculate the possible damage.

I already knew what happened, but I needed to know how bad it was.

"It was a drive-by, but they wouldn't stop coming. There were so many cars, one after the other. Everything happened so fast," he buried his hands in his hair as he slumped down in the chair with his elbows on his knees.

"Who's left?" I asked, the hospital light flickering in sync with my voice.

"I tried to go back outside but every time I opened the door those fuckers were blasting through us like we were paper."

I could hear the sadness in his voice, but it only stoked my anger since he kept avoiding my question. Avoiding giving me the truth of it all. I clenched my fists allowing the pain to fuel me and ask him again.

"Who's left, Cézar?" My voice didn't waver.

"Your mamá had a pulse when I ran to turn on the car, so I put her in the backseat before I brought you out there. She's in bad shape though Celia." My old name came out of his mouth sounding so strange and foreign that it took me by surprise.

"Who is left, Cézar?" I asked him one final time because he was choking on the words I needed to hear so badly.

"Everyone else is gone," his brown eyes met mine and there was nothing but sadness and pain in them.

"Everyone? You checked everyone? You're sure?" Panic ripped through me at the thought of Carolina or my tía bleeding out all alone in our driveway, but he shook his head at me grimly.

"I've never seen a job so overdone, Celia. He didn't leave any room for error with this one. I couldn't even recognize them they were all so fucked up. Some of the guys looked like Swiss cheese. It was bad reina."

"What a joke," I scoffed, "Reina del cártel... Queen of nothing. He painted such a pretty picture, my whole life I actually thought it would come true one day. He was protecting me though, you know?" I said through my swollen, cut-up lips.

"I know princesita, I know," Cézar murmured from the chair in the corner as he looked out the window. "He knew that without sons, his seat had a countdown, it was just a matter of time before Ignacio would kill him for it."

"He understood that women in the Cártel only have one place and that's being married off for an alliance, he would have never let that happen to me though. Not while he was still alive." I scoffed, angry at everything, but mostly at my papá for being so naive to think he had the upper hand on his brother.

"I think he would have liked to have seen you come to power, and I think we could have seen it through if he stayed alive until you were old enough to take his place, but now..." he trailed off.

"Todo está perdido", I said, and Cézar nodded.

"All *is* lost. Now princesita, you and your mamá must lay low, don't get noticed, live quietly. Entiendes?" He asked, and I nodded. "He will not stop looking for you until he can be sure you are not a threat, and even then, he may still find a use for you, and I don't want to think what that could mean princesa," Cézar's words were a warning of the harsh reality I somehow avoided twice now.

Rafael Flores' only living daughter was sure to have a pretty price tag to the highest buyer. Bile churned inside my stomach as I realized how vulnerable my papá left me. I wasn't even sure how rage was the surpassing emotion over grief at this moment, but I knew the bastard was responsible even for how I was reacting to his own death.

He burned into me long ago exactly who he wanted me to become.

"Where will you go?" I asked Cézar, realizing with my papá gone it was likely Ignacio had already taken his seat and pledged his case to the cártel.

With Papá's top men out of the way, the rest would fall in where the green would roll from. The lack of loyalty made me bitter. My papá was cold, but he was dedicated to his men, and always did right by them.

"I have some amigos scattered around a couple of motorcycle clubs out East, thought I'd pay them a visit and maybe find some work," he shrugged his shoulders.

"You? In a motorcycle gang?" I laughed so loudly that my shoulder stung, making me wince. "Hanging up your Armani suits for a leather cut? I'd like to see the day."

"They're clubs, not gangs. And I'm not too good for anything Princesita, your papá changed my life when he took me under his wing, but somehow, I always knew it wouldn't last. Nothing good ever lasts," he muttered.

"I am harshly aware," I cut his words with my own and immediately sighed my regret, "I don't blame you," I softened to reassure him. "I know you would have done anything for him, for us. And I know the pendejo would have asked you to save me instead of him anyway. I'm sure he's proud of you... en el infierno." I mumbled the last bit, and he pressed his lips together in a flat line like he hadn't decided whether he agreed with me or not.

"Listen princesa, one last thing. That boyfriend of yours came running by after I brought you and Jamila to the hospital. I don't know what he found when he got to your tía's house, but you better start painting the picture you *want* him to see before he decides to start turning stones on his own, *eh*?" Cézar's tone changed, and I knew he was right, any breadcrumbs that could lead Ronan to the truth would just put him in danger.

"He's outside the room right now. You know, one visitor at a time and all, and I made a damn good case that I should be the one with you when you wake up," he pulled on his suit lapel proudly and I laughed, coughed, and shuddered from pain all at once.

I would miss Cézar like a crab missed an infected limb after they self-amputated it.

I knew that my papá picked him because he saw in him a son he never had, and I felt that same sibling love I had with Caro with him as well. Now we would just be strangers with a shared history of violence and fucked up trauma. I'd be lucky to bump into him at the grocery store on an odd day.

Cézar stood and awkwardly limped my way, he groaned as he bent down and placed a kiss on the top of my forehead, "Don't look for me princesita. Even if you somehow kill the pendejo."

He dropped a single gold coin on my lap, but it wasn't money. It had the Flores cártel symbol pressed into it, a five-petal flower crest. His relinquishing of it was the greatest insult I could probably endure, it meant he was out.

I scoffed to myself because no one got out, not alive at least.

Rafael Flores would have put a bullet between his eyes for leaving me, whether or not he raised him as if he was his own son.

I was not my papá, and I refused to ask a dead man to do my bidding, I was a dead woman too.

With one last look, he turned the doorknob to leave. Before he could fully get through the door, Ronan was already coming in with an intense burning in his eyes as he looked Cézar's way. Once his gaze turned to me though, that intensity quickly dissolved and transformed into a look I knew as fear.

He rushed to my side.

"Oh shit, Cecilia! You're awake," he knelt by my bed as he grasped my hand on my non-injured side. "I thought I lost you. I heard so many guns going off from my house and I tried calling you but you didn't answer. By the time I came over, they were all dead. Everything was taped off and you were gone!" He blurted out in one frantic breath, and I could see the tears pooling at the edges of his eyes.

I finally allowed myself to break to the one person I knew could put me back together again. The tears poured out of me for the first time in longer than I could remember, and he climbed onto the hospital bed. The pain in my shoulder as he reached to hold me was a dull sting compared to the deep ache inside of my chest.

"I got you, okay? I promise I'm not letting you go," he vowed, and I knew he meant it.

I pressed the button on my side to call for more morphine and let myself succumb to the drug's call as it soothed my pain.

2

CECILIA

18 YEARS OLD

It was two in the morning, and I was wide awake from the same nightmare again.

The one where all I saw was the darkness, not even my fingers right in front of my own face. Everything was hot and I could hear machine guns all around me at a deafening volume. The trauma smorgasbord my lovely mind concocted that promised to continue to haunt me until the day I died.

Ronan mentioned therapy but there wasn't much time anymore these days, and not much a professional could do if you weren't exactly willing to tell them *any* of your life's details.

Graduation was only four months away, so my senior exams weren't too far off. When I wasn't running jobs with Santos - Ronan's roommate - I was working after school a few days a week at a diner to pay my mamá's rent. I put her in a trailer away from town after the drive-by, she was just a shell of the person she used to be.

The only thing that remained was her disdain for me.

She hardly said a word and stayed mostly in bed since she was permanently bound to a wheelchair now. She'd scream at me anytime I stopped by and threw violent fits of rage about my papá.

She almost always ended up hurting herself in an attempt to hurt me. It used to make me sad, but I knew what she was doing. She pulled away so she could drink herself to death without feeling guilty for abandoning her last daughter.

I wouldn't pity her, and I refused to watch it happen.

I thought I was doing the best I could, what my papá and Carolina would have hoped that I'd be doing. Most days I was on autopilot though, as I went through the motions of normalcy.

The reality was, I probably checked out a long while back.

I was drenched in sweat from my dream and Ronan's spot in the bed was empty. I walked to the en-suite bathroom and managed to look up at the mirror - the girl that looked back, she was just a stranger to me these days. My papá's eyes stared back at me until I managed to turn my head to the side in defiance. My long, straight, inky black hair was sticking to my face from sweat; so I fashioned a braid down my back.

Too much like *her* now.

My mamá.

I tossed on a robe over my pajama shorts and shirt then made my way to the living room in Ronan's apartment. *Our* apartment technically, but nothing really felt like mine anymore. It wasn't fancy, just a two-bedroom with some outdated furnishings, but the three of us got by. We were happy, and we sure weren't starving or anything.

It was easy to make money on the west coast with college kids constantly hungry for drugs.

Santos was still up playing some zombie video game on his PS3. He frowned when he looked at me and said, "you good, Morena?" as if he could see the nightmare still written on my face.

He brushed his brown, curly hair away from his hazel eyes where the tattoo of a small "X" decorated his left temple and handed me a beer from the cooler next to him. I took it, cracking it open and letting the coolness drown out the heat inside me as it washed its way down my throat.

Santos was the kind of handsome that left you scared to keep looking for too long. His entire look screamed "bad boy who was going nowhere fast", and a small part of me simultaneously envied and felt sorry for whatever girl would end up lucky to have him. He was all laughs, lighthearted jokes and somehow a good listener to boot.

I'd been wrapped up in this world long enough to know that the mark on his temple meant he had a body count under his belt and that was a whole mess I didn't want to get sucked back into again. Aside from Ronan, he was my best friend. Not that I had attempted to get close to anyone else in the last few years.

Being untrusting, was a lonely game.

Santos and I spent a lot of time together making runs, selling weed and the occasional party drugs to rich kids. In the end we were always just waiting for Ronan, who was trying to find something bigger, something better for us all.

It was the closest thing to family I had at this point, and I knew I was lucky to not be alone, or dead.

"Couldn't sleep, bad dreams." I replied, putting the beer on the coffee table as I sat on the other side of the couch and propped my feet on his lap.

Sometimes it felt like Santos was more my friend than he was Ronan's, we spent more time together than they did.

"Your family, right? You get a lot of dreams of the drive-by?" He looked my way and paused the game on his screen, to show me he had my attention.

I think he felt a kindred connection there. Santos came from gang life and he was Mexican too, but he was born in Ocean Valley. I was honestly not even sure if he knew how to speak Spanish aside from some curse words, and common sayings.

I could tell by the look he was giving me though, that he was wondering if it was one of his cousins or older brothers who may have been responsible for my family's death. It was a harsh reminder of the web of lies I had woven around myself when I told Ronan the police ruled it as gang initiation shooting. It wasn't a complete lie, that technically was what they filed it away as, before they threw the file in the trash without bothering to investigate.

We were just another immigrant family people didn't care enough about to bother disrupting their day over.

"Yeah, I got really lucky," I shivered and pulled the blanket down from the back of the couch to wrap myself up in it.

After the shooting Ronan got this place and moved us all in immediately. Lucky for me, social services didn't give a shit about vaguely legal brown kids, so no one had come looking for me after my family had been killed.

He nodded and we sat in silence for a few minutes, Santos eventually un-paused his game when he realized I had nothing more to say on the subject. The sounds of zombie hordes in the distance somehow soothed me back to sleep in the end.

I woke up to a dark and empty living room and Ronan scooping me off the couch as he carried me towards our bedroom.

"Did the job go smoothly?" I asked him, my voice scratchy and full of sleep.

"Perfect, ended up making more than we planned since Guillermo's guy didn't show up. West siders never cause us any trouble, so we didn't need him. We ended up getting a fifty percent split on the product." He nuzzled his cold nose into my neck and the smell of his bleu de Chanel cologne overwhelmed my senses in the best way as notes of cedar and sandalwood lit me up.

I looked up at him through hooded eyes as I brushed the sleepiness away and licked the dryness from my lips. The bedside clock read four in the morning but the hunger in his eyes told me I wouldn't be going back to sleep just yet.

His thumb gently traced the raised-up scar on my rib, and it scorched beneath his touch. To him it was nothing more than an old injury I'd constructed in a story to cover the truth, but to me it was all I had of my past now.

The only thing that was left of who I was meant to be.

I ran my fingers through his sleek dirty blonde hair, it seemed darker every year now as he aged, and it suited him well. It fell long to one side past his ears, but the back and the sides were meticulously kept trimmed short. He pulled back from me and placed me on the large oak dresser across our queen-sized bed. Stepping between my legs, he pulled the robe off of me in one motion and pressed his lips to mine forcing his way through with his tongue.

I willingly welcomed him and tasted the cinnamon of the gum he'd been chewing.

He let out a low growl into my mouth and crushed me harder against him, letting me feel his excitement through his jeans.

I bit my lip in anticipation and looked into the eyes that always brought me home. They were a forest of green I could wander tirelessly, full of amber specks throughout them like burning rays of sunshine that could consume me, if I let them.

"Were you waiting for me?" He breathed into my ear.

"Yes." I hissed, my heartbeat quickening in response to him, and I palmed his thick hard length through his pants.

He slid his hand through the top of my shorts, eyes widening when he discovered my lack of panties and let out a satisfactory groan, "You *were* waiting, so wet for me already," he dropped his forehead to my shoulder as his fingers made their way down and he unerringly found that magic spot with his thumb.

Heat flooded through me while he worked his way skillfully in a steady rhythm.

I tipped my head back and a soft moan escaped me when he replaced his thumb with the flat of his tongue. He ran it over my clit, making circles and quick motions until my head was spinning from the sensation.

I could feel a finger and then another making its way inside me, stretching me open to prepare me for what was surely coming. He drove them into me at a heady pace, coaxing pitiful whines as I begged for my release.

Ronan gazed up at me with a smirk, I knew the look on my face was giving away how close I was to losing it completely. He muffled my mouth shut with one hand for his roommate's sake while continuing his torture until I was screaming into his palm.

It was like seeing stars with him.

Every time.

"If I could bottle that sound," he chuckled, and threw me onto the bed, his erection at full mast fighting the fabric of his jeans.

I instinctively licked my lips wanting a taste, but he shook his head and pulled his shirt over it revealing his well-defined abs.

"Not tonight, I need to be inside of you. Right now."

I scrambled to follow and undress as well. I got up on my knees in the center of the bed as I waited for him to remove the last bit of his clothes that kept me from him.

He straightened as he stood looking down at me from his six feet of height and every inch of my skin buzzed with need to be touched by him.

I turned around to show him how I wanted to play tonight, and he pulled me close against him, my back to his chest. My skin goose bumped as he tipped my head to the side and planted firm kisses on my neck, trailing up my jaw. He roughly pressed the top of my back until I was belly down on the mattress, pulling my hips up high into the air. The sting of the slap on my ass forced a guttural groan to slip out of my throat from the sharp contact.

"Please," I said looking back at him knowing he could read my mind, but he liked this game too much, he loved the control and I loved giving it up to him.

I was too high from the last orgasm and all I could do was chase the feeling of the next one.

"Please what?" he asked with a half-smile knowing exactly what I wanted, but obviously wanting to make me work for it.

"More, please," I begged, and his hand came down on my other cheek with a burning sting.

I screamed, my arousal gushed like liquid heat between my thighs. He rubbed gently, soothing the burning sting on my flesh and I moaned into the mattress. I squeezed the sheets in anticipation, but the next strike didn't come. Instead, I felt the hard steel of his cock pushing into me and filling me up completely. Once he gave me a few seconds to adjust to him inside me, he grabbed a hold of both of my hips and began to move, deep and slow.

Perfectly in sync, every thrust of his hip sending me closer to oblivion.

"Come for me little flower," he said while hitting that perfect spot over and over until I was left mumbling Spanish obscenities at him with no choice but to let go and unravel once again in an earth-shattering climax.

Sweat drenching me as I struggled to breathe, he flipped me over and placed each of my ankles over his shoulders while propped up on his knees and made his way inside me again.

I moaned at the delicious sensation, he picked up his pace, moving quicker this time, finally chasing his own pleasure.

"Beautiful," he said as he slid a finger inside, collecting my wetness to use it to press into my clit once again.

I almost lost it immediately, the sensory almost an electrifying feeling from how sensitive I was from my previous orgasms.

"It's too much," I gasped for breath and clenched the sheets around me, but he chuckled darkly and closed his mouth around mine to swallow the sounds of my pleasure, never relenting on his pace until I was coming again, and this time taking him with me.

"Fuck, you're perfect," he exhaled and crashed down on the mattress next to me while we both panted and struggled to catch our breaths.

"Te quiero." I said, and rested my head on his chest listening to the fast drumming of his heart.

"I want to get your mom out of that trailer Ceci, I can use the money from that run to pay for a few months in an adult care facility that can handle her needs," he said a few minutes later while staring at the ceiling.

"Really?" I perched up and then straddled his stomach to look down at him, "Are you sure?"

"Cecilia, no kid should be taking care of their parents the way you've had to do with your mom, I want you to focus on graduating and...whatever your plan is after that," he said, awkwardly unsure of his own words.

"My plans are you, pendejo," I punched him in the shoulder, and he dramatically faked the injury.

He looked at me with a million questions and worry flooded his eyes.

I knew my papá's mind tricks were likely still playing in his head, probably on repeat – but my words were the truth. I knew I wasn't on the path Rafael Flores put me on anymore, and I was starting to think that life was never meant for me anyway.

A few days later we headed out to my mamá's trailer on the edge of town. It was hidden away behind a grove of trees with no driveway, far from any mobile home community. It was the only way to stay hidden while I finished high school online, though I honestly wasn't even sure why I was bothering with a diploma anymore. Even if cártel queen wasn't in my future, it was obvious I couldn't make money the straight and narrow way.

Crime was ingrained in my genetics.

We parked the car on the side of the road halfway into the grass and made our way out into the thick clearing of trees. We walked mostly in silence for a few minutes before reaching the hidden trailer, Ronan understood how I felt about having to come here. It was one of those things where it was best to just get in and out, keep it brief.

"You should probably stay out here; God knows she's probably not even dressed and is very likely passed out drunk. She's not going to be thankful about any of this, so don't expect it," I said to him shaking my head as I pressed a kiss to his cheek.

"Yell if you need anything," he said, pulling me in and kissing me deeper before he let me go.

I climbed up the trailer steps and opened the door, immediately the overwhelming stench of shit and death engulfed my senses. I was taken back to the torture sessions against the Cártel's enemies papá would force me to participate in.

I was twelve the first time he had me kill a man.

"Mija, if I was to let this Hijo de la chingada free, the first thing he

would do is rape you and then kill you. Your responsibility in this life is to be the one left standing, every time." His lip curled back, and a darkness shadowed over his face as he handed me the blade. He stood back and watched as I mercilessly stabbed a stranger in the stomach repeatedly, until his insides were promising to fall on my brand new white adidas.

I shuddered the memory away with a cough as I removed my cardigan and wrapped it around my face to shield me from the odor coming from the bedroom. I was here four days ago with groceries and tequila, so she had probably been dead for at least three days.

It definitely smelled like three days.

What the hell, Jamila?

I thought to myself as I clenched my fists, anger turned my heart to stone at the thought of my mamá's cowardice. She was the wife of a dead Capo, suicide was a copout. Though ashamed, I wasn't surprised that she was dropping out of the fight so early and leaving me all alone in this world.

I fought back the tears and opened the bedroom door, the unexpected waiting for me. I dropped to my knees, a hearty sob leaving my chest at the sight. My mamá's throat had been slit open, her camisole ripped, and the five-petal flower that was the Flores cártel symbol had been carved on her chest. Her legs had been tied to the bed, I guess they didn't realize she couldn't put up a fight.

On the wall next to her bed her blood wrote, "¿Dónde estás reina?" - Where are you, queen?

I made my way to my mamá's side and gazed down at her lifeless body. Even in death she was more beautiful than most. Her long hair was black and straight like mine, and her full lips were a dark purple hue fit for a corpse. Her dark indigenous skin was already pale and colorless as if the sun God had never blessed her at all.

She was dead, and it was both a relief, and a new burden entirely. For a few minutes I allowed the tears to fight for their chance to fall as I grieved the finality of my family. It was a mess in the room, which made me wonder if there was something my uncle had been looking for while he was here.

I glanced at my mamá again.

What were you hiding from him, mamá?

What cost you your life?

I shifted my gaze over to her bedside vanity and found her box of jewels containing a few of the gifts from my papá from over the years. She obnoxiously insisted I retrieve them from Tía Larissa's house after the drive-by.

I opened it up to reveal the velvety blue pillow containing a plethora of obnoxious diamond rings and earrings with more carats than I could probably guess. I pocketed them and turned my eyes to the small drawer in the bottom of the box. Once I pulled it out it revealed the prize I'd been seeking, the rose gold chain with a matching pendant of the same flower carved into my mamá's chest.

I pulled it and the tufted velvet lining of the drawer lifted up with the necklace, revealing a small silver key underneath. I put both items in my empty pocket and took one last look at my mamá - her dark eyes, once so rich and alluring, were now dull and lackluster. I kissed the tips of my fingers before using them to close her eyelids.

"Adios, Mami." I whispered as I made my way into the tiny kitchen and propped open the door of the two-burner range.

I turned the gas on and left it running while I searched for something flammable that might be handy. The smell of death was making it impossible to think straight, so I made my way out of the trailer for some fresh air and called out to Ronan.

"Do you have a lighter?" I asked, tears flooding my face without my permission.

He brought his eyebrows together but the question he was clearly thinking didn't leave his lips. He fished for the lighter out of his pocket and tossed it my way, his eyebrows still furrowed patiently, waiting for an explanation.

"I'm gonna burn it down," I answered casually as I unwrapped the cardigan from my face, folding it into a small bundle and lighting it on fire.

"What? Are you crazy?" he rushed over to me to try to stop me from lighting the fabric on fire, but I pushed him away.

"She's dead okay? I just need to clean up this shit so we can go." I picked up a heavy rock and threw it against the trailer window and it shattered without any trouble. The cardigan began to burn in my hand, so I quickly hurled it into the broken window.

Ronan didn't ask anything anymore, and I could feel the rift splitting us apart from the millions of lies and unanswered questions between us. We ran through the trees, and I waited to hear the explosion before I climbed into the passenger side of his black Dodge Charger.

We sat in silence for the twenty-minute ride back into the city to his two-bedroom apartment, my hands were sweating with uncertainty for the future and the mixture of rage and fear colliding inside of me.

Ignacio, he'd taken *everything* from me.

It had only been a few days after I disposed of my mamá, and I was usually alone now. Ronan was mostly out of the house aside from quick pop-ins to shower, change and sometimes sleep. We were going through the motions but the weight in my chest told me if I didn't open up my box of deceptions this would be the end of us.

The timing of it all didn't help either.

Ronan and Santos had been working on the foundation for something big. Something that would make it so that we could stop the dozens of different illegal runs a week with minor payouts, and focus on one thing at a time – most likely guns.

I tried pushing the idea of moving weed, since the cártel almost always had a hand in any weapons traveling through the west coast. It was nearly impossible to make a case while trying to convey naivety and ignorance in the subject though. It was a fight I couldn't win.

Weapons simply cashed out bigger, and money talked loudly.

I was sitting on our beat-up leather couch watching reruns on daytime television when Santos came bursting in through the door cheering and whooping.

"We made it big, Morena!" He danced into the room shouting and laughing. He squeezed me in a tight embrace, kissing my cheek as he lifted me off the floor.

"What happened? Where's Ronan?" I looked out of the apartment door for him but couldn't find him in sight.

"He's moving the car out of the closed garage spot so we can hide the van."

"The van?" I asked, not understanding what he was saying because we certainly did not have a van.

Before he could answer I was already making my way out of the door and running down the stairs to find Ronan pulling a black van into our closed garage parking spot. I waited for him to come out of the driver's side with my arms crossed.

I knew I had no place for interrogations, so I waited for him to offer up information willingly.

"Santos' cousin Guillermo gave us a tip for a tradeoff that was guaranteed to go south. We set up and waited for them. Once the guns stopped going off, we took the van and high-tailed it out of there before the cops showed up. It's gotta be at least a hundred thousand dollars in guns alone, I haven't counted the cash in the briefcases yet." he said breathlessly, a giant smile painting his face as he opened the trunk to show me the loot.

He had this nervous look on his face like he was waiting for judgment, and I tried to feign the illusion of it but this was my world, and he was just now finally emerging into it. If I was supposed to be shocked, I was probably failing at it. That was, until the trunk opened, and I fought to push down the acid rising in the back of my throat.

I eyeballed the dozens of black gun cases with the five-petal flower crest on them.

"Maldita sea!" came out of my mouth before I could stop it, but he didn't notice.

Ronan smiled widely at me, "This is the end of all of our troubles." He lulled in my ear as he put his arm over my shoulder and I realized our expiration found us just as my papá had predicted, maybe just not how he planned.

I rolled out of bed at two in the morning, checking over to see Ronan was dead asleep next to me. By the lack of video game sounds, I could bet that Santos was passed out as well from their celebrations earlier. I pulled the duffle bag he normally used for cash and weed exchanges out of our closet and filled it with as much as I could with just the light of my phone. I could only hope there were at least a couple of complete outfits inside.

I slid into the jeans with the four or five carats worth of diamonds in the pocket and left my phone on the kitchen counter. Grabbing the van keys, I made my way into the garage, shoving the duffle bag into the trunk with the guns. I took the money briefcases and made my way back into the apartment, pocketing a small stack of hundreds for the journey and placed the two briefcases next to my phone.

When I opened the door to leave, I heard Santos from the dark of the living room, "You're gonna destroy him."

But I didn't answer, I couldn't.

Without turning back, I ran to the van as fast as I could with my heart pounding in my ears. Peeling out of the parking lot, I drove off in no planned direction. I plugged my phone into the car's sound system, drowning out my sorrow with music as I allowed my heart to break for the one real thing I ever had.

I drove a few hours before I found the perfect lake to drive the van into. Putting the car in neutral and crawling out as fast as possible while I stood back with the duffle bag in my hand, I watched as it rolled into the water, sinking deep below the surface. I sighed with relief when the last of the bubbles dissipated from the water, knowing Ronan wouldn't be killed by my uncle for stealing and selling his weapons.

Everything that was Cártel property was branded and marked.

Once the weapons were sold it was just a matter of time before they circulated, and Ignacio would put feelers out to find their source. It wouldn't take long for him to trace them back to Santos and Ronan. He would no doubt hate me until the day he died for this, but at least he wouldn't die tomorrow.

I made my way to the country road and stuck my thumb out while I lazily paced towards the undecided future.

3

CECILIA

12 YEARS LATER

"The Ortíz family ruled all of México as one single cártel until Arnácio Ortíz died at the ripe age of thirty-nine, leaving his wife and four-year-old son Augustin. Tradition declared the eldest would take place as jefe after spending their lives being counseled for the position by their papá."

I looked up from my paper nervously, but Papá looked back at me with pride gleaming in his eyes and encouraged me to keep going with a nod.

"Well, it would have been an outrage to allow a four-year-old to sit in the position of cártel boss. Hungry for power, the four top influential families that worked for Arnácio took this opportunity to rise in power. They decided to split the cártel into a delegation of three to keep balance and equality, The Flores family - that was your abuelo," I recited to Papá, "The Ramirez, and the Chávez family. What no one really knew was that his mamá was doing way more heavy lifting in the cártel than señor Ortíz let his lackeys believe."

My mamá interrupted to chime in, "Behind every good man," she sang and my papá smiled affectionately at her.

"Well, she spent the next twenty years teaching him everything there was to know about being a jefe. When Augustin "comes of age" I exaggerated with big finger quotes. "He climbs his way up the ranks until he's earned all of the grunts' loyalty. One day he shows up guns blazing with the whole backing of the cártel behind him and he says, 'I'm here to take what's mine!' but nobody wanted to die. Instead, they all agreed to add a fourth seat to the cártel since Augustin proved his mettle to them, and in the end, everyone knew blood

rights held the most power." Ten-year-old me finished reading off of the paper I had stayed up the entire previous night writing.

When Mamá announced Papá was coming home for a surprise visit, I immediately hopped on the computer and began asking my mamá for as much information on our family history that she could provide.

My papá chuckled and signaled for me to come to his lap, I eagerly ran his way and he swooped me into his arms. "It was a little more complicated than that, quite a few people died. But I think you captured the essence of our history well, mija. That was very good." Papá planted a kiss on my forehead, and I swelled with pride.

"And who sits in the Ortíz seat now?" He asked inquisitively though I knew he knew the answer himself.

"You do!" I giggled. "Papá came in guns blazing too and said 'I came to take what's mine!' Now the Flores family owns all of the cártel." My papá made eyes with my mamá and let out a throaty laugh before saying, "Yes mija. Nothing in this life is given to us, if you want power you have to take it."

The memory was so clear I could still smell the scent of cigar on his suit jacket and touch the smooth, expensive fabric between my fingers. I could feel the roughness of his thick mustache against my face when he cradled me for a hug or a kiss if I focused hard enough. I could hear his strong accent and his deep voice soothing all of my worries away like he always did.

That was the last summer I would spend as an innocent child before my papá would begin to mold me in his image.

I sighed away my grief as I rolled out of bed dreading the day. I didn't have the luxury of dwelling on old memories anymore, I had surviving to do. I checked-out of the small but overpriced rental studio apartment I stayed in the night before when I got into Cove City.

Twirling my mother's old necklace between my fingers, I fished through my dress pocket for the address I had folded up inside. I hailed a cab and gave the driver the location before popping my ear-plugs in my ears to tune out the overwhelming sounds of the city.

I didn't know what I was thinking, but I had completely run out of options. I never stayed anywhere long enough to make friends, let alone trust anyone enough to count on them for help. Five times in the last ten years Ignacio had gotten too close to my trail and almost killed me. Every time I'd escape by the skin of my teeth due to some dumb luck coincidence.

There was the time I picked up an extra shift at work and my mailman, Fred ended up triggering a detonator meant for me. Poor fucking Fred, he was a dick who never knocked hard enough to hear and always made me pick up my packages at the Post Office, but he didn't deserve to die for me.

Then there was the time I almost got stolen out of my own car in a fast-food drive-thru line in Texas, but I had my gun on me and no one batted an eye when I shot Ignacio's men in cold blood in the parking lot mid kidnapping.

Half the time I avoided getting close to people, or making friends in fear that I'd end up finding them dead on a random Tuesday. The last attempt, I was working as a teacher's aide at an elementary school in Philadelphia. He set the entire school on fire, killing twelve kids and three teachers.

I stayed home with a fever that day.

A few years back Ignacio and his son, Carlito, killed the last two jefes remaining in the cártel along with their offspring, making him the only leader of the entire Mexican Cártel. My ugly primo was his sole heir.

I left to keep him safe, but now I was running to his doorstep to beg him for his protection.

It was a cruel twist of fate, and I must have completely lost my mind to think Ronan Zerkos was going to do anything other than try to put me in my grave when he saw me again. He had become one of the leaders of the Black Crow Brotherhood, one of the most powerful and violent gangs in Cove City. Along with two others, Santos Álvarez and Mateo Kane; together they had dominion over all of Cove City.

This place was bigger than you could imagine, full of high-rise buildings, casinos, and strip clubs.

There were no suburbs here. Everything was dripping in sin, and the city definitely didn't sleep.

I'd been in a lot of different places over the last twelve years, but nowhere was quite like this city. Full of lights, and the promise of danger in every corner.

And I was willingly walking into it.

4

MATEO

Ronan Zerkos suffered no one and took absolutely no prisoners. His attitude and alpha demeanor made it easy for him to dominate control of a room with a single gesture of his hand. Our men both feared and respected him, but most of all, their loyalty knew no end when it came to him.

He was the hand that fed, and the hand that dealt the blows if the dominos did not line up.

Now don't get me wrong, there was no decision that we didn't make together, but I knew if you were to ask, most people would think he was the one in charge. It didn't bother me, at the end of the day our wallets weighed the same and I was ninety percent positive my dick was bigger. Actually, make that ninety-five percent.

However, his attitude right now, was causing a pain in my ass I couldn't shake, and his choosiness was going to ruin everything this year.

"They're all fucking *blondes.*" he yelled, pointing at the three frightened girls crouching in the corner. They let out a startled cry as his drink spilled from his glass all over the floor.

I rolled my eyes at the tantrum and Santos casually chimed in to relieve the tension.

"Yo, I like blondes man, reminds me of all the beach girls in Ocean Valley," he sighed, "I miss the beach."

I felt bad for the guy, I knew he would always miss Ocean Valley but we needed him here, with us, and he needed to stay away from that place. Anytime he ended up in Ocean Valley, his hands got bloody, and not in a good way.

Was there a good way?

There definitely was.

But all that murder was starting to get to him, I could see it. I would do anything to keep him from shouldering that burden alone.

I was grateful for Santos Álvarez. He was my brother through and through, and if it hadn't been for his alliance with Los Muertos, I don't think we would have been able to take this city by storm six years ago.

Without him we would have never been able to merge all of the smaller gangs into one giant syndication operation.

The Black Crow Brotherhood.

Álvarez had an older cousin, Guillermo. Before the age of eighteen, Guillermo's cruelty helped him bleed his way to becoming the top dog in Los Muertos, the most powerful Mexican-American syndicate organization on the west coast. It was an impressive operation, and the entire thing was a family affair.

Santos Álvarez watched his older siblings all heading towards the same future with a glimmer in their eyes that would certainly be extinguished before most of them would get to turn thirty.

He was determined to not be a part of it and to keep Guillermo's claws from reaching his younger siblings.

His "dear" cousin would try and sweeten the offer every time he'd round back to Álvarez to try to convince him to the dark side. Santos was a machine when it came to taking lives, and his cousin had a mega boner set on using his skills for his own benefit. But my brother was adamant on breaking a generational curse because even before Guillermo found his place, gang life had been the standard expectation where he grew up.

When Ronan enlisted in the Navy, he instructed Álvarez with a goal, to find something concrete to build a foundation off of while he'd be gone. But Álvarez knew that nothing that was solid, would come without a strong hand behind it, so he made an agreement with his cousin. Six full years as a dedicated member, six years of unquestionable loyalty and he would be free to walk away.

The barter was made, and after those six years, the two gangs would always have each other's backs, as allies across the country.

They struck the deal, and no sooner had he agreed but they'd already begun tattooing their brand on his chest. Santos stayed true to his word, he killed, hurt, and maimed anyone Los Muertos pointed his way. Until the day we came home from war, that's when we freed him from his contract.

Guillermo paid us back with a small army, and everything we needed to set up base and kickstart our empire.

"You want me to take them back?" I asked, a bit unsure how I was gonna tame the beast right this second.

I was trying to deflect some heat off Santos, because the guy looked like he was in over his head right now. It wasn't his fault. It was impossible to tell which year Zerkos was going to want the exact opposite, or the very same thing he once had.

The very thing he'd never really get over.

"Take them back? You want to take Cindy Lou and Mary Kate over here back to the Bratva and the Irish and hope they aren't just gonna kill them when we drop them at their doorstep?" Zerkos asked, and I snorted holding back a laugh because I was pretty positive that definitely was not either of the girls' names, and I wasn't even sure we were fucking with the Irish this year.

Ronan glared at me with a look that was full of sharp knives, and I schooled my expression to a serious one.

"My bad dude. I get it, we're stuck with them. Álvarez fucked up. He'll owe you big next year. Only brunettes. Right man?" I nudged Álvarez trying to coach a response out of him.

"Yeah! Totally man, all dark hair next year." He gave him a big grin and Ronan just shook his head in frustration and downed the whiskey in his glass.

Tensions were usually high this time of the year, when we were starting the selection process for the Black Crows traffic trials. It started as a game we created after a long night of drinking when we first came to power. See, the big gangs were all still around. The Bratva, the Yakuza, the Ukrainians, the Sidhe, the First Command, whatever. We didn't play nice with them, but we didn't go around starting wars either.

The one thing all most of these mafia types had in common was that they all loved the flesh trade. We decided every year we would steal a few nobodies from them. Just a couple of some poor trafficked souls with no allegiance or loyalty that wouldn't be missed.

We spent a few weeks breaking them with some psycho brainwash shit Ronan learned while we were doing special ops for the Navy Seals, and when they totally lost all sense of self, we turned on the charm.

We showered them with love and affection and fought for their attention until they each thought they were safe, loved, and cared for. It guaranteed their undying loyalty to us and assured us they wouldn't betray us to the enemy. We let them each choose one of us to take care of them over the next few months and turned them into pampered little princesses who ate from the palm of our hands and fed us vital intel on our enemies.

The lackeys went crazy over it since we basically turned it into an Olympic event, we had all but created a point system to it. In the end it wasn't so bad, just two or three months out of our year, they almost always were dying to jump on our dicks anyway, and bonus points for getting to siphon as much information from them about their previous gangs as we could.

It wasn't a relationship, and they were made well aware of that from the get-go. In contract form. It was more like a mutually beneficial partnership...one where they lost all sense of freedom and self for a small amount of time, but for the greater good.

We were able to take the Triad's trafficking ring down two years ago. The Cove City PD didn't even so much as thank us when they were taking the credit for freeing over six thousand women and girls. Once our captives' usefulness ran out, we paid them for their time and guaranteed them work for the Black Crows in the strip clubs or bars.

If they wanted to leave the life completely, we sent them on their way with as much protection and money as we could offer. They were always grateful, and in the end the future we promised was safer than the unknown. Most of the girls would rather strip than go back to being forced to suck some rich, John's cock on a Wednesday for chump change. Especially, when that money was just going to go to some asshole's pocket.

We made our home in Cove City, it was the clear choice we all agreed on from the moment we got back from overseas.

We owned the entirety of our high-rise from top to bottom, and every floor was filled with our men for protection. The three of us occupied the glass wall penthouse. We set it up, so the higher-ranked soldiers were positioned on the highest floors, with lower-level foot soldiers near the ground level. This way, any attack on us, would be highly guarded with at least fourteen floors of bullshit and hell our enemy would be forced to deal with before getting to us.

My phone rang and our guy at the door downstairs was telling me there was some broad demanding to come up and see Álvarez. I laughed to myself thinking his last conquest must have forgotten something behind in his room. This was why I didn't let women up here. They always found a reason to come back and hang around and I didn't need some chick distracting me. I told him to let her up and made my way to the triple elevators to let her in.

The door dinged open on the center elevator and a small bronze goddess walked out.

She was probably five-foot-five, but with the heels she was only about a head shorter than me. Her hair was a deep obsidian shining brightly that fell down just past her collarbone without a single wave to it. Her eyes were deep, woeful dark full of mystery and sadness that would have hypnotized me if I didn't let my eyes wander.

But wander they did, as I was only human and the woman who stood in front of me could only have been described as a masterpiece. I turned my attention to her lips, as I appreciated the plumpness of them painted a shiny dark purple. Her legs were toned and a golden-brown hue that shone in contrast to the white skater dress she wore and I briefly wondered where she came from.

No one around here dressed like that.

Cove City was wild but it was also full of executive drones who walked around in black like there was no other color available. Anyone else stuck out like a sore thumb.

"I'm actually looking for Ronan, but I needed to get past your goons," she gave me an innocent half-smile while biting her lip with a nervous look. Like I said, bitches were fucking distracting.

Ronan almost never had a girl around here so I didn't buy it, but I wasn't keeping track of all his lays.

I led her through the doors anyway and told her to follow me into the main room. She called him *Ronan* though, and it had been a long time since I had heard anything other than "Zerkos" when it came to him.

There were only two people he let in close enough to call him by his first name, and we were both in the room right now.

Before I could let thought become a seed in my mind, I heard the shattering of a glass.

5

RONAN

I had given up on complaining and accepted the fact I was gonna have to be stomaching looking at blondes for two years in a row now. Álvarez managing to find a Japanese chick with bleached hair was a precise kick in my shin.

Somehow, I just wasn't fucking shocked.

He was nervously pacing, explaining the reasons he picked each of them and I knew he was doing his best to justify his cause, but I wasn't having it.

"Oh fuck, "I heard Santos behind me.

But it was the shattering from his glass dropping that forced me to turn my head in the direction he stared shockingly at.

I turned to see Mateo standing six feet away from me with none other than the treacherous viper who injected her venom all over my life and stole our future from me.

I felt time stand still, completely frozen.

Exactly like that first time I ever saw her when I was just a ten-year-old boy awkwardly standing at her door.

In three steps I cleared the space between us, and I pinned her to the wall, holding her by the throat as her feet dangled in the air.

I wasn't that boy anymore, and I wouldn't let her hypnotize me again.

"You grew," her voice scratched through from the pressure of my hand against her windpipes, and she drew a sinister smile that made me want to break her neck.

"This is a joke, right? Give me one reason why I shouldn't kill you," I roared, letting my grip on her dissolve as she fell to the floor.

She rubbed her throat casually as she stood, "You're lucky I still like that, asshole." With the narrowing of her eyes I was suddenly reminded of every filthy thing I had ever done to the girl standing in front of me.

I had to mask my reaction to her remark and hope she didn't notice the effect she still had on me.

"Maybe that's what I'm here for," she shrugged.

I arched an eyebrow at her confession, self-destructive had never been her style, she was too smart of a girl for it.

But she wasn't a girl anymore either, and standing in front of me was the woman I once thought I'd share my whole life with. She filled out in all the right places, but aside from that she looked almost exactly how I remembered. Her golden-brown skin glimmered in the most lick-able way possible. I had to force myself to remember that she wasn't mine anymore.

"You came to hand yourself over to the Devil then?" I asked, crossing my arms over my chest as I tried to fight the temptation to touch her soft flesh.

She laughed. She fucking *laughed.*

"You are not my Devil, Ronan Zerkos, no matter what you *think* you may know about how you feel. My Devil goes by a different name and compared to him, you are an ant crushed by the weight of his heel." She spat the words out at me in anger, like *I* was the one who threw everything away over a few hundred thousand dollars.

"What's the con, Cecilia?" I asked her, as the whispering and whimpering of the blondes behind me started making my blood boil in annoyance.

"I am and have been many things since we have last seen each other, *Zerkos*. Con-artist has never made it to the list," she huffed and turned her chin up at me in defiance using the name my men and the city knew me by.

I didn't speak, not yet. I was completely out of words, and I could barely even believe she was standing right in front of me.

After years of looking for her, she was finally right there.

"I need protection," she finally admitted.

Her confession was a sudden surprise, and it took everything in me to hide the instinctual part of me that re-awakened, the part of me that told me I had to protect her. I bit back the urge to ask her who was after her, but I had to know what kind of fucking trouble she could have gotten herself into.

Knowing Cecilia and her ability to attract the strange and unpredictable, I couldn't even begin to guess.

"Who'd you piss off?" Santos asked from behind me, as if reading my mind.

I gave him a cutting look that let him know this wasn't his interrogation and my brother sat back down like a wounded dog. I didn't mean to chastise him but, he didn't understand how to handle Cecilia. She could walk all over him from the very first time she stepped foot in our apartment all those years ago, and I was honestly not sure if he even hated it.

"I can't tell you," she said to him, not breaking eye contact with me in that arrogant style about her that pissed me off to no end.

It was the trait that ruled my life for the better portion of ten years, and it was what forced me to accept whatever she wanted to tell me or *didn't* tell me as an absolute fact.

"Typical. You show up here in *my* city, *my* house, twelve years later asking for protection – after you steal from me. After you steal from *us,* and you won't even tell me from who? I don't owe you fuck Cecilia, get out before I put a bullet in your pretty face," I shook my head and pointed to where she came from.

"No," she said, lifting her chin up higher. "If you want me to leave, you'll have to do more than threaten me. What waits for me is death, so unless you plan to kill me now, and put me out of my misery, you're closer to my salvation than my reckoning. I need your help and you will give it to me, Ronan. I can make it worth your while." She pulled a small silver key out of her pocket and opened her hand to show it to me.

"It's a fucking key, so what?" I asked her impatiently, as I teetered between needing her under me as much as I wanted her as far from here as possible.

"This was in my mamá's trailer the day we found her dead. I know this key is the way to my abuelo's fortune, and if you give me protection, I'll help you find it. You can keep it, it's a thousand times more than what I stole from you, and we can call it even." She raised her eyebrows at me as she waited for a response.

That was a lot of money, even for us, but I wasn't going to let her see that affect me.

"Your grandpa left your mom a hundred million dollars?" Álvarez interjected again from behind, making my skin prickle.

"Probably more but it's hard to say for sure," she looked at him and smiled an eye squinting smile that should have been meant for me, and fury began to cloud my mind.

"And what do you need protection from?" I asked again, interrupting their little moment.

"I can't say," she whispered this time and looked down.

"Cecilia Gomes and her secrets, coming back to haunt me. I'm waiting for the punchline, but I think the universe forgot to write me one," I said through flared nostrils. "No deal," I growled and took a final swig of my whiskey.

"Keep your fortune, as you can see, I'm doing pretty well these days, no thanks to you. Maybe you can use it to stay alive." I was so close to her face I could feel her breath on my skin while my anger boiled through to the surface.

I peeled my upper lip back to fight the instinctive urge to kiss the lips that were only mine for so long. I backed up and made my way to my bedroom leaving her with her mouth parted in shock as she realized her lack of sway on me.

"Santos, please. I wouldn't have come if I had any other option. I just need a little time, just a few months. I just need to get everything set up and legalized to head to Spain." I heard her beg, her voice full of a desperation I had never heard from her before.

It was torture to try to ignore it.

I turned on the exorbitant sound system in my room and let the music blast out in a volume that vibrated beneath my feet. Kane badgered me into upgrading my portable Bose speaker when he found out that was how I had been listening to my music. Music was sacred to Mateo, and apparently what I had been doing was borderline sacrilegious.

I headed straight to the small bar in my bedroom to refill my whiskey glass.

As I slumped on a nearby chair, I tried to make sense of what the hell just crashed at my doorstep. Once the glass was empty, I shuffled my way across the black marble flooring and opened the door to my en-suite bathroom. I stepped out of my dark blue Prada suit pants and briefs and lazily undid the black button-down shirt before turning the water to an uncomfortably hot temperature.

The steam rolled out of the walk-in shower before I moved under the cascade of the water that took up the entirety of the shower ceiling. I wasn't stupid enough to believe anything I said or did was enough to make her walk out of the high-rise. Actually, I would bet on the fact that she was probably sitting on the couch right now, sharing smiles and stories with my brothers like she was an old friend.

I also wasn't stupid enough to realize that if the bitch hadn't left me to begin with, I wouldn't be here right now. After she left, Álvarez gave me exactly three months to drink away my pain, but it wasn't enough. I had a profound numbness inside of me that couldn't be remedied, and I needed to feel something other than the void that was left behind when she walked away.

After I self-imploded and distanced myself from everything I ever cared about, I enlisted in the Navy.

That's where I met Mateo Kane. Our ambitions, convictions, and lack of fear for our own lives made us the perfect desirable candidates for the Seals. We made it into the Special Ops team in record time, and at twenty years old we were *almost* giving Scott Helvenston a run for his money as the youngest ever Navy Seal.

Kane saved my ass more often than I could count and there wasn't a day during our time served that I wasn't pulling him out of the fire. To be honest the guy was a magnet for death, he had a hard-on for it like no one I had ever met before.

One time in Russia, while rescuing a political hostage, the asshole actually jumped out of a twelve-story window. I mean he was trying to avoid a bullet in the brain and got lucky enough that a pool was there to dull his landing – but still.

The corner of my lip turned up in a smile while I thought about the years with both of my brothers next to my side. Santos spent the six years Kane, and I were in the Seals solidifying an alliance with his cousin, the leader of Los Muertos, and walking him through the blueprint of the dream we had for Cove City.

We owned it all here now.

Drugs, guns, cars, it all came from us.

Sure, the Bratva had their brothels, the Irish had their bars, and everyone shuffled a little product here and there. At the end of the day though, everything they were pushing came from us first, they just didn't know it.

Once we called Cove City home, we moved fast. We took the city in just a few nights so that the gangs wouldn't know what hit them. Mateo and I used our time, resources, and skills while in the Seals to find out everything about our future rivals and their leaders.

With the help of Santos and his small loaned-out army at our disposal that was courtesy of Guillermo and Los Muertos, we were able to take them out during a few well-planned attacks. We made it look like they had all killed each other over a turf war during negotiations, it was easy as pie. Eventually, everything fell into place, and the smaller street gangs took note of the new outfit in town and instead of going against us they joined us.

That's when we became The Black Crow Brotherhood.

When you cut the head off, the beast doesn't die.

It does considerably weaken and allow for a bigger beast to take control while they lick their wounds though. We played the smart game so that we could play the long game – syndicates don't vanish, they replenish. We would never be bold enough to believe we could wipe them out here, and if anything, we'd be raising alarms by slaughtering a bunch of bosses. Bratvas and Yakuzas would be flying in by the hundreds to put us in our graves early.

No, Cecilia Gomes was destined to be my undoing, not some mafia piece of shit. Her old man must have been somewhere in hell having a laugh at me.

The joke was on him though, because there was no way I was going to let her walk out of here ever again.

6

SANTOS

"You fucked up colossally. I brought Blondes, you brought the goddamn apocalypse, man." I shook my head at the black-haired jerk.

"So, that's her." He said, not asking. Because there was no way this asshole had been friends with Ronan Zerkos for twelve years and *hadn't* heard about Cecilia at least fifteen thousand times.

She was the topic of conversation at least once a week, even if it wasn't purposeful.

She was the biggest part of his life, and until she could no longer be considered that, he'd never be able to stop.

"That's her." She said, her voice like liquid honey as she brushed her hands down to smooth her dress.

She made her way to the pristine white leather couch and took a seat casually, as if she wasn't a ticking time bomb.

"I don't think you should stick around, Morena. He's not the guy you used to know." I tilted my head at her in warning.

"No, he's a little boy in a brick shit-house body with a chip on his shoulder." She scoffed at me and then narrowed her eyes as she gazed between me and Kane as if examining us. "Why are you all so tall?" She asked, irritated and walked over to the glass wet bar. "Do you have tequila?" She asked again as if the first question didn't matter and I pointed with my glass to the bottle of DeLeón añejo.

The girl had cojones, and I'd be lying if I said I wasn't impressed a little.

"What's with the whores?" She asked, casually gesturing her drink at the half naked girls in the corner and they flinched closer together in fear again.

I shook my head, "That doesn't concern you, Cecilia, you don't get to ask questions here. Why are you trying to leave the country?" I hoped maybe I could convince her to tell me what she wasn't telling Zerkos.

I was always better at getting her to open up and talk than he was.

She sighed and her shoulders dropped, "I need to get away from someone, that's all I can tell you. You have to believe that I'm not hiding it to hurt him. There's just so much in the past that if he goes digging for it, I think he would end up making some decisions that would probably end up killing him. Please, *Santito*" she softened as she raised her hand to reach for me but instinctively pulled back and anxiously ran her fingers through her own hair.

"I can't promise anything." I said, not trying to get her hopes up.

Ronan was his own person, there was no part of me that actually thought I could sway his mind either way, his decision was made the minute he laid his eyes on her again.

"I thought you were the boss too?" she looked up from her drink with a mischievous look in her eyes. "Or is he still the one who runs the show?" She baited me.

I heard Kane choking on his water at her suggestion and he quickly hid his amusement at her gall. I smirked but she didn't sip her drink yet and lifted her eyebrow as she patiently waited for a response.

"We make decisions together," Kane said as he relaxed back onto the couch spreading his arms over the back of it.

"And you are?" She asked him, though I could probably bet she already knew his name.

She wouldn't give him the satisfaction of letting him know he was worth a minute in her mind though. It wasn't like she acted like she was better than you, no– but when she was in the room you just knew that she was. Everything about the way she carried herself exuded a type of confidence that must have been fostered and nurtured since she was a little girl.

Even though Cecilia was an immigrant, and had nothing and no one left, she still presented herself as if she was royalty. Unlike me, I grew up in poverty and had to claw myself out of the depths of gang life, I had to sell my soul to the devil I promised I never would. Even now with money in my bank account and everything I could have ever hoped for at the snap of a finger, I wasn't comfortable living this way. The Black Crows were still a gang, you could polish a turd... but it was still a turd nonetheless.

"Mateo Kane" he stuck out his hand casually, her eyebrows pulled together in the middle as she accepted the introduction.

"Italian?" She asked with a hint of curiosity in her tone, and I couldn't quite put my finger on what wasn't quite right, but I realized I had noticed it the minute she first spoke to me.

"Mom's Italian," he explained.

"Hmm. And your father?" She continued the small talk and I ping ponged between their exchanges trying to solve the mystery I couldn't put together quite yet.

"A useless drunk." He raised his glass in cheer, "Yours?"

"Dead." She said flatly, with a blank look on her face.

"Oh." His smile faded awkwardly, and silence filled the room before she cleared her throat.

"It was a long time ago. You can't dwell on who's not here anymore, or you'll never move forward." She said and finally I realized what had been missing.

"Your accent is gone, morena." I pointed out.

"I don't speak much Spanish these days. Haven't in a few years," she said and downed the rest of her tequila before she poured another double into the glass.

"But you can't take Mexico out of the girl." I said, raising my glass.

"This is a terrible idea." Mateo said, pointing to the girls in the corner. "Also, terrible fucking timing." The last part came out as more of a nervous laugh, but the situation was less than funny.

At this point in the selection for the Traffic trials Zerkos would have spent the last two hours starting the process of breaking their little minds. Instead, all he has done is moan, pout and hide. I dropped to the couch and sighed a long exhale of defeat. I noticed Mateo rubbing his temples with his fingers and I realized the pressure was coming down on all of us if he was getting another headache.

"It's almost always the neck." She said walking over to the back of the couch that was positioned in the center of the massive penthouse living room.

She handed me her glass of tequila to hold and all of a sudden, her little fingers grabbed a hold of his neck and before he could protest, she'd almost taken his head off his shoulders. At first, I was sure she killed my friend from the terrible cracking I heard, but he immediately moaned his satisfaction following the horrendous sound of all the bones settling into place.

"Oh shit." he breathed. "That feels so much better," he said in a marveled expression that had him looking at her like she was a brand-new toy.

He brushed his dark hair away from his dark brown eyes and grinned at her in gratitude. She shrugged her shoulders and relieved me from holding her glass as she continued to sip her drink standing.

"He won't help you unless you start telling him *something*. He's too hung up on the lack of answers you left him with" I said to her frankly.

"And what about you?" She asked me, and dammit if I was just as willing to do her bidding as I was twelve years ago.

I sighed, "More—Cecilia, there's nothing I can do if he's not willing. Zerkos saved my life too many times for me to disregard his feelings right now."

"Doesn't seem like he's hurting anymore." She scoffed and took a swig of her drink.

"You did a number on him when you left," I explained.

"And guess who had to clean up your mess?" Kane chimed in, his sharp jaw creating a hard line as he clenched his teeth at the thought.

"I did what I had to, in order to keep the two of you breathing a little longer. I won't say more than that, and I sure as shit am not here to apologize." She said with that fire inside of her I knew so well coming back to life.

"Maybe he just needs to take his pound of flesh and you can call it even." Kane threatened without so much as looking at her.

"Ha, I have nothing to lose anymore. He can try."

The music that blared from Zerkos' room came to a quiet stop and Kane and I simultaneously looked at each other nervously. Whatever was about to happen next was not going to be good, not for her at least.

7

CECILIA

The heavy metal music stopped, and my heart skipped with it in nervous anticipation.

I was spinning inside, and the truth was, I probably should have poured a bigger glass because I was in no way shape or form ready to confront the only man I'd ever loved, again.

But I wasn't raised to be weak, I was made- and Cecilia Flores was created to be indestructible, my papá guaranteed it. I downed the rest of the shot in one swallow and made my way across the room where glass lined the entire upper half of the walls in windows surrounding the penthouse.

I turned my back to the room and gazed out at the Cove City skyline admiring it for the first time in my life, letting it calm my nerves.

The apartment was insanely obnoxious, full of marble and gold and it reminded me of everything I once lost. Aside from the white foyer that opened up from the elevator, the entirety of the living area was the blackest marble I had ever seen, full of deep gold veins and speckles.

The white leather couch was so large it could easily sit six or seven with extra space and the concrete coffee table was more of an art statement than for putting drinks on, if I could guess.

I suddenly itched with the need to leave a ring mark on it.

Two matching leather chairs faced opposite of the couch and aside from the wet bar across the room the only other piece of furniture was a desk in the corner.

"Why are you still here?" The deep rumble of his voice sent butterflies swirling into my belly and weakening me at the knees, but I squeezed my empty glass for strength and found the courage to speak without letting my voice waver.

"Because you're going to help me," I said, still staring at the open glass in front of me.

"You still haven't given me one reason why I should help you, Cecilia."

I finally turned around and let my eyes gaze into the beautiful specimen he had become.

He was at least six-four now, his towering height demanded the attention of the room. He was only wearing gray suit pants and it was doing terrible things to me that I wasn't even sure I *wanted* to fight off. His hair was still wet from his shower and a heavy exhale escaped me at the realization that the boy I left was now a man.

He was exactly how I'd remembered him, but somehow, he had completely changed. He was polished and yet full of sharp edges, and under his shirt had been hiding a multitude of tattoos that covered him from his wrists all the way up to his neck.

I bit my bottom lip, my gaze trailed down to his V, and when I traveled my way back up, I found his eyes staring straight into mine.

"Call the Diablos and tell Cézar Villalobos to come pick her up," he said as he began to turn around, and the thought alone caused me to lose my composure.

"NO!" I shouted out.

"What? Big brother got tired of bailing you out?" He snarled at me with a hint of jealousy in his tone.

I wasn't sure what he hated most, the closeness that Cézar and I shared even though we weren't really family, or the fact that he abandoned me when shit hit the fan.

"You don't reach out to someone who specifically tells you to never find them again. Not unless you're looking for a fight." I said looking down, my heart breaking all over again at the recollection of the last moments I spent with Cézar.

"Is that all I had to do then?" he said, peeling his lip up like a rabid animal. "Why...should...I...help...you?" he spaced out each word as he began closing in on me.

"Because, you know me," I said softly.

"Know you?" he scoffed angrily. "I know more about my breakfast than I ever knew about you. I was a stupid little boy and you blinded me with your secrets, your pussy, and your lies until it was convenient for you to leave," he said angrily as he narrowed the distance between us and I backed myself into the wall, searching for support with my hands to keep my legs from betraying me.

"I didn't know you then, and I sure as hell don't know you now Cecilia. The only thing I'm certain I ever knew about you was how to make you come." Forest green eyes burrowed into me, his face so close to mine that I could smell the intoxicating scent of the Bleu de Chanel he still wore.

Was it for me? Or had he really changed so little?

He slid his hand up my dress, his fingers just lightly traced up the sensitive spot on my thigh before he cupped my pussy. I widened my eyes at him in surprise from the invasiveness, a million emotions and thoughts colliding and threatening to break me apart. I expected anger, I expected even maybe violence, but I didn't have this in the BINGO card for what Ronan would do when he saw me again.

"Let's see if you can still make my favorite sound?" he whispered into my ears and before I could object, the shock of his fingers sliding against my slickness forced me to grab his biceps to brace myself, my heart thundering in my ears.

"So wet," he groaned. "Still waiting for me all this time?"

But I didn't say a word in response.

The truth would betray me, and I was tired of treachery.

I'd been living too many lies for too long.

Two thick fingers impaled me, rubbing inside me at a slow, delicious pace. He found that magical spot with ease and used his thumb to circle my clit, a flood of arousal threatening to spill down my thighs. I was acutely aware of the number of people in the room watching us when Mateo's stare met mine.

"Look at me" Ronan said, and I peered straight into that emerald forest fighting through the heartbreak that began to envelop me.

I didn't stray my gaze from his. Instead, I narrowed my eyes like a challenge and squeezed his biceps until my nails began to break the skin. It kept the sorrow from escaping if I just focused on the pleasure igniting throughout my body.

He moved against me, like he was trying to prove it to himself that this existed between us once. The whimpers of pleasure were stuck in my throat, I bit my lip until I tasted metal, doing my best to contain the sounds of my climax as he brought me to ruin faster than ever before.

He removed his fingers and brought them to his lips before sucking them clean and said, "Maybe next time then," before he winked my way.

I took a few seconds to catch my breath and glanced over his shoulder to see Santos and Mateo with slack jaws, unable to pretend that they didn't watch me get finger fucked until I came. Embarrassment ravaged through me, and I was suddenly thankful to my ancestors that my skin tone didn't allow for blushing.

"Get on your knees," he said as he reached for his belt, and I frowned in response.

"No," my eyes found Santos , but he was looking at an abstract painting hanging on the wall now. "I'm not your whore." I stood my ground, my eyes shifting to the half-naked women whimpering in the corner, wondering if that was *their* purpose here.

"Want to put it to the test?" he whispered in my ear, chuckling darkly, and then turned to Mateo before he said, "Call Dezmond Junior and tell him to get his ass up here." He hesitated for a second and then spoke again, "Actually, get anyone on the eighth floor and up in here. We've got trials to start."

He narrowed his eyes at me, "If you want my protection, then you're gonna have to earn it like them my little *flower.*" He pointed to the women still huddled in the corner, his words full of venom laced with the promise of revenge.

What were these women going to do for his protection?

What was I going to owe him for mine?

I quickly masked my face to be void of emotion as the room started closing in on me from anxiety.

Coming here was a mistake, I knew it- but it was either the unknown or a body bag, and for now I would take uncertainty over the latter.

8

SANTOS

"Are you fucking crazy man?!" I shouted from across the room while I made my way over to Zerkos, because if *something* was going to mess up the trials, it was going to be *this.*

Not three fucking blondes.

Mateo pulled out his phone and shot a few texts and within a couple of minutes, Dez was stumbling out of the elevators with his briefcase. He was our lawyer, had been since the start of it all, that was the biggest advice Guillermo gave me when we started all of this.

Keep the law close to you and keep a lawyer even closer.

Dezmond Archer Junior was the kid of one of our oldest soldiers. He wanted a different life for his son, but he knew the Black Crows offered a kind of protection that couldn't be passed up. We drew up a contract, paid Dez's way through school and now we kept him on retainer twenty-four-seven. He lived in the building, he only took assignments that were Black Crow Brotherhood business, and we paid him a goddamn fortune for it.

He looked disheveled, like he probably drank too much last night, and I couldn't blame him because I was right there next to him pouring the shots. He was wearing sunglasses inside with a white button-down and some nice suit pants that complimented his slender tall figure. He lifted up his sunglasses over his short brown hair and I had to fight the laugh wanting to bubble out.

The guy was wrecked, and it was my fault. How was I supposed to know we were going to need him today?

With a clear of Ronan's throat, the mood darkened again, and Kane met my gaze from the side. I could tell he wasn't on board with Zerkos's decision by the still stunned look on his face.

We shared plenty of girls between the three of us, don't get me wrong - there wasn't much my brothers and I hadn't seen of each other in the name of a good lay. But whatever the hell that was just now, wasn't that. It was unhinged, angry and full of pent-up hate. The strangest part about the whole thing was that she just took it, like she'd be grateful for anything that came from him.

I wasn't sure if I wanted to think long enough about that to analyze it either.

Cecilia Gomes had always been more of an enigma than I wanted to spend my time dwelling over.

"It'll be a good twist for this year, a fourth," he said without looking back at me, eyes still fixed on her.

Dezmond put his briefcase down on the coffee table and waited for instructions like the well-paid, intelligent man he was.

"And how will that work?" Kane finally spoke, challenging his directive.

"Well..." he trailed, "Maybe this is the year we toss the extras in the dumpster," he hissed, the cowering pile of blondes in the corner cried out from his proclamation as Mateo Kane released a whoop in excitement, and I rolled my eyes at the show they were all putting on.

"I did not hear that," Dez said, plugging an ear bud in and fumbling with his phone.

"You're not thinking straight brother. You need to take a step back and separate the two situations here," I warned him before he did something he was going to seriously regret.

"Last chance Cecilia. Tell me who is after you," he said looking at her, but the stupid look on her face of pure defiance let me know before she opened her mouth, that she was just going to stoke the fire.

"Did you ever consider this world might be bigger than you, asshole?" She shoved at his chest, but it didn't faze him.

He raised his eyebrow at me, and I knew he'd finally noticed her accent as well.

"Tell me this then, where have you been these last twelve years? Because you went up in smoke, like Cecilia Gomes never existed to begin with." He was starting to fume again, and I could tell her answer was gonna be the breaking point of whether or not he lost the rest of his shit.

"You looked for me?" she asked.

"If *that's* what you want to call it," I mumbled and got another annoyed look from Zerkos.

To say he looked for her would be putting it mildly. It took about three months to pull him out of the alcohol induced zombie state he put himself in after she left him. That was the easy part, then came the months of regret that he let her go, the anger redirected at *me* for letting her go. Finally, he enlisted and decided to direct that rage into something a bit more *productive.*

Once he came back it was difficult to keep him focused on building our army for The Black Crow Brotherhood. He was spending all of his time trying to find her, turning over any stone he could think of that would lead him to her. She turned into a ghost though, just vanished into thin air, and completely disappeared without a trace like she had never been real to begin with.

Now she was just showing up at his door like a goddamned gift-wrapped present or something.

"I've been hiding," she said, looking up at him through her eyelashes. "And to be fair, Cecilia Gomes is the longest I've ever been anyone. I'd like to think that's the closest to me I've ever been." She said so gently I feared the words would break like glass once they'd left the comfort of her mouth.

"Talks like a con artist." Mateo circled and suddenly I wasn't sure he was on my side anymore.

Wait, fuck...why was I on this side?

I shook the intrusive thought out of my head.

I walked back over to the wet bar and poured myself a double shot of the añejo, as I tuned out the hauntingly familiar sound of Ronan arguing with the girl that always seemed to be too much to handle.

I recalled all the other times their loud arguing turned into sex at the flip of a switch. All you could hear through the paper-thin walls of our shitty apartment was the muffled sounds of her screaming out her climaxes in the bedroom next to mine.

I adjusted my pants as the unwelcome thought got me hard.

Zerkos paced across the room to the glass top gold framed work desk and pulled a black folder out of the drawer. He pulled a single sheet of paper from it and beckoned her over with his finger as he sat on top of the desk. Dez's eyes perked up from his phone and he watched carefully.

She drifted over with no sense of urgency, testing him, and pushing all of the buttons like she craved the Devil's punishment.

Ronan whistled at Dezmond and finally let him know what he had been called up here for, "We need a legal witness." He explained and Dezmond's face contorted in confusion.

"Isn't it a bit early for that?" he asked Zerkos, but he just chuckled back at him.

"Not for this one. She's already primed," there was a darkness to the smirk he gave him, then he turned back to Cecilia to say, "If you want my protection, you'll have to sign here." He pointed to the pre-drawn-up agreement we used for the trials, she picked it up and read the bottom half of it out loud.

"I hereby relinquish the ability to self-govern in exchange for protection, room, and board? I will do what I am told, I will wear what I am told, I will be where I am expected. I do this of my own volition. Punishment for breaking the rules will be determined by the Black Crows," she said with an alarmed tone in her voice as she waved the paper in his face, "Who the hell would sign this?"

"My men are coming up the stairs in less than four minutes, if you want my protection, you *will* sign that before they get up here. Otherwise, I'll have them toss you out and you can con someone else out of half their life."

The look of hurt on her face from his final words gave away to the first break in her exterior shell she'd been putting up since she had gotten here.

"I'm not going to be some puppet for you to play with," she raised her chin at him, but he scoffed at her response.

"Seems like you don't really have a better option right now. You said death was waiting for you, you're a woman with one card left and you've already played it," Zerkos challenged her once again.

I could hear the seconds ticking loudly in the large gold framed clock hanging in the middle of the wall while Kane paced like a lunatic. If Ronan wasn't already so close to her, Kane would be making circles around her like some sort of wild predator. I took note of the effect she already had on both of my brothers. I couldn't tell if Mateo's opinion was clouded by the memory of how many times we had to pick our brother up from the wreckage she left behind, or if it was a result of what he was seeing right in front of him.

Kane was like a guard dog who was barely held back by his owner's leash. He felt Zerkos' pain unlike anyone else and his love for his brother showed in the way he burdened his grief, his heartache, and his sadness as if they were his own. It was why I loved him too. Mateo Kane reserved that for the most special people in his life, and I was lucky to be considered one of them.

"Oh, Jesus Christ! Sign It!" He exploded as he slammed his hand down on the table, his onyx hair falling down to his face.

Cecilia jumped with surprise, picking up the pen and signing the contract while Kane threw his head back in laughter at the reaction he earned.

Zerkos gave him a nod and Mateo casually made his way back to the couch, crossing his ankle over his knee as he sat.

The guilt was eating at me, and I sighed my disapproval, but it went unnoticed as the three sets of elevators to the penthouse opened up. Twenty of our best men crowded themselves out of the elevators into the entranceway as they waited eagerly to see the women. It wasn't about the women as much as it was about finding out which assholes we would be going up against this year.

With the two whimpering girls in the corner, it was obvious I painted the target well.

There were times where I wondered if twelve years ago, I could have stopped her from leaving and if I *should* have. My abuela always said a woman leaving in the middle of the night had more reasons than you could imagine. I didn't know what to think when I saw her putting all of the money in the kitchen and walking out of his life. I immediately woke him up, but he didn't want to chase her.

He just said that it was a long time coming and she was doing exactly as her father had warned him.

Our enforcer, Fletcher, plowed through the crowd of men standing at the large entryway as he checked in with Zerkos with nothing but a quick glance and tilt of his chin. He held the starving crowd back from the show they'd been so eagerly anticipating for months, waiting for our signal to let them through.

He was a solid enforcer and someone we considered the right hand of our operation, whatever you threw his way he got done without question, and without fail.

He was a six-foot-three mass of muscles.

An overgrown kid who was raised on the wrong side of the tracks. We gladly took him in the minute he turned eighteen. His red hair draped down his forehead in short waves he kept neatly trimmed on the sides and the back with lots of attention. Just like my brother Zerkos, you couldn't catch him in anything but an expensive tailored suit, and both the bastards made it look good.

I glanced over at Cecilia and I could see her nerves were starting to show through her façade as she fumbled with the hem of her dress anxiously. Our eyes met and there was a silent plea between us but there was nothing I could do for her now that she signed everything away on that power of attorney form.

The form was one of the last steps in the traffic trials, after Ronan melted their little minds and offered them the chance to go home, to certain death, they realized sticking with us was their best bet for safety and comfort.

She'd signed it all away without him doing anything.

She was desperate, which meant she was in a lot of trouble.

I couldn't help but wonder if this trouble was going to come crashing at our door the longer she stayed.

Ronan did a big dramatic speech like he always did every year about our power growing as a gang and the guys all went crazy for it. The look on Cecilia's face told me she wasn't even a little impressed though. I couldn't help but appreciate the fact she saw through his bullshit too.

"Get them down in the kennels, Fletch," Zerkos said, "all of them." The loud clang of the chain connecting the three blondes rang out as it clattered against the marble floor from the force of Fletcher's tug on it.

He didn't so much as make eye contact with the three half-naked blondes before making his way over to Cecilia. When he reached out for her, she slapped his hand away and I choked back a laugh, swallowing my drink.

"If you put your hands on me, you will regret it. Do you understand?" She said as if she was seven-feet tall.

Fletcher looked to Zerkos for support, but he wasn't looking at him, he was burning his gaze into her so fiercely I think she would have burst into flames if someone didn't cut in.

"She can walk down there herself man, just put a bag over her head," I broke the silence, and he nodded at me as he put the bag over each of the blondes' heads and then hers.

He gave her his arm, then said, "You're probably going to have to hold on to me then."

An audible growl came from Ronan's direction and the thumping of his blood pressure rising could practically be heard when she put both hands around Fletcher's bicep. He guided her into the elevator while dragging the parade of yellow hair behind him. The three of us entered with them while the rest of the men piled into the other two elevators.

We made our way to the floor directly below ours, but first we spent a few minutes going down and up a few levels to disorient our captives. Once the elevator opened, we made our way through the hall until we got to the apartment set aside just for the kennels.

It wasn't actually a kennel though, it was just a regular apartment, with a kitchen and a living room and everything, except the bedrooms had no walls and were closed in with metal bars, like cages. The entire walk Ronan kept his eyes focused where her hands connected with Fletcher's arms and I was just counting down the seconds before he would explode.

Surprisingly enough, he managed to keep it together through our trek.

Fletcher opened the kennel and shoved the blondes in before removing the bags from their heads as well as Cecilia's. He closed the metal door, locking them in with the automatic mechanism.

"You okay boss?" He asked Zerkos who still looked like he could have probably killed Fletcher then and there.

"They're going to need another bed. Go get one," he said to him, sending him away with a flick of his finger. "Start it up, will you Kane?" He signaled Mateo as he pulled up a metal folding chair and opened it up in front of the kennel sitting on it backwards.

Across the hall was another empty kennel of the same size but with three twin size beds in it. This kennel was as big as a standard bedroom, but there was nothing in it, just three walls lined with metal bars along with one exterior wall. The walls that were present were exposed brick, but that's because they were a fake wall we built to cover the windows that were once here.

Probably wouldn't want anyone looking in here, even if we were fourteen floors high.

Kane went inside the kennel grabbing the hose and started blasting all four of them with water until they were forcibly pressed up against the corner of the kennel trying to use each other for protection.

All except for her.

She was just standing there with her eyes fixed on Ronan as if he was the one holding the hose. I mean shit, he might as well have been.

"Just three more hours of this, ladies!" Mateo yelled out and he turned to us and said, "Go chill out man. Come back when you're ready to get busy, and your head is in it. I've got this." He reassured him and Ronan nodded.

We both got up and made our way back to the elevator.

The rest of the men were gathered in the makeshift lobby we created for the fifteenth floor where the kennels resided. They watched the show from the flat screen TV that played the live camera footage, but we didn't acknowledge them as we waited for the doors to open.

Once we were both in the elevator all it took was a glare for his composure to drop. He slouched down to the floor with his head in his hands, reminiscent of the broken boy I once had to put back together.

"What the fuck am I supposed to do?"

"I think you *weren't* supposed to turn your ex into a prisoner," I said, the disdain still obvious in my tone.

He shook his head at me, "It shouldn't have gone down like that. I didn't think she'd sign. I never knew that girl to be anyone who would buckle or break under pressure. She wasn't supposed to sign, she was supposed to fight me on it," he said without looking back up at me. "She fights me on *everything*, she signed without a second thought. What the fuck is after her?" He said exasperated at the situation, but all I could see was that Cecilia was in more trouble than we could probably imagine if she chose this willingly.

"Now what?" I asked.

"Now we keep playing the game, I need to know what she's running from, and if breaking her is the only way to get any sort of answer, I'll deal with the mess later. Whatever she's hiding from is so bad that she'd sign away her freedom to get away from it. I need to know what that is."

"She'll hate you for it," I said matter of fact.

"Good. She still has a lot to pay for."

"I won't play this game, man. Believe it or not, I don't have a beef with Cecilia, leave me out of it. Where are you going to even tell the guys she's coming from?" I asked.

"She's Mexican, just tell them she has cártel info," he said it like it would even be believable.

"The Cártel is too big for us, and the guys know it, what if one of them touches her?" I crossed my arms in question.

"Why would they do that?" He immediately stood back up and got in my face.

The elevator dinged open, but we didn't get out yet. He kept breathing hard waiting for an answer from me, like I was the one feeding her to the fishes.

"I'm not the enemy *brother*, I'm just presenting all the possible scenarios you just opened our world up to. She just signed a piece of paper that turned her into Black Crow property, *all* of the Black Crows."

Zerkos backed up and slammed his hand on the button to take the elevator back down, I followed him out, back into the kennels.

"Out!" He shouted at the entire lobby and the men scrambled to make their way out and take their post doing whatever it is the fuck they did when we weren't around.

Within a few minutes they cleared out and we turned the corner down the hallway to the kennels, where Kane was still laughing like a mad dog while he power washed the girls against the wall.

Kane chuckled at us once I unlocked the kennel door, "That didn't last very long." He said knowing full well there was no way Ronan was going to stay away from Cecilia for long.

With the hose off, the girls had a minute to catch their breaths, the three blondes huddled together for warmth in their underwear and Cecilia began lifting her drenched and now see-through white dress over the top of her head.

"What the fuck are you doing?" Ronan asked her, his eyes noticeably shifting toward the surveillance camera, and I could see the physical relief on his face that he had already sent all the guys out of the lobby where they could watch the show.

"It's *wet*. I'm *wet,*" she said, cutting the T's sharply as she threw the sopping wet dress onto the opposite corner of the kennel.

Kane whistled with no shame as her lacy black bra and matching panties were revealed, along with a body that would bring any good man to his knees. She was still not breaking eye contact with Ronan and the whistle visibly threw him over the edge as the right corner of her lip turned up into a half-smile.

"There's two hours and forty-one minutes left of the hose. If you want to go to the dry room now, come show me what you'd do for it," Zerkos announced to the room and the first blonde crawled over to him and began to paw up his pant leg.

The second blonde caught the drift and made her way over as they both started to unbuckle Ronan's pants. He chuckled loudly and lifted them up to escort them to the kennel across the hall, muttering about how this year was going to be even easier. The Japanese chick briefly looked at Cecilia then turned her face back to the wall as she decided her fate.

"So, you do the work, and he gets to fuck them?" Cecilia asked Mateo who still hadn't taken his eyes off of her.

"I don't fuck anyone who's not begging me for it," Kane said, drinking her in. "And they all beg, sweetheart."

"Oh, so you're *not* rapists?" She scoffed.

Kane turned the hose back on blasting the two of them into a pile as they were forced together by the pressure of the water.

It was physically uncomfortable for me to watch this happen to Cecilia. We had history, shared time in our shitty apartment playing video games, and drinking beers while we waited for Zerkos to come home, for nearly three years.

Ronan and I had gone to school together, we had known each other for a long time, and when Cecilia's family died, he asked me to go in with him on an apartment for the three of us. I didn't really know her then, but all the time we spent in cars together running drugs up and down the West coast for a few hundred bucks made me glad I took a chance on them those years ago.

Life was different then, everything was different then, and I was just a lost kid trying to make it out of the gang I was destined to die for some day.

Having Zerkos and Cecilia around back then was like I had created a new sense of family, one that wouldn't force me to kill kids, or make them do drugs just to keep the cycle of soldiers in line. When she left, it was like the day my parents told me not to come back unless I was ready to wear Guillermo's colors. I wouldn't be family unless I was ready to devote the rest of my life to Los Muertos.

Her leaving shattered me too, and the worst part was that I didn't have anyone to lean on because I had to be together for my brother while he mourned her.

After a few more minutes I signaled Kane to stop, and I approached her. "You should have just told him the truth, morena," I pleaded with her, even though at this point it was already too late.

She clucked her tongue and turned her chin away from me like the defiant woman I knew her to be.

"Tell me this then, are you bringing something down my door? Should I be worried?" I asked her, hoping for a grain of honesty, and finally, her eyes met mine.

"I think so," she barely breathed the words out as she hung her head in defeat.

I grabbed her by the hand and led her out of the kennel.

I opened the door to the other kennel across the hall where Zerkos sat on a bed uninterested, while the two blondes performed for his attention.

He immediately pushed them off to the floor in a sweep of his arm as he stood to his feet and crossed his arms to question me.

There was a single gray dresser in the room, and I opened the top drawer and pulled out a pair of gray sweatpants, and a white t-shirt, and threw them her way.

"A towel?" She asked, and at this point, I knew she was egging him on, and I was not only aware but entirely on board to get a rise out of my brother.

He was going to admit to me he wasn't done letting Cecilia fuck with him whether or not he wanted to. So, I walked out of the kennel without bothering to close it with Zerkos inside, a quick glance at Mateo let me know he was still at it with the Japanese girl. I grabbed a towel from the bathroom and once I made it back into the sleeping kennel, Cecilia practically ran to me to grab it and then wrapped herself in it.

"Thanks," she said looking up through her long-wet eyelashes, as she dried her body and eventually wrapped her hair in the towel.

She began to step out of her wet underwear casually like she was just home alone, but before I could even look away Ronan was already swearing under his breath and making his way over to her.

"Are you fucking kidding me?" He was so close to her that she had no choice but to lift her head up to look at him.

"You're the one who didn't give me walls, also the cameras," she pointed to the corner where the surveillance camera hung. "You're not really conveying the illusion of privacy here, so why should I try to preserve any modesty I may or may not have left? You haven't even told me how long I'll be in here." With the last word, she unhooked her bra from behind and rolled it off her arms in a single movement and then held it out in mid-air before dropping the lacy lingerie.

She stood there completely naked an arched eyebrow in challenge, she knew exactly what she was doing to him. I had to adjust myself once again otherwise I would have been showing everyone what she was doing to me too.

I could practically see the steam rolling out of his ears and in that same moment Fletcher came in directing two-foot soldiers carrying the twin size bed Zerkos just asked for.

You could almost feel the room shake when he boomed out another excessive, "Get out!"

The guys dropped the bed and turned around without question like good little low-level grunts. Ronan was so close to her he was basically pressed against her in what I could only assume was an attempt to keep the others from getting a peek at her. I glanced at Mateo, and he was all but drooling, jaw slack with his eyes on Cecilia while almost damn near water-boarding the fake blonde.

"You don't seem to have a problem with the *other* practically naked women," she pointed out, but he didn't even acknowledge her comment.

I grabbed a hoodie out of the bottom drawer and handed it to her, "Here," I said, never in my life working so damn hard to maintain eye contact and not let my gaze drift.

She turned the corner of her lip up into a half smile for me and slipped the hoodie over her head before reaching around Ronan to grab the sweat-pants off the bed, before putting them on.

The screeching of the bed that was left halfway through the door made me wince as Ronan tugged it fully into the room with one pull of his arm. He turned his back to leave.

"Maybe next time do the torturing yourself, cobarde." She spat at him, some of her fire, coming back to her.

I had to push myself out of the doorway to keep Zerkos from coming back in, and I moved him away with my hand while I closed the gate, letting the automatic lock mechanism turn.

Once again, we were shuffling through the hallways as we made our way back to the elevator in silence *again.*

Fletcher was waiting for us, but Ronan didn't acknowledge him, so I just shrugged my shoulders, and he knew well enough not to come in with us. Once the doors closed, he shoved me back into the elevator wall, "Are you fucking with me?" He eyes me down through flared nostrils.

"She had enough for now man, you said it yourself, she already signed. She's ours," I interrupted myself before he lost his shit completely, "Yours, whatever. She doesn't need to go through the same shit as the others." I said to him, "You need to get a hold of yourself, Zerkos." I softened my tone as I clapped his shoulder, "She's been here less than three hours and you're completely unraveling. Don't let the men see you like this."

The elevator opened and I walked back into our penthouse leaving my brother in the elevator to ruminate.

9

MATEO

It had only been a few days since Cecilia came to the high-rise. Ronan was coming undone little by little with each passing day. She was like a disease spreading through us, taking over him and turning him into the worst version of himself.

The problem wasn't her though, it was that he couldn't have her.

She was making Santos weak too.

He flat out told Zerkos he was out of the trials this year and wouldn't be doing any of it. Lucky for him, Ronan wasn't the type to put up a fight when we set boundaries. It was probably his best quality as a leader, he understood that if you pushed someone past a certain brink there was a risk that you would never get them back.

Our friendship was too important, and the trials aside, there was a lot more the Black Crow Brotherhood had their hands in, than vigilante human-trafficking rescues. Santos' time was probably better spent teaching the newer guys down on the third floor how to file the guns or working with our lawyer Dezmond to purchase our next real estate investment.

I personally thought his talents were best put to use figuring out which judge we were going to extort next. The law around here was crooked as hell and Santos had a knack for finding people and figuring out what they were hiding from the world. Anytime a new District Attorney or Judge was appointed to our area, it was only a matter of a few days before Santos would show up to their house with an offer they couldn't refuse.

Threats worked, but there was nothing that kept someone in power under your heel like blackmail did, and Santos was good at getting the dirt. All his years spent scuffling in the grime with Los Muertos turned him into someone we valued higher than ourselves. He was the equivalent of a Swiss Army Knife, dressed up as a gang leader.

Now Cecilia was undeniably hot as fuck, but I couldn't comprehend how someone had so much power over my brothers, and it was concerning to see them fold like paper under her weight.

But I remembered the damage, even if they didn't. I was here to help Zerkos get his revenge, and I'd keep reminding him of it too.

I walked out from my bedroom into our kitchen, lured by the smell of something delicious and buttery. My eyes landed on Santos in the kitchen flipping an omelet, and I scrunched my eyebrows at him in confusion.

"Wait, are you cooking for *her*?" I asked, and he shrugged his shoulders at me.

Santos was a damn good cook. It wasn't out of the norm for him to be cooking something up, he was basically the only one out of us who used the kitchen. The problem was that he was especially cooking a meal for one of our *prisoners.*

"So, you *aren't* going to work on breaking her, and you *are* going to cook hot meals for her. Just her. Specifically. Is that right?" I asked him, and again he just shrugged his shoulders at me.

I grunted my irritation at him, and he dropped the omelet onto the plate before setting the pan back down on the stove.

"Listen, I don't expect you to understand, but I don't need this shit. I'm not taking it from Zerkos, and I'm sure as hell not taking it from you either. Cecilia was my friend. I'm not hurting her. We're just as bad as the people we try to save the others from if we do this to her." He grabbed the plate and turned his back to me as he made his way toward the elevator.

Probably taking the bitch her food right now.

I had seen him gut men like a fish, but he had morals whispering in his ear over *this*.

His words were echoing in my mind, and I tried my best to pretend like they weren't phasing me, but I was only lying to myself. And what good did that shit do? The pressure in my head was building up again so I dragged myself back to my bedroom and opened the Cello case.

I stroked the strings with the horsehair bow until the sonata played its way out of me, but the pounding against my brain wouldn't let up as usual.

I used a bit more pressure against the strings, almost pushing a fine line of playing through my emotions and flat out abusing my instrument.

"ARGH!" I yelled, throwing the bow, and knocking the cello off to the side in anger.

I looked up to see Santos standing in the doorway and he lifted an eyebrow at me.

"Fuck off!" I shouted and he pulled up the corner of his lip into a smile and stepped across the hall into his own bedroom.

I picked up my ninety-year-old cello and silently apologized to it for my previous outburst, before putting it back into its leather casing. I reached into my nightstand for the jar of weed and the grinder and began the ritualistic process of rolling a joint. Once it was rolled, I sparked it up and opened up one of my bedroom windows. My phone almost immediately buzzed, and I looked down at it.

Zerkos: I know you're gonna go to the rooftop with that joint right?

I sent a middle finger emoji and took a drag.

I didn't know how that fucker could smell that shit from four floors down, but he could. I exhaled and immediately the medicinal properties of it started easing the high-pitched whining in my ears. My shoulders dropped as I started to relax for the first time in days. Just as I was sinking down into the chair closest to me and closing my eyes to fade away into the depths of my own mind the blaring of my phone's alarm rang out jarring my eyes open.

Every four hours, like clockwork, someone was down there. Food, bathroom, torture, sleep. That was the schedule until they broke. I had already been down there this morning for their usual wake up call, but with Santos bowing out of the game early I was stuck pulling extra shifts in the kennels. I silenced the alarm and reluctantly made my way down.

I could hear the two girls speaking to each other in their language before I even got to the kennels. Chiyo, the Chinese one, was laying facing the wall with her back to the world, while Cecilia laid on her bed. Her entire upper body was hanging off the edge, her head almost grazing the floor as her black hair draped all over the concrete.

"What are you doing?" I asked her while turning the key into the lock of the kennel door before pushing it open.

"Producing dopamine," she answered before getting herself right side up. "Being upside down makes me want to kill myself a little less."

"Well, I guess it's a good thing there's nothing in here you can hurt yourself with then." I let her know, but mentally I was scanning the room to be sure, because that was a possibility I didn't think any of us would be prepared for right now.

I sure as shit didn't want to deal with a dead chick, and Zerkos would for sure lose his mind if she off-ed herself. I pulled the string out of her hoodie completely and she shouted, "Hey!" in protest at me.

I walked over to the Russian girls, Anya and Oksana and took their hoodie strings as well for good measure, before doing the same to Chiyo. Never had this come up as an issue before but you never fucking know.

"Across the hall. Let's go. You know the drill already." I herded Cecilia over to the other kennel across from their sleeping quarters and the look she gave me was almost venomous enough to kill but I just shoved her in carelessly.

I secured her wrists to the cuffs and chains screwed into the wall so that her arms were lifted high above her head. She didn't look away from me the entire time, her eyes searching mine, but for what I wasn't sure. I didn't know what she was looking for in them, because nothing good was left in me anymore. She wouldn't find it here with me. I bent down to lock her feet into place against the wall.

"You won't break me," She spat the words out at me. "Stronger hijos de puta have not broken me; you think you can?"

There was a sinister smile painting her face and I rose up to meet her, grabbing her chin firmly between my fingers, "Either way it'll be fun to try, don't you think?"

10

CECILIA

I had no idea how long I had been locked in here now.

Maybe two weeks.

I couldn't really be sure, everything was split into a routine with short blocks. We were rewarded with food and sleep after a few hours of enduring whatever bullshit way they came up with to physically exhaust us. It didn't seem like there were any windows on this floor, at least not where I could see, so there was no sense of time.

We went back and forth between the two kennels, some days they kept us all in what they called the "torture" kennel and some days they worked on us one at a time, individually.

More than anything, I was just glad I committed to the birth control implant in my arm last year that was keeping me from having a period. This was possibly the last place on Earth I wanted to be while I was bleeding all over the place. I saw what they brought the other three during their cycles and it was dollar store commodities at best.

If I was being one hundred percent honest, that was the biggest form of torture anyone could have put me through.

It was pretty clear there was some sort of tactic there to keep us from forming any bonds with each other. Not that I had any intention of cozying up to the two Russian twats who whispered back and forth to each other all hours of the day and night.

I definitely wasn't looking for an alliance with the Chinese chick who gave me constant evil side eyes anytime she was awake. I didn't need friends here, I just needed to last long enough to convince Santos to help me get out of this country. At this point I had a feeling relying on Ronan was a waste of my efforts.

Whoever he was now was a far cry from the man I knew, and the only thing left between us was stale hatred.

They had wanted to break me, that was for certain.

What they hadn't realized was that they would have to do a lot more than just pluck away at my petals if they wanted me to wilt and die. I wasn't a flower; I was the bronze fucking cow made in the shape of God in the heat of scorching fire. I was the statuette that mere mortals kneeled for reverence in hopes of a rainy day, and I was that same rain that bathed away their sins.

I had forgotten the queen that I had been molded to become, so I would have to thank Ronan for the reminder.

It was time these fuckers dropped to their knees and worshiped.

Twice a day, Santos came in with plates of hot food for me and sandwiches for the others, and of course this only created more evil looks and animosity. I wasn't sure if he was setting me up, trying to get these girls to kill me off, or if he was honestly being kind.

Sometimes I pushed my plate in the direction of the Japanese girl, Chiyo I think was her name, but she seemed afraid to eat anything that wasn't given directly to her. There was also a good chance she didn't speak any English, but then again, the smarter move was definitely pretending you couldn't understand anyone, so who could be sure?

Half the time I didn't even touch my food, hunger just wasn't at the top of my list of things to satiate anymore. There was a sadness breaking me open, threatening the dam I had been building for the last thirty years to crumble and allow all of me to pour out through the cracks.

I was ashamed of the person I had become, a mess of lies with a fabricated past and no family left to mourn me when I was gone. Even now, I couldn't speak the words that would free me, I dug my grave too deep and there was no one strong enough to bear the weight of my bullshit that could lift me out.

Ronan came in two or three times a day as well, sometimes with Fletcher, or someone named Ethan. He would take the girls to some area where I couldn't see past the kennels for hours at a time. They always came back crying and clinging on to them like they were their only hope, and I could only imagine whatever he was doing to them was working.

I didn't know what the end goal was, but I could imagine they wanted these girls mindless and willingly.

Ronan always did his best to avoid me, even when he was stringing me up to the wall he didn't so much as look at me. He and Mateo would do their worst to get any crumb of information from me in whatever way they thought would work, but my mind wasn't some fragile thing waiting to collapse from the weight of his semi-barbaric tactics.

I knew them well because my papá taught me them.

When you were born to be queen of something that was covered in blood, violence, and money, well let's just say even your personality wasn't left up to chance. Even now at thirty, I was exactly the woman my papá had planned me to become, I just didn't have the ruthless army to back me.

Their methods were effective, just not so much on me.

You isolated someone from anything and everything – luxuries, freedom, comfort, even the ability to choose their clothes and what they ate and after enough time the person would eventually crack. This would allow for the brainwashing to start. Provide your captives with small acts of kindness or gifts and soon they would reveal all their little secrets like the rats they truly were.

My lips were sealed, and I had the scars to prove there was nothing in this world that could make me crack under any amount of pressure.

I was a fucking diamond when it came to my secrets.

Santos tip-toed his way into the kennel, softly shutting the barred doors so that they didn't make a sound. His quiet efforts weren't wasted when my cellmates didn't stir from their naps at his entrance. I sat myself up on the bed and smiled at him, the incredible smell of the torta hit me before he pulled the plate from behind his back returning an over-exaggerated smile that was all teeth.

He sat on the edge of my bed and offered me the plate, raising an eyebrow at me in curiosity to see if I would take it.

I reached for it like a starved animal and let out an unrestrained moan when I took that first bite, letting the delicious flavors combine and roll across my tongue before I chewed and swallowed.

"I wish you'd eat everything I brought that way," he said with amusement in his voice.

"You sound like an abuela," I joked, "Keep bringing me my favorite foods and I might take you up on that."

"It only took me a couple weeks to remember your favorite, not bad right?" He confirmed how long I had been their captive, while raising his chin proudly at his own accomplishment and I couldn't help but laugh at his ability to soften every difficult moment.

"Thank you," I said gently as I reached for his hand and squeezed it.

Maybe he knew what he was doing, or maybe it was the guilt eating at him for being a part of this, but Santos was the only thing that kept me feeling human most of the time in this cage.

Santos was nearly as tall as Ronan these days, but he was leaner, and his light brown skin matched the color of his curly chestnut hair that grew wildly out of his head. His hazel eyes were full of a sadness that reminded me of my own, it was the only part of him that gave away the joyful, carefree mask he kept putting on.

That was my favorite part about him though, there was a tragedy buried so deep inside of Santos that the only way he knew how to heal it was to keep others from feeling it too. His easy-going façade was how he coped with his mistakes, and amusingly enough it was completely polar to my cold-bitch exterior I had to use for the same purposes.

"Do you remember that time we almost got caught with all that ecstasy?" He asked me with a mischievous smile on his face.

I couldn't fight back the grin as I recollected the memory of some of the best times in my life.

"The time where you hotwired that McLaren and we drove it off the pier, or the time where I had to bribe the cop?" I asked him, raising an eyebrow as I remembered too many occasions where we got caught, but we always had a way out of it.

He let out a roar of laughter and squeezed my hand, "No! The time where we ran into that strip club while the cops chased us, and you got on stage and started dancing. The owners didn't even care that you didn't work there!"

"I made two hundred dollars during that dance too!" I laughed with him until my sides hurt and we remembered some of our favorite jobs gone wrong.

There were so many times we should have ended up in prison or dead, but yet here we were despite the stupid mistakes we made as kids. He let go of my hand with an awkward air about him, and used it to scratch his head before he reached into his pocket and pulled out a chocolate bar.

He shook it in front of me and my eyes widened as I reached for it, but he pulled it back and shook his finger at me in a teasing way. He put his index finger to his lips to signal me to be quiet and turned his back to the camera completely while he unwrapped it and slid it over to me.

I all but choked on my food laughing at his ridiculous attempt to sneak me a treat, in these insane conditions. It was absolutely outrageous, considering the circumstance but it was also probably one of the sweetest gestures I had seen from Santos.

I happily ate my chocolate in secrecy and handed him the wrapper when I was done, giving him the sincerest smile I had probably given anyone in ages.

You want to push someone to the edge of a mental breakdown?

Deprive them of chocolate.

Santos left just as covertly as he entered, and I was once again reminded of the destitute situation I put myself in when I realized I forgot to ask for a bathroom break.

The days kept ticking away painfully slow, like watching the dripping of pitch before it was shattered with a hammer. It was always the CLANG-CLANG of the metal rod Mateo beat against the metal bars that woke me up from the illusion of a night's sleep. Out of the three of them, he was the morning guy. He was the only one who was ever awake early enough to come down here after the longest sleep ended.

That was the only way I knew the time. I couldn't call it night anymore, there was no essence of time down here, and the lights were always on.

The slamming metal rang out loudly to announce his presence and the three girls rose to their feet on his command, "Just her today ladies, take a seat," he said, waving them down and they all dropped to their respective beds like dogs waiting for a bone.

Mateo's visits were always unpredictable, there was a wildness to him that I couldn't understand.

He was full of uncontrollable impulses, but there was a softness to him that I could see was trying to break through the surface. He put on a show of indifference, but I could see there was a deeper pain fighting against his currents. I had known that he enlisted with Ronan in the Navy, and if I were to put my money on anything, I'd say that maybe he didn't come home completely whole.

His torture sessions were pretty mild though, it almost seemed like a test instead of punishment when he was the one calling the shots. It was like he wanted to see how much I could endure, instead of hoping that I would break. The last time, Fletcher blindfolded me before they came to get me out of the room but it didn't matter that I couldn't see.

I could already smell the difference between Mateo's trademark pine and leather scent, to the peppery cedar of Ronan's Bleu de Chanel. What I did know for certain was that Santos never came down here with them, because Santos smelled like gunpowder and smoke. Like his hands were either busy shooting a weapon or holding a lit cigarette.

It had been Mateo's heady pine scent that engulfed my senses, almost invading my throat.

He chained me to the wall and sprayed me down as usual before pulling out what I could only have assumed was a defibrillator before pressing them to the wet soles of my feet. I'd tolerated plenty of pain in my life, and that shit fucking hurt, but I still knew there was no way it was turned up enough to even jump start a heart, let alone leave a mark.

My torture standards were apparently much higher than theirs, but I played along. I would let out a scream or two and earn their pity and get my ass back on that dry cot again.

Today was a new day, and I was somehow always intrigued to see what they could come up with as they tried to force me to crack. He unlocked the kennel door and with a single finger he beckoned me over.

"You're a tough cookie to crack sunshine," he said, forcing a bubble of laughter out of me.

"Sunshine? What part of my personality made you think that was an appropriate nickname?" I challenged him with a laugh.

"It's not your personality," he said as he looked me up and down shamelessly, even though I was wearing the same gray sweatpants and white t-shirt the others were in. "Your skin reminds me of sunshine," he said tilting his chin up to the ceiling, the smile on his lip fading as he looked up and didn't find the Sun.

To say Mateo Kane was attractive was an understatement, to be honest I didn't know what factory they were building these guys in, but they perfected them. He wasn't as tall as Ronan, and where Ronan's dark blonde hair constantly fell to his eyes, Mateo's was an inky black that he kept perfectly slicked back with shine.

His skin was a beautiful light olive hue that complimented the rest of his features like his strong jaw and his long nose. His full eyebrows suited him and made his eyes burn with a deeper intensity than I thought was possible. In another life, I would have daydreamed of him and let my fantasies carry me away, but these bars were a constant reminder of my reality and who put me here.

The truth was it had been even longer since I thought about being with a man let alone acted on those urges. I'd been una muerta for so long, and dead women didn't need sex.

I had a pretty good success rate with my own hands, probably six out of ten times if we were calculating for data purposes. Sometimes the anxiety would keep me from getting out of my own head and I could never reach that sweet spot, eventually, I would just give up, wipe my fingers, and go to sleep.

Not here in this prison though, not with three roommates just a few feet away. It had been so long at this point that the only material I had was when Ronan made me come on that first day I stupidly came here. I shuddered the memory away and clenched my thighs together.

Such a stupid bitch.

I decided to try and regain some sort of control over my situation, and I offered up a half-smile at his attempt at a compliment. He returned the same with a dimpled cheek and I all but stumbled over my own knees from it.

Fuck. Are they doing this to me?

Panic fluttered through my belly and as Mateo closed the door to the kennels behind us.

I hit him with the side of my hand in the throat.

I made a run for the direction I thought the entrance was but before I could even get to what looks like a hotel lobby, I was struck by an arm in the chest that sent me flying back and gasping for the wind that was knocked out from inside of me. The cool of the concrete almost burned my back from the friction of being pulled as someone dragged me by the ankle, taking me back to where I just came from.

I heard a laugh, "This one is extra feisty, you okay boss?" came from Fletcher.

I made a mental note to remember to pay him back for that one eventually.

"Fuck," Mateo rasped as he stood over me clutching his throat. "You've got a lot of spice to you sunshine. I'm not going to take pleasure in washing out some of your flavor." He chuckled darkly and took my ankle from Fletcher as he started dragging me past the kennels.

"Where are you taking me?" I yelled at him as I realized we weren't going to either kennel, and fear began to take hold of me.

I was thrashing as he dragged me along the floor down the hall to where two doors stood side by side.

"This isn't a punishment for that stunt you just pulled. Just so you know," he croaked at me, but I was too busy trying to hide my panic from surfacing.

"What do you care what I think?" I spat at him, and he lowered down and squeezed my cheeks in forcing my mouth to part.

"Because if I was the one ruining you, I'd go about it in different ways," he threw my head to the side with one hand as he let go, while sliding his other hand against my pussy through my sweatpants, leaving my mouth parted in shock.

He pulled away just as quickly and cleared his throat before continuing.

"One of these were made especially for you." He knocked on one of the doors, "The other...has always been here, it's where *they* go," he said as he pointed his chin in the direction of the kennels.

"Which one do you think you want?" He looked down at me as he asked me with actual sincerity and for a moment, I actually believed him when he said this wasn't a punishment he was doling out.

There was nothing but softness in his eyes.

"Neither?" I asked, my breathing heavy and labored as my ability to hide my panic was deteriorating the more, I tried to imagine what was behind each door.

I thought about how mindless, and desperate for Ronan those women looked when they would come out of here and I narrowed my eyes in anger, realizing I didn't want anything that was meant for them.

He shook his head at me, "I told you, I don't want to wash out your flavor, but I have to." He reached down as if to touch me but pulled back.

"Because he's making you?" I asked him, peeling my upper lip back at his dog-like behavior, and his jaw ticked – clearly catching what I was implying.

"Because you signed," he said, crouching down brushing the hair out of my eyes, and my anger was redirected at him when I remembered the only reason I signed was him.

He was pacing around me like a lunatic, making me overly anxious at that moment. I couldn't have passed a clear thought in my mind with everything that was going on in that room. The way my heart annoyingly thumped so loudly, and the berating tiks of the clock that hung on the wall. His energy was too erratic, too demanding, and the minute he slammed his hands against the table, I lost my footing, my control over the situation.

"I signed because of you," I said dryly and he tsk-ed at me, his thumb brushing down the side of my face until my chin was between his thumb and forefinger.

"No, you signed because of you," he said in his quirky playful tone, but I knew he was telling a closer truth than I was.

I'd been basically walking around with explosives strapped to my own chest for as long as I could remember because I didn't have anything else to lose anymore, I hadn't for a while.

"I'm letting you choose," he barely whispered it as if it was the greatest kindness he could offer me.

"The one for me?" I asked, unsure of myself.

He took a long look at the door and turned back to me to say, "I think that was the wrong choice, sunshine." He mourned as he opened the door to the left and pushed me inside with one motion before shutting the door on me and surrounding me in pitch black darkness.

I could barely hear the muffled sound of his voice and I could only assume I was in some soundproof box because it was mostly vibrations and not words, I could make out. Before I even had time to piece together any thoughts, I was overwhelmed by the deafening sound of what seemed like hundreds of guns going off at the same time.

Panic gripped me and I was thrown back to that moment half a lifetime ago where everything changed, and I realized as I tried to get up and move that I wasn't sure I was in a room at all. The walls and the ceiling, it was all right above me, right behind me and in front of me. It felt like I was inside a fucking coffin.

I was in a fucking coffin.

What the fuck!

I slapped the padded walls surrounding me as I screamed and begged Mateo to let me out, but the temperature started to rise inside. My head was completely spinning as the guns continued to go off over and over again without a second of silence in between to let me relax.

The one person I loved more than anything in this world created a chamber to echo my trauma and my losses. I took a long breath and channeled a deep place inside of myself where all that was left were my papá's wisdom, and his calculated rage.

11

MATEO

I didn't actually have a damn clue what was going on in that closet, aside from Álvarez being too pissed off to even look at Zerkos for the last two days since he finished building it, and mentioned putting her in there. Except for the non-stop pounding ache in my head that only quieted with music, it was completely silent down here.

I figured if it was really so bad in there, I would be able to hear something about it, but she wasn't even shouting or banging on the door.

I sat there for three hours like I had been told to. It wasn't until I opened the door to the room and the heat poured out of it along with the blaring sound of gunshots, that I realized the bastard put her in a soundproof box inside of the closet. She was sitting there with her eyes open; a dry stream of tears marked her face as she tiredly rested her elbows on her knees and clutched her ears with her hands.

She had the most vacant expression on her face, one I recognized from my own nightmares, and there was nothing I could do to stop myself from picking her up and cradling her in my lap as she wept. I wanted to tell her it wasn't me. I don't know why but I needed her to know that her misery was not my doing, that I didn't know what was happening in there.

It seemed pointless though and I couldn't find a way to will the words out.

Once her tears stopped and her breathing became shallower, I took an ear bud out of my pocket and placed it inside of her ears. I thumbed my playlist with one hand and turned on my favorite classical playlist.

She gazed into my eyes for the entirety of the song, feeling every heartbreaking pull of the cello string through as she exhaled into me.

We sat there on the floor for longer than I planned, though it only felt like a blink of an eye. I secretly dreaded the minute reality would take me away from this moment. I lazily ran my fingers through her hair, it smelled like coconut, though I wasn't sure how because there was definitely no coconut shampoo, it was just dial soap we let them use every few days.

I made a mental note to get some coconut shampoo for her, never wanting this scent to fade away.

I eventually decided to stand, picking her up and carrying her back into the kennel and she laced her hands behind my neck. I sat down on her bed to put her down but as I went to get up, she tightened her hold on me, and I understood her silent plea to stay.

This was so completely fucked, there was no way that asshole was going to make me put her through this again, if he wanted to torture his ex-girlfriend, he could come clean up after himself too. I mean, I understood his pain, I made it my own for so long. When she first showed up, I was excited to see my brother get a taste of revenge. She wasn't some Yakuza or Bratva bitch who was going to lead us to the big fish though.

It was too personal, too close to home and Ronan fucked us all when he brought her in here.

It had been over a month now since we locked her up and all I could see was a chick who was tougher than nails and refused to break for him. Every time I looked into her nightshade-colored eyes; I could see her hatred for him growing tenfold with every new thing he put her through in his mission to get answers from her.

I had my own questions too, they were burning inside of me as I shoved them down day in and day out. I wanted to know everything about her, what created a woman like this? Out of what ashes did she emerge from that stoked the inextinguishable flame in her eyes? That look of revenge that could never be satiated, a bloodlust that couldn't be fulfilled.

I wanted to know what kind of music played through her head when she was all alone.

Did someone like her even care about music?

What were her favorite things?

I realized I wanted to know everything I could about what made her tick. What made her, *her.* In that same train of thought I realized I was fucked beyond return now, and it was just a matter of time before Ronan killed me just for looking at her.

I sat next to her while she rested her head against my shoulder for the better part of an hour until she fell asleep and I stood up to make my way out of the kennel without paying any mind to the other occupants. I didn't need to lock it behind me, the doors had an automatic lock once they closed shut.

Before I arrived in the lobby, I heard Ronan calling my way.

"All good?" He asked nonchalantly with his arms folded behind his head casually, though I knew he had likely been watching me through the surveillance for the last hour.

"No. Not all good. Fucking asshole," I muttered the last part as I stormed out of the room to try to avoid giving him an actual piece of my mind.

Before I could make it to the elevator, he was cutting me off and blocking me with his arm.

"You want to tell me what happened over there?" He raised his eyebrow at me, but I shook my head at him.

"You don't get to play jealous boyfriend while you're making me torture her." I pushed his arm off the wall and entered the elevator.

He didn't follow me in, so I closed the door and pressed the button to go back up to the penthouse. When I walked in, Álvarez was in his usual position sitting on the couch with a drink in his hand staring off at the wall.

"He's crossed a line," I said to him.

He just rolled his eyes at me and raised his glass, "I've been saying that for five weeks now man, welcome aboard the S.S. Sanity."

"I don't even think we're working the others right this year. Everything feels off with her here. His attention is everywhere but where it needs to be." I said and Álvarez nodded quietly as he opened up the laptop on the coffee table in front of him.

He pulled up the live feed for the kennel's surveillance which showed her there, exactly as I left her, with her eyes closed and holding on to the smallest granule of peace she was offered.

"Last year they had all broken at this point, remember we joked that he should go work for the CIA with how fast he made work of the Irish and the Odessa?" Santos asked without lifting his eyes from the screen, and I grunted my agreement at him.

"Something bad is gonna happen, man, I can feel it." He lifted his gaze up to me and I could see the concern in my brother's features.

Even though I knew it was his superstitious Mexican bullshit tugging at his thoughts, there was more to it than just bad juju floating around.

Everything was wrong this year.

"We'll sort it out together," I promised him.

"There's no together if Ronan is on this revenge mission. He's gonna destroy her, and then he's gonna destroy himself. He'll take us all down with him." He warned and worry began to fill me from the inside at the idea that it might be true.

All I knew was the life I worked so hard to build with my brothers, without them I was a nobody, with nothing. We may have been kings in the hill we conquered for ourselves but at the end of the day we were all just shadows of the little boys we used to be. We sat on a throne out of the skeletons from our past hoping we could muffle out their cries and screams.

Santos was always just barely drowning in regret from all the things he did in Los Muertos, all the lives he was forced to take that were innocent to their war as he fought to make his way out of something you can only understand if you were born into it.

I thought about my little sister, Andrea and sorrow permeated through me as my mind froze on the image of her lifeless body in her bedroom. I tried to clear it from my head, but I couldn't, I knew I would have to smoke tonight to clear the memory long-term as my heart held on to the feeling of failure.

That feeling was why I agreed to do these trials to begin with, to save a few innocent girls where we could, even if it wasn't in the nicest way possible, a little brainwashing for a couple of weeks and a few months from now they would all be free to live their lives exactly how they wanted, this was a future that wasn't possible if they'd stayed locked up and sold by the gangs who previously owned them.

With Cecilia, there was no justification though, what I saw today didn't have a higher meaning or purpose. What would happen once she gave him the information he was looking for? Would she be free to live her life a few months from now? Would Zerkos ever let her leave? How far would his punishment go? There were so many unknowns and the biggest one that swirled through my mind were the words she spoke to me today.

Because he's making you?

I trusted Ronan with my life, he'd saved it enough times in the twelve years we spent inseparable, and he'd never led me wrong. Something inside me knew this wasn't right and the memory of my little sister was haunting me to make better choices.

"I'll tell him I won't work her anymore." I finally said out loud, "If he wants to keep breaking her, he's going to have to do it himself. I'm not going to be responsible for this."

Santos clapped me on the shoulder like he was proud of my decision and nodded his head in approval. I knew he could see what was haunting me, but he never pushed and I never wanted to talk.

"He's so wrapped up in his revenge and what he lost that he doesn't see the truth. And he won't until it's too late," he said to me.

"And what is that?" I asked.

"She's protecting him from something. I think she always was," he said, and his words brought clarity to my mind that opened my eyes to a possibility I had never even considered.

"That's why she didn't steal the money when she left," I said as I pieced together the pieces of the puzzle I knew, and he nodded at me.

"All he is doing is pushing her away, and she gets further and further from trusting us enough to tell us the truth. If you want my opinion, this is going to blow up all over us." He no sooner said, and the elevator dinged.

I sucked in a big breath in anticipation as I waited for Ronan to make his way in. He looked at us both on the couch watching the surveillance and raised both eyebrows at us. "Say what you need to say, you've clearly been talking." He crossed his arms over his chest as he waited for us to berate him.

"There's nothing to say man, you made up your mind about her..." Santos said.

I cut him off to announce my piece, "I won't work her anymore."

Ronan's eyes opened in alarm at my proclamation.

"Is that so?" he asked me, turning his head like a confused dog.

"Yeah asshole, that was fucked up. If you want to torture her, do it yourself. I don't need one more thing keeping me up at night," his demeanor changed with my last remark as he softened from my words.

He sat down on the white leather chair opposite the couch as he slumped his shoulders.

"I get it," he said, and even though I was kind of taken aback by his understanding, I wasn't completely surprised. He knew what kept me awake in the dark of the night, and he wouldn't fight me on this.

"It wasn't supposed to be like this. None of it was. I don't know what it was supposed to be like, because I lost that a long time ago. But having her here, in our home, all of the time. She's under my skin. She's in my head. Always laughing at me for pulling one over on me when she got the opportunity. And every time I give her the chance to tell me the truth, she reels back farther from it like *I'm* the one who deserves to be punished," he said scratching the side of his head in anxiety and in that moment, I felt for my brother again.

He too was just a lost little boy whose heart was broken by the only real thing he ever had.

I rubbed my temples to ease the pressure building up again, and Santos looked at me with concern, but I shrugged him off.

"It's like watching a wolf with the moon," Santos said to our brother, looking up from the monitor once again. "You lose your fucking mind over her, obsessing non-stop, all day. But if you had her, *really* had her again, and not just locked up downstairs. You'd probably go full lunatic."

Ronan shook his head as he drowned in his self-created misery, and said, "I'm gonna go work out. Call me if you need me." He headed to his room and came out almost instantly holding his gym bag.

"Is that all you do now?" I asked, pushing to get a rise out of him.

He spent most of his time in our gym now, either lifting weights or beating the shit out of the lower-level grunts in the fighting ring. The guy was getting bigger than I even thought was possible for him.

"If I don't take it out somewhere, I'll take it out on her and..."

"You *don't* want to do that?" Álvarez interrupted him, scoffing at our brother's selective methods of cruelty.

"Fuck you," he swung his bag over his shoulder hitting Santos in the head as he made his way out to the elevator.

The gym was on the fourth floor so he wasn't going far, we kept it tight around here so that we wouldn't have to leave the security of the high-rise for a lot of things we needed to do on a daily basis. It was important that we stayed in the high-rise unless we were doing business that required us to leave. It wasn't something we required out of all of our men, but as the ones making the decisions it was necessary for us to not only stick around, but to stay behind to protect our people.

The entire next week got away from me, and most of the next. I spent most days waiting for the alarm to go off on my phone so I could find a reason to be down there with the siren that was taking up all the space in my painful head.

Ronan took Cecilia to her special "room" at least once a day for a few hours at a time. She was getting visibly skinnier now because she barely ate her food, even though Álvarez was cooking her every possible meal if he wasn't sneaking her all the best take-out spots from Cove City.

Ronan rarely stuck around after her sessions in the soundproof chamber were over, always itching to avoid the always present conflict between the two of them.

I walked past the kennels and found him opening the door and pulling her out, but she was so different from the first time I pulled her out of the box. It was as if this had been hardening her instead of breaking her like he planned, and my admiration for her grew because she was a soldier just like me.

He nodded my way as he acknowledged my arrival, I shot my hand out to catch the keys as he tossed them at me and shouted back, "I gotta go pick up some things for tonight."

I nodded back as I walked closer to the one thing that had been running through my mind all week no matter how hard I tried pushing any thoughts of her away. I stuck my hand out at her and tipped my chin in the other direction to signal her to take my hand and follow me.

12

CECILIA

Over the weeks I had grown to feel a mild form of safety around Mateo and Santos.

Well, as safe as someone who was constantly trying to stay aware enough to not lose their mind, could feel. Santos only came around to bring me food, while sometimes begging me to just end this and tell Ronan everything.

At this point we all but played Pictionary to decipher my "big secret" but I still appreciated his company to that of my cell mates.

They were about as exciting as wet cardboard.

The first time I came out of that box I decided I would never breathe the truth from my lips while my heart was still pumping blood. My contempt for Ronan had grown so deeply, I hoped to God my uncle would find me. That they would both end each other and rid me of all of my problems in one fell swoop. It was the practical and efficient end-all if you asked me.

I didn't sleep much now either, I sure as shit couldn't let my guard down around the two whispering girls. They scared the hell out of me, and I wasn't sure if I wanted to know what the Black Crows were doing with them here. The Bratvas had a lot of power.

Too much for the Black Crows to handle.

Mateo came down once a day sometimes, and just sat next to me, letting me lean my head on his shoulder until I fell asleep. He never actually said more than a word or two, he mostly just played classical music on his phone. He was always gone when I woke up of course, but I was grateful for the moments of calm I was given around him.

I looked into his inky black eyes, and he extended his hand to me. I took it willingly as he led me past the kennels, through a living room, into a bathroom where a barstool was placed in front of the sink. I looked at him with confusion, unsure of what was about to happen.

"Sit," he said, tilting his head toward the stool.

I sat on the chair with my back to the sink and he lifted my hair up off my shoulders and placed a towel over them as he brought my head into his hands. I heard the sound of the faucet and I flinched before feeling the warmth of the water touching my head and relaxing from the wonderful sensation. We got showers maybe once every three or four days and the shower didn't get close to warm.

To say that I was in heaven was an understatement.

Then he poured the shampoo into my hair and began to work his fingers through my scalp, lathering it with the delicious coconut smelling suds. I fought back but my body betrayed me, the tear escaped me before I could will it away and I just hoped that he hadn't noticed how weak I had already become.

It was such an insignificant act of kindness bringing me to my knees.

I still knew the game being playedI still knew its rules.

I couldn't pretend like I didn't want to cling on to any small amount of good I could find here though. I was already crumbling. He rinsed the shampoo out of my hair delicately and I didn't know why, but my mouth began to work on autopilot. It was like something inside me just needed to get the words out, just so maybe someone else would know why I was hurting so much.

"My family home burned down when I was eight," I said, barely a whisper out of my mouth and his fingers came to a slow motion as he listened.

"My parents practically threw my sister and I out of our bedroom window to save our lives, the room was already on fire by the time I woke up to falling on the lawn." He cleared his throat and continued to work his fingers through my hair diligently. He squirted another tube into his hand and coated my hair in the conditioner before I spoke again.

"When I was fifteen most of my family was killed in a drive-by shooting. I was locked in a closet for over twenty minutes after I had been shot, while car after car took out the rest of my family." My eyes looked up at him to find his black eyes piercing through me as he started piecing together just how cruel his brother could be.

"I found my *mamá* dead in her bed after I had been living with Ronan for almost three years. That's when I left."

He rinsed the product from my hair and shut the water off before he squeezed the water out of my hair and began to wrap the towel around my head.

"So, what? You're a magnet for accidents, and you left to keep him safe, sunshine?" He asked, and I shook my head at him.

"They weren't accidents," I whispered and reached up for the towel, our fingers grazed just slightly as he let go.

I sat back up, pulling it off and letting the cascade of wet hairs drench my clothes. The distance between us was almost fictional, just fractions from touching. My chest was heaving with my breathing as his fingers grazed my jaw, then he lifted my chin up to look at him.

"Will you tell *me?*" he asked, but I shook my head instinctively.

I tried to look back down but he didn't let me and his grip on my jaw tightened just slightly.

"What will it take?" he growled the words out in question.

"I don't know," I answered, some semblance of the truth willed its way out of me, "I've locked it away too tight."

He huffed a breath out that was full of frustration, but I could see in his eyes that there was understanding there too. He released my chin and tucked a strand of wet hair out of my face behind my ear.

"What if we trade secrets?" he hummed in my ear.

"You keep secrets from Ronan?" I raised my eyebrows in question at him.

If they were keeping secrets from each other, then soon there would be cracks in their little operation. The thought alone made me want to smile at the idea.

He didn't dismiss my question surprisingly, and instead leaned impossibly close to me, and whispered into my ear, "I could think of a few off the top of my head."

Obsidian eyes and that dimple, once again turned my insides into butter before I could help myself and I was squeezing my thighs together to keep myself in check.

Down girl.

"You go first," I urged him on.

"No, that's not how this works," his tone was gentle, but his words were decisive, he was in control of how this was going to play out and he knew it.

"I didn't steal the guns from Ronan, not really. I didn't sell them either."

He stared at me with a curious look on his face.

"What did you do with them then?" He asked me but I clucked my tongue and shook my head at him.

"That's another secret, for another time, and you owe me one already. Pay up." He just threw his hands up and shrugged at me making me realize I had been gotten.

It was hard not to feel angry, even though Mateo had no allegiance to me.

Every time I started thinking he might be a good guy, or that he may just be in my corner for a split second, he would betray me again and shatter the tiniest piece of trust we had built. Like the first time he threw me in that box, and then acted like it pained him to see me after it was over.

It was my own fault though, there were no good guys left, especially in the places I was searching. His erratic behavior still frustrated the hell out of me, and I couldn't tell if it was just a game he played, or if he was just surviving too.

Sometimes I wondered if it was a defense mechanism, to keep people at bay.

Maybe Mateo Kane might have been just as fucked up as I was.

"How long have you been waiting to let that go?" He was so close I could feel the hotness of his breath on my neck, and smell the trademark scent of his leather jacket mixed with pine from his cologne.

His thumb was smoothing down my jaw again making goosebumps appear all over my flesh. I shook my head slowly, refusing to allow him to have any more of me but we were standing so close that our lips grazed, almost electrifying me from the contact.

"We need you to play the part tonight," he said, pulling away and clearing his throat as he cut through some of the fog in the room that felt like a hypnosis, breaking whatever spell he had me under.

"The part?" I questioned, unsure what he was trying to ask of me.

"The others are ready, but I can see through you, nothing that's happened in the last two months has changed you," he said, narrowing his eyes at me like he was unaffected by my vacant expressions and the mask of a broken woman I had been putting on each day.

Two months.

Shit.

I couldn't believe I'd allowed that much time to slip away from me unnoticed.

"And?" I questioned again, not letting my surprise show.

He squinted his eyes like he was in pain and pressed his thumb to one side of his temple before he spoke.

"While I find your resolve incredibly attractive, Ronan needs you broken. Everything will go a lot easier if you play along," he said, half warning, half pleading for me to make the right call.

"And if I don't?" The monster part of me that never backed down reared its ugly head out, mentally slipping on her boxing gloves.

"I'd hate to see him create a worse punishment for you sunshine. Don't speak, do as you're told, and be the trophy we need you to be tonight. Can you do that?" His voice was so soft and his tone so gentle that I was nodding in agreement before I could think twice about what I was agreeing to.

"It's been two months?" I asked him, unable to hide my surprise as I realized how differently time moved when you had absolutely nothing to live for.

"It's been nine weeks," he corrected me, clasping his hand around mine and leading me back to the kennel where the door gaped wide, and the rest of its occupants were gone.

He paid no attention to that as he grabbed the burlap sack on the dresser that I wore on my way down here weeks ago. He placed it on my head, and I instinctively reached out to him grasping his arm with both hands to keep me steady as he navigated me through the halls to the elevators.

After going up and down a few times we finally reached the penthouse again and he removed the sack from my head as the elevator opened up. The place was immaculately cleaned, and the black marble floors shone brighter than the last time I was here with its gold speckles glimmering from the sunlight that poured through the windows.

There were additional wet bars placed throughout the grand living area and more couches and chairs than I recalled the last time. He led me through the room into the hallway where it was divided into three openings. We took the entrance to the left through a door which I could only assume was his bedroom.

It was half the size of the living room, but it was still unnecessarily big, with a large king size bed in the middle neatly made with black satin sheets.

There were two white boxes on the bed along with a small black bag. Another brown bag rested against the box with the LV logo on it and I raised my eyebrows at him in a silent question.

"You can get ready in the bathroom," he said pointing to the En-suite, as he sat on the edge of the bed and rubbed his temple.

I sighed as the nerves started to creep their way inside me as the unexpected floated its head above the water once again and I was forced to drown in the mess I created for myself. I grabbed the bags and the larger box and stepped into the largest bathroom I had been in, since my tía's house in Ocean Valley.

I ran my fingers over the gold details on the clawfoot matte black tub in the center of the room and lazily made my way to the mirror and took a look at myself for the first time in months. Still the same old uptight bastard's eyes haunting me, mocking me for being too weak and letting the pussy in between my legs dictate whether or not I was fit to be his heir.

I opened the bag and found a few bare essentials that would help cover the illusion of a captive and painted my eyes thick with eyeliner and black eyeshadow. There was a tube of mascara, and a few colors of lipstick to choose from and I had to question who did the shopping because there was no way Ronan or Santos picked out black lipstick.

I felt the corners of my lips turn up as I decided to wear black as my armor for the night and coated my lips in the war paint before opening the white box with Versace printed on it. I huffed in annoyance at the unnecessary display of money and wondered if the others would be wearing designer dresses tonight as well.

Lacy black underwear was folded delicately in the brown bag, but even my annoyance was tamed by the contents of what was inside the box, because it was a masterpiece. The dress - no, the *gown,* was one of the most beautiful things I'd ever seen in my life. It was something I would have imagined seeing my mamá wear at a party when Papá was in the mood to show her off, back when we still lived in México.

The straps were barely there and had no purpose at all as they fell down my shoulders, the sweetheart cut of the neckline hugged my breasts and accentuated the curve of my waist and the flare of my hips. There was a slit on the side that ran up high on my thighs as it fell all the way down to my feet along the small trail of a train.

Not terrible.

I took one last look at myself in the mirror, seeing less of my papá and a bit more of the woman who created me instead, unsure who I felt had betrayed me more. As I contemplated which of my parents let me down most, I remembered the biggest victim was Carolina, my sister. I gripped the edges of the sink as I forced back the pools of tears challenging to fall and I bit my cheek until I felt the sting, tasting the metallic liquid in my mouth.

I walked out of the room and Mateo whistled a long exhale as he took me in from head to toe.

"Bellissima," he said in a low hushed voice as he admired me from his place on the edge of the bed.

I arched an eyebrow and wondered if there was more Italian where that came from.

Before I could voice my thoughts, he opened the other box, pulled out a pair of red-bottomed black heels, and held them on the edges of his fingers tips for me to take. He had changed as well and was wearing pristinely tailored suit pants with the tie draped across his neck undone. His hair still required grooming and fell over his eyes like he needed a haircut, and I wondered if he didn't care to keep his hair "just so" and did whatever he pleased with it. Maybe he only cut it when the mood would strike him.

Ronan had the same appointment, I bet even now, every three weeks to keep his hair exactly the same and I smirked to myself as I appreciated their differences. Where Ronan was fire, consuming everything in his path - whether in passion, hatred or anguish - Mateo was an ocean waiting to pull me under until all that was left was waves upon waves of his current washing through me, slowly cleansing me of everything I once thought I was.

I couldn't deny that I didn't just appreciate his company, but I craved it.

Though part of me knew I *had* been broken, and that they *did* get into my head, I wanted to believe that every small intimate moment between us had been ours and ours alone. I glanced around the room a bit and curiosity peaked at the sight of the black grand piano next to the window, was it decoration? An heirloom? Did he play? I let my eyes wander around the room and noticed a few other instruments in their selective cases, and a few guitars hanging up on the wall.

"You look fucking edible," he stood, pulling me close, hooking an arm behind me and pressing his erection against me. "Be good." He whispered, reaching for my hand, "and I promise I'll try to make it better." His grazed his nose behind my ear, his fingers tracing over my black-painted lips, goosebumps running along my entire body from his touch.

A whimper betrayed me, his mischievous grin showing itself before he pulled away. Guiding me by the hand, Mateo led us back into the main room, where a few caterers were setting up and bartenders were getting their things ready. Close to the balcony a makeshift dance floor was set up and a DJ readied his table for the night as he talked to Santos.

His eyes widened in recognition from across the room, ending the conversation and making his way over to us in a few, quick, strides.

"Morena, phew," he whistled, his reaction forcing my cheeks to heat from the attention.

Wrapping his arms around me, he placed an exaggerated kiss on my cheek that though felt platonic, no different than any of the others throughout the years, but still somehow seemed like it was meant more to warn Mateo off, than to greet me.

It was an odd display that had me fighting back an ear-to-ear smile.

"That's what I said." The deep rumble of Mateo's voice cut through the moment, my pulse quickening at the overwhelm of both of them so close to me. "Without the kiss," he added dryly, his point loud and clear.

If Mateo was the ocean, Santos was the air. Everything about him was so light and free, and filled me with life like a lungful of the purest oxygen. Even when the past tried to weigh him down, he could rise above it. Laughing around him felt effortless, even in this own private little hell they had created.

He wore dark navy dress pants with a button-down shirt that was a darker shade of the same color. The bandana sticking out of his back pocket still gave his roots away. If I didn't know he was a ruthless syndicate leader I would have assumed he was dressed for business. His curls bounced in front of his eyes with the slightest movement of his head, his smile stretching from ear to ear.

"Could I have tequila? Please?" I asked him sweetly, wondering how far my freedom would go tonight.

If they were going to give me an inch, I would take a few fucking miles.

"Why not?" Santos said as if he could read my thoughts making his way through the few people starting to gather in the room.

I kept my eyes on the hallway where the bedrooms were, expecting the rest of the girls to come out of Ronan's room at any moment, arm in arm with him.

The elevators opened up time after time allowing different guests in, from tattooed grunts to well-dressed millionaire-looking types and their pedigreed escorts. Eventually, it was Fletcher who appeared with the three women, removing their sacks from their heads as they came out through the elevator doors. Absolutely no one paid any mind to the fact that they were in shackles, but I didn't fail to notice I was given more freedom than my cellmates. They looked nice, well dressed, but I could tell they didn't receive the same attentive care as I had tonight, and a part of me had to wonder why.

I normally didn't see too much of Fletcher, it actually didn't seem like he saw too much of me either, because anytime he showed up to take any of the girls somewhere he did his hardest to avoid looking my way. He guided the three girls to the large white leather couch and sat them there. Like little Barbies, perfectly trained for this moment, they sat there silently staring forward, with each of their legs crossed *ever* so differently.

I shifted uncomfortably, the seconds passing with a painful slowness until Santos returned with a large glass of añejo that I downed with no effort.

I passed my empty glass back to him, flashing him my teeth in request for more. It must have been the dress because with no arguments he shuffled along back towards the bar.

"Waiting for someone?" Mateo asked, surely noticing my millionth glance in the direction of Ronan's bedroom.

"I just thought they'd be coming in with him," I shrugged.

Mateo's hand wrapped around my wrist as he pulled me up to a stand, leading me to the dance floor that had been created for tonight's purpose only.

A few more tequilas went by, the loud bass of the music reverberating through my body, freeing my movements. It was the closest thing to freedom I'd felt in as long as I could remember. and I was starting to feel their influence on me to the point where the loud bass of the music was encouraging me to move freely.

Mateo stayed close behind me with a hand on my hip, swaying to the heavy beat of some pop song on full blast together. Every so often he'd let his hands wander around the curve of my ass or slide up to cup a breast with a soft squeeze.

I reached my arm back and draped it across his neck, bringing him in closer to me as we danced. My eyes drifted to where Santos still stood, my next drink in hand as he leaned back against the bar. His eyes were fixed on me, but there was something different about the way he was watching me tonight.

Mateo's fingers danced around the slit of my dress, his touch light, but electrifying. With purposeful intent, he slipped his fingers through the slit, his warm hands grabbing at the flesh of my thighs. Santos' eyebrows furrowed in the middle, his stare a pointed spear thrown from across the room.

"That's the look of a man who wishes he was in my place right now." Mateo breathed into my ear, his words throwing me off completely.

I shook my head in disagreement, but even I was having a rough time believing myself. Yeah, Santos was looking at me like I was lembas bread, and he was Frodo on his way to deliver the rings, but I knew it was just the dress. Santos would never cross that line, though these days I wished he would, even if it was just to piss off Ronan.

Just to piss off Ronan?

Get it together.

Mateo pressed into me from behind as if to pull my straying thoughts back into the moment. I choked down a gasp at the feel of his hands still exploring my body like we were completely alone and not on a crowded dance floor. We danced another song or two, grinding against each other, never escaping the scrutiny of Santos' gaze.

"I need some air," I told him.

Mateo pointed to the balcony door, where outside, a few people stood in groups, mostly smoking cigarettes in circles.

I looked back at him, wondering if this was a trick. Was he really going to let me go out there?

As if hearing my thoughts, he answered, "What are you gonna do? Jump? We're fifteen floors up."

The balcony was covered in hanging lights high above, a fire pit was built into the middle and there were chairs scattered all around. I crossed to the emptier side, away from people, leaning my elbows on the railing as I looked down below, letting the cool breeze dry the sheen of sweat still coating my skin.

"And whose prize are you tonight, gorgeous?" An older, well-dressed man spoke from a chair to my side.

The hair on both his head and face were fully silver, letting me know he was likely old enough to be my father.

"I'm no one's prize. I'm the curse that slowly drains the life of those who come too close," I said to him in a warning, lifting my eyebrow up when he dared to stand and move to my side.

"A pretty thing like you?" I couldn't tell his motives here but every alarm in my head was going off at this creep's vibes.

I was pretty socially inept at this point, and most people put me off.

Overtly forward men, specifically.

"I have fangs, and trust me, my venom is worse than my bite. *Sir,*" The bite in my tone made no difference, he still inched closer into my personal space.

He stroked his mustache, unphased by my warnings, "A black widow then? Interesting."

"I haven't left a trail of my ex-lovers' bodies just yet, but I get the feeling that would have excited you just the same."

Who did this guy think he was? Maybe I looked like one of the many escorts they'd sprinkled around this party for the purpose of their men getting their needs fulfilled, but I felt like I was being pretty clear.

"Dezmond Archer," he introduced himself, the familiarity of his name itching at the back of my mind. "the first." He clarified as he extended his hand in introduction.

"Well Dezmond, it was a pleasure, but I am afraid that's as far as your pleasure will get with me tonight. I am not for sale." He retracted his hand back with a frown when I refused to take it.

The man's gaze drifted nervously back to inside the apartment, where I found Mateo staring daggers into Dezmond Archer the fucking first. By the time I broke from Mateo's gaze, the older man was already long gone into the crowd. I let my shoulders drop, relief settling in as I enjoyed my moment of peace once again and peered out into the depths of the streets below us.

"Hope you're not getting any ideas." His husky voice growled from behind me.

"I used to think I was too brave to off myself, too defiant, too hard-headed. That it was for the weak, and I was anything but weak. I think I'm ready to admit that I'm actually just scared of what might come after. Maybe it's the opposite. Maybe it's the ones who jump, the ones who pull the trigger that are strong." I confessed my darkness a little too casually without turning around to look at him.

It was like that with Santos. Easy to get tangled up in each other's darkness.

"Was he bothering you?" He asked, his focus only on the direction he'd disappeared to.

I shook my head, "Nothing I couldn't handle myself."

He brushed my hair off of my back, sweeping it over my left shoulder to expose the ink now starting to fade there. His fingers touched the words tattooed over my shoulder blade. The only thing I ever bothered to memorialize on my skin.

"Todos tenemos un poco." He read it out loud. "What do we all have?" He asked me, roughly translating the words inked on my skin as he ran his fingers over the letters gently.

"'De músico, poeta, y loco, todos tenemos un poco.' Just a l reminder, that we're all a little bit crazy. Your Spanish really is shit huh?" I asked him, finally turning around to look at him.

"Yeah," he shrugged, "I don't think it was always that way, but once I learned English in school, my parents didn't bother making the Spanish stick." He said with a kind of sadness I understood.

The loss of culture was like cutting a limb off and watching it slowly rot in your freezer like a self-perpetuated hex, phantom pains somehow still itching throughout the process.

"It's hard when you don't feel like you're from anywhere. Nowhere that's really yours anymore. Nowhere you can call home." I kept my head hung as I stared back out into the busy street.

"You called us home once." He stood next to me, dropping his elbows to the railing.

With a heavy sigh, I accepted for the first time that my mistakes and decisions hurt Santos just as much as they hurt Ronan.

"I did." I looked up to see he had now turned to face me. Staring into his greenish-caramel eyes, I spoke each word clearly, so he was sure to not miss them. "Now he locks me in a box and brings my ghosts out to haunt me." I pressed my hand to his chest and my lips flattened into a line.

"You have to know; I have no part in that. You know that right?" Santos held me by the shoulders with both hands, shaking me as if desperate for my answer.

I brought my hand up to his cheek, softly placing it there. "But you don't stop him. None of you do." Santos expression broke.

I knew it wasn't fair for me to push my hatred and anger towards Ronan onto Santos. "It's okay." I added once my regret turned to guilt, coming to the tips of my toes and pressing a kiss to the corner of his lip.

As much as I wanted to hold resentment towards Santos, I couldn't.

He was the little bit of good I had here, I couldn't mess that up.

I knew if I pushed too hard, he would just wallow in his own misery instead, and I needed his light in the darkness that was starting to swallow me whole.

He cleared his throat uncomfortably, his voice almost a whisper. "We should get you back inside, Ronan should be here soon, and he won't like seeing you out here." He warned.

Though I wasn't sure if he meant out here, or out here *with him.* Entwining my fingers into his, I let him lead us back into the party and the now-crowded dance floor.

Santos guided me to the couch where the other blondes were already seated and waiting. Mateo sat across from me in the large white leather accent chair, and Santos turned back to the bar area before giving me one last longing look.

If it was hot before, the penthouse was now a sauna. Heat rolled out of the elevator and without turning my head I already knew it was him. Ronan Zerkos stepped out in a black button-down shirt with the sleeves rolled up to his elbows and matching suit pants. My mouth dried at the sight of him. How it was possible to hate someone with every fiber of my being and yet still feel betrayed by my own body's response anytime he walked into the room, was beyond me.

I wanted to rip him open and bathe in his blood.

I wanted him under me and on top of me making me scream until I couldn't breathe anymore. I wanted to carve him to pieces, until all that was left was the man I once knew. We had gotten so far from who we had once been.We had gone past the point of no return, the point of fixing things.

There was no way we could ever make it back to each other again. I wondered if he felt the same way; sorrow laced with the weight of regrets from all of the things left unspoken between us. Only he didn't so much as look at me as he cut his way through the room, turning his lips up in a smile when his eyes landed on the blondes seated on the couch.

My blood fervored at the thought of him actually being interested in any of them.

Santos appeared again with another double shot of tequila, and I turned it over hoping it would help me fake my way through the night like I had been asked. I didn't want to spend another minute of my life in that coffin ever again. I could hear Carolina's screams in the background of all the bullets and even though I knew it was a construct of my own imagination, it haunted me louder than anything else that box reminded me of.

13

RONAN

It was probably the hardest thing I had ever done; walking into a room, and looking everywhere but where she was. Even without staring head-on, I knew she was the most stunning creature within these four walls, without a doubt. The dress I picked out fit better than I could have predicted and it took every ounce of restraint I had to not stand there drinking her in.

So, I faked my attention at the others, earning a few *coos* and *awes* from them as I made my way to the couch, sitting on the furthest side of it, away from her.

Yup, this was exactly where I wanted to be, with three fucking blondes in between the bronze goddess who ruled my soul and haunted my every waking moment. There was so much tension in the air I wasn't sure if I was imagining it or if my brothers could feel it as well, but the rest of our guys were clueless and enjoying their well-deserved party to celebrate our successes this year.

Tonight most, or hopefully all three of the blondes would sign their agreement with the Black Crows and we could begin making use of their knowledge. Then we could work on taking down the Russian's trafficking ring.

We'd never nabbed two girls from the same stash before and this year we took a risk with the Bratva that Santos was sure would pay off as soon as they started spilling secrets. The weight in my chest pulled me down like an anchor though, and I couldn't focus on anything but the woman who had already signed herself to us.

Once they signed, we let each girl decide who they wanted to be responsible for them for the next few months. We'd take care of them until a certain rapport was created between us, fostering trust while something of a relationship was built. It was always business for us, though more than once I'd seen Kane and Santos catching clingers before we were ready to turn the girls out to freedom.

It was shitty to do this to these girls, I knew it.

They knew it.

Everyone knew it.

We weren't the good guys.

It was the double-edged sword I swallowed gladly knowing that at the end of the day, all of the cruelty, fake love, and mistrust they experienced at our hands would be the ticket to freeing possibly hundreds of other women from the Bratva human tracking market this year. Yeah, maybe we worked them too fast and too hard, but we didn't have the time to lose, and we needed to be efficient; it was how we were able to keep doing this without any of our rivals getting on to us.

These fuckers spent years brainwashing these women before bringing them to the United States. We had to break the loyalty to the assholes these women somehow felt a need to protect even though they would have thrown them to the wolves at the first sign of a fat stack of cash.

I was pretty convinced the Japanese girl, Chiyo, needed more time in the kennels, but I worried that with the other two being ready, this would create a sense of jealousy. Any small feelings could tip the scales in the work we were doing and we needed the utmost of trust established.

We never got picked by the same two girls because we picked our type before we even broke them, offering them kindness and warmth at every chance so they *thought* they were picking us, but the reality was we were picking them.

If by chance they picked wrong, we had rules in place for that too.

The other could challenge the selection made and they would spend however much time it took *convincing* the captive that they should rethink their choice.

That only happened once, when a Cuban got confused and thought I was cozying up to her, when she should have chosen Álvarez instead. Poor bastard had to spend three weeks going the extra mile with neck rubs and shopping sprees while she was getting the cold shoulder from me before she realized she needed to choose again.

Throwing a fourth into the mix was definitely going to screw things up, but Cecilia didn't know the rules of the game, and as far as I was concerned, she wasn't a player. Yes, she signed herself away to me, but for different reasons and I wasn't going to let the situations mesh no matter how much Álvarez was convinced I would.

Time passed, the drinks flowed freely, and I avoided the demoness to my far right like she was Medusa, and a single glance would turn me to stone. I already felt like it anyway, guilt weighed me down, kept me frozen. I was a mere reflection of the man I had become in attempts to seek the truth out of her lips. There was a sense of urgency that tugged at me, that told the most inner part of me that she was in too deep.

I would do whatever it took to get the answer.

If protecting her meant she would hate me, I would take that hatred tenfold.

Because If death is what waited for her outside of my doors, I would keep her locked away inside until that death came knocking, and even then, it would have to cut through me to get to her.

But for the sake of my own men, and the people that followed us we had to find out what was coming. We couldn't take the chance that this was some small-time bookie coming for a debt, or a drug dealing ex-boyfriend on her tail she'd likely stolen from and took off during the night again.

I was hurting her, to protect her, but I was hurting her for me too. Every time I threw her in that box, I was breaking open a piece of me that I shut away and covered with the hard exterior I built in my time serving our country. I wasn't a patriot like the rest of them, and neither was Kane. We were misguided youths with no future left, who enlisted to get out of the clutches of our past and our mistakes.

Every person I killed, every choice I made to hurt someone was made for me, not for freedom or the illusion of it that was promised by our superiors. There was nothing about us that even whispered red, white, and blue. We knew the truth about war and the cost of it, and we didn't buy into it at all. At the end of the day, it was just a means to an end for both Mateo and me.

The party was in full swing, a mixture of guys and women throughout the room, some of the women were our own soldiers and some were the plus ones of our higher-level guys. Since almost everyone lived here in the high-rise, some floors were meant strictly for business, and some for living quarters.

There were some older members of the Black Crows with full families, they chose to live away from the high-rise to keep their personal and work life separate and we respected the hell out of that too. Shit got messy sometimes and we knew what could wash up on our doorstep if anything we did caused blow-back. Sure, maybe we weren't making announcements about where the Black Crow HQ was, but I doubted it would take much if someone really wanted to find out.

It was clearly easy enough for Cecilia to do it.

The one named Anya kept crawling closer and closer to me until she was almost perched on my lap.

My attention was on Fletcher and even though I wasn't completely paying attention to the words coming out of his mouth, I was at least giving him the fantasy that I cared. Fletcher was a damn good right-hand man, and I never took him for granted, but sometimes he just talked too damn much about shit I really didn't care about.

"Yeah man, I trust you to deal with it." I said and his eyes widened with surprise, and he thanked me for the confidence in him.

Álvarez stood to gather all three of the blondes and take them to the other side of the living area. Dez quickly picked up his briefcase and followed. There was a guest room in the back that we kept mostly empty aside from the bed in it.

He would explain to them the rules extensively and present them with the contract to go over. Once they agreed to sign, he would tag them with a tracker and then bring them out of the room and announce it to the entire party where the rest of the guys would cheer and make a huge fuss about the whole thing while they signed in front of them.

"What's happening?" I heard Cecilia ask Kane and he moved from the chair opposite her and sat down next to her to explain in a hushed tone.

My skin prickled at the thought of him so close to her, but I knew my jealousy had no ground here. I still hadn't turned my neck to acknowledge her presence and it was quickly killing me to pretend like she wasn't here, or that she wasn't constantly taking up all the free space in my mind.

I didn't want her here tonight, nothing about having her next to me made it easy for me to convey an image of power, but I was outvoted and the fuckers I called my brothers kept bringing up the damn contract. The woman made me completely weak, from the way she looked to the intoxicating scent of coconut and vanilla that seeped out from her with the flick of her hair. I knew it, and my brothers knew it.

She was my beginning and my end.

Anya came out first and sauntered over from across the room with a cat-like gait that would have been sexy had it been anyone but her doing it. She was too skinny, and her arms hung long at her side awkwardly. Her face was pretty, but it wasn't the first face I'd look for in a room. I could see she had her eyes set on me as she continued to prowl her way over.

Before she had sat down the door opened again and the other one, Oksana, followed suit almost identical to Anya. I began to notice their similarities for the first time since they had been here and as I stared at their matching cheekbones, and eye shape I began to wonder if the similarities ran deeper.

Fuck.

They were sisters.

There was no way they weren't.

That was going to complicate everything. What the hell was Santos thinking when he nabbed these two?

He was so proud he took more than one from the Bratva, but to me, they looked more like a package deal, than an accident.

I rubbed my temples at the thought of how messy everything felt this year. It was because of *her.* I hadn't been thinking straight from the moment she walked back into my life. Every decision I made was somehow corrupted by the ghost who wouldn't stop haunting me. Anya squeezed in on my right side and Oksana sat on the arm of the sofa pressing against me and I sighed impatiently at the obvious gestures.

Álvarez opened the door one more time and stood at the threshold. He made eye contact with Fletcher and with a subtle motion of his chin he beckoned him over. I dismissed him from the one-sided conversation and like a good little soldier he headed over to Santos and closed the door behind them. Something was happening, but he was clearly trying to keep it discreet.

Shit.

I knew she wasn't ready yet.

Anya muttered something in a heavy accent about me being tense and started pawing at me through my clothes, sliding her hands over my thigh and letting them creep up. I arched an eyebrow at her and leaned back with my arms resting on the sofa, wondering how far she was willing to take it.

Getting my dick sucked by her before she signed in a room full of our guys would be a full-on win against Kane and Álvarez. We always had a big betting pool going every year of who would be the first chosen, and who would be the last chosen, and I didn't plan on losing this year *again,* just because they were all blondes.

I'd fake my way through it if I had to.

The mood changed drastically, the lights dimmed, and the music played a loud and heady tone.

Some people were going at it in the corners without much regard for privacy, but it was nothing out of the average for one of our parties. I was wondering if my little flower was starting to feel out of sorts and embarrassed, but when I stole a glance over her way, she was only looking at one thing, one person, *him.*

Mateo Kane.

They were fully enraptured in conversation. As if the mental daggers I was sending his way could cut through him, Kane met my gaze and rolled his eyes at me.

The fucking nerve.

Finally, Fletcher and Álvarez appeared in the doorway of the guest room and hurriedly snuck Chiyo past the foyer and through the elevator. They made their way through the doors to take her back downstairs without a single other person noticing, except for Kane who caught my gaze again and we had an entire conversation without words.

This year was different, and I wasn't the only one who was nervous.

Oksana was rubbing my shoulders with her knees straddling one of my legs while her sister started to fumble with my belt buckle. For the life of me I wasn't sure why, but I turned my head to see Cecilia belly laughing at something Kane said, not even bothering to look in my direction.

Jealousy was a three-horned bull.

And when it came to her, I allowed it to spear me over and over until there was nothing left of me.

I looked down to see Anya reaching into my pants and I tilted her chin up to force her to look at me.

"Are you sure sweetheart?" I asked her and without a beat she answered in that thick accent.

"Let us help you relax," She pushed my chest so that I was once again leaning back on the couch.

I wasn't hard yet.

There was nothing she was doing that could get me there, but if I closed my eyes and imagined the raven-haired beauty on the other side of the couch instead, I could make it work. I allowed my eyelids to shut heavily in anticipation of the feeling of her hot, wet mouth on me, but it never came.

Instead, I heard a smash and a scream and I opened my eyes to find Cecilia slamming Anya's face into the concrete coffee table repeatedly. Oksana lunged off of me and she tried to get to her sister, but I held her back.

"Kane!" I shouted over to him, who was apparently mesmerized by the whole situation and took three or four seconds to register what was happening before he pulled my girl off of Anya.

Cecilia cackled loudly like a drunken witch, and my cock eagerly twitched awake at the entire scene. I whistled loudly and Ethan, one of our top dogs, was at my side ready for instructions.

"Go to the kennels and give her to Fletch." I shoved Oksana at him, who was wrestling against me like a pissed-off raccoon without looking back at her.

Kane released Cecilia and her eyes widened when she looked at me as I admired her work, she turned around and ran to Mateo's room. I heard the door slam. I didn't need to chase her, I knew she wouldn't be going anywhere and I had a hell of a mess to clean up.

Anya was shrieking like a fucking banshee and when she lifted her head up, I could see why. Her nose was completely shattered, blood gushing down her face and she was probably missing three or four teeth now.

Cecilia fucked her up good.

I ran my hand down my face, annoyance, and pride both battling for dominance of my mood.

"Party's over!" I shouted and it was like almost comical the record-type scratching effect you saw in old-time cartoons when all of the sound abruptly stopped.

Everything flipped like a switch, and they all began to clear out as the music came to a screeching halt.

"Go with Álvarez and take her to the hospital, pay off the staff on shift," I said to Kane.

"And then what?" he asked me, but I was honestly feeling just as clueless as he was at that moment.

"Set her up nice, pay her off too if you have to. Just make sure it doesn't come back on us." I said in a hushed tone fully knowing I was completely unsure as how to handle this fucked up situation.

We were all in over our heads here. Not only did Cecilia hurt her, but she permanently damaged that poor girl's only asset for the rest of her life. It wasn't that I was some fucked up pig who thought her body was all she had to offer. It was that for the last six years we had been doing this, we'd seen it all.

These girls came from fucked up situations, they were stolen young and were kept and moved around until they were sold to the highest bidder for their virginity. If they weren't virgins, then there was a good chance they'd been doing it so long that it was all they knew.

Only once since we'd been doing the trials had a single girl chosen for us to put them somewhere they could reinvent themselves. The security of a safe brothel or strip club was more of a happy ending than most of them could imagine, especially when they had our guaranteed protection for life.

She hadn't signed yet either so there was a pretty good chance she wouldn't want to stay with us now, and there was nothing we could do about that other than let her go. Maybe we could at least hope she would decide to start a new life, somewhere away from Cove City and gangs, but with her sister here I had a feeling it wouldn't be so simple.

"What are you gonna do to *her?*" He gestured his head towards his room as he accentuated the word her.

"Everything," I said through closed teeth.

"Don't say scary shit like that or you're not allowed in my room," he warned me as he picked up whimpering Anya as if she was a small baby and made his way towards the elevator. "Seriously. No punishments without talking to us. Say it," he demanded without looking back.

"No punishments," I said, fury clawing at me from inside, but I knew I had to let it simmer before I went in there and completely exploded.

She was jealous.

The realization hit me like a bullet train.

I had to contain my smile from taking over my face, but it soon disappeared when I remembered she had no right to be jealous, she forfeited that right a long time ago.

"No punishments," I hummed to myself as I paced in front of Kane's closed bedroom door.

Did she lock it?

If she was smart, she would have locked it until Kane got back. I turned the handle to find the door barely even fully shut and I opened it out further letting the door dramatically hit the wall behind it as I entered the room.

14

CECILIA

Fuck.

One minute I was having a halfway decent time, almost forgetting that I was actually someone's captive and not their party guest, the next I was seeing red because that blonde bitch had her hands in my man's pants.

Not my man.

He was actually going to fucking kill me.

Carajo.

I noted the random passing thought in my mother tongue. I was spending way too much time in my own head in that box listening to my papá lecture me and now my Spanish didn't feel as distant as it used to. I ran my hands over my face in anxiety and looked down to see all the black smeared all over my hands.

Great, now I probably looked like a damn clown.

I drank way too much and with how often I'd been avoiding food all together, I knew it hit me faster and harder than normal. I heard the door slam and I knew by the scent of Bleu de Chanel cologne it wasn't Mateo coming in.

I had nowhere to hide now.

I was standing in the corner of the room with my back to the wall when he stormed in, eyes full of rage and no ounce of compassion to be found in that emerald forest of his. He didn't say anything yet, but he closed the space between us in a few strides and I was practically becoming one with the wall trying to create distance between us that didn't exist.

I hurriedly started trying to spew off some sort of defense in hope that it would cool his rage, unfortunately I had nothing else to offer.

"Fuck you!" came out instead though, and even he seemed shocked.

"Don't tempt me, flower. I don't know what you think you're doing, but that little trick won't go unpunished," he said through his teeth moving closer and closer.

I curled my lip in anger at him. "I have nothing left to lose anyway. Do whatever you want to me. Yeah, maybe I'm the catalyst but this was your fault!" I selfishly blamed him for my behavior, and he raised an eyebrow at me like he couldn't believe I was pushing guilt on him.

"You can expect me to play the part of the little doll you want me to be, but you can't force me to watch some whore touching you. Touching the only man I've ever loved. The only man I've ever..." I stopped before I gave away more than I wanted to, but it was too late, and he narrowed his eyes at me in response.

I traced my eyes downward and nervously picked at my nails to avoid giving him the truth.

"The only man you've ever what?" He asked as if everything else that happened was minute compared to what I could possibly say next.

"Can you really look at me and say you'd have no problem with watching some other guys touch me in front of you?" I asked him. "No bullshit Ronan, it's just us," I pleaded, my breaths coming in heavy as I trembled from my words, unsure if I could handle the truth.

"The only man you've ever what?" He asked again with a little more bite, waiting for the answer impatiently.

"Don't make me say it."

His eyes widened in recognition of my truth and embarrassment flooded through me that in twelve years there hadn't been anyone else, there couldn't be. It was always just him, and the thought of getting close to another had never crossed my mind before I stepped inside of this high-rise.

"We don't belong to each other anymore. Your choice, remember?" He said with a scowl, crossing his arms over his chest.

"It wasn't a choice," I barely whispered, the tears threatening to pour out of me as the dam started to crumble again.

He took one last step and he rumbled in my ear, "Help me understand."

But there was no hardness to his words anymore, his thumb grazed the side of my face as he contoured down to my chin and lifted it up.

The tears were flowing freely from my eyes and I gazed upon the beautiful man who continually broke my heart day in and day out. It was a power only he had over me, he was the only person who could make me cry, and he was the only person I could allow myself to cry in front of. It had been that way since I was eight years old and decided my tears were a small part of the control I had in my life.

Before I could respond, his mouth was closing around mine with a bruising pressure and his tongue was parting my lips, pushing its way in with no abandon. My heart thundered in my chest. I let down my walls and gave in to the thing we always did best. It was always easier when we stopped trying to make sense, or use words, and just used our bodies.

A combination of a sigh and moan escaped my throat as I allowed him in, tongues fighting for dominance and the taste of tequila mixing with his whiskey had me forgetting anything but this moment, and the two of us. The kiss was like a jumpstart that my heart had been severely needing to bring me back to life.

There was so much pain in coming back from the dead.

I knew he could taste it too.

His hand found my breast over the dress and he carelessly ripped it to give himself better access as he roughly massaged it. I gasped as his free hand grabbed the back of my head and he tugged my hair roughly to force my head to tilt in his direction.

Heat surged through me from the power of his demands, and I was too caught up in the moment to care about anything else. I knew I was making a mistake, but I would deal with the consequences later. I could feel his the hardness of his erection through his suit pants, I ran my hands down to feel the familiar thickness of his cock.

I squeezed hard.

He groaned a response and pressed into me harder. Ronan unbuckled his belt and I started to reach for him but in one motion he lifted my legs up as he pinned me up against the wall. With fumbling hands, I scrambled to tear the shirt off of him, running my hands over every inch of his sculpted body. He was magnificent, and just for now I wanted to feel his skin against mine and worship every muscle on his body.

I closed my ankles behind him, the heels of the Louboutin's surely digging into him with a piercing pressure as I urged him closer, our mouths never separating as our tongues collided against each other. It had been too long, and it felt too right, and I never wanted to put any distance between us again.

His thumb flicked my nipple and brushed over it with an unbearable heat that was winding my body up as it begged for release. Eventually he broke away from my lips and trailed down my neck with a familiar firmness until his lips found my other breast, pulling it out of the dress and closing his mouth around my nipple.

"More," I groaned it out as his tongue pressed against my nipple.

With just a few steady motions, he had pulled himself out of his pants and was pushing my underwear to the side while he teased me with his cock pressed to my wetness. Teasingly, he slide up and down, coating himself in my arousal and setting off sparks from the friction against me.

He paused, furrowed eyebrows and flared nostrils before stretching his way inside me with one sure thrust. I gasped at the feeling, my nails digging into his skin as I struggled to adjust to the sensation of fullness.

It was like coming home again after being away for so long that you didn't even know if you had a key anymore. But Ronan *was* the key and feeling him inside me again was the kind of pleasure that would haunt me until my last breath.

With our foreheads pressed together, he never took his eyes off of mine, not like he was searching for the girl I was once but like he was trying to figure out who I was now.

He wouldn't be able to find her though, so I closed my eyes to avoid giving it away.

"Look at me." He commanded as he pulled my chin up.

I scraped my nails down his back.

He grunted, bringing his hand up to my neck, not squeezing, just holding as he moved in and out of me. My toes curled and my stomach tightened as I got closer to my climax with each thrust of his hips. His mouth found mine again and he said his encouragement in a hushed tone.

"Let go flower," he demanded as he forced me to come undone in a shockwave that rippled through me, leaving me uncaring of the cries departing my mouth.

My body trembled while he held me up and pumped his release inside of me. We stayed like that for a few minutes as we both caught our breaths before he pulled out of me. The feeling of emptiness was so sudden and chilling but a good sobering reminder of *what the fuck are you doing estupida?*

"Who are you running from?" The broken record stuffed himself back into his pants, and I pulled my dress back down as I adjusted myself.

I was breathless and still high from the mind-blowing orgasm, but he couldn't catch me off guard.

"What are you doing with the women?" I asked instead of answering, the feeling his cum slowly dripping out of me somehow emboldening me.

"That's not your concern," he said, buckling his pants and removing any trace of what we'd just done.

"Looks like we don't trust each other then," I said smiling and crossing my arms, knowing damn well I wasn't going to be spilling any of my own secrets just because he knew how to make me come faster than I could do on my own.

He clenched his jaw, he was holding back his anger. He was made out of so much rage now, and I knew that I was the reason for it all. I was the reason he turned into this hardened version of himself, one that could cut you with a single look.

I was the reason he went to war. I was the reason he was untrusting and always had a gun tucked between his boxer and his pants. I was sure even now if I checked it would be there. But I wasn't scared of him, I already knew he wouldn't hurt me.

Not in the ways that counted anyway.

"Don't be so damn stubborn Cecilia," he said through closed teeth. "That's Black Crow business, it doesn't concern you. That little stunt you pulled back there? That's gonna cost us something," he said but I wasn't sure what he could mean.

"Sounds like your problem," I spat back at him. "Get your dick sucked in private, payaso."

"This building is mine to do what I want, where I want. Just like you, you're mine too now, don't forget it."

"How could I forget? You keep me down there like an animal." I threw the words at him as I stood a bit taller, nobody owned me.

Maybe on a piece of paper he did, but I wasn't really even the name who signed.

I wasn't anyone anymore.

Just a ghost of my past.

"If you want a nicer situation, you'll tell me who you're running from, otherwise I can get you a mailbox for your kennel because you'll be setting up permanent residence down there my sweet little flower." He said the same nickname and even though it had hardly been minutes since he used it last, the contrast in the way it made me feel was almost crippling.

He turned around and began to head to the door and the idiota part of me that was my papá's daughter, the part that refused to back down, decided to poke the bear.

"Did I break your little sex slave's nose?" I chuckled out hollowly.

I could see him pause for a moment in reaction as he white knuckled the door handle.

The loud slamming of the door being shut rang out against the room and I slid my way down to the floor, while my heart and brain struggled to catch up to my growing list of stupid decisions.

At least an hour went by, possibly two, Ronan was likely still pacing the hall outside of Mateo's room. I could hear his steps against the marble floors every now and then for a few minutes at a time followed by some cursing. After a while he would disappear again as if it was taking all of his restraint to not come back inside.

Mateo hadn't come back either and I hadn't seen Santos since before I broke their captive's face, so I was starting to get seriously nervous. I finally decided to make the best of a bad situation and use my surroundings. Taking advantage of my temporary prison, I walked towards his bathroom and turned on the beautiful gold faucet in the clawfoot tub.

I unzipped the ruined dress and let it drop to my feet, reaching down to remove the red bottom heels off of my feet. I tossed them carelessly to the side as the thought of their cost annoyingly tugged at the back of my conscience. I'd spent the last fourteen years of my life struggling to make ends meet, always working a minimum of two jobs at a time. The thought of being someone's captive and receiving gifts I couldn't really afford was a real fucking mind trip cherry on top of the stockholm sundae.

I stepped into the steaming, hot water and I was thankful I was alone so I could moan into the comfort of the bath without any judgment. I melted into the heat of the water and closed my eyes. I wasn't sure how much time had gone by, but the steamy room began to lull me into a quiet stillness I hadn't been able to surrender to since the second those elevator doors opened the first time I walked into this high-rise.

"I feel a little like the three bears from Goldilocks here," Mateo's gravelly voice cut in as I almost drifted into sleep.

I opened my eyes to find him shamelessly observing me in his tub.

That was the thing about Mateo, he never looked away, or pretended like he wasn't watching. It was like he wanted me to see that he was looking at me, and it was kind of a thrill to capture his gaze when I was the object of its attention.

"I might never get a bath again in my life, how could I pass up this magnificent tub?" I asked him in a honeyed voice.

"I think we both know you'll live to fight another day," his expression was serious but somehow, I had amused him.

He had a way of carrying a smile up to his eyes even when his lips were trying to conceal it.

"Ronan might disagree with you," I pointed out to our mutual friend in the hall.

"Has he been in here? Did he do something to you?" His eyebrows pulled together in worry and the concern seemed genuine enough to startle me.

"Yes, and yes, but nothing I couldn't handle on my own," I stated, and his eyebrows lifted up even higher in question, but I didn't give him more than a turn of the corner of my lips.

He walked towards the sink and opened a drawer pulling out a sponge in its packaging and an old Nike shoebox. He opened the box at me like it was going to be filled with treasure and I let out an actual gasp when the contents revealed a plethora of bath bombs, bath salts, essential oils, and bars.

"I knew I should have snooped around first," I joked, and he smiled at me before dropping a fizzy gold ball into my bath.

The dye quickly melted into the water turning it into a masterpiece of liquid gold specks and filling the room with the overwhelming scent of lavender and vanilla. I closed my eyes again and relaxed back into my original position as the bomb fizzled out into the bathwater.

"I went through your bag when you first got here," he said nonchalantly like my privacy was of absolutely no concern, and pulled out the crappy burner I'd been carrying for the last year or so. "You wanna tell me why your contacts list is three people long?" He asked and I couldn't help but laugh.

"What can I say? I've always had a hard time making friends, you saw me out there giving my best to Cocks-Ana," I mused at him.

"No, I think that was Anya's face that you used to tenderize our coffee table with," he flashed me his teeth.

I had to actually look away because that smile was starting to give me a physical reaction and at thirty, I was way too old for that bullshit butterflies-in-your-stomach kind of feeling.

"In my defense, Santos poured me at least six shots," I raised an eyebrow hoping it was a fair defense.

"I think Álvarez would do anything if you asked him."

"Except let me go," I challenged him.

"You didn't come here so that we could let you go Sunshine, you don't fool me. That door has been unlocked all night but instead I found you in my bath. You *want* to be here. I just wish I could figure out what the hell is so bad out there that has you sleeping in a cage here," he said almost angry at whatever possible situation he could imagine had me cornered like this.

"To be fair, *you* have me sleeping in a cage here," I pointed out.

He rolled his sleeves up his forearms, and my mouth watered at the sight of his olive skin against the dark dress shirt that contained him.

"Hmm," he said as he knelt next to the tub and poured a ridiculous amount of soap onto the sponge and reached into the water to pull my left foot out.

He silently scrubbed it into a soapy lather moving his way up my thigh slowly and ritualistically. His arm was fully in the water before he dropped the foot and picked up the other and repeated the process.

"My little sister, Andrea, died when I was a kid." He rasped out and my eyes met his, the pain I recognized so often in them became clearer with his words.

I stayed silent as he continued.

Mateo moved to my side and picked up my hand scrubbing at it delicately then washing up my arms and across my shoulder to the other side to repeat the action.

"She was killed. My piece of shit old man had been drugging her and raping her, I don't know for how long. I didn't know anything; I was a dumb kid who didn't give a shit about anything except myself. Until one day, I came home and found him, his dirty, disgusting body on top of her, crushing her. When I pushed him off, I saw she was already a shade of blue, her mouth was full of foam and bile. She overdosed from whatever he had given her that time."

There they were, the ghosts I'd been looking for in his eyes.

I reached up and touched the sharp stubble on his face, "How old were you?" I asked, wondering how long it had been since his innocence was ripped from him.

"Old enough that I should have fucking killed him for it," he said, his eyes burning with an intensity that made me truly believe he wished he could have.

Yeah, they reminded me of my own ghosts.

He rubbed the side of his head like a bad habit and winced. It was then I realized he was finally sharing that piece of himself with me, like he had promised to.

"Twelve. She was ten."

"You were just a kid. You can't carry that weight," I said to him, my fingers rubbing over the stubble on his jaw gently, the crease between his eyebrows slowly fading away.

It was a comforting lie, I knew full well how easily a child could lose their virtue from the actions of adults. He pushed my shoulders forward and I hugged my knees to allow him to lather up my back, before sliding back down to recline again.

I heard the squirt of the body wash as he poured more into the loofa and his gaze didn't waver from mine while he rubbed it thoroughly over my breasts and down my stomach. My eyes widened in surprise as his hand made its way down my center before pulling his arm out from the water.

There was a lingering awkwardness, but it didn't last as he reached into a cabinet behind him and pulled out a large bath sheet and extended it open.

I stood letting the water fall to my sides and I lifted my arms up to allow him to wrap the towel around me. It took him a few seconds longer than it should and he didn't waste a second of it looking anywhere but at me, all of me.

He exited the bathroom, and I stepped out of the tub letting the water absorb into the mat before stepping on the cool black marble and slowly tiptoeing back into Mateo's room. There was a black t-shirt draped over the bed with a horned goat illustration printed onto it. Mateo crossed back into the bathroom leaving the door open so I could hear the shower turning on.

I thumbed the fabric, feeling the softness of it, allowing the towel to fall to the ground as I slid his shirt over my head. It smelled like him, a comforting fragrance of pine that was so refreshing and somehow reminded me of safety. It was a defeating realization that he slipped through my defenses and crawled his way in with his dimples and annoyingly cavalier attitude.

But despite how hard Mateo Kane pretended to be, I had seen through that cold exterior and saw something gentler, someone who cared a little deeper than they let others believe.

The t-shirt fell past my thighs, and it was somehow the best piece of clothing I had worn in the last month. I nervously fidgeted with the hem of it as I waited for him to finish his shower. Millions of expectations and possibilities flooded my brain for how the rest of the night was going to go, and not a single clue for how it would end other than the depressing surety that I'd be behind those bars again when I woke up tomorrow.

15

MATEO

It was damn near three in the morning when I had gotten back to the penthouse, we spent hours at the south-side emergency room. It was Black Crow property, so we could bring in anyone with any injury for treatment and the docs and nurses knew to just do their job and keep their mouths shut if the pigs went sniffing around.

They knew better than to ask or answer any questions, but bringing in a pulverized Bratva bitch was going to get us some eyebrow raises and some nasty looks from the residents, there was no way around it.

Anya was off in oxy-land when I left her there with Santos, and it seemed like there was no way she'd be coming back to the high-rise. Shit, who could blame her? Her eyes were swollen shut and black from bruising by the time I left, and she was scheduled for surgery in the morning to start reconstructing her nose.

They would need a dentist to do an evaluation, but I had heard some of the doctors say they were going to need to pull a few teeth that had been impacted from the force of the trauma too. She had at least ten stitches on her forehead and about six on her lip going down her chin. All in all, it was unlikely that she was going to look the same, ever again.

My head was pounding, and I was itching to leave that sterile box. Hospitals weren't for me, and we usually had the Doc make house calls for that very reason. When I got back, I didn't expect to find Zerkos passed out, sitting up against the wall next to my bedroom door, or our fiery prisoner naked in my bathtub.

God, she looked incredible in that bath. Droplets of water beading beading over her golden skin, her tits floating above it like perfect globes, begging to be squeezed.

Fuck, this girl was doing things to my mind that made me constantly forget *who* the reason was she was here, and *he* was asleep right outside my door this very second. I let the hot water cascade down my back as my cock hardened at the thought of rubbing that loofa all over her perfect skin just moments ago. She never once told me to stop or pushed my hand away, and she looked at me like...fuck.

That was my brother out there.

And that was the woman who fucked him up so good he went to war over it.

There was a conflict raging beneath me, and I knew the only way to quiet the storm inside me was going to be between her legs, but that could never fucking happen. I fisted my dick in my right hand and closed my eyes. I squeezed the tip with two fingers and then wrapping my fingers around my entire shaft, I tugged up and then down, letting my pre-cum lubricate me as I picked up the pace.

I wondered what she tasted like after a bath, how her thighs would feel in between my teeth as I closed them around her flesh. I wondered if she would whimper quietly or if she would scream when she came.

I kept the image of her in the bath, big black eyes wide open and fixed on mine as I reached lower and lower. There was something about her where she saw everything as a challenge. I'd be damned if that didn't get me hard to watch her face off to anyone and anything these last couple of months. My balls tingled as I got closer and closer and I imagined sinking into that perfect round ass, her raven hair wrapped around my fist tight. I came fast with a low grunt before washing and turning the shower off.

By the time I walked out of the bathroom she was already asleep on the floor, sitting up with her back against the foot of the bed almost identical to how I'd left Zerkos out there. I opened the closet and pulled out a pair of black boxer briefs and put them on before reaching down and picking her up. I gently placed her on the bed and covered her with the comforter before walking around to the other side of the bed. I hesitated, unsure if I should sleep somewhere else but after a moment of thought I decided... fuck it.

This was my bedroom, and I had already come anyway. I could get through the night with her next to me.

When I got into the vacant side of the bed, she was completely turned to her side facing me, her eyes were open and fully fixed my way. “Should I be afraid?” she asked me, and I almost laughed at how unpredictable her mind was.

“I didn’t think you were someone who could be scared of anything, you don’t give me that impression sunshine,” I said, and she hummed.

“I’m not. But I still like to know if I’m heading for a situation that if I was allowed to be anyone else, would I be scared?” she asked almost like it was a philosophical question.

There was a big part of me that was heavily intrigued by what she meant when she said *if she was allowed to be anyone else*, but I didn’t push. I would just file that tidbit away for another time.

“Am I here for the same purpose as them?” she asked.

“You mean, are they here because they broke our hearts over twelve years ago, and then showed up on our doorstep asking for our protection? No sunshine, you are not here for the same reasons,” I reassured her.

“Are you doing something bad with them?” She asked with a bit of concern showing for her cell-mates, even though I hadn’t seen her so much as look at any of them for more than ten seconds at a time.

That little exchange with Anya was the closest she’d ever gotten to either of them.

“No, but bad is a construct. There is no good or evil.” I said truthfully, without telling her much more, and she couldn’t hide the puzzled look on her face that said she was trying to put pieces together but couldn’t. “You should sleep while you can,” I warned her, knowing full well that once morning came, I wouldn’t be able to keep her hidden in this room for long.

She scooted closer to me and laid her head on my shoulder, as if she had gotten so used to it that it was better than any pillow on my bed.

Blackest eyes met mine, and her hand lifted up as I felt her cool fingers against the side of my head. She pressed into my temple with the gentlest of touches and then firmly rubbed her thumb against the spot.

I could feel the headache dissolving for the first time in days and it was hard to pretend like it didn’t mean what it meant to me. She slowed down when I closed my eyes and eventually dropped her hand back down.

She was fast asleep by the time my phone buzzed and I saw a text from Álvarez to our group chat.

Álvarez: We need to talk. Meeting in the morning.

That wasn't going to be anything good, but I was tired as fuck and couldn't think past my heavy eyelids.

Vanilla and coconut surrounded me while I was slowly pulled from slumber.

There was a leg draped over mine and soft skin under my palms that had me aching to rub all over her. Her head was practically on my chest and somehow my arm was cradled beneath her. It felt comfortable, like we had always done it somehow. I took a deep inhale and buried my nose into her hair.

A low growl in the corner of the room forced my eyes to jar open. Ronan Zerkos was sitting on the piano bench wearing the world's meanest scowl, I braced myself for the explosion.

"I didn't touch her," I said in a hushed voice to him.

"I slept outside your room, I know," he said and the puzzled look on my face spoke for me so that I wouldn't disturb her. "Well, either your dick wasn't doing the job, or you didn't fuck her, because Cecilia Gomes screams when she's being railed right." He smirked at me, and his gaze shifted to the security camera on the ceiling.

Only I had access to the footage in this room, but suddenly I wondered if I needed to take a look at the little visit he paid her last night. I made a mental note to review that shit when I was out of bed but then I remembered Santos' text.

"Did Álvarez get back in from the hospital yet?" I asked him but didn't allow for an answer, "What time is it?" I slid my arm out from underneath her.

She stirred just slightly with a soft moan that compelled my cock to wake up as well.

"Yeah, he just got in, it's six-thirty," he threw a pair of sweats at me, the scowl never leaving his face for a moment. "Cover your hard-on and let's go see what we've got to deal with next." He said, getting up from the piano.

I rolled out of bed as quietly as I could and stepped into the pants before following my brother out into the main living area.

Álvarez looked absolutely wrecked, the poor guy probably never got more than thirty minutes of sleep in that hospital chair knowing him. He just cared too much about everyone and everything, he had that tinker bell mentality where he genuinely thought he could make the world a better place if we just believed enough. He had bags under his eyes and even though Fletcher was working on coffee as we walked into the room, he was just a few long blinks away from crashing.

"Fill us in," Zerkos commanded, and Santos nodded.

"She's fucking pissed, yo. Like, that bitch is mad-angry, man. I had to have Emory dope her up pretty well to keep her from shouting about the kennels and the trials. Chalked it up to her being hysterical, but I think we'll still need to answer some questions over there. She was pretty out of it towards the end, but eventually, she had some other doctor kick me out of her room before her surgery. Said she had a family member who was going to pick her up after." he said questioning the last part.

"A family member?" Ronan asked, and we looked at each other.

We were all thinking the same thing. Something was shady here. Human trafficking victims taken from other countries didn't often just have a family member they could call on at the drop of a hat to come pick them up after weeks of being missing.

"Fletch, can you send Ethan to monitor the hospital? See if he can get a good look at whoever leaves with Anya or any visitors she may get," I instructed, and he nodded at me and headed out towards the elevators.

I walked over to the kitchen and poured the French press coffee Fletcher started into four mugs. Black for Zerkos, a bucket of cream for Santos, and a cube of sugar and just a splash of cream in mine. I placed all four in a tray and brought it over to the coffee table where Santos looked like he would collapse any moment. I nudged his mug at him, and he mumbled a thanks but began to close his eyes before he reached for it.

Ronan eyed the fourth mug and raised an eyebrow at me suspiciously. Stupid silent bastard could say a million things with just a fucking look and this one screamed "I know what you're doing", but even I didn't know what I was doing anymore.

I was completely enraptured by this siren, I needed more of her, even if it were just those awestruck thankful looks whenever I gave her a fraction of a kind gesture. I was starting to wonder if the opportunity for freedom arose, would I actually allow her to have it? I'd grown so used to time in her presence and looking forward to small moments together that I wasn't sure what I was doing with myself the other twenty some odd hours left in the day.

They were just the moments in between her.

"She goes back inside the kennels when she wakes up," he said, lowering his eyes to his mug as he drank his coffee.

"You think she's gonna be okay locked in there with the other one?" Santos asked him through his sleepy haze.

"She should have thought about that before she—" I stood up pushing the chair back against the marble with a screech and interrupting Zerkos.

I grabbed two mugs and turned to head back to my bedroom. I was exhausted with the act he was putting on. If I thought I had it bad, this guy was a million times worse. With good reason of course, the two of them had bible-size history between them and apparently, they got off on hurting each other, and themselves, at their own expense.

I walked back into my room to find her wrapped in my black sheets, the shirt riding up her thigh promising to reveal more if she were to just move ever so slightly. I grabbed my laptop from my desk and opened up the program for the security footage for my room and searched for the feed from last night. I popped an ear bud in my ear and scrolled to the timestamp right after she beat Anya's face in.

I wasn't in the least surprised when her face that was contorted in anger from whatever Ronan said to her quickly changed to an expression of lust when he began pounding into her against the wall. However, the sounds that came out of her mouth were a symphony I never thought I'd have the fortune of hearing in my entire life. The whole thing was fast, and full of unspoken regret between the two of them and just as it started it ended with them bickering.

How they spent a moment in each other's company in the past was beyond me, because the two of them were live wires constantly threatening to spark and explode with the slightest contact or friction. And yet neither could stop reaching for the other. I felt for my brother, because even in his hatred for her I could see that, if given the chance, he'd do anything to be able to have her love again. But pride, shame, and a million secrets between them drove them further and further apart the longer she stayed here under his heel.

I closed the laptop and placed the coffee on the bedside table closest to her, and made my way over to the piano bench. I caressed my oldest friend and let my fingers go to work as *Beethoven's* "Moonlight Sonata" moved its way out of me through the keys, the melody taking me to a place only ivory could find. By the time I finished, I noticed she was not only awake but fully sitting up leaning against the headboard, with her coffee in hand.

"That was incredible," she said in between sips. "I kind of pegged the piano for decoration, but now you make a lot more sense."

"I didn't know how you took your coffee, so I just brought it to you black," I told her. "But I can get cream or sugar if you want." I offered but she shook her head.

"Black is great," she said and for some reason, I wasn't surprised that they even took their coffee the same way.

"I don't know if I should take the piano comment as an insult or not," I admitted but she shrugged her shoulders at me.

"It's hard to imagine you as a three-dimensional person sometimes. Not just someone who's locked me up," she said casually, eyes averting me as she looked around the room like she was taking it in for the first time.

"I didn't lock you in here, sunshine," I reminded her again as I stepped closer to the bed at a leisurely pace. "But don't get that twisted, because I'm starting to see why Ronan won't let you get away."

"Then you're just as bad as him," she said, the flare building in her eyes again.

"Wrong," I said, closing the distance between us, "I'm worse."

Her mouth parts but no sound comes out and I notice out of the corner of my eyes her hands are fisting the bed sheets. "I don't know if I want to ask...Why?" She betrays herself and asks anyway.

"Zerkos is just a heartbroken fucking idiot, and his pride is what gets in the way of you two, every time. That's why you clash. But me? I'm doomed to never get to touch, or taste, or feel you. And to never have, is a greater curse than to have and to lose." I said through my teeth, too close to her already and my anger obviously apparent.

Her breathing was heavy, when she responded to my confession and she stared at me with those wide eyes. "You heard him. We don't belong to each other anymore." She sneered at the memory of his words.

She wasn't just sunshine, she was the whole fucking Sun. So far, so unreachable, and when I thought I was close enough to touch, I would burn instead. She was all my sins coming back to haunt me, to push me over the edge so that I would lose control.

I grabbed a handful of her hair close to the scalp and pulled her up. She let out a soft cry but didn't protest, I pressed my face to hers and inhaled the scent of her hair. I dropped her back on the bed and walked over to the dresser where the burlap sack lay and tossed it over her lap, "Put this on." I said.

She was giving me those giant dark eyes once again. That was her tell when she was scared or unsure, no matter how much she pretended to be fearless.

I had learned it well now.

"You're locking me back in the cage," she said, half asking, half already sure of the answer.

"Let's go," I gestured my chin toward the door.

"Please, Mateo. I-I can't go back there, I don't feel like a person there. Please," she whispered the last bit, the tears in her eyes starting to form.

This whole thing was really doing a number on her no matter how well she tried to hide it.

"There are two ways I can get you out of that kennel." I told her, "You can either start telling us the truth..." I stopped for a bit, but she urged me on with a look that told me that option was completely out of the question for her. "Or you go out there and tell Ronan you're mine." Zerkos made it clear she wasn't part of the trials, but at the end of the day she signed paperwork for exactly that, and when she did, she became Black Crow property.

She was mine just as much as she was his, and if she chose me to protect her, I could at least get her out of that kennel. Maybe I could even get her to trust me enough to tell me what she was running from. It would at least keep him from putting her in that box and damaging whatever was left of her any further. The reasons seemed legit enough that they calmed the storm in my head, but I knew the real reason. I wanted her.

It was that simple. I had never wanted anything in my life, not for a long time.

But I wanted her.

"I don't belong to anyone," she said defiantly, turning her chin away from me.

"We can't help you if you don't choose one of us, it's the only way he'll let me get you out of there. It's in the contract." She didn't turn back to look at me.

I chuckled loud enough for her to hear, and she narrowed her eyes at me with a hating look she normally reserved for Ronan.

"You deserve him. You're perfect for each other, constantly pushing the other closer to the edge. Eventually, one of you is gonna fall off the cliff, then what?" I said, unable to hide my frustration.

I grabbed her by the wrist, and dragged her out of my room holding the burlap sack as I practically tossed her into the living room.

16

SANTOS

Sometimes being the sensible one was bullshit.

I spent all night trying to put out Black Crow fires that I didn't spark myself. I had a permanent headache I couldn't get rid of, and to top it off we had more problems than I had solutions. Top of my list was the Bratva bitch who was gonna need a new face on our dime, and the fact she had no allegiance to us doubled our troubles.

"Álvarez, is she gonna be a problem?" Zerkos asked me seriously.

"Which 'she' are you referring to at the moment?" Because honestly, I had no fucking clue.

As of right now, the Black Crows felt pretty vulnerable and if I were to pin it on anything, I'd narrow it down to a couple of broads throwing this whole thing over the edge.

He rolled his eyes at me in annoyance, "The one with a casserole for a face now. Which, by the way, did you notice they were fucking SISTERS?" He practically shouted the last part at me but honestly, I couldn't tell.

White, blonde girls with blue eyes all looked the same to me. That's why they were easy to bone, they were just *so* familiar.

"Hmm," I said starting to close my eyes, I was fucking exhausted, but it didn't seem like Ronan was gonna let me sleep until his anxiety cooled off.

Kane burst out of his room and threw Cecilia out in front of him with so much force I had to stand to catch her to keep her from falling over my chair. She spun her head at me and stared with startled eyes.

"Jesus, fuck, Kane." I looked at him questioningly, but there was a visible shift to his attitude since he left the room.

"You ready to go back down sweetheart?" Zerkos asked her and she cowered into me clenching the fabric of my shirt.

"Morena, please end this. Just tell him what he wants to know," I said in a hushed tone right against her ear, she backed up closer to me and shook her head.

She was just wearing one of Mateo's shirts. I could feel the roundness of her ass as she pressed into me. It was a temptation I absolutely didn't need, and I had to redirect my thoughts immediately so as not to fall into a void of my own destructive thinking.

"You'll let him fuck you, but you won't tell him who's after you? That's rich," Kane questioned crossing, his arms over his chest, the same demeanor coming out that he put on those first few days she was here.

I watched him change over time and soften in her presence. I saw him never taking his eyes off of her through the camera feed. I watched him going down there to let her sleep because it was so fucking obvious that she didn't trust those other three in the kennel, and she was staying up out of fear. I watched him follow Ronan blindly until he finally saw for himself that she was worth questioning him over.

Cecilia didn't just totally fuck with Zerkos by coming here, she had thrown a grenade into the Black Crows that I was starting to worry we wouldn't recover from.

I looked at her with a clear question in my eyes, and she looked down like she was embarrassed. I realized something happened between them, and Kane getting pissed over it, just meant all of this was going to wrench us apart if we couldn't get our shit together.

I gave him the same puzzled look I had just given Cecilia, but he was already starting to pace, which meant we were on the verge of whatever wild card bullshit he was about to pull next. Mateo Kane's anger came out as impulsive outbursts, he'd gotten better at controlling his shit over the last few years, but I could see he was coming undone. It was the kind of quality that made him a fantastic murderer in the name of his country, but not so much as someone who you could predict to fall in line.

Zerkos chuckled from the corner of the couch but didn't say more than that, and he didn't need to. That was all I needed to confirm my suspicions. He pulled out his pocket knife and casually started cleaning under his fingernails.

"Take her downstairs for me, will you Álvarez? I'm suddenly tired of brunettes," Kane said with a look that could have cut through stone.

"I told you both already, I can't make it any clearer, I'm not doing this. Not with her," I said through clenched teeth, annoyed we were having this power struggle in front of her.

I could feel her relax a little at my words, but Zerkos got up and she immediately turned to me and grabbed on to me.

"No! No! Please don't let him take me back there, please Santito!" She begged me.

I instinctively wrapped my arms around her at the use of the old nickname, but Ronan grabbed her by the arm and pulled her away from me. She wrapped her hands around my arms and started kicking at him, but he was much stronger than her.

"I choose Santo!" she yelled out desperately.

It took me a second to realize what she said.

Ronan let her go on instinct but he was scowling so hard I thought he might burst a blood vessel. Kane was clenching his teeth to the point where I could see the muscle on his jawline protruding and his nostrils were blown wide. Angry sneers covered both their faces at her decision.

"No. You're not a part of that," he said coldly, narrowing his eyes at Mateo, who returned the look back to him.

"She signed," I said calmly, knowing I was probably her only chance out of that kennel at this point.

Ronan's jaw ticked and Kane got up off the couch, walked up to her and grabbed her chin with his thumb and forefinger, "I challenge the fuck out of that." He let her go but he didn't do it gently and her head was thrown to the side with force.

He stormed out of view where we could only hear his bedroom door slam. Her breathing was loud and labored as she worked through her nerves, her eyes didn't meet mine or Ronan's though.

"Looks like this is under discussion for now *my love,*" Ronan said, and grabbed her by the arm as he threw her over his shoulder.

He made his way to the elevators and practically forced the door open before going in.

Fucking sloppy shit.

Didn't even put the sack over her head.

I walked over to the coffee table and propped open the laptop. Within a few minutes, I could see Ronan hauling her through the hallways as he walked her past the kennel into her box, opening the door and tossing her in. He closed the door and passed by Oksana and Chiyo in the kennel, giving them a two-finger salute before heading out and making his way back to the elevator.

I closed the laptop and anxiously rubbed my neck. This was a hell of a situation, and I couldn't begin to think of a way out of it for her. I heard the elevator arrive back at the penthouse and Ronan was walking toward me like he was gonna rip my head off.

"You need to chill man," I said to him trying to soothe the beast raging inside him. "I haven't done shit, I've been in a hospital all night dealing with *your* girl's bullshit that's bound to come back and bite us in the ass, I didn't ask for this mess."

His eyes narrowed at me in anger, but I could see that he knew I was right.

"Kane!" He shouted and crossed his arms over his chest as he waited for him to come out of his room.

Mateo appeared at the edge of the hallway and leaned against the wall casually on his forearm as he looked back at him.

"We're gonna do this then?" he said nonchalantly.

"Oh, we're gonna do this," Zerkos closed the distance between them in a few large steps and threw a fist into his best friend's face.

Mateo's head snapped back hard enough to hit the wall, and he covered his nose with his hand as blood gushed from it. He let out a wild cackle like the pain didn't bother him one bit.

"Psycho asshole," He finally said, shaking his head and walking past him as he took a seat on the couch. "It's not like she chose me." He pointed his rage over at me and I raised my hands up in front of me in defense.

He took his shirt off and used it to absorb the blood coming down his nose into his mouth.

"Why did she even *know* to do that?" Zerkos redirected back to him, and I was glad my brother was seeing clearly enough for once to know I didn't plan any of this.

I spent a lot of time thinking about Cecilia Gomes, about how I was doing her wrong.

Zerkos was my friend, shit he was my brother. But she was my friend once too. Every time I went down to the kennels I was thrown back to a time where none of this shit was between us and it was just us having a good time, getting through the trash years of our lives. I had even gotten her to laugh out loud a few times down there when I brought her food and gave her some company for a bit. It was always awkward as fuck with the other three chicks watching us, but I mostly avoided them this year.

Yeah, it was shitty that I picked them out specifically, and wasn't putting any effort into breaking them or doing any of the things we were normally doing at this point in the trials in previous years. I completely jumped ship when Cecilia walked into our penthouse, and there was nothing Ronan could do to get me on board again.

If I was being honest with myself, I was fucking depressed right now.

I spent most of my time in my room playing video games, watching the camera feed, and delegating most of my work to Fletcher, though the poor guy never complained. He was solid as hell, and he always went the extra mile where it was needed.

"She was scared shitless to go back in there, dude," Mateo said and even though he was acting like a complete shithead around her, I was wondering if there was maybe more to his little outburst. "And she *signed*. She doesn't belong to you, she's Black Crow property. And it looks like we're down one anyway." He crossed his arms over his chest at him not backing down.

Ronan cracked his neck without using his hand and sat in the chair across the couch from Kane. "She's not a part of this." He repeated again, some of his temper simmered by the sheer fact Kane didn't give in to his outburst.

Sometimes that wasn't the best way to deal with Ronan. If you let him get his rage out without fighting him on it, we could all move on and get back to how we should be.

Most of our issues were minuscule compared to the dark haired goddess locked up downstairs.

"She helps my head," he said, shrugging his hands into his pockets, but he didn't look at either of us when he said it.

It was a cheap shot, but Zerkos would give our brother anything if it meant taking away some of his pain. I just didn't know if that would extend to Cecilia.

"How long are you going to keep her in the box this time?" I asked, turning my attention back to Zerkos.

"Until she breaks," he said, not looking back at me.

I shook my head and Kane scoffed at his response, "And what are you gonna do when she *does* break? Get all your answers and free her?" I asked knowing damn well that Cecilia Gomes likely didn't have a breaking point.

"I'm gonna continue to do what she's asked of me. Keep her safe," he said with a coldness to his voice that reminded me he was still very much bruised from his past.

I raised my eyebrow at the suggestion that he'd been keeping her safe and he pressed his lips into a thin line, then let out a heavy exhale.

"Believe it or not, asshole. At the end of the day, she's safer here than she is out there if someone *is* after her," his admission made me realize my brother really was too far gone to reel back.

He was completely haunted by her presence here, but the thought of her being in danger out there was one that he couldn't accept, even after she had broken his heart and his trust.

"You big softy," I said flatly, sounding more annoyed than joking.

"And we're sure she's not already broken?" Kane dropped his elbows to his knees where he was seated, and we both shifted our attention to him.

"Are you saying that because she chose me, even though you've been clearly drooling and pissing all over her like we wouldn't notice?" My annoyance slipped out, and like Zerkos said, we were doing this.

I had my right to say my piece as well and let the cards fall where they may. She was fucking with all of our heads, and she didn't even know it.

Or did she?

"I'm saying that because only a broken girl fucks someone who locks them in a box for hours a day," Mateo said, kicking the laptop off the table, his anger and jealousy so apparent that Zerkos couldn't hold back anymore.

"You have a thing for my girl, Kane," he didn't ask, he stated it as the obvious truth it was.

"She hasn't been your girl for a long-time *brother*. And if she had been mine, and walked in here for *me* she wouldn't be sitting in a box downstairs. That's for damn sure," Kane said darkly, his attitude changing again as he got more visibly upset with every word he exchanged with Ronan. "And like I said, she makes my head not hurt."

"Well lucky for both of you, she chose me. So, when you're done throwing tantrums over it, let me know so I can go get her out of there," I turned my cup of coffee and down the rest of it before getting up from the chair, but Zerkos grabbed my arm as I was passing by him, not letting me go.

"She stays downstairs until she tells me who she's hiding from," he burned his gaze into mine and I grunted a response before shaking him off. "And you stay away from her." He pointed to Mateo, who just shrugged before he made his way down to the gym.

I'd spent the majority of the afternoon watching the camera feed in the kennels. Cecilia was still locked up in the box and the other two sat quietly on their beds without so much as glancing at each other. She'd been in the box for almost eight hours now and I knew I was going to have to go down there and get her out soon, despite the shitstorm that would blow back my way.

He hadn't given her so much as water, or a bathroom break and I wasn't willing to dehumanize anyone to that extent, no matter what it cost. I'd gladly face Ronan's wrath for that, for her.

He was too wrapped up in finding out the truth, and the hurt of his past kept fueling him to make terrible decisions when it came to her. Mateo's words kept crossing my mind, and I didn't know why but it angered me to think she'd let Ronan fuck her. Was she really that damaged that she'd let the same person who was hurting her, have access to the most intimate parts of her? Or was it something else? Was there still love there after all this time?

I didn't want to keep thinking about him and her together anymore, as much as I loved my brother unconditionally.

I wasn't sure he deserved her anymore.

I knew why she chose me, I was the safe option.

The choice that she could count on and predict, even if she didn't exactly understand what she was choosing. But under the surface, I was reaching a tipping point, and I didn't feel so predictable anymore. I did my best to hide it and conceal my reactions and emotions, but I could only handle about an hour at a time of her presence. Anything longer and I'd start fumbling at accidental touches and I couldn't take the risk of her, or anyone else watching and noticing the lingering looks.

My phone buzzed and I picked it up to see a text from Ethan.

Ethan: Two giant Bratvas with face tattoos personally escorted what's left of Anya out of surgery into some imported car with blacked-out plates.

Me: Any idea what kind of car?

Ethan: Black, looked like the front had "Aurus" on it, they pulled in and out quick.

Me: Have the guys down in tech look up and see who's imported any Russian cars that cost over $250k in the last year. That should get us a start.

Ethan: Roger that boss.

There was a good chance this was going to turn into a much bigger situation, but I didn't want to hyper-fixate on something I couldn't control. Not yet at least. Maybe they weren't Bratva, maybe she did have family out here, or maybe the Bratvas had a tighter hold on their merchandise than we thought. Were they waiting for us to mess up again so they could take the other one too?

Or maybe they weren't merchandise.

Maybe I had seriously fucked something up this year.

Zerkos locked himself in his room, metal was blaring through the speakers so loudly I could feel the vibration of the music through my walls. I would bet anything that he was drinking himself stupid and watching the feed of her in that tiny black closet, punishing himself for punishing her.

That was their thing, hurting themselves while hurting each other. It was an annoying by-product of them growing up together, where sometimes they acted more like brother and sister instead of lovers.

They knew the other so well they could push a boundary or button without so much as uttering three words to each other. Ronan always said I didn't get to know the real relationship they had, that those last three years were just a sham, a ticking time bomb that was counting down from the moment her father told him that she'd one day leave him. They were constantly at each other's throats, fighting, yelling, and fucking until he'd go off on another job, leaving her with me.

It was like they'd picked up exactly where they left off and the only way out for them at this point was through it. They had so much unfinished business, if one of them died the other would probably stick around just to haunt them.

The problem was that going through it might wreck us all. We were all keeping so many secrets from each other that the entire Black Crow Brotherhood would probably burn before we could get any answers. Guilt ate at me at the thought of endangering any of our people or their family. We had always taken care of our own here.

What tugged at my conscience the most was my own raging feelings. Was I supposed to tell my brother that his girl wasn't as safe with me as he thought she was? I opened up a new tab and pulled up the live feed for the box, it was separate from the feed for the rest of the kennels because Ronan didn't want any of our guys to have access to it. He was so consumed with jealousy and possessiveness that he wasn't even letting our top guys handle the kennels as much as they usually did. It was like he didn't even want anyone else so much as *looking* at her.

She sat there in the corner, arms slack as she rested her head on the corner of the wall, knees up to her chest because there wasn't room to stretch out. She was looking straight at the camera, barely blinking, breathing so softly you couldn't even see her chest move. I decided enough was enough and I was going to go get her out of there.

Before I could act on it, the door to the kennel opened and she was pulled out of it.

17

CECILIA

My eyes were open, but I was somewhere else.

I was at that place in my head where no one could touch me, the place my papá carved out of me like a river cut through a mountain range. He knew it would take more than just blood rights and learning the politics of the syndicate to turn me into reina del cártel. A king had to be forged in heat and be as hard as steel.

As a woman, he knew I had to be twice as resilient. I had to be indestructible to survive those who would stand in my way.

"Your enemy will do whatever it takes to get information from you mija," my papá paced in front of me.

I was fourteen again dripping in sweat, body aching, covered in my own piss as I hung by my bound wrists.

A few of my fingers burned from the nails being removed the previous day and my toes were barely grazed the floor, exhaustion coursing through me, my hunger no longer present as we reached day three in the dungeon.

"You must compartmentalize if you are to rise above them all," he said calmly, gesturing Cézar over.

"And if they kill me for my silence?" I asked through labored breaths.

"Then you will die with the honor of knowing you were not weak, and the Flores Cártel will be stronger for it." His eyes were full of pride as I nodded at him in understanding.

Through all of the beatings, the waterboarding, and psychological torture he put me through, not even a scream escaped my lips, let alone the word 'stop'. We'd been doing this for a couple of years now, Papá said his father started when he was fifteen and he wanted me to be better than him, stronger than him. Personally, I just thought he was making up for the fact I was a woman.

I would always need twice as much to be half as strong.

One weekend every two months, since my eleventh birthday he brought me to one of the cártel dungeons in Tijuana to mold me into the queen he thought I should be. It was the beginning of summer vacation, and I was to be by his side for the entirety of it. By the time I would get home for the school year to start, my nails would have grown back, my scars would be less visible, and I would be ten times stronger than the girl I was when we started.

There was always a part of me that wondered if this would have been my life so early on had we not been forced into hiding all those years ago, when Ignacio burned our home down. But I think this was always papá's plan from the minute the doctor announced he was having a girl.

Cézar uncrossed his arms from the corner of the cell and pushed off the wall with a foot as he grabbed the iron cattle brand off the flickering heat of the torch that was ignited. The five-petal crest was glowing red hot and his eyes met mine with an apology etched into them that was unspoken, I didn't need it anyway. Even without the chains or the handcuffs I would willingly stand here and accept my fate.

It was more than an honor.

I braced for the pain I knew was coming when he tore the bottom of my shirt off and lifted it up to expose my rib. "Respira Princesa," he said. I swallowed a deep breath, but nothing could prepare me for the agonizing pain that would tear through my body.

I could almost taste the hot iron of the brand melting my flesh, I bit my cheeks to force down the scream that was threatening to slip out of me. The smell of torched skin filled the air and warm urine dripped down to my toes, but I couldn't feel much aside from the throb below my breast.

I flickered in and out of consciousness, head hanging down as saliva and blood pooled out of my mouth, but I could hear bits and pieces of Cézar's quiet approval telling me I had done well. Right before I lost control of reality, I heard my papá say, "Welcome to the cártel mija." I heard the clinking of the gold coin thrown at my feet, but I was lost to the darkness before I could appreciate my well-earned trophy.

The door of the coffin opened, and I was blinded by the sudden brightness of the external world. It was hard to say how long I had been in here, but judging by the pressure in my bladder I'd guess it had definitely been a while. I didn't bother to stand or move, so he grabbed me like a rag doll and threw my limp body over his shoulder again, all of the fight, completely drained from me as he crossed through the large lobby that separated the kennels from the bathroom.

He gave me a few minutes to myself and opened the door when he heard the flush of the toilet before picking me up again.

I could almost feel the scorch of the brand on my ribcage searing through my clothes from the heat of his touch against my cold body.

"Are you ready to talk?" Ronan asked as he dropped me onto my bed, but I felt further from it than ever before.

I felt hollowed out and frozen in the past. I could fight the effects of that closet for a few hours at a time, but I was out of practice, and I couldn't last as long as I did when I was young. It stole a piece of me to be locked away in there, and the fact he did it intentionally stung deeper than the scars I bore.

I had no strength to fight him after spending all day in that dark chamber, so I didn't answer. I lay on my side and faced away from him, curling my body into a small shape. I closed my eyes as exhaustion hit me like a ton of bricks and I was too weak to resist the call of slumber, though in the back of my mind I knew it wasn't safe.

I woke up to a sharp stab in my stomach and the fog of sleep took too long to clear. Before I could make sense of what was happening, I felt the same stabbing pain again and again before I could will my legs to kick out in front of me. Oksana was thrown to the ground from the force of my kick, the opaque sound of her head hitting the concrete floor forcing my eyes to finally open.

I hurled myself on top of her and pounded my fist into her face without regard for her life.

"I'll kill you like I should have killed your sister." I spat.

In between fists slamming down her face, I could hear the loud clamoring of the guys rushing to the kennels. It was Fletcher who got in first pulling Oksana out from under me as he dragged her into the opposite kennel, and I heard Ronan telling him to cuff her to the wall. Santos caught me from behind as I stumbled backward and he sat on the bed, legs wide as he lowered me down in between them.

"Shit," he said, "This is gonna hurt a bit," he warned me as he pulled the fork out of my stomach, and I yelled at the unexpected sting of the pain.

I looked down to see the blood dripping down to the mattress from the twelve small puncture holes, but Santos already had his shirt off and folded into a neat bundle that he pressed into the wound.

I groaned a few curses in both languages laying back into his chest as I breathed heavily through the pain in my stomach and the burning ache in my hands. I turned my head to the other kennel to see Fletcher hosing down Oksana again like they did the first couple of weeks when we first came down here. I looked up at Santos' face to see it was filled with worry and anxiety. I shifted a bit so that I could get on my side to look at him.

I groaned from the pain.

He was looking at his hand pressed to my stomach and the blood staining through his shirt.

I reached up and touched the Los Muertos tattoo on his chest, my fingers outlining the image of the masked skull inked onto him. It made me sad to see this image burned into him forever, marking him as one of theirs. He spent his entire life fighting against becoming a part of it and in the end, he still became their property.

Were we all destined from the beginning?

Did none of our choices matter?

Would we always end up in the path that was laid out for us?

If so, that thought alone scared the fuck out of me. I'd long strayed from my path, and I wasn't sure I could even find my way back to it if I wanted to.

The skull was a taunting reminder of how weak we all truly were.

None of us had any choice in how we ended up here, not really. I continued to trace the image softly, letting my mind wander to Cézar and how easy it was for him to stray from *his* path. He was supposed to have protected me, to have put me on my throne. Now he was free of every burden my papá had placed on his shoulders when he guilted him into becoming his right hand as a payment for the debt of raising him as his own.

Santos took his hand off the wadded shirt pressed against my bleeding stomach and gently grabbed my fingers, almost like a warning that I shouldn't be touching him. But as I looked up at the only person who didn't try to break my spirit every day in this hell, I found fear and uncertainty staring back at me.

I brushed his chestnut curls away from his hazel eyes and allowed the corner of my lip to curl up awkwardly into a half smile and to my surprise he returned it. The unfamiliar feeling of fluttering in my belly lasted only a second when my injury throbbed from the rush of liquid dumped on my stomach. I looked down to see Mateo pouring tequila over it before casually offering me the bottle. I took as many gulps as I could before the burn of the alcohol dried my throat and I had to pull the bottle back to cough.

"Easy there, tiger," Mateo said, as he took the bottle back and poured it over me again.

I grit my teeth through it then he pressed the makeshift gauze to my belly with a bit more pressure than Santos used. Santos stared into my eyes, but he didn't say anything, he just sat there holding me, calming me as I used his heart beat and synchronizing breath to find stillness.

"Lock her in the box when you're done," Ronan shouted over to Fletcher and I tensed up, my body going completely rigid in Santos' hands.

"For how long?" I heard him asking.

"I don't care if you forget her in there," he said, my heart dropping with those words but before he could fully turn away from him, he looked back and added more. "Actually, don't let her stink up the box, it's not hers. Take her down to five when you're done." Ronan instructed Fletcher and relief washed over as I realized he wasn't talking about me.

I could see a look of worry etched into Santos' face though and I had to wonder what they were doing on the fifth floor.

"You sure brother?" Mateo questioned him but not in an undermining way.

"Yeah, something's fucking off and I'm going to get to the bottom of it," he slammed the other kennel's metal door so loudly it made me flinch.

"Call Emory and see if she can come by to check out Cecilia," I heard Mateo ordering someone but the pounding in my heart was dulling out all of the voices.

"Down *here?*" Santos asked in a hushed voice.

"Better take her back up," someone answered and in less than a heartbeat, Ronan was scooping me up in his arms and carrying me out of the kennel as if I was completely weightless.

When we were back up in the penthouse, we made our way past Mateo and Santos' doors that stood opposite of each other, into the door at the end of the hall. He nudged it open with his shoe and the room opened up, it was just as large as Mateo's room, but it wasn't as bare. He had a TV hanging on one side with a loveseat in front of it and a wet bar in another corner.

The bed was the biggest bed I'd seen in my life and completely unnecessary even if he *was* eighty feet tall now. Red silk sheets covered it like a fine fitted gown and I ached to feel the cool of it as he sat me down onto the bed. My hands were hot from the pain of my torn knuckles. I looked down to find them bloody, I couldn't find it in me to care that I was dirtying up his fancy sheets, but when he sat next to me my heart took off at a million miles an hour and my breathing began to skip.

The crease in between his eyebrows let me know he was angry, but there wasn't a doubt in my mind that for once it wasn't directed at me.

Maybe at himself this time.

"Let me see," he said, moving my hand off the wadded t-shirt.

The blood was still coming out of the puncture wounds at a slow steady pace, but it didn't look or feel like I was going to die. When his other hand met my waist as he examined my injuries, I let out a stuttered exhale and that line between his eyebrows finally dissolved. We sat like that for a while, just frozen in time while he softly stroked his thumb against my waist and his stare burned into mine.

The rhythm of his breaths slowed like he was trying to lead mine in the same fashion and I allowed myself to match my breathing to his, heavy but stable and slow. There were so many things I wanted to say but nothing I could force out. In so many ways he reminded me of the love of my life.

He was so much like the boy I had given all of myself to, but if I looked too hard I could see we were complete strangers, unknown to each other in every possible way. The heat of his touch was toxic and all consuming, and I was completely paralyzed by the infernal blaze of his light caress.

For the first time since I stepped into this high-rise I wanted to open up and let all the walls tumble down, I wanted him to beg me for the truth again so that I could finally let it all out. I wanted so badly to hope that he could be my knight in shining armor, that he could fight my demons for me and help me conquer them.

But for once he didn't ask, and I wasn't sure if I was relieved or disappointed.

This wasn't a fairy tale, and I knew my uncle had the resources to bring the entire Black Crow Brotherhood to its knees with a snap of his fingers. It wasn't just unfair for me to want him to shoulder my problems, it was cowardly. I wasn't a damsel in distress, I was a queen whose crown was torn off her head and I refused to let anyone fight my battles for me.

My future held three possible scenarios: One where I escaped and hid for the rest of my life in hopes he would never find me. The second where he would no doubt find me and finally kill me, with that smug look on his fat bastard face. The third option was the one where I killed him, but it was currently the most unlikely option of the three for so many reasons, but number one being I had no army to go up against his with.

Trying to kill my uncle was a suicide mission and as hopeless as I felt, I would die by my own hand before giving that *hijo de la chingada* the satisfaction.

"This better be good, Zerkos, I was just about to go to sleep." Her hot as hell Irish accent came tumbling into the room before I could see her.

A gorgeous redhead with a small suitcase walked in unannounced. Her waves long and full, her lipstick almost the same copper color as her hair. She was wearing white high heels paired with a matching lab coat and a dress skirt that screamed a kind of put together I couldn't even dream of being.

I was suddenly overwhelmed with insecurity at how haggard I must have looked in comparison. Leftover makeup from the party smeared down my face and my hair, a wild mess comparable to a rats nest. I couldn't even remember the last time I brushed my teeth if I was being honest, but he didn't look up at her or take his eyes off of me when he spoke to her.

"Just need to make sure she doesn't need to go in for this," he said, revealing the stab wounds and her eyebrow raised up at him.

"What the hell happened to her?" She asked him but I answered instead.

"She's right here, he doesn't speak for me."

"Oh!" She squeaked, "I'm so sorry, um, the girls usually don't speak English. I didn't think..."

Ronan cleared his throat, interrupting her from finishing her thought. "Can you just take a look at her Emory?"

"The girls?" I asked, but I knew well enough to understand she was referring to the others in the kennel.

How many had there been? I was starting to wonder if this Emory might be my best source of information to get some answers on whatever the fuck Ronan was doing with those women. Unfortunately, as soon as the words left my mouth, she looked to Ronan for approval, but he shook his head, denying my request.

She rushed over to my side as she began to examine my stomach, opening up her suitcase and pulling out a plethora of medical tools.

"You know, I like my paychecks, I do. I'm grateful for everything you and the Black Crows have done for me, and I like how well funded you all keep Saint Murphy's Hospital..." she nervously tripped over her words as she fished in her bag for something, and Ronan interrupted her again.

"Spit it out, Emory."

"I saw what you did to that Russian girl, Zerkos," she said without looking at him, keeping her gaze down as she mumbled "I didn't sign up for this."

"He didn't do it to her, I did," I said, coming to his defense, though I wasn't sure why.

Maybe I just didn't want her thinking he was capable of hurting a defenseless girl like that. But maybe he *was* capable. She looked up at me, confusion written all over her face as she waited for an explanation that I wouldn't give.

"I don't think the cord to my ultrasound machine will reach the outlet, can you find me an extension cord?" she asked him, and he nodded. Before leaving the room, he threw me a glance, and for once I couldn't tell what he was thinking at all.

"I'm not pregnant," I said to her, a bit confused at why I needed an ultrasound.

"It's to check for internal bleeding, I want to make sure your vital organs aren't punctured," she said in a professional tone, and I nodded in understanding.

I was dying to ask her a million questions, and maybe fill some of the pieces I was missing here. How close was she to the Black Crows? What did she know was happening with the girls, and why did it seem like she was on board? Did she know what my future held? Did she have a history with Ronan? My thoughts derailed at a rapid pace and my heartbeat quickened at the thought of them together.

Cálmate. *The nice lady is patching you up.*

She was setting a few packaged tools down on a medical pad next to me, and I had to admit I was pretty impressed at how prepared she was at the drop of a hat.

"Do you make house calls often?" I began my interrogation.

"For the Black Crows, yes."

"But not normally for the women?" I pried further, trying to see how far I could push her.

"They don't usually need it, I've come by for wellness checks before though, or if someone gets sick," she started dabbing at my injuries with a cold gauze and I groaned at the sting.

"Mateo already cleaned it out," I said, trying to push her hands off of my stomach, but she laughed instead and just batted my hands away.

"I'm sure the tequila did well, but it's my job to make sure you heal okay," she said with a bit of warmth that showed me that she was actually a good doctor, the kind that was rare to come by.

She wasn't someone doing it for the money, but doing it because she genuinely gave a shit about people.

"What do you know about the other women?" I decided to stop beating around the bush and see what I could find out.

She looked me right in the eye and said, "That they need to be here." She barely answered before she asked me, "Do you want to tell me why you battered that poor girl?"

I turned my head to the side, unwilling to tell a stranger that pure jealousy took over all of my instincts and every piece of control I once had, disappeared in a red flash. I couldn't tell her that I didn't regret it or that I would do it again and again, if I had the chance. I definitely couldn't confess that I wouldn't even blink twice before turning her face into a pizza too if I saw her reaching for Ronan in the same way.

"You don't trust me, that's okay. I don't expect you to, but maybe you could be better about not making so many enemies hmm?" She looked up at me from the wound she was tending to and I pressed my lips into a flat line.

I didn't answer but she went on anyway.

"I'm just saying, I got called in twenty-four hours ago over a twenty-two-year-old female who had been beaten beyond recognition, and now I'm cleaning what looks like multiple fork stab holes in your stomach. I'm smart enough to understand the timing and that the woman who stabbed you isn't the same woman who you gave a beatdown to."

"I rub people the wrong way." No sooner did the words come out of my mouth but Ronan was strutting back in with an extension cord chiming in his opinion.

"You can say that again."

I glared at him but he didn't even spare to look my way, handing her the extension cord so she could plug in a small device that could have been mistaken for hair clippers.

She connected it to her phone, the pressure from it against the still bleeding tiny holes making me wince. Within a few minutes, she exhaled a sigh of relief and gave us the update, "All clear, no internal bleeding, all major organs are okay. It should completely clot within a couple of hours. I'd like to glue the punctures shut to facilitate the healing if you're okay with it?" she asked me.

"Just because it wasn't serious doesn't mean I want you going overboard." She looked at Ronan before she went on, "I want her resting for the next few days. Here are painkillers for it, she will be sore, and I'll send over some antibiotics, twice a day. With food Zerkos, she looks skinny as hell." She side-eyed him and he shrugged his shoulders at her.

"I can't make her eat if she doesn't want to."

She shook her head and gave me a slightly empathizing look. "I think too often we women are pitted against each other. Just remember that. It can be good to have someone in your corner every now and then, yeah?" She gave my hand a squeeze and then began to pack up all of her medical equipment into the bag.

"Walk me out? We need to talk," her tone darkened with her words, and she didn't bother throwing a single glance at Ronan.

I didn't expect the doctor to have a spine after all, and I was impressed that she could channel that confidence to stand up to him.

He grunted, giving me an almost apologetic look before walking out of the room with her. He was barely out of the room, and I was painstakingly maneuvering myself off of his bed as I disregarded the pain medication and hobbled towards the door, clutching my stomach. There was nothing I hated more than not being in control of my mind, and that was exactly what any pain relieving drug did.

The tapping of my bare feet on the marble floor echoed out as I reached the threshold that opened out into the hallway, and I stared at the two doors on opposite sides of the wall.

I sighed heavily, annoyed at myself for having feelings I couldn't begin to process or understand.

I was sure as shit not turning back to the door behind me, and the door to my left had too high of a chance for rejection that I certainly couldn't handle right now. I decided I wasn't done letting myself drown in misery yet, so I turned to the door on my right, and I was somewhat surprised to see it slightly open, the music becoming louder with each step I took.

18

MATEO

I could hear the "tap, tap, tap" of her feet stamping like a steady metronome and I used it to fuel the keys beneath my hands. Her feet slowed during the crescendo, but I didn't let up the pace, my fingers moved faster with a delicate ease I practiced almost my entire life. She stood watching me almost like she needed permission to move at all, and I shifted a few inches on the piano bench as an invitation.

She reminded me of a wild animal.

Prey.

Completely unsure if she should move any further or back to where she came from in a quick hurry. There was a look to her that said if I were to make any sudden moves she may just bolt. Based on her current condition I didn't think that would be possible, but I wouldn't have put it past her to try. I scooted one more inch over, implying the obvious as I finally looked away from the instrument, keeping my fingers in control at all times.

It took her so long to come to my side that I began a new song, another *Sonata* in the book of sheet music that had long retired to the storage portion of the bench. I hadn't needed it for a long time, its secrets had been sealed to my memory permanently since the age of nine.

"What did the doctor say?" I asked as I played the final notes slower than needed.

"You said it yourself last night, I'll live to fight another day," she gave me a soft smile.

I didn't return it.

"Why did you come here?" I tried to keep the jealousy and left-over anger from reaching my voice, but it was impossible to hide it.

"Because the first time I trusted myself to fall asleep without you there, I woke up to someone trying to fork me to death," she dead-panned.

"Fair." I responded, trying to keep my emotions in check, refusing to show how surprised I was at her honesty.

I was never sure what I was going to get with her. If she was going to willingly tell me exactly what was in her head, or if I'd maybe get two or three words I'd have to use to decode a bigger puzzle later. Adding it to my ever-growing list of things that tormented me.

"Did Álvarez lock you out?" I let my insecurities show, not bothering to hide that I envied my brother.

"I didn't check, couldn't really handle the thought of rejection right now. Are you going to tell me to leave?"

I sighed heavily trying to ignore the agonizing ache in my brain as I stood from the piano, extending my hand to help her up to guide her to my bed, the same place she woke up from just this morning.

"Zerkos won't want you in here," I reminded her, but she crawled into my favorite side of the bed anyway.

I picked her legs up off the floor to help her get comfortable without pain.

"He's too preoccupied with the *Doctor* to care," she spit.

I huffed a small laugh out as I realized we'd all somehow managed to end up doing the same dance.

She was jealous, he was jealous, fuck it, *I* was jealous. It seemed like the only person with common sense left was Santos, but I was starting to wonder if he was just better at hiding his crazy. She looked up at me in annoyance from my reaction, but I just shrugged my reply.

"What a tangled web we weave, hmm?" I asked, turning to my closet. "Do you need anything for the pain?" I looked down at her blood covered hoodie as I pulled out one of my t-shirts for her, but she shook her head at me.

"No, do you?" she asked, raising her eyebrows up as she waited for an explanation.

I shook my head at her before I started. "My neurologist says migraines are common with severe cases of PTSD."

"From being in the Navy?" she asked, and I twisted my face, shaking my head at her again.

"I've been getting these for a lot longer than that."

"From your sister," she didn't ask, she said it and I confirmed it with a nod.

Most people thought it was from my time overseas, hell even my brothers thought that. But the truth was there was nothing I'd done or seen with a gun in my hand that fucked up my head. Nothing like the image of Andrea that played on repeat in my head like a constant echo of my failures.

"I don't think I can get this off by myself right now," she admitted, shaking me out of my fog.

I lifted her elbows up over her head and grabbed the hem of the hoodie as I pulled it up and over her head. I couldn't hold back the noise that escaped my throat at the sight of her. It took every single ounce of restraint I had to not reach out and caress her beautiful skin. She didn't cover herself with her arms, she just waited for me to get the clean shirt for her.

"Who taught you to play?" she asked as I slipped the t-shirt over her head, and she slid her arms through the sleeves.

"My mother, she played just about anything. She went to school for it, ended up becoming a musical director at the university she went to and conducting the symphony there. She taught me the piano and the Cello, my sister too." I explained.

"That's amazing, I wish I could do anything artistic," she said looking around the room. "Looks like you play more than just the piano and the cello though."

"I picked up a few things here and there, I guess I'm just like her in that way. I like to compose, and sometimes you just need a full symphony. It's easier to piece things together if I'm the one playing it all," I explained to her.

She laughed and said, "I can't tell if you're really talented or just afraid of not being in control."

I shrugged my shoulders, but I knew the answer.

"Where is your mom now?" she asked.

"Boca Raton, I think. That's where she was last time I followed up on her. She remarried about a decade ago to a car salesman. We haven't talked since I was eighteen." I answered, knowing full well I was crossing a point of no return, sharing far too much of myself and letting her in somewhere she absolutely did not belong.

"Oh," she breathed out. "Because of your sister?"

"Because I reminded her of it all. Because deep down she blamed me as much as she blamed my old man. Because she would have rather it have been me who was at fault. Because it was easier for her to pretend like she could just start over instead of picking up the pieces and rebuilding with me. I was on my own from the moment the police took that piece of shit away, I didn't have a mother anymore after that either." I released the words out of me, in a way I had never admitted to anyone before.

"That's very sad. That must have been really difficult, you were so young," she empathized.

She was probably the only person in this penthouse who understood the pain of losing someone like I did, but my loss suddenly felt shadowed by the magnitude of hers as I remembered her history.

"It shapes us, right?" I asked.

"Either that or it destroys us," She responded looking into my eyes, "I lost my little sister too."

"I know, Zerkos talked about her a good amount," I said, and her eyes widened in surprise. "He keeps a photo of her in his wallet, even now." I let her know, even though it wasn't my place.

I knew whatever they had between them now was completely fucked up, possibly beyond all repair, but she still deserved to know that her sister meant something to more than just her too. Sometimes we were so burdened by the ghosts of our pasts that we didn't realize we might not be the only ones who were haunted. Her exhale came out in a stuttered breath as she fought back her emotions.

"What happened to *him*?" she asked with a bit of hesitation to call him what he was, my dad, the guy who made me.

The scariest part of that acknowledgement was the ever-looming thought that there was a fifty percent chance I would end up just like him someday.

I would end myself before I ever let that happen.

"He's been in prison ever since. I never saw him after he was convicted. What was your father like?" I prodded to see if she was willing to give me anything else tonight, and to my surprise, she answered.

"Just, like...me," and she pressed her lips into a fine line, faking a smile.

I tossed my boots off and put my leather jacket on the bedside table as I climbed into the bed next to her. I leaned against the headboard and out of habit she settled into me, readying herself for sleep. The smell of her hair was a comfort I couldn't rationally explain, but I knew I needed it.

"What happens on the fifth floor?" she asked me, her voice full of drowsiness.

"Bad things, sunshine," I told her the truth without telling her anything at all.

The fifth floor was where we did the heavy load of our work. It was where anyone who crossed the Black Crows was taken when they were captured. The kennels were an all-expense-paid vacation to the Bahamas in comparison to the fifth floor.

Anyone from the Black Crows was allowed to fuck with our prisoners, however they deemed fit. Sometimes Hughes and the others who manned the floor just forgot to feed them for weeks at a time and we'd come back to rotting corpses.

I knew he put Oksana there to scare her, and as much as I didn't give a shit about her, I did have to wonder how safe she was down there. Cecilia didn't press for more answers, and she let out a heavy exhale that let me know sleep wasn't too far.

This time I tucked my arm behind her and pulled her in towards me. She adjusted herself as I brought her head into my lap, my fingers softly stroking the black tourmaline strands of hair splayed across my legs. It didn't take long but soon her anxious exhales turned into soft peaceful breathing and I knew she finally relaxed into sleep. I took my phone out and snapped a photo of her on my lap with my middle finger flashing the camera and sent the photo to the group text.

Your little flower doesn't seem to know what she wants...

ÁLVAREZ IS TYPING...

Why is she out of my room?

ZERKOS

Goldilocks came to my door out of her own free-will. Shouldn't have left with the Doc.

ÁLVAREZ IS TYPING...

I'm coming up to get her as soon as Emory quits bitchin at me.

ZERKOS

Don't be an ass. She's asleep

Álvarez U good?

Yeah...

ÁLVAREZ

Lock my door for me will ya? I can't get up. *Tongue sticking out emoji*

I leaned back onto the headboard, a few minutes went by and I heard the creak of my door opening followed by the click of the lock and a soft shut. I already knew without a doubt it was Santos because there was no way in hell Zerkos would have come in here without ripping her out of my arms. I made a mental note to thank him in the morning.

I knew the only reason he locked the door was to keep Zerkos from blowing a gasket and throwing her back down in the kennels tonight, but I was grateful for it either way.

The morning came fast and abruptly, the sun was shining through the glass of the exterior facing wall and painting the room with a kaleidoscope of reflective colors. I reached over for the remote to close the automatic blinds and soreness hit my entire body like a freight train. I was still leaning against the headboard, neck bent to one side and her head on my lap.

I looked over at my phone and it read four-forty-eight, so I decided to slide my body all the way down the bed, as I wrapped my arms around her fully and curled myself around her. Somehow the pressure in my head wasn't as intense this morning as usual, and it was easy to fall back into sleep.

"Is that a sledgehammer in your pants or are you really happy to see me?" her voice was so smooth it was practically dripping in honey as she woke me up from my sleep.

There was a firm round ass pressed against me as we lay on our sides, and I could feel my cock growing to attention. My arm was already draped over her, so I took her hand under mine, lacing my fingers through hers. I brought them just over my cock where it rested on my leg so that her hand was touching it over my boxer briefs.

"Find out for yourself," I dared her and to my surprise, she squeezed her fist around me.

Even though her hand was too small to connect all the way around, the quick firm touch was enough to drive me insane, wanting for more.

"Oh," she breathed out heavily and pulled her hand back quickly, making a chuckle escape from me.

I liked that she could be dirty, darling, and somehow shy all within a matter of seconds.

"Yeah, oh," I said, pulling her hips back towards me, she ground her ass against me, forcing a growl out of my throat.

"Why Santos?" I asked the question that had been circling my mind for nearly the entire last day.

She let out a heavy exhale before speaking.

"Because I don't think you're someone I want to be indebted to," she stopped for a second and shifted to her back and groaned a little. She looked at the ceiling and continued, "Because you've hurt me."

She finally looked at me when she said the last bit, "Because I know you'll probably hurt me again."

"You think you'd owe me something for getting you out of there?" I narrowed my eyes at her but tried to hide the offended tone in my voice.

"Wouldn't I?" she asked me, and I didn't answer.

"Do you think I'd hurt you again?" I asked her instead.

"Wouldn't you?" she asked again.

"Only in the ways that count," I murmured.

The real truth was that I didn't know. I couldn't predict my moves at all anymore, not that I ever really could. With her around though it was like I was a stranger to myself these days.

My phone buzzed and I picked it up.

Tech got back to me, the car that picked Anya up from St. Murphy's is registered to Alisher Sokolov.

ÁLVAREZ

As in, the Head of the fucking Bratvas?

ZERKOS

The one and only.

ÁLVAREZ

So, either our little guest is somehow involved with the head of the Bratvas, or they're tracking their merchandise hard. This is gonna blow the fuck up.

ZERKOS

You think Sokolov collects all his products personally?

ÁLVAREZ

Fuck. Why the fuck is Kane not answering yet?

ZERKOS

THUMP-THUMP-THUMP

Zerkos's heavy fist slammed against my locked door and Cecilia pulled the comforter over her head, cocooning herself in with a groan of dissatisfaction.

"I saw you two together the other night before I came back," I told her, pulling the cover from her face, and revealing the wide-eyed reaction that I loved to draw out of her.

I pointed to the surveillance camera mounted in the corner of the wall on the ceiling and her mouth parted in an 'O' shape and I barked out a laugh.

"Yes, I'm very good at making bad decisions. I thought we already covered the obvious," she said, covering her face again but with her hand this time, making me laugh.

"So, Zerkos is a bad decision?" I asked her.

"Ronan is all of my bad decisions, coming back to haunt me full force," she stated, all amusement stripped from her face and her voice. "Love is fucked," her accent slipped out a bit with the words that ran through me like an electric current.

"Santos thinks you're protecting Ronan, but he's a big boy, sunshine. You still love him?" I asked even though I knew the answer.

"He hurts me more than anyone has ever been capable of doing. And that's saying a lot." She said with a pause that forced me to nudge her for more information. "But I don't think I'll ever know how to stop."

Somehow, I had a feeling that was the most honest thing she'd said since she stepped inside of our little slice of hell.

I hooked my arm around her waist and pulled her closer to me. She let out a startled breath from the motion, and I felt kind of like a dick when I remembered her stab wounds. Her chest was practically touching mine as it heaved up and down with each inhale. I thumbed the bandaged area on her stomach gently. Her breathing was getting quicker, I could feel the nervous energy dripping out of her as she waited for me to respond but I didn't, I knew if I stayed quiet, she'd eventually open up. She gazed down at my hand and took blinks that were too long before she finally looked up.

Our lips were teetering the edge of kissing but never quite making contact, the two of us clearly so afraid of making the decision.

"I didn't choose you because you scare the hell out of me. You're erratic, impulsive, unpredictable, and all in all you're bad for me." She said each word describing me like they were curses but it just made me hotter for her that she already knew me so well.

"Yeah? And what are you, sunshine?"

"I'm careful, I calculate everything, every option, before I make a decision. I weigh out every possible path before I take it, always have and always will." She blinked slowly as she looked into my eyes.

"That sounds boring. Maybe you need a little unpredictable in your life." I smirked at her as I pressed our foreheads together.

"At least with Ronan I know that we deserve each other's worst. We're toxic, we're killing each other slowly but I think I'm okay with that. Toxic is all I've ever known." She looked away. "Worst of all is the way you look at me. I-I don't want anyone to want me the way you think you do, I hurt people who get too close to me."

"Then hurt me too; I'd gladly suffer by your hand." I whispered as my thumb rubbed against her bottom lip roughly, leaving it red and puffy.

She shook her head like I didn't know what I was saying, and maybe I didn't anymore. Maybe I was all the things she said I was.

Was that such a bad thing?

"Part of me is also afraid that letting anyone else in, might force me to stop loving him. I'm not ready to do that," she confessed looking straight into my eyes, it was all I needed to hear to seal my lips around hers.

Her lips were soft, and I pressed into her firmly but felt her pushing back at me with just as much vigor as she parted them for me. She tasted better than I could have imagined, like summertime and heartbreak. I wrapped my hand around a cluster of her hair to contort her the way I needed her to be. She gasped into my mouth as our tongues swirled together, but it was brief and she pulled back looking at me with confliction dancing over her eyes.

"And how is it that I look at you sunshine?" I asked her.

"Like I can save you, like I'm the answer to something you've been looking for." She breathed out heavily.

Spot on, she had me figured out.

I was addicted to being around her because she fixed something inside of me. She was like being stabbed in the heart to distract from the pain of a knife in your foot.

"I'm not." She said coldly.

"You are. I can feel it. Let me in." I gritted out into her ears.

"Don't you get it? Everyone who's ever gotten close to me has ended up dead!" She cried out showing a sliver of her true emotions for once.

"I'm already dead anyways. I have been for a long time." I whispered tracing her jaw with the side of my finger, "I know what you really fear. I won't ask you to stop loving him." I promised, shaking my head almost as if I was giving her the permission she was looking for.

I stared into her glossy eyes and this time she initiated the kiss, softly, and so timidly that it took all of my restraint not to grab her and bend her to my every whim.

I turned the sound system in my room up with a click on my phone so that a *Gautier* cover echoed through the speakers and into our bodies. I deepened our kiss as she parted her lips for me again and let me take charge of the moment.

There was a soft moan that came from her. It was barely audible, I swallowed it down my own throat while she ran her hands down my chest, exploring the ridges of my abs and trailing her hands up my chest and down my arms.

I touched her softly and with intent as I lapped up every second of being with her. All I wanted was to keep feeling her skin on me while I explored every curve on her body, mapping out her cartography and ingraining it in my memory in case this wouldn't last.

I used my own leg to part hers to find that, of course, she wasn't wearing any panties because she was still just wearing my shirt from the previous night.

She exhaled and it came out frantic and full of nerves. I would bet her heart was racing too.

This was wrong.

It had to be. Because she felt too good, too real.

Reaching between her legs, my fingers finding her already slick and ready for me. I pressed my thumb over her clit, her head tipped back, a whimper falling from her lips as I made circles.

She bit her lip, her leg hooking over mine, giving me the encouragement I needed to keep going.

THUMP-THUMP-THUMP

The asshole banged again, so hard this time that some of the art I had hanging rattled against the wall in their frames from his force. Her eyes were wide open, she looked absolutely flustered, maybe a little bit afraid, and completely turned on. I slipped two fingers inside of her before she could think too hard.

She gasped, I whispered into her ears, “Don’t worry about him sunshine, it’s just you and me in here.”

She moaned her response back to me. Curling my knuckles I hit the spot that made her cry out loud just as the palm of my hand rubbed against her dripping cunt.

I clamped my free hand over her mouth and chuckled at how little restraint she had and how hot it was. It was better than music. I lowered myself down, needing to taste her, to coat my tastebuds with her pleasure. I ran the flat of my tongue along her clit, first up and down and then in circles.

She tasted like honey-dipped in the shadows that she ran from. I wanted to get lost in her darkness and be consumed by her void. She writhed under me, grasping my hair and pulling me closer to her as moans of pleasure left her throat. She bit her lip and threw her head back, closing her eyes as she surrendered to the pleasure being coaxed from her body.

She rode my fingers, her hips moving in sync with me and her eyes burning straight into mine. I didn’t let up until I felt her walls seizing and pulsing around my fingers. Her head thrashed from side to side as she came with the violin crescendo on the speakers. I made my way back up to her, finding her mouth as I devoured the sounds coming from her like I'd been starving my entire life for her.

It felt like it.

Her exhales came out with force as she came down from her high. I removed my fingers from inside her, licking them clean and tasting her nectar, knowing immediately I'd forever be addicted to her sweetness.

I would never get enough of seeing her unravel.

"OPEN UP KANE!" he shouted, banging again, and forcing Cecilia to pull back with a frantic look on her face as she looked up at the surveillance camera in horror.

"He doesn't have access to my room," I assured her, and some of the anxiety seemed to fade away.

"I don't know who he would kill first, me or you," she said, her voice full of fear I had yet to see in her.

Was Ronan Zerkos the only thing this girl was afraid of?

THUMP-THUMP-THUMP

"Should we find out?" I joked, pulling the comforter down and sitting up on the bed.

She looked at me like she was absolutely terrified of the idea of him catching her with me. It was probably the most entertained I had been since I watched her pound Russian number two's face with her fists.

Humor aside, I had no idea what would happen if he knew what we'd just done and a big part of me knew I fucked up royally. The other part of me just didn't care. I had suffered for so long, had nothing to call my own until this bronze Angel appeared in my life as if she was a gift from the gods directly to me.

I dropped my feet to the floor but before I could stand, she ran in a limping hobble to my bathroom and locked the door behind her before I could comprehend what was happening. Probably smart, Ronan didn't have access to the surveillance in my room, *yet.* There was a good chance with Cecilia sleeping in my room two nights in a row that he was actually about to go *Zerkos* and lose all possible rationale.

All he'd have to do is go down to tech and demand they gave him some way to access that footage. Even though we were all supposedly equal as the leaders of our syndicate organization, the motherfucker was big and scary. It was unlikely any one of our IT guys were going to square up to him about their ethics on sharing surveillance codes.

I lazily made my way to the door and unlocked it before moving out of the way for his rampage. Zerkos immediately slammed through it like a charging bull.

He looked around the room, nostrils flaring before asking, "Where is she?"

I pointed to the bathroom with my chin, and almost like she timed the perfect cue, the shower started running.

Santos walked into the room following him, his eyes darting to the bathroom first before acknowledging me.

“Stop fucking with me, she isn’t part of the trials,” he said.

“What fucking trials?” Santos challenged him for the first time in longer than I could remember.

My eyes widened in surprise as I realized his doubts must have been digging deep for him to finally explode like this.

“You got something to say?” Zerkos crossed his arms at Álvarez, but he didn’t back down, he reserved his turn to speak for times like this when he knew the wrong calls were being made.

It was why the three of us worked.

Zerkos was a maniac when it came to a gun, and taking charge, I mean, that was the whole reason we called him that. The guy literally turned into a machine when you handed him a weapon and pointed him at the enemy. Rage issues.

Collateral damage.

From her.

My loyalty to my brothers, my love for violence and bloodshed were what served me in our organization. Álvarez was the common sense that kept us from fucking up and making mistakes. He always had a blueprint of the big picture in his head, so when he stepped up to challenge him like this, well even Ronan knew when it was time to back down and listen.

“Yeah, I do, *brother.* Call it off this year. Your head isn’t in the game, and I checked out of it the minute you forced her to sign. At this point, we’re causing more harm than good. You don’t have two girls down there who are going to willingly help us set some victims free. You have two girls we’ve kidnapped, tortured, who I’d bet at least a finger on, to say that they aren’t broken or ready at all. You’ve got one fresh out of the hospital with a fucked-up face and two months’ worth of meaningless trauma attached to boot. We need to clean this shit up, and *now* we got to worry about Bratvas coming to our door,” Álvarez huffed out at him, putting our brother in his place.

“I think we have bigger fish to fry than where your girlfriend sleeps at night,” I added, scratching the side of my head.

Álvarez looked at me with the same annoyed look he was giving Zerkos.

“Get your shit together, both of you,” he said with one hand against my chest and the other pushing Ronan away as he tried to keep him from advancing on me.

"Guillermo called in a favor. I have to go to Ocean Valley for a few days. Can I trust you both to not kill each other?" He looked between us but kept his eyes on me when he said the rest. "Can I trust you to keep her safe?"

Ronan grunted his frustration but before I could respond her voice cut through instead.

"You're leaving?" she said standing in the doorway, wrapped in a towel, dripping from head to toe as she looked at Álvarez with a devastated look on her face.

I had to wonder how much she just heard and the look Zerkos was giving me told me the same thought was crossing his mind as well.

"I've got business to take care of in Ocean Valley," he said looking back at her, his tone softening completely at her presence.

It was only because I was really looking at him that I noticed the smallest of reactions when he realized she was fresh out of the shower, and I fought back a smirk.

"It's only for a couple of days max, morena, I'll be back by Monday. If I'm fast enough I can be back by tomorrow," he told her, trying to reassure her.

"I don't know what day it is," she shrugged at him.

Something about that wrapped me up in guilt, I couldn't do anything but drop my head in shame.

Zerkos looked away and tucked his hands in his pockets to pretend like he didn't care, but I knew he did.

Normally the girls would break so fast in the kennels that we could move them to the apartments on the lower floors and start giving them back something close to a real-life again. We would even take them out to restaurants and clubs, and we'd have some of the guys run them wherever they'd ask to go. Hell, we even gave them money when they wanted to buy things.

It was a big part of how the process worked, and a few weeks in, they were trusting us enough to tell us anything we wanted to know about where they came from, and who trafficked them.

Cecilia didn't have a breaking point, and the more he pushed her, the harder she became. She was strong but human enough to admit that even though she wasn't broken, she was affected. Hell, even I had a breaking point. The one thing you learn above all when you're learning torture tactics from the U.S. Government, is that the most effective way to get someone to talk, was to find and use the thing they care about most in this world.

The problem with this method was that if Santos was right about Cecilia, and everything she'd been doing was to keep Zerkos safe, then we weren't ever going to get our answers. Because the thing that she cared most about, was the same thing that was trying to break her for the truth.

19

RONAN

To say I was angry would be putting it lightly.

I spent an hour kissing the Doc's ass while I tried to explain the situation with Cecilia without *explaining* the situation with Cecilia. The entire time I was an anxious mess, waiting for her to shut her trap so I could rush back upstairs and claim what was mine again. I told mostly the truth to the Doc, that Cecilia and I had history, and I was keeping her safe from a big bad that she wouldn't let me in on.

That, of course just led to an entirely different lecture from the Doc, about what an idiot I was and that I was endangering the entirety of the Black Crows by "leading with my dick" as she called it.

I just wanted to get back to the penthouse and lay next to her again, even if just for one night. I couldn't get her off my mind, not with her this close to me and certainly not since she let me have her, it was all I could think about, every moment, all of the time. She had burrowed under my skin, crawling inside of me like an itch I couldn't scratch. A need I would never be able to fulfill no matter how many more times I'd have her.

It wouldn't be enough.

Worst of all was that I couldn't deny that we had a moment back there in my room when it was just the two of us. I felt it and I knew she felt it too. Even if she was too stubborn to admit it, I could still see the truth swirling around in those obsidian mirrors of her eyes.

Emory made me pay for her food and a coffee at a diner down the block from our high-rise to explain what was going on. She wasn't even halfway through her food when I got the text from Kane with the photo of her cuddled into him. I just threw a wad of cash at the table and told her I had an emergency. I knew she would probably chew me out for that one too.

Emory was a good friend to the Black Crows, and we treated her right because a good doctor who kept their mouth shut was hard to come by.

Emory came from the trials. She was from our first batch almost seven years ago now. Emory O'Connor was twenty-three when we rescued her from the Irish trafficking ring. Her father sold her to pay off some debts after her mother died of cancer, racking up tons of medical bills and leaving them penniless.

Emory was the only girl we ever rescued that did something meaningful with her life. Not that it mattered what they did after, because it was their freedom to choose how they lived, not ours, and that was the point of the whole damn thing. She wanted more, and I appreciated her hunger. We paid the Doc's way through medical school and in exchange she was contracted to work for the Black Crows for ten years.

We paid her well, and I was pretty sure that when her contract would come to an end in a few years that she would be asking to renew it. She was welcome to work wherever she wanted, and we would fund the hospital well, but she had to make herself available to us for personal calls at all times. It was a tough job, but she was a damn good doctor and a professional at all times, so I knew I would be getting an earful for that move I just pulled on her, the next time she saw me.

I sprinted back to the high-rise so fast that when I burst through the doors our doorman, Nate, almost pulled his gun on me before he recognized me. I took a few heaving breaths with my hands on my knees, and I pulled my phone out as I walked towards the elevators.

Kane: Don't be an ass. She's asleep.

The asshole was baiting me, and it was working.

When I got up to the penthouse, I headed towards our bedrooms, but Santos was already standing in front of Mateo's door with his arms crossed. I raised an eyebrow at him, but he wasn't fazed.

"Move along brother. It's late." He eyed me until I made my way to my room, leaving them unbothered.

I looked at the spot in my bed that had just been occupied by her presence not too long ago. I kicked my shoes off before sinking into it, letting her smell be the only thing I had to simmer the flames building inside of me.

Now here I was in my brother's room *again*, the morning after my woman spent the night in his bed *again*. To top it all off, there *she* was, the creature from Hell I summoned to punish me for all of my wrongs, standing there with nothing but a towel on.

She wasn't at all phased by the fact she was standing in between the three most dangerous men in the city. In fact, she stood there in testament to how little fear she felt for any of us, and my dick throbbed at the sight of the kind of woman she had become.

"It's Saturday," Santos told her and aside from the slight drop of her shoulders, there wasn't really a visible reaction.

Like time meant absolutely nothing to her anymore.

And I was the one who robbed her of that.

She huffed out a big exhale that gave me the impression of relief at the thought that he wouldn't be gone so long. The two of them were always close, and I was glad my brother was someone I could trust with her all those years ago, whether it was to keep her company or to keep her safe. Nowadays, I wasn't so sure anymore, I could see the same hungry look in Álvarez's eyes that I saw in Mateo's.

All I'd done was open up the way for them to get to her.

"You were supposed to be in my room when I came back," I said through closed teeth.

She clucked her tongue at me in her arrogant way, shrugging her shoulders. "I didn't think there was a difference as long as I was with one of you," she narrowed her eyes at me. "I thought I was your little *club's* property," she said, demeaning the entire integrity of our operation.

It didn't matter if it was life and death or over minuscule choices; Cecilia Gomes and I were destined to fight about anything and everything for the rest of our days. I knew that was part of the intrigue when it came to her. I used to think we had been broken because we couldn't stop fighting, but then I realized she didn't *want* to stop fighting. She didn't know how to do normal. She was fucking insane and in the best way possible.

I *knew* that if everything was always perfect, she would have been bored.

Happily-ever-after wasn't her style.

"You are *mine*," I reminded her, grabbing her arm, and pulling her closer to me.

Álvarez took a fraction of a step towards us but he stopped himself. She tried to shake me off of her, but I didn't let go, she looked between Santos and Mateo before she spoke.

"Is that true?" As if rehearsed they both responded "No" in unison and then looked at each other in a silent agreement.

Fucking assholes.

She was almost glowing from the win, but I didn't let her bask in it for long. She tried to shake me off again, but I squeezed her arm, this time hard enough to bruise, forcing her to cry out from the pain. Kane clenched his fists at me, but I didn't care. I dragged her out of his room behind me so abruptly that her towel fell off before we were through the door. My quick pace forced her to move her feet through the hall while she shouted her futile protests.

"What the hell are you doing?" she screamed at me as we made our way back into my bedroom.

I closed the door behind us, locking it so my brothers couldn't get in.

"You think you can fuck with me by getting to my brothers?" I asked her as I threw her onto the bed, her tits bouncing from the force of her hitting the mattress.

"I'm just surviving in the circumstances I was provided, It's what I'm good at. Not everything is about you," she said dryly, not bothering to attempt to cover herself up as she rested her elbows on the mattress.

I couldn't help but take the moment to appreciate the landscape of her body as I engraved the new geography of her changed curves into my memory once again. She didn't miss how long it took for my gaze to return to her face and she bit her bottom lip seductively. It was probably not even intentional but everything about her exuded a sensuality that couldn't be captured or contained.

Her eyes shifted to the outline of my already hard cock through my pants. I undid my belt buckle and her eyes darted directly to my hands as I pulled it off of my pants in one quick motion. She narrowed her eyes at me then turned her chin away. I caged her in between my arms on the bed, but before I could lower myself to taste her, I found myself spitting the metal flavor of blood that coated my tongue from the force of her head against my face.

The pain came after.

It took me a moment to realize what happened, but it was the cackling of her laugh that brought me back to the moment in a heat of pure rage. I wiped my bleeding nose with my hand and smeared it against her face, dragging it down to her chest. I squeezed the most perfect tits I'd ever had the pleasure of holding, forcing a moan from her in response to my touch.

When I leaned down to put my mouth on her skin, she kicked out at me straight in the chest, sending me back into the wall.

She laughed like a maniac once again. I growled as I advanced towards the bed, annoyed and fucking hard as a rock at the show she was putting on.

"What the fuck are you playing at?" I asked her, pinning her legs down beneath me.

She squirmed but couldn't do much under my massive weight. She tried to hit me again, so I grabbed her hands and pinned them above her head.

"You're going to have to try a lot harder than that," she laughed it out like she wasn't afraid of what I could do to her.

My hand found her throat and I squeezed with a bit more firmness than I knew she liked. When I lowered down pressing my mouth against hers, she opened up for me but just long enough to bite my lip, hard enough to put a small tear through it. I grunted through the pain and kept kissing her, letting my blood coat her lips and smear down her chin.

"I told you, I'm not letting you have it that easy," she said, licking my blood off her lips like she was savoring the taste of my pain.

"But you *are* going to let me keep having it," I growled in her ears, more of a statement and less of a question.

She didn't agree but she didn't deny it either.

I snarled at the pain in my lip as I flipped her around and in three swift motions my palm rang out against her ass cheek in an even rhythm. She barely had time to cry out from each slap, they happened so fast that by the last strike the noise that came out of her was a purely animalistic, guttural sound that sent my dick into overdrive. I wanted them to hear her cry out, I wanted them to know that she *was* mine.

Always was, always would be.

The tip of my cock was pressed to her entrance, she was soaking wet and it was starting to drip onto my sheets. The anticipation was killing me, but I wanted to hear her begging me for it.

It was a game we'd played long ago, and I knew she remembered it.

"Tell me," I demanded.

"I hate you." She said in a cold tone.

It was jarring and as much as I knew that she meant it I also was sure there was still something between us. It was the same reason she wasn't saying no. She might as well have said "I love you" and it would have sounded just the same.

"It's me and you baby, you can pretend you hate me all you want but I can feel the truth spilling out from between your legs." She groaned as I pressed into her slickness without entering her yet.

She turned her head to the side, and looked back at me, making me think she was giving in to our game. A sinister smile covered her face and the words that came out of her mouth left me floored. "He made me come," she said with that dark smirk, and I pushed myself inside of her so hard and fast that she cried out again.

She was liquid hot inside, and my mind was racing with images of someone else making her this wet.

Until this morning I had been the only person who had been able to do that, but now my brother and I had yet another thing in common. With one hand pressing the side of her head back down into the mattress, and with the other I brought her hands behind her low back and pinned them together. I moved in and out, thrusting into her repeatedly.

She was cursing at me in Spanish, but I didn't let up the pace. I wanted her to feel what she was doing to me, every single bit of it. Every wicked smirk, every challenging glare, every stubborn way she went against me scorched me up from the inside like lava. I watched as my cock disappeared inside of her at a perfect rhythm that even Kane would have appreciated. The thought of them together making me angry, jealous and closer to the edge than I wanted to be.

"Do you think he can make you scream like this, my little flower?" I asked her, using the nickname that unraveled her every time.

She went lax under me, her cunt pulsing around my cock as her climax robbed her of her strength to pretend to fight me. Spiteful as ever, she still managed to nod the answer to my question, despite the incoherent cries leaving her mouth as she came loudly on my cock.

I pulled her hands back further forcing her to lift her head off the mattress as she arched her back. It didn't look comfortable, but she didn't fight back as I pounded against her until I finally found my release inside her. We stayed like that, breathing heavily while we both made our way back to reality again.

I didn't care for it.

It was filled with the ghosts of our love that guarded the crypt to our past, buried deep in its grave.

She rolled onto her back and leaned back up on her elbows once I'd gotten off her and gotten my pants back up. I threw her the two bottles Emory gave me and she looked at me confused.

"One is an antibiotic, the other is for pain, if you need it. Doesn't look like you need 'em though," I smirked at her, but she didn't return it.

She was too busy staring daggers into me.

"You can stay here until Kane and I get back tomorrow," I told her. "I'll have Ethan take care of bringing you food."

"You're leaving too? Where are you going?" she asked, but I shook my head at her.

"None of your business," I responded.

"I want to stay in Santos' room," she told me, crossing her arms and my lip peeled back on instinct as I fought back a growl threatening to rise from deep inside my chest.

"You are *mine*," I reminded her again.

"Am I?" she challenged me, and my nostrils flared in response.

"Let me spell it out for you, in case the last two months haven't made it clear for you." My hands were holding her tiny little shoulders forcing her to look up into my eyes, "Your body, *mine.* Your pussy, *mine.* I'll keep you safe little flower, don't worry about that." I added, "But if you won't give me the answers I'm looking for, I'm going to find them on my own. Whatever's following you isn't going to bring us down. Not my people." I let her go.

She sneered.

"If none of you are going to be home, I'd like to stay in Santos' room," she said again, but it was non-negotiable.

I'd have Ethan and Fletch guarding the penthouse the entire weekend, but my room had security feed I'd have access to while I was gone. I *needed* to be able to see her if I wasn't going to be close to her, it wasn't just about keeping her safe anymore. After spending years of my life looking for this woman, I couldn't bear to spend a single moment not being able to find her when I craved her.

"You can stay in my room, or you can go back to the Kennel. Take a pick," I could see her rage building again from my words in the way her fists clenched, it was a habit she'd had as long as I'd known her.

"Count yourself lucky I don't throw you back in the box until we get back." I threatened and there was a small shift in her eyes, almost unnoticeable.

Almost.

But I knew her too well and I could peg it for what it was, fear.

"Looks like we're going back downstairs then," she said without blinking as she walked around me, stark naked.

She opened my bedroom door, Kane was standing there, his height towering over her with arms crossed like he he'd been out there the entire time we were fucking.

She flinched for a split second out of surprise but didn't make any attempt to cover herself up at all. His eyes were only on hers for a split second before he let them trail down leisurely to the rest of her body, absolutely no goddamn shame in the fact that he was completely eye-fucking her in front of me.

"For fucks sake," I took my shirt off and threw it at her, but she didn't rush to put it on like I expected her to.

"What the hell happened to you?" He eyed my bloody nose and my torn lip, and I just smiled and shrugged at him wiping some of the blood away with the back of my hand.

"It's called rough sex," I grinned, he frowned at me in response.

"He's making me stay in the kennels while you're gone," she told him like a child tattling on another.

Without moving his head at all his eyes shifted over to mine for a split second before he plastered them back onto her naked body.

"And you want me to fix that for you, sunshine?" he asked her so softly and gently that I could barely hear the words out of his mouth.

I scoffed and he arched an eyebrow at me.

"Don't flatter yourself just because she used you to get her wet for me, she asked to stay in Álvarez's room." The look she gave me was one dripping in venom and outrage like she couldn't believe I had thrown her under like that.

But if she thought I was going to let her get her claws in my brothers like she had done me, she was sadly mistaken.

I was fucked, cursed, long gone, completely mad over this sorceress who had me under her spell. My brothers were still free of her poison though, I could still maintain the illusion of control here as long as they weren't falling apart with every bat of her eyes, or the curve of her hips.

"Hmm," he rubbed his thumb against her cheek. "Too bad he left already, not even thinking twice about our pet." He brushed his thumb down against her lip and left it there for a moment.

"Almost like you chose wrong," he said sharply, turning around and walking back to his room, leaving her mouth agape from a response she wasn't expecting.

Something happened when she chose Santos the other day, like she had picked at an old wound of Mateo's and now it was bleeding open again.

I was sure if his shrink were to pick him apart, they'd tell him he had deep-rooted mommy/abandonment issues to blame for all of his problems. The thing was, it was so much more than his mother abandoning him. It was his sister dying, it was the lack of a halfway decent father figure growing up, it was never having anyone in his corner until he found us.

Mateo Kane just wanted to be wanted, and I could see Cecilia was pushing him further into ruin by slicing at the fragile armor that was barely holding him together.

20

SANTOS

When Guillermo told me to jump, I didn't ask how high, I asked when and where.

It was the bittersweet pill I was forced to swallow anytime he called me up with a favor. Just his name flashing on my caller ID was enough to remind me that I was permanently indebted to him until my corpse became food for the bugs.

I was a king in my own right, at least on this side of the country. But my cousin never failed to put me in my place at any chance he could get. He loved to remind me that I was here because he *allowed* it to be. Los Muertos was a life sentence, you either died for the cause, or you died a traitor, but you'd bleed out for them no matter what.

He saw the Black Crow Brotherhood as an extension of his power, not as an alliance. It was a dangerous line we teetered and if Zerkos found out I was trapped so far under his thumb like this, he would probably start a war over it.

One we wouldn't win.

It was only supposed to be six years, that was the agreement we had struck. But nothing was ever that simple, my cousin was a mastermind pulling too many strings I couldn't see and the minute that tattoo was branded to my skin, I knew I had to play it smart if I wanted to be my own man ever again. He kept me under his thumb, threatening to put my younger siblings and cousins through the ringer. Constant menacing that they would be given the worst of the tasks needed from his gang.

The kids had it the worst, they were forced to kill rival gang children to send messages, and they were always running a corner to sell drugs to the dope heads. It was the sickening part of that life that I refused to accept, and he knew as long as they were around, that he had me too. I would do anything to keep my siblings free from the stain that came with this life.

At this point, I found it easier to go with the current, instead of fighting his demands. He wasn't unreasonable by any means, and his asks weren't ludicrous. Two or three times a year he called me to Ocean Valley, threw a photo my way and expected the job to be done clean and correct. It wasn't like there weren't other hired guns he could use and wasn't like the men closest to him weren't capable. It was a power move to let me know he owned me, and like a dog I came running to the one who held my leash, every time.

I got the call right after I had herded Zerkos back into his room last night to keep him out of Kane's. There was a part of me that was absolutely writhing in agony out of jealousy. She had said it herself that she wanted *me*, but yet she crawled into his bed just the same. *Again*. It was a mind fuck and I had to keep reminding myself that she only chose me because I was the safe option. She chose me because I was probably the one friend she had left at this point.

Friend.

By morning, my plane ticket was already bought, and my bag was packed for the weekend. I wasn't happy to be leaving. Even less happy to see her coming out of his bathroom in just a towel.

Why was I overthinking a shower?

I was even less happy to be telling her I was leaving and seeing the letdown look in her eyes like I was to blame.

And then Zerkos dragged her naked body into his room like she was his property and fucked her loud enough that Mateo and I would hear. Kane stood by the door. His fists clenched so tight you could see the white of his knuckles wrapping around the bone.

I wasn't ready to let anyone into my head yet and realized maybe Guillermo's call was a blessing in disguise. I took the opportunity and headed out as fast as I could.

Ethan was waiting at the elevator, and I lifted my chin up to greet him as I piled my way in.

"Do you need a ride?" he asked me, but I shook my head at him.

"I'll only be gone two nights max, I'll keep my car at the airport, thanks," I said to him as the doors opened letting us out on the ground floor.

"I need you to keep an eye on everything, let me know if anything strange happens, anything odd, or different." He raised his eyebrow at my vague request, so I leveled with him. "Let me know if Zerkos goes Berserk, okay?"

Ethan laughed at the request and said half-jokingly, "You mean more than he already has? Or is there a certain threshold we're tolerating?"

"Just keep me in the know, if anything happens. *Anything*," I stressed, knowing that it was going to be impossible to focus on whatever job Guillermo had waiting for me in Ocean Valley.

I had to trust my brothers to take care of Cecilia and keep things afloat here.

I closed my eyes as soon as I boarded the plane, and let my memories haunt my dreams.

20 YEARS OLD

"Wooooohooo!" Cecilia screamed in the passenger seat of the Audi convertible she somehow talked me into hotwiring twenty minutes ago. San Diego always had that effect on her, in fact, anywhere outside Ocean Valley did.

She always became the freest version of herself when she was away from that place. I knew the sensation well myself, being away from Guillermo's hold on me was the only time I didn't feel like I was free-falling into a pit of darkness.

Her laugh breezed through the wind like a song I couldn't make out the words to. We shared a brief look and her smile stretched from cheek to cheek. I didn't know that I'd seen her this happy before. Okay, maybe that was the ecstasy we sampled coursing through her system, but there was genuine joy there too, maybe just amplified.

We were on a job, and Ronan would have killed the both of us if he knew we were not only high on our own product, but that we were breaking the law while doing it.

You can only break one law at once.

That was his motto, and I never really understood why. Maybe the bail money would be less? The guy went as far as buckling his seat belt if we were lifting a car.

This was a special occasion and it demanded broken rules. We never did this, but after we picked up the batch, Cecilia gave me those dark puppy eyes and I was helpless to her demands. It was just a few days until the anniversary of when her family was killed, if she wanted to take her mind off of it, I couldn't deny her that.

She may have been Ronan's girl, but our connection was different.

I'd never gotten as close to anyone like I had with Cecilia. It was the truest friendship I'd ever gotten the chance to share. Ronan left her with me for weeks at a time, and we had no choice but to rely on each other for friendship, comfort, and running whatever jobs he sent our way.

"Watch the road!" She laughed out again, and I realized I had been staring at her instead.

The danger was that she was absolutely breathtaking. She was my best friend, and she was also the girl of someone I considered a brother to me. I shook the intrusive thoughts out of my head, refusing to let my head take me there again.

Damn, this was good E.

I could practically taste the ocean salt in the air as we drove the convertible next to the shoreline.

"Go faster Santito!" She used the nickname only she dared to call me, and my dick treacherously threatened to wake.

I let my foot get heavy on the gas pedal, forcing a growl from the Audi as it climbed up the speedometer and Cecilia's hair beat wildly in the wind behind her. She screamed louder and threw her hands up in the air like we were on a rollercoaster, and I couldn't fight the grin spreading over my face.

This feeling was the closest thing to freedom I had ever known. Right here. Right now.

With her.

I shook my head again before the darkness could cloud my thoughts over the drugs and as I looked over the rearview mirror, I noticed the cop pulling out behind us.

"Fuck, we've got company. You ready to ditch the ride, morena?" I asked her with a crooked smile on my face and she returned the gesture in approval.

I jerked the wheel to the left taking the nearest alley, forcing another loud whoop from Cecilia as she practically landed on my lap from the turn.

"Put your seatbelt on!" I laughed at her, and she frowned her eyebrows at me seriously.

"Nothing holds me back!" She grabbed onto me as I turned out of the alley into a closed off street too fast, nearly tossing her out of the car. She burst out in laughter again before finishing, "Except maybe death."

I pulled the emergency break, the screeching of the wheels no doubt loud enough to let the cops know exactly where we were. We jumped out of the car and she whisper-yelled at me, "This way!"

I followed her into another alley, and she chose a door at random and just her luck it was open.

"Let's go!" She tugged me in.

I knew it was probably a terrible idea, but I could hear the sirens creeping closer and it was just a matter of time before they followed us in.

The dark hallway trembled from a booming deep bass as we made our way into the building from what looked like a service entrance. We made our way past the kitchen, giggling like idiots as the drug peaked its way into our systems.

The hallway suddenly opened up into velvet carpeting, booths, and purple ropes separating the stage from the on-lookers. It was too dark to see anything but the spotlight on the stage illuminating the steel pole. The cops were right behind us, their walkie talkies giving them away with their obnoxious chattering.

"Let's split up, go sit!" She pushed me into a nearby booth and before I could protest, she was gone, like she'd never been there at all.

I was left mouth opened in the booth before I realized she was smart enough to pick one that was already occupied, knowing that if I had been sitting alone it would have been suspicious as hell.

The men in the booth paid me no mind, as if this was completely normal, and continued to chat business. Nothing illegal, some financial jargon I couldn't decipher. I knew for a fact these guys were clean cut, for the most part. At least when it came to their work.

I rubbed my hands against the velvet fabric of the seat almost ritualistically before I'd realized what I was doing.

That was nice velvet.

Five or six cops filled the club from the same hallway we just emerged from, pointing the flashlights at every John who'd been looking for a discreet show. They earned themselves a few nasty looks and curses before the manager of the establishment made himself known to them as they huddled in for a talk.

Places like this didn't abide by common law, they weren't here to please the men in blue, but they knew they couldn't piss them off either. The manager attempted to direct the cops out of the strip club, trying to keep their clients' privacy intact as they enjoyed whatever show they'd come here to watch. At the same time the club got darker, and the spotlight turned a deep red hue.

Something dark and heavy came on the club speakers, the hair on my arms raised to attention, and every single person shifted their gaze from the police back to the stage. My vision blurred everything in my periphery, my throat dried and my body temperature rose like a fever I couldn't break no matter how much I'd try.

Everything moved so slow.

She appeared out of a dark corner as she stepped into the red light so sensually, her hips swayed as each foot took its place in front of the other. She moved with the beat until her hand found the pole. With all the grace of a prima ballerina, she pulled herself onto the steel, wrapping her legs around it in one fell swoop, dropping an arm behind her as she let her head drop backward. She spun down the pole with a type of seductiveness I hadn't seen from her before.

Sure, I'd heard her and Ronan screwing in the room next to me plenty of times, and a couple times I walked in on them doing it right in the living room. But this was different. And the way her eyes were glued to me as she twirled around the pole made a heat grow inside me, Satan himself whispering in my ear that this was all for me.

She made taking off her shirt look like the Mona Lisa itself, if a painting could get you hard. If you had a thing for chicks without eyebrows, that is. She was a work of art, every curve on her body, and every hair on her head was intentionally put there by a God who knew no mercy for me.

Cecilia was a punishment. She was the harbinger of my agony, and I'd be forced to suffer until I left Ocean Valley and freed myself of Guillermo's clutch. I didn't spend a day wondering what I had ever done to deserve this kind of mystery.

I knew.

Being the right hand of the Devil didn't make me any less guilty than the fallen angel himself. The invisible collar around my neck proved that I wasn't man enough to find my way out of the mess I was born into. I deserved everything that was coming to me.

And falling for my best friend's girl was the creator's way of letting me know, I wasn't out of his radar. No, I'd likely be forced to feel this way until my last breath, or until hers.

It was an unbearable torment.

An insufferable anguish.

To want, and never have. To love, but never speak it.

To hate yourself because of the thoughts intruding in your mind.

To want to swallow the barrel of a hot gun and blow my brains out all over this velvet booth so I wouldn't have to see what came next.

But that top came off and the pants soon followed. She skulked around that stage with an allure about her, unminding that she was in nothing but see-through lacy lingerie as she laid on her back and threw her legs up in the air, doing things I couldn't have ever expected or imagined from her.

I groaned and dropped my head to my hands, my elbow resting on the slightly sticky table in front of me and I heard a chuckle from one of the businessmen next to me.

"That's a hot one for sure, haven't seen her around here before. I may have to order a lap dance and break her in." He leaned into whisper in my ear but his words were loud enough for the whole booth. "I'll let you know how she tastes." I clenched my fists together, fighting the urge to go up on that stage myself and drag her down before anyone else could see her.

She wasn't mine, so why did I have this need to keep her to myself? To keep these lecherous men from staring into the only good thing I ever knew?

She shook her ass seductively and achingly slow but on tempo to the music and the stage filled with bills as the regulars ate her up.

While I swirled deeper into the chaotic void of my mind, Cecilia's dance ended, and the cops shone their flashlights on her as she exited the stage. I could hear the managers telling them they had no business talking to the talent they employed. Either the owners here really didn't care to appease any sort of law enforcement, or they didn't know who actually worked for them.

Either way was a win for us because we needed to get the fuck out of here ASAP and the jar of ecstasy bulging out of my cargo pants wasn't going to help us right now.

They took advantage of the break between dancers on the stage and began to pass by every booth, questioning each patron about where they'd been before the most recent dance. Cecilia made her way to our booth, still in nothing but her underwear as she casually ignored the officers who were stepping their way towards us.

"My lucky day." The guy next to me chimed in with a creepy smile on his face. "How much for a private dance, sweetheart?" He asked her but she didn't avert her eyes from mine.

"Sorry amigo." She exaggerated her accent as she played a part I didn't

know she could. "Lady's choice." She straddled my lap and pulled the already lit cigar from the man's hand.

She took it in her mouth and exhaled the smoke into his face. She pointed to a neon sign on the wall that said, "lady's choice lap dance" and I couldn't fight back the chuckle. How she noticed that and used it to her advantage was beyond me, but it was such a Cecilia thing to do that I couldn't help but be amazed.

She was good at that.

Noticing things that most people overlooked.

She wasn't like anyone else I knew. She was smarter, like someone had made sure she was always aware at all times of all the possible situations that could unfold from one scenario.

It was hot as fucking hell.

Handing the cigar back, she pulled me by the collar on my shirt to stand and pushed me toward one of the lone chairs facing the stage that were meant for lap dances.

"Hey! We've got questions." The officer said to Cecilia, but she didn't miss a beat and their lights in her face didn't intimidate her one bit.

Damn, this E was good.

My pulse beat heavily through my jugular, and Cecilia matched the authoritative tone of the cop with her own,

"Listen, pendejo, unless you're paying for my time, you're not scaring my money away. Fuck off." She spat at him, and the owner laughed a throaty laugh, exposing all the gold in his back teeth that reflected the shine off the even more gold chains around his neck.

"If you lose my girls any money, you will compensate them." The guy warned the cops, and they mumbled a disapproving chorus together but resigned to their defeat, nonetheless.

That's when the real torture began.

I was exposed. The ceiling was too tall, the room too big and open, the spotlights too bright, too revealing. There was so much space, but all at once there was nothing to put between us, nothing to keep us from one another.

I was a weak man.

And she was a bloody bird of prey who would swallow me alive with no mercy.

Her pupils were blown wide, but the dark of her eyes' natural color made it nearly impossible to tell, unless you really knew.

I couldn't quite make out the song that was playing, all I could hear was the thumping of the bass and the loud pummeling of my heart as the blood inside me thrashed against its ventricles in a frantic attempt to self-implode, so that this wretched feeling would end.

I could hear the bass of the song playing reverberating through the club as Cecilia worked me like a pro. Every time the curve of her ass came down on me, I died a slower death, time would freeze, and I waited for some savior to end this cruelty.

But no one came for me.

My cock was harder than it'd ever been in my entire life, and her torturous grinding made me think she knew just how painful this was for me. Or maybe it was all in my mind.

There was nowhere for me to hide.

But either the drugs had her somewhere she didn't care, or she was truly focused on getting us out of here without steel cuffs and a high bail over our heads.

She grabbed her heels with her legs still straight as she folded over nimbly and her ass did something I'd never seen before except maybe in a music video. She straddled me again, this time using her index finger to push my jaw upward and seal the gap between my lips and she gave me a playful wink.

"Slide some bills under my bra, you're not making this believable." She hushed into my ear, reminding me of the serious trouble we'd be facing if we couldn't shake the pigs on our tail.

"Morena, you're making it too believable." I muttered under my breath, but not quietly enough because she threw me a confused look.

"We need to get out of here, I think our best bet is sneaking out through one of the private dance rooms." She shook her boobs in my face and I swear glitter-dusted in the air in front of me.

Where she found the time for that I couldn't tell you, but it was pure genius. She grabbed me by the hand and led me out of the chair, a cop shouted for us, but she didn't turn her head, her voice laced in confidence.

"It's twice as much to watch a private dance, three times if you're gonna bring any extra friends in blue." She chuckled, the pig sighed in annoyance, and she feigned knowing where she was going until we made our way behind a black curtain. It was a small space, not a room, more like a dressing booth with three mirrors and a chair.

"Fuck. How are we going to get out of here?" She hissed in frustration; the excitement mixed with the effects of the E was causing a sheen of sweat to glisten over both of our bodies.

"We may need to wait them out in here." I practically panted the words back to her, as I struggled to catch my breath even though she was the one who had been dancing for her life.

She nodded her head in agreement, our bodies practically touching from the forced proximity of the velvet draped booth. Each mirrored reflection showed me a side of myself I couldn't stand to face, and a side of her I couldn't dare ignore anymore.

"How do we almost get caught every time we're in this city?" She giggled like the situation wasn't severe at all, and I smirked at her attempt to downplay the moment.

"Maybe we're cursed." I whispered the words practically shooting them onto her lips while our chests still heaved up and down against each other from the adrenaline.

"Oh, I'm definitely cursed Santito, you should know that by now." She chuckled but the shadow that cast over her eyes told me that she'd been through enough to truly believe that.

Fuck.

Maybe we were both cursed.

I wanted to grab her by the back of the neck and pull her in tighter. I wanted to lick those beautiful plump painted lips of hers and bite them until they bled for me. I wanted to push every thought of right or wrong away and give in to my crippled heart's desire for her.

But I was the friend.

Not the man she dreamed of a happily ever after with.

That guy was my brother.

The guy who upheaved all his life's plans for this girl, the guy who made sure she had a home and something to call a family after the world robbed her of everything she once had. The guy who worked hard as hell to make sure she had everything she could want or need.

I was just the miserable fuck who tagged along hoping for a scrap of her attention ever since she showed up at our door.

She peered through the crack in the curtain before turning back to me, "They're finally leaving, I think we can leave from the front. You've got the product still?"

I nodded at her and she clasped her hand around mine, causing my heart to bunch up at the base of my throat. She pulled me out of the booth with her and marched straight towards the management that had been speaking to the cops earlier.

"Did they leave the same way they came?" She asked like she had no problem admitting they were after us.

"You should probably wait a little before heading out, I'm sure they'd love a reason to shut us all down. You're welcome to take the stage again meanwhile." The sleazeball draped in gold winked at her and I clenched my teeth together in anger to avoid lashing out at the person who helped us through this.

"Thanks." She laughed out, "but I'm not much of a dancer, that is, unless the stakes are right." She ignored his creepy attempt to recruit her and pulled out the cash she had stuffed into her bra.

"Can I pay you for your silence?" She asked him, and he pushed the money back towards her.

"Nah, you earned it. Think of it as an advance, a working interview of sorts. If you ever change your mind, that is. Ask for Saul." He grinned from ear to ear until I could see the gold glittering from his back teeth again.

"Thanks Saul." She laughed, keeping up her polite pretense and we made our way past the bars and patrons as we headed towards the front door. I unbuttoned my shirt and handed it to her so she wouldn't have to walk outside in her underwear and we both squinted from the shock of daylight invading our sights as I pushed the door open.

"Fuck, I forgot it was daytime." She giggled again, and to be honest so had I. No wonder the club was more than happy to have us in there, for a Wednesday, that was probably the best show they'd ever had.

"I think I parked the truck a few miles east, let's catch a cab." I told her.

Once the taxi pulled up next to the black pickup truck, we piled into the front and a sigh of relief left us both. There was something exhilarating about getting into trouble with her, but even better was the calm that followed once we cleared out of it.

No sooner had I put the key into the ignition, but Cecilia's head fell on my lap with an audible groan slipping from her lips.

I mentally told my dick to fuck off.

"That was good ecstasy. I'm crashing hard." She said before closing her eyes, "Wake me up when we get to Ocean Valley?" She mumbled before dozing off.

The drive went tediously slow without her company to keep me occupied. With her sleeping head on my lap, it amplified my torture, my need to brush away the hair clinging to her face. My heart ached, and my mind tumbled fast into the swirling chasm of my own dark thoughts.

I turned the radio up to drown out the screaming in my head, but quickly turned it back down as she adjusted herself on my lap, threatening to wake.

How long could I keep this up?

How long could I live this way?

The tattoo on my temple was a searing hot reminder of all the good things I didn't deserve, that I had no right to anything worthwhile or genuine. I was a lowlife reaper for an even lower cause, I was an unofficial gang member of an organization I'd spent my entire life running away from.

Guillermo dangled my younger siblings' innocence and freedom right in front of me, like cherries ripe for picking.

If I wanted to keep them away from sin, I had to bathe myself in it. It was the only way.

I pulled into our apartment complex slowly, the sun setting in my rearview mirror. The drive from San Diego was always so tedious that we usually grabbed a hotel for the night, but I needed to lock myself in my room for the next few days and pretend like Cecilia Gomes didn't exist.

Or that she didn't have this effect on me.

Impossible lies.

And the only person I was fooling was myself, and maybe Ronan.

I turned the ignition, shutting the truck off as I gently shook her awake. She moaned sleepily but didn't make any efforts to rise.

"We're home," I nudged her again, this time getting some movement from her as she lifted her head out of my lap and wiped some excess drool from her face.

"Sorry." She laughed nervously like her spit was going to put me off.

She could have been covered in dog shit and she would have still been the most beautiful woman to have ever existed.

We climbed up the stairs that led to our floor and I unlocked the door. Zerkos was home for once and that was a surprise on its own.

"How'd it go? Wasn't expecting you two till tomorrow." He said, rising from the couch calmly as he looked between the two of us, his eyebrows furrowing together in the middle for a brief second as he noticed Cecilia wearing my shirt over her lingerie.

"Had some trouble, nothing we couldn't shake." She closed the distance between the two of them and gave him a sweet peck on the lips before disappearing into their room.

"Listen, uh—" I started but he interrupted me before I could complete the thought.

"Thanks for getting shit done, and thanks for keeping her safe, man.

There's no one else I could trust. We're the closest thing to family she's got." He *slapped my bare arm like he had no issue with the fact she was wearing my clothes, or how she ended up half naked to begin with.*

Maybe he just trusted the both of us that much.

Maybe he shouldn't.

21

SANTOS

The flight was a direct one, but it was always tedious traveling from coast to coast. Cove City was basically another planet compared to the Ocean Valley culture I had known my entire life. As I stepped off that airplane and felt the sun on my skin, I was reminded I was home.

I made my way out of the gate and Guillermo was waiting for me with a grin plastered to his face, three tatted dudes flanked him as I approached. The smile was as fake as he was. We both knew he was just waiting for me to fuck up in some way so he could either put a bullet in my chest, or a leash around my neck.

"Primo!" he opened his arms wide and took me into a half hug from the side, never actually stopping as we walked towards the exit.

"You're bald now?" Guillermo was a good seven years older than me, but he wasn't old enough to be losing hair yet.

He was a few inches shorter than me but built bigger, stockier. It had probably been six months since I'd last seen him. He called me down to torture some rival street gang soldiers they needed to get some information from.

"The ladies love it, man," he said, running his hand over the shiny globe, then pulling out a pack of cigarettes from his pocket and offering me one. I gladly accepted it after that flight. He lit his, then mine, taking a deep drag before looking back at me to ask, "Should we eat? Let's eat."

His Lamborghini Urus was obnoxiously parked on the sidewalk, miles away from any airport parking. He didn't bat an eye to the airport security scowling at him, but he did throw him a small wad of cash before getting into the car. The drive to the restaurant didn't take nearly as long as I expected for a Saturday in Ocean Valley, but Guillermo also drove like an absolutely fucking maniac, and that helped too.

"I've got a few jobs for you this time," he said as the waitress placed the breadsticks in front of us.

I reached for one, it was still warm, and the buttery flavor rolled over my tongue as I took a bite of the delicious garlicky bread.

I arched my eyebrow as I waited for him to give me all of the information I would need to get this weekend over with as fast as possible. This was the first time that being back in Ocean Valley didn't feel like being home, and a part of me had to wonder if it had to do with the morena that was waiting for me in Cove city.

"Take care of this first one for me, do it clean and fast. Get a drink, get your cock sucked, relax a little, and then go eat at my mamá's house...if you can do the job fast enough, dinner might even still be warm by the time you get there." He slid a facedown polaroid towards me and sneered at the plate of pasta the waitress put down in front of him.

"I'll have one or two more for you tomorrow before you go back to Cove City," he said, stabbing at his food without looking up.

"If I'm finishing up early, I probably won't stay an extra night then," I warned him, and his eyes shifted down from his plate of pasta to me. "I have a situation I'm in the middle of dealing with," I explained to him, hoping it wouldn't become an issue.

"I always crave the *idea* of pasta, but then when I get the real thing upfront and personal, it just doesn't hit the same. You know what I mean 'Cuz?" he said, ignoring me and taking a bite out of his Italian food almost begrudgingly.

But I didn't understand, because if I had my pasta, I would devour it entirely. I would eat it like a starving animal who had nothing else on this earth to consume. The pasta was a terrible fucking metaphor of course, for the one thing I couldn't have.

No woman had ever made me feel something. No woman could make me laugh or share ideas and thoughts with me. There had never been anyone I could let my walls down and open up to, no one I could just be myself with. *Except for her*. But she was never mine, and she never would be, and just the idea of speaking these heavy feelings out loud could risk burning down everything my brothers and I had worked to build.

It only took an hour to find the asshole Guillermo wanted dead. Just a ten-minute call back to the Black Crow's tech team and they had the guy's entire family tree and his last three known addresses for me. It took exactly fourteen minutes to kill him, so to say I was making good time would be an understatement.

Triple points for not even having to use a weapon.

The guy was passed out drunk in a recliner watching daytime reruns and I snapped his neck clean before he could wake up. I don't know why Guillermo wanted him dead, and honestly, I didn't want to know.

I wrote my own stories in my head about the people he sent me after, it was the only way I could sleep at night. When I slept. This guy particularly was a child molester, scum of the earth. That's what I'd tell myself so I could get through it. That, and maybe if I did it, my little brothers and sisters wouldn't have to.

Maybe someday the Black Crows would have enough manpower and firepower behind us that Guillermo would just agree to let me go without bloodshed. That dream was a far cry from reality and I couldn't live on the hope of that alone.

I didn't know what the worst was anymore...the killing, or the melting-their-bodies-in-their-own-bathtubs-with-acid part. Either way I was starting to get pretty desensitized to it all. I didn't even remember finishing but before I knew it, I was outside and climbing into a town car with a partition. Guillermo sat across from me, legs spread wide against the seat.

He signaled the driver to roll up the partition with a motion of his hand and it was done in a matter of seconds. I crossed my right ankle over my left knee.

"You get faster every time, primo!" he said laughing. "I know you think badly of me for keeping you around 'Cuz, but you're wasting your talents out there! You're a cold-blooded killer. Look how you shine when someone puts a target in front of you." His words forced me to shift uncomfortably with the weight of my sins pressing up against me. I looked out of the window instead of responding so he continued.

"You belong here with me, with your family. You'll see that soon and I'll be here to welcome you back with open arms." he winked at me. "You're a soldier, not a leader." He said condescendingly and I just smiled at him and nodded. It was pointless to argue unless I was ready to start a war.

"What's for dinner?" I changed the subject.

"Ahh, you know my mamá; everything." We both laughed and just like that we were telling old stories and joking about the family like we were kids again.

I could handle being Guillermo's cousin, I loved my family. What I couldn't handle was being his *soldier*, his weapon, the *family business*.

After I showered and spent an hour convincing my cousin that I didn't need him to send up one of his many willing whores to come fuck me, we headed out of his Hollywood home.

I didn't want some bitch who was being paid to give me attention, I wanted the dark haired girl who looked at me like I was a big gulp of air under the sea. I didn't want fake, cold, uncaring eyes. I preferred my hand to the charade any whore could fake.

Fuck!

I needed to get home, *now*.

It was driving me insane that I couldn't pull my phone out to text her or call her and hear that my brothers were treating her okay. I grabbed my phone and debated checking the feeds. Who the fuck knew where she would be right now?

Would she still be in Ronan's room?

Would she be in Kane's?

Was she in the kennels again?

There was a part of me that wanted to believe she'd be in my room, waiting for me when I came home. I practically laughed out loud at my own insane thoughts. Why the hell would she be in *my* room?

There was a better chance she'd be locked in that box again when I got back.

I tucked my phone back into my pocket and we pulled into my aunt Rosalinda's house. She refused to let Guillermo buy her a nicer, bigger house no matter how rich he got. She didn't want blood, or drug money and there was no way he would ever convince her otherwise.

Walking in and I was greeted by a rush of the next generation of niños running by, screaming at each other and I smiled remembering the days when that was me. How something could feel so close yet so far away.

Time ruined us.

And soon Guillermo would destroy them.

"Ay Santito! You are all man now, mijo." my aunt declared, which was insane because she had seen me in the last six months, and I was a thirty-three-year-old who hadn't grown in years.

I didn't argue though, I just let her fawn over me and returned her affectionate manhandling with pleasant smiles. I was relieved to hear that my dad had been running a fever and my mom stayed home to take care of him, but I had a pretty good hunch it was just an excuse to avoid coming face to face with me again.

It had been at least fifteen years since I'd last spoken to my mom. And to be completely honest that was more than okay with me. They'd written me off just as long ago for not falling in under Guillermo and giving them the cushy life they thought I owed them. They considered my tía stupid for denying Guillermo's money, and they thought the same of me for refusing the 'work'.

Dinner was tolerable, to say the least, and Guillermo tried his best to force his mom to let me stay at his house, but she was having none of it as we had all expected. I was grateful because I was too tired to listen to Guillermo and his backhanded compliments while he tried to convince me to abandon my brothers.

Tía Rosa made up the guest room for me and I thanked her for her hospitality. I made my way to the bed kicking off my shoes and pants, ready to crash for the night. When I dropped my head to the pillow, I realized my phone was still in my pants, but I was too tired to care.

Murder was a tiring business.

Playing nice with family was twice as exhausting.

Just one more day and I would be back home, where I needed to be.

Morning came and I met up with Guillermo for breakfast and my next two hits.

They were both easy.

Easy to kill and easy to dispose of.

I didn't mind whacking either of them, they both reeked of the scum of the earth. You know when you get that feeling in your gut that the throat you slit was for the good of the world?

No?

Well I do.

The first guy was jerking off to some sick shit when I snuck into his house. I didn't even give him the courtesy of letting him finish before I slit his throat. Didn't bother melting him either. When the cops would find him, bloody with his dick out and child porn on his computer, they would toss that case out as fast as they could.

The second guy had a giant bag of Gamma Hydroxybutyrate just laying out in the open on his kitchen counter. I didn't personally know a lot of good guys who kept a personal stash of GHB who *weren't* rapists, so I was happy to off him just the same.

By the time lunch came around I was already mentally ready to go home. I had already booked my flight for the next one taking off in two hours, but Guillermo still wanted to go over some things and food didn't sound too bad either.

He slid an upside-down polaroid at me across the restaurant table and I arched an eyebrow at him. I was good, but I wasn't *-two hours till my flight-* good.I was tired and I was ready to relax.

"Listen 'Cuz I hate to turn you down, but I'm beat and there isn't enough time for me to get another one in before I leave."

He chuckled at me before he said, "I don't think you'll find this one here anyways. It's actually a gift for your friend. Tell Ronan Zerkos it took some time, and with the right motivation I was able to get a general location, but that's it." I wasn't sure what he was talking about at all.

I reached for the photo, but he slammed his hand on top of mine, stopping me from turning it over.

"I'll want something for this, tell him he owes me. And I *will* collect." I narrowed my eyes at him, knowing exactly what he meant when he said he would collect.

Me.

I was the payment.

I fought my upper lip from curling up in anger, not wanting to let him see how he could get to me.

He didn't fool me either. He said it was a gift to Ronan, but he wouldn't be the one asking me to pull the trigger if it didn't benefit him in some way or another either.

This was Guillermo's target too.

I wasn't a fool.

I contained my anger, but was barely able to disguise my shock, the color draining out of my face as I flipped the photo over.

22

MATEO

I was fucking furious. At *everything.* At him, for trying to control where she slept like we didn't even have a say in anything. At Santos, for leaving me alone all weekend with the miserable bastard. At *her,* for sleeping in my room yet-a-fucking-again, and somehow still making me feel like a piece of dog shit stuck to her shoes.

How was it that she was begging Ronan for his cock first thing in the morning–just minutes after she came all over my hand, and then was asking to stay in Santos' room just a few moments later? The girl had no idea what she fucking wanted, and it was driving me up the fucking wall. I thought back to Álvarez's words that first day she was here.

You brought the apocalypse.

Damned if it wasn't true.

Zerkos tossed her in the kennels as soon as she refused to stay in his room, and as much as I wanted to bask in that victory, it was as much of a loss for me too. It had been over two months of me using my hand to get off and it was making me more and more on edge. Even the thought of one of the many tag-along Black Crow groupies that were more than willing to satisfy any of us put me off.

There was only one chick that was doing it for me anymore, and she was hell-bent on making me miserable. I didn't even doubt that she was probably punishing me for all the shit we were putting her through.

I ran my hand over my face in frustration and laid back down on my bed. For the first time in longer than I could remember I had absolutely no desire to play music. There was no insatiable urge digging at me to tune my soul into the beat, and disconnect my mind out from the present.

And I knew exactly why.

She was occupying every single inch of my mind, and like a black hole festering inside of me, she was consuming all of my thoughts.

The lights were too bright and the high pitch whining in my head was pounding into my skull again, but she wasn't here to erase it this time. I'd grown used to her presence, too comfortable with her touch.

I felt bitter at the passing thought that I was being played like a fool.

Con artist.

It was about a three-hour drive to Grimm's Reach from here, we hadn't even left yet and it was almost dark. Zerkos was set on spending some time with Oksana to see if he could get any information at all from her. There was a good chance we wouldn't be back until morning and that thought alone exhausted me. I would have paid any amount of money to not have to go, and I knew he could have taken Fletcher or Ethan with him, but the truth was simple.

My brother didn't trust me alone with his plaything.

I knew as soon as he'd come back up from the fifth floor that we were going to have it out again. But I was tired of fighting it, and he needed to know it too. I could hear his heavy footsteps coming closer from outside of the room and I grabbed my wallet and keys and headed out to meet him. His angry expression softened as soon as he looked at me and I realized I must have really looked like shit for Ronan Zerkos to be looking at me like that, with *pity*.

"How's your head?" he asked with genuine concern.

I shrugged and waited for him to get his things out of his bedroom. We both made our way into the elevator to start our little road trip.

"Oksana hasn't said a damn word down there. I couldn't get anything out of her," he said looking at me, the weight of it all written on his face.

He wasn't sleeping well, and I could tell by the dark circles under his eyes that It was more than just guilt.

"I think we were played."

"By the Bratva?" I asked him, trying to piece it all together in my head.

"I don't know brother, but I'm gonna get to the bottom of it. First, I'm gonna figure out what *she's* keeping from me. Then I'm going to figure out what's going on with the Bratvas." He looked determined, and I hoped for all of us that we could get the answers we were looking for.

"You think he's gonna be okay with you showing up over there? I remember the last time he almost killed you for it." I asked, crossing my arms.

It was one thing to be King of your own mountain, but a good king respected the reign of others. Motorcycle clubs were notorious for having their own silent, invisible armies. Most of them had several chapters across this country that were just waiting for a phone call to ride into battle.

No, I wasn't trying to piss off the Diablos.

Again.

Last time Ronan showed up at their door was when we came home from our final assignment as Navy Seals. It had been six years since he had seen her, and according to every single corner of the internet we traced, Cecilia Gomes was a ghost.

Motorcycle clubs were too unstable, with too many hot heads making decisions and of course, everyone was armed to their teeth. All it took was bringing up her name and guns started waving around. Zerkos couldn't take a goddamn hint, so Santos had to drag us out of the compound before we were in over our heads.

I'd give them that though, those fuckers were loyal to their President.

The ride was too quiet, my brother was clearly choking on all the shit he wanted to say to me, but he was holding back because he felt sorry for me. He felt guilty because he thought the headaches were a side effect of our time overseas.

But I'd been having headaches since I was a kid.

My portable CD player hooked into my backpack snuggly to keep it from skipping. I just bought the new Offspring *album and* "Original Prankster" *blared through my headphones as I stepped through the crunchy autumn leaves. It was my favorite time of year because it meant Christmas was coming.*

I bought Andrea's present back in July and I'd been hiding it for months. It was the hot pink Tamagotchi with purple buttons I saw her eyeing during the summer fair and dad refused to buy it for her because he said she already had too much junk. She cried the entire night in my bed and the next day I snuck out and used my entire year's savings to buy it for her.

I had it wrapped in my dresser drawer in a box with a bow and everything. I kept it locked because Andrea was a little snooper, and I didn't want her to spoil her own surprise.

I opened the door to our house and kicked off my shoes, hanging my backpack on the hook and taking the CD player out of it as I ran up the stairs.

Once I got to my room, I removed my headphones off but before I closed the door, something makes me hesitate. A feeling, a tiny noise in the distance.

Andrea stayed home sick with dad today, maybe she wasn't feeling good.

I heard some grunting and opened the door to inspect her room, and instead, I found my dad with his back to me. There was a whistle, almost like an alarm in my head when I saw him. His pants were dropped around his ankles and he was pushing into the bed over and over and I wasn't sure he could hear me, but I also couldn't be sure that I was even saying anything. Everything was so loud. The television was on, but it was static on the screen and the intense siren of the cable searching for a signal overwhelmed my senses as I made my way into the room.

"What are you doing?" I said, cutting through the fog of the high-pitched whining.

He didn't turn back to look at me so maybe the noise was too loud for him too.

I moved into the room and see it's Andrea under him and I yelled again this time louder, "What are you doing?" I push him off of her once my brain focuses and realizes what's happening.

He looks at me, his face filled with rage. We both look back at Andrea who isn't moving, her face is already blue, and foam is pooling at her mouth.

"Look what you've done you useless shit!" He screams at me, the force of his hand throwing me against the floor so hard the side of my head hits the metal frame of the bed.

The warm liquid drips down the side of my face and the high-pitched noise gets too loud to fight off. I close my eyes to try to get relief. I try to stay awake. I know I need to help Andrea. The heel of his boot connects with my rib and then my chin and the pain is just too much to not give in to the call of darkness.

I'm awake but my eyes are closed, my head hurts too much to take in the outside world right now. I can tell it's too bright by the way it all speckles through my eyelids. That ringing is still there and a bubble of anxiety trapped itself in my chest as I tried to force my senses to not get overwhelmed by the sound.

There's talking in the distance but I'm not able to make it out. I push away the hundreds of sounds in my brain and attempt to make out the words hanging in the air.

"Why isn't he cuffed to the bed anymore?" I think it's my mom, it's a familiar voice.

"We ran a rape kit, it did not match your son Ma'am. He isn't a suspect.

It did match your husband though. We've taken him into custody." I can hear my mother start to break down, her sobbing almost on the verge of hysterical.

"Shouldn't he be charged as an accessory or something?" I hear my mother through her cries.

"Mrs. Kane, we have no reason to believe your son had anything to do with the murder of your daughter. His injuries lead us to believe he may have tried to intervene." I hear the rough but caring voice tell her on my behalf.

"I need a minute alone with my son please," she says to the man.

His footsteps are followed by the sound of the door shutting.

All of a sudden, her heels quickly tap against the hospital floor, and I feel her cold hands pinching at my face. She plugs my nose for a few seconds but let's go before I feel lightheaded. She lifts my eyelid up, but I don't move at all, she sneers at me before letting my eyelid fall back down.

"Waste of space," she spits out at me.

I can hear her breathing heavily and I want to know so badly what's going on in her mind right now. I don't understand why she wants me to be punished for this. Why does she think I'm to blame? Maybe I should have done more.

Maybe I am to blame.

I don't open my eyes, my head hurts. I can't possibly handle coming face to face with her right now.

I shook the memory out of my head like an oncoming migraine as I jostled awake in the car.

"Good dream?" Zerkos chuckled.

"Hardly," I crossed my arms over my chest and propped the seat back to an upright position.

I looked down at the navigation app, it read that we were about ten minutes out from our destination. I let a big exhale out as I tried to contain my nerves, but I knew one thing for sure, my brother and I needed to be united when we walked in there together, and the only way that was going to happen was if we cleared the air.

"I didn't fuck her," I told him for the second time in three days, hoping that counted for something.

He only raised his eyebrow at me, barely taking his eyes off the road at all.

"Maybe the only reason you didn't fuck her is because, I interrupted you?" he asked, his tone void of any emotion and I worried we were slipping into risky territory here.

Did she tell him what we did?

"Maybe," I confessed, and his eyes shifted off the road to me considerably longer this time and I had to grab the steering wheel to keep us on the road. "Do you want a brother who's going to lie to you and keep you ignorantly happy or do you want someone you can trust unquestionably?" I asked him, a bit angry that he'd get pissed off at my honesty.

"Can I trust you unquestionably?" His nostrils flared out angrily with his words.

He yanked the steering wheel and swerved off the road bringing the car to a screeching halt. He was looking dead ahead at the road, refusing to turn my way when he said, "Get out Kane."

His voice was almost monotone, but I'd learned enough in the last twelve years to know that this was when his rage took over, when he seemed most void of emotion.

"Brother, don't be ridiculous. We're hours from—"

"GET THE FUCK OUT, KANE!" He took his pistol from the cupholder and pointed it at my head.

I was dumbfounded, but I knew my brother well enough to know he didn't point a gun unless he meant to kill. I raised my hands above my head and opened the car door, unbuckling the seatbelt with one hand while the other stayed raised like I was dealing with a wild fucking bear or some shit.

I got out of the car and realized the fucker wasn't completely insane, ready to strand me in between Grimm's Reach and Cove City. He threw the pistol in the back seat and got out as well. Relief ran through me as I realized he wasn't planning to bury me here. He crossed the front of the car in a few swift steps, the power in his gait was enough to let me know what he was coming after.

I felt the heavy weight of his fist against my cheek, and he knocked me back a few steps before he got another good hit in.

I caught the next hit and returned one back with my free hand and the asshole laughed at me instead. My next punch landed again, and it encouraged him to throw one more in and that was the one that split my lip open. I spat a wad of blood on the ground and grabbed Zerkos by the shirt and pulled him in closer.

"If we fight, there isn't a winner. There's just two dead fuckers on the side of the road and an entire organization we leave in Santos' hands." I told him looking into his green eyes, our foreheads pressed together throwing me back into the days when we were forced to be this close in order to best our enemies.

He snarled and turned his head to the side. He pushed me away with a hard shove and walked around the car again, opening the back door and grabbing the pistol.

I raised my eyebrow at him as he walked my way and pointed the pistol near my feet.

He fired each shot with an intense burning in his eyes that begged him to point a little more to the left.

When the click of the empty clip sounded out, he threw the gun at my feet with an angry yell before returning to the car.

I let him sit there, fuming, for probably a good ten to fifteen minutes. When I could finally see his shoulders moving a little less and his breathing started to steady, I opened the car door and planted myself in the passenger seat once again.

His eyes turned back to the road, and he didn't say anything else but now I felt compelled to lay it all out. There was no one else I could talk to about it anyway, no one else who would understand the torment I was dealing with day in and day out. Except maybe the other man who was just as cursed as me.

"She makes me feel things brother, things I didn't think I was capable of feeling anymore. Not since Andrea." Our eyes met again for a split second, and I didn't see an ounce of anger or hatred in them. "She drives me insane, I'm not sure I'm even in control of myself anymore." I kept going, "Nothing hurts me when she's around. Except for her, she's good at hurting me, and the worst part is that I like it."

"It's absolute madness, isn't it?" he said as the corner of his lips fought a smile, "The way she does that? She doesn't even know what she's doing, and I think that's the part that I love the most." He looked at me. "You get why I'm so fucked now don't you?" he asked.

"I do," I told him, and he turned the key and began to drive once again.

"Stay away from my girl, or I will kill you, *brother,*" he said, and my stomach dropped.

We pulled into the gravel drive that took us into the Diablos Locos compound, and a skinny kid, probably barely eighteen years old, wound the gate back for us to pull through.

"Who you here for?" he asked, chomping on a piece of gum.

"I'm here to see your Prez," Ronan told him.

The kid said something into a walky-talky and pointed us in the direction he wanted us to park.

Too late to turn back now.

23

RONAN

I'd only ever been here once before, the first time was before we had even established ourselves as a noteworthy gang, let alone an actual syndicate operation. I was young, brash, and thought the number of men that fell under my bullets meant something.

It didn't.

The Diablos gave me the firm reality check I needed.

An hour in their compound six years ago, and they showed me that you couldn't be shit in this world if you didn't have an army behind you, willing to die for you. The Seals were loyal, and we never left a man behind, but only in the name of our country. It didn't matter to us, the military was just an outlet for both of us to focus our rage, and our grief.

It served a purpose in its own way.

I had no desire to join a motorcycle club, not by a long shot. But I couldn't deny that their devotion to their leader was what inspired and motivated every action that led us to create the Black Crow Brotherhood. After almost getting killed by the Diablos years ago I knew I needed to find my own army, and I knew I would need to earn their trust and fealty in my own way.

A king was only a king if he could prove himself worthy.

To say I was feeling brave would be an understatement. There weren't a lot of motherfuckers out there that I could say made me nervous anymore. But this son of a bitch and I had a history almost as ancient as me and my girl I kept locked up in the kennels, and I wasn't taking no for an answer this time.

The scrawny kid was wearing a leather cut that said PROSPECT on the back of it, and I chuckled to myself as I wondered if he was savage enough to make it all the way someday. You either swallowed the world or it chewed you up instead, and to be fully honest...the kid looked hungry, but he also looked like a damn good meal. He waited for us to park and personally escorted us to the clubhouse entrance.

"Wait out here first, we have Church in session," he said, and Mateo gave him a confused look.

"What the hell are a bunch of one-percenters doing praying?" he asked, and the kid laughed.

"It means they're meeting. Important stuff. Club business you know?" he explained putting his hands in his pockets and shrugging.

"You don't get invited to important meetings?" I asked him, a bit curious myself at how it all worked over here.

"I'm just a Prospect. Once I earn my patch, I'll be able to sit in Church with the rest of them," he grabbed the edges of his leather vest proudly and gave a big cheesy smile.

"How old are you, kid?" Mateo asked.

"Seventeen," He grinned at my brother.

"And your parents are cool with the career path you've chosen?" I asked him, crossing my arms, wondering what the hell a *kid* was doing in one of the most notoriously violent motorcycle clubs in the country.

"Wouldn't know. I've been in the foster system since I was born. Never stayed anywhere longer than a year, at least until three years ago. That's when the Prez found me stealing from a grocery store and told me to come by. He took me in, and gave me a clean place to stay and three meals a day. I've never lasted anywhere this long, but if he lets me, I'll stay till the day I die. I think I'd be dead if it wasn't for him. I owe the Diablos everything."

"Prospect, go do your homework and tell Veneno to take post at the gate," the voice came from inside and the kid almost jumped from surprise.

"You got it Prez. You've got visitors," he headed inside leaving Kane and I standing on the porch of the clubhouse.

"Gringo," he said, opening the door, "I thought I told you I never wanted to see your face again?" Cézar Villalobos said coming through the swinging double doors looking one hundred percent like the mean asshole I remembered.

He was just a little bit shorter than me, but the two inches I had on him didn't make him look any less intimidating. The copper tone of his skin was a deep, rich shade and his black hair was trimmed to a close fade all around. It made him look even meaner, more dangerous than I had remembered.

"You keep saying it, but I think you actually miss me," I gave him a half-smile and lifted up my shirt to show that I was unarmed.

He looked at Mateo and waited for the same gesture before he said anything else.

"Good to see you're not a boy waving his new toys around anymore, Zerkos. Entra." He said as he opened the door to the clubhouse. "What the fuck happened to you two?" He asked of our clearly bloody and beaten faces, but Mateo shrugged, and I didn't bother giving him the satisfaction that this was just another aftershock of Earthquake Cecilia.

The clubhouse itself was an impressive set-up. From the outside it looked like a giant farmhouse but once you got inside the whole place looked like it was gutted and redone. The floor was a beautiful oak with a light stain on the large wide planks.

To the right there was a massive kitchen fully stocked with an authentic brick oven and a professional built in griddle. The entire back wall was lined with stark white cabinets and just a few feet away was an island that easily sat twelve stools around it.

To the left was a large sectional couch, a couple pool tables, and all the way in the back wall was a large bar with hundreds of bottles of liquor lining the shelves. Dividing both rooms was a set of stairs that went both up and down into what must have been a basement. On the left side, there was a door just before the bar with another much larger upside-down cross hanging above it.

"Let's step into my office," he said, running his tongue over the diamond on his top canine like a bad habit before turning around.

He signaled us to follow as he made his way to the room with the upside-down cross. A few members were walking out of the room, and they stared at us as we went inside. I didn't belong here; it was clear with my Prada suit and my Versace shoes.

Kane, however, looked much more in his element than I had ever seen before, his black leather jacket, and boots made him appear right at home. Even the intentional rips in his pants that I never for the life of me understood, actually fit right in with the other bikers.

The room was large, the walls were painted black, and one side was filled with old leather vests framed and hung up. Another wall was filled with photos of the MC throughout the years, members aging, and disappearing into different portraits as they were replaced by the new generations. A table that easily sat twenty men spanned across the room with a large upside-down cross about four feet tall hanging on the wall behind the head of the table.

There was another door through the room, and he unlocked it and held it open as he gestured us in. It was an office, plain with not much but a desk, a few chairs, and a filing cabinet.

"You look tired," I told the ornery bastard.

"It's always something, isn't it? Figured you of all people would understand that, pendejo." He threw a half-smile at me, as he let me know that he knew *exactly* what I'd been up to these last six years. It was true though, there was always something and that was probably the first time in my life Villalobos and I were on the same page.

"If you're here for the same thing as last time, don't bother sitting. I don't know where she is, and to be honest, I hope it stays that way," he said looking at me, but I took a seat anyway.

"No, not looking for her anymore. I have questions I need answered," I told him, sitting up as straight as possible since he hadn't sat down yet himself.

"And I can guarantee you I don't have answers for you, boy," he said *boy* in the most condescending way as if he wasn't just eight years older than me.

I raised an eyebrow at him, and he gave out a sigh like he was already exhausted by my presence.

"Look, ever since I distanced myself, the people around me tend to drop dead a lot less. You catch my drift, clown? I need it to stay that way. I've got people to look after these days, the family I've chosen. I'm not calling this shit to my door anymore," he reasoned with me.

I could understand where he was coming from.

"I have my own people to look after too, that's why I'm here for answers. I need to know what kind of danger might be dropping at *my* house. Catch *my* drift?" I asked, crossing my arms, and not backing down.

KNOCK-KNOCK

"Yeah?" he shouted past us toward the door.

"Come party Prez, we're gonna rip that bastard's patch when the sun comes up tomorrow," a voice sounded out.

"Have a few drinks, hang around for the night. I've got a proposition for you come the morning," he said vaguely as he proceeded to stand and leave us in his office.

I looked to Mateo for his thoughts, but he just shrugged his shoulders. I knew the asshole was gonna make me work for it, but I was already annoyed at how far Cézar was going to push my buttons along the way.

There was nothing unpredictable about their MC's party, from the fishnet-clad women in booty shorts with unimpressive fake tits, to the cheap booze that flowed through their bar. But that didn't mean I didn't allow myself to have a few too many shots and try my hand at getting what I needed from Cézar. He was good though, anytime I'd catch him off guard and try to strike up a few inquiries he'd practically pull his dick out, and soon enough there would be a slut on the other end.

And I mean, good for the guy, that was a lot of blow jobs in one night to avoid conversation. I'll give him props for that because I sure as shit had a hard time sticking around to wait for him to finish to get a few words in.

Kane sipped his water casually in the corner until I got too drunk, and he asked Cézar for our lodgings for the night.

Morning came with a painful reminder of why I didn't drink before a job anymore, and why I didn't drink anything that cost less than four figures a bottle. But there was a sweet little thing in the kitchen pouring coffee and grilling up bacon and I wasn't disappointed to wake up to the smell of food.

"It's almost time Pres, we got everything loaded up in the van, who's riding?" A lean, clean-shaven guy no shorter than six-five marched through the kitchen.

His face was tattooed to resemble a skull, the black over his eyelids and nose, and the bony smile inked over his lips.

I didn't remember seeing him last night, but then again, I didn't make the effort to strike up a conversation with anyone here but the man in charge. His hair was cut short all the way around with a fade to the scalp in the back. He had the word MUERTE tattooed on his throat and his entire arms were blacked out in tattoos from what I could see.

He was an intimidating motherfucker, and he knew it too. No one tattooed *death* on their neck if they didn't mean it.

"I thought we could talk this morning," I said to Cézar as I sipped my coffee.

"You've got some bad timing boys, Calaveras and I've got plans today that can't wait," he said, getting up from his chair, shoving the last few bites of his breakfast down. "You're welcome to stay here and wait though. Unless..." He trailed off looking at the grim reaper standing in front of the door.

The guy shook his head at him as if he knew exactly where his president's head was at, as they communicated in silence.

"Or you can help me out, earn a favor from Diablos, maybe even get some of that information you're after." He stood waiting for us to answer as he baited me with what I needed.

I looked at Mateo who tilted his head at me. I knew what he was thinking, we came all the way out here, might as well play the bastard's games.

"What's the job?" Kane asked the question for me.

"It's a drive out a few hours, got to set some things right," he answered vaguely but Mateo wasn't satisfied, and neither was I.

"We aren't riding into something blindly, you either tell us all the details or count us out." He crossed his arms as he waited for an answer and the guy named Calaveras stepped in closer.

"I've got a rogue president a few states over who needs his patch stripped like a hotel bed. Grimm's Reach is the founding chapter of the Diablos Locos, which means it's my duty as president to make sure all chapters stay in line. If someone's doing dirty, I've gotta keep it in check, either the whole chapter goes down, or the president does," he explained.

"What's too dirty for a one percent club?" I asked with genuine curiosity.

I thought the whole point of being branded as outlaws was to not have any limits.

"We don't deal in flesh, and we certainly don't deal in *kids.* This motherfucker is doing both. I've got more than half his members holed up in our clubhouse spare rooms." He pulled out a pack of cigarettes from his back pocket and lit one in the office but tilted his chin towards the door to signal us to follow him out.

"And the other members of his club?" Kane asked, letting him know that detail didn't go unnoticed.

"They apparently didn't have a problem with it," Cézar spits out through clenched teeth, and Calaveras put his hand on his shoulder in an attempt to calm down his president.

"So, no such thing as innocent bystanders then?" Mateo asked, and I followed where he was going.

He wanted to know if there was a limit. If there was anyone, he *couldn't* get rid of. He had a wildness dancing through his eyes, and I could tell he was out for blood tonight. She'd sunk her claws in him almost as deeply as they pierced through me, and he needed an outlet.

"Cannon fodder," Calaveras spoke in a raspy unused voice that made me wonder if silence was his usual preference. "They go with La Flaquita tonight," he put his index finger to his lips in a signal and winked at me.

I'd been around Cecilia long enough to know who he meant.

His deity of Death.

Mateo let out a loud whoop and I knew there was no chance I could hold on to his leash tonight. He had a lot of pent-up energy and aggression to let out and this was probably the best way for him to do it.

"I want a Bike," he looked up at Calaveras, and Cézar chuckled at him.

"Better watch out Zerkos, or your boy might just cross over to the dark side." He tossed keys in the air and Kane caught them with ease. "Calaveras will ride with you in the van." He said to me.

I pressed my lips into a thin line, he was doing it again.

He was making sure I had no way to get what I needed from him until the job was done, no chance of even leaving moments of silence in a car ride between us.

At the end of the day, Cézar Villalobos and I would always clash.

The fact that he held a piece of my girl's heart I would never be able to understand, or claim for myself, made my resentment for him grow even stronger.

24

CECILIA

Queen of absolutely fucking nada.

I paced the cell like a neurotic animal caged in a zoo enclosure, looking for a way out but knowing damn well I was doomed. They'd be gone *all* night.

All of them.

Something about that just made me feel uneasy, insecure.

It was crazy, but at least here, with them, I was protected. Sure, I was living in a prison cell with someone who didn't even speak, and maybe I was too damn stubborn to take the easy way out sometimes. But Ronan Zerkos didn't own me, and if it took sleeping down here to prove it, I would do it again and again.

He thought he had the right to control everything I did, everyone I… I bit my lip at the thought of Mateo's hands on me this morning, the feeling of his hard erection pressed up against my hand and how quickly he made me come undone with just his fingers. I closed my eyes as I remembered the feeling of Ronan inside me, wildly pounding into me with so much passion I thought I would burn from his touch alone.

He took everything I dished out and begged for more and it was the epitome of everything we stood for.

Constant whiplash.

A teeter-totter of love, and hatred that never touched the ground to let us off.

We *were* destined in the stars, no matter what my papá said.

I had a taste of his blood and I wanted more. I wanted to bathe in it and baptize myself until I became new. I wanted him to suffer for my sins the way I'd been suffering for protecting him all those years ago. How dare he think that this was about some *guns*, some *money?* Puta madre.

Men could be so fucking stupid.

"ARGH!" I screamed, throwing my plastic cup of water against the wall, causing Chiyo to jump off her bed in surprise.

"Sorry," I said, sitting down on the concrete floor.

It was cold enough that I could feel it through the layers of the gray sweats I had been accustomed to wearing the last couple of months. The lack of underwear didn't help my frozen-ass situation, but I preferred it to the idea of those three jackasses picking out my underwear again.

"So, do you not speak English then, or are you actually the mastermind I've pegged you for?" I asked her as I realized this was the first time we'd been alone together.

Oksana was still on the fifth floor as far as I knew, and I had a feeling they wouldn't be letting her out until one of the guys got back. Chiyo looked at me and just shook her head. I pressed my lips into a thin line and narrowed my eyes at her.

I wasn't fully convinced, there was no way.

Right?

Where did he get these women from?

The day drew out longer than any day I'd ever spent in my life. Maybe it was the fact that it was the first time none of them had come down here. Had I really become so attached to their presence? I could literally hear the seconds ticking on a clock hanging on a nearby wall and it was slowly making me more irritated.

My rage was bubbling up inside me, roaring to come out and I didn't have anyone to direct it to except the poor badly bleached blonde huddled into the corner staring at me like I was neurotic. Maybe I was.

The lack of any stimulation was what drove me insane. At least when they were putting me in the box, or physically torturing me, my mind could work a way to pull me out of the present. Moments like this, where it was just fucking *boredom* though, that was what actually made me feel fucking psychotic.

I tried to shake the crawling feeling under my skin as anxiety cocooned around me like a prickly wool blanket again. I knew the cameras were on and I couldn't let them see how much I was struggling. If they knew this was a bigger punishment than anything else they'd done to me before, I would be fucked with a capital F.

I heard Fletcher whistling the little theme from *Kill Bill* like he always did and jumped back into my bed before he came into view. I laid on my side and pretended to be asleep, I wasn't in the mood to deal with one of the assholes' grunts. I heard the jangling of the keys and within a few seconds, the bars were slamming shut and ringing out through the empty concrete floors.

Fletcher walked through the room without even glancing at me, his red waves falling in his eyes as he carelessly dropped a plate with a cold sandwich at the foot of my bed. I kept my eyes closed as he made his way to Chiyo. He placed her plate at the side of her bed and sat down, dipping the mattress with his weight.

With a gentleness I had never seen from him before, he carefully tucked a lock of her bleached blonde hair behind her ear, and whispered, "Perfection."

She lowered her head with a smile, there was a shyness to her that reminded me of myself. Just a kid, with a stomach full of butterflies over a blonde boy who cared too much. These days it didn't seem like he cared at all, and I wasn't even sure I knew him anymore.

It felt like I was intruding on an extremely private moment between them, but I couldn't stop watching and I had no plans to look away. I was bored as hell and it was so sweet to watch something so innocent unfold right in front of me. His hand draped over hers as he brought her fingers to his lips and softly kissed each one.

They sat in silence, the barrier of language differences making it impossible for them to communicate but at the same time proving it was transcendent. There was something there, something so tangible and real that broke all laws of common sense.

There was love there.

And it made me fucking sick to witness it.

I was jealous.

Not of her or of him, but of the fact that they had found love together while here I was running from it in every corner.

He picked up the sandwich and brought it to her lips, she smiled at him with her hands folded in her lap as he fed her each bite, giving her time to chew before lifting it back up to her mouth again. He continued feeding her this way until the entire sandwich was gone, and every so often he would pick up her glass of water and give her a drink to swallow the dry sandwich down with.

Once she finished the entire thing, he put the plate on the floor and climbed into the bed with her, wrapping his arms around her as he took the position of the big spoon.

I must have fallen asleep watching the show because when I opened my eyes, Fletcher was already gone from the kennels, and Chiyo was fast asleep on the other side of the cage. I didn't even know what time it was, but I was itching to get out of here and hoping the guys would be home soon. At least when they were around, I had something to focus all of my anger into.

It was easier to tell myself that, than to admit the truth.

That I felt something.

I heard a loud crash far off and the sound of multiple guys yelling through walkie-talkies in another room coming through their radio feeds. The ever-familiar sound of guns firing off in the distance jarred me into the present moment. I rushed over to Chiyo. I'd learned to stay calm through these moments with practice.

Being able to handle complete chaos had become my own personal superpower.

I heard shouting from a distance, and my brain ran a million miles an hour when I couldn't discern the words from the two languages in my brain. I shook her awake and before she could yell from surprise, I clamped my hand over her mouth and pressed my fingers to my lips in signal. She nodded her head in understanding, so I let go, and grabbed her and pointed under the bed. "Get in, ok?" I asked her, hopeful that maybe she comprehended the message I was trying to send.

Her eyes were full of fear and darting towards the kennel door. Guns were going off like crazy and getting louder and louder and I knew we were running out of time because there was absolutely nowhere to hide.

"Don't say a fucking word." I told her again trying to get the point across as I gave her a pleading look pressing my index finger to my lips again as she laid on the ground under the bed.

I grabbed the blanket on her bed and draped it over the edges so that it fell to the floor, covering the gap and hiding her from plain sight.

But we couldn't both hide, not for both of us to make it.

An empty cage would get searched, but maybe if I was in the open, she had a chance. If I could give her that chance, then it didn't matter what would happen to me. The reaper had finally come for me and probably the only thing that would save my soul from damnation was maybe this one act of humanity I could provide this innocent girl.

I couldn't allow Ignacio to take her as well.

I accepted my fate and sat on the bed patiently until the guns got so loud it was obnoxious, borderline painful. Fletcher appeared and my heart leaped with a relief that was just as quickly doused by a wave of fear as a gun came into view, pressed to the back of his head.

The gunman stayed silent, he was a tank of a guy and towered over Fletcher with a face that resembled a bulldog. There was an automatic rifle strapped to his back on top of the pistol he held in his hands, finger boldly on the trigger. He grunted and pushed Fletcher with one hand, forcing him to stumble forward into the kennel door.

He looked wrecked, his face purple and already swelling from some sort of cruel beating. The way he clutched his side let me know he already received a courtesy bullet. His eyes widened in alarm, and I could see he was frantically searching the room for Chiyo as he fumbled with the keys. His blue eyes found mine and I did the slightest of tilts with my head in the direction of the empty bed.

His shoulders dropped with a sigh of relief. Looking at the burly guy behind him, I could see the defeat as it washed through him before he underhand tossed the keys inside of the kennel towards my bed. He sealed his fate, and I couldn't hide my shock with the move.

"If I let her out, my boss will kill me. You might as well do it, because I won't betray him." Fletcher said looking back at the kennel hopelessly, and before I had a chance to even appreciate his sacrifice the bulldog's laughter rang out, followed by a single gunshot.

"NO!" I screamed out from shock but also to silence some of Chiyo's whimpering from underneath the bed.

Fletcher's body fell to the ground with a sickening thud, and the giant man kicked his body to the side as he stood in front of the cage's door. He pointed his gun at me with one hand and held up five fingers with the other. He started folding one finger down at a time. Before he got to three, I stood and grabbed the keys, dropping them once before I got to the door.

With shaking hands, I tried to focus on the one person I might be able to save tonight from my uncle's brutality. I remembered the door locked without the keys and if I could do this well, I could keep Chiyo alive a little longer. I turned the key in the lock and pulled it out quickly, throwing it back into the room as I pushed my way through the cage door and threw my knee into the bulldog's balls.

He barely grunted in pain, but it was just the second I needed to close the door behind me, hearing the lock as I tried to faked a futile attempt to run for it. Before I could take three steps, he was yanking me by the hair. I felt the intense burning of my hair being pulled, forcing a scream from my throat that turned into a yelp as he slammed me against the wall.

The force of the impact against my back knocked the breath out of me. Panic and the pain from colliding against the wall had me stuttering my breathing as I struggled with tiny sips of inhales.

I was fighting to take a single full breath when he knelt down in front of me and knocked the gun against the side of my head, darkening my vision. His pale blue eyes were the last thing I saw before I succumbed to the dreadful pitch black nothing.

25

RONAN

This motherfucker was testing my patience and I couldn't tell if he was egging me on to pump me up for the job we were about to do, or if he got his kicks from watching me squirm. Cézar rode his bike to avoid any chance of me having any sort of discussion with him and I wanted to punch his stupid face in for it.

Though the car ride with Calaveras was quiet and long, I was plenty satisfied knowing Kane's ass was going to be numb and completely destroyed by the time we got to their compound.

We followed behind the bikes as the two of them rode together like old friends in the front. Eventually, Cézar threw his arm out to the side to signal us to pull off onto the side of the road. We turned our headlights off, Cézar swung his leg off his bike gracefully and I could make out the "LOBO" patch that curved around his club's name on the back of his leather cut.

"Lobo?" I asked Calaveras and he answered in his ghostlike voice.

"Road name," he vaguely explained, and I was glad I didn't bother with small talk during the ride.

Clearly, this guy couldn't manage full sentences. Maybe he didn't need to.

"Because of his last name?" I asked him, looking up at the only guy who'd ever towered over me.

"Because he's always got the pack's best interest in mind." Damn if that wasn't enough for me.

I didn't want to respect the bastard. I knew he would always look at me like some kid who would never be good enough for Cecilia. His people certainly respected him though, and I was having a hard time pretending like I couldn't see why.

He walked over to the van and opened the trunk revealing a beautiful stash of weapons that made any good soldier's mouth water. I reached for a Glock 23 and loaded it up before putting it in the back of my pants as a backup. I grabbed a few knives and tucked them away into my boots. I grabbed another Glock and kept that one in my hand and I looked at Mateo to see he was making the same selections. I smirked at him turning up the corner of my lip because this was the shit we lived for, this chaos was where the roots of our bond sank into.

"We're going to go through the thicket of trees, it's about a ten-minute walk and we'll be able to sneak into the compound unseen this way," Cézar said, pulling out a single flashlight from his pocket and turning it on as we marched through the tall grass into the dark clearing.

The caw of a crow in a nearby tree made Mateo jump back with fright and Calaveras cracked up laughing so hard that he was slapping his knees and wiping tears from the corners of his eyes.

"You almost shit yourself!" He cackled.

Mateo and Cézar simultaneously shushed him like a badly behaving child. Watching such a giant, fearsome guy laughing so freely and wildly actually put me in a better mood. I ended up letting out a few chuckles myself as I slapped Calaveras in the back in a friendly manner.

"There are ten members left here, everyone else who didn't want to stick around while their Prez did disgusting things to little kids, packed their bags and found a new Diablos chapter somewhere to call home." He pulled out a piece of paper from his pocket and it was a blueprint of the clubhouse just a few hundred feet away from us.

"They'll probably be off their asses drinking and on whatever drugs. Shoot first, ask questions later, but if there are any cut bunnies around leave them out of it," he warned.

"Cut bunnies?" Kane asked him, raising an eyebrow.

"Anything with tits and a hatchet wound." He explained before continuing, "Do you see this door here?" He pointed to the drawing on the paper. "This is the basement door, I need one of you to make sure there are no victims here, can you do that?" He looked at both of us, but Mateo answered first.

"I'm on it, I'll sneak in through this side window." Kane pointed to the piece of paper.

"This pendejo here though," he started and pulled out another folded-up paper from his vest's inside pocket this time. "You don't shoot to kill, not yet I need to take his patch while he's alive." He explained, unfolding the photo of a long-haired man.

We all nodded in agreement after Cézar asked if we were ready and we moved silently as a unit. Mateo signaled us with a finger to let us know he was heading towards the back of the house to find a way into the basement.

"I'll go in through the other side, count to ten, and then burst in," Cézar said to us and we began our countdown as he took off to the opposite side of the clubhouse that Mateo went in.

"Eight, nine..." I said and the mass of muscles next to me shouted, "TEN!" as he ran back for momentum and threw his weight into his shoulder as he slammed into the clubhouse front door.

There was no time to think, as soon as the door broke open it was pure chaos. Tits, beers, and bullets were flying everywhere. The scum that was leftover in this MC clearly didn't even give a shit if they accidentally killed one of the women they were about to fuck.

I kept a mental screenshot of the guy we weren't supposed to kill, and aimed both of my guns, shooting them off at the same time. Calaveras was stabbing some dude in the throat while I took out four of them with clean headshots. A few more guys poured in from a back hallway, thankfully too wasted to be shooting straight. I took a knife from inside my boot and threw it with as much force as I could.

Right into somebody's eye.

There were four guys left by my count, and from what I could see they were all hiding from their fates. "Come out, come out," I sang, loving the way the adrenaline rushed with a righteous kill.

I'd be sleeping like a baby tonight knowing we rid the world of these fuckers.

A bullet whizzed by so close, I could feel the heat against my skin. I pulled the last knife out of my boot and threw it in that direction without paying too much attention. The scream let me know I hit a target.

I walked toward their bar and found my knife wedged in some bald guy's thigh.

"Please, please, don't do this!" he begged, but unfortunately for him, today I was judge, jury, and executioner.

I pulled my knife out of his thigh and cleaned it off on his shirt before putting a bullet between his eyes. The girls who didn't get shot by these fuckers were running out the door, Mateo was already out there waiting for them, with a few kids in tow.

I contained my rage, reminding myself that no one who was guilty was going to be surviving the night.

I didn't even bother to ask the other guy if he had any last words before I took him out too. A crashing sound drew my attention to find Cézar throwing the very guy from the photo down the clubhouse stairs. He stepped down behind him, kicking him down the rest of the stairs before dragging the man along the floor by his greasy hair.

It looked like the guy was practically dead already, but Cézar had a point to make and I sure as hell could appreciate that too. The crime was too big, and death was too good for this grimy piece of shit. Villalobos took out his phone and passed it to me. "Record this shit," he said, pulling a cigarette out of his shirt pocket and lighting it with a deep drag.

First, he took the guy's leather vest off and threw it into the ground. "I'd take your President patch, but to be honest, I think we'll just burn your whole clubhouse down." He said reaching for an open bottle of tequila that sat on the bar.

Cézar took a big swig then pulled his knife out and in a single motion, he grabbed the skin on the guy's chest where the DIABLOS LOCOS MC emblem was tattooed and sliced down like he was taking a filet. Cézar tossed the patch of flesh on the ground in front of him, a wild and erratic sob leaving his victim's mouth.

The guy was shaking violently from shock, his oily, dark hair was dripping with sweat. To most, that would have been sufficient punishment, but the overwhelming smell of fear and piss in the air seemed to fuel Cézar to go further. The biker fought to remain conscious, but he was probably better off letting go. I wouldn't want to be on the other end of Cézar's wrath tonight.

I knew, because that same demon I saw hiding behind that crooked smile, lived within me as well.

Kane burst through the front door not paying any attention to the wild mess and the dead bodies, his eyes were frantic, scanning the room until he found me. He heaved big gulps of air in and out of his lungs to catch his breath before he spoke, "We gotta get the fuck out of here brother."

I pulled my eyebrows together in question, he waved his phone at me. I felt the pockets of my pants and realized I left my phone in the van.

"What's happening?" I yelled at him, overwhelmed at the incoming flood of things to deal with.

I turned my head just in time to catch Cézar pulling the guy's tongue out of his mouth and slicing it off with one clean motion. He dumped the rest of the tequila over his body and tossed a lit match over him before exiting the clubhouse.

"The high-rise was compromised. Too many fatalities. I think they came in from the rooftop," Mateo said, still struggling to breathe.

My brain was slow to process his words and too many thoughts were racing in my head, trying to make sense of what was happening at the moment.

"She's gone Ronan, they took her." he shouted, slapping at my face to knock the haze out of me.

It worked, but instead my rage was misdirected, my fist flying directly into his face mechanically, out of sheer reflex.

"What do you mean she's gone? Who took her?" I yelled at him, but he seemed to be fully out of answers for me.

It was probably the first time I had seen Mateo Kane look freaked out and unsure in my entire life.

The fire was spreading through the clubhouse, Calaveras pushed us out through the door since we were both frozen in place.

"Lobo," I yelled out for him as he piled the three remaining women into the van with the rest of the kids. "We need your bikes, we don't have time to go back to Grimm's Reach. I have to get to my men, now."

He threw the keys in my direction, nodding in understanding, "I appreciate the help, Zerkos. It's good to have trained guns on jobs like this. Sorry, it didn't pan out so lucrative for you. You need a favor, just call it in. The Diablos owe you."

That wouldn't be good enough. He owed me a lot more than a favor.

"I need more than that. I need answers," I said through clenched teeth, pulling him toward me by the shirt.

"I'm grateful for the help, amigo, but the life I come from doesn't allow me to spill secrets. I hope you can appreciate and understand that," he said with a look that let me know he never planned to tell me a damn thing tonight.

"Cézar, I have to know!" I shouted.

"Listen, the things I've done to that girl. I wanna keep that shit buried with the rest of my skeletons you understand?" But I didn't understand, and Kane was charging at him before I could register what he had said.

"What the fuck do you mean the things you've done to her?" My brother in arms asked, taking the words straight out of my mouth and earning himself a look from Villalobos that said 'now he'd seen it all'.

"I didn't peg you for someone who shared Zerkos," he glanced between me and Kane.

My upper lip curled up at the insinuation.

"Settle down, both of you. I didn't mean it like that. She was my family, and I hurt her in more than one way. The best thing I can do for her sake, is keep my mouth shut and keep her secrets," he said.

I pushed him away with a frustrated growl. I pulled the glock from my pants but the familiar feeling of a chamber pressing up against the back of my head let me know Calaveras had a quicker draw than I did. But I didn't care, "I came here for answers, I'm not leaving without them."

Cézar let out an obnoxious laugh that had me clenching my fists together, my nostrils flared wide in anger. "I don't know if it's hilarious or completely sad that you still know nothing, gringo." He said matter-of-factly.

I shoved him again and it earned me a look from Calaveras that said he wouldn't tolerate me laying my hands on his President again.

"I need to know Cézar," I pressed again.

"I'd say, she doesn't trust you, or she loves you too much to give you the truth. Either way, I would consider it a blessing amigo," he said.

I didn't move. Didn't change my expression. He raised his hands up in defense, letting out a sigh of defeat, "Suit yourself, *kid.* But don't say I didn't warn you when you start meddling in shit that's too big for you. No one makes it out of the Flores family alive. *No one*. That's all you'll get from me," he said.

I threw the Glock on the ground, unsatisfied but well aware that was the most I'd get out of Cézar Villalobos when it came to Cecilia.

My heart was pumping so wildly I could hear it pulsing in my ears as Mateo and I both threw our legs over their bikes, the sound only masked by the throttle of the motorcycles.

I didn't have time to process Cézar's words but I made a mental note to remember the name Flores when this clusterfuck was dealt with.

It only took a few seconds to steady myself as I adjusted to the purring of the engine beneath me and we pulled out of the compound, the heat of the fire blazed behind us as we rode back to Cove City. It was going to be a long ride, and the weight of the world was coming down on me. I left her there, by herself, vulnerable. If anything happened to her, *it was on me.*

Whoever took her didn't know the monster they just unleashed.

I'd go to the ends of the Earth to find my girl.

Now that I had her back, I didn't plan to let her go ever again. Like a rabid hellhound, I would do whatever it took to exact my vengeance and make sure she was safe. She was all there was, all there could ever be. And no one would take her from me.

26

CECILIA

I woke up to the shock of cold water hitting my flesh, and as my body naturally reacted my back hit the cold metal bars constraining me.

I groaned loudly from pain, my entire body ached from being forced into the smallest shape I'd ever had to put myself into, the pounding in my skull reminding me that I didn't get here willingly. My tongue was swollen and dry and my throat was screaming for a drop of moisture. I tried to fight through the pain at the front of my head, eventually working to force an eye open, the other no doubt, was swollen shut.

There was barely any light shining in, but the cold, dampness of the area quickly let me know I was in some sort of basement, or underground area. There was a constant, steady drip in the distance but I quickly worked to tune it out, knowing it would eventually drive me insane and break me if I spared it any of my attention.

Whoever dumped the water on me was long gone, and for some reason, something was telling me it was the closest thing I'd get to a shower for the foreseeable future.

How long had I been knocked out?

The last thing I remembered was throwing the keys back in the cell hoping I could save Chiyo. And Fletcher. Fuck, he was definitely dead, there was so much blood. My uncle finally caught up to me and even the deadly Ronan Zerkos couldn't stop him, because he took a day off.

A laughable thought really, but it was likely the reality we were living.

The corner of my lip curled into a small smile, the thought that I'd finally gotten what I'd been hoping for in the end. How many times had I prayed to Santa Muerte to let Ronan and my uncle end each other accordingly, for chaos to rain down on the cártel and his silly brotherhood.

The memory of Fletcher's frantic gaze crossed my mind and my smile quickly soured and turned into a scowl at the thought of how many innocent men must have died at the hands of Ignacio tonight.

Because of me.

My hands were bound in front of my knees with a zip tie that was digging into my wrists so tightly that some dried blood was already forming at the edges. I couldn't reach to feel the bars to my side but the ones above and behind me let me know I was in a kennel. A *real* kennel, one probably just big enough for a labradoodle or some shit.

"Hay alguien ahí?" I shouted but it came out barely a whisper through my dried-out vocal cords, and I grunted trying to ease the need to not lick the water droplets still on my arms.

"Kill that cocksucker!" I heard a childish voice to my left that made rage boil inside of me.

I expected there to be others down here with me, prisoners of my demented uncle just like me. But knowing his depravity didn't end at children made me wish I had the strength to tear out of this cage and rip through him with my bare hands myself.

"Kill who? How long have you been here?" I asked, hoping this kid could at least let me in on how long I'd been out.

"Kill that cocksucker! Cocksucker!" The little shithead repeated, and I couldn't help but let out a sob of relief.

My companion wasn't a child, it was a fucking Parrot!

"How long have you been here, little guy?" I asked my new friend, knowing full well that his verbal range probably started with and ended with "Cocksucker".

"Whore!" The little asshole shouted, and I tried not to take it personally.

"What's your name?" I asked him, "Cómo te llaman?" I added, just in case.

"Pluto! Pluto!" he chirped out and my eyes nearly popped out of my head in surprise.

This little dude was smart as hell, and I instantly felt sorry for whatever future must have been planned for him. I knew the world of the Cártel and any other big dick syndicate enough to know that this bird wasn't heading off to a forever home.

"I guess it's just me and you Pluto," my raspy voice pushed out as I hung my head between my knees to keep it from pressing against the top of the kennel.

"And the Lion. Cocksucker," Pluto said, and I immediately began to fear my fate.

If there was a lion down here with us there was a good chance, I would be its next dinner. My good eye began to adjust to the darkness, and I could barely make out the shape of the coop a few yards away my little pal was stuck in. It was too small for him to even stretch his wings open, let alone experience flight and my heart instantly broke for him.

"Chiyo?" I called out, wondering if they had gotten to her, regardless of my feeble attempt.

"Chiyo! Chiyo!" Pluto repeated but no one answered, and I let out another sigh of relief.

I could accept little victories, at least *someone* out there knew I was taken, but the problem was, would anyone care? Ronan didn't want me there to begin with, Mateo looked like he could have thrown me to the wolves for asking to stay with Santos. Santos wasn't even in the same zip code anymore.

Shit. Was I?

If my uncle had gotten a hold of me there was a good chance I was already back in México. I was a dead bitch regardless of the country I was in, so I guess those details didn't matter.

The loud rumbling of my stomach distracted my thoughts. I was normally able to tell how fast time was passing with my hunger, but since I avoided the last meal Fletcher brought me, I was clueless. It could have been hours since they had taken me, but the bottomless pit I felt in my stomach told me it was probably longer than that.

The water was starting to dry on my skin, but my underwear stayed soggy making me that much more uncomfortable. Whoever stuck me in this kennel took off my sweats and put some off brand wanna-be-fancy lingerie on me, and that didn't float by me well.

"Fuck!" I screamed in desperation as I tried slamming my body against the kennel, and the zip ties cut deeper into my flesh causing new wounds.

"Fuckidy Fuck Fuck!" sounded out from my left, but even the bird's fantastic sense of humor couldn't dig me out of the sinkhole my mind was starting to create at a rapid pace.

"She is stronger than all of us." My papá's praise rang loudly in my aching head, but it was the image of Cézar sitting in the corner that stayed etched into my memory.

There was disapproval in his features that I couldn't explain this time. He sat through all of my torture sessions, he even dished it out when my papá forced his hand. Was he angry because he thought my papá believed I was stronger than him?

Or was he angry because he didn't think I should be going through this?

Papá walked away from the dungeon leaving me strung up by my hands as he nodded to Cézar who made his way up towards me. With a flick of his pocket knife, he cut the binds that held me up and I fell to the floor in a heavy pile. I was fifteen now, and played this game with both of them long enough to know that showing weakness was the biggest mistake I could make. I quickly stood to my feet, stumbling as they burned from waking up after ten hours of hanging by my wrists.

I swung my fist at Cézar's face, but he quickly ducked and threw one back into my stomach. Blood poured out of my mouth, but I didn't let up, I rammed my head into his stomach pushing him into the wall with all the force left in my body. I swung fist after fist into his chest, his face, before realizing he wasn't fighting back anymore.

"What are you doing?" I asked him, knowing this wasn't how we did things.

The point was to get me too weak to fight back, so that if I was ever in this position and given a chance, that I could take it and win. But if he wasn't trying then the point was moot, and I had no reason to kick Cézar's ass if it meant nothing.

"I don't want to do this anymore Princesa." He said to me with a pained look on his face. "I don't like watching you get hurt like this."

I hit him again and again, and though compared to his size I knew my blows weren't lethal, but he was starting to feel them as he winced after each strike.

"Fucking hit me!" I cried back at him as I continued to throw my fists against his face, his stomach, his chest, or any part of him he left open for me.

"Stop Celia!" He grabbed me by the shoulders with both hands as he shook me and spit a wad of blood out to the side. "I don't like hurting you like this, hermanita." We huffed our labored breaths together for a few moments, my upper lip involuntarily peeled up in anger.

"Then send someone in who can handle it." I scoffed at him. "Don't come to me with your pity bullshit because I'm not here for it, you had your time in

this dungeon the same way I am now. Are you feeling remorse because I'm a girl, or because we're family?"

"My time was nothing like this. And your papá never put his hands on me the way he does you, the way he makes me hurt you. This isn't good for any of us." Cézar pushed me away with one hand as he wiped the blood dripping from his nose with his free one.

He made his way to the door and walked out, leaving me strained for breath, exhausted, and completely confused.

Cold water drenched me once again, this time I gasped loudly from the unexpected shock of it as I tumbled out of the darkness of my own mind. That was the last time I had seen my papá and Cézar before the visit that took every single person I loved away from me.

Cézar was supposed to be family.

My papá raised him like he was his own son, but when hell came tumbling loose, he was gone just like the rest of the "loyal" men who followed him.

He was just as dead to me as the rest of my family, and if I ever saw him again, I'd put the bullet in him that I owed him for abandoning me.

27

MATEO

On borrowed bikes, we rode almost twice as fast as the speed limit all the way to Cove City. Ethan's call let me know a good amount of our men were dead, but since they came from the roof our guys from below flooded the thirteenth floor before they could get any further down. My heart was pounding a fierce beat at the thought of what I would find when we got up there, even though I knew most of it was likely already cleaned up.

Ronan and I parked the bikes right in front of the High-rise doorway. I tossed the keys to Nate, barely giving him enough time to react and catch them. The lobby floor was covered in reinforcements, but if you asked me those idiots should have been perched on the rooftop instead.

"Get these bikes back to the Diablos Locos in Grimm's Reach," I said to Nate, who gave me a brief nod. "And get me one just like it before you get back here." I hadn't been on anything with two wheels since our deployment, and the freedom and rush that came with the rumble of an engine between your legs was almost as good as the right pussy.

Almost.

"Fletcher, Senior, meet me in tech," Ronan barked out directions to the room with a sure voice. "Where's Fletcher?" He doubled back. Ethan's brow furrowed in the middle before he spoke.

"He's at St. Murphy's, in critical care. There was nothing the doc could do for him here. By the time we got to him, I didn't think there would be any blood left in him. I don't know how she got out, but she kept him alive."

"Who?" I questioned, trying to figure out what happened here when we didn't have enough details.

We were going to need every surveillance video pulled so we could piece the puzzle together.

"The Japanese girl, she was out of the kennel, keeping pressure on his gunshot wound and screaming some crazy shit by the time we got to him."

"And where were *you?*" Ronan pushed him in the chest with a single finger but the strength in it alone knocked him off his balance.

"I was in tech, getting information for Santos, boss." Ethan hung his head.

I could see the remorse in his expression. He wasn't where he had been instructed to stay while we were gone, and now he was carrying the consequences on his shoulders.

If this was a full-fledged attack there was no way he alone would have made enough of a difference. Zerkos needed to reign his temper in and out his focus where it mattered.

"You need to chill. No one is to blame here, and if you want to point fingers, point them towards ourselves. We're the ones who left them here, unguarded." I put myself between the two of them, Ronan's nostrils flaring hard with each exhale.

"Tech Lab. *Now!*" he gritted out through his teeth again, and the two of us followed him.

Dezmond Archer *Senior* was the oldest member of our gang, not only that but his history as a gang banger dated more than four decades now. He was born into it, hell, he had his own side of this town and he ruled it for a long time. When we came around, he saw the opportunity to be swallowed like a mom-and-pop shop bought out by Walmart, and he didn't miss his chance. He was happy to join our ranks and merge his men with ours for a fat cut and an early retirement without the guaranteed early grave that came with being a boss. It was just too sweet a deal to pass up.

He had no real voice when it came to decisions, but Ronan respected the hell out of him and tried to include him in anything that meant anything around here. Sometimes this gave him the impression he still had power, when the reality was that he wasn't even a henchman anymore.

When I saw him talking to Cecilia during the party, I didn't get a chance to ask him what he was doing, but it pissed me off to see him try to get so close to her. Ronan would have probably shot his aged kneecaps off if he had even known the old bastard was coming onto his girl. But old perv-like habits aside, the guy was harmless, and one look was enough to steer him away from her, so I figured I'd keep this secret for him.

For now.

Tech was on the sixth floor, and those guys were as protected as it got. They alerted everyone they could as fast as possible to the attack but had any of our enemies made our way down here, we would have been fucked. We had the best technical team money can buy, our hackers were as good as Anonymous and could get us intel on nearly anything we wanted. There hadn't been a challenge we'd sent their way that we'd been given disappointing results for yet.

The doors opened up but there wasn't anything but a steel, safe door once you stepped outside the elevator. Ronan entered the code, 356937, it was a phone word that spelled out flower and for some fucking reason that was the first code to enter. Once the code was accepted, a slot opened to receive his thumb print followed by a laser that would take his retinal scan.

Aside from Myself, Santos, and Ronan the only other fuckers with access to this room were the guys who worked past the heavy steel doors. There were only a few of them, but they all lived on this floor in their own separate apartments past the tech HQ.

"I want two men in each elevator at all times now. Send the command down," I instructed Ethan.

The locks slowly undid themselves one at a time as Ronan continued to enter different passcodes for each additional manual lock that came after the retinal scan. Fifteen in total, and to be honest I didn't come down here often because I couldn't face letting him know I didn't have them memorized. How could I? The expectation was insane, a few of them changed every six months, and the other half changed even faster than that.

The only code that stayed the same was 356937.

The door opened with a loud hiss that reminded me of an airplane depressurizing, and before the door was fully wide, Taylor was standing there ready to guide us through what happened.

Taylor Constance was an epic hacker; she was almost six feet tall and what she lacked in decorum she made up for in intelligence. She kept her hair in a G.I. Jane buzz cut that reminded me of our time served together. The three of us went through basic training together nearly twelve years ago and even though we went our separate ways once Ronan and I got into Seals, we never lost touch.

Once we were out, she came to find us, and we were better for it too. A shady operation, with unlimited technical resources and the money to back it up? It was a wet dream for her, perfectly packaged as a powerful syndicate and she immediately signed up.

"The whole thing was wild boss," she started out, leading us to the array of monitors covering the walls of the technical lab. "They were here for maybe fifteen, twenty minutes total? Whatever they wanted was either in the kennels, or they ran out of time before they could get down any further. I think they didn't expect they would need to get any further down."

"You suspect they knew where the girls were? So, they came here for them?" I asked her, and she twisted her face in an unsure way before responding.

"That's my best bet. We're still translating some of the audio grabbed from the surveillance, but I can play the video back to you from the moment their helicopter landed on the rooftop. They didn't bring enough men to get further than a few floors, and the fact they didn't come up from the bottom makes me think they either came for the kennels, or for you boys, and just your luck you weren't there." She stated in a matter-of-fact kind of way, but Ronan scoffed.

"Or lucky for them," he corrected, she shrugged her shoulders.

"Alright, let's start from the top shall we; here's when the helicopter lands and they take out the four guys guarding the rooftop." She looked at Ronan disapprovingly, like she couldn't believe we didn't have more men at the top.

How were we supposed to expect something like this though? We didn't even have a landing pad out there, that motherfucker ruined our rooftop bar, and it was going to take weeks to clean the debris from the infinity pool.

Taylor continued walking us through the attack, making sure to thoroughly reprimand us anytime she saw a flaw in our security as the reason for the whole thing progressing or whenever they got through another layer of our defenses. There were thirteen of them total that came out of the chopper and they made quick work of our unsuspecting guys. A few tore through our penthouse shooting their automatic rifles into our furniture before they ransacked through our things.

My heart broke as a guy with a face like a goddamn dog tore into my room and released dozens of rounds into my most precious instruments. My Cello splintered into thousands of shards of wood right in front of my very eyes, and the piano collapsed after enough bullets hit the legs hard enough to break them. I felt Ronan's heavy hand on my shoulder, as if to say he knew what I was feeling at this very moment. I etched that ugly bastard's face to my memory because no matter who he was, he was going to choke on breathing his last breath with my knife in his throat.

It was a promise.

Once they got past the penthouse our men were already starting to flood up the stairs and take on these fuckers. They were big though, each one of them towering over our guys, and they were well trained. Not just with the guns they were using but with sheer brute force. Dogface was easily twisting heads off of necks like little Barbie dolls. And a few of the guys around him had been shot multiple times but weren't going down so easily.

What the fuck were they on?

It was like listening to that story in elementary school back in the D.A.R.E program where they talked you out of doing drugs by telling the story of the guy who was on PCP and ripped his thumb off before jumping out of a window and beating up a bunch of cops. It seemed like a crazy story they told at every single school to ward kids off of drugs, but after watching these guys take bullet after bullet and keep going, I was wondering if that was exactly what was going on here. Maybe they were just fucking mutants.

"So, this part was interesting," Taylor spoke up and pulled up a second screen on the side with footage of the Kennels.

It showed Cecilia looking alarmed, like she could hear something happening, then all of a sudden, she was shoving Chiyo under the bed and covering it with a blanket. Fletcher and a few others were waiting for the elevator to open, and the last three standing giants came out swiftly.

The first guy reached out for the first head he could and immediately twisted it, throwing the body like a ragdoll over his shoulder. Fletcher got a shot into Dogface's stomach, but it doesn't phase him. The guy throws his fist into Fletcher's face and then breaks his hand to remove his gun from his hold. The rest of our guys that have made it to the kennel's lobby were fighting the other two when Dogface shot Fletch in the side with his own gun.

Even Zerkos flinched watching our close friend and most trusted man getting hurt because we weren't here to help.

The other two giant assholes make a mess of our men but the other surveillance from other floors shows the flooding of our men as they try to move through the stairs and make their way to the level where the kennels are at. The three men yell at each other in another language and they must have realized they were running out of time, Dogface fucker kicks Fletcher and forces him to stand and lead him to the kennels while the other two stand back and guard the entrances and exits.

Yeah, they came here for the girls.

Or they came here for her.

She came here for protection, was this who she was running from?

The ugly fucker nudged Fletcher to open the kennel door but instead, I see the moment he resigns his fate and decides loyalty was worth the price. He throws the key into the kennel towards Cecilia and Dogface guns him down right there. Cecilia screams but he doesn't give her time to react before he uses his fingers to count down and give her a warning.

The panic is written all over her face but there's something else there too.

There's a strength that says she knows this isn't how she dies, that this isn't her time, and that she's stronger than whatever he threatens to put her through. There's a calmness to her as she picks up the keys and jams them into the lock, turning it and just as quickly squeezing her way through before shoving her knee into the bulldog's junk. She tossed the keys back into the kennel, but he didn't realize it or assumed she was the only one in there and didn't bother to check.

It was a calculated move, and she saved two people in the process of it.

He threw Cecilia against the wall so hard that both Ronan and I tensed up at the sight of someone putting their hands on her like that. Then, I see red when he knocks her out with the butt of his gun. He throws her over his shoulder while the two others try to hold back our men. They get back into the elevator and try to beat our men back up to the rooftop, but it turns into a free for all shootout. Dogface throws Cecilia into the helicopter and for one split moment, I saw the face of our enemy inside, waiting, before they lifted off.

"Scan that face," I pointed to the monitor at the sinister man standing in the middle of the helicopter yelling at the remaining two men as they lifted off.

"Already tried boss, no results. Just like Ronan's girl, this fucker has three or four ghost identities but none of them are the real one. Someone's gone through a lot of trouble to hide them." Taylor said with a disappointed tone.

"I need to go see Fletcher in the hospital, he can't be there alone," I told Ronan, but Taylor cut in again.

"The other girl is with him."

"What?" Ronan's eyes practically bulged out of his head learning our entire team let one of our captives freely walk out of here.

"Doc's orders boss. Apparently, she wouldn't unglue from Fletcher's side, and since no one knew what the hell she was saying Emory decided the fastest way to save his life was to bring her along. There are a few men guarding his operating room, and I'd take a wild guess that she's not a flight risk." Taylor said matter of factly like she knew something we didn't as she tried to calm the beast rising in Ronan.

"You don't take wild guesses, show me," Ronan demanded, and she sighed heavily at the idea of breaching someone's privacy, but it wasn't her call to make anymore.

She pulled up another feed that showed Fletcher climbing into bed with Chiyo, soothing her until she fell asleep.

"What the fuck?" Zerkos and I said in unison.

"Did you know that was happening?" I asked Taylor and she shrugged her shoulders.

"How long has it been happening? I don't know, how long have I been seeing this? Probably closer to five or six weeks. Red fell hard for her, kind of impressively romantic if you ask me. Breaking the language barrier and what not." She shot me a look that let me know she'd seen what I'd been up to as well but she knew better than to say it in front of Ronan.

Ronan grunted and spun on his heels to turn around and leave the technical lab but Taylor grabbed his shoulder, spinning him back to face her.

"I wasn't done. I said I couldn't tell you who that fucker was, doesn't mean I can't find out." She said, crossing her arms.

"Hold on, Santos just landed. I gotta call him and fill him in," Ronan said, turning away and walking towards a quiet corner to make the call.

Santos was always the calm one out of the three of us, but I knew the bond he had with Cecilia was probably going to cause an eruption over this.

He would blame Ronan, he would blame me, and he would go on a rampage until he got her back.

My head was spinning and pounding at the same time, the stress of losing Cecilia creating an intense pressure in my skull that wouldn't be relieved now, no matter what I did to try.

All my crutches, my vices, my solace, they were all taken.

Along with her.

I'd get her back even if I had to burn this whole city down to do it.

Now that I'd had a taste of her, I wouldn't let her go, I was just as condemned as Ronan when it came to her, except I was reveling in the wreckage that trailed behind her. I knew I needed more of it, more of her. Without her I would sink into the bottomless ocean of all consuming guilt that made its home in the void of my heart.

No, she'd made her home there too now.

28

SANTOS

There was a war brewing deep in my mind.

From the moment Guillermo slipped me the photo of Cecilia across that table, a million questions swirled through my head like a tornado cutting through a forest.

Who the hell was Cecilia Gomez? Why did Los Muertos want her dead? What did she do that deserved a hit being put on her? And how the hell was I going to get out of this one?

There wasn't a foreseeable way out unless I wanted to take that bullet for her myself. Cecilia Gomez was destined to die by my hand. Even if I somehow put it off, it was just a matter of time before Guillermo sent his own men to cash in whatever bounty her head would earn them. There was an unfamiliar feeling creeping inside me, a loathing created from the mere essence of distrust her name coated my tongue with.

Out of everyone, *everyone*, I didn't expect the betrayal to come from her.

I simmered and brewed until I reached my boiling point on the flight home, doing everything I could to keep my shit together and not get arrested for attempted terrorism for just needing to get home faster. I paced the aisles until every flight attendant eyed me suspiciously, and one eventually got the nerve to ask me to take my seat, the air marshal making himself known, flashing me his badge, and giving me a warning nod.

There was no way out of this for me, and unfortunately for Cecilia, she put her trust into the most damaged of the three of us, it would be the root of her demise.

Once my phone came back on, hundreds of notifications, missed calls, and SOS texts popped through, urging my attention. My stomach sank, and I texted Ronan immediately, knowing that trying to go through it before talking to him was a worthless waste of time.

I just landed. Catch me up

Half a second after my thumb hit the send button, his name flashed on my screen. "Fill me in," I said, answering his call.

"We got hit," he said, speaking quietly but the hurt in his voice rang loud and clear. "It was bad." He breathed out without giving me anything to go on.

"Do we know who it was yet? Is anyone hurt?" I prodded for more information while I ran through the airport, grateful I decided not to check my small bag at the last minute, so I didn't have to wait for baggage claims.

"It was fucked, they came from the top brother. Thirteen dead, six injured. Fletcher is in intensive care, nothing is guaranteed for him right now." His voice was wavering and cracking like he was doing his best to stay strong. Somehow, I knew this wasn't the worst of it.

"What else?" I asked him, almost knowing damn well exactly what was going to come out of his mouth next.

"They took her," he didn't need to say who, it was obvious by how broken he sounded. The war in my mind waged on and I struggled to feel any sort of relief under the overwhelming sense of failure.

She came to me for help.

I failed her.

"I'm hitting the road." I hung up and got in the BMW 760i that was waiting for me in the lot. As if the universe sensed my urgency, every light turned red, and traffic became as impossible as ever. I gripped the steering wheel tight, trying my best to focus my rage. The nearly twenty-minute drive turned into forty, and it gave me far too much time to get lost in my own thoughts. I specifically told those assholes to take care of her, and they fucking lost her? Whoever hit us had to have known we left the high-rise, or they would have never been so bold.

I muscled my way through the clusterfuck of soldiers and family members all evacuated into the lobby waiting for instruction or some message from their leaders. They looked to me for some crumb of information or a sign that everything was going to be okay, but I didn't have it. I had no idea what the hell went down here yet, and I wasn't going to be the one making any speeches about what I didn't know. It would have to wait. My phone buzzed, and I pulled it out to see a text from Guillermo.

15

GUILLERMO

Fuck. The asshole was giving me a countdown. This meant Cecilia had fifteen days to die by my hand before the Black Crows would no longer be considered allies to Los Muertos. He would use it as a reason to come after us, and he would send his own men to finish the job I couldn't do. There were too many lives at stake in this building, and after the shock of the attack, I knew the priority was keeping our people safe and making sure they felt protected.

I got through the three thousand security codes and locks that waited for me at the technical lab, and when the door hissed open, I pushed my way in. I marched straight to them, and as if I'd been possessed by a demon, I watched my arm fly directly into Mateo Kane's face.

"Holy hell!" He shouted as he ducked away from the next swing.

Zerkos grabbed me from the back, pinning my arms behind me, but he didn't need to. I knew that was the only shot I could get with him before he could put me on my ass. I was the smallest of the three of us, and though I was a cold-blooded killer who could use a soda can as a weapon, I knew they both outmatched me when it came to brute strength. I breathed heavily through my nostrils, shaking off Ronan and crossing my arms over my chest to show I was done.

"Fuck." Mateo continued, "That's like three times this week now fuckers, I'm not gonna let you keep getting free hits on me." He pinched the bridge of his nose where previous bruising was now darkening from the impact of my fist.

He would though, it was just in his personality to do so.

He and Ronan got into it again apparently, no doubt over *her*. Maybe it was a good thing she was gone, maybe we could focus on things that mattered, things that the Black Crows needed to do to keep thriving. We had so many plans half-cocked, that were on a permanent freeze since the minute Cecilia walked back into our lives.

It was about time we went on with our usual programming.

But then the thought of her being alone and afraid somewhere hit me like a freight train, and I purged all those whispering, wicked thoughts from my head again.

"I wanna know what the fuck was so important that you idiots thought it was a good idea to leave the high-rise without leadership while Allisher Sokolov is hunting for whoever stole his merchandise?"

"You think this was Bratva retaliation?" Ronan asked me, as if the thought never occurred to him.

"I can't be sure, but it's a good guess. Whoever it was, they knew the three of us were gone and used it as an opportunity to attack." I looked back at Zerkos, realizing he thought this was clearly something else. "You were thinking this was someone after her?" I wondered what my brother would think if he knew just who was after her.

"If what you're saying is true, and someone had intel that we were gone. Well then, that means, we either have a rat in our forces, or it's someone big enough to be able to monitor us." Kane said, taking the wadded tissues from his nose once the bleeding finally stopped.

"Or both," Zerkos said, letting his distrust show. The very same trait was created by none other than the same witch he was doomed to pine over for the rest of his days.

"Well, I'd say let's start with the Bratvas then, Cecilia can't be mixed in with anyone big enough to have infiltrated our forces or monitor us." Mateo said confidently, and I scowled, knowing it was absolutely possible.

I wasn't ready to share what I learned yet though, mostly because I didn't really know what any of it meant yet. All I knew was that Cecilia must have been mixed up in something big and dangerous to have Los Muertos sign her death warrant, and I couldn't risk my brothers trying to stop me from doing what needed to be done. The look in Kane's eyes promised me she had just as much of a hold on him as she had on Ronan, and I knew right then I couldn't trust him with my secret.

Taylor played the surveillance back for me, my heart nearly breaking as I watched our most loyal guy get gunned down to protect the girls. I looked back to Zerkos and Kane, who seemed just as devastated watching it for the second time around.

"Taylor, you said that the asshole from the chopper had three ghost identities, what were they?" Mateo asked when the last bit of the clip played, and his complicated little mind began to compose a symphony out of the puzzle pieces in the video.

"Anton Rabinovich, Adrik Kuzmin, and Aleksandr Bugrov." She listed out, and he rubbed his temple to alleviate his constant headache.

"Ok, let's try something different. Run a search for Anya and Oksana and use the same last names," he said.

"These are all very common names, we're going to get thousands of results," she warned him.

"Then go through them all until we get what we need." I cut in, the coldness of my tone shocking nearly everyone in the room. The realization set in for them that I wasn't taking this issue lightly.

Ronan scowled at how I spoke to one of his long-time friends, but I didn't give him the satisfaction of letting his gaze affect me. They fucked up royally while I left the Black Crows under their watch, so now we'd do things my way a bit until we got this shit fixed.

Taylor nodded at me, understanding the severity of the situation, and sat down on her tech throne, promptly getting to work. "It could take longer than a day, but we'll drop everything and prioritize this. I'll let you know as soon as I get anything."

"We're looking for anyone that matches these two faces." Mateo showed her close-up photos of the Russian sisters we'd harbored under our noses the last few months, and another thought came to me.

"Let's go pay a visit to the fifth floor." I looked at Ronan, who gave me an approving nod. Dezmond Senior followed us back out of the tech lab but knew better than to come with us to the fifth floor.

29

RONAN

Santos' unfamiliar, cold behavior was putting me off. The minute he entered the lab, I could tell something was wrong. It wasn't that he was so predictable, but I knew my brother inside and out. I could tell there was something lodged deep in his core, festering, and rotting him from within.

He was keeping something from me, as if we needed any more fucking problems on top of everything else. No doubt he was likely feeling a lot of guilt and resentment for leaving, with the timing of the attack. From that little outburst with Kane, it was safe to say he also blamed us for it. I refused to live in a state of regret. I had too many people to worry about to ruminate over decisions I had already acted on.

I turned to Taylor before locking the tech team back in their secure little bat cave, before giving her one more instruction. "Flores," I said, and her eyebrows scrunched together in the middle as she waited for the rest. "It's not as urgent as the attack, but when you get a chance, dig up what you can for me on that name, I think it's a family of some sort?"

Taylor let out an exaggerated laugh and stuck her hands on her hip in a display that was far too feminine for her personality. "You boys are really asking for God's work here today, aren't you? Sure, I'll look up one of the top ten most common Hispanic names in the history of history and tell you what I find," she said in a sarcastic tone, rolling her eyes before muttering, "Fucking idiots," under her breath and shutting the safe door to the lab.

It had been exactly three hours since the attack on our home, but it already felt like fifty without knowing what was happening to Cecilia. I was trying not to self-destruct from the grief eating at me, so I did my best to keep moving forward. Any little thing could lead me back to her, and I wasn't going to miss a single detail this time. I waited too long for Cecilia to return to me.

Losing her twice would surely destroy me.

Being without her was like catching on fire and dying from smoke inhalation instead. It was painful and all-consuming. It was suffocating, it was toxic and the burning ache inside me wouldn't be extinguished until she was safe in my arms again.

Santos led the way into the fifth floor; Mateo and I flanked him as we made our way to the Hellmouth of our operation. The men tipped their heads down as we passed them, they said nothing, but I knew we would need to address them all before the day was over.

We needed to reassure them that retaliation was coming, and that security for our families was guaranteed. But first, we had to get all of our information straight and figure out who we were retaliating against. I had a pretty good feeling the bitch that stabbed Cecilia with a fork knew more than she was letting on.

The fifth floor was a work of art, in my opinion. We removed all the flooring and poured concrete down the same way we had done in the kennels. It was a completely different atmosphere once the elevator doors opened you up into the level. It was resemblant to a prison, nothing but six-foot by six-foot cells with a cot, a bucket to piss in, and a drain in the middle of each one.

For the blood.

If you somehow found yourself down here, it almost always meant your days were numbered. This was the final resting place for the people who challenged or went against The Black Crow Brotherhood. This is where we put our enemies down. If you pissed us off enough, we shoved you in a cell with someone else. There was nothing like arguing about who gets to shit in the bucket and who gets the bed, to force you to see things a bit more *clearly*.

As it was, there hadn't been a woman who had found herself down here in the almost seven years since we created our little organization. There had never been a need, every single syndicate organization we considered our enemy, overlooked the women around them.

They put collars around their neck, and they only served them for the purpose of breeding, or fucking. It was misogynistic and idiotic, because some of my best men, were actually women. Taylor Constance and Emory O'Connor were just two examples of powerful women we didn't take for granted around here, but on every floor, you were guaranteed to find a bad bitch willing to take on the city, with or without us at their back.

There was a first time for everything and stabbing my girl in the middle of the night was definitely a surefire way to get you on my enemies list. I had a creeping suspicion this chick wasn't as innocent as she had been playing us for, and we would get some answers today. The soldiers who worked the fifth floor nodded their heads to us as we made our way past them and walked on, cell after cell, until we reached hers.

She was sitting on the cold concrete floor instead of using the cot, and there was an air to her that reminded me of Cecilia's uncrackable strength. Her upper lip curled up as she lifted her head to see who was walking toward her cell, and I had to admire her lack of fear. She put on a hell of a show these last two months, but whoever the hell she was, had started to break through to the surface.

"Who are you?" I asked her, and her lip turned up in the corners.

"You're not ready for the answer to that yet, Ronan Zerkos." Her thick accent wrapped around each word tightly like a boa constrictor ready for a meal. She knew my name. That tidbit of information was something we made sure our captors wouldn't know until it was safe to share with them. It wasn't possible that she knew my name, but yet here she was, saying it like we were old friends.

"What are you doing here?" I asked her, and she opened her arms to show the cell surrounding her, as she looked to her left and right.

"You know what I mean. I'm not stupid, I know you had something to do with the attack this morning." I gripped the bars tight as I spat the words out at her.

"Oh. Was that today?" She clucked her tongue, "So sad I missed it." She let out a dark chuckle as she stood up and made her way over to me. "I'll have to catch the next one so I can make my way out of here."

"If you had something to do with the death of my men, make no mistake bitch, you will die here. Tonight." Her eyes widened in surprise. She didn't think I had it in me to hurt a woman, but she was wrong. Maybe not with my own hands, but if she was responsible for the death of my men or for putting Cecilia in harm's way, then I would gladly put a bullet through her skull.

She entered this high-rise and we believed she was a victim, someone who needed to be saved, and someone who would help us save others. That's where I was wrong. I could see now she was just another snake who slithered her way into our home and her scales were starting to show.

"You will find that killing me will not prove to be very beneficial to you Ronan." She closed the distance between us with her cat-like gait and wrapped her thin fingers around the bars of her cell. "Not while you have a rat, hiding in your crow's nest." She whispered, and then laughed loudly before turning her back on me.

"Susana Sokolov," Santos said, holding his phone up in his hands with a dark smirk plastered over his face.

Gotcha.

Taylor always came through.

It was my turn to laugh now, but she didn't turn around to look at me. She was clearly startled by her identity being revealed and needed a moment to compose herself.

"Susana, Oksana." Mateo sang repeatedly as he walked around her cell, tormenting her. Dried blood was still coating his face from Santos' hit, and God dammit he looked like the perfect lunatic.

"So, tell me. What were two Bratva princesses doing in a trafficking ring, playing the part of a captive?" I asked her, and she finally turned on her heels to look at me.

"The fun just got started my dear, I'm not going to spoil the ending." She laughed confidently, but she was close enough, so I reached my hand in the cell and gripped her throat between my fingers. I squeezed tightly knowing that her oxygen was completely cut off, and her windpipe was on the verge of being crushed.

"Just kill her dude, we don't need her. Let's go pick her sister up at the hospital." Mateo lied with a confidence that came natural to him. She didn't know that her sister had been picked up by Daddy yet, and we were sure as shit going to use it to our advantage.

Santos cocked his gun behind my head, and I saw in my peripheral that it was aimed right in between her widened eyes. Daddy Sokolov trained her well, but not that well. I could smell the fear on her, and if she didn't start talking soon, she was gonna be stenching up the whole floor.

Every minute that passed, was another minute that her monster of a father could use to hurt my girl. I could only hope they didn't know what she meant to me yet; maybe it was better they thought she was a nobody. Being useless was safer than being desirable in our world.

"Wait. How can I be sure you'll let me go if I tell you anything?" She asked, her composure crumbling away as her voice rasped from the pressure of my hands. I released her, realizing she wasn't as tough as she was playing out to be.

"We won't let you go. But if you give me what I need, I won't let my friend here put you six feet under, *for now*." I told her, watching the defeat consume her.

The whole level had gone silent, listening to our exchange and the audible click of Santos releasing the safety of the gun, caused all of the color to drain from her face.

"If I tell you, you might as well kill me. My father will do it himself if he finds out." She said fearfully through the bars as she clutched them tightly.

"Your father took something that belongs to me, and I intend on getting her back." I told her plainly, as I crossed my arms and waited for her to decide her own future. Her eyes widened in realization as she understood just exactly who I was talking about.

"I told you Ronan Zerkos, you have a leak. I can't risk them letting my father know that I've told you anything. The Mexican girl isn't worth this." She began to turn away from me and walk towards her cot. I was losing her, but maybe if I put a little more pressure, I could get her to crumble.

"Hughes!" I called out to one of our guys who kept the cells in order. "String her up, whatever makes her talk. No limits." The last words I said looking her dead in the eyes so she could understand she had no power here.

"Wait!" She begged, knowing Hughes had already had some time with her and by how rough she looked, I could tell she wouldn't want a second round. "If my father hasn't realized she meant something to you yet, if he thought she was just merchandise, then maybe you have a chance to get her back."

"And if he realized she wasn't a prisoner of mine?" I questioned.

"He would have already called you to make a trade for my sister and me. He doesn't realize he has something you value." She sat on her cot without looking up at us, the defeat etched into her face as she dropped her shoulders and rested her elbows on her knees. "There's a strip club, Sapphire. My father will be keeping her there in the basement with the other girls he's auctioning. He'll show her off and sell her to the highest bidder as soon as he can. He doesn't like to keep whores wasting away in his possession. Too expensive to feed."

I clenched my jaw at her calling Cecilia a whore, but I didn't react. My girl was somewhere out there starving, alone, and afraid. I had more important things to direct my anger towards.

"There's at least three Sapphires in the city. Which one?" Kane jumped in, getting as much information as possible while she was still willing to talk. She looked over at Hughes, who looked more than happy with whatever outcome would be produced from this exchange.

We kept a few psychos on hand to take care of the work that needed to be done that no one else wanted to do. Hughes was one of them. As far as I knew, he had no conscience, and he slept eleven hours a night, which let me know he was born to get his hands bloodied. Men like him were what made our organization solid.

"The one on the southside," Santos cut in, "Where I first found you and your sister."

She nodded at him, "But you have to be smart about this. He'll expect a raid, and he'll know I led you to him if you don't do this right," she warned us, and Mateo scoffed uncaringly.

Personally, I didn't give two shits if her father killed her, as of right now, I wasn't even sure what was keeping me from killing her either. I was hoping I could keep the bitch talking long enough to get Cecilia back. There was a fear in her eyes when she spoke about her father though, and it made me question if she was as guilty as I assumed her to be.

Maybe she was a victim of him too.

"And what do you suggest, Susana?" Kane asked in a sobering tone, using her real name.

"You have to buy her back if you want to do this without a war."

She was right.

I beckoned Hughes with a curl of my finger, and we walked away from her cell together, Mateo to my right and Santos on my left just a few paces behind me.

"Hey! What about me?" She yelled at us from her cell and the three of us turned our heads to look at her.

Santos brandished his Glock back in her direction, closing one eye as if he was aiming for her head before letting a *pew* under his breath, faking the shot.

"No one, except you, comes in here. Understood?" I laid out the new rules turning back around, Hughes nodded, but I needed to ensure he fully comprehended. "No exceptions. Not someone coming to get their anger out on any of these fuckers, not someone bringing by a meal. No one comes inside this floor but the three of us."

"You got it boss." He said without so much as curiosity or a need for reasoning behind my actions.

"Good man," I said, clapping his shoulder with my hand and walking away with my brothers next to me.

"We can't tell anyone anything until we figure out who's feeding the Bratvas our intel." I explained, and they both nodded understanding the severity of our situation. If the rest of our people knew there was a rat in our forces helping our enemy bring us down, it would be a shitshow. Discord would fill every level of our high-rise until our men were either too afraid or too untrusting to follow us, which was a risk we couldn't take.

As we made our way out of the fifth floor, Dezmond Archer Senior was addressing our men. I scowled at the audacity. These weren't his men anymore; maybe a long time ago, some of them had been his, but he signed them over to us, and with that, he threw away his leadership.

It was a slap in the face to watch him reassure our people that everything would be fine, and retribution was guaranteed. Santos, Mateo and I stood behind him as he finished his words, conveying an illusion that we supported and backed him.

Inside I fumed.

I felt Santos' hand on my shoulder and met his gaze to see the silent message he was sending me.

Not now.

There were too many things at stake here. We had a traitor we needed to uncover, we had made clear enemies of the Bratvas, and we had a community to keep safe. Most importantly, I had a bronze goddess to rescue. If Dezmond Archer Senior was getting his kicks off at playing the big man for a few minutes, it wasn't worth it to make a scene and lose the support of his men that would come with it.

I sent a text over to Taylor, asking her if she could figure out how to get us on a buyers list for the Bratva, and we made our way to the penthouse as we waited for a response.

It was trashed.

Bullet holes decorated every wall and surface, complementing the wood splinters that covered the ground from all of the broken furniture. Our people were already hard at work, cleaning it up and putting everything back together. There were Crow Sluts playing at interior designers as they decided what furniture would replace the bullet-infested sofa that was once the grandest piece of furniture in our living space.

"I'm going to check on Fletcher. Fill me in if you find anything else out," Santos said, shocking the hell out of both me and Mateo.

"You don't want to work out how we're gonna get Cecilia back?" he asked, bringing his eyebrows together in the middle. I was just as confused as he was. Our brother spent the last few months refusing to do anything that would harm even a single hair on her head. Now he was just gonna act like getting her back wasn't top priority?

"You got this," he said, and I couldn't hide my surprise.

"O-kay then," Kane shrugged, noticing the strange behavior but letting him turn around and walk away, there was nothing more he could do anyway. Once he headed out to the elevators, he looked back at me, "Who can we trust?"

"Fuck, I don't know. Aside from the two of you and Taylor, it could be anyone." I walked to the wet bar and poured myself a neat glass of Blanton's. I turned the whiskey over and let the smooth nectar coat my tongue and burn my throat before I looked back at my brother to see him judging me with one eyebrow lifted.

The asshole didn't drink a drop of alcohol, never had, and never would. He was too afraid of becoming his father. He seldom chastised us for our terrible drinking habits, except when we used it as a crutch to block out our problems. It was "The road to darkness," as he called it, like a fucking Jedi or something.

"Don't," I shot him down with one word as I poured another and held it in my hand.

Our phones buzzed, letting us know a group text came through, and since Mateo's phone was already in his hand, I didn't bother pulling mine out. "What's she saying?" I asked, knowing our smartest friend already had our needed answers.

"She sent over a phone number and said it's better if we don't contact ourselves.

The types who buy women, normally send over their sleazy lawyers to broker the agreements and get on their books. It would be smart to have Dez make the call," he read her text out loud to me.

"This should keep the Bratva bitch out of the hot seat too, they'll be directing us straight to the strip club to come look at the girls," I pointed out, and Mateo nodded in response. "Call Dez, set it up. Just tell him we're looking for new girls since the others are gone. Don't mention Cecilia, don't let him in on the plan."

"You really don't trust anyone right now do you?" Kane asked.

"Brother, if I'm being completely honest. I don't even trust Santos right now. Ever since he got off that plane, something's different. Something's wrong," I said, rubbing my chin, the coarseness of my stubble irritating me.

"You noticed that too then?" he asked, letting me know that nothing got past him. I had to focus on what mattered, and right now, that was Cecilia's safety. All I could hope for was that we could get to her before someone else tried to buy her out from under us.

30

CECILIA

"Céci!" Carolina's laughter rang out in my head through the foggiest dream. I couldn't picture her face anymore, it was just a faded blur now, but her childish voice was still so clear in my memory.

"Caro hurry up!" I shouted back with a giggle as Ronan chased us in my tia's backyard. She squealed sharply in my ear as he stomped closer to her with a loud roar.

He was twelve now, and these games were way too immature for him, but he never seemed to tire from entertaining Carolina and not once acted as if he was outgrowing her. She squeezed my hand, and with another scream, we both took off running with Ronan right on our heels.

What should have been a dream felt more like a nightmare, just the memory of how my sister sounded was enough to trigger painful feelings that were locked away deep inside me. The shock of water splashing on me, paired with the way my heart splintered open when I got lost in my own mind, was a type of hell in itself.

My back radiated with the kind of pain I couldn't block out of my mind anymore. Being forced into the tiny cage quickly became the most agonizing form of torture I'd endured to date, but I tried not to compare.

Every form of torture felt terrible while you were living it, but with the right training, it wasn't hard to put it to the back of your mind. Maybe that's why some women had a million babies, after the abuse ended, *poof* amnesia would resolve all of their problems.

Once I realized no one was coming to let me out to use the bathroom, I knew I only had a few hours before my resolve would break, and I would just piss myself. At that point, it wasn't even the worst thing I was dealing with, at least I was only wearing underwear. With the asshole throwing buckets of water at me every hour or so, I had to assume it was either to keep me awake or to rinse the pee off the dog cage so it would run down into the drain in the middle of the floor.

It had been quite a few hours, from what I could tell, and once my eyes finally adjusted to the dark, I was able to make out most of my surroundings down here. It wasn't even until the third time I received a bucket full of water to my face that I realized that the asshole was doing it further down the basement as well. Once I tracked his footsteps, I was able to see the little dark area with the others. There were a few girls in kennels just as small as mine on the most distant side of the room.

Their cages were pressed against a wall forming a line in a curious way. They didn't move much and refused to make any noise or answer when I called. I feared some might be dead, or maybe they had just learned the easiest way to survive was to go unnoticed.

They were smarter than me.

But mostly, I'd just given up on self-preservation.

Once the water jerk would leave, I tried to call out, but aside from my little planet-named bird friend's incessant comments on fellatio, there wasn't even a trace of sound that came out of the basement.

Aside from me, of course.

Every time my nap was interrupted, I resorted to screaming for Ignácio to man up and come deal with me himself, but apparently, he didn't have the balls to face me yet. I was expecting a grand supervillain theme and a well-prepared speech that would certainly drag on too long for our first encounter in over twenty years.

He never came though, and I was on bucket six or seven now of water to the face. Fuck. My methods of keeping time weren't working for me. How long was a bucket of water anyway? Twenty-four Pluto "cocksuckers"?

No, at least thirty.

I groaned from pain, and from the wreckage of my own mind collapsing in around me as I tried to come up with a new method of telling time. My wrists burned with a tenderness that let me know the zip ties cutting into them were starting to inflame that whole area, and if they didn't get attention soon, I'd probably be at risk for an infection.

By the time I had counted over forty buckets of water splashing over me, I had pissed myself at least six times, and my stomach was playing a louder tune than Pluto could sing to me; I could barely feel my limbs anymore. Aside from the few drops of liquid I managed to lick off of myself every time he splashed me, I hadn't had a real drink of water.

I wanted to break down and cry, I wanted to crumble. I had broken into too many pieces, and my entire soul had become fragmented. I wanted every shattered part of me to come back together so I could return to being the girl I used to be, but I knew that was a fantasy. For starters, I didn't even know who the girl in question was anymore. She was more of an idea really, someone my papá snuffed out and buried in the darkest corner of my mind, never to be found again.

To top it off, I was beyond starving.

It felt like my stomach was starting to eat my body from the inside out in pangs, yet somehow, I didn't crave food at all. It was a mental teeter-totter, and I knew I had hit around the thirty-six-hour mark when I stopped feeling hungry all together. The problem was that if I got too weak, I wouldn't be able to fight back.

And if I couldn't fight back, then I may as well have just laid down and died right there.

"Danger! Danger!" Pluto warned and I focused my eyes on the steps as I waited for the bucket asshole to go another round with me. Except, this time, there were two of them, and they were much larger than the bucket guy. I immediately recognized the bulldog-faced piece of shit who stole me from the high-rise, and from the look he was giving me, I could tell he remembered me too.

I clenched my fists and schooled my expression, sure I was scared as fuck, but I wasn't gonna let them know it. Not showing my fear was the biggest weapon I had against any of my enemies, I knew that well. The other guy had a scar from his cheekbone that crossed his entire face and ended at his jawline, but not in a sexy way. Somehow you could tell he earned that by being the ultimate piece of shit. He was ugly and he knew it. Those types of men scared me the most, they had a way of trying to take what wasn't theirs by force.

Willingness wasn't something they had the pleasure of witnessing often.

They walked straight towards me as they talked to each other in a language I couldn't understand but sure as shit could recognize as Russian after a few seconds of listening.

After two months of being objected to Stabby and Pizza face's non-stop chatter, I could pick out a few words here or there that the two men were saying. Relief filled my entire body in a rapid rush that forced a laugh to bubble out of me deep from inside my throat. They looked at me with a scowl, but I didn't care. Ignácio wasn't here for me yet, this was just some Black Crow Brotherhood bullshit I ended up getting caught in.

Bulldog kicked the kennel to stop me from laughing, and Scarface pulled out a syringe that instantly made my stomach drop and my laughter go quiet. I shrank into the back of the kennel, knowing it was useless. I had nowhere to go, but at least they were too big to get in here.

Scarface grabbed the top of the kennel and lifted it all the way up to his massive six-foot-five height before a grin formed over his face. He turned the cage towards the floor and there was nothing I could do to stop myself from falling as he shook and hit the back of the kennel like a nearly empty ketchup bottle, until I let go of the bars.

I dropped to the ground and tried to scurry away, but my limbs were sore, stiff, and I couldn't feel much of my legs. I lifted my foot and threw it up to slam into the Bulldog's balls, the tingling of my nerves went off like a thousand ants had crawled down to my feet making me scream as he clutched in pain.

Scarface grabbed my hair and pulled me back against him so hard that the wind got knocked out of me. He laughed and jammed the needle into my neck, shooting the poison straight into my veins with a sharp sting.

He released my hair and dropped me to the floor, the pain in my legs shocking my extremities as sensation began to return to my body. I took a step away from Scarface and looked around at my options, but whatever he gave me quickly made its way into my system, clouding my brain.

They both laughed, but it came out as a drowned-out warbling and everything was in slow motion. I took a step and stumbled, they didn't reach out for me.

Maybe this was my chance to get out.

I tried to run but my feet felt like clouds under me, and one step turned into me falling hard against the cold concrete floor. Blood pooled around my mouth from my teeth biting into my tongue, but I couldn't feel much pain. I knew my face was likely purple from the impact of hitting the ground, but it was hard to do anything but laugh at myself and close my eyes. I was so sleepy now, and this was so comfortable.

It'd been such a long time since I'd really slept.

I heard one of the guys yelling something in Russian, and I was hoisted back quickly. I felt the hot breath of the giant animal in front of me, before my brain could register the very real fucking lion that was charging at me. His chain kept him a mere inch away from biting off my head, and I laughed out wildly, not even recognizing my own voice before spitting out the blood collecting in my mouth on the ground for the kitty to lap up.

Then there was the burning tear ripping through me as the Bulldog removed his belt and struck my back with it in three sharp flicks of his wrist. "Crazy Bitch." He spat out, in a thick accent as he wrapped the belt around my throat and tightened it until I could feel my eyeballs swelling from the pressure around my neck.

"Two options. You become cat food." He pointed to the impatient lion that paced the back wall of the basement. My head was spinning, I felt like I was on the verge of losing consciousness, but he tugged on the long end of the belt to get my attention and my eyes flickered open again, my pulse beating heavily in my ears.

I was uncomfortable in every possible sense of the word and couldn't fight the sob that broke out of me. Being drugged was officially my least favorite thing in the entire world, only just above being stuck in a dog cage for God knows how long. Scarface petted my head as the Bulldog laughed at my defeat.

"Or you go put on show." He said, pointing up the stairs. "Become other man's problem, yeah?" He asked me, as if the second option was a blessing, though, for a brief moment, I considered it might be.

Especially since being eaten alive definitely didn't sound like a good time or something I could talk or fight my way out of in my current condition. My brain was shutting down from whatever they gave me, and my body had long given up. If it weren't for Scarface holding me by the head, I would have probably fallen on my back.

I could feel the blood trickling against the open gash that had torn my back open and silently thanked the drug for keeping me from feeling the pain as much.

The ground looks so comfy right now.

I was starting to slobber, I couldn't make out words anymore and I wasn't sure if that was because they weren't speaking English or maybe it was that I wasn't. I nodded my head up and down and hoped they understood what I meant.

Suddenly, their hands were all over me, undressing the little bit of dignity that separated me from them as they ripped my underwear off me.

"Stop!" I screamed but the Bulldog held my wrists in his one giant hand as they both worked to force me naked. I had made it thirty years without getting raped, and today was not going to be the day.

I kicked out against Scarface, getting him right in the balls, but he didn't even flinch from the pain. He slapped me across the face so hard I could see the spirit of a Tweedy bird making laps around my head like an old-school cartoon. I was so high, it was like swimming through an ocean of thick tar.

I was fucked.

The tears flowed freely down my face and the sob that broke through my throat almost cracked the smallest hint of sympathy from my captors' faces. But they'd been through this too many times, they'd grown cold and unfeeling when it came to their tasks.

Scarface pointed to the lion again, reminding me, "Cat food?" And I shook my head fiercely. They grabbed me by the arm and walked me to an area of the basement I hadn't seen before. A shower head came out of the wall, and a drain was on the ground, but aside from that, you'd have no idea that it was supposed to be a bathroom of sorts.

The water was cold, shocking my broken skin as it made contact with the lash wound, and I cried out in pain from what the drug couldn't numb, but they didn't ease up. Bulldog held me by the hands as Scarface began to scrub my body with far too much force.

The abrasive loofah scraped over my skin, and I screamed and thrashed in agony while he went on and on with no mercy. He scrubbed every inch of my body with it until I was raw and aching, despite the horrendous drug that was fighting for dominance to numb every part of my being.

They cleaned my hair with just as much aggression, and my soul grieved while I remembered Mateo washing me with so much care and gentleness, as if I had been a porcelain doll in his collection. The two brutes pulled in opposite directions as they brushed it wet, combing with force to tear through the tangles of hair that had matted while I'd been in their possession.

The towel was cheap and rough against my tender skin, scratching me as they rubbed it over my body, drying me and leaving me exposed. My fear of what they'd do to me quickly faded as soon as the realization hit me.

I was merchandise, and they were treating me as such.

Once I was no longer wet, they began to redress me in clean, lacy black lingerie that was almost identical to the one that they put me in when they first brought me down here. The thought that they just had a storage room with the same lingerie in multiple sizes for all the women that would come in and out made me sick. My revulsion mixed with the drug that was starting to eat away at my malnourished body and there was nothing I could do to stop myself from throwing up. Nothing but bile came out, there was nothing inside me anymore.

Once the bulldog let go of me, my legs gave out, dizziness swept through me and sweat coated my body from getting sick. Scarface picked me up like a child and made his way up the stairs with me in tow. The new room spun, and my vision struggled to catch up until it was too late, and I was already being secured to a chair that was welded to the ground. They cut through the zip ties and before I could even get a chance to rub my wrists in relief, they handcuffed them to the back of the chair behind me.

Rayos. This was really happening.

My eyelids were heavy, and my breathing was labored as the drug began to win the fight.

I felt a kick to the chair that jolted me awake, drool spilling out of my mouth as I struggled for coherency.

I recognized "Putting Holes in Happiness" by *Marilyn Manson* playing in a distant room loud enough for me to hear the heavy sounds of the electric guitar.

How long was I out?

I looked around the dimly lit room and it was now filled with countless other girls like me.

No, not *like* me.

These girls were much younger.

They looked broken, just shells holding air in the place of their empty little souls as they wasted away internally. My heart pulled inside its cage, but there was nothing I could do for these girls.

There was nothing I could do for myself.

My head was beginning to throb from the drug, its effects dulling as it began to fade away from my system. Right when I was about to thank some supreme being for letting clarity come back to me, it was as if the Bulldog noticed too, and he marched toward me with a determined look on his face.

"If you no fight so much, we wouldn't be problem." He said in broken English through clenched teeth before shoving another needle into my arm again ignoring my weak protests. I sobbed in defeat as he pushed the toxic substance into my body despite my pleas.

I would have been good.

I would have done anything to not feel like that. My thoughts were coming in slow and my head tripled in weight as I let it loosely hang down.

I'm a cloud, just a little cloud.

Maybe I could float away.

31

MATEO

My palms were sweating from anxiety, the thought of this mission going wrong lingered in the back of my mind like a constant threat. We couldn't mess this up. I needed Cecilia back just as badly as Ronan, and though I didn't think I could ever tell him that, I kind of knew I somehow didn't need to.

When Santos told us he was staying back, Zerkos' fists went on autopilot, and I had to push him out of the house before he used up all his good rage on our brother. Neither of us knew what his problem was, but if it wasn't strictly Black Crow business, he wasn't talking.

He had holed himself up in his room and was wallowing in some sort of misery that I couldn't figure out. My brother was hurting, and we needed to get to the bottom of it before it turned into another issue that would surely explode right in front of our faces.

There were already too many to deal with as it was. We had a security problem, we had a Dezmond Senior-trying-to-pull-rank-on-us problem, and we had a Bratva problem. On top of all that I had a Cecilia problem that was surely gonna be the death of me, and possibly the end of me and Ronan. Except, now I had the taste of her burned into my memory like a brand on my soul and I couldn't let her go.

I refused to.

She was the peaceful silence I had been longing for all these years. Unlike music, she could take away the pain permanently. The melody of her voice could drown out the sounds of my regret and self-loathing. The headaches had been the permanent reminder of how I failed my sister. But with Cecilia around, I could finally quiet all those screaming reverberations of my remorse so that all that was left was her. Cecilia felt like home, it was something I hadn't experienced in too long to just let it slip through my fingers.

I couldn't let her go to waste.

I refused to let her go unloved in all the right ways.

It'd been three days now since they had taken her, and Ronan and I both knew what that meant. Our chances of getting her back were becoming slimmer by the hour, she could have already been bought by anyone. Dez reached out to the Bratvas to arrange a buyer meeting, and we headed for Sapphire as soon as they passed him the location.

That was the plan, Dez was the buyer, I was his grunt, and Ronan was playing driver tonight. He was pissed when Dez told him the plan, but even he knew it was too risky for him to go inside. Too many people knew Zerkos as the face of the Black Crow Brotherhood. If the wrong person recognized him, it was only a matter of seconds before we were all dead and they rained down another attack at the high-rise to get Oksana-Susana back.

Maybe it was better that Santos stayed back, who knew if they would attempt another strike on us. Now that we knew someone on the inside was feeding them intel, we could use the rat to manipulate whatever outcome we wanted this way.

Ronan's jaw clamped tightly as Dez went over the plan for the fifteenth time in the car ride, but he nodded his head and breathed through his anger instead of taking it out on our lawyer. We'd be patted down once we got inside, so we couldn't do this with weapons, we had to do it their way. Taylor was in the lab waiting patiently for the text to wire over funds to the Swedish bank account, so all we needed now was to see our girl and make the purchase.

Dezmond Archer Junior and I made our way through the club, first going through an extensive pat-down process, followed by a metal detector wand. They checked the list for his name, and once he was confirmed they let us through the strip club. Tacky red velvet lined the floors, and a royal purple fabric covered every booth and chair in the room.

There was an elevated runway that ran down the center of the room, and cocktail tables had been set up on either side of it. Expensive-looking men sat at every booth, most with masks covering their faces, and I wondered if we fucked up, coming in exposed. It was too late to worry about it now, we just needed to find Cecilia and get the fuck out.

Scantily dressed women passed each table and took requests for drinks. Dez placed an order to keep the illusion of normality, but I waved her off when she got to me. She raised her eyebrows like I was making a big mistake, so with a heavy sigh of defeat I gave in to her demands.

"Tonic and lime," I said, wondering if she'd honor it, or if the drink was going to come back spiked. Obviously, they preferred their business transactions to happen with a cloudy head and a foggy mind, but I wouldn't give them the satisfaction.

I tipped my chin towards Dez in approval, a signal for him to continue drinking as he kept the pretense up in case someone was watching us. I stirred my drink, watching the ice cubes clink against each other. I was unwilling to test even a sip of it in case there was booze, or something stronger lacing it.

Once every rich fucker in the room was on their second or third drink, the lights in the room turned off completely and a bright white spotlight shone on the stage. A voice boomed out from somewhere behind the curtains announcing the auction was about to begin.

I curled my fist anxiously and released my fingers over and over again as each girl stumbled onto the stage with a look of stupor that let me know they had been drugged to oblivion prior to this. They were young, barely a few years older than Andrea had been when my father killed her.

It was taking every ounce of personal restraint to not stand up and kill every mother fucker in the building for having a part in this horror show. Dez cleared his throat and shook his head at me in a silent warning, as if he knew exactly what was going through my mind at that moment.

I started to wonder if I had been the right man for the job as each victim stumbled through the stage until their new owner claimed them for themselves. My mind couldn't help but go to that dreary place where nightmares lived side by side with my own memories.

I curled my fingers tightly against the glass in my hand while I waited for each girl to get auctioned off and escorted from the stage. As the night slowly dragged on, panic began to creep in. There couldn't be that many left, so, where was she?

Was I too late?

My mind was already running through every worst-case scenario that could have happened.

Maybe she had already been sold, or worse, she was dead.

I pressed my fingers to my temple to relieve the incoming migraine and hoped to God I was wrong.

"The next one is a special treat," said the voice behind the curtains through the microphone and every hair on my body stood up. "She's a little older, but this exotic beauty is a fighter if you're looking for someone to go a few rounds with." He laughed out and confirmed what I already knew.

My girl with skin like sunshine was next.

Head in the game. I thought to myself as I waited for Cecilia to come out on the stage.

Someone pushed her through the fabric, and she stumbled forward, falling but unable to crash down on the floor as a makeshift leash held her up and she floated, choking in mid-air. I immediately recognized the piece of shit with the bulldog face who destroyed my instruments. He pulled her to her feet while the other hand stayed tightly around the leash that fastened on her neck.

Cecilia's head wobbled and her body swayed, I knew she was too far gone to even realize what was happening to her at that moment. Anger wasn't a feeling I enjoyed, unlike Ronan I didn't thrive from it, I survived in spite of it.

My fury was the only thing that made me feel truly out of control in my own body. It reminded me of my piece of shit old man, and so for some reason I thought that if I could keep myself from getting to that place, that I wouldn't turn into him. But at that moment, the rage curdled my blood as her eyes squinted from the spotlight blinding her vision and the ugly piece of shit nudged her forward another step.

The bidding paddles flew up and my eyes went wide at how many buyers had been waiting for someone just like her to be brought out. These sick fucks got off on girls like Cecilia, the ones who didn't give up, the ones who put up a fight before they forced them to give them what they wanted with violence and pain.

I kicked Dez under the table and he lifted up the paddle to get our bid in. One by one, paddles came down as the price increased, but it didn't matter if it drained every bit of our finances. We would leave here with her, even if it made me a poor man.

At a million and a half, the last paddle went down, and I sighed an anxious breath of relief out of winning her away from the savagery of the men in this room. Dez nodded to me and got up to complete the transaction, I texted Taylor to let her know the purchase would be going down.

I followed him into a small office room where I stood back, continuing to play the part of his lackey as he hashed away the financial portions of the deal with a masked man sitting at a laptop. I feigned disinterest to keep up the charade and did my best to look away the entire time.

Once the wire was completed, he led us through a narrow hallway and unlocked a room where Cecilia stood with a dark bag over her head in nothing but underwear. Her wrists were handcuffed behind her, and a giant scarred-up motherfucker held her by what I could now see was a leather belt secured against her throat.

I pumped my fingers in and out again and I twitched my nose, knowing we were only a few moments away from getting out of here. I couldn't let my impulsive behavior fuck it all up when we had gotten so far, when she was so close to being free. Ronan would no doubt kill me if I fucked this one up.

The guy pulled a key out and undid the handcuffs before he released the belt around her neck. Her head came down heavily on her shoulders and I resisted the urge to reach out for her. I waited for Dez, and after what felt like too long, he finally called out to me.

"Get her and put her in the car." He doled out orders and I nodded, stepping toward Cecilia just as the big asshole pushed her forward, nearly knocking her down if I hadn't been there to catch her. I heaved her over my shoulder with ease, unable to hide how eager I was to get out of this hell hole while also making a silent promise to myself that the big fucker would die by my hands too.

Once we were out of the room and back into the narrow hallway, I grabbed her off my shoulder and brought her to my chest not looking back as I walked out. I texted Ronan to get the car ready and I looked for a sign for the exit as I paced down the corridor.

"I got you Sunshine, you're gonna be okay," I said to her in a soft voice, but all that came out of her was a moaned grumble that broke my heart a million ways.

"Wait. Pluto," she mumbled out, and I hushed her in case anyone could hear her talking to me.

"They'll feed him to the lion," she barely made the words out, but I was only more confused now than ever before.

"You're not making sense Sunshine, it's the drugs. I'll have you home soon," I reassured her.

"Home?" She asked and snuggled closer to me, burying her covered face deep into my neck. "Santos?" She asked, and my heart shattered again.

"Mateo," I hummed into her ear, and she pressed tighter into me, making my pulse rise a million miles an hour.

"Please, get him," she groaned out again.

I didn't know who she was talking about, but Ronan would beat me into the next life if he knew I wasn't following the plan. She seemed desperate to get whatever was down there. I pulled the bag off of her head, even though Dez had said to keep it on until we got outside, and my heart broke doubly. One of her eyes was swollen shut and purple, her face was a rainbow of colors in multiple areas. There were cuts and scrapes all over her. Her eyes were sunken deep, but they shined glossily as she recognized my face.

"I'm sorry Sunshine, we have to go," I told her, my resolve nearly crumbling seeing the devastation on her face from my denial.

Before she could plead any further the Bulldog-looking piece of shit that destroyed my instruments, the same one that had been leading my girl by a leash on that stage, came flying out of a door. Instinctively, I dropped Cecilia to the ground as he stomped his way over to me and swung his fist out with confidence from his size. He was too big though, and I was quicker. I dodged and rammed my knee into his head in the same motion as he tried to duck from my swing and then shoved him against the door.

The asshole punched me in the face, knocking me off my balance, and forcing my back to hit a fire extinguisher that was attached to the wall. I pulled it off with a jerk and smashed it over the bulldog's head forcing him down to the ground with the impact. I hit him with it again, a sick crunch played in my ears, and I smiled at how music could be found even in the strangest of places.

I lifted the fire extinguisher again and brought it down on his head, once, twice, then a third time for good measure. The fourth was to stop the twitching. Once his skull was liquid goo on the velvety floor, I picked her back up into my arms and ran through the rest of the building towards what looked like an emergency exit.

I kicked the door open and Zerkos stood outside the car while he waited for us. "Where's Dez?" he asked, with a confused look on his face, rushing towards Cecilia.

"He was right behind me," He tried to pry her from my hold, but she recoiled into me.

"It's me, Céci," Ronan said with a gentleness I had never been a witness to in the twelve years I knew him. He reached for her again, but she clung harder to me and screamed a raspy protest in my ear.

"No!" She cried painfully just as Dez came bursting out of the door in a hurried pace.

"Get the fuck in the car. Get the fuck in the car. We gotta go go go," Dez chimed frantically as he ushered us all in and Zerkos was begrudgingly forced into the driver's seat again. I went to put Cecilia in the backseat when I noticed the open gash splitting her back apart from the top of her left shoulder, all the way down to her right hip.

"Shit," I muttered, climbing in behind her, trying to handle her as gently as I possibly could, so that I didn't cause her any additional pain.

"What is it?" Ronan demanded in an unhinged tone.

"It's just worse than what we could see. Get us the hell out of here. What took you so long, Dez?" I slapped the back of the passenger seat where he was sitting.

"They tried giving me some shit, saying the transaction didn't clear and I had to wait until they could see it on their side," he said from the front, and I looked into the rearview mirror and met Ronan's gaze.

Yeah, right.

I'm on to you motherfucker.

Zerkos peeled away from the strip club parking lot, and my pulse was beating a heavy sound in my ears. Every single nerve in my body was shot from tonight, and even more so from the last five minutes.

Cecilia fell asleep almost immediately with her head on my lap, and I gently combed my fingers through her hair and breathed deep gulps of relief into my lungs.

Once we made our way back to the high-rise, Ronan stopped the car at the door and got out without saying a single word, throwing the keys at Dez to finish parking. I followed him inside with Cecilia in my arms. He kept glancing at me with a scowl etched into his face, he was no doubt seething, but I hadn't done anything wrong. If anything, he should have been thanking me.

"I think it's Dez," I said once we got into the elevator.

"It's believable," he responded dryly, and we both muttered a soft "fuck" before the doors dinged open into the penthouse.

We made our way in, and before Zerkos could start demanding I take her to his room like I would have expected, Cecilia began to shake in my arms and foam began to fill inside her mouth.

"Oh shit," I called for Ronan's attention, but before I could set Cecilia on the couch he was already dialing for Emory. I laid her on the bullet-ridden sofa and turned her to the side so she wouldn't choke.

"She says we need to get her to throw up if we can, in case they gave her pills." He shouted back at me and I frantically ran to the bathroom to grab a trash can.

"Sorry about this Sunshine, it's for your own good," I said softly, but not quite enough and Zerkos raised an eyebrow at me even though he looked fully occupied with Emory on the line.

My hands were trembling at the familiar image below me. I tried to shake my sister's face out of my memory. I steadied my shaking limbs and shoved my finger into her throat, she pushed my hand away moaning a weak "No."

I couldn't let her decide her own fate here. I sent my finger down her throat again and this time I didn't let her frail little hands control me, I wiggled my finger until I heard the heaving and bent her over the trash can. Nothing came out, so I tried a few more times until it was certain.

"Nothing's happening," Zerkos told Emory over the phone and with a few quick words he disconnected and made his way into the elevators. I could hear each tick of the second hand on a nearby clock, so unbearably loud, almost mocking me, while I was left alone with her to spiral into the chasm of my mind.

Her body shook and convulsed right in front of me, but there was nothing I could do to keep her here. I shook her and screamed her name until defeat crashed over me, forcing me to realize I had been cursed to watch the same fate the universe laid out for my little sister, with Cecilia as well.

"Don't give up, Sunshine. I need you, okay? Ronan needs you. Santos needs you." I whispered to her as I held her tightly in my arms, doing my best to not let my emotions take the reins though I felt closer and closer to spiraling out of control.

"MOVE!" Zerkos came crashing out of the elevator with something small in his hand as he ran through the foyer and jumped over the couch. I darted out of the way and without a second thought he shoved the tiny white container into her nose and pressed it in. "Start a timer," he instructed me, cool as a cucumber. Even though we trained together, it still impressed the fuck out of me that he could keep such a level head when he was so emotionally invested in the situation.

I let my head and my heart get in the way too often.

He began giving her mouth to mouth, and I told him every time sixty seconds passed. Once we reached the four-minute mark, he got another little nasal sprayer out of his pocket and activated it into her nose again.

"What is that?" I asked him.

"Narcan," he said and almost immediately she took a big gasp of breath, her eyelids fluttering open. He tossed the nasal sprayer on the ground and gave her mouth to mouth again, but this time it was mostly a kiss.

"Heroin?" I asked him, and he shrugged. Clearly, he was just as clueless as I was, but whatever it was, the Narcan worked.

"Emory said she'll be by in the next day or so to check on her, but she's pulling an ER shift at Saint Murphy's and can't leave tonight," he explained.

She began shivering on the couch, so I lifted her head up and laid it back down over my lap while Ronan covered her with a blanket. She tried to say something, but a dry cough came out instead.

"Water?" he asked her, and she nodded her head in the tiniest, almost unnoticeable way. Zerkos stood and filled a glass from the dispenser in the fridge before putting a straw in it and bridging it to her lips. I lifted her head up slightly so she wouldn't choke and reminded her to take small sips.

"Everything hurts," she rasped, still not opening her eyes.

"It'll get better now. You're safe baby," Ronan encouraged, but she scowled at the sound of his voice and curled in towards me. Zerkos growled and I cut a look at him that meant *not now* and somehow, for once, it worked. He stomped away heavily before the sound of his door slamming rang out through our penthouse making her flinch in response.

"I'm going to bring you into my room, is that okay?" I asked her and she nodded, her teeth chattering hard while she trembled against me. I lifted her up and carried her through the hallway. Glancing in the direction of Santos' room to find the door open as he stood there in the doorway, a blank expression on his face while he watched me take her into mine.

With the most care I could offer her, I gently laid her on the bed, stomach down, and I unhooked the bra they put on her. My gut churned in the worst way, as I examined more closely the brutal gash splitting her open. It cut across the entirety of her back diagonally, ripping apart some words that had been inked onto her shoulder. I walked to the bathroom and pulled open the medicine cabinet, removing the cheap, unopened first aid kit.

I soaked the gauze pads in the saline solution and gently dabbed them over her back, each time I made contact with her skin she groaned in pain. I thought about the possibility of her back sticking to the sheets, or to a shirt if I were to put one on her so I adjusted her onto the bed so she could comfortably sleep on her stomach while her wound dried.

Then I remembered that she was still recovering from being stabbed in the stomach just a few days ago, and my guilt intensified. She'd already suffered under our hands so many times. How could I claim to care for her, if I was just going to continue to let bad shit happen to her? I made a vow right then and there that I would do whatever it took to never allow something like this to repeat.

Doing my best to keep it brief, I hopped in for a quick shower to wash the Bulldog piece of shit's brains off of me and then turned the lights off before crawling into bed next to her.

Tonight, was a shitshow.

But at least it felt like home again with her next to me. I tried and tried, but couldn't fall asleep yet, too much adrenaline, fear, and rage was coursing through my system, and it needed somewhere to go before I started bouncing off the walls.

I'd watched plenty of people overdose since my little sister died, but it never made it any easier and every single time brought me back to that moment. But with her, it was somehow the most scared I'd ever been since I could remember.

Fuck, war had somehow become less frightening than the thought of losing her.

I rolled out of bed and found Zerkos pacing the hallway, his adrenaline no doubt still fueling him on as well.

32

RONAN

I had no way of sleeping.

How could I, when I had endangered everyone that I was responsible for, and almost lost her completely in a matter of hours? I got a text from Taylor telling me to come down to tech and she only sent it to me, which could only mean that maybe she had something on my personal request.

Unfortunately, Kane was snooping like a little bitch and read over my shoulders, deciding he wasn't going to miss out on any sort of new information. Álvarez was still sulking in his room like someone shoved an icepick up his ass, but I had no intention of poking the homicidal bear. If he was gonna brood, he could stay there the whole week for all I cared.

I'd had enough of secrets.

"I don't know how I'm supposed to feel about her always choosing everyone else over me." The confession bubbled its way out before I could stop it, but my brother needed to know this was eating me alive.

"It's because you keep trying to cage her in whatever way you can. You're so afraid of her leaving again, you haven't stopped to think that maybe she's here by choice now." He looked me in the eye.

"What, so just absolve everything, forgive all the deception and secrets?" I asked him, and the thought that I was getting advice from him on a girl I'd known my whole life was laughable.

Did I know her though?

"Maybe just try to move past it, stop trying to put limitations on what she can do, where she can go, who she can *fuck*." He emphasized, making my blood boil at the insinuation. "She wants to be free, so let her."

"Let her fuck you, you mean?" I clarified with my own question knowing he wouldn't directly admit it.

"The difference between me and you is that I love exactly who she is. You love the idea of who you had. I'm not asking for more than she can give. I'm taking whatever she's willing to spare. I just want her, a little or as much as she's willing to let me have." I was having a hard time swallowing down his words. I couldn't accept that he was right in any way because it meant admitting that I didn't know the Cecilia in front of me anymore.

"You love her?" I repeated his confession back to him, not missing a beat before he realized what he'd said a little too late.

"I think somewhere along the way I realized she wasn't like anyone else this world could give me." He was looking at me, waiting for me to call some sort of truce to this. But I didn't know what he was expecting, I would just share my girl with him?

"Except the world gave her to *me*," I cut through him as the elevator opened to the tech level and he grabbed my arm to stop me from getting out.

"If you can't give her what she needs, you will lose her. And believe it or not asshole, I'm actually cheering for you here. You don't have to lose her. *So don't lose her*." He looked me dead in the eye and I shook him off of me, as I began to enter the codes.

Once we made it past the safe door, we could see Taylor seated in her chair. Chair was putting it mildly though, it was a fucking epic throne. It was reminiscent of a captain's seat in Star Trek, but instead of the vastitude of open space, it was an array of screens that somehow never failed to let me down.

She was in full concentration mode, so I cleared my throat to announce that we were inside. The rest of the team was gone and that struck me as odd, even for how late it was. They normally slept in shifts so that at least three of them could monitor the live feeds at a time, you never caught one of them alone.

I wasn't a micromanager, technically this lab was Taylor's responsibility. Anyone employed here was hers to deal with, and I never worried about the ins and outs of this place. I signed their paychecks but as far as I was concerned, they were her team. Not mine. But still, it was strange to see not even an extra person in here.

"Pizza party for the rest of your team somewhere?" I joked at her.

"Um, something like that." Her mood was nervous, and her vague response immediately set off red flags.

"Why'd you send them away?" I asked as I caught on.

"I found some *seriously* sensitive stuff, and I knew you wouldn't want just anyone seeing this. I only watched a few seconds myself before I realized what I was watching," she said, her face pale and full of worry. I began to sweat while a million possibilities began rushing through my head.

What the hell could have been so bad to have her this spooked? Taylor Constance saw the same horrors we did out there, so if something had her looking at me this way. I knew it had to be rough.

She glanced over at Kane and shifted her eyes back at me, but I nodded at her. Her loyalty was unmatched, and I appreciated that to no end, but Mateo Kane was my brother and whatever secret Cecilia was keeping from me, he deserved to know as well. I knew whatever it was, there would be no way I'd be able to go through it without him anyway.

She nodded her head in understanding before she began to explain. "This was a hell of an ask, and someone sane likely couldn't have done it."

"Good thing he didn't ask someone sane, did he?" Mateo smirked and took a seat in a nearby chair.

"Alright, buckle up and I'll take you the whole ride through the way my mind worked this one out." She pulled up some google articles, reddit posts and underground media videos, and began to lay them all out across the many screens.

"When you told me to look up Flores, I literally wanted to shoot you in the dick. But, after a few hours of digging up hundreds of thousands of Flores census archives, I decided to go a little obscure. Reddit can be a hell of a tool if you don't know what you're looking for." She mused and highlighted the page.

"It wasn't what I found, but what they didn't want us to find, over the years there had been a couple hundred posts made. Nothing too specific, just some ramblings that sounded illegitimate and vague as hell. The interesting thing is, they had all been removed from the main server, every single post."

Mateo leaned forward in his chair to give her his full attention, and I couldn't help but feel my interest pique. Anyone with the power to remove information from an internet server is a lot higher up the chain of anarchy than I could have imagined Cecilia being tangled up in.

"So, what were in these posts?" I nudged her.

"Like I said, speculations, paranoid conspiracy theories, He-said-she-said-they-saw type of stories. All involving some Ortíz cártel family. I found some old photos of newspaper articles that talked about them, but even though it's hard to search it ain't news baby."

"Apparently everyone below the Texas border can tell you who the Ortíz family is. I called a girlfriend whose mom was born in Tijuana and she spent about two hours telling me every story under the sun. This is the real deal shit, *the* Cártel. That's why, aside from a few deep underground media videos of live executions that have been server trashed as well, there is *nothing* to find. Not unless they wanted you to find it. Which they don't, by the way." She said, crossing her arms.

"And what does that have to do with Flores?" I reminded her of what I sent her after since it seemed like this was going to be taking a few detour routes before we got to the main exit.

"Well, that's why I was getting all these deleted hits when searching for Flores. My friend's mom said when she was young The Ortíz Cártel was practically Greek mythology to them at that point, the Cártel had been split into multiple families, and eventually, the Ortíz head was killed off by one of the other heads, ending their long line, and rule over the Cártel." She looked at me while she waited for me to beg for more information, but I was starting to get annoyed, and she wasn't giving me enough to keep me calm. Maybe she was procrastinating because she didn't want to get to the point, I'd never seen Taylor so uncomfortable with digging up some dirt before.

"That's where the Flores family comes in, they don't just kill off the Ortíz line, but they take over their seat in the Cártel. They acquire all of the money, and assets, the paid off military men and police working for the Ortíz, and merge with their own. Fucking powerful shit. Throughout history even the presidents worked for the Flores family because they had so much military power behind them, it was easier to keep them paid and happy than to start a civil war. The Cártel kept the cities protected, and justice was served by their principles. Nobody interfered. That's fucking wild right? Can you imagine a government so fucked that the gang leaders are secretly in charge and puppeteering the politicians?"

"Can you get to the point? You sent your team away over village gossip?" I asked, not hiding my annoyance one bit. Kane kicked out at me with a deep scowl on his face that told me not to piss her off.

"Take a seat asshole. And stop rushing her," he came to her defense, and she nodded at him in gratitude.

"Well, once I knew what I was looking for, it wasn't so hard. I started searching through Mexican records of politicians with the last name Flores and there we had it. Rafael Flores, political affiliations with nearly every single president for over twenty years, listed as a member of The Congress of the Union. Basically, way too many hands in way too many baskets to avoid the last name for me. Can't find any information on any relatives, living or deceased for him though. He wiped himself off the radar so good, I'm honestly impressed. Nearly fucking impossible to find a photo of the guy, but I did find a few older ones, all side profiles." She split one of the screens as she pulled up the image of a Mexican man shaking hands with another. Both men looked incredibly put together like they both knew the world of politics like the back of their hands.

"No clearer photos? This shit is more pixelated than trying to play a nintendo64 on a 4K TV." Mateo rang out, and I had to agree. These pictures were no good to me.

"The photos don't matter because he's dead. Killed in a drive-by shooting nearly fifteen years ago." My eyes went wide while the gears turned in my head faster than I could process it, there was no way. It was a coincidence. I only met the guy once, but I would have recognized him even in those shit quality low-resolution photos.

"Bring back the photos," I told her, and she rolled her eyes as she pulled them up again and I stared into the much younger version of the man I once thought would become my father-in-law. I dragged my hand over my face while every terrible thought my mind could conjure up began to consume me. My vision went black and the noise around me felt muted and hushed. The sizzling buzz of the electronics in the room was the only sound coming through and connecting with my brain.

My knuckles were a stark white as they pressed through my skin from the violence that yearned to pour out of me and I clenched my fists to relieve the desire. Who the fuck was she? I let a Pandora's box into my life, into my heart, locked up, full of secrets while she chose to never once share any piece of the truth with me

Her father–the coldest motherfucker I had ever met in my entire life–was Rafael Flores, and he was probably the most dangerous man in Mexico while he was still alive. The ache of her betrayal had grown into rage, and it clawed its way out of me. I knew if I didn't get rid of this energy somehow, I would end up with someone bleeding under my fists again.

Taylor waved her hands in front of my face to get my attention, but I couldn't quite make out what she was saying. I stood up from my chair and shoved her away from me, earning a "Hey!" from both her and Kane.

"I wasn't done, you know?" she announced as I turned my back to leave the room. I didn't care. I needed to get my ass to the gym now, I needed to turn a punching bag into dust and fabric with nothing but the force of my fists.

It was no wonder she was looking for protection. Daughter of the head of the Cártel, I could only imagine how much someone would have paid to get their hands on her. She was a trophy, and whoever had *truly* killed Rafael Flores all those years ago was likely still after her. Though hard to say who wasn't after her. Being the kid of the most powerful man in Mexico was probably painting a huge target on her head for anyone Rafael may have pissed off in his wake.

I hit the bag over and over without relenting, not bothering to wrap my hands so I could feel every blow splitting my knuckles apart as I dealt it. I allowed the same woman to ruin me twice now and it was a mistake I couldn't repeat. My heart was breaking all over again, but even stoking the tumultuous rage that throbbed inside me, I knew I would allow her to continue to break me over and over again. Because I would always come back to her, I would always look after her. From the first time I ever saw her, I knew she was mine to protect.

33

MATEO

Pop –The bubble I had made with my gum echo-ed loudly and awkwardly through the empty tech lab.

"You can go," Taylor said flatly, and I smirked at her show of loyalty to Ronan.

"Nah babe, you said you weren't done. Plus, Zerkos practically told you to brief me in his stead, didn't you hear him?" I shot her my dimpliest half-smile and shook the hair out of my eyes as I folded my arms behind my head.

I threw my feet in the chair in front of me and settled in for the rest of this story. I knew my Sunshine was hiding something big, but hot damn, I wasn't expecting cártel big. Knowing she was mixed up in something so fucking dangerous, even though I wasn't quite sure how, somehow made her even hotter.

I wondered what my shrink would have to say about that one. I made a mental note to call Barb in the morning and bring this up. She loved when I got all self-aware on her.

"No, I didn't, *babe*," she shoved my feet off the chair as she barged through my legs, nearly knocking me off the chair with her sheer strength reminding me that she probably got more pussy than I did. At least these days that was true.

There was only one that I was interested in.

"Finish it," my tone became harsher, and her expression morphed from one of annoyance to one of fear. I didn't care if people thought Zerkos was the leader, but I refused to let anyone treat me otherwise, least of all Taylor Constance.

Sure, I had a broken mind, but Ronan was a lost little kid who got thrown into a war with a broken heart and Taylor had no sense of self-worth from spending the majority of her life in the closet, too afraid to be herself. But the three of us looked out for each other, and never once did I let them down in all of our time together.

She knew better than to withhold from me.

"Well, wipe that smug look from your face, cuz we're getting to the bad shit. I'm gonna hop over the crap you don't care about because I know you. You don't give a damn about the technical details," she said, pointing a remote to one of the screens, getting some financial records up.

"To make a very, very long story short, I dug up as much as I could on Rafael, finding some ghost identities that tied to some bank accounts, one of those bank accounts led me to this warehouse." The remote clicked and she pulled up an aerial view of a warehouse from a satellite.

"It's just a packaging and processing plant for some popular Mexican candy *Paleta Payaso*. It's a clown on a stick in case you're wondering. I googled it," she turned on the image on the largest screen for me to see the chocolate-covered clown face on a popsicle stick.

"Obviously, that's not all they're doing in there, so naturally I hacked my way into The Lacrosse." I twisted my face in confusion, letting her know I didn't have a clue what some indigenous sport had to do with this, "It's a satellite that's powerful enough to see some underground areas. I was in there for a total of sixty-three seconds before they booted my ass out and we almost risked the FBI dropping down our roof next." I shot her another look, shocked that she had the audacity to make jokes.

"Ok, too soon, I know. I'm using dark humor to cope, don't kill me." She raised her hands in the air defensively, and I was starting to understand why Ronan went all *berserk* and left before she got the point.

She'd been cooped up in here, way too long, and the info dump was just falling out of her mouth like rapid fire at this point.

Note to self; *Taylor needs a vacation*.

"What'd you find?" I tried to steer back on track while her attention deficit riddled brain went everywhere but where it needed to.

"Listen, I'm pretty scared of what I've found, if this family has the heavy hitting power they do, I don't want to be on their shit list. But I'll tell you what I didn't find. I *didn't* find an entire underground network system full of intricate tunnels leading all over Mexico as well as through the border. I *didn't* find dungeons upon dungeons full of drugs, money, weapons and holding cells. I most *definitely* did not find a video of Mr. Flores torturing a little girl." Her voice wavered with her words as the seriousness of the situation began to settle in.

"What the fuck did you say?" I asked her because it sounded like she said this Cártel family was torturing children.

"I was able to hack into the mainframe of the security system for one of their dungeons. I don't know what the deal with it is, but it's like the whole thing is completely unmanned. The live feeds show it's just sitting there abandoned, or maybe locked up since the dude is dead now, but no one is there. There's no way anyone is there, they would have booted me and shut down the whole thing within a minute of me forcing my way into their system. The fact I was able to spend hours trudging through their surveillance history let me know that place was a dead zone. But when I went digging through the server? I found all sorts of hell in there. I watched maybe five or six seconds of it before I stopped and told Ronan to come down here, no one has seen it yet." She opened up the file and clicked on one of the many surveillance videos named after a random series of numbers. CF113 came on, and right away I recognized her.

She was so young–maybe thirteen at best– but I knew that dark hair and the "eat shit" look in her eyes that she gave to anyone who wasn't serving her every whim.

She was hanging by the wrists in iron shackles that were fastened to the dungeon's stone wall. Her toes didn't touch the ground, letting me know her little body was probably in excruciating pain from the positioning.

The man, the same one from the previous photos, stood across from her. He was decades older in the videos, but I could see clearly now that it was him, Rafael Flores. I feared for the young version of Cecilia, and I fiercely needed to know what she could have possibly done to earn herself a place as a prisoner to the Cártel when she was just a little girl.

I was losing my calm, anger was taking over me as the man walked closer to her and he reached out his hand like he was waiting for someone to place an object in it. That was when I noticed they weren't alone in that dungeon. No, resting against the wall, looking calm and with a "no fucks given" attitude, was none other than Cézar fucking Villalobos.

He grabbed a cattle prod from a wall laced with weapons and handed it over to Flores who didn't hesitate a second before pressing it against Cecilia over and over again until urine dripped down her legs freely. Watching her tiny body shake from the electric current running through her, wave after wave with no pause forced bile to the back of my throat.

The high-pitched whining in my head threatened to explode alongside my rage. I looked into the face of the motherfucker in disbelief. I had risked plenty of my own men's safety just days ago by abandoning the high-rise and helping him on his renegade motorcycle club mission.

The thing's I did to that girl.

Cézar's words repeated in my brain, and I nearly broke my teeth from clenching my jaw so tightly. I had thought he was implying something sexual happened between them, I thought he was trying to get under Ronan's skin. But there he was, leaving a permanent mark in her mind and her spirit that I could now see clear as day for what it truly was.

Emptiness.

Nobody that had been meant to care for her had ever given this girl a morsel of love, affection, or security. And while I knew how that could feel, I didn't know it on the level that I was seeing here.

Taylor grabbed a nearby trashcan and heaved loudly into it, apparently not lying when she said she only watched five seconds of footage. She wiped the tears from her eyes as her gaze met mine and she tried to play off like this wasn't fucking her up to watch, but I knew better.

This was as dark as it got, a world where kids couldn't get to be kids was hell incarnate. Unfortunately, I had already seen hell, and it had only numbed me enough to come back here to suffer the rest of my bullshit reality.

My stomach churned when Cézar released her from her shackles and she immediately slammed her knees into his balls. A glimmer of hope surged through me as he collapsed in pain, but my gut sank once the head of the Flores family plunged his fist deep into her belly, throwing her against the wall.

Cézar took a seat on her chest as she collapsed to the ground under his weight, his legs pinning both her arms down while she shook her head side to side violently without ever screaming a single plea to stop. Almost as if she knew what was coming, she took a big breath before Cézar threw a piece of fabric over her face and Rafael Flores began to slowly pour a large container of water over it.

"Fuck," I mumbled, my stomach feeling queasy watching a thirteen-year-old little girl getting water boarded in a torture dungeon.

"Turn that shit off, that's a fucking kid," Taylor reprimanded me as if I was enjoying watching this any more than she was.

"It's not just a kid Taylor. It's her. Cecilia," I explained.

"Oh...Shit!" She said, her eyes widened with realization, and she took a seat again as if this was now the most important assignment she had ever been given.

"Turn up the volume, he's saying something." I instructed her, not being able to make out what this Devil in disguise of a man was saying.

Cézar had thrown a few more punches at her until she stopped coming back up, and she sat there, beaten, broken, and abused. As she looked into the man's face, Taylor adjusted the sound so we could listen.

"Can you translate?" I asked her and she nodded her head.

"It's when you have nothing left, that you have to find strength to end your enemy." She paused the recording to speak, "Or they will end you, make no mistake."

He opened the door, and a teenage boy entered the room, tattoos already covering his young face as he tried his best to fit into a life that was clearly too much for him, too soon.

"You said you needed a job kid, Necesito sangue." He spoke in half English, throwing a knife into the space between him and Cecilia. The kid only looked back at him for a split second before deciding.

She didn't move at all, not at first, and then the kid immediately lunged for the knife on the ground, and she took the opportunity to slam her fist into his face. Her knee shot out in between his legs violently, causing blood to pour out of his mouth. I instinctively cupped my own jewels feeling the need to protect them from the brutality.

"Now tell him why he's going to die today *Mija*," Taylor translated Rafael Flores' words as they came out of him with a look of pride in his face as Cecilia ripped the knife from the kid's hand and stood over him.

"Because you thought you could kill Celia Flores, asshole," Taylor translated, looking at me, eyes full of shock. I turned my gaze back to the recording to see Cecilia, her eyes full of that devouring darkness that ran through her soul as she drug the blade across his throat and sat on his chest the same way Cézar had done to her, just moments ago.

Rafael leaves the room, but Cecilia stays perched on the dead kid's chest until most of the blood drains from his body. Cézar kicks off his spot leaning against the wall once again, this time he makes it over to her with a smirk and extends a hand for her to grab. He pulled her up to stand and kissed her affectionately on the forehead before supporting most of her weight as they walked out of that dungeon together.

I fought the urge to relieve my stomach of its contents as well, as my head tried to wrap around what I had just watched. "Celia Flores," I told Taylor, and without needing to give her any additional instructions she began her research again. "1992, maybe '93." I remembered that she was two years younger than Ronan and myself and waited for her to dig.

"Tons of results, but the good news is, it's easy to filter now that I know I'm looking for a ghost. Just gotta clear any of the ones with social media, photos, essentially any relevant information aside from birth records. Oh, interesting," she stopped and looked back at me from her chair. I took it as an invitation to lean in closer.

"This one's got a death certificate in 2000," she pointed to the screen and my gut sank with the confirmation I heard on the video with my own two ears.

Cecilia Gomez didn't exist, she was the ghost of Celia-fucking-Flores, daughter of the head of the Cártel. She had been my prisoner for the last two months, and I had never questioned the stone wall she put up any time we worked to break her, and that was our first mistake.

Stronger hijos de puta have not broken me.

I fought the bubbling of manic laughter stuck in my throat at the thought of our own stupidity. The truth didn't hold back with how hard it hit me when I stepped aside to think of all of the hints she had dropped, but we weren't listening. What we put her through was child's play compared to the hell her father had been dealing her. And based on the number of files in that folder, that shit had been going on for years.

How many hours did she spend being tortured in that dungeon? How many kills had her monster of a father forced upon her before she had a chance to understand the stain that taking a life left on you? She should have been playing with barbies, but instead, she was slicing the throats of whoever her father deemed deserving.

Of course what we did to her didn't come close to leaving a mark on her, let alone breaking her. She was born into a world that had stolen her youth and instead prepared her for the very thing we had been trying to do.

I hated the man in the video almost as fiercely as I hated my own old man, and the knowledge that he was already dead only made me angrier and more bitter while I came to terms with the fact that somebody else had stolen the opportunity for me to remove him from this earth.

Ronan obviously already made the connection just looking into the face of her father, that was clear enough to me. But as the world stood still and my mind worked a million miles a second, I realized Santos was right from the beginning.

She was protecting him, both of them. She knew Zerkos was brash and headstrong enough to try to take down the entire Cártel over the videos in these files alone, and that surely, he would lose a million times over.

I didn't steal the guns. Not really.

I sagged into the chair with defeat as my brain puzzled together every crumb of information she dropped while she had been here. Of course, she didn't steal the guns, Zerkos told me that was the job that was supposed to be the start of the brotherhood. Santos' cousin Guillermo tipped them off to a Cártel deal that was set up to go wrong, as long as they could make it there in time, before the cops showed up, there was going to be a van full of cash and weapons for the taking.

I slapped my own face hard enough to shock me back into the present moment as Taylor watched me silently. She didn't steal the guns, because they were Cártel property, so in a way, they had belonged to her. But most importantly, she didn't steal them to sell them or to ruin Ronan's life. She saved both their asses by getting rid of Cártel weapons before those idiots redistributed them into the streets.

Ronan was rampaging, and he hadn't even seen the worst of it yet. I knew there weren't any words that could explain the severity of what I just watched. The only way for him to understand was to see with his own eyes.

34

CECILIA

Sleep was basically an illusion at this point. However many days I spent locked up in that basement, unable to get more than an hour's rest at a time, ended up doing a number on my circadian rhythm. I woke up in Mateo's bed, with the moonlight brightly seeping into the glass that lined the exterior wall of his bedroom. I groaned at the pounding in my head and rolled to look at the ceiling only to feel an excruciating pain burning through my back.

Puta Madre!

Had I slept all night into the next day? Had I slept an hour?

The scent of pine and old leather coursed through my senses as I rolled to my other side to see him there next to me. His raven hair draped over his eyes, and a serenity displayed on his features that I hadn't had the pleasure of experiencing for myself yet. Where did he go when all the worry had been smoothed out of his face? Where did that peace come from?

I spent the last few months fighting my brain and my heart, letting them wage a battle against each other while I sat on the sidelines as a mere spectator. Falling for Mateo Kane was a mistake. I knew it would be, and somehow in the end, I'd suffer for it one way or another. But right now, I couldn't stop myself from letting those feelings rise to the surface and take over the empty space that had been carved out in my chest. He came for me. As alone as I felt in this vast world, I couldn't deny what I had witnessed with my own eyes.

Mateo saved me.

My head throbbed from the drugs that had been continuously shoved into my system, and my body ached from being pent up in that tiny cage. My pulse quickened at the thought and worry began to tumble its way into me.

What if they put me back down there now that I'm here again? What if Ronan shoves me back in that closet?

Maybe I just needed to get the hell out of here before I let myself become anyone else's plaything. I thought about going to Santos and demanding that he help me, but another thought crossed my head before I could act on it.

He wasn't there last night.

I was really fucking out of it, but not fucked up enough to know that I saw Ronan and Mateo last night. Not Santos.

I groaned loudly as I rolled my way out of the bed, unable to avoid feeling the pain slicing through my back. Something tugged at my arm, and that's when I noticed the IV connected to the inside of my elbow, hanging from a metal hook over the bed. Pulling the needle out slowly, I hissed with discomfort as I freed myself from all the tubing, fully aware the empty saline bag was likely the only reason I didn't feel like death walking at this very moment.

My feet hit the floor, but my legs gave out underneath me before I could take a step.

Rayos.

I looked back at the bed to make sure Mateo was still fast asleep.

That would have been embarrassing.

I used the wall to help myself stand again, and inch by inch, I made my way to his en-suite bathroom.

Que Chingados?

My face was every array of color imaginable under the black and blue spectrum, and my bad eye was just now starting to open up. My black hair was dull and lackluster, riddled with knots and tangles throughout. My neck sported a colorful purple and yellow hue in the shape of the leather belt I had been dragged around by for most of the night.

Gathering the courage I needed to face my newest demon, I spun away from the full-length mirror and sipped a large inhale before turning my head to inspect the rest. A gasp tumbled its way out of me as I stared into the flogging gash that split my back open like a fault line.

My eyes pooled with tears, and I reached behind to graze my fingers along it, but it was more sensitive than I could have imagined. I pulled back immediately and turned around.

Monstrua.

I hurt a lot of people in my life, and I somehow had also been on the receiving end plenty of times as well. This was a new kind of horror I hadn't seen yet for myself, and yet somehow it was the clearest reflection of who I was inside, now shining on the exterior.

How fitting.

"I was waiting for you to wake up to call the Doc. Are you ready?" Mateo's soothing, deep voice cut through the fog of my self-deprecating thoughts.

He stood at the entrance of the bathroom leaning an elbow on the wall, his eyes full of a sadness that I knew was directed at me. I nodded and wanted to respond but my voice cracked, and my throat burned when I tried.

"Don't talk yet. Do you want to eat something?" He asked me sweetly, and I nodded again.

He took his shirt off and handed it over to me. I painstakingly put it on, feeling the fabric burn against my fresh wound while I fought a wince. He grabbed me by the hand and walked me to the kitchen. If he noticed my awkward limp, or my clear discomfort he didn't mention it, and I appreciated it. Being weak was not my strong point.

Being helpless, even more so.

He pulled the stool out from the island for me and then walked to the other side before opening the refrigerator.

"I'm uh, I'm not the one who usually cooks. But everyone else is asleep so it looks like you'll have to settle." He looked back and gave me a smirk. As terrible as every part of me felt, I couldn't help but return it. There was just something about Mateo when he gave you a smile that wasn't totally coated in crazy that could melt the ice inside you.

I took a quick glance at the oven clock, and it read a little past one-thirty. Either I slept an hour or two or I slept a full day, and by how trashed my body felt, I honestly didn't know for sure. Mateo dropped a glass of juice in front of me and put a straw through it before pushing it towards me. "Little sips," he instructed, and I nodded again.

I couldn't control the moan that came from the deepest part of my soul as the orange juice coated my tongue and slid down my throat. It was the first thing I'd consumed since I'd last been in their care. And though their version of kennels was a five-star hotel compared to the basement of the assholes who had taken me, I wouldn't have considered it being cared for in any way.

"Not too much!" He pulled the straw from my lips, and I groaned in protest. "Don't want you getting sick." He pulled out a carton of eggs, some butter from the fridge, and a pan out of the cabinet before turning the gas on the cooktop. Before I knew it, there were slightly overdone scrambled eggs in front of me and a bottle of ketchup. I raised my eyebrow at him, but I couldn't stay silent on this one.

"What the hell is wrong with you?" I laughed out in a raspy voice that resulted in a dry cough and a pained look I couldn't fake away.

"There is no better way to eat scrambled eggs than with ketchup. Trust me," he said confidently as he crossed his arms over his chest and dipped his head at me to try the food.

"This is an abomination. Haven't I suffered enough?" I joked, but his attitude deflated, and he turned back to the fridge. Before he could grab the ketchup from the counter, I snagged it and squeezed a glob onto my plate.

"Let it be known, I wasn't scared of anything," I announced, and he let out a hearty laugh at my proclamation. He cocked an eyebrow as he waited for me to judge his terrible food preferences. Maybe it was the fact I hadn't eaten in days, or perhaps the lunatic was right. That shit was good, but I wasn't going to let him know.

My ancestors would be rolling in their graves over this one.

"And?" He asked when I didn't say anything after my second or even third bite.

"It'll do," I responded without looking back up at him, but my face betrayed me when the smile tugged on the corner of my lips.

"You're damn right it will," he shook his head at my refusal to give him any more than that and he began to clean up after himself while I finished my food.

"How long was I gone?"

"Three days."

"And how long have I been asleep?" I asked again.

"Give or take a day, you were really heavily drugged," he said, and his expression turned serious before he continued, "You actually overdosed. Ronan saved your life."

"Oh." My thoughts were running wild, *Ronan* saved me?

Ronan who couldn't spend two seconds around me without treating me like I was the worst person to ever walk this Earth–Ronan? Ronan who hate-fucked me like it was the only way he could tolerate to be around me without murdering me?

No. Absolutely not.

"There's something else too." He scratched the back of his head nervously and I pushed my empty plate at him, this time it was my turn to wait for a response. "It's hard to explain, but... it's probably better I tell you instead of waiting for Zerkos to come back up." He wasn't rushing to tell me whatever it was, and the silence kept dragging on until I could practically feel my anxiety floating around in the room like a tangible thing.

"Spit it out! You're making me nervous," I rubbed my arms, trying to figure out what else could have happened that I didn't remember.

"We know who you are, Celia Flores." He looked straight into my eyes as he said my birth name, and there was something hypnotizing about the way the dark vortex of our gazes collided when we looked at each other like this.

Like there was only us in the chaos of the entire universe.

I was drowning in the pitch black of his stare before I could snap back to reality and focus on the words that came out of his mouth.

It was like the ground had been removed from right under me, I was floating, waiting to free fall and lose everything once again. I hadn't been Celia Flores in twenty-two years, I certainly didn't expect the name to be casually tumbling out of Mateo Kane's mouth.

"What did you call me?" I shook my head slightly, hoping maybe I could still play it off with denial, and maybe he didn't have enough proof to back it up.

"Don't lie to me, I won't ever tell you a second time. You have no reason to lie to me and you never will. Do you understand?" His serious tone sobered up any lightness that still floated through the room as he growled out at me, stunning me with his command. He pulled his phone out of his pocket and a low-quality video played on it but I only needed a few seconds to know what he was showing me in his hand.

"Turn that off." I looked away, tears pooling in my eyes as I did my best to contain them, but my body was wrecked, my mind was torn, and my soul was fractured.

Somewhere in the remnants of that war raging inside me, my heart had been protected by the thick layer of ice I built around it long ago. Now, I felt every emotion I'd suppressed since I was a little girl, slamming its way through the dam. The after effect of the drugs heightening my emotions as they battery rammed their way out of me.

A sob fought its way out and Mateo put his phone away quickly.

"No, no, no Sunshine," his voice softened as he rushed around the kitchen island and wrapped his arms around me. I melted into his embrace, letting go of the pretense for once while he let me cry on his shoulder.

"Ronan has seen that?" I asked without looking at his face after we returned to his room, sitting back down on his bed.

"He's probably watching them right now. *All* of them. Then he'll probably turn a punching bag into dust in the gym again," he said, and my eyes widened in reaction. I had no idea where Ronan and I stood anymore. I wasn't ready to forgive him for everything he'd put me through, but I wasn't stupid enough to think I was faultless.

And he knew everything now.

He was probably furious.

"I have to get out of here," I started getting up as I frantically looked around for my things as if this had been some sort of one-night stand but there were no shoes, or my belongings anywhere to be found in his room. That's right.

I was a prisoner here, not a guest.

"You're not going anywhere," he said, carefully pushing me back down to the bed. "You asked for protection, and you'll have it. I promise I won't let anyone hurt you ever again. That includes Ronan."

His eyes told me that he truly believed the words he was saying, and I wanted to as well. The problem was that I hadn't trusted anyone in over fifteen years. How was I supposed to start now?

"I-I can't face him." I looked down while I shook my head because I couldn't face him either. He'd seen parts of me that no one else was meant to, and if he'd seen enough, he'd know that my soul was too dark and corrupted, there was no salvation for me anymore.

He knelt down between my legs as I sat on the edge of his bed, and he tilted my chin up with his index finger. His gaze washed away all of my thoughts and I was suddenly lost in this moment, just between the two of us.

"I've yet to see something you can't handle. Let's not start now." His words had talons and they sunk deep into my flesh with their truth. While they stung, they also ignited the fire within me I needed to prepare for whatever Ronan would throw my way. I didn't think things could get worse between us, but that's because I never imagined a future where he would find out.

I couldn't resist the gentle way Mateo's thumbs caressed my collar bone, his eyes burning deep into mine while he filled me with encouragement and strength. He dropped his forehead to mine and this time I knew I didn't need to fight against it.

"Before they took me…" I began, but our lips were already practically touching from our closeness. "Did you mean what you said?" I asked, too afraid of repeating the words myself.

"I don't say anything I don't mean." His hand found the back of my neck and he somehow urged me even closer. "But you'll have to be more specific."

"That you weren't here to stop me from loving him," I was breathing so heavily, I was practically panting from our proximity.

As if it was a new ritual, I wasn't wearing any underwear and with him almost kneeling between my legs I was having a hard time focusing but I just kept my gaze fixed on his lips.

It was fucked up to want him, I knew it. But I couldn't stop myself anymore, I was feeling things that made me question every black and white way of thinking that had been indoctrinated into me. There were plenty of reasons why this was a stupid bitch of an idea, number one being the angsty blonde pile of muscles who slept just a few feet down the hall.

But we didn't belong to each other, and Ronan himself said that to me not too long ago. Every time we slept together it was chaotic and hot as hell, but it was messy and left my brain and heart hurting and begging for answers I couldn't give them.

Mateo's thumb grazed my neck gently as he dropped his eyes to my bruised throat. He let out a low hum as he caressed the purple and yellow skin below his touch. "I killed him, you know?" He said looking deep into my eyes, and I shook my head, unsure what he was referring to. "The motherfucker who took you, the same one who brought you out on that stage with his belt around this beautiful neck. I killed him."

My brain was going a million miles an hour with thoughts of Ronan and Mateo colliding, it was too much to think about. My head was screaming at me, and my body was sweating out of a physical need for more of whatever the drugs those assholes had given me.

"Turned his brain to mush." He whispered in my ears like the words were an aphrodisiac, and shit, I guess they must have been, because I had to squeeze my thighs together to relieve the exploding need inside of me.

Was that a declaration of love?

I gave up and decided to just feel.

I locked my lips around his, and he pressed back with a crushing demand. Just like the first time he kissed me, I felt weak all over. He tasted like despair wrapped in sin and I ached to burn in hell for him, for the deaths he took in my name. Before our lips could even part to deepen the kiss, someone cleared their throat in the distance and my heart nearly jumped out of its cage.

"Hope I'm not interrupting. I came to change out your fluids and check on you," the doctor said, making her way into the room as she cocked an eyebrow at Mateo and her heels clicked beneath her.

He shrugged his shoulders and before I could protest, he was pulling the t-shirt off of me for Emory to see. She gasped in horror and ran over to me with startled eyes like this was the worst thing she had ever seen in her life.

I wish it had been the worst thing *I'd* ever seen, but unfortunately, it didn't even scratch the surface. It was just one of the most permanent things I'd endured. This one would physically mark me forever. It was gruesome, but I had done far worse to fewer deserving people than myself before I even turned eighteen, and in some sick way it felt like a righteous punishment.

"Lay down on your stomach," she instructed as I lifted my arms up for Mateo to pull the shirt completely off of me, feeling the burn in my cheeks as his eyes shamelessly wandered over me. "They didn't tell me about this over the phone." She said being completely honest about the fact she wasn't prepared.

"Didn't you put the IV in me?" I asked her, thinking she had already been here before.

"No, I talked Zerkos through it over the phone. He wanted to make sure you were comfortable," she said with a convicting tone, and I looked away, pushing my guilt down. I hadn't done anything wrong. "How are you feeling after the Narcan?" She put her doctor face back on.

"A little nauseous, my head is killing me, and I would probably suck a dick for another jab right now if I'm being honest," she eyed me suspiciously with those words, but it was true.

It was the worst, most terrible, fantastic poison I'd ever had the misery of enduring in my life. Ever since I woke up, all I could think about was getting back to that floaty place where my memories didn't haunt me, my past wasn't chasing me, and I had never hurt anyone.

"I'm kidding," I said with a flat tone hoping to ease her worried expression, but I think we both knew I wasn't, and I didn't really have any reason to bullshit Emory. She didn't care for it, and I didn't have the energy.

The doc took out her equipment ritualistically, set up a new IV drip, and attached it to the top of my hand. I groaned at the annoying feeling of the needle, but I knew I was still severely dehydrated and was thankful after just a few minutes once my headache began to dissipate. She checked over the rest of my body, making sure there were no other areas of concern, and applied an ointment to my wrists where the zip ties cut into my flesh.

"I want to clean and dress the wound, but before I do, I want to make sure you're comfortable. I'm gonna be honest with you Cecilia, I don't want to give you painkillers for this after you overdosed," she looked at me as she began to pull out her kit from her bag in the same way she did when she cared for my stab wounds. "I'm going to numb the area with lidocaine injections so that we can do this without pain, okay? You're going to feel multiple stings."

Mateo slipped his hand into mine and I nodded my head, but I didn't expect the needle to come so fast and burn so painfully deep. She made quick work and I squeezed tight against Mateo's hand with every stab of the needle across the fractured skin. After probably fifteen pokes, my back was starting to feel some relief as the medicine worked its way under my skin and numbed the pain.

Emory cleaned my back in detail and Mateo sat silently. He knew who I was, but he wasn't running away in fear. He wasn't screaming in anger or channeling it through his fists or his fucks like Ronan. He wasn't hiding and keeping away from me like I felt Santos doing. He was here, by my side. And while I was having a hard time keeping a grip on my reality, I knew that meant everything.

"Don't bandage me yet," I rasped out and she looked at me curiously.

"I'd like to shower while I'm still numb," I explained, and she nodded in understanding.

"I can leave a few syringes with you, and if you can't stand the pain then you can have one of the guys administer it again. It would be a pretty impossible thing to get wrong," she said as she pulled out extra syringes and Mateo helped me back to a seated position on the bed. "I'll leave the extra bandages so someone can wrap you up after you're clean."

When the IV bag was almost empty I shoved my hand in her direction in a silent request for her to remove the needle from my skin and looked away. Yup, I was definitely okay with mid-level torture, but couldn't handle the sight of a needle.

There was no point in trying to win them all.

I grabbed the shirt and bundled it up in front of my chest to cover myself as best I could, but at this point, I had little dignity left in my reserves. No, the Bulldog and Scarface drained it all out of me. A small smile tugged at the corner of my lips when I remembered Mateo saying he killed the Bulldog.

"A word Kane?" She said to him after she packed all of her items back up into her little doctor briefcase and stood by the bed in the same way she did with Ronan the last time I saw her.

"No," he said to her, shocking the hell out of me as he still held my hand and didn't spare a glance in her direction at all.

"Fine. I'll say it here then. She just went through something immensely traumatic. Keep your dick out of the equation if you care about her," she said angrily, then mumbled something about thinking I was Ronan's girl on her way out of Mateo's room. I exhaled heavily, the awkwardness from our unfinished kiss still clearly hanging over us.

"Do you want to help me with that shower?" I asked and he nodded, pulling me up by the hand and I let my shirt drop to the ground as I stood up off the bed.

I made my way to the bathroom slowly, Mateo was already adjusting all the shower settings and waiting for me to hobble in. I couldn't help myself, I turned my head back towards the mirror behind me again, mesmerized at the atrocity that was now permanently branded onto my body forever.

"It'll heal. And it'll fade," he promised, seeing the look in my eyes through the mirror as our dark stares found each other again.

He extended his hand my way and I took it willingly as he opened the large shower glass door for me. He was still shirtless from giving me his, and now that the pain was no longer screaming for my attention, I could direct some of it towards the perfectly sculpted abs that adorned his body and the lickable V peeking out through his shredded jeans.

He undid his pants while leaving his boxers on and followed me into the shower, promptly removing the detachable showerhead from the wall and using it to avoid getting my back too wet now that the doc cleaned it. The hot water felt amazing against my bruised and battered body and all I wanted was to make permanent residence inside that shower.

Mateo cleaned every inch of me with a loofah and soap while I stood, my only job was to keep myself upright and I felt like I was truly nailing it. I was expecting a repeat of the last time we were both in this bathroom, when he scrubbed me in a most deliciously sensual way, but it seemed like the doc's words got to him and he was holding back. His sight was fixed on my eyes as if nothing else mattered, there was something unsettling about that, like he could see into my soul now and he knew exactly who I was.

Rayos.

Nobody was supposed to know who I was, I'd grown accustomed to it that way.

He left the water on but helped me out of the shower and draped a thick, luxurious towel around me that somehow was still warm. He pulled a packaged toothbrush from a drawer and tore the wrapping off before putting the toothpaste on and handing it to me. I winced at the pain of moving my shoulder but fought through it as I brushed my teeth and he slid back into the shower.

He removed his soaking wet boxers and began to wash, while I stood there, unmoving, watching. The fogged glass didn't do much to hide the monstrous beast that had been fighting through his boxers as it was sprung free and jerked to life. My lips licked instinctively, and I wasn't sure if I was supposed to look away, or was I supposed to leave the bathroom? I couldn't even bring my head up at this point to stare at anything but it, and I knew he probably already noticed exactly where my eyes were directed.

I heard a dark chuckle, and I turned my head to the side, heat flooding my cheeks from getting caught, but so what? How many times had he seen my body now with no remorse or sense of shame? He was built like a fucking God, and I wasn't going to pretend like it wasn't doing anything for me because lies didn't serve me anymore.

As if he knew exactly what he was doing to me, he lingered in that shower, spending way too much of his time and effort lathering up the giant thing hanging in between his legs. I might as well have pulled up a chair and taken photos at this point, I made no effort to preserve any innocence between us and look away as my eyes trailed back up to find his were still very much fixed on me.

Once he dried off, he slipped on a fresh pair of boxers and instructed me to lay on the bed again, with my back exposed. He strategically placed the gauze on as much of my back that was physically possible then wrapped a medical bandage around my entire torso. He even went as far as wrapping it across my shoulder where the gash ended right above my collar bone.

I was a glorified mummy from the waist up, except the bandage was pushing up on my tits like an eighteenth-century corset and if I tried hard enough, I could have probably licked my own cleavage at how far up they'd been squashed.

"What time is it?" I asked him, wondering how much longer I had until real life came tumbling down and I would have to worry about Ronan rampaging his way in here to demand the answers he clearly already got on his own.

I was a little angry that he couldn't leave well enough alone and went digging behind my back. I knew I didn't have that right, and it was my screw up entirely but I absolutely needed someone else to blame right now, and fuck it, he'd do.

"Nearly three-thirty," he grabbed a remote next to his bed and clicked a button that had darkening electric shades sliding down covering every inch of glass in his room.

Mateo opened his closet to pull a shirt out for me and I extended my arms forward to help him dress me, already so used to the way he cared for me and not at all opposed to being on the receiving end of his devotion.

Even the deadliest nightshade could appreciate the kindness of a raindrop.

I kneeled on the bed and waited for him to make his way around the room, that was when I finally noticed all the instruments were gone.

"Where are your things?" I scrunched my eyebrows in the middle while I looked around the room curiously, like they might appear at any moment.

"They um, they were casualties," he pressed against his temple as he made his way to the bed and scoffed. "I can't believe I said that, Fletcher's in fucking intensive care. They were just instruments."

"Fletcher's alive?" I practically yelled, my shock, so apparent but how could I have thought anything but the worst when I saw his body lying in a pool of blood too massive for anyone whose heart was still beating? I heard the way his body hit the ground with that sick lifeless thud that I knew and recognized all too well.

There was just something about the noise made by a soulless vessel when it fell to the floor.

Nothing else could create that sound.

"Yeah, you saved both their lives when you threw that key back in the kennel and distracted that ugly fucker." Relief drenched me in a powerful wave with the realization that my efforts weren't in vain and that at least something good came out of my misery.

"Good," I said, pressing my lips into a flat line. "That doesn't mean you aren't allowed to be upset that your things were ruined. I'm sure some of those instruments were irreplaceable."

"Maybe that's the lesson I needed. Maybe that was my punishment for leaving something so rare and beautiful unguarded," he said, looking straight into my eyes as if he wasn't talking about his piano or the cello anymore. "Let's sleep now, Ronan will want to talk to you as soon as he wakes up." He turned off the lights with those words and covered himself with the blanket before turning away from me and leaving me feeling a sense of rejection I knew would eat away at me all night.

"Thank you, Mateo," I barely whispered before laying on my side facing the opposite direction. Sleep would come easily, sure. But it would only be another hour or so before the bucket of water woke me up again.

35

CECILIA

I was in the middle of another dream where my sister and I were children again. They were happening often now, and my heart ached at the memory of my favorite person, constantly haunting me and telling me that I'd failed her. In the dark of the dream all of a sudden, her face morphed into another, and I felt hands groping and reaching for me from all directions.

Hands that reached and grabbed me without permission, touching every inch of my body. Hands that roughly undressed me, and stole away my will, my ability to fight back. Hands that washed me with too much vigor and didn't care that I was crying out in pain. I heard my name being called but I couldn't respond, the drugs were making me drool and my tongue was too swollen to answer.

I'm here! Please get me the fuck out of here!

How did I end up in this box again?

I crawled back against the cold concrete until I felt the lion's hot breath against the vicious split crossing my back. The sharp sting of cold water hit me once again right before he could bite. I woke up gasping for air in a panic, but Mateo was already there holding me by the shoulders, like he'd been trying to coax me out of the nightmare for a while. I looked over his shoulder to see the phone brightly lit, four eighteen mocking me on his lock screen as another sleepless night passed by.

"You're okay now. You're okay," he reassured me, but I shook my head, knowing that I wasn't, that I'd never been, and would probably never get to *be* okay ever again.

Still, I just kept moving forward anyway.

I was piling trauma on top of trauma as if it were the thread that was stitching together the shell of the person I'd become. With gentle hands he held my face, pressing his forehead into mine, breathing deeply as he continued to murmur the soft encouragement.

But that wasn't what I needed. I needed to feel something other than the blemish those monsters left on me. I didn't hesitate this time, I kissed him with no reservation left in my body. I knew now that Mateo wouldn't hurt me. He continued to prove it to me over and over again and I wouldn't fight him on it, not anymore.

He broke the kiss, "We shouldn't." A frown forming above his eyes with his words, "You heard Emory."

"She doesn't know me, she doesn't know what I can or can't handle." I responded as I climbed over him and straddled his waking erection.

"You just went through hell," his frown didn't let up.

"I've been going through hell since I was a child. Don't deny me this. I can feel their hands all over me, touching me without my permission." I was starting to break, and I didn't want to do it in front of him again, but it looked like my body wasn't going to give me a choice as I began to shake from fighting the tears. "I don't want to feel them on me anymore. I want to feel something else." I fought the cracks tearing at my edge, "Please, Mateo."

He leaned forward, abandoning all reservation and initiating the kiss, his lips pressing into mine, softer and warmer than I expected. I surrendered to the heat of our connection, moaning against his tongue as it collided with mine, wiping away every worry that clouded my brain. There were too many emotions, too many feelings, and too many dark callous thoughts. In a sudden movement, he repositioned us so that we were both sitting now, me on his lap, firmly against his erection, and him with his back against the headboard.

"There's no going back if we do this. I won't let you get away, I won't let you leave. Do you understand what that means?" There was a wild look in his black-as-night eyes that somehow burned brighter with his question.

I nodded, knowing damn well I would have agreed to anything to liberate my mind, to replace this feeling with anything the only thing that could fix me. The only thing I so desperately needed.

Him.

Mateo kept one hand behind my neck, trailing the other between my thighs. My heart spiked, the anticipation already more than I could handle, my breath hitching at the light touch of his fingers barely grazing over my already dripping center.

I gasped at the teasing motion, feeling a smirk draw at his lips from my reaction. Two could play that game, I didn't think twice before reaching into his boxers and wrapping my hand around his thick, veiny shaft. I pumped up and down a few times until I let my thumb rub against the tip of his cock in a slow, torturous way that left him growling in my ear.

"Tell me that you want this. Because once I bury my cock deep in that pussy of yours, you won't ever forget what it feels like to have me inside you again." He gritted out, lifting my chin up to look at him.

"I want this. I need you." I confirmed again what we both couldn't deny.

He pushed my hand off his erection and in one smooth move he grabbed my ass with both hands and lifted me off his lap, just enough to guide the head of his dick into my entrance.

There was no follow through. He held me there, suspended in the air, too many questions floating through his chaotic mind, keeping him from pulling the trigger.

With a quiet whimper I squirmed against him, desperate to feel more.

I knew we'd lose this moment if he kept trying to follow with logic. So I decided for us, instead. I dropped my hands to his shoulder, pushing down with all my weight, feeling the delicious thickness of his size stretching me with a slight sting.

Biting my lips through the feeling of fullness, I stopped halfway, not wanting to do something he wasn't a hundred percent on board with, but also not wanting him to take this away from us. I raised my eyes to meet his.

"Do you remember what I said the first day you showed up here?" He growled against my lips, holding me in place, not letting me come down any further.

I shook my head at him as I waited nervously, needing so badly for more, for anything, as long as it came from him.

"I told you I didn't fuck anyone who didn't beg me for it, Sunshine," his lips curved, a dark, twisted smirk displaying.

I felt his hands on my ass, squeezing tight before pulling my cheeks apart. Fighting the moans and whines became the hardest game of all, attempting to stay quiet while he proceeded to continue his torment, teasing the swollen clit between my legs until I gave him what he wanted.

"Please...Please...Please," I chanted, not caring how desperate I sounded.

Whatever shame I might have felt for begging didn't last a second after he thrust his hips up, stabbing into me with his full length. I gasped, his size more than I had been prepared for. Mateo laid there, unmoving, giving me the time I needed to adjust to him inside me before I began to move.

He guided my hip with one hand, and with the other, touched my clit, making circles with his fingers that had my head spinning and my body begging for release. With each stroke he took more control, moving me to his own tempo as he sped and slowed our movements at his own demand.

"You're a fucking marvel." He whispered in my ear, "I wish you could see yourself bouncing on my cock like this."

I didn't need to see, I could feel it, I was a symphony, and he was conducting me in the most melodic way. I was riding him but somehow, he was the one in control. The crescendo was building, and all I wanted was to unwind that tight coil that had been building in my core, but it wouldn't unwind. No, it would explode and shatter out of me like a window breaking through a hurricane. I'd been drowning on my own for so long, but now I was fully submerged in the ocean that was Mateo Kane and I never wanted to come up for a breath again.

His fingers worked magic between my legs, as if they had been charged with lighting. It took only a few more precise pinches and I was gasping and whimpering, biting back my screams. He thrust into me mercilessly, coaxing an earth-shattering climax out of my body that pulled him right under the waves with me. I could feel the pulse of his cock through his orgasm, his release emptying into me, his gaze never straying from mine.

"No way around it now," he husked, grabbing my face with both of his large hands and pressing his lips to mine once more. "You're mine."

My brain had completely shut off at this point, and my body was being driven by the primal urge to be with him, to bring life to this connection between us. I ground against him, no end in sight as he continued exploring my body with his hands and my mouth with his tongue, his cock stirring back to life inside me.

We began to move again, slower this time as he let me control the speed. I moved lazily, closing my eyes, and really getting to know every inch of him as it claimed its way deep inside me.

Mateo ran his hands over the bandages that covering my nipples and snarled against my mouth in disapproval even though he was the one who wrapped me. I brought my hands to the top of his shoulders and focused on the pleasure building deep within my core again as I tipped my head back with bliss.

"Fuck...Yes..." Mateo groaned as he lowered his back to the bed and let me grind against him in a meticulous way that had another climax quickly begging to be unleashed. "Use my cock to make yourself come, Sunshine," the filthy words made me clench around him tighter.

I could feel my wetness mixed with his cum starting to drip out of me with every bounce and thrust, but I didn't care, and by the look on his face, I would have wagered he didn't mind too much either.

He moved his attention back to between my legs, but I was still too sensitive from the previous orgasm to be touched.

That dimpled smirk showed it self as he moved my hands out of the way, rubbing those sensitive nerve endings regardless. I held my breath from the hot intensity of his fingers against my clit, and unravelling into another mind-bending, full-body orgasm that, for once, had me unable to scream, or make any single noise.

I collapsed on his chest from exhaustion, his panting heavy, chest rising and falling against my weight as we synced our breathing.

Mateo pulled me closer to him, squeezing me even tighter into his chest. Was he planning to sleep like this, his dick still inside of me? My questions were answered at the first sound of his snore. Closing my eyes, I surrendered, letting sleep take me away again for another torturous hour, before the next bucket of water would surely come.

It was nearly six when I woke up again, this time I managed to do it a little quieter than the last, or maybe he was just that tired from all my wakeups, because Mateo stayed well asleep next to me. I could feel a heated stare lasering in, and I didn't have to look at the shadow sitting in the corner to know who was there. I struggled my way into a sitting position, trying to hide how much pain I was in.

"You let him fuck you," he said, the coldness in his tone was enough to splinter me into pieces, but why he cared, was beyond me.

"Actually, I think technically I fucked *him*," I said the words like a weapon, sharp and ready to wound, but regretted it immediately. I don't know why I cared if it upset Santos that I slept with Mateo, but I couldn't ignore the hurt in his voice. Even if I didn't think he had a right to be.

I wasn't anyone's.

I wasn't a prize to be won or a princess in a tower who needed claiming.

They all seemed to be trying to figure out who my body belonged to, and they were going to have a harsh reality check once they realized that person, was me.

It was impossible to look past the fact that when I needed Santos, when I came to him for help, he stood by while they threw me in that cage and let Ronan hurt me. I looked back at the black-haired mystery next to me and sighed heavily knowing I had already forgiven Mateo for everything he'd put me through the last few months, even if I didn't think I was ready to tell him that just yet. So did Santos deserve to be blamed for Ronan's mistakes?

Groaning as I slid my legs against the satin sheets, I worked my way off the bed so as not to wake him. I almost fell once both my feet hit the ground, my legs not quite ready to walk just yet. Santos moved toward me as if to help, but then frowned, correcting himself instead. I hissed from pain as I clutched the wall and used it to get myself up.

"Promise me you won't tell Ronan yet," I looked him in the eyes, some part of me knowing it wasn't fair to pit them against each other.

I needed to tell Ronan on my own terms. I couldn't risk him taking this out on Mateo.

Not over me.

He growled out a wordless response and darted his eyes towards his sleeping friend.

"Let's go," he said, tugging at my wrist and pulling me towards the door.

"Where?" Was all I could muster, but my brain was going a million miles an hour and Santos' strange demeanor was making me anxious. I tried to fight the panic that wanted to claw its way out, but even though I knew damn well he wasn't fully capable of putting me in that box, there was something about him that wasn't right tonight.

"We need to talk–*now*," the coldness tone in his voice confirmed my fears were right.

36

SANTOS

I had eleven days to solve a problem with no solution. Cecilia looked like she had been on the receiving end of a brutal beatdown, which was upsettingly tugging at every decent part of me, telling me to hold her and make sure she was okay. But I wasn't an honorable man, and this wasn't a decent job, so it was easy to drown out those voices trying to control my thoughts as I tried to maneuver the situation.

I was the villain now, and I had a hit to fulfill.

Worst of all, was knowing I was a puppet in a much bigger show than I thought I was part of. Worse than that, was knowing how many innocent people were at risk if I didn't hurt the only woman whose presence I had ever truly enjoyed. The only woman who I considered my equal. There wasn't a way out of this one. Not for me.

I opened the bedroom door quietly, tilting my chin towards the hallway, wordlessly gesturing her out of Kane's room.

"We're taking a walk," I said, still keeping the cold mask in my voice so she wouldn't be able to tell how much all of this was killing me.

I walked towards the foyer where the three elevators waited for us, listening to the tapping of her bare feet against the cold marble as she followed me. I kept my gaze away from her, but I could still feel her stare searing through me.

Just a short moment later the elevator opened up to the rooftop patio. It was still a mess here, but at least the blood and bodies had been cleaned out of the pool. There were tables, chairs, and sun loungers all splintered away into pieces from the damage of the shoot-out, and not a single bottle survived in the bar.

She walked in front of me, taking in the state of the rooftop, slowly examining every destroyed piece as if she was somehow responsible for it. She wasn't, but none of that would matter anyway. Glass was still piled around the bar top and the stools. I nudged her to walk further away from it, as if preventing her from cutting her feet was somehow important right now.

Was there a nice way to kill someone?

I begrudgingly pulled the pistol out from my pants and pressed it to her lower back. She didn't turn around, but she halted, as if she could feel the gun and knew why I led her up here.

"Walk, Morena," I pushed her forward with the revolver, and she continued to walk across the rooftop until we made our way to the edge, overlooking the city.

"Are you at least going to give me the courtesy of an explanation? Or letting me look my killer in the eyes?" I scoffed at her request, pulling the gun back, but still keeping a tight hold on it as I let her turn to face me.

"You don't seem surprised," I pointed out the obvious, I didn't know what I expected. Maybe a hell of a lot more than whatever was this calm that washed over her.

"I've been waiting for death to catch up to me for a long time, Santito," she hissed the nickname out, only this time it was coated in venom. "I didn't expect it to come from you though, that's for certain. But I guess that's neither here nor there now, isn't it?" she said in an unattached way as she turned back around and leaned her elbows against the four-foot ledge. Letting me know *exactly* just how little she feared me, or her own mortality.

"A lot of people want you dead, Cecilia," was all I could muster. I was teetering a fine line. Anguish, guilt, and sorrow overwhelmed every inch of my heart. But as much as I missed my friend and wanted to take her into my arms and kill the men who hurt her. I was going to have to hurt her even worse.

"That I know, but does that list include you?" she asked without looking at me, at this point I wasn't sure if I wanted her to, either.

My facade was starting to crack, and if I didn't hurry up, there was a good chance I was going to call the whole thing off.

"No. This isn't any more my choice, than it is yours."

"What will you tell them?" She turned around, tilting her head to the side curiously.

I wasn't sure yet. Maybe I'd plant the gun in her hand and leave her up here, like a clear suicide. It wouldn't be too unbelievable after all that Ronan put her through, but the pain of that would crush him and I couldn't let him live believing he was responsible for that. All I knew was, I only had thirty minutes or so before Taylor figured out I'd looped her feed of the rooftop.

"That's not your problem to figure out," I said, putting the gun in my pants pocket as it weighed heavily in my hand from the pain of my responsibility.

She cocked an eyebrow and took a few casual steps toward me.

"Maybe it could be my choice then? Maybe you don't have to carry that burden. Maybe I can step right off this ledge and all your problems will be gone," her hands pressed to my chest as she looked up into my eyes, and I was suddenly lost, captured by the all-consuming void of her stare.

Even battered and bruised she was a vision of every dark desire and dream I'd ever conjured up. It was hard to believe there was once a time when I was a young, naive boy who thought I could actually be this girl's friend.

Friend.

What a joke. That would never be enough, and I knew now my soul would fester and rot if I had to go on with the charade I'd been keeping up for the last fifteen years. I'd once said she would be the grenade that destroyed us, but Cecilia wasn't a grenade, she was a nuclear bomb. Her damage would last long after she was dead and gone from our hold. We would never be the same again.

How could anyone be?

I'd once thought this woman was the closest thing to my salvation I would have ever known. But she would never be mine. And what I thought was my lifeline was just a mirage in the scorching desert, slowly draining me as I walked closer and closer to my own death.

That was the worst part about all of this. The relief I knew I would feel once I pulled that trigger because I wouldn't have to continue to endure the torment of not getting to have her. I wouldn't have to suffer through watching my brothers possess what so clearly would never be my own.

I was better off if she was dead.

"Why would you do that?" I looked past her, down into the street, wishing the gun was still in my hand so I could squeeze it to keep my limbs from shaking.

"Because I see you, as plainly as you see me. Your dark, your depravity, the way your soul is stained the same way mine is. People like us, were lost to that darkness, and we know our seats in hell are reserved. I've never killed someone I cared about though, and I won't let you either," her eyes were locked on mine, clearly seeing the confusion in mine from the words she just uttered.

As if she knew the weight of taking a life.

She held my face in her hands, not allowing me to look away, "I know I deserve this. You saw those videos with your own eyes."

"What videos?" I couldn't feign my alarm, breaking out of her hold as I stepped back to examine her face for any hint of a clue. If there were videos that meant my brothers were keeping something from me, which meant my circle of trust was getting smaller by the minute.

"Hmm," was all she said, looking away like she *still* wanted to keep secrets even when I was out here promising her certain death. She still couldn't give me the trust I deserved from her. The trust that I had fought for and earned.

I grabbed her by the throat and pushed her against the concrete ledge, it was the only thing that stood between her and a fall that would guarantee her end. But there was no fear in her eyes, no ounce of hesitation, even though her throat was already purple from someone else's aggression.

"Why did you come here, when you knew he couldn't forgive you?" I asked her, clenching my teeth together as I waited for her response.

"Because I knew you could," she said, not looking anywhere but into my eyes.

"Wrong."

Ronan had already come completely undone from her presence here in the last couple of months, and Mateo was obviously too far under her spell to see clearly. Not to mention the blowback that was sure to happen once Zerkos realized his best friend fucked his girl. I myself was running the risk of losing all prospect of sanity and rationale anytime even the mention of her name was spoken around me, I feared if she wasn't gone soon, we would all be in trouble.

This had to be a sign.

It *had* to be.

I pulled the gun again and stuck it right under her chin, forcing her head up so she'd have to look me in the eyes again. I could feel her pulse racing under my thumb as I still held on, just tightly enough, around her bruised throat.

"Do it," she coaxed me with barely a whisper. "I've been waiting a long time to be free."

"We don't get to be free, Morena," I pushed her into the wall so hard she had no choice but to sit on the ledge, her back to the dawn breaking. "All we get is another layer of hell after this one." She was hundreds of feet from the so-called freedom she desperately craved, but all it would take was a nudge to end her right then and there.

Do it coward. The villainous voice inside me cheered me on.

Instead, she wrapped her legs around me, using her heels to pull me into her, my hands still clutching onto her face tightly as she stared at me with what looked like desire glossing over her eyes. She licked her bottom lip, some hesitation still glimmering in her eyes letting me know we were teetering a dangerous line.

"Don't do it," I warned her through gritted teeth.

"What do I have to lose?" she asked, I wanted to answer *everything*, but before I could, her lips were on mine, pillowy soft even though they were still a bit cut up from whatever they'd done to her in that trafficking ring.

She urged me even closer, and defeat powered over me. I gave in and pressed into her body, my hand leaving her chin and grasping the back of her head while I tangled my fingers through her hair. She moaned a soft rally as my tongue slipped through the part in her lips, and the sound both jarred my cock awake and snapped me back to reality.

I broke away and turned around without looking back, marching straight through the doors, and leaving her there. If I didn't kill Cecilia Gomez, she was going to be my ruin. That much I was sure of. The only problem was, there was now something more urgent pressing into the back of my mind, and I knew my conscience wouldn't let me kill her until I'd gotten the truth.

There were videos.

Videos of what?

I made my way down to the tech lab, knowing I'd have to answer to Taylor's wrath from jamming up her rooftop feed, but she would also have the information I needed.

37

CECILIA

Well...that was a whole bag of crazy I didn't have a reaction for. I craved death more than any creature that ever walked this Earth, but somehow, I knew Santos Álvarez wouldn't be the cause of my demise. I thought surely, he was enraged by the truth of me he'd seen in those videos, that he was coming for me because he couldn't bear to let someone as vile and disturbed as me, continue to live. Someone who ruthlessly killed whoever my papá would point my way or throw into a dungeon with me.

Solo los que son fuerte aguantan. Only the strong endure.

And I fucking endured.

But his confession that he hadn't seen them was too suspicious, telling me I needed to dig deeper into this, and figure out what was going on. This was something else, and I was gonna get to the bottom of it before he ended up doing something he would regret.

I knew Santos well enough to know that whatever was bothering him would stay that way until one of us pried it from him and he likely wouldn't give us the chance. I sighed heavily as I sat on that ledge, mourning the friendship we once had. It seemed I didn't have anything else to lose any more.

Santos was now just another name on the ever-growing list of things being Celia Flores had cost me. Or maybe he'd just changed too much for me to realize I'd lost him long before I came back here. We all changed over the years, and I was better off finding out exactly who these men really were now, than to cry over the boys they used to be.

Clearly, I didn't have a clue.

I turned myself around, feet dangling in the air as I challenged death herself and basked in the glory of the sunrise. I ignored the sickening feeling in my stomach that stirred inside me just from the scenery of the height alone. I'd been locked up in some form or another these last couple of months and just getting to *exist* and breathe in fresh air, was a freedom that made me want to ignore even the basic survival instincts that were screaming at me to get down. I kept waiting for Ronan to come bursting through the door and put me over his shoulder to drag me back into the kennels, but he never came.

He was keeping his distance too, but at least with him, I knew why.

Once the pink rays began to fade into the true morning light, I decided I had enough of this so-called freedom. I resigned to my fate and decided to head back inside. Before I could even turn around on that ledge, Mateo's husky voice was in my ear forcing goosebumps all over my flesh at his proximity.

"There you are," he whispered, planting a soft kiss on the sensitive part of my neck, and I tilted my chin up towards him to give him better access. "How'd you get all the way up here?"

"Would you believe me if I said I ended up here on my own?" I questioned him with a smirk.

"Absolutely not Sunshine, after the attack, the elevator doesn't even work without our thumbprints now. But if no one is dead, and you're alright, you can keep this one secret," he said with that dimpled smirk and I turned my head and planted a kiss on his lips, my cheeks heating from the memory of last night. I felt his lips pulling into a smile letting me know his thoughts were in the same place.

"Something is going on with Santos," I said to him, unsure of how much more I wanted to give away.

"Ever since he came back from Ocean Valley," Mateo confirmed exactly what I had been thinking. He helped me spin around on the ledge so that I was still seated but facing him now, and he stepped in between my legs.

"Ronan is a loose cannon who makes his problems everyone else's. Santos is the exact opposite... he bottles it all up until all he can do is collapse under the weight of his own bullshit," he said.

"And you?" I raised an eyebrow as I tried to figure out where in that spectrum he fit.

"Somehow, I ended up as the psychopath with the healthiest form of communication methods. You can thank my therapist," he grinned this time, showing his teeth, and I couldn't help but return the expression. His hands were immediately on me, one over my breast and the other clutching the back of my head almost painfully as he pulled a kiss from me.

"I want you," I breathed out, pulling back from him, and reaching my hand into his sweatpants to find that the monster hiding inside was already awake.

He groaned out woefully and dropped his head to my shoulder.

I stroked my hand up and down, squeezing his length, feeling the thick, delicious vein that led all the way up to the tip.

"As much as I want this, we can't do it here, we need to go inside before Zerkos comes crashing through that door," he said, his voice full of regret, but I knew it was just a matter of time before I had to tell Ronan. And why shouldn't he know? I was as much Mateo's as Ronan was mine.

Whatever the hell that meant.

"It *would* be pretty fucking awkward if I walked in on you two like this wouldn't it be?" The low bravado of his voice announced his presence as if I had summoned him myself.

"Shit," Mateo mumbled, his forehead still on my shoulder as I pulled my hand out from his pants.

I raised an eyebrow at Ronan, who stood on the other side of the rooftop, leaning casually against the door with a frown on his face.

"Don't stop on my account," he pushed off the door with his foot and casually made his way over to us one step at a time, so goddamn slow I realized I was trembling the closer he got.

I hopped off the ledge and put myself in between them once I saw Ronan's hateful stare wasn't focused on me anymore but directed at Mateo. He was just inches away from me now, the anger etched into him so deeply that I had forgotten why I wanted to cause any pain to this beautiful creature in the first place.

The emerald forest in his eyes was nearly succumbing to the ring of fire around his pupils and it threatened to swallow it whole from the inside, making it so his eyes almost looked yellow.

"If you wanted to be a Crow-Slut, you should have just told me from the beginning, I would have provided much cushier accommodations. The whores stay on the third floor," he lashed out at me with his words and before I realized it my hand swung out to strike his face, he caught my wrist before I could make contact.

"Try that again. I dare you," he growled out through his teeth.

Never being one to back down from a challenge, I swung out with my free hand. He captured it as well bringing both wrists high above my head as I struggled to free myself from his hold. I squealed in anger at how his size could make me feel like a doll, a plaything in his possession.

I fought and pulled against his hold, the tear in my back burning but not stopping me. When he didn't budge, I swung my head back and bashed my forehead into his nose, forcing a pained cry from him. He brought both of my wrists into just one of his hands and grabbed my ass with the free one, pulling me against him.

"You were expensive, so unless you have a couple mil lying around, I'd behave, or you *will* regret it," he promised vengefully into my ear.

"I thought you owned me before, you spent a lot of money just to own me again," I smirked back, narrowing my eyes at him. Shit, I was royally fucked if he spent that much to save my ass.

Being indebted to Ronan Zerkos was not part of my plan.

"You're not gonna hurt her," Mateo said firmly from behind me, forcing both Ronan and me to break our staring contest and look back at him.

"I don't need to hurt her to prove a point," he huffed as he walked me backward until my ass was on that cold ledge again. My eyes widened from the shock of it against my bare skin.

38

RONAN

I spread her legs open as I stepped in between them. Giving her all of my attention, I tried forgetting about the friend I'd called brother standing to my side who'd been entangling himself deeper and deeper into my girl's web. She looked up at me through hooded eyes, her lashes long and dark as she waited for me to make a move. She was unbreakable, and now I knew exactly why. But at this moment I was the predator, and she knew damn well to play the part of prey.

I didn't understand what was going on between her and Mateo, and as much as it made me jealous enough to want to put a bullet in my brother's pretty face, it was also relieving in some ways. It was reassuring to have someone who could feel her pull and her influence in the same way I did.

It was comforting to know I wasn't the only one being driven completely mad by just a look this sorceress could bestow on us. But that didn't mean I was okay with the way he touched her like she belonged to him.

I thought about the way she reacted to me in her drugged-out state when we rescued her from Sokolov. Insecurity flooded through me as I remembered her body recoiling in a mixture of fear and anger around me. She was neither of those things now, her pupils shot, and her desire nearly palpable.

Her eyes darted to Kane, and I closed whatever distance was left between us, pressing hard against her body, and forcing a whimper from her lips. I was tired of how much space constantly separated us, it was painful to be so close and yet so far away from her.

"And what point is that?" She thought she was egging me on, but her voice was coated in lust and there was no hiding the electricity between us.

"That you'll be mine till the end," I pressed my forehead into hers, breathing her in, thankful just to touch her once more. Not wanting to risk the pain of losing her again, I could temper my jealousy.

For now.

"Tell me I'm wrong. Tell *him* I'm wrong," I said through clenched teeth, and her eyes darted to him before she shook her head in refusal.

"Good girl," I muttered the praise in her ear, pulling a shudder from her body. The way she could still physically react to me let me know I was right, I still owned a piece of her heart and I couldn't throw that chance away. If I had a granule of her affection, I would tend to it until it became a field again. Because if the last three days taught me anything, it was that I couldn't exist without Cecilia again.

She was worse than any drug, any injury, any curse that could ever plague me on this Earth. She was my undoing, and I would unravel in her presence until there was nothing left but the fibers of my being. How I failed to see all the darkness in her before was beyond me. She wasn't the cause of the splinters in my heart, she was the pitch-black shards themselves that were lodged inside me.

The kind of woman Satan himself would fear.

After all, if you're going to dance with the devil, you might as well lead.

And my girl knew how to tango.

I pulled her by the back of her hair, exposing her throat to me and forcing a gasp from her lips. I sunk my teeth into her neck as she cried out in pain, her hands clawing at my shoulders, giving me back equal parts of what I dished out.

As I ran my tongue up her bronze neck, her feet instantly wrapped around my waist, pulling me against her. I grazed my lips along her jaw, a half-smirk I couldn't hide if I tried to, as our lips found each other, and I pushed my way into her mouth with a groan.

My cock was straining against my pants at the sight of her. Even with bruises decorating her body she was the most sinful temptation, a product of hell itself. No, she was its queen, and I would just be the hound at her feet to do her bidding. Content with whatever scrap of herself that she could toss my way. I didn't want to believe that Kane was right, that if I stopped trying to control everything, she would stop pushing me away. Was

I just supposed to put up with the fact that my brother got to touch her in the same way I did?

If I could trust him with my life, then could I trust him with hers?

"You saved my life?" She whispered into my mouth, and I nodded a response. I didn't think she remembered the night we rescued her, I thought she was too far under the drug's hold. The memory of almost losing her caused my emotions to course through me wildly, and I never wanted to feel the way I did during the days she was gone, ever again.

"Every single time, Flower," I promised. "I'd go to hell to bring you back."

"That doesn't sound like someone who hates me."

"No, it doesn't," I confirmed, and she pressed harder into my ass with the heels of her feet as I reached in between us, until my hand found her center, slick and waiting for me.

"Was this for him?" I asked, running my fingers over her clit as I teased her, trying to sound more curious than envious but it wasn't working.

"If I'm yours, can't he be mine?" she asked, kissing me again, but this wasn't the time to figure that out.

I shoved my fingers in and curled them, pulling a moan from deep within her throat as she arched into me, and locked her wrists around my neck. I responded by taking my free hand and grasping the back of her neck as I leaned her over the edge, causing her eyes to widen as I bent over her body. She was so close to free-falling from that ledge, but it wasn't fear dancing through those dark eyes, it was exhilaration.

I pulled my fingers out from inside of her and brought them up to my own lips to taste her sweet nectar. I finally turned my attention to my brother, knowing damn well he already crossed that line anyways.

"Nothing tastes quite like her, right?" I shot him a half-smirk, narrowing my eyes at him, daring him to answer, but he just folded his arms over his chest and leaned back to watch the show. A smile of contentment fought to let loose over his face, but he was playing the long game.

And he played it smart.

I freed myself from my pants and in one swift motion the hard length of my cock was pressed to her entrance, and she urged me on, digging her nails into my forearms. I pushed myself to the hilt, groaning in satisfaction at feeling the molten hotness of her pussy surrounding me, closing in on me so tightly all I could do was revel in it while we both adjusted to each other.

She impatiently ground her hips against me, trying to take pleasure in any way she could.

"Patience little flower, I'm going to make you scream." I whispered the promise into her ear while I brought my hand to her hip, still keeping her dangling over the ledge as I pulled out and slammed my way in hard enough to pull a cry from her lips. I kept up the pace, grinding her clit against me every time we made contact to give her the friction she so craved.

"Oh Fuck!" she cried out as her orgasm took her by surprise with the last thrust and the shockwaves of pleasure that crashed through her were enough to send me over the edge as well.

We came together with ragged breaths, and I lifted her back up to a seat on the ledge before pulling out from inside of her, not bothering to deal with the mess as I stuffed myself back into my pants. I began to turn away and she grabbed my face with both of her hands, and a scowl appeared on her face.

"This means nothing," she said, her words, a dagger lodged deep inside of me, and pulling it out would only leave me worse off.

"Whatever lies you want to keep telling yourself. We have quite a lot to discuss, *Celia*. Clean up, I'll have breakfast waiting in the penthouse," I said bitterly, marching towards the door and leaving both of them up there, unable to look back—a chaotic inferno blazing through my mind, burning away at my soul.

You don't have to lose her. So don't lose her.

Easier said than done.

How do you keep a forest from burning when you're the one holding the pyre?

How do you explain to the forest that it's just the fire's nature to burn?

I made my way back to the penthouse, placing an order on an app at a nearby breakfast place for the works. She looked so tiny, frail and beaten—nothing like my fierce girl. Despite how furious I was at the weight of the secrets Cecilia had been keeping from me, I was struggling to feel anything but relief at having her back here with us again and I knew I had to keep her safe. Knowing she *came* from this world only made it so that it would be significantly harder to protect her than I previously thought.

If the Cártel found out she was with us, they would come to collect.

I needed to hear it from her.

I just needed the truth now, it was too late for anything but that.

I walked past Santos' room, the door was open, and he was sitting on the edge of his bed, elbows on his knees and his hands running through his hair.

"You were just gonna keep all of that shit from me man?" he said, his voice coated in a darkness that made the hairs on my arms stand.

"I hadn't decided yet. You've been acting... off. I thought maybe you needed time," I confessed, not at all bothered by the decision I made to protect him.

"Hmm," he huffed out and followed it with a laugh that chilled me down to my bones and made my gut churn. "Funny how that works, huh?"

"What's going on with you? Talk to me," I stepped into his bedroom but didn't go any further than the door.

"I deserved better from you. You know she's screwing Kane, right? You can't be that stupid," he looked at me with a sneer etched into his face as he waited for my answer.

"I'm...working through it," I said through my teeth, earning another look from him.

He raised an eyebrow at me, and I exhaled through my nostrils in annoyance. When I didn't say anything more, he began to put a jacket on, and I blocked the doorway with my arm before he could get past.

"You're not even going to see her?" I needed to figure out what was going on with him, and maybe if anyone could get through to him, it was her.

"Yeah, I saw her already. Naked in Kane's bed this morning," he pushed my arm out of the way and walked past me towards the elevators.

And I was supposedly the one with anger issues.

But for the first time in a long time, I wasn't feeling that burning rage inside me anymore, the one I saw so clearly in Santos now. The kind of anger that rooted so deeply inside of you, and it would consume you from within like a hunger, until that dark craving went satisfied. I needed to know what was killing my brother. Because what was ruining me was the ghost of Cecilia. Kane was right, she wasn't the girl I once loved, and I owed it to her to find out who she really was.

The thought that she was here right now because she wanted to be, kept circling my head over and over. Maybe she was here more out of necessity than desire, but she *did* want this. But she also wanted him. And that was too many levels of screwed up to consider. I quickly made my way to my room, putting on "Devil's Dance" by Metallica to play through my sound system while I hopped into the shower, letting the cold water hit me, jarring all my nerves awake as I used the shock of it to clear my head of all this noise.

39

CECILIA

Bouncing between the wild range of emotions these guys were throwing my way was giving me whiplash. I felt like a Goomba stuck on a treadmill while Wario threw bananas and bombs my way, I had no way to avoid them without getting off.

If I was being honest with myself, I wasn't necessarily sure I wanted off.

Between Ronan's possessive hold on me, and Mateo's attentive care, I was starting to feel more alive than I had in so many years. Like the broken pieces of who I once meant to be were beginning to come together again, joining to heal, and form the scar tissue that would fix my fractured soul.

I didn't wait for Ronan to get inside before jumping off the ledge and following him in, unsure if I could even look at Mateo at this very moment. Was I embarrassed? No, that wasn't it. It was just *weird*. Maybe because of the fact that I didn't know how to say no to Ronan.

And saying no would be a lie.

Sex was supposed to be private, wasn't it? Sure, he said it himself that he wasn't going to stop me from loving Ronan, but surely this wasn't what he meant. And what the hell was Ronan doing? He said he was proving a point, and maybe I was dumber than I thought because it went way over my head.

"That was so unbelievably fucking hot," Mateo whispered in my ear, bringing his hand to my low back as he walked next to me. He tucked a flyaway strand of hair behind my ear, "I think watching you come is my new favorite pass-time. It was even better in person."

Goosebumps covered my body from his words, and I turned my gaze to the ground, the heat in my cheeks was absolutely unbearable and I realized the "point" must have also gone over his head.

If Ronan was trying to tell Mateo that he and I would never stop, then Mateo just basically responded by saying "and"? I didn't know what to make of any of it, or how to feel about someone being okay with sharing me? Did that mean he would expect me to be okay with sharing him too? The thought made me nauseous, and I grabbed Mateo's arm, he looked at me in alarm at my expression.

"I'm not okay with you putting your dick in another woman," I blurted out with a possessiveness to my voice that made me unsure of who I even was anymore.

He chuckled at me, "No, of course not. I'd be too afraid of what you'd do to *their* faces." And there was that look again that always brought me to my knees, I bit my lip, and shrugged off the fact that I could *somehow* still be cringe as fuck when it came to men, of all things. I understood how to run a criminal organization better than I knew how to deal with dating or navigate jealousy.

Was this dating?

No I don't think we could call this that.

The elevator opened up when we got back down to the penthouse, and I exhaled in surprise to find Santos on the other side of the door. He looked extremely annoyed, and I would bet it had something to do with the fact that I was probably thwarting his plan to avoid me again.

Of course, my own nature made me want to dig through whatever was wounding him, so we could fix it together. Like we always did.

"Can we talk? Please?" I asked, feeling Mateo squeeze my hand as if he could feel the pain between me and Santos.

"I'm on my way out, *Celia*," he muttered while giving Mateo a look that was sharp enough to cut. Mateo's eyes widened in alarm, and if I took a guess, I'd bet it had been a collective plan to keep Santos unaware of my past. Though why, I wasn't sure.

"Unlikely," Mateo's sunny disposition shone out momentarily as he draped an arm over Santos' shoulder and ushered him away from the elevator and back towards the apartment. "Nowhere to go. We're on lock-down didn't you hear? Only food comes in." He laughed, pushing Santos towards his bedroom. I followed and mouthed a "thank you" to Mateo, which he returned with a wink.

Now to deal with the brooding Mexican.

Too afraid to invade his space, but too far gone to turn back, I found myself frozen, standing just a few inches past his door.

"We used to be able to talk about everything," I said, and immediately realized it was quite possibly the wrongest thing I could have said.

"Then why'd you keep this from me for so long? You never said *anything*. Now it's out and convenient for you, you want to talk to me about it?"

"I was protecting you," I whispered so quietly, that even I had trouble hearing myself.

He scoffed in response, and I knew why.

Santos betrayed Los Muertos thousands of times to me. He shared with me every crooked thing he'd known them to be responsible for. Every scheme his cousin involved him in, even when he was just a child. We spent months planning every possible way to make enough money to get as far away from Ocean Valley and away from Guillermo's hold on him. He thought the trust between us was mutual.

Wasn't it?

I'd been telling myself for so long I'd been protecting them, but what *would* have happened if I had just been stupid enough to tell them everything?

I couldn't even contemplate an alternate reality where I could live that kind of carefree life. Even now, knowing that the three of them finally knew my secrets, was overwhelming. It was hard to fathom who I could truly be if there was nothing holding me back anymore. No story I had to adhere to.

No secrets to keep.

"I learned pretty early on that telling anyone meant signing their death warrant," I tried to stand convicted in my choices, but the tone in his voice was breaking my heart and filling me with well-deserved guilt.

He hadn't looked at me yet, and I knew exactly why. He'd seen them. Maybe not all of them, but he'd seen enough to know what kind of darkness lived inside me.

I stepped forward.

"Can you look at me?" I pleaded with a trembling tone.

"Stay the fuck away," he raised his voice as he backed up and my mouth gaped open.

"Santos," I whispered, shocked at his reaction.

"I don't even know who the fuck you are," he cried out desperately running his hands through his overgrown curly hair.

"Don't do that, you *know* me," I pleaded with him, stepping forward slowly, but he backed up again and shook his head in warning.

"No, I know the mask you've been putting on to fool everyone into thinking that you're just like everyone else. *I don't know you*," the insult cut right through me as he continued to back up and a tear fell free from my eye.

"Santos, I need you. Don't do this," my strength was fading, and I knew I would break apart soon enough without him. He had been my rock here, and now he couldn't stand the sight of me.

"What does that even mean huh?" he raised his voice with his hands in the air, the spontaneous movement forcing me to back up into the bed and fall back. "You say shit like that, and it fucks with people's heads you know?"

He was practically yelling now, and I tilted my head at him in confusion, unsure if this was about something more that he would admit to, "It's the truth. You know it is. We were family once."

"Oh, *now* I know the truth? How many people have you even killed?" He growled through his teeth. I didn't think for a second that it was a matter of judging how many lives I had taken, I knew Santos Álvarez played the executioner plenty in his life. The tattoo marking his temple may as well have been a tally sheet of bodies and his demons glared right back at me through that hazel stare.

No. It wasn't about knowing how dark the stain in my soul had been. It wasn't even about knowing if there was any sort of salvation left for me. It was about figuring out which version of me he preferred. The innocent one, or the one he could relate to.

"I don't know," I replied honestly.

"Because you've lost count?" He asked, his nostrils flaring in anticipation.

"Yes."

"We spent every single day together. How could you keep this from me? You knew what it meant to me to escape that kind of life, and yet there you were living it!" He said in an angrier tone, one I could have never imagined he was capable of using.

"What was I supposed to say? Hey, I'm Ronan's girl, my dad owned the Cártel by the way, and I've spent my entire adolescence being groomed to take his place someday. Turn on the TV please," I said, crossing my arms and standing back up to meet his eyes.

"Anything would have been better than the lies you fed us!" He screamed at me, the pain from his raw emotions too real, the wounds that I created scarred into him now, so visibly.

"All I needed from you was a few months so I could get the fuck out of this country. It didn't need to be this way. I didn't want this to hurt you, it wasn't my intention," I said, my heart breaking right inside of my chest.

"So, you would rather I never found out, than live in a world where you had someone you could trust? You're not capable of trusting though, are you?"

"It's not about trust!" I tell him as much as I tell myself. "It was about keeping you both alive!"

"You fucked with my head for the last time Morena. I don't know what you want from me, and I certainly can't give you anything you need," his lip peeled up in displeasure, and I felt every piece of my shattered soul splintering into a thousand new shards.

"It would have been better than the way you're looking at me now. Like I'm so fucked up and beyond redemption. Like you've lost hope in me. Like I'm evil," my eyes were pooling with water, but I refused to let another treacherous drop fall.

"Maybe you are evil. I can't fucking tell anymore," he said in a hushed tone that crushed my soul and I begged again.

"Santos, please," I reached forward for him.

"Just get the fuck out! All I feel for you is hate now. I hate what you did to him, and I hate what you're doing to me!" His hands pulled at his hair in distress, and I recoiled from the sting of his words. Maybe he just needed time to heal from the hurt I caused him, but for so long he had been the person I ran to when my heart was breaking the way it was now.

"You don't hate me Santos Álvarez. I don't believe that for one second," I tried to find the strength in my voice to say what needed to come out; what I hoped had been the cause of his pain, because deep down I was afraid to admit it was the cause of some of my pain too.

"I think you're scared," I approached him, and he sneered.

"Scared of what Cecilia? Or should I say Celia?" He used my name like it was a curse against all humankind, and maybe it was. Maybe, if you said it three times the ground would break open and the gates of hell would open up and swallow all of us down into the fiery pits of despair.

"Does it matter? You haven't called me by my name for as long as I can remember," I crossed my arms and when he didn't respond I continued.

"I think you're scared that maybe you're wrong. Scared that maybe what you saw in those videos were the worst thing you've seen, and you can't do anything to change it. Maybe you're afraid, because now your idea of who I am might be tainted and you can't stand to be around me longer than necessary to find out. Or maybe it's that we're so alike, that it actually petrifies you." I kept getting closer with each word I spoke until we were finally chest to chest, and I tipped my chin up to look into his eyes.

"How do you figure?" He narrowed his eyes on me.

"You understand now, I've always known the ruined pieces of our souls were the same," I tap on the tattoo on his temple letting him realize that I've been aware of *exactly* just how consumed by the shadows he was too, "and I think you're afraid of how that makes you feel. How I make you feel."

"How I feel? I feel like I don't know who you are at all," he said in a cold tone as I bravely tried to call him out.

"Maybe neither do I. Maybe all I have is the person I am when I'm around you guys. I don't want to lose that too," I confessed, reaching for his face as I tugged him into a kiss. His lips crushed into mine with the desperation of a man who had been making up for lost time, but just as quickly he broke away and pushed me off of him.

"See what I mean? What the fuck are you doing this to me for? This doesn't get to happen for us. This is the knife in my brother's back. You don't get to come between us. I won't let you ruin this," he grabbed me by the arm and dragged me to the doorway, once we crossed the threshold, he practically threw me out.

"Stay away from me, Morena. Or I *will* kill you," he warned before shutting the door in my face.

Fuck, that stung.

It felt like all the oxygen had been pulled from my lungs, and I struggled to find the will to inhale life back into me. I wanted to crawl into bed and forget I existed for the next fifteen years. But I didn't have time to react or even recover from that blow before Ronan came strutting out of his bedroom in nothing but gray sweatpants and wet hair clinging to his face. That emerald forest in his eyes clearer and more alive than I could remember ever seeing.

He made a B-line towards me and pulled my chin with his thumb and index finger before pressing a soft kiss to my lips that sent butterflies to my stomach in a sickening flutter. I turned my cheek in defiance, letting him know my momentary lapse of sanity was over, and I wasn't so easily forgiving of what he put me through the last two months.

"Let's eat. You owe me the truth. All of it," there was no anger in his expression anymore though, like the truth somehow mended a piece of him, and I nodded in agreement. We walked into the kitchen where a Game of Thrones-worthy spread was laid out over the massive island. As much as I wanted to bash his face in with a brick, he was right. I did owe him the truth.

Okay, maybe not the face. He was too pretty for that.

There were at least three different types of croissants, and probably two dozen donuts from the pink frosted with sprinkles kind to the chocolate covered with cream. I grabbed a plate and filled it with donut holes and nearly died when I saw the churros. They didn't look authentic in any way, but I would settle for now. I had just received a serious upgrade from an actual dog kennel to this.

"What do you want to know?" I asked him, unsure if he wanted to spend hours trailing over every detail.

"Everything. Eat first," he said, scraping avocado onto a piece of toast and then smothering it in sriracha.

I sat down once I'd decided on my assortment of foods, though I wasn't sure my stomach would, in any way, fit even half of what I'd put on my plate. But I could try. Once I'd eaten my second chocolate croissant, Ronan finally let me focus on talking instead of eating. We went over what he thought he knew about me, and I corrected every piece that had been a fabrication made for the purpose of keeping him safe.

I told him about the things I went through as a kid, not just the house burning down, but how my papá trained me to replace him. Even though he had seen it for himself I wanted him to hear it from me. He had that look in his eyes, like what I had been through was hurting him, but I wanted him to know that my past didn't break me like he thought it should have, it *forged* me.

"And the day we found your mom dead?" he asked when I finished.

"My uncle killed her, slit her throat. Painted the walls with her blood. I couldn't take the risk of you or anyone else seeing that. Let alone the police," I scowled as I thought back to that day, that was the lie that toppled them all. That was the searing hot divide that began to crack us from within, as it threatened to end what we had.

"Fuck Céci. You didn't even let me be there for you. You didn't even get to grieve," he shook his head, his eyebrows drawn into a frown on his forehead.

"I regret it, if it counts for anything," I pressed my lips into a hard line as I stared off at nothing in particular. He placed his hand over mine and stroked his thumb against my skin gently. My eyes filled up with the threat of weakness again, but I was too tired of being strong. It was exhausting. Ronan had always been that safe place I could go to when I needed to break, when all I could do was crumble.

The lies had broken us, and the truth would finally heal us.

But healing was painful.

And we had so much of it to do.

I jerked my hand out of his hold and hardened my gaze on him. I couldn't keep denying how much I wanted us to be whole again, but it was impossible to forget all of the hurt he caused. I needed so badly to be loved by the man who could overlook all of my flaws and still see me as something worth caring for, but I was far from forgiving. As if he could read my mind, he scooped me off the chair and placed me on his lap, inspecting me as if it were the first time.

"Stay with me tonight," it wasn't a question but there was hesitation and insecurity behind his voice. We'd been picking at each other's wounds at every chance we got for the last few weeks, the habit had begun to sink in deep. He knew damn well I was fully capable of saying no just to hurt him. I'd gotten so damn good at pushing him away just to see if he'd finally go.

If he was so easily forgiving me for all my lies and deceitfulness, then could I forget the last couple of months? Could I forget the monster who hurt me, even if I had a hand in forging him?

"No," I said coldly, pressing my hand to his cheek. My response forced the line in his jaw to harden and become more defined as he clenched his teeth.

40

MATEO

I couldn't fight the shit-eating grin plastered on my face once I came out of the shower to find Cecilia sitting on Ronan's lap. There was a settling peace that came from seeing them no longer at arms against each other. The little bit of right in a world that had gone so wrong, if anyone deserved a happily ever after, it was him.

"So, what's on the agenda for today?" I chirped as I walked into the kitchen, scooping a donut off of Cecilia's plate and giving her a wink that encouraged a frown from Ronan. Just because I was confident that Cecilia wouldn't pick between the two of us, didn't mean I couldn't have some fun with him in the process.

He was too easy, and it was too entertaining.

She got up from his lap, and I realized I might have completely misread the mood in the room. I shrugged it off, pulling up a stool and sitting down while interrupting whatever it was they'd been going through. If they couldn't sort this out, the least I could do was try to keep it from getting worse. Ronan was good at digging his graves deeper than they needed to be, and if he couldn't own his shit with Cecilia, it wasn't just him who'd be losing her.

I didn't see a possible outcome where I'd get to keep her if he didn't.

"We've got a traitor problem to deal with, urgently," Ronan's eyes burned with intensity as they met mine and I nodded at him.

"One of your guys are feeding intel to the Bratva?" She asked me, biting her lip like she already knew the answer.

"That's how they took you, someone told them we'd all be gone, and they came from the top," I told her point-blank.

"Well, who's getting greedy about power? Who's acting like they want more?" She asked, not bothering to hide how good she was at this, and it was so obvious how deep in this life she was. Ronan and I shared a look again and this time he answered.

"I have a pretty good idea. It's an Archer, I'm sure of it. I just don't know if it's Junior or Senior making waves."

"Or both," she added, and we nodded in agreement.

"But I can't just go off executing one or two of our founding members. It could cost us a lot of support if we went into this without concrete evidence," Ronan sighed heavily like he wished he could.

"Well, what if we could get this concrete evidence?" She looked between the two of us with a mischievous look on her face.

"What are you suggesting?" Ronan asked, but I had a feeling I already knew where she was going to go with this one.

"What if we set a rat trap? Give them the kind of cheese that they can't resist," she said casually as she shrugged her shoulders.

"You're not playing bait. I just got you back," he growled out clenching his fist and pounding it on the marble countertop.

"It's my decision, not yours," she said with conviction powering her vocal cords.

"Why would you agree to that?" He narrowed his eyes at her suspiciously.

"Because *your* rat problem became *my* safety concern. In case you're oblivious," she rolled her eyes at him in a dramatic gesture that had him scoffing.

"What if we tagged her?" I suggested, earning a wicked glare from him. "We should have tagged her anyway, the minute she signed. If we had, it might not have taken us this long to get her back," I pointed out.

"You mean like a tracker?" She asked, scrunching her eyebrows in the middle, and I nodded. "I'm not opposed to it, there's probably at least two or three in me right now anyway. My papá was crazy paranoid that my uncle would kidnap me or my sister one day."

"You're okay with it?" Ronan asked her, the surprise in his tone hard to miss.

"I mean, I just spent the better portion of a week starving in a dog crate, and I wasn't even kidnapped by the asshole I'm running from. I've kind of resigned to the fact that I need help," she shrugged her shoulders awkwardly.

"And you'll let me help you?" he asked her quietly, and I smirked at this gentle side of him that showed up out of nowhere. It was as if there was a completely different version of Ronan that had been dormant since she betrayed him, and he had finally woken up. However, this rendition of him could still put nine bullets in me in under three seconds.

She eyed him suspiciously like she was still adjusting to this version of him as well, one that wasn't so sharp and full of hate. I was too. It was like this guy had been hiding under a mountain of pain and somehow, she was able to pull him out of it just by being back here again.

"Am I free from the kennels?" she asked. "Free from that box?" Her eyebrows pulled together like she was thinking about keeping that grudge just a little longer.

I wouldn't blame her for it either.

He pulled her back onto his lap and wrapped his arm around her waist, keeping her pressed to him, giving her no option but to straddle his legs.

"You're not a free woman, because I'm never letting you go again, Cecilia Gomez. Or Celia Flores, whoever the hell you wanna be. But I'll never lock you up again. I swear it," he looked her way, the blazing burden of regret burning in his eyes with the weight of an apology he had yet to give her.

"Good, because if you try, I'll have my boyfriend over here kill you," she laughed, looking at me and I shrugged in agreement.

I wasn't going to correct her.

"You wouldn't have to ask him. You want me gone, I'll drain every ounce of my blood in my veins and let you bathe in it. You want to make me pay? I'll give you the knife myself so you can cut me open as slowly as you want. Call it nothing short of eternal bliss to meet my end by your hands, as long as It can stop this pain, gnawing at me from not having you."

"Fuck," she whispered before pressing her lips onto his briefly, "I'm still not staying with you tonight." He frowned, realizing his words weren't enough.

"If he's your boyfriend, what am I?" Zerkos asked, breaking away, glaring at me.

She moved her head to cover my face and force his attention back to her, "You're my sunrise, and my sunset. There's no distinction of where you end or where I begin. You're the only home I've ever truly known, the only home I'll ever need." Her tone changed drastically before she continued, "But that doesn't mean I'm just going to forgive you."

He burned his stare into me again before he turned his chin away from us.

She grabbed his face with both hands to force his gaze back to her, "Hey, don't do that. Don't make this about something it isn't."

"How can I not? How can I not feel like there isn't something missing in me that makes you want him?" I could hear the hurt in my brother's voice, and while I never intended to fall for her, I didn't have any intentions of letting her go.

"Because how I feel about him has nothing to do with you. It's not because of you, that I care about him, it's because of how he makes *me* feel," she pressed a soft kiss to his lips again and slid off his lap as she stood up.

"And I can't make you feel that way too?" He asked with a pained look on his face that nearly split my heart in half.

"No, but he can't make me feel the way you do either," she said, caressing his cheek with her thumb before lowering her hand to her side and looking at me.

"You'll have to choose one of us eventually," he threatened, crossing his arms over his chest.

"Not if you don't make me," she whispered, shaking her head at him before looking at me with those hopeful eyes.

I wouldn't ask her to choose.

I'd never had anything good in this life that was mine, I meant it when I said that I would take as many pieces of Cecilia that she'd let me have. Maybe he wasn't as desperate as I was.

Maybe he was just greedier.

Either way, I got it. If I could have all of her, I would. But I knew better than to think my brother wouldn't always have a piece of her heart. I was just the lucky bastard that ended up worming my way in there too, claiming a sliver of it for myself.

Would she let me go, to keep him, though?

That, I didn't know.

"Let's go get you chipped then," I said, trying to avoid letting my mind fall into a dark place where my insecurities would bury me alive. I stood, reaching my hand out to her.

"I thought we were on lockdown. Where are you going?" Santos' voice cut through from behind us as he emerged from the hallway, his eyes not missing the way Cecilia's fingers entwined in mine.

"Nowhere outside the building," Ronan answered first, making the decision to keep him out of the loop, probably waiting to see if he could prod the moody bastard to tell us what was stuck up his ass the last few days.

"That's all you're gonna say? So much for equals," he retorted, narrowing his eyes at him.

"You've been brooding," I said, and I noticed the way his glare cut to her but she averted his stare and shifted her gaze to the ground.

"Fuck this," he spat out. The clanking of the decorative cast iron vase hitting the marble floor rang loudly from the force of his kick before he made his way to the middle elevator.

"Hey!" Zerkos shouted out at him.

She took a sharp, stuttered breath, causing Ronan and me to make eye contact, a kind of silent message between the two of us. It was agony to see her feeling any hurt or pain. There was something inside of me that wanted to do everything I could to keep her from ever feeling that way, ever again. The way Ronan looked at me let me know he felt the same.

She'd had so much sorrow in her life.

I just wanted to take some of it away.

I wanted to experience how she could be if just a *little* of her burdens were lifted. And I would, I'd stand there all day carrying the brunt of them if it meant she would feel even the smallest bit of freedom.

I tightened my hold on her hand and dragged her to my room to change. She was still wearing just a t-shirt, and I didn't need the rest of the men in the building ogling her like hungry wolves. I didn't turn back to see Ronan's expression, but I could probably take a couple of guesses that he was either scowling or foaming at the mouth. He'd threatened to kill me at least twice already, but at this point, he may as well have been saying, "I love you, let's share."

My brain was not getting the message.

All it could hear was the sound she made coming on my cock and my fingers, or how soft and shallow her breathing got when she was right on the edge.

I tossed a pair of black boxer briefs her way along with sweatpants that were way too big. "We'll get you some clothes," I said to her, and she lifted an eyebrow at me.

"You sound like you wanna keep me?" She questioned with a tilt of her chin and a smirk on her lips.

I advanced on her, grasping the back of her neck, and bringing her in towards me.

"Sunshine, I'm fucking mad about you. Keep you, isn't close to what I want to do to you. I want to wreck you, ruin you, devour you until all that's left are the echoes of the pretty screams that come from your mouth when you're crying my name out in the middle of the night."

Her eyes widened at my confession and her body melted into mine in surrender.

"I want to worship you, the way you deserve to be worshiped. Touch you, the way you deserve," I reached my hand into her shirt grunting in disapproval when I felt the bandage wrapping her torso, covering her soft flesh, and keeping it from me. She let out a soft chuckle that almost sounded like music coming from her throat, and my dick twitched awake.

If God had a sound, it was her laughter.

"Hmm. Best not start something we can't finish Sunshine. We both know he'll come barging in if you stay in here too long," I kissed her lips feeling the smile carving its way into her mouth like the most beautiful sight I'd ever witnessed.

"He's not stupid, he knows." She pressed into me.

"He's not okay with it." I traced my fingers up and down her arm.

"Well, would you expect him to be?" She asked, practically laughing.

"You and I both know if we push hard enough, he'll give in. He won't lose you again," I moved my fingers down to her thigh, pulling a shiver from her while I teased going further.

"And you? What do you get?" She asked as if it wasn't obvious, and I frowned at her lack of awareness.

"I get you," I closed my mouth around hers, parting my lips to allow her in as I let my fingers dance around her slickness as if she were my instrument to play. She let out a gasp and let her head drop to my shoulder while I continued a silent type of torture, using my brother's cum mixed with her own wetness to pleasure her again.

"What if you get tired of sharing?" She groaned out in pleasure when I sunk two fingers deep inside of her. "What if I can't give you what you need?"

"Doubtful. I've never had anything good in my entire life, and you're by far the best thing this world has to offer. I'm not an ignorant man, I'll take what I can get," I shoved a third finger in pulling a cry from her that forced me to use my other hand to clamp over her mouth.

"Shh," I warned her. "I may be willing to share, but that doesn't mean he gets to see you when you're like this for *me*," I curved my fingers hitting that spot inside her that had her legs turning to Jell-O, she let me take the brunt of her weight into my arms as I continued to pleasure her.

"Now, come on my fingers. Show me how much you like this, Sunshine," I whispered in her ear.

"Oh! Shit..." She cried out, squeezing, and digging her nails into my biceps as her walls pulsed around my fingers, gripping me like a vice.

Her eyes locked on mine as if she knew how much I needed to see that dark abyss in her gaze while she crumbled in a wave of pleasure. Pulling my fingers out of her, but not once daring to look away, I took each digit into my mouth, licking them clean.

"He was right, you know? Nothing quite like it."

"I thought you said you didn't want to start anything you couldn't finish?" She gave me a dark smirk, raising one eyebrow up in challenge.

"I don't know about you, but I could have sworn you finished," I gave her my best-dimpled smile and she clucked her tongue at me.

"That's not what I meant," she said, slinking down my body, undoing my belt as she got to her knees. "I want to taste you. Te quiero," she breathed out as she pulled my achingly hard erection from my pants. Fisting me in her hand, I groaned at how even the simplest touch from her could feel like agony and bliss all at once.

"You're going to end me," I dropped my head back while she took the tip of my cock into her mouth, feeling her tongue as it swirled across it wildly.

My breathing became shallow and she moaned with my length in her mouth. The feeling of her cheeks hollowing out as she attempted to take as much of me in as possible, doing things to me no other woman had been able to before.

I looked back down to find her eyes fixed on me, desire and lust rampant in her gaze, driving me closer to that place where only the blinding quiet of pleasure lived. I gasped as she grabbed hold of my hips and pulled me into the back of her throat, the sounds of her sloppily running up and down my length making my toes curl when she only came up for air when she absolutely needed to.

"Oh fuck," I whispered, tugging at her hair, and pulling her back slightly to look at her, drool dripping from her mouth and tears spilling from the corners of her eyes. She'd never looked quite so beautiful than at that moment, a creature made just for me, spun from the very fibers of hell by the Devil himself. She kept up a torturous pace, making sure every inch of me got the attention it deserved until I could feel my balls pulling up and tightening.

"I'm close," I warned her, "Open." I instructed her but she wasn't the type of girl you gave orders to.

She answered by squeezing my ass and pulling me deeper into her mouth. I bottomed out as she relaxed and hummed contentedly and I emptied myself inside her, shooting deep into the back of her throat with a groan. She swallowed and licked her tongue over her lips in satisfaction, as if she'd just had the best meal of her life and I helped her to stand, pulling her body against me.

"One wrong move, one twist of events that would have spun our lives differently, any little thing that would have happened another way and I wouldn't have you here right now, with me. I can't say I'm sorry for any of it Sunshine, our lives have gone exactly how the fates had intended," I said seriously, running my nose up her neck and burying my face behind her ear, falling prey to the intoxicating scent of coconut that exuded from her. I tucked myself back into my pants and redid my belt as she found her footing again.

"You make our misery sound so much more romantic that way," she smiled a crooked grin at me, and I shrugged, lifting the boxers and sweats I pulled out for her.

"It's a gift." I grinned, "I'll give you some time to yourself." I rubbed my thumb over her lip, cleaning a stray drop of cum before walking out of the room.

Ronan's harrowing gaze found me as soon as I turned the corner out of the room. He was exactly where we'd left him, in front of the exuberant display of food he ordered for her, but the look on his face said he'd been busy self-condemning in his own mind since we'd gotten up.

"So, didn't matter how many times I said I'd kill you for touching her, did it?" He shifted his gaze to his plate, his insecurities shining brightly.

"Brother, you might as well end me now, because there's no way in hell, I'm going to spend the rest of my life the same shell of a man you've been these last ten years, all because I decided not to take a chance on a good thing," I crossed my way to the couch and propped my legs up on the coffee table, keeping my gaze fixed on him. I respected him too much not to give him the honesty he deserved, but that didn't mean I was going to give her up. The thought alone made my skull pound with intensity.

"*My* good thing," he growled through his teeth, his anger seething through him visibly.

"*Ours*," I smirked at him, and he frowned deeper. "Just because you found her first doesn't make her only yours."

"What, and you're just some enlightened asshole who has no problem sharing her between the two of us, because why? It makes her happy?" He asked angrily, unable to conceive the idea that, yeah, maybe I was. I pulled my pocket knife out and began flicking it through my fingers, nicking a knuckle or two as it scraped over them carelessly.

"Maybe I see that we feed different parts of her soul, give her different things that she needs. Maybe, I'm secure in knowing that no other sick bastard alive can give her what I can, just like I can't give her what you can. And no, not just the two of us," I said, removing any trace of humor from my expression so he could see that I was serious about this, that for her, I *could* be all in. With my brothers, I *had* no reason to be jealous because I needed them as much as I needed her.

"What, you wanna share her with the whole brotherhood? Why stop there? Let's call the Bratva too, maybe they'll pay us back for half of what we paid?" He practically shouted in anger, and his accusation blurred my vision, his suggestion sending me into a pit of blackness that I didn't come out of until I heard the gasp leave his mouth.

"You're a lunatic you know?" He yelled as he pulled the knife out from the chair he was sitting on, lodged just a centimeter or two away from his face.

"Maybe, if you opened your eyes, you could see this thing going on with Santos was a lot bigger than just Ocean Valley," I said, and the look of shock grew on his face at the new possibility he hadn't conjured in his mind yet. "Those two have been pining over each other since the minute she stepped foot in here. Our girl is hurting, and so is he." Before he could respond, Cecilia came out into the living room looking between both of us like she knew she missed something pivotal.

"Tracker?" She asked, tilting her head to the side, and cutting through the tension in the room.

"It's kind of hot that she wants it, right?" I asked him and he shook his head at me before dropping his forehead to the counter in defeat.

Whatever, it was hot.

41

RONAN

No.

She fucking said no.

It felt like I was being eaten alive by my own frustration, consumed entirely by the choices I made, and the choices she made for us. But it didn't matter that she hid everything from me for the entirety of our relationship. It didn't matter that the Cecilia I knew was a fabrication, a make-believe fantasy, a role that she played to get through that chapter of her life.

Because she was fucking right.

All her lies had merit. Everything she hid was to keep me safe.

At any point, if Rafael Flores thought that I was a liability, he would have put me six feet under. I also watched enough of those videos to know that he would have probably made her pull the trigger, as a lesson.

Who was I kidding? I watched *all* of the videos, all two hundred and fifty-six of them. The man was a monster, but even now I could see she didn't think of him that way. And how could she? He was her father, in her mind this was always how it was supposed to go. This was the path he laid out for her.

Her destiny.

I was worse than him because I should have protected her without question. I should have kept her safe and instead, I let my rage take the driver's seat while I played tricks on my mind, telling myself that it was for her own good. I didn't deserve her forgiveness. That's what made it even more painful to see her look at Kane the way she did.

He'd earned that.

I'd spend every day trying to earn it too, now.

I got up from the table, grabbed a clean t-shirt from my room, and headed to the elevator, pushing the down button. I knew I wouldn't have to look far to find the other asshole. My brothers gave me shit for pouring all of my emotions into a punching bag, but at least my rage never left a permanent scar on anyone.

Maybe just a few black eyes.

When Santos got like this, he didn't spend hours in the gym sweating it off until his muscles screamed at him. You wouldn't find him channeling these feelings in a healthy way like Kane did with his instruments. No, the sick bastard went down to the fifth floor to cut his demons out of him by bleeding others.

He always picked the most deserving of them to feel his wrath. The ones who were absolutely not going to make it out of here no matter how many secrets they spilled, or how many promises they made. The ones who were marked for death because the weight of their sins was too heavy for us to allow them back out into the world again.

It wasn't just about him though, the minute Kane mentioned the tracker, a thought popped into my mind that I couldn't shake, I needed to confirm my suspicions for myself before I could make another move.

I stepped onto the fifth floor, hearing the pained cry of a desperate man echoing off of the concrete floors and bouncing through the metal bars. Hughes stood in the corner, giving me a hesitant look.

"You didn't try to stop him?" I asked him, and his face twisted up in conflict.

"I'm not getting in his way when he's like this. Sorry boss," he looked away and I couldn't blame him. We didn't pay him to deal with Santos' shit. He kept it together for the most part, but we'd noticed a pattern the last couple of years. Anytime he went to Ocean Valley, he came back real murdery.

This time seemed worse.

I stepped through the walkway looking to the cells on my left as I admired my brother's handiwork. There was a guy laying on the ground in a puddle of blood with both his arms slashed from the wrist all the way up to the elbow, his cold dead stare looking past the cage like he was searching for salvation. But every man who found his way here was guilty of more than one unforgivable atrocity.

I didn't pity them.

Nor would I get in my brother's way.

But I couldn't risk him offing the girl, just in case, he got a little too bloodthirsty.

The next holding cell had a guy with a knife handle sticking out of his ear, the blade clearly embedded deep into his brain. The unfortunate fuck who shared that space with him must have tried to put up a fight, because Álvarez straight up disemboweled him.

He didn't usually get that personal unless you really annoyed him.

I picked up the pace and hurried my way past all the formerly living prisoners until I found Santos about two cells away from Oksana. Or maybe it was Susana now. I didn't actually give a fuck either way.

He had some guy pinned to the ground as he bashed his face in with what looked like the remnants of Hughes' coffee thermos. The girl screamed in horror, my head nearly imploding from the unending screeching. I approached him slowly, knowing that when Santos got like this, he tended to see a little...red.

I rested my hand on his shoulder as I stood behind him, keeping a small distance between us, just in case.

"What do you need, brother?" I asked in a low, soft tone.

He turned his head to where my hand rested, and he snarled, peeling his lip up in discontent.

"What I *need* is for the people who are supposed to have my back, to not lie to me," he raised his voice in anger.

"It's not like that Álvarez, nothing's that black and white," I tried to explain but his rage was getting in the way of his reasoning. I knew that feeling well myself.

"Black and white enough for you and Kane to decide what's worth telling me. When did we start keeping secrets? Or is that her poison affecting us all?" He narrowed his eyes at me, and his accusation confused me even more.

He wanted to blame Cecilia for the way we were all coming undone, but I could see the truth in his eyes after Kane's little revelation this morning. He *was* jealous. If he felt a lot more for her than he ever let on, then I could take a guess these feelings had been around much longer than since my girl reappeared out of the ashes of her past.

"You tell me, when *did* we start keeping secrets? Ever since you came back from Ocean Valley you've holed yourself in your room like a hermit. If you'd come to me, I would have told you whatever you wanted to know. But something is eating at you, and if you can't tell me what it is, then you deserve to feel this way," his eyes widened in surprise at my words, but he knew I saw through his bullshit.

He opened his mouth to speak again, but in an almost animalistic move, he turned his head to the side and snapped his mouth shut, clicking his teeth together.

"I'm busy," he said, pushing past me and walking back towards the entrance. I barked out a laugh loud enough for him to hear so he'd understand he wasn't fooling anyone here.

"Sure, let me know when you stop being *busy* brother, and we can finish this conversation," I chuckled again, purposefully antagonizing him in hopes that pushing his buttons would at least force him to open up to me, even if it was out of spite or rage.

He stormed out of the fifth floor without looking back at me, and I turned my attention to Oksana, whose fear was starting to fade from the scene she'd witnessed.

"Why do you think your daddy hasn't retaliated against us over you yet?" I asked her, "I mean, he obviously knows where we are. Surely, he has the men to take this whole building down if he wanted to. Am I wrong?" I cocked an eyebrow at her while I waited for a response.

The look of disdain on her face said it all, but she decided that wasn't enough and spat at me, nearly getting it on my shoes.

"Don't be like that. It's not *my* fault he doesn't love you. I mean he probably thinks you're dead though, since we gave your sister back," I lied, she didn't need to know how Anya ended up back where she belonged. "Does he really need you when he's got another just like you who can take your place?" I kept poking to see if I could crack through the facade she put up every time we came here to get information from her.

"Maybe he's just waiting to make the right move," she spoke, her accent rough and cutting through each word sharply.

"You don't sound so confident," I smirked, knowing I was seeing right through her.

"My sister, he trusted her more. My job was to marry for the benefit of the family and then kill my husband. You kept the wrong sister."

Swallowing the hard knot in my throat from her words, I pushed down my feelings so I wouldn't feel pity for her. I remembered Fletcher was still in a drug-induced coma in the ICU and any ounce of empathy I felt was soon gone.

"Why were you locked up in that trafficking ring when we found you? And if you don't tell me, I'll get my friend back in here to get the answers out of you, and you've already seen his methods," I pointed to the rest of the room where the bodies lied lifelessly.

"Are you ever going to let me go?" She crossed the cell and made her way to the tiny cot that was now her bed.

"That depends, you can either be useful to me, or you just end up as the filth we gotta wash down the drains later. Like the rest of them," I jerked my head again towards the bodies Santos left behind. "Maybe if you're *really* useful, I can send you far away from here. Where even Daddy won't bother you," I whispered the words like they were dangerous, and her eyes grew large at the idea, like that was something she might actually want.

"A new life?" She crossed her legs with the question.

"If you help us," I nodded.

"He is smarter than you think, he knows I am alive. He's been one step ahead of you the whole time."

"Of Course," I said, realizing that if Anya was the favorite there was a good chance Sokolov wouldn't be wasting any more of his men on Oksana. She walked towards me and stuck her arm through the space between the bars, letting out a heavy sigh. I yanked her through it, nearly slamming her face against the metal as I examined her underarm and noticed the small bulge.

There it was.

"Fucking hell. He's known where you were this whole time," I stated matter of factly, and she nodded in disappointment. I couldn't imagine how difficult it must have been to think someone was coming to save you, but they never came. She cried out loudly as I tightened my hold on her wrist through the bars and pulled out a pocket knife, slicing fast and deep enough to push the tracker right out of her before sliding it into my pocket.

"So, let's try again. Why were you locked up in that trafficking ring?" I crossed my arms over my chest as I waited for an answer, hoping I'd given her something worth betraying her family for.

"How many girls have you stolen from my father over the years?" She retorted with her own question.

"Probably six, eight with you and your sister," I had to admit, even though we liked to switch up who we targeted most years, we almost always tended to grab a Bratva trafficking victim. They were always on our heels, trying to nab any little bit of power from us they could. Always trying to take back what we fought for. If they took a mile of the city from us, we snatched it back the next year with interest. It sort of became a cat and mouse situation, and since they never really came out of hiding it was easy to keep fucking with their plans.

"My father counts every penny. If you think he hadn't noticed before, you're a fool. He planned this, and you walked right into his trap," she looked at me like I was an idiot and honestly, I felt it. I should have seen this coming, we all should have.

"So, he sent his daughters off to slaughter in hopes of catching the butcher," I twisted my face in anger at only myself, and how stupid we'd been. Little boys playing at gang leaders, not paying attention to the bigger picture.

"Exactly, and when my sister realized we weren't going to be resold and that it was all a game to you, we decided it would be easier to charm our way to freedom so we could then give our father all the information he'd need to bring you down."

"Except, now she's free, and no one is coming for you," I turned around and began to walk out of the room. I still needed to sort things out with Santos, but this was a start. If we didn't deal with our Bratva problem soon, it was going to end up at our doorstep again. That was a risk we couldn't take for the sake of everyone who lived here under our protection.

"Are you going to help me?" She shouted at me as I made my way out of the prison-like level.

"I'm not killing you yet, I'd say count your blessings, Susana."

As if it wasn't enough that she was refusing to forgive me, the universe kept plaguing me by forcing me to catch her and Mateo pawing at each other every chance they got. As soon as the elevator door opened, they were pulling apart awkwardly like we were all pretending this wasn't actually happening.

I felt like I was losing my damn mind.

Kane cleared his throat and grabbed her chin with one hand, pulling her head to the side to expose the tracker embedded in the back of her neck. I boxed her into the corner of the elevator, both hands placed on the wall on either side of her head.

"How does it feel to know that I will always be able to find you, no matter how far you run?"

She got on the tips of her toes and whispered into my ear, "Oddly comforting." Cecilia winked at me before ducking under my arm as the elevator dinged and the doors opened back into the penthouse.

T*wo days.*

Well, technically two nights. Two entire nights where she slept in Kane's room after I asked her to stay with me. I didn't know what it was going to take to earn her forgiveness. It wasn't like before when sex was just sex, and we could go back to hating each other the moment it was over.

We'd gone too far past that.

We'd exposed too many layers of ourselves, and her secrets were out into the world now. We couldn't go back. Not to the way we were when we were just kids, and definitely not to the toxic mess that we'd become since she walked into this high-rise. There was only one way out of this for us, and it was by walking through the fire. I owed it to her to fix this.

I owed it to *us*.

I burst into Kane's room, the door slamming into the wall behind it from the force of my entry. He barely looked up at me from playing the guitar as he sat on the edge of his bed. I had one of our guys go pick it up for him a couple of days after the high-rise was raided by the Bratva. There was a deep sadness within Mateo that was exposed when you took music away from him.

It was an easy gesture to rid him of some of his pain.

And it was important to me that my brother wasn't suffering.

As if knowing exactly what I came in here for, he tilted his chin towards his bathroom and continued to play "Where is my Mind" by *The Pixies* on his new instrument.

The hot steam rolled out of the bathroom in a cloud as I opened the door and stepped inside.

"So much for alone time," she mocked from within the opaque glass that separated the shower and divided us.

"I heard no such thing," I stepped closer, and she peeked her head out of the barrier.

"Oh. Hi," she breathed out, her hair plastered to her wet face as the water crashed over her.

"Hi," I mused back, stepping closer and closer before I stood just inches from the shower entrance.

"Well, are you just going to stand there?" She arched an eyebrow in challenge, and I took it for the invitation it was, quickly shedding all my clothing. Her eyes drifted down as she took all of me in for the first time since we'd been apart for so many years. She probably didn't even realize she was doing it, bitting her lip before her eyes made their way back to mine. Those dark glossy orbs always threatened to consume me, exposing me until all that would be left were the ruins of who I once was.

"This doesn't mean anything," she whispered it again like it was more for her than for me as she dragged a loofa over my chest.

"You keep saying that my little flower, but I'll keep reminding you, this means *everything*," I said, tucking a wet lock behind her ear.

"I still hate you for what you did to me," she looked down, avoiding my eyes and I lifted her chin up so that her stare could see the truth searing inside me.

"I'd rather feel your hate than not feel anything from you at all. As long as you let me spend the rest of our lives trying to make it right," I brushed my thumb over her lips, too nervous myself to seal the promise with the kiss I so desperately wanted to take.

But I'd already taken too much from her.

It was time I fixed the damage I caused.

I took her hand into mine, pulling the soapy loofa from her and running it over her body, worshiping every inch of the woman she'd become with the attention she deserved.

"Turn around," I told her, but her eyes grew in alarm.

"W-wait a minute," she stumbled backward as she tried to put distance between us, but she couldn't hide the pained look on her face as the water hit her from behind. I narrowed my eyes at her, unsure and confused about her reaction. Grabbing her wrist I pulled her into me, our naked chests pressed together as droplets of water ran between us.

"Let me take care of you," I murmured into her ear, "Let me try to fix this." I pleaded, all strength escaping me as my voice broke with my words as the inevitable feeling of defeat washed over me.

"It's not that; It's- I- I..." she kept stuttering over her words, but I could see in her face she didn't have the resolve to keep any secrets anymore. Whatever was bothering her was something she didn't know how to or maybe even *want* to conceal. I made the decision for her and turned her to face the wall, and that's when I saw it.

The wound split her back from top to bottom, from her left shoulder down to her right hip. The skin was angry, red, and irritated and though it had been a few days since it happened, the smallest of her movements was enough to get it bleeding again.

I placed my hand on her right shoulder blade, and her body trembled in my hold. I couldn't see her face, and even with the water drenching both of us, I could feel her shaking under my hand. I lowered my head until my forehead was pressed to the top of her head, and I whispered into her ear.

"I *will* kill every single one of them," I vowed turning her back to face me, her eyelashes beading from her tears mixing with the shower water spraying from above. I pressed a kiss to her forehead before I made my way out of the walk-in shower, grabbing a nearby towel and heading out of Kane's room.

There was a lot of fucking work to do.

And a lot of Bratva scum to kill.

"I know you want to focus on the Bratva," she said, sitting on the kitchen counter while eating a bowl of cut-up dragon fruit. "But it would behoove us...me, to get some ducks in a row first before you tried to start a war."

"What kind of ducks you lining up, Sunshine?" Mateo asked, taking a forkful of her breakfast, and eating it straight out of her bowl.

"The kind that guarantees my safety, the kind that lets me sleep a little better at night," she said looking up and shifting her gaze between the both of us. "I need you to take me to him."

"No!" Mateo said before I had the chance to.

"Absolutely fucking not, no fucking way. I'm not taking you to see that piece of shit. Not after what I saw him doing to you in those videos," I told her, eyeing Kane as he nodded his head in agreement with me.

"Contrary to what you may believe, he was never the villain. Family looks different when you've been raised by Rafael Flores," she tried to reason, but it wasn't enough. Villalobos was just another Devil in my eyes, and in some ways, he was worse. I expected him to have loved her like a sister, but he damaged her, then abandoned her as if she never existed. What kind of monster could do that to their family?

I didn't budge and she sighed, "Look, I need him, we need him. We need the numbers if you want to go up against the Russian Mafia. This building is big, and it's impressive, but from what I've noticed it's a bit empty Ronan. You need more soldiers."

She was annoyingly right, and I hated how that was becoming a regular thing these days. She was so unbelievably smart, and she knew how to lead better than the three of us put together.

Almost like someone had been prepping her for that very thing.

Fucking hell.

"You think he's just going to jump on board with this even though he's been practically ignoring your existence for the last fifteen years?" I asked her and Kane nudged her for the answer when she didn't immediately respond.

"I won't give him the choice."

42

SANTOS

Eight

GUILLERMO

I had just over a week to deliver Cecilia's head on a platter and absolutely no bright ideas to work around the task I'd been given. The longer it took for me to do what needed to be done, the more I contemplated my own ending. It would be easier that way. At least I wouldn't be around to watch Guillermo bring down everything and everyone I've ever cared about.

Fucking coward.

The intrusive thoughts screamed at me.

Everything made sense the moment I watched those videos, and all the pieces came together. Guillermo didn't give a shit about Cecilia, he was following orders from a much higher chain of command and for all he knew, Ronan was still heartbroken and would have relished the thought of putting her under.

My cousin probably thought that he was killing two birds with one stone and earning a favor from Zerkos while doing it. Now we owed the Cártel a death, and Los Muertos would come collecting it in the next week if I didn't have her head.

At the end of the day, Los Muertos was just an extension of the Cártel. An Americanized base my primo created for the purpose of selling out to the bigger bad. He assured the Cártel they'd have no need to step foot on U.S soil as long as they kept them stocked with weapons, drugs, and cash. Guillermo would make sure business was always handled.

Which left me with handling the business now or incurring the wrath of the entire *Cártel* and bringing it down on the Brotherhood's steps. Was I supposed to kill the one person who'd ever really mattered to me? The same person who was now the cause of all of my suffering? Was I supposed to sacrifice all of the lives in this building so that she could live?

I could. But she still wouldn't be mine.

It felt like a sickness, the way my thoughts, no matter where they were, always circled back to her. Like an infected limb, I had no option but to ignore it until the time would come when I'd be forced to amputate it or die.

Would I die for her?

A hundred times over you fucking idiot.

I was sitting on my bed, trying to wrap my head around how I was going to go through what needed to be done when I heard a noise and turned my head over to my open door. At the same time, I saw her leaving Kane's room in nothing but his t-shirt as she pranced away.

What the fuck is happening here?

I groaned in frustration, unsure why it seemed like the only person who couldn't be happy was me.

Well. I did deserve it.

There was nothing I'd done in this life that ever-merited accolades.

And that's what Cecilia was.

A reward.

A prize.

Something I'd never be good enough to claim as my own.

It was bad enough I had to spend every waking day suffocating in her presence now, pretending like there wasn't this hatred bubbling up inside me. Hatred over the fact that she'd never be mine, loathing for how she lied to me while calling me her best friend. Disgust towards myself for not being able to see coming what was now my doom.

But now she and Kane were inseparable, for some reason they were hitting it off way too well. Even if Zerkos blew a gasket every time he found them so much as sitting next to each other, neither of them seemed to put any effort into concealing what they were becoming.

It was fucking annoying.

He didn't even know her.

I knew her.

But I guess everything I knew had been a lie, so in the end, maybe he *did* know her better than I ever did.

Maybe that's why they looked so obviously in love, and when night time came, they practically sighed like teenagers before heading for Kane's room. Always shooting questionable glares at Zerkos.

How I was going to go through with what I needed to do without those two stopping me was a constant thought in my head as well. They hardly left her alone to do Black Crow business to the point where Archer Senior had long forgotten his place and was starting to take more than what belonged to him.

Either they didn't notice, or they didn't care.

Like her presence here was polluting their thoughts and the only thing either of them could focus on was her.

I pulled at my hair with a groan.

She was all I could focus on too.

But my grave had already been dug, and the clock was counting me down to my last breaths. The risk of not doing what needed to be done was too great, the price to pay was too high and for once in my life, I needed to do the right thing.

So why did the right thing feel impossibly wrong?

I flicked open my tanto blade and twirled it around my fingers like a nervous habit. Not being careful enough to avoid nicking myself as I secretly wished it would do more. I moved from the bed and sat down in the black leather chair in my room, the PlayStation controller at my feet as I pressed the blade of the knife to my wrist.

Do it.

Everyone's problems would end.

I would be free of the morena who cursed my dreams like the wicked witch she truly was. I would be free of my obligations to Los Muertos. My brothers would be free of all the burdens that came with being attached to someone like me.

A waste of space.

A tragic fool who'd never been loved by anyone else.

"Aghhh!" I screamed, stabbing the blade down on the leather fabric of the chair and dragging it down, wishing it was my own arm instead.

"Are you chill?" Kane asked from behind the door, tapping his fingers on the wood as if privacy was something any of us ever cared about before.

"I'm fine," I lied, breathing heavily through my nostrils.

"We're heading out for a bit, we may be gone for the night," he said, piquing my interest.

"We?"

"Yeah. She's coming too," he explained what was already obvious and I waited a beat before responding.

"I'm guessing I'm not invited then, or you wouldn't be telling me."

"Bro, you are acting a million kinds of off. Do you even want to come? You've been treating Cecilia like she's a goddamn leper, and she's noticed, in case you didn't know. You're hurting her fucking feelings asshole," he said, and I scoffed.

"No, I don't want to come," was the only answer I gave him, and he pulled the door to shut it all the way, my heart hammering viciously in my chest. They were keeping me out of everything, it was infuriating but I knew I couldn't blame them. I was visibly coming undone and there was nothing I could do to even hide it.

The truth was, I *wanted* to go.

Even sadder, I desperately needed to be asked if I wanted to go.

To be told my presence would be missed.

I wanted to be with my brothers, I wanted to soak up the girl whose laughter I could still hear in the wind as we wreaked havoc in a much less demanding world, during much simpler times.

But I had a murder to plan, and a betrayal to fulfill.

Or maybe I needed to go casket shopping.

Either way, I wouldn't waste the time they were gifting me.

43

MATEO

The drive to Grimm's Reach was barely tolerable. Between Santos' moody aura stinking up the whole car without him even being here, and the fact Cecilia and Zerkos could barely look at each other without bickering about the A/C or the music playing, I was ready to get the fuck out of this negative car and stretch my legs. I sat in the back with Cecilia, for one, to piss off Zerkos, and two, because why would I pass up a chance to try to finger her in the backseat?

Once we arrived at the Diablo's compound, I could feel a visible wall being put up around Cecilia. She was covering herself in armor, and her change in attitude sent a powerful surge of excitement through me. I craved the unpredictable, and right now she was feeding the monster that lurked beneath my surface.

"Give me a gun," she demanded from Ronan, and he scoffed, turning back to look at her.

"First of all, no. Second of all, if you go in there waving a gun around, you'll be dead in less than three seconds. Trust me," Ronan said to her sternly, clearly remembering the first time he'd ever been here all those years ago. She let out a laugh that was a bit unhinged but fit the mood suspiciously well.

"Well, good thing I only need two seconds to make the point I need to make," she extended her hand out for the gun.

"No," he said again, and she flared her nostrils back at him.

"Scared I'll turn on you?" She let out a half-smirk.

"Baby, always," he said, grabbing her by the hair and stealing a kiss from her that should have had me clenching my jaw with jealousy, but instead, it just left me turned on. She pushed him away roughly and stuck her hand out again.

"Uh-uh. No way," he laughed out, but her change in tone let him know she wasn't here to play around.

"I swear to God Ronan Zerkos, give me a gun or you will regret it," her threat was empty, but Ronan lifted his eyebrow up with hesitation and let out a heavy sigh of defeat.

"Your fucking funeral then," he groaned as he placed the gun in her palm. I would have given her one too, but she didn't ask me. She probably knew she could get anything from me, but I think she enjoyed challenging Ronan too much. She squeezed my thigh and the corner of her lip turned up in the tiniest amount before she released my leg and grabbed the gun with both hands.

"Do you know how to work the safety?" Zerkos asked her.

"I know my way around a pistol better than I know my way around you these days *baby*," she spat back at him, for once owning the double life she had been living. She put the gun inside the back of her pants, and we pulled into the compound, where the same kid with the Prospect leather cut waved us through.

"Are you coming, or not? I don't care either way," she baited him, using her confidence in knowing full well I had her back no matter what she was planning to do once we got in there.

The prospect tried to stop her from walking through the doors before he could alert his president, but she just pushed him away with one hand, and the kid stumbled back in surprise. She shoved the door open and in the same moment two shots rang out from the gun Zerkos had given her, all hell immediately threatening to break loose.

Over a dozen guns pointed our way but before my brain could register what was happening, I heard the pained shout coming from Cézar. "Stand the fuck down!" he shouted to his men, that's when I noticed him clutching his leg and the blood dripping from his shoulder.

Cecilia put two bullets in Cézar Villalobos in less than two seconds of entering his clubhouse and it took every part of me to not let the smile break free from my face. It wasn't lethal but I was betting it hurt like a bitch, and that was the least he deserved. I lifted my gun up to back Cecilia, not knowing what the hell kind of point she was trying to make here, but still a hundred percent down for the chaos.

I looked over at her with wide eyes but the girl I thought I knew wasn't there anymore. There wasn't an ounce of fear coming from her, this was the woman her father shaped her into, this was the little girl ruthlessly molded in a Cártel dungeon.

"I came to collect, pendejo," she said pointing the gun at him, and I looked back at Zerkos and mouthed *what the fuck*? To him but he just lifted his shoulders and gave me the same look right back.

"Back down little girl, I can't let you keep pointing that gun at my Pres," the enormity that was Calaveras stepped up to her and put himself between the two of them. She didn't flinch though, and instead, she put the pistol right under his chin like she didn't give a fuck about the size difference between them.

"Take a seat gigante, this is your president's comeuppance. You can either be a good little grunt and listen to him, or I'll shoot him dead right here, and you can bet your ass he'll let me. Because that motherfucker owes me his life," she pushed the gun until Calaveras had no choice but to crash back into the couch behind him, and then she looked back at Cézar.

"So, what's it gonna be Pres? Your life, or your life?" She asked him, letting out an icy laugh as she used his title exaggeratedly so that it came off as the condescending remark she'd intended it to be.

"What the fuck is she talking about Pres?" A dark-haired, equally large motherfucker wearing a leather cut with "Sanguinero" on it spoke, but pressed his hands down to encourage the others to lower their weapons. Cézar stayed silent as his men looked at him, and he looked at her.

"There's a reason why he's not talking right now boys, it's because I'm in the room. Which means unless I ask him to bark, your Lobito will stay quiet like the good little dog he is. I'm talking about the fact that your president has two options right now, he can leave you in the capable hands of his VP and do his *fucking* job like he was sworn to. Or..." Cecilia trailed off in thought, but Sanguinero took the opportunity to speak.

"We're a family. We ride or die for each other. If he's got business with you then it's our business too."

"Lovely, I was betting on that. I could use more muscle behind me. It looks like as of right now the Diablos Locos belongs to the Flores Cártel until further notice." Conflicted voices spoke over each other in anger all at once, but it didn't break her cool composure at all.

"You think we're just gonna let this stand?" Another guy chimed in from the corner and Cecilia didn't blink before putting a bullet in his kneecap. Calaveras stood up and Cecilia stepped forward to match him, power, and control exuding from every pore of her body.

"I said stand down!" Cézar shouted and Cecilia smirked something sinister at the deadly-looking motherfucker looming over her.

"Try something, I promise you any harm comes to me, and your President won't hesitate to put a bullet in his own skull on my account, but not before he puts one in yours as well. We were both brainwashed in the same tub, he knows where his fucking duties lie."

He looked towards Cézar for some sign that Cecilia was fucking crazy, but he bowed his head silently and I knew she wasn't lying, the whole room did.

"Why the fuck would he do that?" Sanguinero asked.

"No one ever pays attention to the part that says no one gets out alive!" She tapped her finger to her head to suggest the thought should have crossed his mind. "The only way out is death." Clearly, all of his men had known his history if the mention of the Cártel didn't surprise them.

"You can go down to hell with him and do my bidding, or you can watch him burn by himself. But Cézar Villalobos belongs to me, until I decide otherwise," she said, crossing her arms and turning her chin up. "And I've been missing my number two boys, so I might be keeping him for a while."

"Pres," someone said quietly, possibly the poor fuck who had just gotten shot in the knee cap. Calaveras looked to Cezar again and Cecilia sighed heavily.

"I understand it may take some time for you to get used to the idea, but I won't tell you twice. When I'm in the room, you don't look to him for approval, you look at me. Understand?"

Calavera let out a low growl in disapproval, and Cecilia took it for the challenge that it unmistakably was.

"I don't think you understand the position you're in. You want to *ride or die* for your number one? Well, let me be the first to tell you that your number one is my number two. Has been since the day I was born, and until the day my miserable existence ends, he will continue to serve me," she threw a coin at Cézar, and he scowled at her but gripped it tight in his hand. "You lost this, payaso."

"I didn't want it back," he looked away and she marched over to him and grabbed his chin between her fingers to force him to look into her eyes.

"We both know this is scarred into us deeper than a fucking coin," she let go and began walking away like she owned the place. I was fucking impressed. I was hard, and I was mesmerized all at the same time. She was the kind of woman who breathed fire, who turned men into a smoldering pile of ash with nothing but the sheer power that ran through her veins. I could feel the layers of who I once was scorching away in her embers, from simply the heat of basking in her glory.

"I hope you enjoyed your freedom, Lobito. We have work to do, you left me with quite a mess." She announced, walking over to the bar and grabbing three shot glasses.

"Where the fuck is your doctor? My brother is bleeding all over the place," she said angrily to Calaveras as if she wasn't the one who just shot him.

"He'll be here in five. He said to keep pressure on the wounds. All of them." The Prospect said looking at Cecilia's other casualty as he pulled the phone away from his ear to tell us.

I ripped my shirt off and tore it to pieces to bandage up these asshole's legs and Cecilia bit her lip at me from across the room at the sight of my abs on display.

I smirked knowing that my shirt died for a good cause, if it gave her that reaction. Though I wouldn't call becoming a bandage for fucking Villalobos a good cause, you couldn't win them all. I still hated the fucking guy for all the shit he put her through in those videos. *All those years.*

As much as Cecilia was putting on a badass fucking front for Cézar's men, I could see there was actually worry etched into her expression for him. By my guess, she'd probably be upset if we just let him die. If he was important to her, then unfucking-fortunately for me, he was somehow important to me too.

Ronan looked shell-shocked for the first time in his life and his jaw was practically spilled out on the floor in awe from the entire exchange we just witnessed. I knew a mood would follow along with that, because he couldn't handle the thought of not knowing every single part of what made Cecilia, *Celia*. It was time he got over that and realized he needed to get to know every version of her, as she was, right now.

He was dwelling on a long-lost idea of a damsel in distress he had put on such a high pedestal over thirteen years ago. She was damaged as fuck, but she wasn't a damsel, and she wasn't in distress. If anything, she was a harbinger of terror and madness just like the rest of us. It was just one more reason why I knew we were bound together by so much more than just my feelings for her.

She walked over to a console table pushed up against the wall. There was a photo hung of what looked like the Virgin Mary, but a skeleton took place inside the dark robes instead. There was a statue replica of the same photo sitting in the center of the table, with some trinkets and bones scattered around it along with a few black candles. She poured a shot into one of the glasses, leaving it on the table next to the bony lady before she grabbed a matchbox and lit one of the candles.

"Sit him the fuck up, get him off the floor," she commanded as she walked over to him holding a bottle of tequila in one hand and the two-shot glasses in another while Calaveras hoisted him up onto the couch. She lifted his legs and moved a nearby chair under them, elevating them to help reduce the bleeding.

I came in behind her and wrapped each bleeding hole with the bandages I fashioned, and he let out a loud groan as I tightened and applied pressure.

Cecilia poured two more shots and handed one to her second in command, he accepted it willingly though the scowl never left his face. "Salud," she said, raising hers in the air before shooting it down her throat and slamming the glass on a nearby counter. "Lighten up, Lobito. If you'd kept your mouth shut, none of this would be happening. If it was up to me, I'd be drinking expensive wine somewhere in Seville right now, but unfortunately, this is what happens when you put your faith in men."

"You didn't have to shoot me princesa. I would have agreed to it without the bullets in me," he gritted through his teeth like he was having a hard time dealing with the pain, and she could clearly see it. She laughed and poured him another shot that he grabbed without hesitation.

"I didn't shoot you to convince you to help me, you know better than that. One bullet was for leaving me behind fifteen years ago. The second bullet was for the loose lips. Rafa would have killed you for both," she snorted a laugh.

"You think he'd be proud of me?" She raised her eyebrows in question at the thought of her father and his opinion of her but Cézar just groaned a response.

It was hard to figure out if she loathed the guy, or if she idolized him. Hell, maybe it was both.

A parent could do a number on a kid.

"What's next then?" He raised an eyebrow at her before turning his shot over, seeming completely unaffected by the burn of the alcohol, and the holes she put through his body.

"The Black Crows have a Russian Mafia problem."

I could see the tips of her fingers turning white from her grip on the shot glass tightening, and the look in her eyes told me she was reliving some of her time in that basement.

"Consider it my problem too."

She shuddered as she snapped out of it, "And now I'm making it yours." She narrowed her eyes at him as she crossed her arms over her chest waiting for him to deny her, but he didn't.

Suddenly a kid in scrubs came bursting through the door, nearly knocking me aside as he rushed to Cézar's aid. But the dutiful president waved the young, blonde doctor aside and forced him to tend to the other guy Cecilia shot. I mean, to be fair he looked way worse off, and he was starting to turn white from the blood loss.

"*That's* your doctor?" Cecilia nearly laughed out, earning a less than intimidating scowl from the young doctor donning a leather cut over his hospital scrubs just like the rest of the men here. Except his said "MÉD".

"I'm a first-year medical student," he narrowed his eyes at Cecilia, and she threw her hands up sarcastically in defense.

"My apologies Médico," she fought a smirk as she turned back to Cézar and murmured loud enough for me to hear. "Should I be concerned for you?"

"Believe it or not, without you around, life-threatening injuries were pretty few and rare for me. Even in a one percent club. But Méd can handle it, his dad had him patching us up before he was even out of high school. His old man would have been proud."

Before I realized it the doc finished up with the other guy, had an IV drip going and everything in the corner of the room. He was fast, but Cézar was officially looking worse for wear, and Cecilia moved to sit next to him, holding his hand in hers and talking quietly between them.

I guess if he ended up dying, they might have some things to air out between them. I could understand that. Villalobos was too tough and too ornery of a bastard to die so peacefully. He had too much chaos in him, just like I did. Guys like us needed to die wild. Not on a fucking leather couch, in a remodeled farmhouse with fucking *oak* floors.

"Hey. Open your eyes asshole," I shook his shoulder, my eyes darting over to Cecilia who bit her lip nervously and looked at me with a flash of fear in her eyes.

"He's gonna need blood, he's lost too much. He shouldn't have let me patch up Rico first, I didn't realize he'd been shot twice," Méd glared at

Cecilia, realizing how important he was to the room and allowing it to make his balls grow twice as large.

He probably wouldn't be so gutsy had he been here five minutes ago.

"I'm gonna need to run some quick tests to find a blood match." The doc said and Cecilia immediately tisked him, rolling her sleeve past her elbow, practically shoving it in the doctor's face.

"No need, we're a match," she said plainly, gathering the entire room's interest.

"It's not the first time one of us has drained the other of nearly all their blood," Cézar explained with a grunt as the doctor began to clean Cecilia's arm with antiseptic and poke her with needles. "We found out we were a match pretty early on."

"Rafa nearly shit when he realized all he needed to do was keep Cézar around in case I lost too much blood," she said it too casually like she was telling childhood memories, and maybe it was. Perhaps it was too hard for her to see how much fucked up trauma lived in her past, Rafael Flores somehow normalized it for them. Seeing who she was around Cézar was a glimpse into a piece of her I didn't think I'd ever know.

This was her...*Celia Flores.*

The real her.

"Can you ask Emory to make the drive out here? I'd feel better if she checked on him," she looked up at Ronan with puppy dog eyes that would no doubt get him bending to every one of her whims, but I didn't blame her. She just wanted to keep the little bit of family she had left alive.

I would have given anything to be able to do the same.

He nodded in response and pulled out his phone as he stepped outside.

44

CELIA

Originally, I had no intention of staying the night in Grimm's Reach at a motorcycle club compound, but Cézar looked like shit and I wanted to wait until a *real* doctor looked at him.

Okay, maybe I was being an asshole about their club doctor, but the kid looked seriously young, and his hands were pretty damn shaky. Not a reassuring quality in someone who's trying to keep criminals alive.

It was nearly eight at night, and despite the fact their president had been shot, and I'd just declared ownership of their little, *whatever* this was, it looked like a party was almost always on the agenda for the Diablos once the sun set. She pulled into the compound in one of those bright blue electric car cabs with her typical oversized medical bag and her pristine white pencil skirt and blazer.

I literally ached to be that put together.

But I was kind of a hot mess at all times and as I looked down at my shredded black jeans and faded *System of a Down* t-shirt, I knew I'd outgrown my style a long time ago. Who had time to define personal fashion sense when you'd been either running for your life, or held captive by your asshole ex?

The same asshole who was looming over me now like a bad mood I couldn't shake. The added testosterone floating around the motorcycle club must have been getting to his head. He was doling out death glares at anyone who so much as walked by me. I could at least appreciate the fact that he let me hold my own when I walked in here. It was nearly impossible to be taken seriously as a threat when you were a woman if there was a man constantly trying to fight your battles for you.

She knocked on the door and the prospect opened it up for her, she smiled at me as she entered the room, and I couldn't help but return it. Emory was too genuine for me to pretend like I wanted to hate her, and she was right. I needed to make an effort to have at least one friend, clearly Santos wasn't willing to fill that space anymore.

Women didn't need to find enemies in each other. This world was already constantly pitting us against each other as it was.

"Have you fucked her?" I said under my breath just loud enough for the two men on my side to hear, not turning my head either way so that they'd know the question was directed to both of them.

It was weird to want to know that, but there was a part of me that wasn't even sure if I'd be upset if either of them said yes. She was really attractive and honestly, I'd probably want to fuck her too if I was that brave.

I was *maybe* gay in the sense that I could look at any woman and appreciate her for her beauty, her body, and her personality. But put a vajayjay in my face and I definitely wouldn't know what to do with it.

I *for sure* liked cock.

Mateo spat out his drink, choking and coughing while Ronan growled out, "No," without skipping a beat. I turned my head a fraction of an inch towards Mateo and raised one eyebrow while I waited for him to finish getting his shit together.

"No!" He said between coughs like he was laughing at me, and I turned my head back to the room, all the attention on the beautiful redhead sauntering towards my brother.

"I assume the old dying man is who I'm here to check on?" She said in her snarky tone that I was kind of growing to love. She just didn't give a fuck about being polite, she knew her worth, and she didn't take any shit from anyone. The only person she really seemed to answer to was Ronan.

"Old man?" Cézar rasped out, wincing in pain. "Blanca I can promise I'd run circles around you if it wasn't for the bullet through my leg." He winked at her.

Emory granted my brother a nearly lethal side-eye, barely stopping to entertain his antics before opening her bag of tricks.

"Unless that's your thing, then I'll gladly let you call me Papi eh?"

Gross.

Watching Cézar flirt was tragic.

I turned and walked towards the bar, knowing at least now my brother was in good hands and would make it through the night. I didn't have to look back to know my guys were following behind me, I could feel their presence there. Yeah, I liked knowing I could be powerful enough to handle any storm I was fronted with, but it also felt good to know there would always be someone holding my umbrella.

To have them watching my back like there was nothing else better they could want to be doing.

I never thought this was a loyalty I could have, without buying it of course.

My mind immediately went to Santos, as if I'd been programmed to think of him now when I thought about the other two. Kind of how I couldn't think of Ronan without thinking of Mateo, or vice versa.

They'd all wormed their way under my skin, into my heart somehow, finding all the vulnerable pieces of me I'd laid bare and accepting them for what they were. They'd given me exactly what I needed from each of them so I could survive with what was left of me.

I took three or four shots of tequila with Ronan before Mateo cut me off, forcing me to drink water as well, but at this point, I couldn't complain. It was probably my sixth shot of the day, and even though it had been stressful as hell, it was not going to be a good look if I threw up here.

Especially on the fancy wood.

What was with these oak floors? This place was creepily nice for a one percent stomping ground. Out of nowhere, Ronan grabbed my chin and stole a kiss from me, practically forcing my mouth open as he slipped his tongue through my lips and shoved it deep inside.

"I'll be back," he said heading toward the bathroom, and before he'd even disappeared from view Mateo was mimicking the same action, kissing me just as deeply in front of the entire MC like he didn't care what they thought about any of this. He pulled a joint out of his pocket and whispered in my ear.

"Want to join me outside?" He twirled it in his fingers, and though it sounded like a great idea considering how tense my world had been feeling lately, I'd had too much to drink, and that joint was a one-way ticket to the spins.

"Next time," I said, giving him a quick peck on the cheek and he walked out of the front door. Through the farmhouse windows I could see him sitting down on the porch swing as he inhaled his joint and blew out the smoke.

"Will he make it then?" I asked Emory as she walked over to me and sat down on the barstool.

"He will indeed. I'm glad you called me, I had to open one of the stitches in his leg. There was still a good amount of bullet fragments in there but I was able to get them out," she explained, grabbing one of the already poured shots of tequila and downing it without any expression.

Okay, Doc.

"Oops," I said with a guilty expression painted on my face.

"*You* shot him?" She asked.

"He had it coming," was all I said, and I appreciated her for not trying to pry any further.

"He'll recover completely in a couple of weeks, just needs to take antibiotics and watch out for an infection now, the med student can take over from here," she smirked at me.

"Well, thank you for coming out here, I know you did it for Ronan, but I appreciate it," I said to her, and she smiled at me.

"Look at you, making an effort. That's growth," she let out a genuine laugh, the playful side of her so much different than her icy, professional demeanor. "Listen, I know it's not in my place to say but, Ronan was very clear about what you mean to him," she said, her expression growing a bit more serious now.

"Meaning?" I asked, wanting her to cut the shit and get to the point.

"I saw you and Mateo." She fumbled her words, delaying the next bit, "Promiscuity, it's a really common trauma-based response-"

"You're right," I cut her off, "It's not your place," I cut her a glance.

Emory's eyes grew with fear, her response a stuttering of sounds that made no words.

I didn't like it, for once.

God damn it, I *wanted* her to be my friend, and though I had gone through life without any, I knew you weren't supposed to scare your friends into telling you whatever you wanted to hear. "I'm not lying to either of them, I'm not hiding anything," I clarified.

"Well then, you must be living out every girl's fantasy," she joked with a laugh, "Or nightmare."

I let my lip curl up in a smile before hustling a cigarette from a nearby biker and pushing my way through the doors to join Mateo outside. He eyed the Newport in between my fingers and lifted an eyebrow up as if he wasn't expecting it.

I shrugged my shoulders, "Sometimes the heart wants what the heart wants."

Six shots in, and it was nicotine.

"I'm seeing you in a whole new light today." His husky voice threw my stomach into a swirling spiral.

"Is that a good thing or a bad thing?" I questioned him anxiously.

"I thrive in mayhem. Keeps me on my toes." He brought the lighter to the cigarette in my mouth.

"I may end up being more than what you bargained for," I exhaled the smoke through my lips before straddling him on the bench.

"I sure fucking hope so, Sunshine." He said, flicking the end of his joint onto the ground before pulling me into him. He buried his nose into my hair, taking a deep breath before whispering into my ear. "I waited a long time to find you, it would be such a disappointment if your presence brought me anything less than pure havoc."

The melt-my-panties smirk was gone, in its stead was a smile that was the most genuine I'd seen on his face since meeting him. I ran my fingers through his hair, as if to feel if he was actually real.

"I hope I don't make you regret those words, crazy boy." I shook my head at him before climbing off his lap and heading back inside before Ronan came hunting for me.

The party died down once the Doc declared the wounded were medically ordered to stop drinking or they'd bleed through their bandages, and Cézar genuinely seemed to not be listening on purpose to get her attention. He was a smooth bastard and maybe it was part of his plan because she eventually had to go tuck him into bed to make sure he'd get some rest.

An Old Lady to one of the older members set us up in two different rooms and I told her to put the guys in the other together so I could have one to myself. I didn't want to deal with Ronan fuming about me spending another night in bed with Mateo, so it was just easier this way.

When we got home, I had every intention of claiming the extra bedroom on the other side of the penthouse to myself, and I was hoping neither of them would have an issue with it. A girl needed her own space for all intents and purposes. A place away from all the sulking and testosterone sometimes.

Did that mean I was starting to become a permanent fixture in their space?

And was that the wisest thing?

45

SANTOS

7

GUILLERMO

I grabbed the half empty bottle of tequila on my bedside table I'd been nursing all day and lifted my head just enough to take a big swig, most of it ending up on my chin and shirt.

Fuck.

I was drunker than I'd realized.

I wasn't honestly sure where the last few days had gone either.

I needed to keep my wits about me if this was going to work the way I'd planned. I rolled my way out of bed, practically crashing to the floor that somehow ended up closer than it normally was. I could have sworn this bed was taller.

Fuck it.

Poorly constructed plans always ended up a mess, but half-cocked was better than no cocks at this point. I needed to get this ticking time bomb out of this building before it blew everyone inside up.

But which one of us was the bomb?

In a way this was all in my hands.

I could end the threat right now.

I pulled the spare Glock out of the drawer of my bedside table, releasing the safety and letting the cool metal of the heavy piece slide inside my mouth. Would anyone really miss me? Would they actually care if I was gone? I already felt like I'd lost everything and everyone that meant something to me. I allowed every cynical door in my mind to open up and let the dark thoughts I normally fought back, flood out and take control.

You will never be deserving of the life you want.

Coward.

Do it!

Pressing my eyelids together tightly, I took a big exhale and squeezed the trigger.

The click of the empty chamber echoed far too loud in my silent room and shame cascaded down my entire body. A fucking assassin who can't even kill himself.

Fucking worthless.

I pulled the empty clip out of the gun and tossed it against the wall with force, unphased as it crashed into the mirror hanging opposite my bed. Hundreds of reflective shards spilled over the floor. It was tempting, but the mess wasn't appealing. I hurled the empty gun across the room as well, letting it fall to the pile of glass.

The least I owed my brothers was a relatively clean death.

Maybe spraying my brain all over the bed wasn't as clean as I thought it would be, but there was something about a slit wrist that just wasn't as appealing. I didn't want to fade peacefully as my blood slowly drained out of me, I didn't deserve that kind of end. I needed the shock and the bang of a bullet splitting open my brain and taking me away from all of this.

Take me away from her.

The room was starting to spin so I quickly sat up, unsure when I'd ended up laying on the cold floor. Instantly, I heaved out all the contents of my stomach onto the ground next to me. It was mostly tequila anyway, I couldn't really remember the last time I had the urge to actually eat anything. I grabbed the bottle again and took a swig, swishing it through my gums and teeth to get the bitter taste of vomit out of my mouth.

Stumbling as I stepped over my pile of puke, I grabbed my phone and made it to my bedroom door. I pushed my way through Kane's room and was surprised to find him alone on the bed with his new guitar this late.

Wait, was it late?

"Where is she?" I mumbled out.

"What?" He asked like he didn't know what I'd said, stopping his strumming.

"Where is she?" I yelled this time.

"Wow, you are trashed, dude. Have you been drinking all day?" He said with that judgmental tone he got any time he saw us settling our feelings with liquor.

"What time is it?" I asked, fighting the heavy weight of my eyelids.

"Nearly two in the morning, drink some water. Go to sleep," he instructed with a stern parental concern.

"Where...Is...She?" I said again pausing between each word to make sure they came out clearly even though I was slurring beyond my own control.

"You've barely said two words to her since we got her back from the Bratvas, you sure you want to see her now?" He cocked an eyebrow at me like I was an idiot.

I was.

"What, do I need your permission now to talk to her?"

He scoffed at me, "I'm not stupid Álvarez, you've been coming into my room every night while she's slept here."

"And now Ronan's made you give her back to him then?" I sneered at the thought and immediately lost my footing and fell. Kane walked over to me and grabbed the tequila bottle out of my hands before I could argue.

"No, if you'd been around at all you'd know she's asked to stay in the guest bedroom," he said as he made his way to his bathroom. "Maybe if you had the balls to talk to either her or Zerkos yourself, you wouldn't be sinking into the pit of despair you seemed to have fallen face first in." I could hear the sound of my Añejo being poured down a drain and I groaned in anger.

Probably for the best though.

"Get your shit together. This isn't a good look," he crossed his arms as he looked down on me and then used his foot to roll me out of the room. Once my body was past the threshold he shut the door on me, clicking the lock loud enough so that I'd know I wasn't welcome.

He was right.

I'd been watching over her almost every night.

She woke up often, and she woke up screaming almost every time. Kane slept heavily and almost never noticed except for maybe one or two times. It started to become a habit, keeping an eye on her at night. It's not like I was helpful, and it's not like she even knew I was there, but it felt like someone needed to see her this way.

This raw, fearful version of her that she didn't let anyone else see.

It took me back to our days in the apartment, where she'd wake up from her nightmares and come to me for comfort. I would stay up late playing video games no matter how tired I was, some nights I'd even make coffee to make sure I'd make it to her witching hour. She'd appear in the doorway with that glazed look on her eyes and sweat drenching her hair and I knew she was lost to her past without having to ask. She'd sit next to me, have a beer, or tell me about her dreams with her feet on my lap, and eventually, she'd fall back asleep.

It was so innocent, but even then, I knew it was more.

I was doing too much.

I was going too far for someone who wasn't and would never be mine.

Using the wall to steady myself, I crossed the hall and grabbed my Glock off the floor, brushing away the pieces of glass and sticking it in my pants. I pulled out my phone and read over the text that had been sitting there, unsent, for the last four days.

This was it. The thing that would ruin all of it, all of us. The guillotine needed to drop, and I had to be a man for once in my life and do the right thing. Make the right call. I hit send and the reply came almost immediately.

Meet in the parking garage in 30.

ARCHER

I stuffed my phone back into my pocket and heard the distant sound of her struggling in her dreams again. Cracking the door to her new room, I saw her lying there, twisting and turning as she fought against someone in her mind.

How she could be fearless and strong while being fragile and soft was the biggest enigma. Or maybe she wasn't, the realization that I didn't actually know her was more painful than I'd wanted to admit. There was a time I'd given up all my secrets to her because I thought I was worthy of the same from her.

But I wasn't.

I was just a fool.

An insect caught in her web as she spun me into her next meal.

This was a stranger lying in front of me. Someone I didn't know, I didn't recognize at all. An actress who played the part so well I couldn't tell where make-believe collided with the truth of who she actually was. But as I stared at her now, I knew I was failing at fooling myself, because she was perfect in every way. It was the worst kind of anguish to know that the sum of our parts *did* fit together so well. We were two puzzle pieces so clearly crafted by a cruel God who never meant for us to be whole.

Two kids who had their entire childhood ripped away from them by cruel men who served even crueler purposes. Men who molded children into weapons and used them for their sadistic bidding. Families who only cared about how we could serve the "purpose", because money was always more important than happiness.

"Mmm...No!" She mumbled in her dream as she thrashed from side to side, and it pained me. I couldn't touch her, couldn't reach out and soothe her, couldn't wrap her in my arms and tell her that it was going to be okay.

That was never my job.

I was just the idiot who was always in the way, always there.

Was I ever even her friend?

My mind was taking advantage of my weakness, filling my head with the most vile black and white thoughts I couldn't shake out.

Was I meant to be her end?

Or was she somehow mine?

46

CELIA

I stared at the ceiling in the plainly decorated extra bedroom on the other side of the penthouse while I laid in bed. Another dream of Caro blending with my time in captivity haunting me back awake. I told Ronan I needed space and he didn't fight me on it, it seemed like he wasn't fighting me on anything anymore. It was slightly uncomfortable to see him submitting to every wish or demand I made, and I knew it was the guilt eating him alive.

I'd have to let it go eventually, I loved him too much, and this behavior wasn't sustainable. I didn't fall in love with a doormat, I fell in love with a man who pushed me to my limits and kept every spark inside of me alive.

My time with the Bratva was still proving to have temporary lingering effects as I continued to wake every two to three hours, gasping for air when the water would splash me awake through my nightmares. Except for this time, it was the dream with my sister again, the one where everything is pitch black, but I can hear Carolina's desperate cries and the sounds of bullets ripping through her little body as the cars drove away.

I knew I could easily sneak my way into Mateo's room if I really wanted to, and even worse I knew that sleeping next to Ronan would likely soothe all of my anxiety and fears that played in my mind on repeat. As much as I thought I needed to be alone, I couldn't lie, it was terrifying to be only a few feet away from their protection.

It felt like miles.

But I was dead set on making Ronan earn his forgiveness even if my heart screamed "liar" at me. The insecure part of me that went unloved for far too long, was starting to feel like I was suffocating Mateo in his own space. I'd slept in his room every night since I'd come back here. That was really the main reason I fought to take over this room. But even as I ignored the pain in my back, staring into the nothing, I wondered if alone was really something I could handle anymore.

I spent so many years fending for myself, so many years on the run, being the only person that I could count on. Now for some reason being alone felt like torture. There was also the nagging thought that'd been consuming me ever since Santos put that gun to my back. Did I somehow lose the only friend I ever truly had since my sister?

It was always at these odd hours of the night that I could count on Santos being awake, playing some video game in our janky old apartment. How the sounds of zombie hoards and machine guns on the PlayStation could always lull me back to sleep was a mystery, but I never thought too much to question it. We were living in different times now, and my best friend couldn't even stand the sight of me anymore.

His unsteady breathing alerted me to his presence, and I turned my head to find him sitting in the white leather chair in the corner of the room as if I'd conjured him up out of my own twisted thoughts.

"Come here often?" I tried to joke, but even in the darkness, I could see the scowl etched deeply into his features.

"Get dressed," he said coldly.

Oh, it's that mood.

Here we fucking go again.

I was wearing pajama shorts and a top, and if he was going to threaten to kill me again, I really didn't want to bother with putting on different clothes for the ceremony. He pushed himself off the chair, stumbling towards me and I tilted my head at him in confusion.

"Are you okay? You reek of booze dude," I laughed but even shit faced his reflexes were on point and he immediately had his gun pressed underneath my chin, lifting my head up to look at him.

"Don't fuck with me Morena."

"Santos," I breathed, "There's no clip in your gun." I whispered out the obvious fact, he was holding half a weapon in his hand and was in no way threatening to me at all. "But I'll go wherever you want me to." I blinked up at him, wrapping my wrist around as much of his forearm that it could and he curled his lip, his anger only rising the more I kept my cool.

He was drunk, and on a downward trajectory. This entire week had been hell without having him to confide in, to talk to, to tell me that everything was going to be okay because we'd get through it together.

He pushed past me and walked over to the night stand next to my bed, opening the drawer and pulling out another pistol.

Good to know. *Apparently, if I want a gun, I just need to open a drawer.*

"Hands," he said, and I sighed a heavy exhale before giving them to him. He secured the zip tie around my wrists fast, taking me by surprise. Every part of me quickly wanted to protest and fight back, my red flags were raising high, but it was Santos. If there was anyone I trusted in this world to keep me safe, it was still him.

Wasn't it?

"Let's go," he tapped me with the mouth of the weapon, and I slid on the fuzzy slippers Mateo bought for me, before opening the bedroom door. Once we got to the elevator, he pressed the 'G' and I turned to look at him.

"Not going up this time?" I asked, but he didn't answer, like looking at my face was somehow going to piss him off further. The elevator took its time making its way down each and every floor of the high-rise until we reached the parking garage. The humidity rushed its way through the doors of the lobby like a suffocating blanket I couldn't pull off and it became hard to breathe.

"Where are we going?" I asked him, forcing the crease between his brows to become more prominent. He took the black bandana out of his back pocket, folding it into a thin flat shape before wrapping it over my open mouth and tying it behind my head, keeping me gagged and unable to speak.

This wasn't right.

A tear pricked its way out of my left eye, and I quickly brought my bound hands up to wipe it away.

"Walk," he pushed me, causing me to trip over my feet and fall on the rough concrete of the parking garage. He huffed and grabbed me by the arm, lifting me up to my feet again and we both walked. I kept my gaze down as we walked, unsure if there was anything I wanted to see anymore.

We walked through the damp garage, no sounds but the slow dripping of a nearby leaky pipe and the tapping of our feet against the concrete.

"No shit, that pretty little cocksucker is what all this trouble is about?" I lifted my head to see the old creep who called himself Dezmond Senior leaning against the trunk of a black Range Rover and my heart nearly stopped.

"No questions. Can you get rid of her, or not?" His voice was colder and rougher than I'd ever heard before. This wasn't a Santos I knew, every sane part of me told me I should be scared and every muscle in my body was shaking from fear, no, not fear. His betrayal was quickly settling in, and anger was taking the place of the panic that wanted to rise inside me.

"And what do you get out of this?" He asked Santos.

"No questions," he repeated in the same solemn tone.

"Well, what do I get out of this then?" The bold Archer continued to ask questions, despite the fact Santos looked close to putting him six feet under.

"What do you get? How about when Ronan finds out you've been consorting with the Bratvas, I'll let you go far enough away from here that you don't hear your son's skin being fileted from his limbs piece by piece." His nostrils flared wildly, and his chest rose and fell heavily with his breathing as Dezmond Senior's eyes widened in shock.

"There must be some mistake, I-" Archer tried to backpedal but Santos quickly interrupted him.

"Call your contact. Now!" He waved his gun at the old man's face and with trembling hands he pulled his phone out and made the call.

"An-O..." I tried to call out his name, but the bandana gagging me got in the way.

He turned sharply to face me while Dezmond Senior made the call. "For what it's worth, I *am* sorry Cecilia. I wouldn't be doing this if there was another option." I had so many questions, and my biggest fear wasn't the unknown future I was headed towards right now, it was the possibility I wouldn't be getting an answer.

If the Bratva were involved there was a good chance I was going straight back into the hell I just came from. I reached out to him with my bound hands, but he stepped back and pushed them down with his own.

"The Cártel wants you dead, which means Los Muertos put a hit out on you. Either you die by my hand, or you die by someone else's, but you *will* die Morena. If I don't get you out of here, the entire Brotherhood goes down with you. I can't have that." His eyes went soft with his explanation, and I wished to God, he hadn't given it to me.

It would have been much simpler to do this with hatred in my heart instead of the sympathy I now felt for him.

I would have thrown myself to the wolves too.

Hell, if he cut me free, I would probably go willingly. I'd known enough about the way the dynamic between Santos and his cousin worked to understand, I was endangering every life inside that building by staying here.

This was a message from my tio.

There was nowhere, or no one, I would be safe with.

And no one would be safe from me either.

Not until one of us was dead.

I nodded my head in understanding at him, the terror starting to lift its way off me as I remembered the piece of comfort buried under my skin. His plan would only last as long as it took for Ronan to find me again.

He *would* find me again.

Right?

Had I caused too much damage? Had I put too much of a distance between us? Maybe it was time I just accepted my fate. Maybe I could look at the situation with the Bratva as an opportunity, they could sell me to someone and perhaps that was the best way for me to finally disappear from my tio's radar.

We hadn't broken eye contact this entire time, and I'd never wanted to be able to read someone's mind more than in this exact moment. I inched closer to him, and he raised his eyebrows up in warning. I took one more step until I could place my head on his chest, the closest thing to an embrace that I could manage with my bound hands. He cleared his throat and kept his arms pinned to his side uncomfortably.

"They will send the meetup location," Archer said as he put his phone back into his pocket and walked our way, "If you want, I can take her myself. I'd love to get a chance to sample the merchandise before it goes on sale." He licked his lips and my stomach churned at the words but before I could express my disgust, my ear was ringing from the shot fired out next to my head.

"Why you gotta to say some shit like that, old man?" Santos yelled out with a groan as he put the gun back in his pants and Senior dropped to his knees, clutching his throat in his hand. The blood was pooling through his fingers and coming out of his mouth as he choked to death from the hot metal lodged into his neck.

"An-o..." I said again, I stepped in front of him, and he turned his head to the side, away from me. I placed my hands awkwardly on his chest, dropping my forehead to the hard muscles that coated his lean body. My head moved harshly with his heavy breathing and before I realized it, my whole body was shaking from the tears that were pouring out of me.

"You don't get to do that," his voice cracked with the same anger that filled him the day he lost it in his room.

"It's not enough you've got the both of them, but you wanna see if you can still keep stupid, needy Santos wrapped around your fingers too? *'He's such a good friend, he'll always do anything for me.'*" His tone was cold and bitter as he grabbed my hands off him and lifted them above my head.

He walked me backwards with a sneer carved on his lips until my back hit a concrete pillar. I winced in pain before looking down to see we were standing just over the dying Dezmond Archer Senior, his blood pooling around my slippers while it soaked into the faux pink fur.

I didn't speak, it wouldn't matter, It would just come out garbled against the fabric and it didn't seem like my words would matter even if he understood them. I was starting to see this pain for what it was, but how was I supposed to have known? I never once stopped to ask myself what Santos meant to me, because it meant questioning what Ronan had been to me too. But things were different now, and I knew my feelings for Mateo existed outside of my feelings for Ronan.

And Santos?

Well, all I knew was that I couldn't fathom an existence without him either.

Maybe without any of them.

His nostrils flared as he slammed my wrists against the pillar, a painful groan escaped my lips and I looked up at him in shock.

"I don't want to be your friend anymore, Morena. You understand?" He spoke through clenched teeth, and I nodded even though terror was starting to creep its way back inside of me. Dezmond made a gurgling noise as his body finally gave into the surrender of death, which seemed to annoy Santos even more. He pulled his gun out again and shot him in the forehead for good measure.

He slid the barrel of the gun against the side of my arm with a tedious slowness, I bit through the bandana and winced from the heat of it against my skin. "Good," he said.

"That's what it feels like being around you, every second of every damn day." His voice steadied, but this was a man drowning in pain.

No longer the carefree breeze my heart once knew, but the dark and dangerous miscreant he tried hiding away. He moved his weapon down, trailing it across my stomach and I hissed through the fabric around my mouth in anticipation.

"You don't know what it's like," he continued, sliding the Glock down to my legs and trailing it up the inside of my thigh, the scorching heat tempered out to a dull warmth that awakened every nerve in my body to attention.

"You don't know what you do to me," he growled out, slamming my wrists back again.

I cried out once more, less from the pain and more from the shock of his confession, and the things his words, his touch, were doing to me. His jaw set into that hard line while the mouth of the Glock rested at the apex of my thighs and a whimper freed itself from my lips.

He dragged the gun inside the opening of my pajama shorts, resting it just over my pussy, the anticipation was almost painful, and my heart thundered in my chest.

I rubbed my thighs together for friction, pushing the tip of the gun against my center to try to relieve this feeling. My whole body was starting to feel so uncomfortably hot I felt like I was going to explode if he didn't do something, anything at all.

I wanted to reach out and touch him, grab him, but my hands were still pressed firmly against the pillar under his tight hold. The bandana was starting to soak from my saliva as I kept mumbling incoherently with desperate whines, unsure of what it was I really wanted to say.

Stop?

No.

"Le-ase..." I moaned through the wet fabric.

"Monsters like us, we're drawn to each other. I could never understand why I couldn't shake you from my head all these years." He looked down at me, his expression still cold, and hard to see through. "You and I are made from the same sins. Born from the same wretchedness. We come from the wicked."

"It's the reason why you're dripping all over my piece, instead of crying for help," he whispered, and I moved my hips in frustration, grunting in disappointment from not being able to communicate what I needed from him.

I wanted him to do it.

Cross that line.

Change things forever.

Mateo and I created something out of nothing, that was easy to do. With Santos, we needed to destroy everything we knew if this was going to happen.

I needed this to happen.

And I could see in him that he needed it too.

He rubbed the tip of the Glock back and forth against my clit, coating it in my own juices as he breathed angrily, but didn't dare look away from me. He wanted me to tell him to stop, that we shouldn't do this, but those lies wouldn't come from me.

I wanted everything that was owed to me now.

And that included him.

Blinking up at him, I stepped my feet apart, splashing through the sticky blood that now completely surrounded us. He let out a breath that sounded like hesitation, but by the time he inhaled again he forced the barrel inside of me.

"Nhm." I moaned out at the intrusive object filling me up and he narrowed his gaze, studying me, like he really couldn't believe what he was seeing even though he was the one wielding all the power here.

He was right.

We were mirror images of each other. Damaged, fucked up beyond salvation by the brutality our families bestowed onto the world.

He pulled the weapon out slowly just to slam it back in, forcing another muffled gasp out of me. Nothing surprised me anymore, not the fact that I was getting off to a loaded weapon that had just been used to shoot the corpse I stood over. And not the fact that it was Santos Álvarez holding that same gun covered with my arousal.

He pulled it in and out of me, building a tension I desperately needed to release. I encouraged him, bucking my hips and moaning in anticipation every time he drew it out of me. I was close, and my mind was flying high, somewhere else entirely even if my eyes were still locked onto the beautiful, tortured creature who stood in front of me. He pulled the gun out completely and stuffed it into his back pocket, moving his head side to side as he continued to study me.

I cried out a pathetic moan of defeat feeling the sudden emptiness he left me with.

"We don't deserve happiness," he whispered down to me, his wild curls falling in front of his face. Maybe he believed it in some deep fundamental place inside himself, but he didn't fool me.

"We've done nothing to deserve it. Don't you agree?" He undid the button on his jeans, still keeping my wrists roughly pinned above my head with his left hand while his right reached into his pants and pulled himself out. I could make out his thick girth in his fist along with the sparkle of silver reflecting underneath his shaft, and I burned something terrible to feel him inside of me.

"We deserve every miserable second we have coming to us, Morena." He breathed out raggedly as he stroked himself up and down, pinning his body so close to mine, all I wanted to do was rub myself against his thighs like a cat in heat to ease some of this torturous feeling.

There was something so dangerous about him like this, so vulnerable and yet so deadly. We could cross this threshold and never look back, fabricate something out of the ashes of how our story began. I could see it in that hazel stare of his, that he was still too scared. Whether it was of the future between him and Ronan if we made this happen or if it was that he was simply afraid of getting what he wanted, of having something worth anything for himself.

Maybe Ronan was just the excuse he used because he couldn't handle the idea of being wanted. The promise of joy.

Life can't disappoint you if you always expect the worst.

But that's no way to live.

"A-nto," I moaned out again through the drenched bandana, but he ignored my plea and continued to fist himself, more anger than pleasure rippling through his features as he eventually climaxed, thick ropes of cum shooting onto my stomach and my pajamas. He quickly put himself back into his pants and his eyes widened with a sobering realization as he let my hands drop in front of me.

"Have one of your boyfriends finish you off," he peeled his lip up in distaste at the word boyfriends and I stood there, looking a bit dumbfounded while I stared awkwardly at him, still desperate for my release. He pulled the bandana out from my mouth, so it hung loosely on my neck.

"Go!" He said through clenched teeth,

I shook my head. He was having second thoughts, but I wasn't. He was right, I couldn't stay here. I couldn't risk innocent lives because I was too afraid of the world out there and the monsters that hunted me. As if he could read my mind, he bent down and fished Archer's cell phone from his blazer pocket and stuffed it into his own. He tugged me by the zip ties, my slipper getting stuck in the pool of blood, forcing me to fall down into it. He pulled me up with a bitter look on his face before unlocking the Escalade and popping the trunk open.

"Come on," he tilted his forehead towards the open trunk as if to say he was giving me the kindness of choosing for myself. I exhaled a heavy sigh before climbing in awkwardly with mostly my legs since my wrists were bound in plastic.

Normally I wouldn't have given it a second thought about Santos Álvarez, if you asked me about men I feared. But laying here in the trunk, my wrists secured, while he drowned out any possibility of a conversation with "505" by The Arctic Monkeys on full blast through the speakers, I was afraid. I wasn't sure if that fear was for myself, or for him; For what Ronan would do to him, and for how this would warp his soul.

But the one thing we both knew, and could agree on, was that I couldn't stay.

47

MATEO

Nothing like waking up at two in the morning to a phone call from Taylor in the tech lab to tell us something weird was happening in the parking garage. She'd always been pretty damn good under pressure, so to hear that kind of panic was alarming.

I rolled down to the tech lab, realizing too late that I couldn't get in on my own without my list of passcodes, which I handily kept inside Santos' or Ronan's brain. I pulled out my phone and dialed Taylor.

"Hey, I'm out here. Let me in." Just a few minutes later the pressurized door hissed open, and I pushed my way in. "What's going on? It's a bit early for a wakeup call."

"Maybe I'm just paranoid, but I figured one of you would want to see what I saw. Since Ronan didn't answer I'll take second best." She spit out the insult nonchalantly like she gave no fucks.

"Ouch," I said moving in next to her as she pulled up the feed from the camera in the elevators showing Santos directing Cecilia at gunpoint, her hands bound, and her mouth gagged. Hot as fuck, but concerning, nonetheless.

"When did this happen?" I asked, watching the two of them go inside the parking garage.

"Maybe forty minutes ago. It was hard to wake you assholes up. Normally Fletcher is around to handle this kind of bullshit," she sighed, we all missed the guy, but he was finally on the mend and would be coming home soon. "It's always something with you guys and this girl, isn't it?" She raised an eyebrow at me, knowing how much I loved the drama.

"I'm an addict, what can I say?" I smirked until the recording showed Dezmond Archer Senior appear. They talked a bit, but it didn't take more than a few minutes before Santos planted a bullet in his throat.

I watched the whole video before deciding to move into action, hoping at some point my brother would have regained clarity and backed out of whatever the fuck he thought he was doing here. I was raging, and not from watching Santos fuck Cecilia with a gun, but from the fact our brother was up to something sinister. His deceit was so clear from his behavior since he'd been back from Ocean Valley.

"Hey, uh... delete that shit," I told Taylor.

"What?" She asked in a confused type of outrage.

"You heard me. Don't let Ronan see that shit," I said with a stern voice as I turned back to leave the tech lab.

I called Santos about sixteen times before I made it back to the penthouse and gave up trying to get through to him, knowing he was on his own mission clouded by whatever was compelling him to betray us all.

I burst into Ronan's room and gave it my best to shake the bastard awake. Seeing his phone out and the dozens of missed calls from Taylor let me know she wasn't lying about having tried him first and failing.

"Wake up asshole!" I yelled out and almost like he'd been conditioned, his eyes jarred open wide with a scowl that carved into his features. "Santos took Celia." I didn't wait for him to fully sink into conscious mode before dropping the news on him, we needed to move into action. We already wasted too much time just by being asleep.

Zerkos slid into clothes faster than I thought possible, pulling out his phone to dial the bastard we'd called brother. "Argh!" He screamed out after the fifth time of going straight to voicemail.

"I've got Taylor setting up her tracker location to get sent to our phones. Let's go." I instructed him and he nodded before we made our way downstairs.

"Did you see anything?" Ronan asked Nate, who sat in a chair calmly behind the lobby desk.

"You mean, like Santos taking the girl?" He asked with a frown, like he didn't realize that was something out of the norm.

"Yeah, like that. Asshole." Zerkos seethed and our doorman shrugged. It wasn't his fault and it certainly wasn't his problem, but Ronan was going to find anyone to blame that he could until we had Celia back again.

As soon as he shoved through the doors to the garage, the black SUV screeched to a halt right in front of Zerkos without finding a parking spot. Santos' eyes were wide with surprise and full of fear at seeing the both of us, anger clearly present in both of our faces.

I only lingered back a few seconds behind Zerkos, but he didn't wait for Álvarez to get out. He pulled him out of the driver's seat and threw him onto the floor, practically on top of the corpse of Archer Senior. The brute percussion of his fists cascaded loudly in the concrete chamber of the garage and as I walked closer, I could make out Ronan hitting his face repeatedly, no efforts coming from Santos to stop it.

"Hey, he's not even blocking you," I called out, trying to calm down the rage bellowing through Zerkos but immediately remembered him in my room just a couple hours ago. "He's shitfaced. Did you drive this drunk?" I yelled, my own fury knowing no bounds as I counted all the ways he might have risked her life.

"Is this what you've been plotting you sneaky little shit?" He spit out as he pulled our brother up by the collar and socked him in the face one more time.

"Where is she?" I asked Santos as I crossed my arms over my chest, raising an eyebrow at him questioningly, still unwilling to accept he would have put her through any situation that could hurt her. He spit a wad of blood out just before Zerkos let go of his grip on his collar, dropping him down to the puddle of blood spread over the ground.

"I don't know."

"Probably not the best answer," I shrugged my shoulders at Ronan, and he hit him again and I flinched at the sound his fist made connecting to bone.

"What do you mean you don't know? What the fuck were you thinking?" Zerkos yelled out as he kicked Archer Senior's body over.

"I had to get rid of her," Santos said quietly, the smallest slur still in his speech.

I blinked back widely at his confession, but I didn't need Ronan to dish out this one. I took the satisfaction of feeling his face crunch under my knuckles.

"Where did you take her?" I barked out at him, hating the way the anger poured over me, hating the way it connected me to my piece of shit old man.

"The Bratvas. Guillermo put a hit on her," he looked down as he said the words, "I needed to get her out of here."

"And you didn't think we could handle this as a team?" Zerkos was practically foaming at the mouth, and I didn't blame him one bit. We didn't keep these kinds of secrets and it was concerning that Santos was in a headspace where he thought he was making the right decision by doing so. "You're fucking pathetic."

"What the hell happened here?" I narrowed my eyes at him as I gestured to Senior's corpse, but he refused to look at either of us.

"You either tell me or we're going up to the lab where we can all watch it, together." Zerkos sneered at him, and Santos' eyes widened, neither of them knowing I already prepared for this exact situation, but I let Álvarez make his choice anyway.

"Okay! Okay! I don't know man, I had a feeling he was our rat, I told him I needed help getting rid of someone, so we met down here. Then the old creep starts saying some shit about sampling the merchandise and I kind of lost it."

"Why do you care what he was gonna do to her if you were so desperate to get her out of here?" I asked him, even though I already knew the answer. All these secrets needed to end, and it started with him admitting to the one he'd been keeping for nearly fifteen years. "You think wherever she is, they aren't hurting her right now?" I yelled.

Santos dropped his head to his hands, and though part of it had to be from how hammered he was, I was almost positive he was crying.

"That bad huh?" I asked the poor fool.

"What's that bad?" Ronan asked as if he was really just that daft when it came to perceiving other people's emotions.

Such an only child.

"You don't understand. None of you fucking understand! It's fucking torture!" His face was still buried in his hands, and even though I was livid, my heart hurt for my brother. Fifteen years of pretending that your heart didn't belong to someone was a special kind of hell in itself.

"So, what, you just get rid of her and move on?" I asked the stupid bastard, but he shook his head.

"No," he took a long time to finally look at me, the gloss in his hazel eyes telling me exactly what he was planning to do when he got home, but we'd interfered.

"You're a stupid fucking idiot," I reached my hand down to pull him up from the spilt blood, but Ronan slapped my arm out of the way.

"What don't I understand?" He asked him, his nostrils flaring like he already knew the answer but needed to hear it for himself. Santos looked at me, but I raised my hands up, this wasn't my fight. Zerkos and I were still on unsteady ground when it came to Cecilia, but it looked like the fucker was gonna need to learn how to stand on a wobbly bridge if he was gonna survive.

"It's not my fault! I can't help it! She's fucking *everything*," Santos screamed at Ronan, slightly startling him with the outburst.

"So, you've just been playing me for a fool all these years?" He pushed our brother until he was practically laying back in the blood.

"No! I- I never crossed that line. I would have never," Santos crawled backwards as Zerkos prowled towards him, realizing how far Santos' betrayal really went.

But could we be held responsible for the person we fell for?

Santos looked like a broken disheveled version of the man I used to know, haunted by his own feelings for a woman he never meant to desire. His behavior was obvious now that I could see it for what it really was. We were alike in that way, but I refused to believe she wasn't meant for me. She wouldn't have wound up here if that were the case.

If she was solely meant for Ronan they would have lived happily ever after a decade ago in some suburban neighborhood with a picket fence and a cul-de-sac. Fate worked its cruelty mysteriously, and I held faith deep in my bones that Cecilia was here because she was meant for us, all of us.

She healed something in every single one of us, and I knew there was something she needed to take from the three of us just as equally. Only these idiots were too stubborn to allow themselves to see that, they were too caught up with what was socially acceptable, and they thought the idea of her belonging to just one of them made their dicks look bigger.

I knew the truth, a woman like her, she didn't belong to anyone. She was Lilith incarnate and we were simply the demons on the end of her leash meant to do her bidding.

"I trusted you with her, above everyone," Zerkos was yelling, and anyone could tell it was taking all of his self-control to not beat into Santos any further. He really couldn't handle any more of it, he was the smallest of the three of us by far, and compared to Ronan, he was downright tiny.

"You think I don't know that?" He cried out looking up at our brother standing over him.

"You think I didn't want to be what you wanted me to be for her? You think I want to feel this way? I'd rather fucking die Ronan, so go ahead and put me out of my misery so I don't have to do it myself later." He spit out another bloody wad and turned his head to the side, like he didn't care to see our expression after dropping that kind of bombshell.

The thought of Santos taking his own life because of the way he felt was a guilt I couldn't live with, and the fact all of it was over a girl and what he was forced to do in the name of Los Muertos was even worse. Except she wasn't just some girl, and if I put myself in his shoes even for a split second, his actions didn't seem so out of sorts.

I pulled Ronan back by the shoulders and shook my head at him, hoping he'd drop his feelings for now so our brother could have a chance to process his.

"Pull up her location Kane," Zerkos instructed, his tone just a touch calmer as he breathed through the pain of losing her yet again. As I logged on to the tracking app there was an obnoxious buzzing of a phone pressed against the hard concrete floor. I looked over at Santos and he pulled a cell out of his pants and handed it to me. I pulled the phone out to see a few missed calls from Dez as well as a text from a random number with a location sent over.

"Maybe it was a good thing you killed him when you did, he would have probably done the same to you at some point tonight." Ronan said to Álvarez, softening his tone as he extended his hand out to help him stand.

"Dez keeps calling. You think he's involved or just missing daddy?" I asked, holding up the phone and waving it.

Ronan and I both looked at each other and simultaneously raced to the lobby, but my heart sank as we pushed through the doors and found Nate dead and a few bullet holes on the door.

"Fuck!" I yelled out, my breathing short and ragged, I dropped my hands to my knees while I took in the situation.

"How would he know?" Santos asked as he hobbled into the lobby looking like a bag of soggy shit, and I felt kind of bad for the guy now that I was getting a good look at him in the light. Ronan's fists were heavy as hell, I knew firsthand. I kind of never wanted to be on the receiving end of them ever again if I could help it. But then, if it meant I could keep her, well I'd take as many of them as I needed to.

"Fifth floor, let's go," Zerkos barked out, keeping his cool and dialing out another number on his phone. "Hey, meet us in the armory in ten. We need you." He hung up the phone and we bypassed the elevator taking the stairs up to the fifth floor. There was too much urgency, even Santos who was seriously struggling to keep up, decided that waiting for any of the three elevators to drop down to the lobby was going to take more time than we had to spare to get our girl back.

"Dez is calling again," I said to Ronan, and he slowed down a couple steps to match my pace.

"Don't answer. I don't want him to do anything rash, It's better if we don't give him the satisfaction of knowing that we know." He had a genuine look of concern on his face, and I didn't blame him. Santos really sunk us in deep with this one. Generally, I almost always craved this kind of disorder, but for some reason, with her life on the line, it wasn't something that sparked any excitement anymore.

I just wanted her safe, with us.

"Taylor, can you see if Dezmond Archer is in the building?" Ronan spoke on his phone as we approached the fifth floor. "Keep us posted." He hung up and turned to me. "Call someone down to man the lobby. Send at least five men down." I nodded to him while I began setting up the instructions to our soldiers.

Once we entered the fifth floor, Ronan and I waited for Álvarez to catch up and we walked down the now empty cells together. I came down here when I heard of the mess he made here the other day, and I was honestly really impressed at our crew with how fast they cleaned that shit up.

"Change of plans blondie." Ronan called out to our remaining prisoner. "You're going home today." Her eyes went wide with his words, but not in a good way. Instead, there was fear brightly shining through them.

"No! You said I would get a new start!" She pleaded with him as Zerkos grabbed the keys from Hughes and unlocked the cell. He grabbed her by the wrist and pulled her out of the cage, and though she pulled against him she was far too small to make an impact. Hughes handed him a pair of handcuffs and Zerkos snapped them on behind her back.

"It's not personal," he hissed in her ear before shoving her towards Hughes.

"Need a couple of favors, can we count on you?" I asked him.

"You know it, boss," he reassured us with a nod.

"Tie her up a bit, get her in the trunk of the Escalade, see if you can get rid of the body in the garage on your way back. *Try* to avoid being seen, let's keep it between us for now, yeah?" I asked him, slapping his arm.

"The body?" He asked me, eyeing Ronan then doubling back when his eyes caught the state of Santos.

"Yeah, you can't miss it." I gave him an awkward grin and another tap on the arm. He picked up Oksana and tossed her over his shoulder like a sack of potatoes and made his way out.

"Keys!" I shouted back at him and tossed them over his way in time for him to catch it.

"Now that's dealt with," Ronan said, and he eyed me suspiciously.

I cocked an eyebrow at him, not sure where his head was going this time.

Normally Santos would be the quicker one, but he was still pretty shit-faced and now he was injured to boot. Zerkos was just too fast when he pushed our brother into the open cell and shut the door, letting it lock in front of us.

"What the fuck man?" Santos cried out from the floor.

"You're no good to us right now. You're a liability. Sober up. Maybe we'll come back for you after I figure out if I can still trust you," he said to him before turning around to walk out of the room.

"You can't fucking leave me here! Are you kidding me right now Zerkos?" He yelled out again, shaking the bars in his hands. "Kane!" I looked back at him with my mouth open, and as much as I wanted to help him, get him out of that humiliating cell, Ronan wasn't wrong.

He was a liability right now.

We couldn't fuck this up.

We couldn't risk losing her again.

48

CELIA

The car ride wasn't quick, at least six or seven songs played to completion before we arrived, wherever the fuck I was now. Santos sent a text out on a phone as he opened the trunk, eyeing me with a look of uncertainty before throwing a cord around my ankles to tie my feet together. He hitched me over his shoulder with a grunt.

"I can carry *you* if it's easier," I snorted out, but he didn't find the humor in my joke. We were outside some warehouse, nothing else nearby and not a single car driving on the secluded dirt road that connected to the building.

And I was starting to regret my decision.

"I have to go Morena, they can't see me here or they'll think you're some sort of trap." he said looking down at me as he laid me on the ground on my side, too many visions of regret shadowing over his eyes. He brushed a strand of hair behind my ear, our gazes locked as my heart thundered in its cage.

This was likely the last time we'd see each other, and all I could think about was that we'd never gotten a chance to be anything more than this.

Contrition.

Fate took with the same hand she dished out.

He broke his stare, rising to stand as he pounded on the rattling tin door behind me. With one last look he turned around and got in the SUV.

By the time the door was lifted up noisily behind me, Santos had already cleared out and was likely back on the main road.

A lanky blonde stood over me, shouting back in Russian into the warehouse.

"Well, what have we here?" A crisp accent cut through the dimly lit space as a man in a gray suit stepped into the little bit of light that shone from above.

He barked out an order in his native tongue and the mountainous, scarred up motherfucker from the basement appeared in front of me with a snap of his finger. It was a small comfort to know that Mateo had killed the other one, in fact, I hoped they were friends.

I hoped he mourned him.

"Where is your handler?" The man who exuded confidence and leadership asked.

"Smart enough to not stick around Bratva shit," I said, spitting on the ground. The scarred-up giant's hand met my face with a deafening sting that had me seeing stars, skin burning hot from where his hand connected with my cheek.

It would have been easy to be afraid here, to cry and beg to be free. But as the giant Bratva cocked his hand back as if to hit me again, his other hand tightly clutching his weapon, I could only feel my own hands steading with my breathing. No. Fearful wasn't the type of woman I was shaped into becoming.

I wouldn't beg.

There was no God who would receive the pleasure of my reverence.

There was no man I'd ask to save me.

When La Madrina would finally come to collect my soul, I'd take her by the hand and gladly cross that threshold, when my time came.

This wasn't my time.

The silver-haired man gave out orders in another language and the giant asshole began tearing at my clothes. I instinctively kicked out at him, to absolutely no fruition, he felt like he was made of stone, practically indestructible as my attempts to hurt him went unphased.

He grabbed me by the throat and lifted me until my toes could no longer touch the ground. I grasped at his arm, my throat raw and burning from the sheer power of his left arm and then I noticed his right hand held a syringe.

"No! No! No! Please! Anything but that!" I scratched out as I bargained, and I tried to slap his right arm away from me. The man in charge whistled to get his dog's attention.

"I think she can be reasoned with, Lev," he gave a subtle nod to his man, who apparently wasn't named, "Giant-mountain looking motherfucker" *or* "Scarface", and he dropped me back to the ground, before pulling me up by the shoulders. He slipped the straps off of my pajama tank top and didn't fight back a growl at me while I once again attempted to keep him from taking my clothes off.

"Undress little one," the Bratva leader spoke to me, a crooked smile on his face as he sealed my fate, "Or we can do it for you." He gestured back to his man, Lev, standing over me with the drug-filled syringe in his hand.

I let the top slide down my body and pushed it past my hips with the silk matching shorts and I stood there, bare. Unashamed of my body but unwilling to hide my sneer, so he could see just how disgusting he was to me. I'd been through his gauntlet once before, I wasn't afraid of being taken advantage of, or that one of his men would rape me. No, this was purely transactional for them, he wanted a good look at what he'd be getting rich off of.

Again.

"Now, what is your name, little doll?" He stepped into me so closely I could smell the lingering vodka on his breath, tapered by the smell of an inferior cigar.

My papá had good taste in everything he put into his body, this guy here consumed for the hell of it, maybe addiction, but not for the taste. The price tag was high but the product itself was inferior.

"Does it matter?" I asked with a snarl, and he smiled.

He scraped the back of his index finger down the side of my face, and I turned my chin in defiance, unable to hide my revolt at the gesture. Lev stood at my back and pulled my arms behind me, using a single hand to keep them tightly bound against my spine so I wouldn't be able to lash out at his boss.

I wasn't an idiot.

I would behave here, for now. I knew my chances were only good as long as I was able to stay sober, which meant I needed to play obedient and keep that syringe the fuck away from me.

He tugged at my chin, pulling it side to side as if he were checking to see if there was something disagreeable about my features. His fingers traced their way around my collar bone, then down my breasts. The touch was brief, and he dropped his hands to my hips as his palms rubbed up my sides.

His thumb stopped right below my right breast, and he thumbed the ancient, raised scar in the shape of a five petaled flower. I let out a hitched breath I could no longer suffer to hold.

His face twisted, and a sinister smile curled up on one side as he continued to rub the brand on my skin against his thumb.

"And here I thought you were going to be my ticket to tearing apart the Black Crow Brotherhood," he chuckled and shouted out to one of his men in Russian before turning back to me.

"Looks like that will have to wait for a better opportunity someday." He winked up at me as he peeled his face away from my breast, "Someone's been looking for you, little one. You, my dear, are going to make me a very rich man today." He winked and before he could fully turn around, one of his men were already holding up a phone behind him.

My stomach dropped and I felt the giant warehouse closing in on me faster than I could breathe.

"Whatever you think this is-" I started but he cut me off.

"Is exactly what it is my dear, I've seen a few of those five petal flower brands in my time. *You* don't belong on this side of the border." The insult stung more than the rapidly settling realization that I'd soon be reunited with my tio. There was always someone who thought the Cártel had no business in the States, like we didn't have a place at the table with the other syndicates.

If I was queen, like it had been intended, I would prove them all wrong. I would build my throne out of the skeletons of all the men who once doubted me. I would reign through the ruins of my papá's legacy until I built something better on my own.

Yeah.

If I made it out of this again, that's exactly what I would do.

Rain hell on all of the men who saw me as nothing but a pawn to advance their own empire.

If I made it out of this one.

"Sorry little one, you behaved, but I'm not a man of my word, and I need you sweet for the trip." The boss breathed out too close to my face and his man jabbed the needle deep into my neck. The heavy sensation settling into my body quicker than before.

49

RONAN

"You think I made the wrong call?" I asked Kane as we walked side by side out of the fifth floor.

"No. I think him coming would have been a big mistake," We waited for the elevator, even though we were only going down two floors. We both stayed silent the whole time until finally I couldn't hold it in anymore.

"You knew this whole time how he felt about her?" I looked at him, wondering if he would lie to me too.

"I'm not oblivious like you. I could see the same pain in him that I was trying to hide myself," he stared back at me, and even though I still had a lot to say about whatever the hell was going on with my brothers and Cecilia, he was still my family. They both were. That was why Santos' treachery cut so deep.

"No more lies. No more secrets," I told him, and he nodded at me.

"Agreed," he said right as the elevator opened up into the armory and just as I had asked, Ethan was already waiting for us.

"What are we doing?" He laughed out as he tossed a semi-automatic my way, and I couldn't fight the smirk forming on my face as I caught it. That was my favorite part about those bastards. Ethan and Fletch were always down to ride, no matter what kind of hell we were marching into. Except Fletcher only woke up from his medically induced coma less than twenty-four hours ago, and we owed that man a debt I didn't know how we'd ever pay back.

"It's a big ask, it's Black Crow business, but it's also personal," I warned him, but he shrugged his shoulders and tossed another semi towards Kane.

"Please tell me we're going after some Bratva dicks," he jumped up and down like a boxer pumping himself up for the next round.

"They've got my girl again. I want to do it without bloodshed, but I also fully intend to be prepared for it." I looked at him and stuck my hand out to see where he stood, "I understand if you wanna sit this out." He clasped my hand and gave out a howl that was Mateoesque in its own way and Kane himself grinned at his excitement.

I pulled the Kevlar vests out of the cabinets and passed them down, strapping on extra ammunition anywhere I could fit it on me. Grabbing a few pistols and knives each before we all made our way down.

"Taylor's got a number for us," Mateo said as he lifted up his phone to show me the text.

"For Sokolov?" I asked and he nodded. "Make the call, I'm not letting her spend one night away from here. Not again."

Kane dialed and put the phone on speaker as soon as the elevator opened up to the lobby. My heart thundered with every single tone that sounded out until the click of the call connected.

"I was not expecting you so soon, Ronan Zerkos." Allisher Sokolov's slimy voice came out of the speaker.

"You have something that belongs to me. I have something that belongs to you. I figured we could do this clean Sokolov," I mouthed, *'let's go'* to the guys and we made our way to the parking garage where Hughes waited with an extremely over tied-up Susana.

He tisked loudly on the line before responding, "Yes, you do have something of mine. But it turns out, I don't seem to have anything of yours." I waived Hughes off as we piled into the car, and he began wrestling with the corpse of Senior.

"Cut the shit old man, I know you have my girl. I'm coming for her, so we can do this the easy way, or the bloody way." I would unleash every layer of hell onto the Bratva if I didn't have Cecilia in my arms again tonight.

"Ah, but that's where you are wrong. She may have been your girl but she did not belong to you. I have returned her to her rightful owners now, no need to thank me. She made me a very rich man." Sokolov elaborated calmly and Mateo snatched the phone from my hand.

"What did you do?" He yelled out, his composure completely gone while his emotions got the best of him.

Sokolov let out a hearty chuckle and Kane reached in the trunk of the Escalade and pulled Oksana up by the throat.

"Papachka!" She begged with a sob and the line went quiet.

"She is not my favorite daughter. Has she spilled all my secrets yet?" He asked flatly, like that was the only thing that mattered.

"But I'm betting an inch off my dick that she's your prettiest one now," Kane laughed out in a cold tone.

"You will pay for what you did to my eldest daughter, make no mistake about it. I know where you live now. I will take your crows out one by one until there's nothing left but feathers to pluck off the ground." I hung up, his threats were useless, and I no longer needed him if what he said about Cecilia was true.

"Should we go to the location on the phone?" Kane asked me.

"No, we follow the tracker. If we head for the meet up spot, we'll likely put too much distance between us. We can't risk the Cártel taking her out of the country." He plugged his phone into the nav system in the car, and Ethan turned the ignition.

She was already more than an hour's drive away and I had no idea how we'd wasted so much time. Every minute was a goddamn mile, and if I didn't hurry, there was a chance we'd be going up against the Cártel.

Three men, against the most dangerous organization known to man. The odds weren't in our favor, but I'd die tonight if it meant keeping her out of harm's way. The tracker moved at the same pace as we did and at this rate we would never catch up.

"If you don't move faster, I'm taking over," I warned Ethan and he let his foot get heavier on the gas, taking it up to ninety miles an hour on the speedometer.

My palms were sweating, every part of me was shaking in anticipation, and fear. If she had been with the Bratva that would have been an entirely different ball game, but now she was being hand-delivered to the same people she'd come to me seeking help to hide from.

I'd failed her.

I had no right to call her mine if I couldn't even keep her safe.

Oksana was whining something awful in the back and my blood was boiling from the anxiety creeping through me. "Shut her up or toss her out. We have no need for her anymore," I yelled back at Kane who made a dramatic shushing gesture with his fingers towards her.

"Are we going south?" Kane asked Ethan who nodded in response. "Call Villalobos, maybe he'll help," he said, sounding hopeful. But no, I didn't want assistance from the same asshole who so easily hurt the girl I loved for so many years. She may have trusted him, and I was a cruel bastard myself, but I didn't trust that Villalobos was someone we could count on when it came to Cecilia.

His track record showed it, and until he proved me wrong, I didn't need him around.

"We're doing this alone. We just need to hurry, maybe we can intercept before she ends up in her uncle's hands," I told Kane and he didn't bother arguing.

Finally, her tracker slowed down to a pace where we could catch up. I didn't have faith that the universe was on my side for once, but I had to believe that someone up there was looking out for me, maybe. Or maybe someone down there. Who knew for sure? People like us weren't gifted with God's grace and half the time it seemed like we were in competition with the Devil himself.

"Is she stopped?" Kane asked as he looked over my shoulder from the backseat.

"It looks that way, step on it E," I told him, even though he was already going well over the speeding limit. The excitement over the possibility of catching up to her before she was handed off to the Cártel was intensifying, and I could barely contain myself from stepping through the floorboards of the car and Fred Flinstoneing this bitch all the way to the location the GPS marked her at.

I'd get her back tonight.

Regardless of who tried to stand in my way.

50

CELIA

Cowards.

All of these men were weak. They had to drug a woman in order to get them to bend to their will.

Pathetic.

My whole body was stone, sinking into the ground before I felt one of the Bratva lackeys picking me up and stuffing me into another trunk. I don't know if the drive was unbearably long or if it didn't take any time at all. I was having trouble remembering to breathe and my head was so heavy.

Eventually we came to a stop on the side of the road. There was some muffled conversation just outside the car, and then, the trunk opened, and his stupid grin was there egging me on. *Carlito,* my primo, the newest heir to *my* throne. The Russian man took a briefcase from my ugly cousin, which was no doubt filled with money he'd paid for me.

The transaction went quickly–or maybe it was the drugs. Before I knew it, my hands were tied behind my back, and I laid face down on the backseat of an SUV with the bandana once again over my mouth. Someone had at least bothered to get my pajamas back on, so I could at least be grateful for that. My head was spinning but the heroin was slowly tapering off from the intense effects of the initial jab.

Fuck it.

I had one shot at this, and I wasn't going to waste it. If my uncle was stupid enough to think I was a one-man job, and to send his weakest link for me, then I was going to make sure he regretted it. I turned my head to the side so I could see the scar on his face in the rearview mirror as he tried his best vocals out. I kept my breathing steady, knowing my best advantage was the fact he thought I was likely out cold.

I quietly brought my knees into my chest, doing my best to stay as low and silent as possible so he wouldn't notice me, and one by one I laced each leg through the open loop in my arms, bringing my bound hands in front of me. I breathed heavily, the small movement enough to get my heart rate skyrocketing, intensifying the high beyond my control.

I counted to ten in my head.

One.

Two.

Three.

Four.

My cousin sang out the lyrics completely wrong and terribly off tune, so I decided to just go for it, wrapping my bound wrists over the driver's side and choking him back into the seat as I pulled with all my might. He rasped out a plea while my zip-ties cut into his neck and he released the wheel fighting to get me off of him, but I knew my only chance out of this was through his death.

He scratched at me, drawing blood out of my arms and when I looked back up through the windshield the pole in the median of the road was headed right towards us. Or really, we were headed straight to it.

I wasn't prepared for the impact, and I was probably lucky to have been trapped behind the driver's seat, but the force of the SUV hitting the pole was enough to knock the wind out of me. The airbag went off in the front, crushing my wrists into his face and as the white powder exploded into the air I cried out from pain.

When I opened my eyes, the pole was nearly halfway into the hood of the car, the engine no doubt fucked to all hell. Carlito was groaning in pain, and I could either finish him off or try to get my ass out of Dodge as fast as possible.

With the heroin still clouding my mind and loosening my muscles I made my choice and lifted my wrists off his neck and the driver's seat, opening the backdoor with my burning hands. I jumped out of the car, immediately feeling the current running through my body, the shock enough to drop me to the ground in a pathetic pile of Celia goo. I crawled away from the car, spurts of electricity still jolting through me little by little.

One hand and one knee in front of the other, I drug my body across the road.

I heard my primo's gargled scream as he rolled out of the vehicle, the shock from the open current of the broken lamp post coursing through his body as he took a single step.

This was my fucking chance.

Except, my limbs were heavier than lead and I knew If I stood up there was a chance I would pass out from the drugs. We were on a country road and there wouldn't be another car coming by for hours. I rolled down, the sinking feeling of the ground swallowing me up and taking my mind away from the present.

It was one blink.

Two max.

It didn't even feel like I had taken a breath since I laid down, and maybe there was a chance I'd been holding it in all that time. Carlito was standing over me and before I could even roll my head over to spit at him, he was dragging me by the arm, my legs scraping along the asphalt while he didn't allow my feet the chance to steady under me.

"Chinga tu madre," I cursed out, but he ignored me, dragging me along for the next several feet of the road.

"Are you going to play nice, or should I put you to sleep again?" He turned around sharply to ask me, my heart beating violently against my chest.

"I've never played nice, pendejo," I slurred out and he smirked, realizing how vulnerable I really was. He let go of my arm and pulled the gun out of his pants and slammed it against the side of my head.

I guess sleep it was then.

"Wake up," I heard before feeling an aggressive nudge to my side. I looked around to see I was laying down on the sidewalk in front of a Motel Six. "Walk." He said, nudging the gun against my waist nearly forcing me to collapse again.

"I need to hold on to something," I slurred out, but he pushed me forward again and through the softening numbness, I could feel the sharp sting of my knees scraping on the ground.

"Go," he said after unlocking the door with the number thirteen on the front of it.

I always liked thirteen.

He turned the knob, opening the door and I practically pushed him off to the side, running through the threshold and dropping straight down onto the bed with a loud groan. He huffed in annoyance but just sat down on the spare chair next to the console.

"Did the big man in charge tell you not to kill me then?" I mumbled out but didn't look up at him when I asked the question. I knew the easiest way to break Carlito down was to not give him the recognition he was so desperate for. The recognition his own papá would never give him.

"He has special plans for you, prima." He dragged a shitty motel chair in front of the door and sat down.

"Oh? And here I thought he just wanted me dead because he was too much of a cobarde to keep ruling my empire while I'm still alive." I laughed out, letting the comfort of the bed give me the smallest bit of solace.

"I don't know what they want with you," he snarled and looked off to the side, giving me a better look at the ugly scar that permanently altered his face. The same scar that my papá bestowed on him when we were just kids, when he thought he could insult his future reina.

Idiot.

He was giving too much away, and he didn't even realize how weak it made him look.

The anger in his voice said it all. My tío Ignácio didn't trust his own son with his master plan. I chuckled out a hollow laugh and covered my mouth with my own hand to muffle the sounds of my joy.

"Laugh it up, maybe he just wants to stuff himself inside that tight pussy before he puts you six feet under."

"Que perro asco," I made no acknowledgement of the attempt at a threat as he suggested the disgusting incest-y scenario.

If that was the case, I would "Million Dollar Baby" the shit out of myself before I let that happen. Drowning in the blood of my own severed tongue in a shitty Motel Six sounded like a better time than letting his wrinkled old cock anywhere near me.

"Well, if you don't kill me," I told him, still looking up at the ceiling like he wasn't worth the effort of turning my head. "I sure as hell am going to kill you primo." I warned and he scoffed, reaching for the remote on the console where the outdated television sat, turning on the TV guide before settling on cartoon reruns.

"Oh shit," I moaned out, reaching for the trashcan next to the bed and I hurled out the contents of my stomach. Carlito stood up like his reflexes were something to be impressed by, but if I had wanted to actually do anything to him, he would have been too slow to even fend off my puke.

Okay, maybe I wouldn't kill him *now.*

"What's your problem?" He asked, raising an eyebrow up, "You're not pregnant, are you?" His eyes widened at the possibility, and I laughed.

"Oh? Is that a line you won't cross?" I deadpanned at him, surprised that he had a limit. "No, asshole, I was drugged by those Bratva hijos de la chingada." I spat. "What the hell are you doing on this side of the border anyway? The Bratvas called, and you came running like a dog with a bone." I finally glanced over at him, narrowing my eyes as I waited for his response.

"I'm up here dealing with business," he crossed his arms and looked away as he answered, an obvious tell that he was lying.

"No, the fuck you aren't," I laughed out again hoping to push his buttons, "That's what Los Muertos is for. You wanna try me again, cuz it sounds like someone's papá is trying to get rid of their golden boy." I laughed an even wilder laugh and he quickly stood up, towering over me on the bed with a look that was full of rage and insecurity.

It seemed like my guess was right, and Tío Ignácio was pushing Carlito away. Maybe he was afraid of being usurped, and I wouldn't blame him. I knew enough about our history to know that crowns were rarely passed down, they were usually taken by force in blood.

But the truth was, that even the momentary thought that Carlito could be smart enough to steal my tio's position was laughable. It was clear that he didn't trust my primo around any position that presented power. There was no love between father and son.

My papá once told me Ignácio was sterile, and that the majority of the animosity he felt about me being reina stemmed from the fact he envied the family we had. There was a chance Carlito wasn't even his, which was why his own mother had been dead for as long as I could remember.

Which left Ignácio believing he'd been raising someone else's son, against his own wishes for the last thirty some years.

That must have been a bitter pill to swallow.

And I was here to soak it all in and use it as fuel.

"Cállate, zorra." He was above me faster than I could react and the sharp sting of his palm against my face was nearly sobering.

I grasped my jaw and rubbed the sore spot as I slinked off the bed, he stood again, preparing himself for the worst.

"I need to pee," I said, and he crossed his arms over his chest.

"No."

"You're going to stop me from peeing?" I rolled my eyes, "Who knows how long we're going to be here and it's not very clear when I might get the chance again. Is that alright with you?" I asked and he opened the bathroom door as if to check for a secret way out.

"It's a Motel fucking Six. There's one window." I lifted my wrists up, a silent plea to cut off my zip ties but he scoffed at me again.

"Figure it out." He huffed out, so I barged past him and locked the door behind me.

Okay, I needed to think fast now.

I turned towards the shower and started looking around the tiny rundown bathroom for anything that would work as a weapon but there wasn't anything here except a bar of soap.

How hard would I have to hit him to kill him with a bar of soap?

Alright, next plan.

I sat down on the toilet to pee, looking for anything that may be a little more lethal for my mission. I looked over the toilet and an idea came to me. After I finished, I pulled the lid off from the tank and put it in the corner where the door would hide it once it was opened again. I let out my best high-pitched scream and unlocked the door for Carlito.

"What? What is it?" He rushed with a slightly concerned look on his face that was almost laughable. He really was a fucking idiot.

"There's a fucking snake in the toilet!" I pointed to the closed lid and he, like a goddamn amateur, proved why his father was keeping him at a distance. He wasn't charged with the job of bringing me in because he trusted him, but out of sheer fucking convenience over the fact he was nearby.

I reached behind me for the tank lid and cracked it over his head, the edge of the porcelain shattering to pieces but not enough to take him out. I raised what was left above my head again and dropped it down on him and didn't wait to see my results. My feet never moved so fast in my life, and I tossed the chair out of the way like a WWE wrestler as I opened the motel door and ran out.

I didn't look back, I put one foot in front of the other and ran back towards the country road and kept going until it felt like my stomach was going to explode from cramps. There was a lot I could tolerate, but physical exercise was not it, I was in the absolute worst shape of my life, and it showed.

The black Escalade was going too fast for my comfort from the direction I was running toward, and I slowed down, too afraid of it being my uncle already here to collect me. But even before the SUV came to a screeching halt sideways across the road right in front of me, Ronan was already jumping out of the passenger side and pulling me into his arms.

He crushed me into his body tightly and I pressed back into him, never in my life having been so grateful for the bottomless well that was his heart; somehow, he had still been able to find love for me, after everything. Not in spite of it, but *because* of all the things we'd gone through together.

"Are you hurt?" He asked, both hands cupping my face while he let that look of fear break through his features. Though it had been years, and he changed and grew so different, it was the same expression I recognized from when he rushed into my hospital room, after most of my family had been killed in the drive-by.

I shook my head and sealed my lips around him desperately, locking my arms around his neck. Just as he whipped out a pocket blade and cut my zip ties a bullet hit the Escalade and we both turned our heads to find Carlito hobbling over, blood drenching most of his face with a gash so large I couldn't help but be proud of myself. Mateo burst out of the back of the SUV and planted a bullet right in Carlito's leg, forcing him to drop to the ground with a pained cry.

"He's mine," I flared my nostrils at Mateo and reached my hand out for a weapon.

The weight of his Glock was comforting in my palm as I wrapped my fingers around it and the three of us walked towards my now somehow uglier primo. The gun was too heavy, and my hands throbbed from the car crash but I held on tightly as I approached him. Blocking out every ounce of pain so I could dish out the start of my revenge.

He propped himself up, preparing to stand as blood freely pooled out of him from multiple wounds, but before he could lift his hand to shoot again Ronan put a bullet in his hand, forcing him to drop his weapon.

"I said he's mine," I hissed at him, but he grabbed me by the back of the neck and pulled me until our noses were practically touching.

"I will never apologize for keeping you safe. It's why you came to me after all, right?" He lifted an eyebrow and the smallest hint of a smile carved into his face.

It had been a long time since I'd felt anything but rage from Ronan and

I couldn't lie that small expression didn't make my stomach flutter all the way up my throat. I returned half a smile and pushed him out of the way as I marched towards my primo so I could deliver him his death.

"Say your prayers primo, but I think God forsook us a long time ago," I pressed my gun to his forehead. Standing over him, I kicked his gun out of reach while he clutched his hand to his chest.

He spat at my feet, "Chinga tu madre."

"*My* mother? I mean, I didn't like the woman either, but she was definitely better than yours, I think." I scratched my head with the gun before pointing it back at him; he swallowed a hard lump before breaking down.

"Don't kill me!" He pleaded with a sob. "I can be useful, I'll tell you whatever you want to know."

Pathetic. No wonder Ignácio was desperate to get rid of him.

"Then *be* useful, where can I find him?" I pushed the gun deeper into his forehead, hard enough that if I pulled away, the indentation would still be there.

"He stays in the Guadalajara villa. Prima, *please!*" He cried from the pain.

"WHAT?" I screamed out, my rage fuming out of me uncontrollably at the thought of him living in the home I grew up in, the same house he set on fire twenty-some years ago. "Why the hell is he there?"

"It's the only place he has access to. Rafa put everything in your name a few years before he died-"

"Before you killed him," I corrected. "He doesn't have access to the dungeons?" I asked my loose lipped primo.

"He's got a few factories down south, but everything else locked up tight when Rafa died. The dungeons won't even open without you."

I laughed wildly at the revelation. "So, he's got *nothing*?" The smile on my face probably looked completely out of place, but holy shit. This was unbelievable. "So, you've really been roughing it these last fifteen years huh?"

My primo groaned in pain, "Celia, I need a hospital."

"Sure, sure. Just tell me one last thing, my papá*s* men?" I asked.

"Went into hiding. Most of his numbers are in Los Muertos, but he's built his own following over the last fifteen years too. The presidente fucking hates him, which makes it hard for him to get away with what he needs." He cried out, raising his hands above his head, and I finally saw the mangled-up mess that was his shot-off hand. The middle fingers were barely scraps of bone with flesh dangling off of it, while the thumb and the pinky were intact.

"Carlito you're a fucking idiot." I said, flipping back the safety with a loud click.

"He won't stop. He's expecting you. He'll send her after you." He said in between pained cries, but it wouldn't save him.

"Vete al diablo." Those were the last words I spoke to him before delivering him to the hell he deserved.

He was never meant for this life, but unfortunately, he was just too dumb and ambitious to ever get out. Stupid and ambitious was probably the most unfortunate combination a man could be. He could never see far enough to comprehend that he wasn't going to make it anywhere on that hamster wheel my tío kept him in. So, he just ran as fast as he could, never quite reaching that carrot being dangled from the string.

Did hamsters eat carrots?

I don't know. I never had a fucking pet, and that was probably for the best. But once his body fell back, I reached into his pocket, pulled out his phone, and dialed the most recent number.

I heard the click of the call connecting, but no one spoke on the other line.

"Don't bother coming for me today, I've already handled your sorry excuse for a son. Not before he told me more than you'd ever want me to know, of course, so I guess you're welcome. I'm coming for you old man, and when I'm done, I'll be wearing your teeth around my neck." I hung up the phone and tossed it over Carlito's corpse.

"We're way too close to the motel, let's get out of here before they call the cops." I said, turning to face Ronan and Mateo, who were both donning very different expressions. Expectedly, Mateo looked intrigued, excited, and *turned on*. Ronan was confused, unsure, and *hurt*. He didn't know this version of me.

He was going to need to make room for her too if he wanted to love me.

I looked up at Mateo, realizing the entire day was quickly catching up to me. The adrenaline from killing someone execution style for the first time since I was fifteen years old was fizzling out of me. "My legs are Jell-O," I told him, and he let out a soft laugh at my honesty as he caressed my cheek gently with his thumb.

Ronan picked me up like a fucking princess and placed me in the backseat of the Escalade. I smiled at Ethan, who waited for instructions while

Mateo sat in the front passenger seat, and that's when I realized what was missing.

Or rather, *who.*

"Where's Santos?" I asked Mateo. Ronan practically growled while climbing into the backseat next to me.

"All of this happened because of him," Ronan gritted, not breaking his gaze from mine. The intensity burning deeply in that forest of his.

"No, that's not true-"

"Cecilia, he lied to us. He betrayed us. He betrayed you. He risked your life," he held my chin between his finger and his thumb.

"He didn't have a choice. I would have done the same if I was him," I whispered, "I don't blame him, and neither should you."

The muffled sound behind our seats caught my attention, and I looked back at the trunk to see Oksana tied up and gagged.

"What's that all about?"

"I was gonna trade her for you, before Sokolov told me he sent you off. That's his daughter, turns out he doesn't want her though." Ronan rested his ankle over his knee calmly next to me, but his hand clutched my leg tightly, like he couldn't risk letting me go.

I frowned at his words, "Untie her."

He raised an eyebrow at me but complied.

Oksana crawled towards the far back of the trunk and rubbed her wrists before removing the gag from her mouth.

She looked pretty terrible, but not that it was a competition because I was pretty certain I'd had a worse week than she did. The fear in her eyes said enough for her, and I let her have her privacy to recollect her dignity as I turned my head back towards the front.

Ethan drove in the direction of Cove City, but all I could think about was how many times I'd fallen under the cruelty of lesser men who believed they were owed greatness. I would bet that Oksana here knew a little something of that too. Maybe I could use that to my advantage.

She wasn't my enemy. Men just liked to paint women against each other for their uses. Well, that could work both ways.

51

MATEO

The drive back was tedious.

I wanted to be right there, next to her, feeling her skin under my hands so I could be certain she was okay. But I knew that she and Ronan needed to get back to a better place, to work through whatever was still keeping them apart.

I was confident that if I gave her the space to be with him, she would still return to me. I didn't see this as a competition or some prize we had to fight over. I saw the end game, and it was her.

Once we arrived back at the high-rise, that ominous feeling of uncertainty crept up, and it seemed like it was affecting all of us. Senior's body was gone, and the evidence of his death was cleaned up. Hughes needed a raise, that was for damn sure. But I also knew the sick fuck enjoyed the messy jobs.

"Go with Kane upstairs, I have to call a meeting with our top men. I need to explain the Archer situation to all of them," he said, scrubbing his face with his hands in anxiety.

"You did nothing wrong. None of you did. Your men will see that. The Archers betrayed the Black Crows and endangered every man and woman in this building by consorting with the enemy." She got on the tips of her toes and pressed a kiss to his lips.

"Well fuck, maybe you should address the men then," Zerkos joked.

"Don't tempt me, I'm officially in the market for soldiers," she told him, raising her eyebrow sarcastically, but it was enough to get my attention.

"You meant what you said then? You're going after your uncle?" I asked her.

"I won't spend the rest of my life running anymore, the only way out is death. I've always known that. For a long time, I just accepted it would be him over me, but I'm done with that now. I'm done letting weaker men control my future. He's outlived his life expectancy," she explained.

Ronan met my gaze, and I could practically read his mind. He wanted to know what this meant for them, if she'd leave him to fulfill her destiny, if there was room in it for him. So, I ended that train of thought for him before it could rollercoaster into something else.

"Then we'll help you kill the bastard," I told her. She narrowed her eyes at me suspiciously.

"You'll go to war with me?" She asked, pressing the palms of her hands flatly to my chest.

"No sunshine, I'll go to war for you. I'll be your weapon, if that's what you need, or I can sit back and watch you get your hands bloody. Whatever you choose," I reassured her, looking into the obsidian tunnels of her eyes, and Ronan growled behind me. "He will too." I smirked with a nod towards him, and she rolled her eyes at me with a smile.

"Put her somewhere decent for me, please?" Cecilia turned to ask Ronan just as Ethan opened the trunk to let Oksana out. He nodded his head at her, and she reached in to give him one more kiss.

"Take her to the apartments on seven, keep some men out front" Zerkos told Ethan just as I pulled Cecilia away and walked her back inside.

"Where is he?" She asked me while we walked inside through the lobby.

"Let me take care of you first," I reached down and raked my hand through her hair before lifting her chin to look at me, "You look like you've had a rough day." I leaned down and rubbed my nose against hers, "Let me make it a little better." She sighed into me as I embraced her, feeling those walls she worked so hard to keep up softening at my touch.

"That sounds nice," She nodded up at me.

Once we got back up to the penthouse, we made our way into my bedroom. I closed the door behind me as she walked in, looking around like it had already been so long since she was last here, instead of just the other night.

"Take your shirt off," I instructed her.

She turned her head back and cocked an eyebrow my way with a mischievous look on her face.

"I want to see how your back looks." I explained with a knowing smirk, shaking my head at the bronze vixen in front of me.

She let out a heavy sigh like the reminder of the permanent mark on her skin was a deeper burden than the actual pain of it. I grabbed the edges of her top and helped her lift it up, she lifted her arms to get it out of the way, and it was revealed.

It was hard to look at.

Hard to stomach.

Not because of how brutally painful it looked, or that she was scarred forever now. But because it reminded me of an atrocious failure.

Our negligence.

Instead of protecting her, we'd let someone do this to her.

She turned her head over her shoulder with a sorrowful look stained in her eyes.

Barely letting the pads of my fingers graze the skin around the hardening wound, I ran them gently and slowly across her back, pulling a shudder from her.

"Lay down," I instructed her, and she fell flatly on the bed, stomach on the mattress with a huff and a groan, the day's exhaustion surely settling in.

I perched myself over her, running my hands softly down her back, lightly stroking my fingertips down, then moving them back up. Placing my lips on her neck and all around her back, I made my way south, achingly slow with a tenderness I didn't know I had control over.

But she was meant to be savored.

Worshiped.

"I'm sorry," I said, and before I realized it, I repeated it after every kiss, like a prayer, chanting it into her skin. "I will never let anyone hurt you again."

"That's a hell of a promise to make," she breathed out as I lowered my hands down her body.

"Cross my heart and hope to die," I rumbled into her ear.

My hands covered each firm peak of her ass, and unable to stop myself, I squeezed, eliciting a wanton moan from her, commanding my dick to attention. Her eyes stayed closed, but as I thumbed the waistband of her shorts, she lifted her hips in the air, and I obeyed her silent command, moving them down her legs and throwing them aside.

I pulled her up like a rag doll and brought her over to my shower, sitting her down on the concrete stool and turning the water to a fine mist over us. Slipping my own clothes off I threw them over my shoulder, missing the hamper but trying not to let it bother me. I lathered up a loofa and began at her feet, scrubbing every inch of her that had been tainted by someone else's hands today.

I couldn't erase what they'd done.

But I could try to remind her she wasn't so easily broken. I knew first-hand that she wasn't just the strongest, but the most dangerous woman I'd ever met.

Once I'd cleaned her of the mark today left on her, I washed, then pulled us both deep into the shower mist. She looked up at me, beads of water lingering on her eyelashes as she batted them away with slow blinks.

"You're making it damn near impossible not to fall head over heels for you," she bit her lip, and I smirked in response.

"Then my plan is working," I kissed her neck, trailing up behind her ear firmly.

"You don't know what you're doing," her eyes locked onto me, "I won't let you go, if you're not careful," it was a threat somehow, but even with the vicious way her gaze cut into mine, it sounded like the sweetest promise. The one thing I could look forward to in this brutal life we lived.

"Well thank fuck, because I'm reckless," I released the words, making space to devour her instead. As I forced my way through her lips, our tongues tangled in a frenzy and she pressed her body against mine. Her throat let out frantic whines as she rocked her center against my thigh for friction, making me even more desperate to get inside her.

I let my hand fall between her legs to rub two fingers against her clit, moving back and forth and coating my fingers with her sweet, slickness. She dropped her head back and clenched her hands around my bicep and shoulder as I coaxed pleasure out of her in slow circular motions.

"Fuck," she cried, squeezing harder and pressing her nails firmly into my skin. She let out a disappointed groan when I pulled away, curling the corner of my lip into a smile.

"Open," I instructed her again, and she parted her lips as I slipped the same fingers into her mouth, "See why we're all so desperate for a taste of you." She closed her lips around my fingers and didn't break her gaze from mine as she licked her own arousal off my fingers.

I grabbed her ass with both of my hands, lifting her off the ground, and she crossed her ankles behind my back. She pressed deeper into me, so that my hard cock was straining against her wet pussy. She moaned from her chest while I continued to kiss her and walked us both back into the room, letting the air dry the water on our skin.

I sat her down on the bed again and stepped over to the nightstand, opening the drawer and pulling out a small bottle of massage oil. She gave me that uncertain suspicious look I was growing to love, and I commanded her to lay on her stomach again.

She didn't challenge me.

"I told you I wanted to take care of you," I squirted the oil into my palms and rubbed my hands together to heat it before rubbing it on her shoulders, making my way down her sides while sneakily getting a handful of her luscious breasts. She moaned encouragingly, and I continued my way down her body, rubbing the oil at a tediously slow pace. Making sure to give attention to every single muscle on her body, as long as there wasn't a healing wound near it.

"I'm turning into putty," she slurred out after about thirty minutes and hummed appreciatively.

I dipped my fingers where her legs split open and slid my oil-slicked digits against her wet cunt. She let out another soft whimper, still pent up from not getting her release in the shower, and I chuckled loud enough for her to hear me.

"You're not playing fair," she whined.

"Who said anything about playing fair? I'm playing to get even," I scoffed out, sliding a finger inside, eliciting a gasp from her before she jerked her head back to look at me.

"Get even? *Como*?" She widened her eyes at me.

"We could have been doing this from the beginning, but you chose to keep your secrets. Maybe, I want a little bit of payback," I winked at her, sliding another finger inside as she moaned and raised her hips to meet me.

"We wouldn't have been doing this from the beginning if I hadn't kept my mouth shut. Don't kid yourself," she breathed out, and I pulled my fingers out, narrowing my eyes at her. She was fucking right. There was no alternate universe where Ronan's ex would have come in here spewing the truth about her past and ended up in my bed.

It just wasn't plausible.

"Stop torturing me Kane, or I'm going to make you regret it," she gritted out, using my last name as a weapon, and the amusement stripped from her face.

I plunged three fingers deep inside her.

She fisted the sheets below her, biting her lip as she turned her head back to look at me again. I moved in and out of her slowly, rubbing my thumb over her clit until she finally shattered in my hold, her climax overpowering her. She cried out loudly, but I could only relish the moment briefly as I realized for once, that there wasn't music playing in the background to drown out her noises.

Then he appeared at the threshold of my door, his arms crossed over his chest while he stared at Cecilia, naked and wrung out from her orgasm. That hurt puppy look he'd been wearing all week was still clearly plastered on his face, and if anything, it cut a little deeper right at this moment. He just stood there, like he didn't know if he wanted to explode from rage, take her away, or kill me.

He'd threatened it enough times now.

She was breathing heavily under me, her face plastered to the mattress, but then she finally looked to see him standing there.

He turned to leave.

"Don't go," She whispered softly, reaching her hand out to him, deciding all of our fates. "Please."

Instead, Ronan closed the door behind him and stepped further into the room.

52

CELIA

My heart pounded wildly under me as Ronan inched further into the room, that sharp, twisted look filled with hatred still burning in his eyes. I pushed myself up until I was standing by the foot of the bed and Ronan began to sever the distance between us.

I was practically shaking, every muscle in my body trembling as he closed in, and I felt the heat of his breath coming down on me. He hadn't left yet, and he wasn't skinning Mateo alive. That was progress, but now they were both here, too close to me; I had to admit I was at a loss. I didn't know what to do with myself or either of them. I suddenly had too many limbs, or maybe not enough, and I didn't know what to do with either of them.

As if he could hear my anxious thoughts, Mateo cupped my breast in one hand while standing behind me and used his other hand to twist my chin towards Ronan. "Are you gonna deny our girl what she wants?" He asked him, the words *our girl* turning my stomach over with a sickening swarm of butterflies.

"Is this... what you want?" He turned his chin sideways, waiting for my answer, and I nodded.

"Say it then," Ronan said through clenched teeth, the anger still apparent and obvious.

"I want you," I said, looking up at him, then back at Mateo, "Both of you."

His upper lip peeled back, and he looked like he was going to take a step back, so I reached for his shirt, fisting it in my hand, "Stay."

"You're asking me to watch you with someone else," he gritted, clenching his fists.

"Not watch," I breathed out, lifting his shirt, and pulling it over his head.

"She wants you to fuck her, while I make her scream," Mateo clarified, sliding his hands between my legs.

I was still sensitive, but every pore on my skin was burning, every part of me painfully throbbing to be touched by the two men surrounding me like predators.

"Has Ronan been *here*, Sunshine?" He asked, his pinky teasing around the entrance of my puckered hole, just a light feather touch as I nodded, my eyes still glued to Ronan's and his lip curled up on one side.

"You'll find there's nowhere I haven't been, brother. Every inch of her has been claimed by me," He spoke assertively like the suggestion was offensive to him in some way and I tried to block out their bickering.

Mateo responded by plunging his fingers deeper into me and letting his pinky press firmly against that tight ring until it pushed its way through.

I dropped my head against Ronan's chest while Mateo continued torturing me, quiet pants leaving my mouth. His pecs vibrated with the growl that came up his throat, and he lifted my chin.

"Look at me," his voice rang out with authority, and I obeyed without hesitation. He conquered my mouth with his, moving his hand down to my throat, giving it just the right amount of pressure to force another moan out of me.

Mateo teased my nipple with soft tugs, and Ronan reached with his free hand to cup my other breast.

His roughness countered Mateo's gentle touch, winding that coil deep in my core tighter and tighter, their touch alone enough to make me want to unravel. We broke our kiss, and he released my throat. The automatic need to swallow air into my lungs forced a loud rasp out of me with the gulp of oxygen I dragged in.

"Don't hurt her, or I'll make you watch instead," Mateo threatened from behind me, his stare icy cold as he fixed it on Ronan.

"What you may not know about *my* girl, is that she likes the pain," Ronan seethed over me, and I cut in before they got carried away and ruined the moment.

"Cut it out! Play nice or don't play at all. I'll kick both of you out and finish this myself," I said sternly, pushing Ronan away as he pressed me closer to Mateo.

"I can't do this. It kills me to see someone else touching you like this," his voice broke as he pushed away from the both of us. "It hurts," he admitted.

"I get it," I lamented, pressing my lips into a flat line as I admitted defeat. "I wouldn't be able to watch another woman touch you either. That would be torture," I exhaled as I looked down, my heart again thundering deep inside my chest.

"But you still want him?" He asked, unable to mask the hurt in his voice, and I nodded my response.

"I told you, my feelings for him, they're separate from what I feel for you. They aren't one in the same. Please don't ask me to give him up, because I can't," tears welled in my eyes at the thought of Ronan forcing me to choose between them. There wasn't a world where I could live without any of them now, even Santos, who was a chaotic mess, and refused to follow through with his feelings. Even if he thought killing me was the answer to fixing the pain in his heart.

I needed all of them.

"It's all of you, or none of you. So, figure it out," I staked my claim, throwing the words out into the universe like a curse that would bind us all to fulfill it, and pushed him aside as I made my way out of Mateo's room.

"*All* of us?" I heard Ronan ask.

"You really are a fucking fool," Mateo said, barely audible enough for me to hear as he seemed to follow behind me into the guest room.

The loud slamming of a door made me flinch before I entered the room, grabbing a solid black skater dress hanging in the closet. I slipped it over my head before I opened my newly claimed underwear drawer and rummaged through it, finding nothing but fancy lingerie that either Mateo or Ronan provided me with. I rolled my eyes, wishing for something more comfortable but slipping on a pair of lacy black underwear.

I heard the gentlest rapping at my door and turned to see Mateo standing at the open threshold, leaning with his elbow on the frame and running a hand through his overgrown inky black hair. He was donning a freshly raised red spot under his right eye, and I sighed as I approached him.

"He's such a fucking dick," I said, carefully brushing his hair out of the way and examining the future black eye.

"Yeah, but we love him," he said with a grin, pushing two dimples deep into his cheek. "You okay?" He asked, brushing his fingers down my arms, and I nodded.

"I'll be fine. This is all the product of my own doing. Reap what you sow right?" I looked up at him and shrugged, but he pulled me in by the waist for an embrace.

"You think he's like this because of you?" He asked me, and I shrugged again.

"Hard not to, he wasn't always like this you know? Not how I remember him." I let him squeeze me closer and rested my cheek against his bare chest.

"Do you think that the woman you are today, would love the sweet unbroken boy he used to be? I remember that boy too, you know? Before the Navy, the world, and you changed him. He would have never made it through any of this." He paused, "Or do you think he needs to be the hard man that you forced out of him? The one that makes you the only person who can stand up to him. Do you think the Ronan you knew could handle the truth of who you really are?" He raised an eyebrow at me, and even though his expression was still soft, I knew Mateo well enough to know his playful side was put away right now.

"No," I admitted the truth I already knew deep inside. "We were doomed from the beginning. I mourned our end from the moment I met him. We were too different, miles apart and constantly drifting away from each other."

Mateo stroked my hair as he tried to comfort my breaking heart. "Give him time Sunshine, he's bound to come around," he told me, placing a finger under my chin to lift it and meet my gaze.

"And if he doesn't?" I asked.

"Did you mean what you said? That it was all or nothing?" He asked, raking his fingers through my hair, and tucking a strand behind my ear.

"It feels that way. I need both of you," I told him, and he nodded.

"Then it looks like I have no choice but to force him to come around," he said with a soft smile that forced me to reciprocate the gesture. "But your heart doesn't hurt for just the both of us, does it Celia?" Mateo pressed his lips to mine, the way he used my real name, doing something to me I couldn't explain.

"How do you see through me so easily?" I asked him, blinking the tears back before they could fall.

"Because I've noticed the way you look at him. Because I feel the way your heart beats faster when we mention his name," he said, placing his hand over the blue jay fluttering against my chest. "Because I don't get to see the real you unless the three of us are around."

I kissed him again, grateful to have someone who understood what I needed, and worried I might not deserve him.

"I want the real you. All of the time, even if I have to share her."

"You must be make-believe. I think I conjured you up straight out of my dreams," I said to him, cupping his face in my hand.

"Maybe out of a nightmare, I'm not a prince charming. You'll see that soon enough too," he stroked my cheek with the pad of his thumb.

"Prince charming is a misogynistic piece of shit who probably can't even shoot straight. Be good to me, to *us*," I paused to emphasize. "And I don't care who else gets bloody in the process," I assured him.

"Good," he growled into my ear before his hand came down firmly on my ass, the surprise forcing a yelp out of me. "Because I'll carve up any other man who so much as gets in your way, and I'll deliver his balls, in tribute."

"A romantic," I smiled at him, and his hand dropped to find mine, bringing them both up to his lips as he pressed a kiss to each one.

"Just a humble servant, my queen," he winked, and my thighs automatically rubbed together in response. It'd been a long day, full of too many *almosts*, and all that left me with was a lot of pent-up sexual frustration.

"Can I feed you?" He asked me, and I shook my head. The nausea from the heroin was overbearing, and the thought of food made me want to hurl.

"I need to see him," I said, and he let out a heavy sigh but didn't fight me on it. He pulled me by the hand, and I grabbed a pair of slip-on converse I'd left by the door as we made our way to the elevators.

"Where is he?" I asked, and Mateo responded by pressing the number five on the elevator touchpad before another screen popped up asking for his thumbprint. "I thought you said bad things happened on that floor?"

"Well, lucky for us our boy cleared the level out before we locked him in there." He answered, and I twisted my face at him, unsatisfied with that answer. "It was just a precaution, to keep him safe from himself while we were out getting you. He was a mess. Do you want to tell me what happened?" He asked, but I shook my head and let out a heavy exhale I didn't realize I'd been holding in.

The doors opened, and we entered the dimly lit floor. Concrete covered every square inch of the place from floor to ceiling, and I wanted to say it was reminiscent of the Kennels I called home for the last two months, but no. There was no essence of comfort or pity etched into this place, and I could smell the blood and bleach that had recently gone down the drains in each cell.

This place had a closer feel to my papá's dungeon than anything else.

My dungeons, soon enough.

Mateo whistled, getting the attention of a burly guy who sat on a fold-out chair reading a book that I couldn't quite make out the title, but the cover had a half-naked dude on it.

Interesting choice. Zero judgment.

"Hughes," he called over the guy, and once he stood, his height towered over us. "Take a break," Mateo instructed him, and the guy tossed him a set of keys with a nod before exiting the floor.

"It's cold in here," I rubbed my arms, using the friction for heat as we walked down the narrow hallway, passing each empty cell one by one.

"I'll let Zerkos know you think the prisoners have it rough," he winked at me, and I rolled my eyes at him in annoyance.

"Don't get smart with me, crazy boy," I slapped his chest with the back of my hand and I walked in front of him, reaching the final cell. Santos sat on a flimsy cot that didn't even seem big enough to hold his size, his elbows on his knees with his head dropped down and his hand clutching the back of his neck. I stopped in my tracks and nearly stumbled over myself as Mateo walked into me.

"We can go back if you want," he said, noticing the effect seeing Santos had on me. I shook my head at him.

"No, he's been avoiding me long enough," I told him, and he nodded in understanding.

"I'll be right outside then, I'll give you some time alone with him."

"You won't stay?" I asked, a bit surprised.

"Sunshine, I'm still livid over the danger he put you in. Just seeing his stupid face makes me want to knock all of his teeth out," he smiled at me, and I snorted out a laugh.

"Well don't do *that*, he'd look awfully ridiculous without them," I told him before pinning my body closer to him. He whistled again, getting Santos' attention. "When will you let him out?" I asked him.

"That's not up to me," he confessed, which meant it was up to Ronan.

"Hey asshole, you've got a visitor," he told him, Santos' head barely lifting and turning enough to look at the both of us. He said nothing, just stared at us.

Mateo pulled me in, his hands pressed to the small of my back as he parted my lips with his thumb before plunging his tongue deep into my mouth for a showy kiss. He smirked knowingly, turning his head over to look at his friend, who was clutching the cot's frame, his knuckles white and his eyebrows formed a deep V.

Mateo inserted the key into the cell door and opened it just enough to push me inside before slamming it shut and walking away leisurely.

"If she comes out of here in anything less than perfect condition, and without a smile on her face, I *will* let Zerkos kill you. *Brother*." He chimed out without turning his head back to look at us.

53

SANTOS

The buzzer brayed annoyingly from Mateo opening the door to leave the fifth floor, spiking my nerves. She stood there, leaning on the bars, biting her lip as she looked at me nervously. I hated that this was where we stood now, too far gone to turn back and too afraid to move forward. To top it off, I was the spineless piece of shit who put her in danger.

"Why are you here Morena?" I asked, looking back down, my guilt and shame still too heavy to bear.

"I wanted to see you. Make sure you're okay," she said softly, starting to toe her way closer to me.

I kept my head down, knowing the minute she saw my face, the only thing she would feel for me was pity. I didn't want her sympathy.

I didn't deserve it.

The truth was, I relished the feeling pounding through my face and my ribs. Even as my eye swelled shut from the force of Ronan's fist against it, and I felt the blood dripping down the cut on my brow bone, I enjoyed this pain. I needed it, because I needed to be penalized. I didn't know when I'd become this feeble, piece of shit excuse for a man, but I needed to atone.

I owed it to all of them. Not just her.

"Can you look at me?" She asked, her voice sounding a bit more commanding.

I lifted my chin slightly, curls falling over my eyes but not hiding enough of the damage.

She gasped loudly, bringing her hands to cover her mouth in horror, "Ronan did this to you?"

"No Morena, I did this to me," I admitted the real truth, yeah, maybe Zerkos threw the punches, but I did this to myself. "You're with Kane now then?" I asked her, wondering how devastated Zerkos might be feeling.

She tilted her head sideways and furrowed her eyebrows at me like she didn't understand the question. "He's with *me*. What's your deal? You wanna act like you don't care. But I know you do. You want to pretend like we can ignore what happened. But we can't," she said, kneeling on the ground in front of me, "You fucked me with a gun, Santito." She said the words, and a chill ran down my spine. "*And I liked it*," she whispered, bringing her hands to my thighs, and pulling herself closer to me.

"What are you doing Celia?" I pulled back, eyeing her suspiciously.

"You were right. I don't want to be friends anymore," she practically crawled on top of me, and I fell back onto the cot on my elbows, my forearms holding me up as my upper body hovered over the shitty bed.

"I was drunk, I didn't mean-"

"Don't fucking lie to me," she cut me off, her voice filled with a dark, assertive tone I'd never heard from her before that sent goosebumps down my arms.

"You sold me out. You thought sending me away would be easier than dealing with your feelings for me." She pushed my chest down until I laid back completely. I was trapped under her carnivorous hold as if I were Frodo and she was the spider Shelob, ready to spin me into her next victim.

"What are you doing?" I breathed out, suddenly overwhelmed by her proximity as she preyed on me.

"Finishing what you started." She slid her hand over my pants to my already hard cock and squeezed hard enough to make it hurt.

"Ahh," I gasped, then reached out to wrap my hand around her throat. She smirked at me like it wasn't a threat, so I squeezed. She moaned and rubbed her hand against my erection again; I dropped my head back in defeat, laboring for my breath as she reached inside my pants.

"Fuck," I begged, but I wasn't sure what I was asking. It was everything I had ever wanted or thought about for the last fifteen years. "You're Ronan's. Stop. I can't," I barely said, and she squeezed again, forcing me to cry out one more time.

"I will not live the rest of my life letting other men dictate who I'm meant to be. What I can do. Or who I can fuck," she was angry, maybe at me, maybe at everything, and rightfully so. But denying the abundance of lust glistening over her eyes was impossible. It was suffocating now that it was directed at me.

It was like waiting for the sunset your entire life, only to find out you were afraid of the dark.

No.

It was like dying of thirst and being offered gasoline.

I wanted that drink more than I'd wanted anything else in my life. But the fear that it would kill me, had me paralyzed, too afraid to reach for the cup sitting right in front of me.

It could have been water, it could have been petrol, but I was too chickenshit to find out for myself. I pushed her off me; harder than I intended to, and she wound up on the floor looking up at me, with that look of hurt on her face.

"Don't you want me?" She asked, the confidence wavering out of her.

"You're *all* I ever wanted. You're the *only* thing I've ever wanted," I finally voiced the words I'd been too afraid to ever own all these years.

"Then stop thinking. I'm right here. I won't lay myself out for you again," It was like hitting a brick wall full force, the way her words slammed against me, becoming what I needed to push every fear, every doubt out of my head.

She was right.

She was here, offering herself up to me like a lamb to the slaughter, and I was worried about the "what ifs". It was already too late; we had already pushed those boundaries, and our past had gone up in flames. There was nothing but cinders left, and we would never be able to return to what we once were.

Our friendship was gone. Now all that was left was to finish killing it completely so we could become something new; to move forward from this. We were never meant to be friends, but our past and our circumstances painted us into that corner.

I snarled, moving towards her too fast, and she flinched back.

Good.

She needed to understand that when it came to her, I couldn't hold myself back, and I never would. She should be afraid because my feelings for her were dangerous, erratic, and nonsensical. I'd go to hell and back for this woman, and with the same dagger, I'd send us both there to stop the world from ever keeping us apart again.

My love wasn't safe.

My love was brutal, it was a poison, and if she wanted it so badly, I'd force her to drink it on her knees.

I pulled the tanto point knife out of my pocket and flipped it over, her eyes widening as she crawled back towards the wall. Once her back hit the concrete behind her, she winced and used her hands to pull herself to stand.

"If we do this, there's no going back," I warned her, and she nodded, eyeing the blade in my hand but pushing the fear out of her expression.

"I don't want to go back. There's nothing for me left in the past," she reassured me, and I pushed her against the wall with a hard shove.

"You might come to regret that," I said before sending the edge of the knife down the front of her dress, not bothering to pull it away from her so that every inch I went down further scratched into her skin, leaving a red mark. She sighed like the world had come off of her shoulders. "You like the danger." I acknowledged a new side of this girl I would've never pictured before, and she nodded.

"I've been in danger my entire life. It's the only thing that lets me know I'm still alive, and not in hell burning for my sins," she breathed out, and I ripped the rest of the dress until it was left hanging from her arms. I pushed the blade under her jaw, pressing it tightly against her neck.

"Then I'll keep reminding you we're still here, very much paying for all of our mistakes. You won't burn in hell Morena, because when I'm done with you, I'll be the one who owns your soul," I told her, and she pressed her throat against the knife, forcing a small cut on the side of her neck.

She moaned, and I lifted the blade, leaning down to lick the droplets of blood forming.

She looked up at me, and for a split second, like she could still feel the hesitation powering over me, she kissed me. It was a feverous kiss, hot, messy, teeth clanking as we fought for control over one another until finally she gave in and let me lead. I knew who she was; I knew this was the most violent woman the world had ever shaped. But she didn't come to me to exert her power over me.

She came here to bend to my will.

"Please," she begged me as I broke free from our kiss, reminding me to turn my thoughts off and to focus on the beautifully wrapped gift that ended up locked in this cell with me.

I smacked the flat steel side of the blade against her still-covered pussy, and she quivered against me with a hiss, lifting away from the wall. I brought the knife's edge to the top of her panties, but she pushed me away.

"Fuck off, these are brand new," she said, pulling them down her hips and stepping out of them, and I smirked, pulling them up and crumbling them in my hands.

"Open then," I commanded, parting her lips for me with my thumb. Pulling her jaw open from the inside, I stuffed her underwear into her mouth, "Can you follow instructions?" I asked, and she nodded silently, eyes full of wild, unapologetic desire.

And it was aimed at me.

"Spread your legs," I directed, and she took heed while I kneeled in front of her. I was exactly where I was always meant to be. That very place I spent every night I lay awake thinking about. I was on my knees in front of the most beautiful creature to ever walk this Earth.

It was a privilege to bow before her.

To be the one to get to bask in the sounds of her pleasure as I licked my way up her thigh and pressed my lips to her center. She gasped as I lifted her foot and placed it over my shoulder, raking my tongue over every inch of her beautiful cunt while I savored her.

"Mmm," she mumbled through the fabric lodged in her mouth as she trembled above me, clenching her fingers tightly over my shoulders as she held on. She bucked her hips, pushing herself deeper into my mouth, and I speared two fingers inside her without hesitating. I found that button inside her with ease and rubbed my fingers along it while savagely sucking on her clit like It was the best meal I'd ever had.

"Oh -od!" She tried to cry out, but it came out as muffled garbage through the panties, and I pumped my fingers harder through her climax, feeling her walls tightening around me. She fisted my hair and pulled tight, dragging me up her body, but I wasn't ready to let her take charge.

No.

I needed this.

I needed to own her, leave a mark on her, to make her mine.

I'd spent too long fighting this feeling, the urge to finally give in and lose control was unbearable, and there was nothing to hold me back anymore. I pulled the remnants of her dress off her shoulders, letting the scraps drop to the floor as I undid my belt. She let out a hitched breath when I pulled my cock free from my pants, her eyes not missing the piercings lining the underside of my shaft as she licked her lips subconsciously. I turned her around in one swift motion to press her front against the wall.

Then it was there.

I only barely heard about it, I'd spent the entire week consumed with my own bullshit, and I hadn't even bothered to check on her. She turned her head back to look at me, as if she already knew.

I wanted to know what was going through her mind, but knowing Cecilia, it was likely something ridiculous about this wound making her unattractive. Her eyes glazed over, the serious expression on her face cut through me as she waited for my reaction, making me angrier than I could imagine.

She didn't say it, but I knew she thought it. I pulled her by the hair, bringing her head back to look up at me.

"You better not be thinking something stupid Morena," I said before lining the tip of my cock to her entrance and pushing it in slowly. Letting her feel each individual bar that went down my Jacob's ladder as it entered her. Her eyes widened, and she let out a muffled moan with each inch while gazing up at me, my hold on her hair still tight, as her neck pulled back, straining her throat.

She looked so fucking sinful.

Every torturous moment in the past made this one even sweeter as I relished the feeling of her around me. Her pussy was so tight and hot, there had never been another that could compare; there was *nothing* that felt like this.

"I want to feel you come on my cock," I whispered in her ear as I pounded into her, smashing her breasts against the concrete wall without mercy.

She nodded and mumbled something incoherently, and I reached down to rub her clit with my fingers again, pinching and moving back and forth as she shook her head side to side.

Her orgasm came out like a guttural cry as she struggled with the underwear still lodged in her mouth, and I felt wave after wave of her muscles contracting around me. She practically melted in my arms, and I held her up as I continued to slam into her over and over, until I soon followed her, shooting my cum deep inside her with one final thrust.

She breathed heavily, her fingers still clutching onto any ridged ledge on the wall she could find, and I pulled the panties out of her mouth. The wet splotching from them hitting the concrete echoed through the cells as I threw them on the ground before turning her around. I wiped the drool from the edge of her lips, sinking my tongue deep into her mouth and she moaned into me, rubbing her hands up my chest as if to feel if I was really here.

"Now what?" I said, breaking the kiss. Not sure where we went from here.

"Now we self-destruct so we don't ever have to look each other in the eye again," she joked, forcing a smile out of me as she casually adapted to this transition much easier than I ever could.

What happens when the dream girl isn't a dream anymore?

I guess you spend the rest of your life protecting that.

Keeping her at all costs.

"I mean-" I started, but she cut me off.

"I know what you mean. I'm going to handle Guillermo," she said, dropping her arms, and I pulled the filthy shirt off of me and handed it to her. Archer's blood had long dried, and as dirty as it was, it was better than the shredded dress that no longer had any use lying on the ground.

I raised an eyebrow at her as she pulled the shirt over her head, unbothered by its state. "You're going to handle him?" I questioned her.

"I'm tired of running. Running from weak men and their quiet threats. I'm louder, meaner, smarter, and I don't send sicarios to do my bidding either. I'll rip his throat out myself." Her voice had that authoritative tone from when she first entered the cell, the same one that sent a chill down my spine.

"And how do you plan on doing that Morena?" I asked her as she sat on the cot casually, as if she hadn't just declared war on the Cártel. I admired her ambition, but as far as I knew, her army was three. Yeah, maybe Zerkos and Kane counted for at least twenty each, but that wasn't enough against Los Muertos.

"I'm taking back what's mine," she announced, and before I could question any further, Mateo slammed open the door down the hall and walked down the aisle towards us, whistling. He stopped in his tracks once he reached my cell, not missing the way Celia's dress laid on the floor next to her panties. He gave her a grin, and she looked down, the closest thing to a tell that meant she was blushing because her skin tone didn't allow it.

"You get what you need?" The asshole asked her shrewdly as he unlocked the cell door, and she fought back a smile but failed.

I used to be the only one able to do that; I didn't know how to feel about whatever it was they were becoming.

What did that mean for me?

"You ready to head back up?" He asked her, but she looked down, fiddling with her fingernails. He laughed louder than necessary.

"I'm not going to take pity on you just because you've got his cum dripping down your legs, let's go."

I eyed him suspiciously. I wasn't sure how he could brush off the fact that I'd just fucked her like it meant nothing to him. Clearly, something was going on between them that even Zerkos acknowledged him as someone he could depend on to care for her well-being.

So why was he being so nonchalant about this?

He tilted his head towards the entrance and winked her way, "Come on, I promise I can make it worth your time." He extended a hand to her, and she stood up from the cot.

I followed her, but Kane tisked at me and put his hand over my chest as if to say I wasn't going anywhere.

"Not you traitor. Ronan's deciding what to do with you still."

I frowned at his words, but Cecilia grabbed my hand as she tried to pull me out of the cell.

"Either he comes out, or I'm staying with him. What's it gonna be?" She tapped her feet as she waited for his answer. Kane lifted her chin and gave her an exaggerated kiss, running his hands up her body.

"Don't make me into the bad guy, Sunshine. I much prefer it when we leave it up to the other two assholes," he said as he pulled away, and she gave a solemn smile.

"Deal," she said, looking back and mouthing the word, "Sorry."

I wasn't sorry.

How could I be when everything led up to this?

54

RONAN

"You took her to see him?" I asked Kane, trying my best not to let the anger take over.

"I'm not in charge of shit anymore," he shrugged, walking past me. I clenched my fists, but before I could take a step, Cecilia was already pushing me away from Kane.

"Put your hands on him one more time and you'll never touch me again. On either of them for that matter," she proclaimed, nearly knocking the goddamn wind out of me with her words.

"How could you do that to him?" She asked, obviously having seen the damage to Santos.

"If Taylor hadn't called us down, you would have probably been hog tied and delivered to your uncle on a silver platter because of him," I pointed towards the elevator as if it was Santos.

"I don't know who the fuck Taylor is, but isn't that the whole point of why you put that chip in me?" She asked, crossing her arms.

"After the shit he pulled, he's lucky I didn't string him up and hang him from the rooftop for all our men to see," I seethed, my nostrils flaring as I thought about heading back downstairs just to lay him out again.

"Ronan Stop!" Cecilia yelled, "You've found your rats, killed one of them, there is no one else to blame anymore. I kept my secrets and Santos did the same. You can't hold it against him and not do the same to me."

"Oh Flower, I *am* holding it against you, and as soon as I have the chance I *will* punish you for it," I said, pulling her in as I hooked my arm around her low back, but before I could close in and seal my lips around hers, I noticed what she was wearing. "Why the fuck are you wearing his bloody shirt?"

"Uhh," she stammered out, and Kane smirked, looking away. "Would you have preferred it if I walked past your men naked?" She asked with a funny look on her face.

"What the fuck are you talking about?"

"No more secrets, right?" She looked at me, and I nodded, scrunching my eyebrows in the middle. "Well, I've slept with all of you. Am sleeping with all of you? Well I guess not sleeping," she laughed out, the thoughts coming out of her mouth like word vomit before she could seem to catch them. "Do what you want with that." She shrugged and began walking towards the bedroom, which she'd claimed as her own.

She pulled the t-shirt off her head and threw it on the ground before she made her way through her door. Kane followed me as if he had every right to be staring at her naked body.

"I'm sorry, what?" I asked her, unsure if I'd actually heard what I heard.

"Is that a problem?" She turned around too quickly, forcing me to bump into her tiny frame and hold her up, so she didn't fall on her ass.

"Yeah, that's a fucking problem. What the hell do you think you're doing?" I grabbed her by the arms, and she frowned her eyebrows at me.

"I guess I must have missed the memo that we were exclusive when you had me locked up in that cell a few floors down."

"I don't recall us ending, I recall you running away." I pointed out and she sneered at me.

"So what does that make of us, when you're getting your cock sucked by a Bratva princess?" Her lip did a funny quivering thing when she mentioned the Russian sisters.

"Well it seems like it's all free rein then?" I asked, and she looked even angrier at my response.

"That depends on whether or not you ever want me in your bed again, but sure, *free rein*," she repeated without breaking her composure.

"That's a dangerous game you're playing Cecilia. You think we're all going to stick around while you make fools out of us?" I gritted out, furious and trying to concentrate, but she was completely naked, and still marked up red in places where one of my brothers recently had their way with her.

Or did they fuck her together?

Did they give her what I refused?

It felt like I was being consumed by the heat her body was exuding, and like the center of my universe, she was pulling me closer to her orbit. It was impossible not to stand close enough to touch, feel her breath on me, and reach out and caress.

But here she was, covered in another man's marks as she toyed with my feelings.

"Are you punishing me?" I asked lower, hoping my brother couldn't hear me.

"Ha!" She exclaimed loudly, making me flinch, "Though a great punishment that would have been. No, my darling, this is not your retribution. This is just the way the fates dealt our cards."

I didn't respond, I couldn't invoke a single thought in the whirlwind that was bashing through my brain.

"You talk a lot of shit about how 'you'll always have me' and that I'd never deny you or being yours. Well, that may be true Ronan, you will always own a piece of my heart. But I haven't been whole, ever. Not even when you thought you knew me. I've always just been the remnants of the girl that my papá split me into. The other pieces of my heart belong to them, I've already given them away." She gestured out the door as if they were both there, but it was just Kane. The continuous reminder of Santos' betrayal, still far too evident.

"And if I say no, if I don't agree?" I asked, needing to know what my options were.

"Then I'll leave, and it'll hurt, and I probably won't ever be okay again. It won't be what I want to do. But I'll have to because I won't tear the three of you apart. I won't be the thing that comes between you and fucks up the love you all have for each other. Either you're all on board, or I'll leave, which based on the countdown Guillermo's given Santos, doesn't sound like the worst idea," she stood her ground firmly even if her ultimatum was fucked up beyond belief. She had the nerve to say this was about not coming between us when that was quite literally exactly what she'd fucking done.

"You've been nothing but a pain in my fucking ass since the minute you walked back into my life," I gritted out, knowing damn well that was exactly why I loved her.

The truth was it wasn't her fault.

I put her in this situation.

I hand delivered her to both of my brothers like she was a goddamn gift as I pulled back and pushed her away from me.

"Would you have me any other way?" She smiled sincerely, but there was pain behind it, like losing me, maybe all of us, would be something she couldn't come back from.

"All or nothing huh?" I asked again, and she nodded her head.

I turned back to look at the idiot standing by the doorway, and he quickly looked away, like he was trying to pretend he hadn't been a part of this whole thing.

"And you're both just fucking dandy with this?" I asked him.

"I don't know about Álvarez, but I'm in for whatever this is."

"It doesn't mean I love you any less. No one is forcing anyone's hand here, but I think I've made my terms pretty clear. Take it or leave it, that goes for all of you," she said, looking back before walking out of her room.

"Where the fuck are you going? This isn't over," I shouted back at her.

"No, I figure it's not, but it seems like the rest is between the three of you. My room doesn't have a shower, so that's where I'm going, alone," she said, the last part directed at Mateo, and I once again fought back my jealousy from taking over my fists.

"Hey! I've been playing nice!" He said, pouting his lip shamelessly while he drank her in as she stood before him.

"Yes, you have been a very good boy," she tapped his cheek with her hand, then stood on the tips of her toes to press a kiss to his lips.

"Now figure your shit out. If you have to know, I choose the option where I walk out of this with the three of you. I've been completely alone for half my life now, I don't wish that on anyone, and I certainly would prefer to never do it again," she laid down her truth too brutally before walking away, and it was something I'd never stopped to consider.

She'd essentially been on the run since the minute she left me. Jumping from city to city, never making friends out of fear she'd be responsible for their death. My heart hurt at the thought of her out there all alone, searching for a family to call her own. There was a time all I wanted was to be able to give her that, and here she was showing me what her idea of family meant now.

They were my brothers. I didn't know a life without them now, and I'd considered them family by every meaning of the word. Even though their betrayal stung something deep when it came to Cecilia, I knew I could still count on them to want the best for me and to have my back.

And now they had hers too.

Was I being unreasonable?

Was I being selfish?

"You look like you're about to have a stroke. Sit down," Mateo instructed me, lifting his chin to point to the bed in the room. I dropped down on the edge with a heavy sigh, not ready to look him in the eye yet.

"I don't know how to get through this," I said, dropping my head to my hands in defeat.

"You've always trusted him with her, to keep her safe, to keep her happy, has that changed?" Kane asked, like it mattered to him that I didn't hold this against Santos. My lip peeled up, and he immediately regretted his words. "Okay, maybe safe wasn't the right choice but definitely the rest." He shrugged.

"I trusted him to keep his dick out of her too." I snarled, and he flinched back, raising his hands in defense.

"That's a tall order, I mean, have you looked at her?" Kane laughed, and I looked up at him so he could see how much I wasn't finding the humor in this.

"Listen, all I'm saying is, fifteen years of wanting someone and not going for her because he loved *you* too much. That's fucking respectable, I didn't even make it three months." He shrugged.

"Cecilia, Celia, whatever her fucking name is, she's special. She's worth it. And she's way too much fucking woman for any of us alone anyway, so there's no point in wasting your time trying." Kane said as he kneeled in front of me and placed his hand on the side of my arm.

"I can't lose you, brother." He continued, "I love you ugly bastards so damn much, you're the family I chose. But I can't lose her either, she's the best damn thing I never deserved. I'll do whatever it takes to convince the two of you to not screw this up for me. And regardless of what you believe, she *is* safer with the three of us," he added, and I scoffed.

"Let's ask that to the guy who just tossed her out like trash," I spat back at him, and he raked his hand over his face.

"He lost himself a bit. Sometimes the right thing is the wrong thing, and sometimes the wrong thing feels the best. If she forgives him, that's enough for me," Mateo said, making me feel like an even bigger asshole for the beatdown I had given our brother.

I groaned as I let my back fall onto her mattress, running my fingers through my hair and kicking my shoes off. Kane walked towards the other side of the bed and opened her bedroom window before lighting a joint. I rolled my eyes but didn't bother to reprimand him this time. It wouldn't fucking matter anyway.

He then walked out of the room but returned in less than a minute with my best bottle of scotch in hand. Pulling the cork off with his teeth he spat it out onto the floor, not bothering to pick it up before handing it to me.

"So much for not supporting drinking our feelings?" I egged and he shrugged, sitting on the bed next to me.

"I'd actually call this a celebration." He smirked, "maybe we put some rules down, some boundaries?" He asked.

"It wouldn't matter, she would break them all anyway," I said with a sigh as the liquor worked its way through me.

Kane laughed like he already knew her as well as Santos and me, and for once, it made me smile instead of fume with rage.

Maybe I could get through this with them if I could just stop feeling like I was losing her. Maybe I was gaining something bigger than I'd ever had before. Perhaps I needed to close the circle of our family. Stitch it up so no one else could enter what we had made ours.

Ours.

I didn't realize I'd fallen asleep, but I woke up with my throat dry, and Kane curled beside me. I pushed off the bed and pulled my phone out of my pocket to see it was barely one thirty in the morning. I pulled the comforter over Kane and left him in Céci's bed as I hunted for my girl.

I opened the door to Santos' room, but it was empty. Across from his door was the sure bet, but even as I opened Mateo's door, I was surprised to not find her there either. Confused, I headed down the hallway to the final option, having a hard time believing I would be seeing her there, but sure enough, miracles existed.

She laid there on my bed, and if I hadn't seen the kind of violence, she was capable of with my own eyes, I'd say she looked like an angel. She wasn't clothed, and I could smell the coconut on her freshly washed hair from the doorway. The way my sheets tangled around her glowing golden-brown skin made my dick throb and I was desperate to touch her.

I undressed down to my boxers and crawled over her, running my hands over her soft skin to ensure she was really here before I settled next to her. She groaned, a sleepy sound turning in towards me.

"What time is it?" She whispered without opening her eyes.

"Late, why didn't you come get me?" I asked, wondering why she chose my bed of all places but not me.

"The two of you looked too cute cuddling together. I didn't want to disturb you," her hands reached up to palm my chest, and I let out an exhale of relief.

I pulled her over me, so her top half was practically using my chest as a pillow, and I wrapped my arms around her tiny frame.

"Mmmm." She mumbled again, "I missed this." She said, finally opening her eyes, those obsidian mirrors reflecting at me, showing me all of my mistakes. "I missed you."

I could have said a million wrong things at that moment. I could have let my anger speak for me, I could have told her that missing me was all her fault; this was always here waiting for her if she hadn't been so goddamn stubborn. But the past didn't matter anymore; there was only one way we could make it through this.

"I'm not going anywhere," I vowed for the second time in our lives. "I've got you. I'm not letting you go."

She softened into my arms with my promise, and I knew I was risking something I wasn't sure I could deliver. But for her, I would try.

I would never stop trying.

She smiled at me so big I almost saw her teenage self-looking up at me from the past. My heart tugged something awful, I knew then and there, I wouldn't just give her the world if she asked. I'd gladly be the bridge to hell she'd walk upon to keep her feet from blistering once she'd set all of her enemies on fire.

"Kiss me," she breathed out through her sleepy fog.

"Are you done fighting me?" I asked, wondering where this left us.

"Baby, I'll never stop fighting you," she smirked, and I pressed my lips to hers, pulling her in closer until her heart was beating directly above mine. She was right, because we wouldn't be us if she weren't always on my heels, challenging me and fighting me until I became better out of the sheer need to give her more.

"Just as long as you always come back to me," I said, pulling my head back to look at her.

"Siempre," she promised, grinding her hips against me, waking up my cock with just the feel of her hot bare pussy over the fabric of my panties.

"I'm gonna fuck you the way I should have when you first walked back into my life," I said, reaching for her throat and pinning her under me until I was pressed against her again. She looked up at me through hooded eyelids as she parted her legs and wrapped them around me, and I sank my tongue into her mouth again. Tasting every bit of the fire that lived inside her as it fought to consume me. "Does it hurt like this?" I asked, remembering the healing wound on her back, but she shook her head at me.

"It doesn't matter. I want to feel it all, so long as it's you dealing it out," she said, slipping her hand into my boxers and wrapping her fingers around my length.

I groaned out at the feeling of her soft hand as she pulled me out and rubbed her thumb against the head of my cock, spreading the beading precum throughout the tip. I dropped my head to her chest with a growl as she teased, and I squeezed my hand a bit tighter, cutting off her air while she played with me.

She made a soft sound as I tightened my hold on her, her eyelids fluttering as she gazed up at me with her hand pumping up and down on my cock.

"Flower, you look so beautiful this shade of blue," I whispered as I lined the tip of my cock to her entrance and only let go of her throat once I'd fully sheathed myself inside her. She gasped and ground against me again, searching for friction while the proof of her arousal soaked into the sheets beneath us. Her head thrashed from side to side and I watched my cock drive in and out of her mercilessly.

"Ronan!" She cried and I pulled out and slammed back into her, finding the rhythm I knew would get her turning into a screaming mess in no time.

I found one of her hands under the pillow and laced my fingers through it, gazing deep into her eyes with every thrust. I marveled at how we could find these instances of pure intimacy even in our most carnal moments; it was something I'd only ever been able to do with her. It was the only time I could ever slow to feel the beating of my own heart.

As if without her, I was only existing, and now I was living again.

A being of flesh and blood that was bound to her soul.

I released her hand and reached down to the swollen bundle of nerves between her legs, swirling her clit with my fingers as I took no mercy in reminding her why we were made for each other. My other hand raised to her throat again, but I didn't squeeze; I just left it there, cupping her neck gently as I drove in and out of her.

"Please!" She shouted while I teased her with the promise of what she craved.

"Louder, I want him to know what he needs to live up to. I want them both to know, if they can't make you scream like this, then they have no right to your bed or your body." I caressed my thumb against her jugular as I waited.

"Oh God! Please Ronan!" She yelled, and I finally squeezed, cutting off her airway and watching as she struggled to surrender.

She dug her nails into my forearms, and I lifted each one of her ankles to my shoulders before reaching back down to pinch her clit one final time, sending her over the edge with a desperate cry. Her walls spasmed, squeezing my cock like a chokehold that had me spilling my cum deep inside her.

"Mine?" She breathed out like a question, leaning up and dropping her legs to my sides as I claimed her lips again to answer her.

The revelation was sharp, almost painful, but it was true.

She was never mine, but I had always been hers.

55

CELIA

We were running out of time before Los Muertos would come for me or Santos, maybe the whole brotherhood? They were barely a blip on my papá's radar when I was just a girl. A few kids in a street gang who liked to tell others they repped the Cártel. Rafael sent plenty of men to warn them off, threatening them to stop affiliating themselves with him before something bad happened.

But the bad happened to my papá instead and Guillermo finally got what he wanted in the end. He wasn't just a piece of the Cártel, now on this side of the border, he was the Cártel. But I would take that back from him too, along with every stolen piece Ignácio hid away.

The lack of communication on both sides was highly apparent though. According to Santos, Los Muertos wanted me dead. According to Carlito, my uncle wanted me alive. I could only guess because he wanted the rest of my abuelo's fortune, and I was his only ticket to getting inside that dungeon.

But the countdown continued, and even though they hadn't let Santos out of the fifth floor, he'd let Mateo know exactly how many days we had left before I was expected to be delivered.

Four.

Which meant we needed to work fast. Ronan had given Cézar a few million dollars to purchase some property that was practically on his compound but owned by the state. These would serve as temporary living arrangements for anyone who worked for the Black Crows and their family who lived in the building.

We'd spent the last two days arranging everything for evacuations, meeting after meeting with Ronan's top soldiers to dole out tasks, so that everyone knew what they were responsible for, when the time came to move out.

Since people would be in and out, packing, and transferring over to Grimm's Reach, there was just no way to keep the lockdown in place and maintain the security measures they established. The high-rise was open, and the elevators were free to use and access.

A terrifying feeling almost.

You didn't realize how much a lack of freedom also translated into safety.

"You can't keep him down there much longer. Your men are going to doubt you if you don't present a unified front," I said, between bites of my bagel as the three of us sat around the kitchen island eating breakfast.

Ronan growled under his breath.

"She's not wrong," Mateo said, snagging my bagel and finishing it in one bite.

"Keep stealing my food and I'll have to start getting stabby with you," My threatening side-eye must have lost it's edge, his response only a shrug of his shoulders.

"But then your nose wouldn't do that adorable twitch it does when I do something that annoys you." His grin forced my stomach to do that sickening fluttering again.

It was too easy with Mateo. Too easy to fall in love, too easy to trust, too easy to just be. Whatever version of me I pulled out for the day, he welcomed her into his arms.

It was unconditional, and part of me feared I didn't deserve it.

Ronan kept grumbling nonsense about Santos paying for his damage, but If I was the damage, then I could say he'd had enough.

"There's a party on the second floor today," Mateo said with an uncertain look, and Ronan's eyes narrowed before he let out a deep sigh. "There was no way I could talk them out of it, not with Fletcher coming home in a couple of hours, and not with the move. The Crows need this," he reasoned, and Ronan nodded in agreement.

"It's dangerous though. Not the right time," he scratched the back of his head.

They'd lost a few of their older members with the news of the Archers' betrayal. The proof was too blinding to ignore, but old men set in their ways refused to believe concrete evidence right in front of their faces. The next generation of soldiers stayed put, loyal to the leaders they'd followed for half a dozen years.

"My opinion may not mean much, but I think this party may be important. For morale, you know?" I said with a shrug as I spread the cream cheese on the other half of the bagel and put it on Mateo's plate before splitting another one for myself.

"Who said your opinion doesn't mean much?" Mateo asked, with no hesitation as he picked up the other half of the bagel and began digging into it, and I smiled at him.

"All I'm saying is, Fletcher chose to give up his life instead of helping the enemy. That speaks loudly, and his return should be celebrated."

"You're right. With everything we're putting our people through, this may be a dumb idea, but it might be a necessary one," Ronan finally agreed, "Shoving all the Crows into one room for a party is probably the safest I can keep you anyway." He turned to Mateo, "Make sure there's at least a dozen men working the exits and you have my green light. Tell everyone else to stay armed, just in case."

Mateo rolled his eyes at Ronan, "Yeah sure, that sounds super stress free."

"And Santos?" I asked again before we derailed the conversation.

Ronan did a dramatic exhale and dropped his head to the table.

"Is this actually about him sending me off, or is it something else?" I raised an eyebrow at him.

"It's all of it. It's the lies, the deceits, the secrets. The years of it. That kind of betrayal cuts deeper than you could ever understand," he said through grit teeth, a little too much emphasis on the word ever, and I knew he was still dwelling over the scars I'd left on him from my own secrets.

"Keeping him locked up down there isn't going to solve any of that. It won't fix it," Mateo said to him, that serious tone he used so selectively to let us know that something mattered to him.

"You make sure the men are prepared for tonight. You go with Taylor to get some more clothes and something for tonight. I'll deal with Álvarez," he said, handing out objectives to each of us.

"Who's Taylor?" I asked.

"You'll like Taylor Constance, our tech wiz. She's sarcastic as hell, isn't afraid of anyone, and will tell you how sexy you look with every outfit change," Mateo laughed.

"Sounds like my kind of girl," I said with a grin.

Ronan added, "More importantly, I can trust her to keep you safe for a couple of hours."

"Just don't go adding her to your harem, I don't know if I can handle sharing you any more than this," Mateo joked, but Ronan's lip just twitched up in a display of dissatisfaction he was so clearly fighting to contain.

I bit through my top and bottom lip to hide the smile on my face because Ronan was definitely running through the possibility of that scenario in his head, and it wasn't being kind to him. I slapped Mateo on the chest.

"I'm all booked up. Three holes, three dicks," I said with a shrug, pushing myself off the seat and taking my plate to the sink.

Mateo spat out his coffee, coughing as he choked on the drink, though most of it landed on Ronan.

"Watch it, little flower," he growled out through clenched teeth, standing up and pulling me into his body.

"I may have allowed this, but that doesn't mean you won't pay for it every time I have you to myself." His coarse fingers rubbed against the underside of my jaw, pulling a shudder from my body with the threat of his words.

He captured my lips, cupping my face with both hands, urging a moan from me. We broke away, my eyes darting to Mateo at my side, who currently looked at me like I would become his next meal soon.

"It's cute that you think you're allowing it," I smirked, teasing him just to get him riled up for the day.

The truth was that it *was* all in his hands. With the ultimatum I put out into the world like a spell, I left none of them any choice but to be mine, or not at all. I'd only ever been with one man in my entire life, and somehow this week, I'd worked my way up to three.

Oops?

My *papá* once said that a single man on earth would never be good enough for me. I wager this wasn't what he intended though.

The guys reluctantly waved me off as Taylor and I got into a black Jeep Wrangler with the doors and top removed. They seemed to trust this girl with my life, so it was easy for me to say that I did too.

"Did you really let those fuckwads put a tracking device in you?" She asked me as we pulled away, handing me a pair of sunglasses.

I shrugged.

"I've been running for too long. Feels good knowing that someone will come after me if I disappear this time around," I told her, and she gave me a sad look but nodded her understanding.

"I ran a long time ago too. No one ever came for me," she said, peeling out of the parking garage and turning on the radio. Mac Miller's "Self-Care" played on her sound system, and I smiled, knowing right then we'd be friends.

"We've got all day, right?" I asked her, not bothering to hide the mischief I was already planning.

"What have you got in mind?" She asked, and I somehow was able to convince her to make the drive to the Diablos compound.

I threw the doors open to the white farmhouse earning a few scowls from the bastards who thought they were tough shit, that is, until they realized who walked in and those scowls quickly morphed into expressions of uncertainty.

Maybe even fear.

I smirked in satisfaction.

"You know, you can call before you show up." My adopted brother rasped as he sat in a chair that was reminiscent of a throne. From the way it was positioned in the room it demanded the attention of every eye that gazed past it, to the way the others were coordinated around it. I knew that no one else had dared sit there before. So of course, being my papá's daughter, I came with a backbone made of steel.

"Levantate," I commanded him with a tilt of my chin, he fought his upper lip curling up in anger, and got up like the good boy he was, making me smile. I didn't have to treat him like garbage, and to be honest, this was mostly just making up for lost time-sibling rivalry and all that shit. But he did owe me for leaving me, and I wanted my pound of flesh.

I took a seat in the enormous Iron chair, doing my best to hide my discomfort once I realized what a piece of shit his throne actually was. Taylor stood at the doorway of the clubhouse watching the entire exchange with a curious look on her face. Cézar stifled a laugh as if he knew how uncomfortable his president's chair was and hobbled his way to a nearby seat, not bothering to fight me on this since he was still healing from his fresh injuries.

"So, what do I owe this visit, hermanita? We're going to help you with your Bratva problem. Your Crows are moving in." He crossed his ankle over his knee and leaned back casually.

"I've decided I want to take back what's mine." I narrowed my eyes at him as I waited for his reaction, but as always, he was good at keeping it locked away. There weren't many people who got to see him free from the burden of leadership and duty. I knew the few instances I earned in my own life were because we were family, not because he was bound to me by the scars we bore.

"Took you long enough." He said without an ounce of inflection to his voice.

"Que?" I asked, surprised at his response.

"It was only a matter of time before you realized it would come down to either you or him. The ugly bastard sure as shit always knew it." He licked the diamond on his canine before continuing, "You're supposed to be the most feared woman on this side of the world reina, it's about damn time you started acting like it."

"Hard to be feared, when you're all alone." I reminded him.

"Since when do snakes hunt in packs? You have me for your fight if that's what you came here for." He pulled a cigarette out, twirled it between his fingers before tapping the filter on his thigh like a nervous habit.

"It's not. I'm a long way from that fight still. I came here for what's owed to me." I tossed him the key I found in my mamá's possession the day she was killed, "I have a feeling you know where this goes to."

"Of course I know where this goes to Celia. I was burdened with every goddamn secret your family threw my way. *'There will be a time'* Rafa would fucking say, like the only thing that mattered to him was me staying alive long enough to share all the Flores mysteries with you." He scoffed in annoyance, like it wasn't his family too.

"So what, you've just been waiting for me to come ask?" I questioned him, pulling my eyebrows together in the middle.

"No hermanita, I'd been hoping you were dead and that I'd never see your face again for as long as I lived." He confessed and I laughed out hollowly to cover up how hurt I truly felt. I stood up from the chair and crouched in front of him, placing my hand on his cheek.

"And how I'd missed you so, *brother*. The pain of losing you carving an actual hole in my heart and soul that could never be replaced by anyone else. While to you, my absence meant your freedom." I smiled but my sorrow couldn't be masked through it and he saw it as clear as day.

"You will always be my family. But our family was poisonous, Celia. I just wanted to be a free man. I don't regret it." He muttered and turned his face away from me as if he was ashamed of how he felt.

"Once the Crows have settled in, you'll take me then?" I asked.

"Yeah, I'll take you." He agreed. I pressed my lips to his cheek before standing and making my way out of the farmhouse, getting back some of the strength I needed to push forward into my plans. Taylor followed me out without questioning anything that had happened inside or why we'd come here at all, earning even more points from me.

Spending the day with Taylor Constance was something I didn't know how badly I needed. It had been so long since I'd enjoyed the company of a platonic friendship, to feel that closeness of sisterhood, not since...Caro...

Taylor's snarky, sarcastic ways kept me laughing the entire car ride until my cheeks burned from soreness. We made sure to get plenty of snack breaks until it was time to finally break down and do the dreaded shopping that Ronan expected us to be doing.

She'd told me about how she played a part in the guys rescuing me both times now, and she'd also apologized for being the reason they now knew all my secrets. I had no reason to hold it against her for even one second though, if anything, I valued her loyalty to them *and* her honesty.

She talked about her past since I wasn't sharing mine, about how she came from a deeply religious family. She spent so much of her life in the closet out of fear for what they'd think when she told them the truth. When that day finally came, they all turned their backs on her. She spent a few years homeless before enlisting in the Navy out of the need for a warm bed and free meals. "Better than prison," she joked.

She said meeting Mateo and Ronan nearly twelve years ago was like being struck by lightning.

"I just knew that the three of us would always be family after that. We'd saved each other's backs too many times, we could overlook our flaws and just accept each other as we were. You know?" I nodded back to her because I did. That was exactly why I loved them too.

All of them.

I was realizing now too they were the family I'd chosen after the world ripped away the one I was born to.

After spending a couple of thousand dollars on far too many clothes I was just going to be packing away and stuffing into a box in the Diablos Locos compound, and after convincing Taylor to do the same, we finally headed into the last store.

"What are you wearing tonight? What's your look?" I asked her, and she laughed at me.

"My look? This is it babe," she opened her arms. She was sporting black cargo pants and a camo t-shirt.

"If I have to buy an outfit for this party, then so do you," I gave her a look that let her know there was no way around it, and she conceded with a heavy sigh.

"Well, what's your look?" She asked me, crossing her arms.

"Um... The-I've been a prisoner for two months and I have no fashion sense- look?" I said with a shrug, and she laughed.

"Okay, let's find something that will have these guys drooling over you." She rummaged through the boutique's racks pulling things out and shoving them back in.

If that was the game we were playing, then I was in for it. I walked over to another rack and began rummaging through it to pick out an outfit that would suit my new friend.

Once we'd made our selections, we swapped hangers and headed for the dressing room. I eyed her choice suspiciously, the black faux leather fabric catching my eye.

"You can't be serious," I heard her from the booth beside me.

"I want to see!" I yelled out, "I think you forgot pants for me." I told her, and she laughed out.

"No, that's the fit sweetie," she said, opening her door, and I did the same. We both checked out the fruits of our labor in the mirror, Taylor rubbing her temple like she was embarrassed.

"What? You look hot as fuck," I told her.

She stuck her hands in the pocket of the navy-blue dress pants secured to her shoulders with matching suspenders. Underneath was a white crop that showed the bottom of her black bra.

"I look like gay Huckleberry Finn" she said too casually.

Laughing louder than I intended to, I corrected. "Some people like that!"

"You however," she pinched her fingers together and pressed them to her lips for a kiss before spreading them open. "Chef's kiss," she said, admiring her own work.

She was right though, and she was way better at this than I was. The black faux leather dress hugged my hips, snatched my waist, and lifted my boobs to my chin. This was engineering at its finest. The fabric was shiny, form-fitting, but wasn't too clingy and left plenty of cleavage for the world to see. She'd paired it with wedged, thigh-high boots with straps and buckles that went all the way to the top, and I'd never felt taller or more badass in my life.

"Yeah, yeah. You're an artist," I said, pushing her back into her dressing room. Even though she wasn't into the look I picked, she still demanded on keeping it, as long as I insisted on paying, which was fine because it wasn't my money anyway.

"What time is this party?" I asked her, wondering if she'd heard from Ronan yet. That's when it dawned on me that I had no way to communicate with them if we were separated. We hadn't really been apart, unless, of course, someone was forcing it on us, but I was a little sad at the fact I didn't even have a phone to shoot them a text if I missed them.

"Oop. We're late actually," she said, waving her phone in my face, showing me the twelve missed calls between Ronan, Mateo, and Santos.

Well, at least he was out of the cell. That was worth smiling about.

We got back into the jeep and headed toward the high-rise, but Taylor's eyes kept darting to the rearview mirror anxiously.

"We have a tail," she said. After a few minutes of driving, I checked the mirror to confirm the black town car following us.

"Gun?" I asked, and she tilted her chin to the glovebox.

"I'm gonna try to shake them, I don't want to bring shit down to the building." She warned me, and I nodded in agreement. She jerked the wheel sharply into an incoming alley, the back wheel of the jeep floating in the air for a split second before touching back on the ground, and a shot fizzled out behind us.

"Bold little shits," she said before pulling down her sun visor and revealing another pistol strapped to it. "Grab the wheel," she said as the car turned back into the main road, and she shot behind us into the car following us. That's when I noticed the two motorcyclists coming up on both sides.

"Take the next right," I told her. She turned her head without a second to spare before she took back control and spun the wheel too fast again, that rear wheel staying lifted longer than I was comfortable with.

I leaned out of my window just in time to put a bullet in the motorcyclist's chest right as he pulled out his weapon. The towncar tried to swerve but was too close behind and crashed right into the bike and their man as they came to a screeching halt. The other biker turned his wheel back towards the accident and gave up the pursuit.

"Okay then. You're hot as shit, you can handle a gun, and homegirl can flourish in high pressure situations. I'm starting to see what all the fuss is about," she joked as we made our way back to the high-rise.

"Too bad I come with a target painted on my back," I rolled my eyes.

56

CELIA

It was such a relief getting back to the high-rise I didn't realize the place had somehow cultivated a sense of home in me. Not to mention, Santos was at the door waiting to greet me. I wrapped my arms around his neck, and he returned the embrace, burying his nose into my neck with a deep inhale.

"I'm so glad you're a free man," I said, pulling his chin down to examine how his face was healing.

"Morena, with you around, I'll never be a free man again," he said, dropping his forehead to mine, "But it's good to be out of that cage." The deep rumble of his voice was enough to make my knees tremble.

They were setting things up for the party on the second floor, and the music was already blaring through the building. I headed upstairs to change into the outfit Taylor chose for me, and by the time I made it back downstairs, all three guys let me know her choice had been made well.

"Oh, fuck me, Sunshine," Mateo breathed out, stepping towards me, but Ronan's heavy hand stuck out in front of him and pushed him back as he closed in on me instead. I gave him a smirk because I could see the progress for what it was, and his attempt to not kill his friends *did* impress me.

"Are you sure you don't want to just go back upstairs and let me rip this dress off of you instead?" He whispered into my ear with absolutely no attempt to actually keep his voice down. Maybe it was the dress, but he was really just looking for an excuse to call the whole thing off.

It was extremely hard to convince Ronan not to cancel the party after Taylor told him about our little hiccup on the way home. Too bad for him, even as he tried to sabotage the event, Fletcher walked through the doors, and chaos reigned over the entire Black Crow Brotherhood.

The sound of champagne bottles popping echoed throughout the giant space that was cleared out for the party, and the screaming and cheering would die down just in time for someone else to start it all up again.

The music played loudly, everyone settling into the mood of the party. The drinks flowed freely, the girls pranced around from lap to lap of any soldier who paid them attention, and my guys loomed over me like dark protective shadows.

"I'm glad to see you're on the mend," I said as I approached Fletcher with a sincere smile, the girl named Chiyo under his arm looking nowhere but at him.

"Thanks to you. You saved both of our lives," he said, pushing the red hair out of his eyes.

"You can owe me one," I said with a wink.

"Deal."

I went to turn around but felt his hand on my shoulder pulling at me to turn back his way. I didn't miss the way Mateo stepped forward or the way Ronan's lip peeled up before he took his man's hand off my shoulder.

"Sorry," he said, lifting his hands to show he meant no harm, "I just wanted to say, if there's anything you need, I'm your guy."

"Thank you, Fletcher," I said before walking away with all three of my guys forming a V as Ronan and Mateo flanked my sides, Santos at my back.

"Did your guy just pledge himself to me?" I turned my head to Ronan, seeing if I could get a rise out of him, but apparently, it wasn't something that made him self-conscious of his authority.

"Looks that way my little flower. I don't blame him," he shrugged before signaling three fingers to the bartender. "You're the kind of woman any man would follow into battle." He turned the corner of his lip before passing the shots around to each of us but Mateo. He glared at Santos, so I elbowed him in the abs, nearly bruising myself on the hard ridges of his muscles.

Tomorrow we would move the last of our things, and car after car would transport everyone to the Diablos Locos compound in Grimm's Reach. It would be a fresh start for the Black Crows, away from the Bratva drama and out of Los Muertos' radar until we could deal with Guillermo. So tonight, we would drink, be merry, and celebrate.

All three men did their best to have a good time but were constantly peering at the exits, double–no, triple-checking, with all their men posted at their stations. There were maybe sixteen people in the entire crowded room who were privy to the danger we were all under, it was a tricky game to play.

What was best for the people?

Joy or safety? Sometimes too much safety could strip away any chance for happiness.

I knew that well.

The heat in the room was overwhelming as countless bodies pressed together, sweating and dancing on what was now claimed as the dancefloor.

"Hey, ditch the possessive assholes. Come dance with me," Taylor said, her voice coming out of nowhere, and by the time I turned my head to see her, she was already putting the next shot in my hand and pulling me by the other.

I turned it back and threw it into Santos' hands before she could tear my arm off the socket and followed her into the crowded center. We danced to one song which and eventually turned into three, the drinks starting to work their way through my system. Her body was replaced by Mateo's in a single blink, his presence crowding me in a away that felt secure, possessive, but *so good*.

It didn't take long for Ronan to give in and join us, his tall figure cornering both me and Mateo in.

"Hi," I said with a smile.

"I told you I wasn't going to watch you with them," he growled into my ear as he pulled me in closer, but Mateo just moved in with me.

"So, what are you going to do instead?" I baited him.

"Don't tempt me, I have a right mind to fuck you in front of everyone here so that they know exactly who you belong to." He squeezed my ass through my dress, a lightning storm beginning to brew at my core.

I gave him my best seductive glare, "You gonna keep holding that million over my head then?" I said, knowing damn well he didn't have it in him to actually consider this a debt.

"Million and a half." He grinned, "But no, baby, you belonged to me before I bought you," he said, sliding his hand up my dress, the knowing smirk on his face once he realized I had no plans to interfere. His eyes widened as his fingers pushed my panties to the side, dipping inside of me, feeling just how slick and ready I was at the mere feeling of their presence surrounding me.

It was overbearing, thought consuming, borderline despotic how unprepared I felt when they all directed their attention at me. As if my thoughts had a tether, Santos' eyes found me from across the room, he sat with his back towards the bar, his elbows resting on his knees as he watched the three of us.

"Is she wet?" Mateo asked with a deep, breathy voice.

"Isn't she always?" Ronan smirked, less attitude than I expected to find in his tone. Maybe I'd finally get what I wanted, perhaps they could actually share their toy for the night. Mateo's hand groped over my dress, cupping my breast firmly as he stood behind me, kissing my neck, neither one of them caring how many of their men could see.

The floor below us trembled, both the men preying over switching to high alert before I'd even blinked. They'd been trained too well and knew it for what it was before my head had a chance to wrap around it. The floor rumbled again, this time so strong that Ronan whistled, gesturing the DJ to cut the music off. Smoke filled the air far too quickly, Mateo tightened his hold on me as Ronan yelled directions to every person around us.

"What's happening?" I shouted.

Santos threw a bar stool against the floor-to-ceiling windows, only cracking the second story glass, demanding more of his strength to break through it. Crows flocked in disarray, panicking, and running all around the room in search of an exit, but all of the entrances had been locked tightly, not allowing any of us to leave. Smoke overwhelmed the room, every person coughing and choking, some collapsing onto the ground as the poison seeped into their lungs.

Glass spilled all over the floor, Black Crow soldiers clearing as much of the pointed shards off the windows as best as they could. The fresh air wouldn't be enough to keep us safe now, we'd need to jump.

"Get her out of here!" Ronan yelled to Mateo while he gestured to an open window.

"No! Not without you!" I stood my ground, knowing he wouldn't dare leave until all his people were safe, and possibly until he killed whoever was responsible.

I had a few guesses, but at this point, we'd conjured up such a mess, that it was impossible to know if this was someone here for me, for Santos, or if this was Bratva retaliation. A gunshot flew past my head, the bullet shattering into a full liquor bottle on the bar shelf. Ronan's reflexes were on point, and he was immediately handling a Glock in each hand, firing back simultaneously at our attackers who hid behind the safety of innocent Black Crow Members.

People were taking too long to jump down, too afraid of getting hurt or of what may be waiting for them on the ground once they did. They were starting to cram outside the window, afraid of the shooter, the toxic smoke that filled the air, and the uncertainty holding all our lives hostage at that moment. Bodies began to push as people panicked and lost regard for the well-being of others.

Santos was still helping others get down, Ronan shooting into the air vigorously as he missed our attacker for the sake of not shooting down any helpless victims. Mateo kept his gun in hand as he held me against his body, and that's when I noticed that the exit doors to the second floor began to swing open.

There were too many to count, as dozens of men filed through each door with a coordinated precision. Bulletproof vests on their chests and motorcycle helmets covered their faces as they entered the makeshift ballroom with their automatic weapons in hand. The image of the skull masked with a bandana over its mouth inked onto their Kevlar armor drew my attention, sinking my heart deep into my stomach.

Los Muertos had come.

Just like they promised.

Have you ever gotten the feeling the Lord Almighty only kept you around because you were the most entertaining show to watch? Maybe your misery was what pushed him out of a depression, perhaps it gave him the motivation to bless the rich with more wealth and to strike down the poor for the sake of laughs. I felt like I was on the fifteenth season of *Supernatural* and we needed to cancel before God really blew this bitch up.

If there *was* a God, he definitely knew I liked it rough.

But he was taking it a bit too literally.

There was no Misha Collins to bring me back from the dead either, so as far as I knew, you could only kill me once.

As soon as the rapid fire from their bullets began, Mateo's body was on top of mine, crushing me to the ground. People around us began to push each other, forcing some to fall down the second-story height before they were ready to leap themselves. There was no denying that a broken leg was comparably better than a bullet to the head.

"Get her out of here!" Santos echoed Ronan's earlier plea, screaming at Mateo, his nostrils flaring widely and his tone darker than I'd ever heard.

Mateo looked way too close to complying, I could see different scenarios running through his head as he tried to decide on the right thing to do.

"I can help! Give me a gun!" I yelled out through the chaos, and he nodded, kicking over the body of one of their men and pulling a pistol from their holster to give to me.

"Stand behind me," Mateo shouted back, and I followed.

I looked for Ronan to find him walking straight into the fuckers who wanted us dead, two guns holstered at each of his sides and one in each hand as he shot bullet after bullet, without mercy, at every man who wasn't ours.

It was the hottest fucking thing I'd ever seen, he looked like some sort of vengeful superhero, except superheroes didn't use guns, and they definitely didn't kill.

The entire floor shook underneath us, and my eyes widened to find Mateo staring right back at me.

"They're trying to blow the building up!" Someone screamed out, eliciting more panic from the remaining Crows who hadn't leapt for their lives.

Suddenly, blood began to pool out of Mateo's mouth, and he began to choke. I looked down to find him clutching his stomach, already too bloody from the bullet that tore through him.

"I got you!" I yelled at him, taking the brunt of his weight as he crashed into me. I sat him down, leaning his back against the inside of the bar and finding a towel to press into his wound. "We gotta get you out of here, okay?" I said to him as calmly as possible, not letting him see how badly my hands were trembling.

"Sunsh-" he coughed out more blood, and I tried to silence him, pressing my fingers to his lips, but he swatted me off. "Sunshine." He finished the word before spurting out more blood through his lips. "Get out of here," he urged me, but there was no way I was leaving without him, without any of them.

I glanced around the corner of the bar again to see most of the Black Crow members had jumped, fallen, or been pushed to safety. There were a good number of men on the ground bleeding from gunshot wounds, and even more towards the entrance that suffocated from the poison, unable to make it to the windows for fresh air in time.

As I looked, I found that was exactly where Ronan was headed, the cloud of smoke where gunshots rang and bullets fizzed out rapidly, hitting what remained of the bar.

I shouted for Santos, who was providing cover for Ronan, but there didn't seem to be anyone who could help me, everyone who'd been left behind was either injured or dead.

"Hey, crazy boy, I'm gonna need to roll you out of that window okay? It's gonna hurt like a bitch," I warned him, doing my best to stay focused on keeping him alive so that I wouldn't crumble into a pile of tears and call it quits right here and now. He grabbed me by the wrist, his voice so quiet I could barely hear him through the sounds of bullets and shouting.

"Get. the fuck. Out." He struggled to say before blood began to spray out of his mouth again, but I ignored him, reaching up behind his arms as I dragged him through the floor towards the nearest broken window. He was heavy as fuck, even though he was nowhere near Ronan's massive bulky size; I was breathing heavily from moving him just a few feet.

That's when I felt the blade on my neck.

"Up," I heard the voice behind me, too close to my ear as his hot breath lingered on me. My blood went cold, and Mateo's eyes went wide as they fixed behind me. He was turning white from too much blood loss, and I feared we would never make it to a hospital to save him in time.

Before I could turn back to look at the face of the man holding me at knifepoint, a boot came from behind me, kicking Mateo over the shards of glass on the open window. His body fell to the ground with a heavy thud.

I heard the screaming before I realized it was coming from my own mouth, followed by the pained grunt forced from my chest as the stranger behind me threw his elbow into my gut.

"You've been a lot of trouble, zorra. You cost me my best hitman," he said, pressing the knife into my neck with too much force, and I winced from the stinging of the sharp metal cutting into me.

"He was never yours," I rasped out, knowing exactly who the fuck stood behind me.

"Guillermo let her go," I heard from behind, and he turned us both around to face the room. Ronan was being held with a gun against his head by two goons with their heads still shielded by motorcycle helmets. Santos stood in the middle of the room with his gun pointed at Guillermo while three of his men had theirs pinned on him.

I swallowed the lump in my throat.

"I've let you play out this little fantasy long enough. Your little vacation's over. I'm bringing you home primo," his breath was on my ear as he spoke, the revulsion in my stomach intolerable as he pressed too close to me.

He tilted his chin just slightly as a signal to his men. The two holding back Ronan as he wrestled against them moved their guns to his stomach and fired shots into him. My body recoiled from the sound, and I howled out for him as he dropped to the ground and Santos began to shoot at his cousin. Guillermo pulled me back harder, tightening his hold as I fought to get free.

To run to him.

He laid there on his side, breathing heavily; a scowl formed into his expression as his eyes searched the room for me.

"Enough is enough. Let's end this and go home," he said, pulling a syringe out and shooting it into my neck.

I prepared for the worst, but as I screamed and struggled against him, it wasn't the slow sinking feeling I had almost become accustomed to.

No, it was far worse.

My tongue froze mid-scream, turning into a mumble, and my arms dropped heavily to my side. Guillermo laughed a dark, sinister sound as my face collided with the floor. He pulled me back up, my body stiff, paralyzed, but my eyes still open, my lungs still breathing. Whistling casually, he grabbed my wrist and dragged me across the room on my back, and my eyes darted over as all five men closed in on Santos, throwing fists and feet with all their might.

I choked out a sob as he pulled me out of the room, my heart splintering into a million shards as I took one last look at Ronan's body lying there, unmoving, in a pool of his own blood.

Had I always been destined to die at the hands of a weaker man?

Didn't seem like I had much of a choice anymore.

57

CELIA

Lo juro por Dios que, this is the last time I end up in the fucking trunk of another sedan.

Fucking cock-sucking hijo de la chingada.

Guillermo's lackeys had barely shut the trunk before they opened it again, this time to throw Santos in with me. I watched the needle slide into his neck, and the same medicine they used to immobilize me was now coursing through his veins as well. His gagged screams of protests turned into mumbles just as his tongue froze inside of his mouth.

There was nothing worse than staring into the face of someone you loved and seeing nothing but pain, knowing that there was absolutely nothing you could do to make it better. We laid there, staring into each other's eyes, crammed into that tiny, piece of shit trunk Los Muertos had stuffed us inside of for what felt like an eternity. An awkward tear rolling down our cheeks every now and then that we could only ignore and pretend we didn't see. Time moved slowly and eventually my muscles tingled with an intense burn when sensation began to return to my body.

I wiggled myself closer to Santos, resting my forehead on his chest. He moaned a muffled sound that was filled with pain. He was hurting, physically and in every other way possible. Mateo and Ronan were dead, and we were headed towards our end too.

The realization was a blade dead center in my chest.

It was all my fault.

I would have gladly met my demise a hundred—no a thousand times over if it meant the boys would have survived. But it was too late now to make those kinds of compromises and I had cost them their lives. I deserved this, they didn't. My sobs were an incoherent mess of sounds echoing off the trunk that caged us in together.

They were gone.

They were fucking gone.

My ocean, my fire. Both snuffed out from right in front of me and there was nothing I could do to stop it from happening. Nothing I could have done to save them.

I wanted to drown. I needed to burn. Instead, I was trapped inside my own body and locked in this trunk, forced to do nothing but feel and come to terms with my loss.

Our loss.

They'd been glued to each other for half their lives, and in a matter of weeks I destroyed it all. I wasn't the rain that mortals knelt for, I was the deluge that swept all of existence from the Earth.

The question of whether or not we'd be able to survive without them briefly crossed my mind before I realized we wouldn't be surviving at all. We were headed towards the inevitable muerte. Death.

By the time the paralytic ran its course through my body, the car came to a stop, and we were forced to take an undignified piss break. Being groped and manhandled by Los Muertos grunts was the better alternative to peeing myself. Santos tried to fight, earning himself a few more sucker punches to the gut and two more syringes of muscle freezing bullshit before they tossed us back into the trunk.

I was sore, stiff, and every inch of my body burned by the time we made it to the West Coast. I could smell Ocean Valley before they'd even bothered to open the goddamn trunk. The salt in the breeze and sound of the waves crashing was undeniable. And then a surge of emptiness washed over me, where home just didn't feel like home anymore. That place you once had belonged to was now lost in the drawer of your mind and filled with the rest of your nostalgia.

Home went by a lot of different names in the last thirty years. México, Ocean Valley, my 2003 Ford Mercury.

I knew better now.

Home wasn't a place. It was a person, or rather, people.

And I'd never be home again.

I would never smell the scent of Ronan's cologne on his neck. I would never feel Mateo's strong fingers dancing over my flesh. Grief would drive me and Santos apart. I could already feel my heart turning cold, feel myself losing the will to fight.

I cried so much that by the time we finally came to a stop my skin burned, and my throat dried out from the tears I lost. Santos never looked away. His eyes stayed fixed on mine as if to prove that he could endure my pain. Afterall, it was also his pain. Those were his brothers, and he was mourning them too.

He looked defeated. Like all the fight had been taken from him with the sound of those two bullets hitting Ronan's stomach. I couldn't get the vision of Mateo's lifeless body hitting the grass two stories below me out of my mind. I just replayed the night in my head trying to figure out how it could have gone so wrong. The Russians, the cártel, they were more involved with each other than we were aware of.

And I brought nothing but death to the door of all of those who cared for me.

I was still completely immobilized when Guillermo's men slung me over their shoulders and carried me into the old house. It must have been right off the shore because I could feel the sea salt on my skin the minute the fresh air wafted into the trunk. I couldn't focus on anything in the present. My brain kept taking me back to the first moment I stepped into the Black Crow's building. Ruminating over every choice and decision I had made since the age of eighteen.

I spent so long running away. Maybe if I hadn't been such a cowardly idiot, maybe if I would have just owned up to my duty, claimed what was mine, none of this would have happened.

Maybe I'd just already be dead with a few less casualties involved.

Whatever oversized brute was carrying me didn't bother to be gentle, forcing my head to bounce off his back with every step he descended. We were in some sort of basement, and my limbs were starting to burn again from that feeling that let me know I'd have all of my sensations soon.

"Can you stand yet?" I heard a voice behind me I didn't recognize. They were talking to Santos. I couldn't make out his answer, but I heard the clinking of the metal chain and the unmistakable sound of handcuffs closing.

Funny how the sounds that correlated with trauma permeated deeper into our memories than the joyous ones. A thousand happy memories couldn't wipe away the existence of one bad moment.

Then it was my turn. Multiple hands slung me about until I was chained to a metal pole, my arms up and joined together at the wrists bound to a hook. Mirrored opposite to me was Santos, just two or three feet away. If we both reached hard enough, we could have touched our toes together.

A box was placed under my feet, taking the pressure off my arms and reducing some of my pain. A small kindness in this hell. My eyes met Santos' again, nothing but sadness staring back at me. But I had no tears left; I'd cried them all out during our journey.

Guillermo's henchmen left us without another word, the heavy sound of their boots marching up the stairs and the slam of the door confirmed we were alone. It was dark, only a single, dim lightbulb hung from its electrical cord and it was somewhere out in the distance, inside another room with its door wide open. It was too far away to make any difference for us, though it wasn't a very large basement.

Then again, it didn't need to be.

It held the two of us just fine.

A large metal table was positioned to our right, and a small sink was pushed against a wall, years of debris and dirt staining what must have once been white porcelain.

Between the two poles that kept Santos and I apart was a drain.

I fucking *hated* the rooms with a drain.

Nothing good happened inside these rooms.

The chances of me coming out of this basement alive significantly reduced the minute I realized its presence.

"Morena," Santos grumbled, lifting his head up from his chest.

Fuck.

He looked like shit, reminding me that I probably looked no better.

His face was bruised and cut up to hell, but the pain he wore wasn't physical.

"I'm sorry Morena," he mumbled. The dry well inside of me somehow found a way to pull from the reservoirs, my weakness cascaded down my cheeks once more.

Was he sorry that we were in this mess?

Or was he sorry that they were both dead, and we were now alone in this world?

Did I even want to survive this if there was no one waiting for us out there?

"We're gonna get out of here, okay? We'll kill him together," I lied, already deciding then and there I would do whatever it took to guarantee Santos' life.

58

SANTOS

My bullshit karma had finally caught up to me, except the trifling bitch didn't care who she hurt in the process as long as I got what was mine too. I practically killed our men, murdered my brothers, and there was a good chance Celia was only here so that Guillermo could force me to watch him kill her.

As a punishment.

Or maybe this was how I'd go too.

We weren't left alone long. Soon the basement door opened again, and the sound of high heels clicking delicately down the stairs followed heavy boots.

"Carajo, you weren't lying," a female voice spoke, and Celia's head jerked up, her eyes went wide like she recognized the speaker.

She yanked at her chains violently, turning abruptly with eyes jarred open and nostrils flared while she searched around the room for the voice.

"I didn't think we'd get the chance after Carlitos failed so horribly," the voice whispered.

"I was hoping this pendejo was gonna do it for me, but it looks like I'm gonna have to teach my primo a lesson, Lina." Guillermo stepped into the light, and behind him stood a woman.

One whose hair lacked shine, and whose aura seemed smudged and polluted by whatever hardships life had placed in her way. Her eyes were a chestnut brown, and her hair matched the color of the freckles on her skin.

They didn't look much alike, but side by side you could see the similarities.

Impossible to deny that they were sisters. She was, in every way, so much like Celia, and yet somehow there wasn't a single shared trait I could pinpoint.

"Carolina?" Celia seethed, her voice raspy from the journey and the chains clanking loudly.

"God damn," she chuckled, stepping towards her sister. "You look like dog shit Celia. Here I've been hating you for half my life when maybe you did me a favor. Has it been a rough fifteen years hermanita?"

"What the fuck?" Celia screamed, throwing her body with no success as her chains barred her from much movement. "What the fuck?" she continued to repeat, thrashing against her restraints while her sister threw her head back and laughed.

Celia's expression briefly showed a glimpse of something that looked like pain before she masked it over with a steel hard gaze. She cocked her head back and spit a wad of saliva on her little sister's face. Carolina reached her hand up silently, and with no command needed, Guillermo placed a tissue in her hand.

It begged the question of who was in charge here.

"Is that any way to greet the sister you left for dead?"

"Left for dead? You were all buried by the time I left the hospital. Instead of finding me you've been hiding, conspiring against me? I can see Ignacio raised you. Una rata just like him." Celia yelled, not bothering to reign in her emotions.

"Tío said you'd say all those things. Told me you would try to poison my mind with Papá's sentimental lies." Carolina stepped closer to Celia; a sharp surgical tool was in her hand now.

He'd spent the last fifteen years brainwashing her.

Poisoning her against her family.

In a way, that almost meant he'd won.

"If you think I'd waste a second of my time letting you hear words Papá meant solely for my ears, you're delusional," Celia taunted her. "You did get one thing correct though, hermanita, Ignacio was right, you should have killed me when you had the chance. Because if I get out of here alive, I'm gonna rip you apart with my bare fucking teeth," Celia roared, thrashing against her restraints while her sister cackled like a mad woman.

The back of her hand slapped violently against Celia's cheek, the sound echoing throughout the basement.

I couldn't believe this was the sister I had heard so much about. The sister whose death broke Celia in half and even left a stain of sorrow on Ronan's life. This same fucking bitch was somehow behind my cousin's brutality, the murder of my brothers, and so many of our men.

"You still think you're better than me? Still think you're worthy of Papá's favor even though all it got you were scars? We'll see who's ugly, you spoiled bitch," Carolina shrieked, dragging the knife across the side of Celia's face, stopping just before reaching the corner of her lip.

Carolina's eyes widened like she couldn't believe what she'd just done, but Celia's expression remained cold and unchanged, like she hadn't even felt the pain of her skin splitting open from the sharp blade. The blood poured freely down her jaw, staining her chest and dripping down the black leather dress she still wore from the Black Crow Party. She lifted her chin up again, a sinister look filled with nothing but hate burned straight from her eyes into Carolina's.

Celia smirked.

She actually fucking smirked, pushing more blood out of the side of her face. Carolina retreated back with shock at first, but Celia's reaction only forced more anger from her. She lifted her hand as if to slice the other side of her face.

"Dame una sonrisa hermana."

"Stop. Wait," I shouted as loud as I could, getting their attention. "Don't hurt her, don't fucking hurt her... please. You can do whatever you want to me. Just don't hurt her," I begged.

"And what kind of satisfaction am I supposed to get from that?" She laughed and just as her arm came down to cut, Guillermo stopped her with his own hand.

"I can use this. I need to teach this pendejo a lesson anyway." He yanked her back by the forearm and she winced, rubbing the sore spot that he squeezed too tightly. "You want to take all her pain? All her punishment? I'm going to make you regret not killing her so badly that you'll ask me to do it yourself when the time comes to let her go, primo."

"You want to teach him a lesson, amor? Consider this the first one," Carolina declared, her accent heavier than I'd ever heard Celia's in the entirety of our friendship. "You can have the other half," she said sinisterly.

She walked over, standing directly in front of me before digging the knife slowly across the side of my face, mirroring Celia's new cut. I groaned from the pain, biting the inside of the opposite cheek to distract from the sharp pain of her blade.

"Stop it. Fucking stop it," Celia screamed, shaking in the chains.

But it wasn't enough, Carolina smiled proudly at herself and looked to Guillermo before sending the knife down the other side of my face, cutting my eyebrow and sending the blade down my cheek. The burn was intense, and the blood spilled out too fast, forcing me to squeeze my eye shut to keep it from dripping into my vision.

It only made the blood pour down faster.

"Fuck!" I cursed loudly and she cackled, the sound antagonizing Celia as she struggled against her restraints even harder.

"Honestly, this is a gift. Think how hot you're going to look when this is healed." She giggled. "Oops, you're probably not going to get to see it by the time we're done with you."

Blood ran down my face and my vision reddened. It dripped into my eyes, my mouth, down my chest, and didn't stop. She raised her arm to slice again and Celia shrieked, but Guillermo held her back.

"Corazón, they need time to heal, or they'll bleed out. They need time to learn their lessons, understood?" he asked her, earning a bitter look from the youngest Flores sister before pulling her back and standing in front of me. "Ay primo, this could have been so easy. You were my best soldier. I still have hope for you though. Maybe once all of this is done, you'll come back to me. Once you've learned the real meaning of family."

"I'll let you teach him your lessons amor, but he's not yours anymore. Los Muertos is mine, and so is Santito here." She bared her teeth at him, confirming who was in charge.

But was it her, or was it his dick, following the tightest cunt it could find?

"Get the brand," she told him, a growl escaping from his chest that she ignored.

Guillermo disappeared into one of the back rooms behind a closed door. The clanking of metal tools falling on the ground only making Carolina more and more irritated. He came back into my line of vision, the brand almost as big as my face scorching red hot at the end of the rod. The five-petal flower glowing bright as it taunted me, promising me the pain of eternal damnation.

"No! Stop!" Celia begged and screamed repeatedly.

I bit my tongue to keep the scream from forcing its way out, tasting the liquid metal pooling in my mouth while the smell of my charred skin invaded my nostrils. I couldn't fight my body, and the warm stream of piss dripped down my legs as I convulsed from the pain of the brand blistering away at my skin.

The burning ache over my heart throbbed violently, the overwhelming nausea from the smell of my burnt flesh fought against the need to close my eyes and fade into the darkness.

"Now everyone will know who owns you." Carolina smiled with satisfaction as she pulled the brand back, revealing where it now burned into where my Los Muertos tattoos once was.

This said everything it needed to.

Los Muertos was part of the Flores Cártel now. Everything my primo had ever wanted. He wanted to rule it, and he found himself at the mercy of a woman. She didn't know it, but he'd never kneel for her.

They'd never work.

"I guess I don't have to take you to the bathroom now," my primo laughed.

Celia let out an unhinged cackle, the sound of her cold laughter shocking me to my core.

"Cállate! Did you already lose your mind?" Carolina spat the words out.

"The problem is you keep trying to take the things that are mine, in typical little sister fashion. But that isn't your brand hermanita, it's mine. And you just proved to the entire world that he belongs to me by putting *my* symbol on his flesh."

She wasn't wrong. Because I *would* kneel for *her*.

He sent his heavy fist into my stomach, stealing all the air out of my lungs with the sharp hit and forcing blood out of my mouth. I lifted my neck, tilting my chin back to try to keep the blood from obstructing my visions while I tried to look into my primo's face. I breathed noisily through flared nostrils, my anger consuming me in a way I never thought it was possible to feel.

He narrowed his eyes and painted a sinister smile on his face, like he truly believed everything he was doing was for the good of our family. He turned on his heels and walked away, leading Carolina out of the basement with one hand on the small of her back. He knew nothing about family.

We were so fucking far from it.

My family consisted of two dead gringos and a dark haired beauty with half a Black Dahlia wound cut into her face now.

And I'd make sure we were all avenged before this was done.

"We'll kill 'em together, eh morena?" I asked her, ignoring the agonizing pain in my mouth while tasting the blood making its way through my cheek and grazing over my tongue.

I forced myself to stay conscious by shifting my focus from the burn on my chest to the cuts on my face, each time the pain became too much to bear I tuned one out and surrendered to the other.

Her chin lifted up slowly before her eyes fluttered open to look at me.

The blood streaked down her face. The stream of red dripping much slower now from the cut on her cheek. She wore a lethal expression. There was nothing but the promise of death in her gaze, and she made her intentions known with just one look.

"I'm gonna do more than kill them," she rasped out, her teeth coated in crimson as she spoke her curse into the world. "I'm going to tear them apart until Death herself can't recognize them. I'm going to ruin their souls, so la Flaquita refuses to take them into the comfort of her embrace and usher them into the afterlife."

Her gaze hardened into a look I didn't recognize from her.

This wasn't the woman I knew.

But I had the feeling I wanted to get to know her as well.

59

MATEO

There was nothing that made you want to die more than that feeling between lucid and unconscious being disturbed by the frustrating sounds of hospital machinery. The beeping piled on top of the obnoxious nagging of a woman you didn't love, trying to wake you up from a heavy dream was more than any person on the verge of crossing over could tolerate.

"Kane. Wake up, Kane. Mateo, Mateo." She shook at my shoulders until I could no longer ignore her. "I really need you to come back to me buddy, you're scaring me."

"Ugh, let me fucking sleep Emory." I pushed her hand off me only to feel a deep soreness pulling at my stomach. "Fuck," I wheezed, opening my eyes to the sterile white walls and fluorescent bulbs of one of the rooms in Saint Murphy's intensive care unit.

"Thank fuck," she said in that subtle Irish accent. "I've been trying to wake you up all day, Mateo. I thought you weren't coming back from that one."

"From what one? What happened?" I groaned out, trying to sit myself up but she stopped me.

"Don't move, you're still recovering from surgery. I pulled a bullet out of your stomach. You're lucky it didn't hit any organs, but they found you bleeding out on the grass, and you needed a lot of blood. I can't believe you're actually alive right now."

She couldn't hold back her emotions, the tears streaming down her face as she clasped her hands together, almost in prayer.

"We lost so many of you." She shook her head.

Then everything came back to me.

The party. Celia in that fucking sexy as hell dress, sandwiched between me and Ronan. Los fucking Muertos infiltrating the Black Crow headquarters and shooting down more than half our men.

"Fuck," I groaned, trying to sit up once again, but the Doc placed her hands heavy on my shoulders to stop me.

"I mean it Mateo, I will sedate you again now that I know you're not brain dead," she warned me.

"Where is everyone?" I said, my voice hoarse and dry. "How long have I been out?"

"It's been five days. Like I said, you lost a lot of blood. The Crows that are left made their way to the Diablos Locos compound." She looked apologetic, like she was trying to empathize but with something of this magnitude it was too hard.

"Where are Ronan and Santos? Where's Cecilia?"

"We didn't find her body or Santos'." She slipped a medical glove on her right hand before following suit with the left. "Ronan..." She wiped her eyes with the back of her forearms, trying to hide her tears from me.

"Where is he?" I asked her, panicking at the thought of our girl missing and the thought of Los Muertos having taken Santos home.

"Ronan is still sedated." She reassured me at the sight of me visibly unraveling from the possibilities. "Taylor found him with two bullets in his stomach, bleeding out. You lost more blood, but he was worse off. With his temperament, I knew better than to wake the giant up before he was healed enough to go out destroying the villages," she said.

She checked my vitals, running the cold stethoscope over my bare skin and jotting notes down onto her chart like she could so easily disregard my urgency.

"Unplug me Doc."

"You need more fluids Mateo. What do you think you're going to do if I let you out of here?"

"I'm gonna get my girl back." I gripped her wrist in my hand, tugging her towards me to let her know this wasn't negotiable.

"I thought she was Zerkos' girl?" she asked, a frown forming on her face while her confusion challenged me.

"Then you better wake him the fuck up too," I said, leaning close.

She pulled the IV's out of my arm, but before I could get up she placed her hand on my chest.

"I'm not stupid. I woke you up because I knew you were well enough to hopefully not kill yourself by going out there. I know they need help. But I can't turn down Zerkos' drugs yet. You and I both know he'll kill himself to save them. And that's just the thing Kane, he *will* kill himself if he wakes up now. He got shot... *twice*."

Shit. If I was lucky to be alive, then the sentiment doubled for Ronan. But all I could think about was her being out there again, surrounded by enemies.

"I can't help them alone," I told her.

"You're not alone," César Villalobos' voice called out from the corner.

I leaned my head around Dr. O'Connor's body to see his smug fucking self, sitting in the chair, ankle crossed over his knee with his motorcycle club vest on. He had the need to announce what gang he belonged to at any given time of the day—like anyone fucking cared.

"Fuck me," I groaned.

"Who the fuck do you think convinced the pretty Doctor here to wake your bitch ass up pendejo?" He smirked but it only lasted a second or two, like he quickly remembered the situation.

"You got enough men to help us get them back?" I asked as Emory finally gave in, helping me into a sitting position.

"Yeah, I got the men." The cocky bastard stood up putting a cigarette in his mouth and just as he was about to light it, Emory snagged it from his lips.

"You're insane if you think I'm going to let you light this in here." She stomped over to the trash and broke it in half before dumping it in.

"Are you?" He paused, tilting his chin. "Insane?" His eyes hooded over, and he wet his lips with the kind of audacity only someone like Villalobos had.

His tongue ran over the diamond glued to his canine.

She stared at his mouth unblinking, like she was stuck in a trance. I cleared my throat, breaking the hypnosis he had her under, and she shook her head, walking back in my direction and tucking her red hair behind her ear.

"Why are you helping her? You left her to die once, why's it any different this time?" I needed to know.

Otherwise, I wouldn't be able to trust him. Not with her life on the line.

"I didn't leave her to die, I left her with *him.* I left her to put this shit behind her and try to live a normal life, something I knew I'd never get a chance to do. I'm not sorry and she doesn't expect me to be." I could tell he was annoyed that I'd even say something about what he did to her.

How could I think anything but?

The things I'd seen him do to her, the things he *failed* to do for her.

Too many people had let Celia down, and I wasn't going to be one of them.

I ran my hand over my face before grabbing the hospital bed to pivot my legs onto the floor. Emory and César both rushed to me as if I was seconds away from breaking and if I was going to be honest with myself—I kind of fucking felt like it.

"We have to wake Ronan up." I looked past the doctor, my words meant for César alone.

He nodded like he agreed, and Emory tsked loudly.

"I swear to fucking God Mateo, I'll put all of you to sleep. If Ronan so much as moves the wrong way, his internal stitches could open, and he'll die. Do *not* make me wake him up."

"You don't understand Doc. If I go without him, *that'll* kill him. Ronan would rather die out there trying to save her, then spend one more second in this hospital, asleep, avoiding our problems. I know my brother," I reminded her.

"This is wrong." She shook her head. "At least give yourself time to get your legs back under you. You can't help him if you can't help yourself," she bit back at me.

"Fuck. Fine. Help me up then," I told her, but it was César who came to my aid first, though I wasn't sure it was a love for me that did it or a need to keep the Doc from touching me any more than she had to.

Something happened between them while I was dying.

But the only thing I cared about was getting Santos and Celia back.

60

CELIA

Carolina hadn't shown her face down here again.

After Guillermo had made the decision that all my punishment was to be given to Santos, she didn't bother to grace us with her presence anymore. As if it was only my misery she'd been interested in witnessing. It had taken me a full three seconds to wrap my mind around my sister's betrayal.

Grief, shock, and happiness, along with complete and utter rage filled its way into my body before I could process the truth.

Puta miserable.

Not only had she been alive the last fifteen years, but she had watched, maybe even had a part in our mother's death. She wasn't ignorant to the attacks Ignacio had attempted over the years or the lives he had taken to try to get to me.

My papá was right.

Power changes everyone. I could almost hear his voice in my ear.

"How are my two favorite lovebirds?" Guillermo chirped as he stomped down the stairs.

It was impossible to know how long we'd been here. I couldn't dissociate and wait for it to be over or for death, because it wasn't happening to me, it was happening to Santos. I was apparently on a fucked up journey, trying to figure out what the cruelest form of torture was.

Each time I found it, a worse version would show itself to me, letting me know it could *always* get worse.

Watching one of the men I loved with all of my heart, suffering and bleeding, was the most painful violence I'd ever endured. But my screams did nothing for Guillermo except urge him on. It showed him that his plan was working and by hurting Santos, he hurt me. And somehow that was worse than the physical pain itself.

Santos hadn't spoken a word to me in days.

I didn't want to be protected if it cost me his love.

Or worse yet, if it cost me him.

I screamed and begged every time Guillermo or one of his men came down here and sliced that knife over his flesh, again and again, until he went pale from losing blood. They burned him, scarred him, and pummeled him senselessly all in the name of loyalty and family, hoping this would bring him back to them.

Maybe it would.

Maybe every hit that was supposed to be mine forced him closer and closer back into Guillermo's poisonous reach.

"What do you think primo? You ready for me to cut you down and get back to work?" Guilermo teased, dangling the keys to his restraints in front of his face.

A dance they did every few days.

Santos raised his chin slowly, a large vertical scab began to form over his eyebrow and the top of his cheek, while another crossed from his ear to the corner of his lip. My own matching wound itched just from staring at it. His shirt had been cut off and every mark Los Muertos had put on his body was now on display.

The five petal Flores brand ruined his gang tattoo, the skin was angry and raised up, red all around and likely nearing infection.

"I'll never work for you again, Guillermo," he said through a crooked mouth. "You might as well kill me here and now."

Guillermo chuckled as if he noticed how Carolina's cut had deformed his speech.

"Oh 'cuz, that's where you're wrong. I won't kill you. I'll keep you both here, barely alive, for as long as it takes. Years if I have to. I'll feed you old bread and dirty water until you hate her almost as much as you hate yourself. But I will prove my point, and you will do the job I've asked of you." He stepped closer to him. "Eventually, you'll be begging me to let you put a bullet in her brain to free you."

Santos snarled, yanking the chains that kept him bound to the pole across from me.

"I even heard my men talk about how loud she moans every time they wipe her cunt when they take her to the bathroom. How she begs them to let her get on her knees for them to be free." I clenched my jaw shut, looking away from Santos, hoping he didn't believe the lies.

I would do just about anything for his freedom.

Not for mine.

"Just let her go," he mumbled, forcing Guillermo to bark out a laugh.

"Primo you're not getting it. *She's* the reason you're here, sewn up with half-ass stitching." He plucked at a gash on his arm, forcing a pained moan from Santos. "Looks like this one needs to be closed up again," he said before slicing a knife over the old cut, tearing even deeper into his flesh this time.

Santos hissed, his eyes filled with a hatred I'd never seen before, all of it directed at Guillermo.

He grabbed a short blade, less than half an inch long and placed the handle between his fingers. Closing his fist so that nothing but the sharp edge of the knife stuck out from his knuckles he slammed it into Santos' stomach, once, twice–

"Please! Guillermo stop," I shrieked, seeing the blood pour down his waist.

He stopped striking, dropping his head back in a psychotic laugh and twirling the blade through his fingers.

"Little cártel princesses, begging me to make their lives better," he sighed. "There's really nothing that makes me quite so hard." He cut again, opening another old wound in his primo's arm.

My voice was scratchy and worn out from screaming, pleading with this monster to stop hurting Santos. I couldn't even remember the last time I'd even felt the urge to pee, my tears were taking everything from me.

"Please... Please," I chanted between sobs as he cut into Santos repeatedly, with such brutality, I thought for certain he had every intention of ending him this time. "I'm sorry... I'm sorry." I shook my head. "I'll do anything, please. Whatever you want. Please Guillermo, stop hurting him."

"Anything, now?" He turned to face me with a calculating look on his face while he seemed to weigh out his possibilities.

"Just stop hurting him, please," I begged again.

"You do realize that *he's* taking *your* punishment right now? How you gonna do me better than that?"

"Celia, *stop*," Santos growled, making Guillermo laugh.

"Celia, stop," he mocked. "You're right, maybe he's had enough of this for now. I can torture him in other ways. I'm ready for that anything now, morenita," he said before pulling at the chains that kept my arms hooked to the pole above my head.

I dropped to my knees on the cold concrete floor, my wrists were still cuffed together, and my body ached from hanging.

"Here's the rules zorra. You use your teeth; I'll fuck him up. You try anything funny; I'll fuck both of you up. You do a good job, make me come, make me feel like a special boy, and I'll let Santito here have a whole day without pain. How's that sound?" He brought his fingers under my jaw to lift my gaze up to him.

"Celia don't you fucking do it. Celia!"

Santos snarled and growled like a caged animal, his chains rattling while he screamed with ferocity for me to stop.

There wasn't a choice here.

Anyone who could even think there was, would be a fucking idiot.

I nodded my head, doing my best to avoid Santos' stare and his defeated pleas.

61

GUILLERMO

How many men could say they had not one, but both Flores sisters sucking at their cock? Rafael must have been rolling in his fucking grave the minute her cute little face nodded up at me, eyes filled with tears. She was still the prettier of the two, even if Lina had fucked her face up. It was scabbing up nicely, and at least she didn't cut all the way to her mouth or through her cheek like she had with Santos. That would have made what was about to happen a little less pleasant to tolerate.

I had spent years trying to get Los Muertos on Rafael Flores' radar. I was young, but I was smart and full of plans. I knew the west better than anyone and I knew what it would take to thrive out here. Flores shut me down time after time, warning me to keep the cártel out of our little street gang's mouth.

His final message came in the form of a tape. I'd sent one of my boys over to him, to see if Flores could use him for a job. Instead, he sicked his little bitch of a daughter on him and dumped his body on his mamá's lawn with the video proof. The little bitch killed him before he'd even had the chance to attack.

Guess I had the last laugh now. Los Muertos and the cártel were one in the same.

Ignacio Flores wasn't a quarter of the man Rafael's ghost was. Which made him easy to manipulate and even easier to fool. Los Muertos was rebranding itself as the Flores cártel right under his nose and he didn't even know it.

Once we figured out a way to get Lina's money that her old man had hidden away, we'd be able to buy more men, more guns, and more drugs. Then once we had control of it all, we could kill Ignacio and any of his men who refused to follow us.

And then I could finally get rid of Carolina. She was fun at first. Ignacio dropped her at my door when she was fifteen, said she wasn't a kid anymore and that he didn't have time to keep raising his brother's orphan. She was a doe-eyed little thing, and I corrupted her to my needs.

But goddamn was she clingy, and sometimes I think she forgot which one of us was actually in charge. I kept her satisfied with money, sex, and the idea of power. Everything a little princess bitch could want to stay happy, but enough was enough. Thirteen years with the same woman by my side was more than I'd granted my own mamá.

That wasn't to say I was monogamous. I smiled remembering the last time Carolina had found another woman in my bed and the bloody mess I had to clean up. An idea flashed through my mind for a second—the image of Carolina and Celia in a battle royale to the death, in bikinis, bloody and violent.

Yup, that did it.

I cupped my hard-on and gave it a good squeeze, my bulge already in front of her face and primed for her.

"Make it as good as you make it for him, okay baby?" I encouraged her before pulling myself out of my pants.

Santos' cursing and shouting was damn near killing the moment, and I found I could no longer ignore it.

"Hold on darling. Let's set the mood." I yanked my shirt off, shoving a wad of it into my cousin's mouth so that his obscene yelling became muffled.

The scab on his face stretched apart, threatening to bleed again.

Celia trembled, most likely because all she'd had to eat this week were a few pieces of stale bread, and even that had been shoved down her throat by force. Stubborn whore would have probably killed herself out of spite to not let us do it on our own terms. She was Rafa's daughter no doubt. Lina, not so much.

As if the coffee grounds were the same, but someone didn't brew it quite right.

Now that I was here, standing in front of the real thing, it was easy to see why Rafael had put all his energy into his oldest daughter. She would have made a fierce fucking jefa. The girl had an abyss of hate burning deep into her soul, and just one look at her eyes was enough to force you to reckon with your own sins.

And she was on her knees for me.

Her eyes searched over to my cousin, an expression on her face that told me she was desperate for him to look at her. To see the sacrifice she was making.

And the stupid idiot was looking away.

"Mira," I hissed at him, grabbing her jaw and shoving my dick in her mouth.

She gagged, closing her teeth around me and I pulled out, slapping her face with the back of my hand hard enough to knock her onto her side. She was so frail and pathetic; a couple hits would be enough to take her out. But what would be the fun in that? I stuffed myself into my pants again and pulled up the zipper.

I pulled the microblade out again and jammed my fist into Santos' stomach two more times.

"NO! Stop," she cried. I stomped over to her and grabbed a fistful of her hair, yanking her up to my eye level.

"Then quit fucking around, or I'll kill *him* just to prove a point to you, zorra." I sent my fist into her stomach before dropping my hold on her hair.

She doubled over in pain, coughing and whimpering while Santos muffled protests through my shirt. I grabbed her chains and lifted her up onto the hook once again, keeping her dangling just above the ground. I walked over to the table of tools and picked up the pliers.

"Abre la boca pendejo." I forced open his mouth, pulling the fabric out before shoving the dirty tool into his mouth and clamping it over one of his back molars. "Hold still and it'll hurt less." Celia thrashed and screamed, calling me an animal, getting my cock hard once again.

Santos stood still like a good boy, exhaling heavily through his nostrils and moaning in despair as I yanked the tooth out with nothing but brute force. It came free with a sharp tug, and I threw the bloody thing at the cártel princess' feet before shoving my shirt back inside my primo's mouth to clot the bleeding.

"Let's try this again. For every tooth I feel, there will be a tooth I pull. Got it?" I dropped the rusty pliers onto the ground before lifting her off the hook and letting her fall to the ground again.

A V formed heavily between her brows. "With finesse, okay? I don't want some high school blowjob bullshit, show some enthusiasm." She looked up at me with disdain. "Well?" I asked, drawing a smirk. "Pull me back out." I crossed my arms over my chest, satisfied with myself while waiting for her to comply.

I could practically see the steam rolling out of her nostrils. I bet she was biting her tongue so hard right now to keep herself from spitting venom at me. I let out another provocative chuckle, pushing them both over the edge. She knew any wrong move would just be a punishment for him instead.

This was the best form of torture.

"*Now* Celia," I harshened my tone. "Show my primo how little it takes for you to get on your knees for another man." She got into position, a disgusted look on her face like she was determined to sour my mood. "I would have taken C minus work before corazón, but you wanted to act like a brat. Now I expect a B plus at the minimum."

Santos was still breathing loudly through his pain, but I'd be able to tune it out once she started choking on my cock. I grabbed a fistful of her hair and brought her closer, her fingers shook as she unbuckled my jeans.

"No need to be nervous little Flores, it's just like any other cock. Except bigger." I laughed, grabbing it at the base and helping it find its way into her mouth.

"That's it, nice and big. Wrap those teeth up good for me. Show Santos what he's missing out on." But my primo was still looking away, refusing to acknowledge that I could so easily take anything he cared about and ruin it for him forever.

He'd learn soon. As much as Lina hated her sister, this wasn't about her. This was about teaching Santos a lesson. And I'd teach it over and over again until it stuck in his mind. It wasn't the worst blow job I'd ever gotten, but I was having to work twice as hard to get myself off with her lack of enthusiasm.

I slammed her head back and forth, ignoring the gagging sound she made every time my cock touched the back of her throat. Tears trailed down the side of her face, but with a bitch as cold as Celia Flores had been trained to be, I could proudly say it was the sheer size of my cock doing it.

Back and forth, using her gargled breaths as motivation to get me where I needed to be until my orgasm broke through me. My cum shooting straight into her mouth while I held her head in place to make sure she got every single drop.

"Now swallow like a good girl." I tilted her head back to force her eyes up at me.

She spat my cum at me and it landed on my abdomen. I pulled the shirt out of Santos' mouth and wiped myself clean before shoving it back through his lips again. His disgusted gagging fuelled my laughter.

With one hand I grabbed Celia's chains and dragged her back over to her post, lifting her up and dropping her onto the hook again to keep her dangling in place.

"I think I'll like this new routine after all," I declared, giving her cheek a few firm slaps before walking my way back up the stairs and turning off the lights.

62

MATEO

Thanks to the miracle that was strong painkillers, I was now mobile again. A full twenty-four hours awake with hospital monitoring and I convinced the Doc to let me go with César and his men out west. Her only caveat was, Zerkos could only come if she did.

Watching Ronan wake up from a medically induced coma was like seeing a bear get its head stuck in a trap. Emory wanted to sedate him again because his wild trashing in the room was enough to make her think he'd open all his stitches.

"Zerkos, if you can't settle down, I *will* put you back to sleep and you *will* stay back," she threatened.

"Stay back?" His nostrils flared, and I could see his brain begin to piece together the memories of the party before the attack. "Celia. Shit. Fuck!"

He swung his legs as if he was just going to magically jump out of the bed and be healed but immediately yelled out in pain.

"Fuck." he roared.

"Yup, that's what two bullets in your gut feels like big guy. Settle down or you *will* fucking die Ronan. Do you understand?" Emory chastised. "I'm letting you go. I'm not letting you be stupid about it. This entire thing is already idiotic to begin with." Her emotions began to rise, and her voice squeaked. "None of you have even talked about the possibility that they're already dead."

The room went quiet, and regret covered her face.

"I'm sorry... I just mean, it's been ten days. What are the odds you aren't sending yourselves off to die?" The redheaded doctor couldn't keep it together any longer and her tears started to fall.

"I'm grateful for the tears doll, but we both know none of us are worth your sadness," Ronan told her, and I watched her eyes dart over to César. "But if you ever fucking say some shit like that again, I'll put you under myself, okay Doc?"

César growled under his breath.

"She's not fucking dead. Her tracker is still active, still showing her location," I said.

"Has she moved?" César asked.

"That doesn't mean fucking shit. We're doing this Lobo." I used his road name as a way to trigger his ego.

"I've got sixteen chapters of Diablos Locos ready to ride west. Get yourself together Zerkos." He nodded at him before tilting his chin at the doctor. "A word, Doc?"

The two of them left the room, the silence between Zerkos and I said far too many of the things we couldn't voice out loud. What if she *was* dead? What if they both were? What if we'd lost everything we had, and every chance of happiness was out the door now?

We stared at each other as if we could read our thoughts but neither of us had the answers we were looking for. I could hear César's voice booming in the hall just outside Ronan's room.

"It's too fucking dangerous Emory. I got my own doctor. I'm not letting you risk yourself."

"He's a *medical student*, they deserve better than that. What if someone gets seriously hurt? I'm a grown woman, *papi.* I make my decisions."

Emory pushed back into the room, the door slamming against the wall before bouncing back closed.

"Give yourself a few hours to get moving again, then we can head out. It's at least four days driving with the stops we'll have to make to keep you comfortable," she said before walking back out again and giving César a cold set of side eyes.

"Taylor has rounded up our uninjured who are willing to come too," I caught Ronan up.

"This isn't Black Crow business. They shouldn't be risking their lives like this." He shook his head.

"They made it Black Crow business when they broke into our home and shot our people during a celebration, brother. Our men have a right to retribution."

"You're right," he said, stunning the shit out of me.

"What the fuck was that?" I said with a laugh.

"I'm learning I can be wrong too. It's not too late to change." He tried and failed to move, so I helped him into a sitting position.

"Well shit, remind me that your reset button is just two bullets to the gut then."

He elbowed me in the side, forcing a pained grunt out of both our mouths from the excess motion.

"Let's go get our girl then, Kane," he rasped out with a smirk.

63

CELIA

"Oh, fuck Celia, you're getting so good at this. You'd be so fucking proud primo. She's using tongue and everything." The pig couldn't help himself but lie to try to hurt his family.

There was no way anything I was doing felt good. At this point, I was barely drinking enough water to survive as my own form of self-harm. My tongue must have felt like rough sandpaper. But he played this game, once a day coming down and forcing me on my knees in order to kill a piece of Santos.

It was working.

Every day Santos seemed closer and closer to taking that gun and putting a bullet in my head. Maybe not for the reasons Guillermo expected but out of mercy. Six times he'd come down here now, which meant it had been six days of this. Impossible to tell how much longer we'd been here before that. There was no method of telling time before he put his filthy cock in my mouth.

But today was the day I was done.

There was something in the air, something tangible I could almost feel.

A warning from La Flaquita.

Either I'd die trying to get us out of here or I'd actually do it. But I wasn't going to let this be our lives. I couldn't allow Guillermo to dictate how my end would be written. I was determined to go out fighting, despite being stuck here with a mouthful of the short end of my luck.

I'd played nice long enough, through these little visits, he'd quickly begun letting his guard down. So typical of a man. As soon as blood rushed to their cocks, they lost all sense and logic. I wasn't stupid. I'd wait until he was close, head so dizzy and filled with pleasure that it would take him a while to register what was happening.

He always let me know when he was getting there too. He gripped my hair tighter and egged Santos on, encouraging him to glance my way.

"Come on primo, she's begging you to look at her. Do you guys talk about it when I leave you alone to yourself?" he asked, thrusting deeper into my mouth.

He didn't need to gag him to keep him from shouting anymore. We'd all resigned to our fates and accepted it.

And there his fingers went, gripping the back of my head and yanking tight like he was on the verge of total bliss. I relaxed my throat and let him as far back as I could before I bit down. And I clamped my teeth shut like there was nothing that would stop me from having his manhood as my next meal.

He screamed a bloody screech, making me fearful someone would come down here. Guillermo yanked at my hair, but I didn't let up, ignoring the pain and biting down until I could taste blood and feel his flesh ripping under my teeth. He went flaccid in my mouth while I relentlessly chewed through his dick. Finally ripped at my hair hard enough to take a fistful from my scalp.

I screamed, my mouth full of blood, when he sent his fist flying at my face. Santos was screaming at me to let him down and his cousin flailed wildly on the floor with his mangled cock still out. I positioned myself under Santos to give him just the leverage he needed to get his chain off the hook and get down on the ground. Guillermo was still crying and screaming, but his eyes went wide once Santos' feet touched the ground.

"Morena, stand back," he said before throwing his neck to the side and cracking it without the use of his hands.

"Primo help me. Fucking bitch," he screamed. "My fucking cock!"

Santos kicked his foot down into his cousin's stomach with no hesitation and no impression that he'd been starved and beaten for days on end. He swung the chain across Guillermo's face, ripping a chunk of flesh as the heavy metal slapped against his skin. It knocked him back, forcing his head to hit the ground again. In a cat-like move, Santos swung his leg around the floor, positioning himself behind his primo and using the chains keeping his wrists bound to choke the ugly bastard.

"If you kill me, my men will just come down and kill you too."

"They can try," Santos hissed.

"Where is she? Where is Carolina?" I yelled, stepping over his fucked-up remainder of a dick and he yelled out again, making me wonder why his men had yet to descend on his behalf.

It almost seemed like his brain was hashing out the same thought, and I watched a look of worry spread across his face as the sound of machine guns went off upstairs. Santos' eyes met mine and he tightened the chain against Guillermo's neck.

Either our salvation was upstairs, or it was someone who wanted Guillermo dead just as much, and there was a good chance we'd die in the process too.

"Hold him still," I told Santos, crawling over to the table and grabbing the same rusty pliers he used on Santos nearly a week ago.

I shoved my chain into his mouth, to force it open while he flailed and thrashed. He was bigger than Santos and I combined, but the damage we'd already done to him was enough to give us the advantage. I sat on his chest and forced the pliers in and with all the effort in my body, I heaved upward until a tooth came loose from his mouth.

Blood pooled in his mouth and he choked on it, but I just reached back in and pulled another canine out, this time with a bit more ease now that I had an idea of what I was doing. I was low on energy though, and it was almost enough to make me lightheaded.

"I think I'll make a necklace," I told Santos, throwing him the teeth. "Finish him." I stood up and grabbed a seven-inch knife off the table of tools. Then it got quiet upstairs. I eyed Santos, but he didn't hesitate. He ripped through his cousin's throat with the knife, not stopping as he serrated past his vocal cords and then through his spine. Blood covered his face, his chest, his lap and it took me a while to realize that the feral scream wasn't coming from our victim but from Santos' mouth instead. I stood there, unmoving as I watched until finally, he sliced through the last bit of flesh that kept his primo's head attached to his body before holding it up like a trophy. Blood flooded down fast. There was a lot more than you'd expect for something as small as a head.

Santos' chest heaved up and down with heavy, labored breaths before he dropped the head to the ground. I pushed away Guillermo's corpse with my foot and climbed onto Santos' lap, wrapping my arms around his neck. He buried his face into my neck and broke down into a hearty, woeful sob.

We rocked back and forth, holding each other for comfort for what felt like a moment frozen in time.

Then the basement door swung open and light spilled down the stairs. My heart rose up to the top of my throat, or maybe it was bile I was holding back from flashes of Guillermo's head getting ripped off before my very eyes.

It took everything to breathe through the nausea, but my nerves only skyrocketed at the sound of heavy boots slowly stepping down the basement stairs. Santos pulled me behind him, kicking his cousin's corpse even further away as if he could hide it from whatever enemy would be coming down for us.

"Sunshine?"

My heart nearly exploded.

I must have been hungrier than I thought because I was hallucinating a dead man's voice. Santos looked up too and then, there he was, coming down the stairs, blood splattered onto his face and his clothes.

"Mateo?" I blurted out, tears flowing down my face as my heart made sense of what was happening before my brain could.

He took large strides to get to me, cradling my face in his hands and disregarding all the fresh blood covering me. He pressed his forehead to mine, and I let out a banshee cry as I allowed myself to feel the nameless kind of emotion that came with knowing that someone would always be there to rescue you.

I was a miserable bitch, and I did not deserve this kind of loyalty.

"I thought you were dead," I finally blurted through hysterical sobs.

"It would take a lot more than that to rip me away from you, beautiful," he said, pulling back to take a look at my face.

He brushed my hair behind my ear, shaking his head in disapproval, as he ran his gaze over my features, his thumb traced over the scar on my cheek softly. And then his eyes shifted to Santos picking up his primo's head off the ground, and he let out a long exhale. He looked better now that some of his wounds were starting to heal, but the brand on his chest was still a bright scorched up mark. He had so many poorly stitched cuts he looked like a Mexican version of Frankenstein's monster.

"Shit, brother, you look fucked up. Let's get you both out of here." He heaved Santos up, propping himself under his shoulder on one side and I followed suit on the other.

Mateo frowned like he didn't need my help but before he could utter a word of disapproval, the basement steps squeaked, and a shadow lingered at the top of the stairs.

"Thank fucking fuck," Santos said and I turned my gaze to the doorway to find Ronan standing there, jaw sharp and flexed with worry as he stared down at the three of us.

My knees gave out at the sight of him. I dropped to my hands and knees and scrambled up the stairs on all fours before I found myself at his feet. Collapsed and crying, my entire chest ripped open, heart bleeding in offering at his altar.

"You came for me," I barely whispered as he swooped me into his heavy embrace.

"Every time flower, every time."

I shook violently in his hold, his arms wrapped around me, squeezing me tight in his embrace. For a few seconds I forgot where I was, because I was home. Ronan groaned, it sounded like agony, and I looked up to finally see how pale and drained of life he was. Looking back, Mateo didn't look much better, and Santos was worse off than both of them.

"Los Muertos?" I asked, wiping the tears off my face.

"You got your big brother to thank for that," Mateo grunted while he and Santos used each other for support to make their way up the stairs.

I frowned, shaking my head and looking at Ronan.

"I don't understand."

"There's some wingless Black Crows up there too, but he brought a hundred and fifty Diablos to Guillermo's door. A few Los Muertos escaped, but it looks like we got all the ones that mattered." Ronan shifted his gaze, and I followed it to see Santos was holding Guillermo's head in his hand like a bowling ball. Fingers hooked into his eye sockets.

We made our way out of the basement to find bodies scattered all over the house. Bikers clad in leather vests were dragging them into a corner making a neat pile of corpses. The sun shone brightly through the windows, but even so, I wasn't prepared for the shock of the daylight once we crossed the threshold.

I shielded my eyes from it until l could make out César's shape in the distance, leaning against a van with a cigarette in his mouth. He frowned seeing the state I was in, but I couldn't help but smile to see him here for me, risking himself and his men for my sake.

"You do love me," I said as we collectively made our way towards the van.

He chuckled, flicking his cigarette to the ground.

"Familia eh? Don't say I never did anything for you, princesita." He grinned, bringing me into his chest and placing a kiss on the top of my head.

"I thought I knew what family was supposed to be, now I'm not so sure anymore."

"What's that supposed to mean?" César asked.

"Carolina. She's alive. This was all her," I said, hating the words as they came out of my mouth.

"That was the woman we saw leaving then. Fuck!" César cursed, kicking the side of the van.

The joy that came with being reunited was short. Everything felt cold. I should have been exploding with happy emotions at the sight of Ronan and Mateo, but between the weakness and thoughts of my sister, I felt like I was crashing. There truly was nothing that could have prepared my heart for the overwhelming joy that came with seeing both of them alive. But instead I was frozen.

Mi corazón. Broken and full at the same time.

Alone, surrounded by people who loved me. I felt nothing. My heart, draped with a layer of ice, and every time I looked at Santos and found his gaze awkwardly shifting away it cemented the feeling deeper into my soul.

"We're gonna get both of you better okay, sunshine? Fuck, I'm so glad to see you." He was crying, he was actually fucking crying and maybe if my soul hadn't shriveled up and died inside of me I'd still be crying too.

He looked to Santos and found the same empty shell of a stare coming from him. Mateo pressed his lips into a fine line and nodded his head like he understood we'd need time to sort ourselves out from this.

"They're mostly all dead now, except your sister," César explained.

"I'm sure she scurried off to Ignacio to warn him. Her time is coming too," I said as he helped me into the backseat of the van.

Mateo climbed into the front with César while I sat between Santos and Ronan, staring out the window as the car slowly began to move. Ronan's head dropped back onto the headrest of the seat, and he winced from pain with every bump the tires hit.

"You doin' alright?" Mateo asked, looking back.

It was meant for Ronan, but his eyes scanned all three of us. Ronan's hand on my lap squeezed, and I placed my palm over his for comfort.

"Emory and the cavalry are waiting to know where to meet. Then she'll be able to give the three of you medical attention," César announced from the driver's seat.

"Emory is here?" I asked, not feigning my surprise.

"She said the Diablos' doctor wasn't qualified for the level of damage Ronan was risking." He shook his head. "So where to, sister?"

"Send your men south," I told him. "We're crossing the border tonight."

The conversation ended there, and we rode in silence for nearly another hour. I stared out at the scenery. It wasn't until I felt Santos' finger lacing through mine and the gentle squeeze of his hand that I realized I was crying again. I broke free of both of their hands in order to wipe my face dry. Ronan didn't miss it. He took my chin between his index and thumb.

"Tell me what happened in there, flower," he whispered. "Let me help make it better."

I wanted to tell him that just by coming, he already had, but instead Santos spoke.

"Nothing happened," he bit out, like lying was somehow going to save me the shame of what had already happened.

I wasn't embarrassed.

It wasn't me who got taken advantage of.

It was the stupid pendejo who thought he could trust to shove his dick into the open mouth of a piraña with the expectation that it was somehow going to come out still whole.

I turned to face him, hardening my stare and dropping my voice down to a cold octave. "Nothing happened?"

"That's not what I meant," he said in a hushed tone, and César turned the radio off completely, the silence in the car becoming damn near unbearable.

"Then what did you mean? Because you couldn't even stomach looking at me Santos. You looked away every single time. Why couldn't you look at me?" I raised my voice to a yell.

He sighed, looking out to the road again, like he couldn't voice out his reasons.

"Santos?" I shouted and César cleared his throat uncomfortably.

"I couldn't stand to see you that way. That's not who you are. I didn't want to see you like that." His voice broke and a tear fell down his fucked-up cheek.

He turned completely away from me once he noticed my gaze fixed on the scarring flesh.

"I needed you to see," I said desperately, and he whipped his head back at me.

Ronan's grip squeezed around my thigh. His head was still dropped back, eyes closed, but his face was wet.Mateo looked out the window and I couldn't hear a single breath in the car.

I'd broken all my men.

César's gaze met mine in the rearview mirror, and with a single look he gave me back the strength of our family. He nodded like he understood the entirety of my experience, and for some reason I felt it in that moment. All of our pain and suffering, it was always unified even when we were far apart.

"I needed you to see that it was my choice. That he wasn't making me into a victim because I was doing it of my own volition. I was saving *us*. I don't regret it, and I'm not ashamed. I'd do it a million times over if it kept his blade away from you," I spat out, crossing my arms over my chest.

"I'm sorry." he said, regret being the flavor of his sorrow.

"I did it because I love you, Santos. And I would have done the same for any of you fuckers in this car." I attempted to keep the bitterness from my tone, but I was tired of being looked at like I was some poor thing who'd been beaten.

I was a fucking survivor. I'd proved it over and over again.

There wasn't shame in that.

"So what's the plan, reina?" César asked, changing the mood in the car.

"Guadalajara. If we're gonna do this, we're gonna do it right. First we get what's mine, then we go home, hermanito."

I leaned into Ronan. He let out a low, pained sound and wrapped his arm around me, bringing me into his chest. He dropped his head over mine and I let the comfort of his embrace soothe me for the rest of the ride.

64

RONAN

We were exhausted, broken, and beaten.

But I'd never felt more whole in my life, and in that van, I promised myself I would do whatever it took to make sure that we stayed this way. I wasted too much time before I realized it. She was right. Together we were complete. There was no way out of this without any of them. Well, maybe without fucking Villabolos, but even that pain in the ass was starting to grow on me again.

He was the only family she had left, even with Carolina rising from the fucking dead. She somehow managed to end up a major cunt, which probably meant she was better off dead.

We ended up stopping at a hotel for the night so Celia and Santos could clean themselves up, and Emory could properly look at everyone's injuries. The Doc insisted on sharing a room with Celia and forced me to stay with César and Santos with Mateo. I wanted nothing more than to sleep with my arms wrapped around my girl again, but she denied the opportunity immediately, and told Celia just how bad the extent of my gunshot wounds were.

She sided with the fucking Doc.

But now it was a new day, and we were in the car ready for whatever would come next. Celia was showered and her hair was brushed silky straight, so black it looked hot to the touch from the sun scorching above us. The scar on the side of her face was red and bright. It looked painful but it wasn't as deep as Santos'. She untucked her hair from behind her ear to cover it up once she noticed me staring.

I grabbed her chin with one hand and tucked her hair back again. She challenged me with a look, exaggerating those damn lines in the middle of her brows. I placed a gentle kiss on the scar.

"So what will this key open?" I asked while César pulled into a small bank outside the city.

"All of the secrets Jamila refused to take to the grave with her," he answered.

Celia was tired of secrets; I could see it on her face. The fact that her mother likely had a million more hidden somewhere only that little key would open was infuriating. How long had Celia been carrying that thing around her neck, too afraid to find out on her own? Or better yet, why had her mother kept this from her?

The thought briefly occurred to me that maybe Jamila had somehow been the better parent out of the two. Doing what she could to keep her daughter away from the violence even if it meant keeping her away from the money.

No matter how you looked at it, it was blood money.

And accepting it meant also accepting her father's sins as her own.

"How do you know this?" she asked him.

"I've been here before, when I was just a kid, before Ignacio burned down the villa. Your mamá wasn't a secretive person, but the few times she brought me here, something was just off. I'm betting my life that key opens up a box here. I saw it too many times in her hand to think otherwise."

It was just a bank, nothing out of the ordinary and nothing suspicious about it. It smelled like old paint, and there was a single teller behind the counter.

"Nombre?" the clerk asked.

"Jamila Gomez." She gave her the alias that belonged to her mother.

She shook her head and denied her request, so Celia tried once again with the Flores name instead, along with the rest of her identifying information she still knew by memory. The teller searched and searched until finally her face lit up with a match.

We walked through metal detectors, all of us setting it off and relinquishing our guns into plastic tubs. The clerk led us down a hallway filled with lockers and took out her own set of keys, opening up a small door with a 131 on the front. There was a single box inside, made of metal, big enough to hold a few letters.

We followed the clerk again, past the lockers, to another door which she unlocked with an electronic keycard before pushing open and guiding us inside. She told us in Spanish to take our time and to shut the door once we retrieved everything we needed from the box.

"I'm really fucking anxious." She exhaled, holding the key between her index finger and her thumb, tapping it against the key slot on the small metal box the clerk placed on the table.

"Do you want to be alone?" I asked her, and she responded with a hard glare.

"Never again, I'm just... nervous." She looked down at the box before looking back at me again. "What if there's nothing there?"

César laughed. "I wouldn't put it past Jamila."

She stuck the key in the box, shaking out the last bit of her nerves with a little dance before she put her hand back on the key and turned it. She opened the lid and the four of us crowded around her, waiting to discover what should have been seen fifteen years ago.

There was an envelope and a torn piece of paper. Nothing else.

"She's really going to kick me down one more time even in death, isn't she?" She exhaled deeply before picking up the little piece of paper.

"What is it?" Mateo asked.

"It's coordinates," César said, reaching over his shoulder and grabbing it from her.

He plugged the numbers into his phone while her hands trembled with the envelope in her hand.

"I don't want a letter. Someone else open it. There is nothing she could possibly say to me that I would want to hear right now." She tossed it on the table, shaking her hands frantically like she was drying the water off of them.

Mateo picked it up, ripping the envelope open to reveal what looked to just be a bunch of documents. Santos picked one up and looked it over before handing it to her.

"It's just birth certificates," he told her. "This one is yours."

She took it from his hand and set it on the table without a single glance.

"Whose is that?" she asked about the one in Mateo's hand.

"Carolina's. This one belongs to big brother here. I thought your last name was Villalobos?" he asked him, shuffling the papers around.

"It is," he said, his annoyance obvious.

"No, this says César Ortíz. Your mom was Maria Villalobos, but your father was Diego Ortíz," Mateo said as César ripped the document from his hand.

"What the fuck?" Celia looked pissed. "Did you fucking know?" She stepped up to her brother and I flipped over her own birth certificate, her mom's name bright and clear.

"You've said a lot of dumb shit before princesita, but this one takes the cake." He shoved her shoulder, and Mateo and I both shifted towards him.

He eyed both of us, raising his hands up in defeat, before he'd even gotten a point across.

"None of this makes sense. Diego was my tío's name, he was my mamá's brother. Her last name was Gomez." She ran her fingers through her hair, like she was trying to make sense of all this new information.

I picked up her birth certificate again.

"No." I shook my head, handing it over to her. "This says her name was Jamila Ortíz."

"No." She shook her head in disbelief. "That would mean—"

"We're cousins," César finished, but Celia continued to shake her head.

"It means that it's technically, *his* cártel. No?" Mateo asked.

César wrapped his hands around Mateo's neck and slammed him into the wall. His nostrils flared widely for a few moments before he decided to finally speak.

"Listen here pendejo, I'm only ever going to say this once. You ever repeat those fucking words again, I don't care what you mean to her, I'll gut your gringo ass alive. Understood?"

"Roger that, hermano." Mateo said with an exaggerated American accent, pushing him away.

"I was four when they took me in, I kind of always knew I was Diego's son. I think you knew it too. We knew we were already family, but it always felt like brother and sister, so why mess with that? There was no way I was a random stray, Rafa? He was too cold to just take in some pup from the street. I knew there was no chance I was his bastard either, she would have hated me if that was the case, Jamila was good to me. They never talked about Diego, and she always sent me those sad eyes if someone brought him up." He scratched the back of his head.

"Why so testy about it?" Mateo asked.

"Something deep in my gut tells me my dad didn't want to be a part of this shit. I don't either. I just wanna finish this war for her, go home to my club and live the rest of my miserable life. Is that too much to ask?" He turned back to her. "He raised you for this shit. You've bled for this, princesa. This isn't my empire, it's yours. And I'll kill anyone who says otherwise."

"Tia Larissa wanted as far away from this desmadre as physically possible. That's why she moved to Ocean Valley. Now it's clear it wasn't just because she was protecting my mamá, but because she'd seen the carnage of it all first hand. She grew up with this too." She lamented, piecing together her family's history.

César simply nodded.

"How many times did we hear Diego's name but nothing about him? No memories, no stories. They buried him just like they buried all the lies and secrets they thought we weren't old enough to handle." Celia's voice shook with anger.

"Age had nothing to do with it princesa, it was about the fact that no one wants to be the person who shares the painful truth. They'd rather absolve themselves from the burden and leave it up to the universe, or some higher power to bring you to find it yourself." César said with a sneer.

"God didn't bring me here. Revenge did." She peeled her upper lip and he nodded in agreement.

César pulled a lighter out of his pants, flicking the flame on and touching the corner of the paper to it. It quickly lit, and he dropped it to the ground, letting it burn to completion on top of the stained concrete floor. The flames triggered the smoke detector and an alarm went off, causing the sprinklers to pour down on us in a heavy torrent.

We ran out of the room, leaving the empty box on the table before collecting our weapons and running out of the bank at rapid speed. We piled back into the car in a rush to avoid the angry bank teller cursing us down.

Celia stared blankly at the piece of paper that had her birth name written on it after we left the building. Her eyes didn't unglue from it the entire ride out to the middle of nowhere.

Because of course the GPS took us to the fucking desert.

The mystery coordinates, on the random piece of paper in a fifteen plus year old safety deposit box, took us to the middle of nowhere.

Why the fuck would it not have?

And of course we all fucking followed it, with the insane hope that none of this was a trap or a terrible idea. When we arrived it was practically dark already. We left the headlights on to provide us with a fraction of visibility to find the exact location we needed.

Celia and César took turns digging at the precise location where X marked the spot—figuratively of course. Celia insisted that the three of us were far too injured to be exerting ourselves that way and refused to risk us opening any stitches. Villalobos grumbled something about not wanting to deal with the Doc's wrath.

She hadn't come out unscathed though, her scars weren't so visible this time, at least not all of them. But they were still very much real.

Santos could barely stand straight. His entire upper body was draped in markings of all textures, shapes, and sizes and for this very reason he was now wearing a long sleeve turtleneck in ninety degree weather.

We were coming apart at the seams, just as we were figuring out how to become whole.

"Fucking finally. Carajo," César shouted from the bottom of the hole.

The sound of the shovel hitting metal over and over again rang out until finally the two of them were able to get it loosened from the soil. The box was big enough to hold a body, though I wasn't sure if it said more about me or them that it was my go-to measuring format. There was at least a sixty percent chance there was a body in there.

"Put it in the car so we can get the fuck out of here. Let's go home," Celia said.

Her face changed when she said home.

"You don't want to open it now, jefa?" César asked.

"It doesn't matter. Now, later—I already know what's inside." She shrugged, walking back to the car.

65

CELIA

I don't know why I called it home. Statistically speaking I lived less of my life in the Guadalajara villa than I did in Ocean Valley, but that sure as fuck wasn't home. I was feeling a million ways out of sorts. Coming back to the land that made me caused a magnitude of feelings that couldn't be described. Feelings of knowing, in my heart of hearts, that la patria was the center of who I truly was at my core.

The urge to sink my roots down into the soil to reconnect was immense.

And then came the shattering feeling of inadequacy. I was an imposter. A pretender, and they would all see it. Not damn near Mexican enough. They would all know just by looking at me. Would they hear it in my voice too? I tilted my chin up to force the tears to be reabsorbed into my eyes. I was fed up with letting them fall.

"Wait, we should open it first." Mateo said.

"Whatever's inside will still be there when we get to the villa. I've had enough of my family's secrets for one day." I tried helping him lift the chest into the car with little success, finally allowing the boys to tag in for this one.

I looked over to César as he shut the trunk. "What's that little favor gonna cost me?" He knew I was referring to him burning his documents, I didn't have to specify.

"I didn't do it for you, reina. I did it for me. When Rafa died, I felt *relieved*. I was a shit brother because I wanted my freedom so bad that it didn't matter what it would cost me. I don't care what some stupid piece of paper says, you're my sister. The throne was always yours. I have everything I want in Grimm's Reach. I just want to be free to go home when this is all over." I swung my arms over his neck and squeezed him tight.

He lifted me off the ground into his embrace and it was the first time in fifteen years I felt the loss of my papá as sharply as the first. Cousin, brother, it didn't fucking matter. He was the only family I had left willing to go to bat for me. And we were going up against our own blood.

"You're supposed to be my number two though."

"You don't need me for a number two guy, you've got three of them." He gestured over to my men, standing back and letting us have our moment.

Maybe he wasn't wrong about that.

The question was, did they want to be?

The drive back was filled with silence, so many what ifs and what nows still unspoken as we followed what seemed to be the path that was laid out for me. Or maybe I was still fucking delusional and leading us to our deaths.

There was a strange familiarity in going back to your childhood home. The only bad memory I had of this place was of my last night here. The air felt thicker as we drove through the gates and past the gardens. A row of cars followed behind us into the Flores property and I turned my head nervously before Ronan reassured me.

"They're Crows and Diablos."

"They were waiting for us?" I asked, scrunching my face together.

"César told everyone you were supposed to be the first person to walk inside," Mateo explained from the front.

Great. No fucking pressure or anything. Not momentous at all.

They all stood outside, some a hundred and fifty men, while I walked through the villa doors. There were plenty of bedrooms and accommodations here for all of them until we went to war. Between this and the guest house there were at least fifty rooms and most of them had multiple beds.

"Now what?" Calaveras' gravelly voice rang high over my head.

"Now we recoup. We lick our wounds, we plan well, and I get my papá's men on my side. Then we kill the hijo de la chingada." He and the Diablos who'd overheard all nodded in agreement as we walked through my family's villa.

Flashes of celebrations, meals, even weddings for cártel families that were held in this property ran through my memory. My papá made this a home, but looking back this was no place for a kid to grow up in. None of us were sheltered from the violence or the blood. Even Carolina knew it well, but we were desensitized early on. He was my papá, I would always love him. But now that I had grown up, I could acknowledge that he made plenty of mistakes. There were some I was determined to never repeat.

Bringing children into this world was one of them.

I sat with my arms crossed on a metal bench while César and Santos used the shovel to attempt and pry the box open. It was three in the morning and far too late for this bullshit, but they refused to end the day without knowing what all of this was for.

I couldn't blame them.

But I showed no trace of surprise when they finally forced the lid open, the smell of the past seeping out first before the contents became visible.

"What's this?" Santos pulled the leather journal out of the metal box first, a wave of nostalgia hitting me as memories of my papa with that thing stuck under his arm filled my head.

"Secrets. Blackmail. Currency of the cártel," I explained.

The Ortíz ledger was the reason why Augustin Ortíz was able to take the cártel in one fell swoop. He knew every dirty secret, every sellable crime any family had committed. And he used it like a leash to control his grunts, his own people. Following suit my papá had no choice but to continue in tradition. After all, why risk something new when you knew the old and tried way worked best?

No, this was what paid for their loyalty. Protection from their past.

"Jesus H. Christ," Mateo said in disbelief as he stuck his hand into the box, hundreds of diamonds slipping through his fingers and falling back into the heaping pile they came from.

"This is the kind of money that's gonna fuck with the economy when you put it back in circulation." Santos scratched the back of his head.

"That's the point. Then she'll own the fucking country."

It was easy to make this place feel the way it used to again, despite the fact my rat of a tío had tainted it with his presence not too long ago. I was here with the three men that I loved the most despite their aversion to me.

I knew the problem. I wasn't a fucking idiot.

Between them thinking I was some fragile little fucking paper doll, and them trying to distinguish the boundaries between the four of us, everything was a mess. At least they'd now finally come to realize that there wasn't a choice between the three of them. It was all or nothing. I meant it when I told them that, before the attack on the highrise.

Three weeks had gone by and all of our scars had begun to fade. Ronan was still in terrible shape which meant Emory was constantly on his ass to make sure he wasn't overdoing it. "No sex for six weeks," she reminded him. "Unless you want it to be your last time," she said like the evil Irish witch she was.

Which meant Santos and Mateo weren't touching me. I guess that was my own fault when I said all or nothing, but that was definitely not what I had meant. Things were just different now, and something told me they were waiting for Ronan to make the first move.

Which left me sexually frustrated and constantly on edge.

How was I supposed to concentrate on a war when there was so much sexual tension and testosterone just fucking floating around in the air at all times? I finally put my foot down and kicked Emory out of my room. I needed space to decompress and process all the fucking trauma I'd been trying to put behind me since it clearly wasn't going to leave me alone until I went through it.

And man did I need to go through it.

Dark humor was starting to become a dangerous coping mechanism, and no one was laughing at my suicide jokes anymore. It didn't matter. I learned long ago the only person who was capable of putting me six feet under would likely share the last name Flores. And now there was a good chance that Flores wouldn't be me.

"Why is Emory telling me I have to share a room with Santos and Mateo now?" Ronan rumbled into my ear from behind, sending goosebumps down my neck.

I was folding newly purchased clothes and tucking them into the dresser.

"Well, I was hoping she would have taken the hint and boarded up with

César, but it looks like she's really making him work for it," I said, turning around and placing a kiss on his cheek. "You can sleep with me. If you promise to be good."

"How do you expect me to sleep next to you and not fuck you until my guts split open again?" He pressed me against the dresser, the hard steel of his erection strained against his pants.

I looked up through my eyelashes and bit my lip. Ronan was fucking massive. And now that I couldn't find a single reason to hate him anymore, all I wanted to do was let him crush me under him and suffocate me until I saw stars.

"Well, you best be a good boy, or I'll have you swap rooms with one of the others." I smirked and he pressed into me harder. His fingers wrapped around the back of my neck, and he forced my gaze up at him.

"You might be their queen, but I'm here to remind you that my hand around your neck has always been your favorite collar," he said, stroking my throat gently with his thumb.

"What do you call a man who owns a queen?" I asked.

"One lucky motherfucker," Mateo answered from the doorway, breaking the staring contest.

The disappointment from Mateo interrupting our moment was brief. Reality checked me hard, even with Ronan's undeniable sex appeal, and my cunt practically dripping just from the idea of being touched.

Ronan was lucky to be alive, and I wasn't stupid enough to risk his recovery.

As if my letdown was obvious, Ronan chuckled again, this time moving his hand to the front of my neck while the other roamed the waistband of my jeans. He turned us both to face Mateo. Santos stood behind him.

Had they been there the whole time? Had he brought them with him?

"You're telling me you fought this hard for both of them, and neither have taken care of you? You deserve to be fucked within an inch of your life. But I'll settle for mine if I have to. Tell the Doc to get a blood donor ready." His hand traveled south, reaching into my thong and stroking against my center.

"Oh fuck," I whispered, dropping my head back against his chest.

He continued his teasing, making circles on my clit before dipping inside of me, two knuckles deep. He groaned in my ear.

"You're so fucking wet." He thrusted two fingers all the way inside before pulling them out, forcing my eyes open at the shock of him leaving me desperate and needy.

By the time I turned around he was already sitting on a velvet chair in the corner of the room, forearms on his knees as he settled in. Mateo and Santos still hesitated at the door.

"I'm so tired of you all treating me like I'm made of glass. You didn't break me, and neither did he. If somebody doesn't fuck me soon, I'm going to go insane." Mateo was first, behind me all too suddenly before his hands traveled up my body, under the fabric of my shirt. His coarse hands massaged my breasts, kneading them softly before turning his attention to my nipples.

My eyes were still stuck on Ronan, sitting in the chair.

"Close the door or get out," Ronan told Santos in a commanding tone.

"I thought you didn't want to watch me with anyone else," I antagonized while immediately regretting my inability to hold my tongue even when it benefited me.

"I was wrong." His gaze hardened my way. "I want to watch them split you open. Then once I've heard you scream enough, I'll clean you up with my tongue."

He leaned forward in the chair and nodded to Mateo, who began to move his hands once again at Ronan's instructions.

Rayos

I felt like I was going to combust from every small touch. The sound of the door closing made its way to me, but before I could look over Mateo's shoulder to see if he'd come in or not, Santos was already there, pressed to my other side and pulling my jaw in his direction for a kiss.

I opened my mouth, parting my lips and letting his tongue dance its way in before reciprocating the movements myself. He swallowed my moans just as Mateo's fingers flicked around my nipples.

"Take her clothes off," Ronan said.

Santos didn't delay, he broke our kiss, pulling my shirt off and throwing it on the ground while Mateo worked to undo the buttons on my jeans. I helped him, stepping out of each leg as he rolled them down my calves. I reached for Mateo's shirt, taking it off of him and turning to Santos to do the same.

He grabbed my wrist in his hand to stop me and pinned my arm to my chest before forcing my back against him.

"Where do you want her?" He asked into my ear but the question wasn't for me.

"Bring her to the bed." Ronan leaned back and crossed his ankle over his knee.

I didn't miss the bulge in his pants and his refusal to adjust it.

We made our way to the bed, where Ronan had the perfect view. Mateo's fingers danced up my spine, forcing a shiver from my body. Once he got to the band of my bra he unclasped it, exposing me to all three of them. I heard the faintest growl coming from the corner but it was hard to tell if it hadn't come from the other two men.

"Take your shirt off," I told Santos, but he ignored me.

"Lay her on the bed. Head towards the edge." Ronan was in charge, and I had no problem with that. I couldn't look away from him. He was hungry, in every sense of the word, and somehow he was going to make do with what I gave him.

I was on my back. Mateo had me boxed between his arms as he hovered over me, and Santos stood above my head.

"I want to hear her choking on her screams," he told them.

Santos pulled me by the shoulders, letting my head dangle off the edge of the bed and before I could figure out what was going on I felt Mateo's hot, wet mouth on my center, lapping up all of my anticipation.

Santos chuckled like he knew exactly how to fulfill Ronan's demands. I heard the unzipping of his pants and shifted my focus from the vortex of pleasure that Mateo was drawing out from between my legs. His tongue fucked me continuously, only stopping to provide more attention to my clit every now and again.

"Open your eyes," Ronan commanded, but it wasn't him I saw once I did.

It was Santos' engorged and overly pierced cock, throbbing as it waited to enter my mouth. I moaned, parting my lips to let him in. I barely had time to inhale, and with this position he slid all the way down my throat with ease, filling up my airways and blocking all possibility of me breathing. I felt each bar of his Jacob's ladder against my tongue, the cold steel making it impossible for me to not try to wrap my tongue over each one as he sheathed himself inside of me.

A tear dripped from my eye, rolling down onto my forehead and soaking into my scalp. Santos wiped it before pulling himself out from my mouth.

"What are you doing?" Ronan asked before I could.

He didn't answer, he just scratched the back of his head anxiously before shaking his head and locking his gaze onto mine.

"I want this," I told him, lifting up and turning onto my elbows, turning back to look at him.

Mateo had come to a full stop, seeing the tension between Ronan and Santos and completely clueless on how to fix it.

"I promise, I want this," I told him, turning towards him.

66

SANTOS

It was as if I was constantly being punished.

I wasn't ignorant enough to say things like, "I didn't know for what". The list was endless. I had sins that had expired by basic statute of limitations, but that didn't mean I didn't need to repent for them.

Her mouth open, my cock deep in her throat.

All I could see was Guillermo.

Her sacrifice.

My fucking shame.

Not being able to do enough to keep her from his brutality.

It had been eating me alive, and though she'd left me to commiserate without pushing, I knew I'd eventually have to face her, face myself, face my regrets.

She turned fully, folding her legs under her and sitting on her heels on the bed. She didn't look back to see what Mateo was doing, she stayed focused on me.

"What is it you see when you look at me Santos?" she asked, her voice not wavering.

I scanned over her body, from the scar on her face, to the small brand below her breast. Both scars matched mine. That meant something.

It had to.

"I see the strongest, most beautiful woman I've ever known," I answered with the truth.

"What else do you see?" she asked, knowing I was holding back.

"I see my failures. I see all the ways I should have protected you but wasn't able to." I cupped her face, thumbing the scar on her cheek.

I would have taken both of them if I could have.

"Take your shirt off," she told me again, this time her voice rang with authority.

"Celia," I warned her.

They'd seen the extent of my injuries, but now that they were healed it was different.

I didn't look so much like a victim as I did a monster.

Not even a monster but a monster's plaything, covered in holes and crooked stitching.

"Take your shirt off," she gritted out, her fingers gripping the hem of the fabric.

I inhaled, wrapping my fingers over hers and letting her guide the shirt over my head. I held that exhale at the bottom of my lungs and waited for any of them to say something, anything, to confirm how disgusting I knew I now looked.

"Fuck man." Mateo was the first to break the silence.

She ran her fingers over the areas where skin was puckered and raised up, scar tissue doing its best to heal wounds that had been ignored.

"Ask me what I see when I look at you," she said quietly.

"Morena." I sighed again, wishing I could make her understand that it wasn't about how I looked, but how I felt.

And I felt like a monstrous failure. Her fingers lingered over the raised up scar in the shape of the five petal flower.

"I see a man that belongs to me. A man who selflessly sacrificed himself for me. A man who gave me everything, including the courage to keep going. Their hatred and their insecurities may have left a permanent mark on you Santos, but all I see is a declaration of love. That scar on your face is the same as that brand on your chest and both of them say 'property of Celia Flores to me."

This woman was a titan, and I was a mere mortal, searching for a place to worship her even if just in evanescence. I would let her have me for as long as she considered me worthy.

"All of this is my fault," I reminded her before looking up at the rest of them.

Ronan ran his fingers over his face like I was ruining the moment, but she seemed unfazed by it all.

"I'm so tired of figuring out who's to blame. We've all fucked up tremendously. Isn't that enough?" she asked.

"I haven't." Mateo smirked and she actually laughed, cracking the serious mask she wore and making my heart flutter with nostalgia.

I used to be able to do that to her.

"I guess that settles it, you can both get out," she said, turning back towards Mateo, locking her arms around his neck, and pressing her lips to his.

"Sorry sunshine, you're not calling the shots on this." He spun her around, one hand gripping one of her perfect tits and the other traveling down to her hip.

He shoved his knees between her legs, spreading them apart from behind and putting her on display for both Ronan and me.

She moaned loudly, dropping her head against his chest and grinding her pussy against his thigh.

"Somebody touch me, please." Her eyes found Ronan's who then found mine.

How we had gone from him wanting to punch my lights out for loving her, to asking me to fuck her was beyond me. It was time I dropped all my insecurities. I could do it if Zerkos could too.

I climbed up onto the bed and on my knees I made my way towards her. She was dripping all over his thigh, a look of need glimmering through those black eyes of hers.

"Please," she whimpered again.

I turned my face to Zerkos.

He gave me a crooked smile.

"Fuck her so good she doesn't know whose name to cry out."

I pinched her chin between my thumb and the side of my index finger.

"Is that what you want, Morena?"

"Please."

67

CELIA

It was nearly unbearable, having all of them watching me, craving their touch, and not getting it. Mateo sensed my need and rolled my nipples between his fingers again, flooding me with an aching desire for more.

"Please," I begged.

Ronan chuckled louder. "I regret not doing this sooner."

Mateo sat, bringing me down on his lap with his erection pressed at my ass.

"I'm going to fuck you here, Sunshine," he whispered in my ear.

He wasn't quiet about it though, and Ronan tossed a bottle of lube his way with a smirk. Santos peppered kisses down my neck, his fingers dancing their way down my belly until they found the slick folds of my pussy right against Mateo's thigh. He moved his leg out of the way, getting ready for what was going to come next.

Santos' fingers made contact with my clit just as Mateo's lubed up fingers skirted the entrance of my puckered hole. First one finger slid through, eliciting a full body shudder from me while Santos sparked bursts of pleasure from me.

I moaned again and heard a wheezed grunt coming from Ronan.

Mateo inserted one more finger just as Santos speared himself inside my pussy, fingers scissoring their way in and rubbing against my walls. I cried out, an unexpected orgasm bursting its way out of me before I was ready.

"You weren't supposed to come yet, Sunshine," Mateo whispered in my ear.

I clutched his thighs, digging my nails into his flesh as I rode the last of that wave and forced him to hold me up from behind. He gave me the courtesy of letting me catch my breath before he hitched my legs up, wrapping my knees over his elbow and splaying me open for Santos and Ronan.

"Do you want him to fuck your ass, baby?" Ronan asked me.

"Yes." I nodded at him first before turning my head back to Mateo.

He shoved his tongue into my mouth, a passionate sloppy kiss to distract me from the burning sting of his way too thick of a monster cock pressing against my puckered hole.

"Fuck!" I bit out, breaking our kiss as the head pushed its way through the tight barrier before sliding in. "Shit. Shit. Shit." I breathed, recognizing how long it had been since the last time.

Santos dropped his head down my center, licking this way through my most sensitive area while Mateo continued to work his way inside me. With a few more thrusts he had bottomed out, and the confusing sensation of fullness paired with the emptiness I still felt with my pussy unoccupied was too much to bear.

"I need both of you, please," I gasped, yanking my fingers through Santos' hair to pull him up to my face level.

He wet his bottom lip. Any reservation he may have had before was now gone. I could see it clearly. We'd wasted too much time holding back before, and all it got us was regrets and scars. It was time to claim what we wanted and burn anyone and everything that stood in the way of it.

I practically screamed once Santos pushed himself inside. Each bar of his piercing drug along my walls with every inch he sunk deeper inside me. He knew exactly the type of madness that thing caused, and he knew how to use it well. He pulled out completely before he'd had a chance to go more than one or two bars in, and with a violent thrust of his hips, he impaled me.

The noise I made wasn't human.

It didn't stop them from continuing their torture.

Mateo still held my legs under the knees, and Santos' hands roamed everywhere they could find within reach. Thrusting back and forth once they'd found a rhythm that worked for them both.

"I can feel your dick piercings," Mateo groaned, making me wonder what that felt like for him, if it felt this good for me.

"Fuck," Santos breathed out, picking up speed.

"Wrap your hands around her neck." Ronan gave one last command and I waited to see which one of them would oblige.

Mateo froze, but I knew it was in hesitation. I gave Santos my most seductive stare, challenging him to dare to disobey. He didn't have it in him. His hand found its way to my throat, pressing at the side to restrict my blood flow. Mateo did the rest of the work, moving my hips in sync with his thrusts so that each time my hip came down I would come down onto Santos as well.

The position had his dick hitting my g-spot every time he skewered into me, but with his grip around my neck I wasn't able to moan, to cry, or scream. My breathing was shallow but the winding in my core grew tighter as my body got closer and closer to release. One hand still on Mateo's thigh, the other gripped Santos' forearm, and I squeezed, knowing an earth shattering climax was just around the corner.

My vision went hazy from the pressure around my throat, and I closed my eyes to lose myself to the colorful bright spots in my eyes, feeling the next climax tear through me like an avalanche.

"Not yet." I heard Ronan's muted voice telling Santos when he tried loosening his grip on me.

Another thrust. There was no distinction between the end of one orgasm or another. I couldn't keep my eyes open. I didn't know what any part of my body was doing at any point in time. I was simply in pleasure, like diving into the bottomless ocean. A moment where all that mattered was how good I felt and how good they could make me feel.

And we were all in it together.

I exploded again, this time hearing Ronan's approval and Santos moving his hands just in time for a guttural cry to rip its way out of me. He pulled out in a single move, his piercings rubbing every right spot along the way, prolonging an orgasm that felt like it would never end. A flood of liquid poured its way out from between my legs and onto the sheets, my body convulsing with tremors as I collapsed onto Mateo.

"We're not done," Mateo spoke from behind, forcing my eyes to flutter back open.

He was right, they weren't.

Santos looked determined, cock hard in his hand as he stroked up and down, playing with the bars of his piercings every time his fingers grazed over them.

"Fuck, that thing is so hot." I let my brain vomit voice itself out loud through my mouth.

I was panting hard, but I was a puddle of cummed out mess, unsure if I even had it in me to satisfy the two of them. I was already three deep and they hadn't even come once yet. Mateo let my legs go, dropping me to my knees on the bed while he stayed inside me. He placed his hands between my shoulder blades, letting me know he wanted me to drop down.

I obliged, lifting my ass up into the air as I pressed my chest to the mattress, turning my head to continue watching Santos pleasuring himself. Precum gathered at the tip, and he rubbed his thumb along it, spreading it around and coating his length in it. He didn't need it. He was still plenty wet from being inside of me.

Before I knew it, my mouth was watering. Watching his hand work his manhood in a way that had his eyes burning into mine as he chased his own pleasure was riveting. With every thrust of Mateo's hip against my ass I felt myself creeping closer to unraveling all over again. No time to get my bearings or recover, I was shaking at the first contact Mateo's fingers made with my clit, giving me the friction I needed to find my release again.

This time I took him with me, feeling the way his cock pumped inside of me while his cum filled my ass. He pulled out slowly, aftershocks surging through my body and forcing an awkward twitch from me as I wriggled against him. As if my pleasure was enough, Santos took two more pumps of his fist before ropes of his cum were landing on the bed, warm droplets landing on my face while he moaned through his climax.

The three of us breathed heavily, taking our time to come down from our high as gently as possible.

"Spread her legs," Ronan demanded and Santos was there in an instant, flipping me on my back while Mateo held me open like a buffet.

I raised up onto my elbows, watching Ronan struggle to get off the chair on his own before slowly making his way towards us. Mateo stood, giving him his arm to help him down onto his knees.

"Fuck me," Ronan whispered before his head disappeared between my legs.

He was making good on that promise.

The flat of his tongue raked against my swollen, abused clit but he didn't care. He licked up every drop of arousal that coated me before shoving his tongue deep inside, doing the same to all of the liquid heat that threatened to spill its way out of me again.

"Oh God," I cried, every nerve ending on my body was still too sensitive, but he didn't seem to care.

His tongue moved in and out of me as he cleaned every inch of my ass and pussy with his mouth. It was too much. I shook my head back and forth, whispering obscenities in Spanish until there was nothing left but for me to come once more, violently shaking in his hold while Mateo kept me spread apart.

"Fuck!" I cried out, clawing the sheets below me desperately.

Once I could finally stop hearing the blood pumping through my ears, I rose back up to a seated position and looked at Mateo and Santos.

"Help me undress him," I told them. "Get him in the shower." I nudged my head towards the en suite bathroom.

Santos was up first, lifting Ronan from his knees while Mateo did his best to remove his shirt without putting him through too much pain. He was healing well, the Doc said so herself, but he was still supposed to be receiving assistance with day to day things like this.

I headed over to the bathroom, stepping on the cold tile floor before walking through the glass doors of the shower and turning it on. Hot water sprayed from the showerhead, instantly filling the room with a plethora of steam.

"Sit." I gestured to the concrete stool across from the showerhead.

All three followed but only Ronan took a seat, knowing my words were just for him. I filled a loofah with soap before dragging it across his body, starting with his shoulders and being mindful to not put pressure on his stomach. He leaned against the tile wall, closing his eyes and seeming unbothered by how cold it must have felt. I bent over and turned to scrub his massively muscular legs.

"Will you tell me what happened? When Guillermo had you both?" he asked, his eyes remaining shut.

"I got on my knees for him," I told him. "To keep him from hurting Santos any more than he already had." His eyes jarred open and looked past me.

He was looking at his brother's scars again.

"How can I make it better?" It was so Ronan of him to ask me that.

Ever since we were children, he was always looking for a way to make things better, to fix whatever it was that was keeping a smile from my face. But it wasn't up to him or Santos or Mateo to make it better. It was only up to me. I was the one who decided how damaged I was going to be from this, not them, and certainly not Guillermo.

"By letting me get on my knees for you," I told him, not wavering my gaze from that emerald forest that burned so brightly in his stare.

I lowered down in front of him, the water hammering into my back like a hot massage that pressed against my muscles. He was hard and ready for me, and there was no way I wasn't going to be savoring all the best dick of my life in one day. I wrapped my lips over my teeth and lowered my mouth onto his erection, licking the shiny head of his length before sending it further into my mouth.

He groaned, grabbing a fistful of my hair and pulling.

"Fuck flower, I forgot just how good that mouth of yours feels." He let out a desperate grunt and I looked up to find him watching me intently, not a care in the world about the two other men enjoying the show behind me.

He pulled at my hair, letting me know he was going to take control and I relaxed my throat, readying myself for it. He thrusted deep down my throat before pulling all the way out to slam again. I closed my eyes, but a picture of Guillermo's sick smile flashed over my vision in the dark.

"Look at me," he said, as if he knew exactly where I'd gone.

I choked out an inhale, opening my eyes to find him looking down at me with nothing but admiration.

"I love you," he said, pulling out of my mouth.

"No, stop. We're not done, you're not done." I shook my head, but Santos pulled me up from behind and began washing me with the same loofah before I'd had a proper chance to fight about it.

Mateo helped Ronan up, but he walked out of the bathroom on his own. The two of them stayed, closing in on me while Santos continued to lather me up.

"It's okay to not be okay, sunshine." Mateo cupped my cheek. "No one expects you to pretend like you're fine."

"I *am* fine," I said through clenched teeth, my nostrils flaring widely before I pushed through them, dripping wet with no towel as I made my way out of the bathroom.

"Fuck!" Santos cursed just loud enough for me to hear.

Ronan stood there, as naked as I was, but seeming ten times less bothered than me.

"Let me try again," I said nervously.

He shook his head.

"Another time, I just want to sleep next to you again. I want to hold you in my arms."

"I love you Ronan," I said the words that had taken too long to come out of my mouth again.

"I love you too, Cecilia. Celia. Whatever the fuck you want to be called these days."

"I'll settle for your majesty." I smirked, grabbing a towel that hung from a chair and using it to dry myself.

"Then come sleep with me, your majesty." He reached out and I accepted his hand, letting him pull me closer.

I helped him onto the bed, thankful that all the wet spots were at the bottom towards our feet and making a mental note to change them in the morning when I wasn't completely fucked out of energy. He laid on his back, and I propped the pillows up just slightly for him, making sure he was comfortable and settled in.

I nudged myself into a nook at his side, draping one leg of mine over his and laying my arm over his chest. My head found a comfortable place on his arm, and I closed my eyes to appreciate this moment, wondering for a second what the fuck was taking the other two so long to shower.

Ronan ran the tips of his fingers up and down the side of my arm, the gentle touch sending a wave of goosebumps down my spine.

Guadalajara was quickly becoming home again, because home wasn't a set place.

I didn't know that I'd ever get tired of saying so.

68

CELIA

To be queen I needed more than just a throne, I needed an empire. Which meant I desperately needed people I could trust. As of right now that list was small. I required more men, my father's men, more importantly. The ones that went into hiding when my tío betrayed my papá.

The metal chest we'd dug up in the desert contained the Ortíz ledger along with millions of dollars in gold and diamonds. Blood money certainly, but my hands were far from clean. I could play differently, but I couldn't change the game. My skin was thick, I was primed for this.

If I had any uncertainties about it, then I should have passed the torch to Carolina.

We'd been settled into Guadalajara long enough now that I'd made contact with a damn good lawyer and paid him everything it took to get Celia Flores out of her grave and back in tip top health. Apparently not such a difficult task. I'd also found out that since I was the only living heir of the Flores and Ortíz families, that I was filthy fucking rich.

César didn't want my money.

Apparently he *was* too good for my blood money. A laughable thought if you took into consideration that he ran a one percent biker gang.

Club. Whatever. Los Diablos Locos weren't to be fucked with, and I was happy to be making allies this early in the game.

I'd procrastinated long enough. We'd been here for weeks and for the most part we had healed. It was time to see who'd stand at my side. Time to see who'd give me a chance to prove myself to be better than both the men who came before me.

The Ortíz ledger was thicker than my thighs. An old leather cover sealed the documents, but the binding was four metal rings, allowing the holder to add to it over time. This is what secured the cártel for the Ortíz family long ago, and this is what my papá gained by marrying my mamá. She was an Ortíz, and everything I'd known about how the Flores family took control was a lie. She was a pawn, as women often were, moved across the board to further the interest of men.

Weak.

Diego was the oldest, but he died before I'd ever been born. Which meant there was a good chance my abuelo arranged to marry my mamá off to the Flores family as his only option for not losing everything upon the death of his line.

As if women ruling was so out of the question.

Their errors would be my gain.

Now I had all of the Ortíz money, the Flores name, and my papá's cojones hanging from my legs. And that ledger, I had that ledger, and it was probably my most powerful weapon.

The cártel was successful because it was a well-oiled machine built on lies, secrets and the never ending struggle for control turning the gears day by day to function. Every blackmail, every dirty skeleton in a closet, every confidential piece of information that might only be privy to the military? It was in that ledger.

It was why my tío wasn't able to make nice with the politicians down here. He had nothing on them. This ledger had generations of crimes with statute of limitations that didn't run out. One secret outed, and that family's name would be tarnished for good.

I had a lot of stops to make, but I was starting with papá's arms dealer.

"Celia. This is a surprise. I had heard rumors but..."

"Yes, quite a surprise, I'm sure." I walked right into his kitchen. It was about the size of Mateo's closet. Tiles were missing from the floor where dirt rested in its place instead. The walls were concrete and stained, and a simple calendar was nailed to the wall above the tiny old oven. Time had not been kind to the Riveras, or maybe it was my uncle.

Dominico's daughter, Gabriella, stood just past the hallway, she must have been in her early twenties now. I vaguely remembered her as a baby when I was just a young girl. She had blonde hair, and her eyes were blue even though both her parents had dark hair and dark eyes.

I pulled out a wooden chair and sat down, gesturing to both of them with my hand to sit. They made their way across the table from me. Dominico looked behind me, eyeing the men directly on my six, guarding my back. I chuckled. "Don't worry Dom, they're harmless, unless you give them a reason to shoot. Sit, let's talk like old friends."

"Like old friends?" He raised an eyebrow up.

They both took a seat. Gabriella looked at me from underneath her eyelashes as she kept her head tucked down. I didn't mean to be intimidating, I just knew that acting like the biggest fish in the room was the only thing that actually made it true.

"I'm going to cut the pleasantries. I'm here to tell you I've come into possession of Rafa's ledger, the Ortíz ledger. I am not here to offer you the option of death or generations of indentured servitude to me. I am not my papá. I am better than him, and I intend to *be* better than him. I will not blackmail you into my corner."

"What is it you offer then, if not blood?" He looked into my eyes, his wrinkling hands fell heavy on the table. He must have been in his late sixties now. In his prime he was a feared and respected officer in my papá's army. Not to say he couldn't be feared now, but I'm sure he was a much easier kill these days then back then.

But he had all the knowledge and connections I lacked.

"What my papá didn't give you, a choice." With my words he looked to his daughter and squeezed her hand. "If you stick with me, I will provide for you better than Rafa ever could. You will feel my protection twice over and my loyalty. My papá ruled through fear, I plan to rule by earning your respect. If you decide not to back me, I won't press you, I won't come back for you, and I won't kill you. I will leave you and all of your descendants to live or die in peace." I looked at Gabriella and tilted my chin down at her in recognition.

"That simple?" He eyed me suspiciously.

"That simple. However, this ledger, as you can imagine, is very precious to me. It stays in my possession at all times. If I were to be a casualty in this war that will *no doubt* come to fruition... Well, it would be a shame if Ignacio were to claim what isn't his. Wouldn't it?" My gaze at Gabriella turned into a menacing one so that my message could ring loud and clear.

It wasn't a threat; it was a promise.

If my tío got ahold of this ledger he would use it to trap every single one of my father's soldiers permanently, through as many generations as he could until he was dead and gone. I was offering freedom. I was offering a life where I wouldn't hang the threat of revealing their dirtiest secrets out into the world if the opportunity struck.

Because there were many. You didn't sign yourself over to the cártel if a life of clean money was something you could easily attain.

"If you help me through this fight, you can retire, without worrying whether or not your daughter is going to be stuck under my heel. That's a promise. Your secrets die with me." I stuck my hand out in an offering and raised an eyebrow at him. "Maybe this ledger even ends up falling into a fire at some point. Maybe we can rebuild on a truer loyalty."

"Rule with respect, huh?" he said as he clapped his hand against mine in agreement. "You've got yourself a deal reina."

"No offense Dom, I'll take you by my side any day. You're as fierce as they come. But you're an old man these days, and aside from your connections, I just need your voice." He scowled, taking offense at my bluntness. "What I mean to say is, Gabriella over here looks mighty hungry." I smirked at her, and she returned a matching smile that let me know I was reading her right. "She's all grown up now. Maybe she wants to fight too?" She didn't look to her papá for approval and right then I knew she was my type of girl.

"I do," she confirmed with a steady voice.

"Good girl." I shook her hand as well and stood from the table. "Then we're in agreement. Contact the men under you, and I'll send over more information in regards to finances and where we'll be meeting soon."

"I look forward to it. My men will be ready as soon as I give them the go ahead."

I nodded my approval and made my way out of his home without looking back, my men surrounding me as we walked through the threshold and made our way to the next name on the list.

Every conversation went the same. Old men, tired of hiding their families from my tío, hoping for something to come along and end their bad luck streak. I was just that thing. Soon my papá's entire council was behind me, and every connection he had was ready to back me. Well, at least those who hadn't betrayed him for Ignacio or gone running to him the minute todo se fue a la verga.

There was only one place left to go, the place that still lived in the back porch of my mind. Where I tucked away the little girl I had once been and became the woman I was today.

69

MATEO

A retinal scan and a digital fingerprint of all five fingers were needed before the main doors opened. We were in the absolute middle of nowhere. It was as empty as it got out here in the desert, aside for the five by five metal barrack with steel reinforced doors sticking out of the ground. The doors opened with a mechanical hiss, sliding inside their compartments and allowing us to enter.

She looked calm, comfortable. Like she was in her element. But I'd watched enough of those videos to know that behind those doors was also the place where her monsters tried to eat her. She of course had ended up eating them instead, but nonetheless, no child should have faced the burdens Celia Flores had been made to bear.

It was a tiny steel room with a trap door on the floor, we turned on our phone flashlights and the stairs presented themselves.

"There are many entrances, but to unlock them I have to open the main door and turn the system on then send power to all the other doors," she explained.

The stairs went down into another room, and there an elevator, with far too many digital screens on it, waited for us. First another retinal scan, another fingerprint on one of the glass screens on the wall. Then a device came out of the wall holding a piece of glass that reminded me a lot of a microscope slide. She reached her hand out to us.

"Who's got a knife?"

Santos was the quickest, placing the blade in her hand. She gripped it tight, pressing the sharp edge against the pad of her index finger until blood pooled around the blade. She squeezed, the droplets of blood straight onto the glass. She pressed a button, and the device withdrew back into the wall, the lights turning green and the elevator opening up.

"No fucking wonder he couldn't steal this from you," Zerkos snorted out.

"He is just a pretender, playing at being the boss. My papá worked hard to make sure that his empire would only be accessible to me." Her eyes seemed to darken as she turned toward him. "Now he will feel the full force of my fury. He's going to pay for what he did to my family, for turning my sister against me, and for all the lives he's taken."

The elevator opened, and the screen read negative fourteen, which meant we were a long way down. Far below civilization—where no one could hear your screams. It opened up to a massive room, the walls lined with large stones and a cold concrete slab floor. Several hallways split off in different directions letting me know this place was bigger than it seemed. This wasn't somewhere you wanted to get lost.

She seemed to know exactly where she was going, head held high like none of the trauma she suffered here had been anything but a stepping stone on the way to becoming who she was always meant to be.

She even looked like she fit the part. She wore a black two piece suit, fitted to her curves from every angle. She wore her long black hair slicked back into a low ponytail and her lips were painted a captivating black.

Battle colors.

"How soon can you get Taylor down here working?" she asked Ronan.

"She's just waiting for you to give her the word." He had no problem deferring to her, it was an odd thing to see because Ronan Zerkos didn't defer to anyone.

"We should be able to track him down within the week," she said confidently.

"How do you figure?" I asked.

"This dungeon is the central hub. There's sixteen total throughout México. Four of them never got locked down when my papá died, that's what he's been working with this entire time. The other twelve I can open through the command station with Taylor's help." She walked over to a large table dusting it off to show a map. "Every dungeon is connected to this one, through a tunnel system. Once I open up all the doors, he'll know

I'm here. Either he'll go scurrying like a rat and go into hiding, or he'll take the bait and come straight to me."

"Is that what you want?" Santos asked her, the scar on his face was finally starting to lose its shine.

"I'm not afraid of him anymore. Let him come, less work for me."

Ronan's phone rang, breaking the intensity of the moment. He stepped away to take the call and I turned back to her. She looked as beautiful as ever, radiant. *My sun*. She wore her makeup heavier than usual, to cover the scar on her face.

The scar didn't take away from her beauty.

It enhanced it.

It told the story of her strength and her refusal to die in a world that wanted nothing more than to bleed her out. Fuck. She was a goddamn reckoning, and she was coming for them all. It was an honor to be considered worthy enough to stand at her side and watch it happen.

But all I wanted to do was reach out and touch her. Slide my hands between her legs and bend her over one of the desks and fuck her senseless. She was so wound up from the stress and the crushing weight of all the expectations that came with being her father's daughter.

I couldn't do that.

Not in front of her men, her soldiers.

I knew she played a calculated game and that to be respected she needed space.

But I hadn't touched her in days, and I was ready to die because of it, I was sure. She cocked an eyebrow at me like she could read my thoughts. She shook her head and turned abruptly to say something to César in Spanish. Then Ronan stepped back into our circle with a pissed off look on his face, his jaw muscles ticking hard like the whole world pissed him off.

"Something's happening in Cove City," he said to me before looking over to gauge Celia's reaction.

She didn't have one. She wasn't just damn good at the game, she was a prodigy, carefully cultivated by a monster of a man who genuinely thought he was doing the right thing. The life was a wicked game, and we are all just pieces on a chess board, waiting to be knocked over.

"You're leaving then?" César spoke for her as if he could sense her lack of words was due to anxiety.

"I gotta sort some things out. I'm surprised your men haven't called you. The Bratvas are sending threats, and the Crows are spread thin in multiple directions and with no purpose. I gotta figure out the future for my men." He looked at both me and Santos, the question was there in his eyes, but he couldn't ask it.

I shook my head.

"It's you brother, it's always been you. Go handle it and come back to us." I tilted my head before slapping my hand on his shoulder, giving him my vote of confidence.

"You won't go with him?" she asked, concern spread over her face.

"He doesn't need us, morena," Santos said from a chair, his arms resting comfortably on his thighs with his shoulders hunched forward.

"And I do?" Shit, she was offended. "Fuck that," she spat out. "All three of you can fucking go. Deal with your Crows desmadre and then come back together." She waved her fingers between the three of us angrily.

César choked out a laugh like the asshole he was. Santos huffed out a response, and Zerkos smirked, seeming happy enough to not be on the biting side of her anger for once.

"If you're opening up these dungeons, you'll be exposed, vulnerable for your uncle to try something. I'd feel better if at least one of us stayed," I told her, finding myself with a shovel in hand, ready to dig my own grave.

"You don't think the hoard of bikers can protect me from the big bad wannabe cártel jefe but you can?" She pouted her lips seductively and stepped closer to me, running her index finger from the center of my sternum and slowly dragging it down.

My breath hitched as she got lower. I could hear César pretending to suck something out of his teeth to distract himself from the moment.

She was dangerous as fuck when she wanted to prove a point.

"Or that the men I've collected who've sworn their allegiance to me, who've dropped to their knees for me, they aren't capable of keeping me safe like you can?"

"That's not it, sunshine," I said with an exhale, feeling frustrated that her past had shaped her to believe that having people who cared for you somehow made you seem weaker. "It's that there are three men in this room who would likely eat a bullet if they found out something *else* happened to you while we were gone."

Her jaw clenched hard, a familiar mannerism of Ronan's. Little moments like this always reminded me that they'd grown up together. Now I saw it for what it really was. It was her behavior not his. He had been mirroring *her* all this time. It made me wonder if she'd learned it from her father.

She was calculating her options.

Damn, I loved a smart woman.

"Everybody out." She didn't even have to say it loud, and the room cleared out fast. All the little techie nerds that were already working to reinstate all of the built-in systems promptly stood and vacated to God knows the fuck where.

César stood as well, and she stood with her arms crossed, waiting for the room to empty completely.

"Are you not going to say anything?" I asked Santos, who still sat on a foldout chair, ankle over his knees and hands behind his head.

"Nah." He chewed on the toothpick pressed between his back teeth.

Of course he wouldn't, so I would be the only insane one who wanted to suffocate her because I couldn't handle the idea of her being on her own without her. Even though history would prove...

Either way. That wasn't fucking fair. Ronan wouldn't disagree because he was never going to be saying no to Celia ever again. And Santos, well... I didn't really know what his fucking deal was. I figured he was just handling the post torture shit poorly. Wouldn't blame him. He didn't talk much about it, but she did. She'd told me in confidence. Every day Guillermo would ask him if he still wanted to protect her, still wanted to take her pain for himself. Every day he gave him the option to swear himself back to Los Muertos, to kill her instead.

Every day he took what was meant for her, and they'd hurt him instead. And every day she watched. I hated that she had to do what she did, but I respected her for it. But Santos, he was still haunted by it and having a hard time looking past anything but his own failures.

70

CELIA

Things were different between me and Santos now because we were different now. We no longer saw the need to keep putting on the mask we did with everyone else. We saw each other at our worst, we saw all of each other's flaws. I knew exactly who he was inside, and he knew the same about me.

It was comforting in a way, to have someone you could be your truest self with.

It was like letting go of a breath you'd been holding your entire life.

When you wore a mask at all times, you kind of forgot what your real face looked like. If I took too much time to think about it, it always sent me into a spiral of panic. An identity crisis that never resolved itself. I'd spent my entire life pretending to be whoever it took to get me through the next chapter, and I ended up forgetting who I was underneath the mask.

Santos saw through it now.

And he couldn't hide from me either.

The problem was that at my core, I wasn't sure who was behind the mask anymore. I felt like an insecure little girl with no personality and a watered down version of her culture that'd been forgotten through years of Americanization. *Assimilate or die*. It was a rough game, but by the time I realized what a good job I'd done blending into the crowd, it was too late. I was a thirty year old orphan with a second-grade education level in the country I'd impulsively moved 'home' to.

Oh, fuck. It was happening again.

I lowered down to a squat on the ground, hovering my ass just an inch from the floor while my head dropped between my knees. I took deep breaths, but the room just closed in on me faster with each exhale, and all I could hear was the high-pitched electronic sound coming from the computers.

And then Ronan's shoes appeared on the ground right in front of my face. I lifted my gaze up to find him there, head tilted as he waited for my eyes to follow all the way up to his. His hand extended out as he reached and caressed the side of my face, his Bleu de Chanel scent reminding me that it didn't matter who I was because he'd find a way to love all those versions of me.

Maybe they all would.

"Let me leave the golden-doodle with you, flower. I'll sleep better knowing you won't be alone in that big house." He smirked, navigating through my ego in a way that only he knew how to do in order to get me to acquiesce to his needs.

My heart slowed down with each stroke of his thumb against my cheek, and I used it as a guide to steady my breathing.

"You'll take Santos with you, to keep you safe?" I asked and he huffed out a laugh.

"Yeah, yeah. I'll take Álvarez to keep me safe." Their eyes met, but neither one showed any expression.

They still weren't seeing eye to eye, which was insane because at this point I thought we'd chalked everything up to water under the bridge. Maybe I was the only one standing on the bridge though. Poor Mateo wasn't even aware there was water to go over, he was so faultless in everything.

"Then yes, I'll keep the golden-doodle." I smiled back at Ronan.

"Did we get a dog?" Mateo asked and finally Santos cracked a smile.

It was just going to be a couple days, but it also just felt like we'd just all gotten each other back. How was I supposed to cope when they would be so far away? Yeah, I *would* have told them all to go too, because I was a stubborn puta and every time I cut myself I ended up pouring salt in the wound, and then I followed it with tequila and lime.

Ronan and Santos got on a plane the next day and left for Cove City. César was tempted to follow, a threat to the Crows right now might as well have been a threat on the Diablos Locos compound. But he'd also told me about the trust he had in his VP and that he knew he could hold down the fort.

I wanted that kind of faith in my own men.

I was just getting to know them though; it would come with time. I needed to be patient. I was building an entire fucking empire from the cremated ashes of what once was. It was an impossible expectation to think I would have all my pieces on the board this soon.

I sighed. I would take borrowed soldiers until then.

"Why don't you take a breather," Mateo rasped into my ear right as I reached for my phone to shut off the alarm. "Just a day or two off from being the big bad queen of Mexico and let me work on unwinding you for forty-eight hours." He pulled my back into his chest and dropped his nose to my neck.

"If I was a man, and you were a woman. I would have assumed you were conspiring against me, and I'd be awfully suspicious of you trying to distract me for so long." I stretched my neck out, giving him the space he needed to pepper kisses down my throat.

I arched my back, pressing my ass to his morning wood.

It was only six in the morning. I could give him a few hours, maybe not the forty-eight he asked for, but I could give him some of me. His hand caressed down my ribs and trickled their way down.

"The guys..." I breathed out just as his fingers traveled down to the waistband of my pajama shorts.

"They're in Cove City. I can promise you I can make it so good you won't even remember they aren't here," he said seductively, his fingers dancing over my underwear and giving me the softest friction.

Just enough to drive me crazy.

"That's not what I meant. It's just. It's..." I couldn't put my finger on it.

"It's what, sunshine?" he asked, like he didn't understand.

But his hands were moving with a mind of their own, and though my brain was struggling to figure it out, my body said, cállate idiota!

"It feels like cheating if they aren't here. I don't know, we got to this place where it felt like there was understanding, but with both of them gone. I don't know. It just feels off."

He hummed into my ear like he was thinking about it, his fingers sliding inside my panties through the side and with zero hesitation he plunged them in. Finding me already soaked for him.

"I can fix that." I could hear the amusement in his voice, like he was really proud of his problem-solving abilities.

I gasped as he pulled out and used my arousal to coat my clit. He rubbed back and forth with the gentlest touch, like he already knew it wasn't about how fast or hard he did it in just the few times we'd been together.

This one took notes.

He was a good boy.

He moved in circles, my head spinning with his fingers and just as I closed my eyes to relish in the moment, I heard the loud dialing of his phone blasting on speaker.

"What?" Ronan answered.

My entire body temperature skyrocketed.

"What are you doing?" I hissed, trying to turn.

"Our girl needs to get off," Mateo said bluntly, and Ronan made a grunting sound on the phone.

"So why are you calling *me*?" Ronan said in his classic annoyed tone.

Mateo was unphased, plunging his fingers back inside of me and forcing a moan straight out of the depths of my chest.

"She's concerned about the ethics of it all," he said, pulling his fingers from inside me in order to assist me in fully removing my clothing.

"Get out," Ronan barked over the phone.

"He's busy. He's with people," I yelled at Mateo, who only chuckled.

"He's never too busy for you, sunshine. Tell her you're never too busy for her Zerkos."

"The dog's right, flower. I'm never too busy for you. Now turn on the camera and show me my girl," he growled out.

Mateo barked out a laugh, hitting a button on his phone as he propped himself up on the bed, running it over my body like he was showing Ronan everything he was missing out on.

"Where's Álvarez?" Mateo asked.

"He's here. Maybe if you make her scream, I'll let him come watch."

"Oh fuck," I gasped, the torment of his words building a heat inside of me from just the thought of the two of them watching while Mateo had his way with me.

It was so incredibly wrong.

So why did it feel so fucking right?

71

RONAN

"Hold the phone between her legs, I want to see how wet she is," I told Kane.

"Aye, aye," he chimed before lowering it from her face.

He thrusted his fingers inside her. I could hear her mewling in the distance, but the way she thrusted her hips told the bigger story.

"Slow down," I said, leaning back into the chair.

I looked up to find Santos still sitting at the end of the table, his eyes awkwardly averting mine. He didn't need my fucking permission to be with Celia. It wasn't about that anymore. It was about the fact that he was supposed to have been the one person I could have trusted with her life.

I never wanted to be wrong about it.

Now I was stuck here with him, because I trusted Mateo with her more than I trusted him. And that was saying a lot. Mateo Kane couldn't even keep a fish alive.

There were a thousand unspoken things between us. Most of them absolute bullshit that I would have rather just resolved with our fists.

But the guy was ugly enough now as it was. A visual reminder that he had been punished plenty for his sins.

I couldn't tell if his appearance was actually bothering him. He was going to be wearing his mistake for the rest of his life on his skin. Then suddenly it didn't feel so fair that I was here, asking him to feel remorse when Celia had somehow found it inside her to forgive me for the hell I put her through.

"Santos can't hear her brother," I chuckled, giving him a smirk.

He looked even more nervous.

Suspicious of me.

Untrusting bastard.

She cried louder the minute he lowered his face to her cunt, his tongue lapping at her clit and just as he covered it up he raised the phone to show me her face.

Fucking radiant.

She had one arm raised up high, her fist wrapped around the bar on the headboard of the bed. The other hand squeezed her breast and her teeth dug deep into her bottom lip from whatever it was Mateo was doing to her.

She was holding it back.

"Come on, don't make me say it." Her eyes sprung open, and she looked straight into the camera, even though she couldn't see me.

She bit her lip even harder.

"Fine. But I want you to cry out Álvarez's name for me when you come for me, flower."

"Fuck! Santos! Shit!" she cried.

Her body convulsed in violent quakes and the bastard finally turned his head my way.

He was fighting a smile so badly It was probably going to constipate him.

"I hope you didn't call me just to waste my time with one?" I egged Mateo on.

He flipped the camera to selfie mode to show me his face, glistening from her juices just as he rose up from between her legs. I would have given a million dollars to be there right now, in his place.

It was all I'd been able to do since I'd gotten shot. Emory had a million rules in place to make sure I didn't drop dead from internal bleeding or post-surgery complications. Gun to my head, dying while fucking Celia Flores didn't sound like the worst way to go. I couldn't fuck her for another two weeks and the doc had strictly prohibited me from getting off in general. Something about not getting my heart rate up too high. So I feasted on her pussy every night that I could.

And oh how I missed my favorite meal.

He was gloating.

Rubbing it in my face because he knew.

I would have done the fucking same.

He flipped the camera back and pointed it down just in time to let me see his cock slowly filling her up. It was the perfect fucking view and I had to clench my jaw tight in order to keep it from going slack.

We didn't have that much time, our men needed answers soon, and I'd just kicked them out to watch my best friend fuck my woman.

He was fully sheathed inside of her, his free hand roaming up and down her body, paying extra attention to her breasts and tracing gently around her nipples.

"Oh fuck," she moaned through the speaker.

"Does that feel good baby?" I asked her, getting her eyes to open for me again.

They somehow looked darker when she was drunk with lust.

"Yes," she hissed, her head bouncing up and down with each slam of his hips against hers.

Then his hand lowered to her clit, and she shook her head.

"No-no… I'm too sensitive still," she pleaded.

He listened, like the obedient little soldier he was and moved his hand away.

"No. Go back," I commanded.

Santos' shadow loomed over me, and I felt his stare behind my shoulder as he watched my phone.

He made a circle on her clit, and she whined and thrashed. Mateo thrusted harder and she sobbed something unintelligible that wasn't English or Spanish until she came down from her climax.

I shut the call off.

I didn't feel good about lying to her, but if I had told her the truth, she would have tried to stop me. Santos smelled my bullshit the minute I opened my mouth to tell her there was an issue that needed dealing with out here, but he didn't call me out. Instead he hopped along for the ride, probably hoping to catch a glimpse of the shitshow that was coming. I had one reason and one reason only for coming here.

"Let them back in," I told Santos, crossing my hands over the table and cracking my knuckles anxiously.

I did not want to fucking be dealing with this, but I had to. What was meant to be a trip to Cove City, ended up being a stay at the Diablos Locos compound in Grimm's Reach. This was where all of our members were taking residence ever since the Los Muertos attack on the high-rise.

No one felt safe going back.

I didn't blame them.

So here I was, using César's church room to conduct a half-ass Black Crow Brotherhood meeting with our members. They filed back in slowly, too many bodies in the small room and these were only the members who were privy to decisions we made, not just any soldier

I was anxious.

But this had been coming, I knew it from the moment she walked back into my life. I'd just been pretending like there wasn't a countdown above my head the entire time. It was now flashing zero.

Time was up.

"Zerkos!" Ethan yelled, hair still wet from a shower.

He greeted Santos with a bear hug, not giving much notice to the change in his face. I embraced Ethan, slapping him hard on the back and Fletcher followed behind, hooting and making animal noises as he bounced on his toes and pushed his way into the room.

"It's good to see you both." I nodded as they made their way in the room.

The rest of our men gathered in, taking seats where they found them. The remainder stood shoulder to shoulder as they waited for me to address them. The last four months had been nothing short of a fuckstorm, but the Black Crows could rebuild from the ruins, they deserved that. I just wasn't sure if I was the one who could stack those bricks anymore.

"This compound is cozy and all boss, but people are ready to go home. Wherever that is. We've been in limbo for too long now and we need a purpose. We need to take out the assholes who hurt our families," Fletcher spoke first, nodding to Santos when he said family.

He was just now back at a hundred percent, and if I were him, I'd want blood too. We needed more than that if we were going to go after the Bratvas. We'd need everything we had and more.

"Everything's wrong right now. I know that," I started, getting the attention of all the men in the room. "I'm gonna do whatever it takes to make sure every ounce of blood gets paid back in double."

"Dez has turned some Crows against you. They don't whisper loud enough for us to know who they are, but we've all heard the whispers, Zerkos." He used the nickname the city knew me by.

The name of the man I was before she came back to me.

Men began to talk over each other, but they were all practically saying the same thing.

They were worried. They had more than enough proof that Dezmond

Archer Junior was now working with the Bratvas to get payback for Sokolov's daughter's face. We also never gave the other daughter back. Not our fault for lack of trying though, apparently she didn't want to go home.

Daddy had done enough damage that the Diablo's compound was cozier than a Bratva penthouse with all the fixins.

And now we had a major target on our back. Our rat problem became a traitor problem and we were down quite a few soldiers. Permanently. The attack on the high-rise killed too many of our people. Out of those who came out unscathed, quite a few decided to leave the life.

Who could blame them?

Not knowing which day was going to be your last and learning to be fine with that was a skill in itself.

Not something either nature or nurture could prepare you for. It was something that was burned into you with the flames of time. For Celia that was a cattle brand in her father's hand. For me it was a black dog tag and all the men I once watched die in the name of freedom.

"We're not ready to attack them head on right now." The second the words left my mouth a chorus of disappointment rang out from half the room while the other chimed in louder to my defense.

We were already divided.

What was I holding on for?

Like a kid who wouldn't share a toy even though he was done playing with it.

Except the Crows weren't a toy and these were people's lives at stake.

Santos stuck his index and middle finger in his mouth and whistled loudly, quieting the room.

"We wiped the floor with Los Muertos, why can't we do the same with the Bratvas?" Bruno, one of our heavier hitters asked.

"It's not that simple. Los Muertos wasn't even half the amount of soldiers as I would expect the Russians to have. They were distracted, the Russian's are waiting for us. Not to mention, we had over a hundred Diablos holding our hands on that fight."

"They won't help us again?" he asked.

Santos scoffed out a laugh.

"No. Los Muertos was a mutual problem. I'm not in any position to ask anything of any Diablo. They didn't fight that battle for us, they fought it for Celia."

Most of them still didn't know the full weight of the truth. They'd heard bits and pieces about how Celia wasn't just some random bitch in the trials, how we'd had history. They deserved the full weight of the truth, but they needed to prove they could be trusted. I could count the men in this room that deserved my unrequited loyalty with less than four fingers.

"Didn't we bleed enough for her?" It was Hughes who spoke next.

His face had the kind of coldness I hadn't seen from him in a long time. It made me realize I hadn't thought to ask what everyone had lost that day yet.

"It can't be now," I told them again. "Sokolov will have to wait. Until Celia has the full force of her army behind her, until she's the only person alive who can challenge the cártel throne, I can't—"

"I think you're too cunt-struck to see clearly Zerkos. Ever since you brought that bitch into our lives, it's been nothing but bloodshed. Either you do right by your people and use her to eliminate our target, or you lose the right to call yourself our leader." He stood up, nostrils flaring, and fists clenched tight.

Yeah.

There was a good chance he was working with Dezmond Rat Junior.

Fletcher stood, chest to chest against Hughes like he would have jumped to defend my honor. I didn't need that from him.

"Sit down Fletch." I stood myself. "He's not wrong."

Some voices gasped, the ones who had already been privy to the history between me and my girl. The ones who had overheard too much about just how deep the root of our problems stretched out.

"I *can't* be your leader anymore. The more I think about it, the more I realize it isn't right. How am I supposed to lead you when I'm following her?"

"You are?" Ethan asked.

"I am," I said without blinking. "She knows the game better than any of us, and I'd give my life for hers a million times over. I won't rush a revenge that I know she's calculating." I hardened my eyes at Hughes, knowing the fucker was going to take that juicy tidbit of information back to Dezmond.

Voices rang out over each other once again in confusion as my men tried to make sense of the news I'd just dumped on them.

"What does that mean for us? What about you?" Fletcher asked Santos.

"I go where she goes," he said, his eyes barely shifting to me. "Wherever he fucking goes too."

"Fuck," Ethan barked, taking in the seriousness of the situation.

The room dropped into complete silence.

"Me too." Fletcher looked up, brushing his red hair out of his face.

A few voices rang out with confusion, and he waved them off.

"I owe her my life, and if she's someone you consider following then I don't see why I can't do the same." He seemed so sure of himself.

"You don't even fucking speak spanish," Hughes shouted but Fletcher just shrugged.

"I'll learn. It's better than sticking around a lost cause with a rat for a boss." He was insinuating that if I wasn't the leader, Dezmond would certainly reap the opportunity.

He would, and he'd lead them all down a dangerous path, aligning them with our enemies who were really just waiting for the right opportunity to knock us down, wipe us all from the map. The idiots didn't see that. The Black Crows had taken money, power and opportunities from every major syndicate in Cove City. The thought that they'd align themselves back with us now that we were broken instead of using it as an opportunity to kill us off for good was laughable.

Then all hell broke loose, and the room suddenly became divided. They were choosing sides. Something I'd never asked them to do. Hughes stepped up to me, his chest pressed to mine and his nostrils flaring wildly. He was pissed, and I'd been so far up in my own bullshit I couldn't even figure out what it was that I'd done to piss him off.

It was a good thing I was stepping down.

Maybe I *wasn't* cut out for this shit.

Life was simpler when I was the one taking orders.

Ethan spread us apart before spit went flying everywhere from how hard the man was seething.

"Get the fuck out of here." Santos pointed to the door, with his gun in hand once the distinction of who would be aligning themselves with Hughes and Dez, and who would be coming to Mexico was decided.

To join the fucking cártel.

72

SANTOS

"Faster," I shouted at the remnants of traitors who scurried out of the compound.

It would be a game of speed now between us to recruit soldiers to our side, see how many men Ronan would want to take back home. Saying it was weird, not saying it was… well, wrong for one. It *was* home.

Because she was there.

I wasn't sure if the surreal part was that it was with her, or that I was finally getting to live in the place where my family came from. Reconnecting made you feel like an imposter somehow, like an outsider intruding in.

Which meant Kane and Zerkos were feeling a thousand times more weird about it, poor gringo-ass motherfuckers. I made a mental note to put some effort into checking in with them about all of these changes. Culture shock was a real fucking thing, and I wasn't even sure the last time I'd seen Mateo eat anything not seasoned with mayonaise.

"We should end this thing with Archer Jr. before it gets out of hand," I told Zerkos without even looking back at him, gun still pointed at absolutely nothing since the last of the Crow traitors had evacuated.

"Killing him won't end this beef with the Russians," he said, his jaw clenching tight, making me realize Archer was just a fly on his food.

He wasn't threatened.

That was a mistake. It was always the smallest bugs that left the worst bites.

"Killing him will stop it from getting worse. Stop the men that up until five minutes ago were considered our family for the last seven years from getting killed in the process too." I scowled, my anger rising to the surface.

"Do you all feel that way?" Ronan asked the room.

"He needs to die brother," Fletcher said plainly.

"Traitors don't get to live," was my only contribution.

The rest of the men in the room all gave their silent agreement.

"How do we find him?" Ronan asked, accepting the fact he couldn't declare he wasn't the boss anymore while still trying to hold authority over our men.

We were all equals now.

"If he's cozying up to the Bratvas then he's hiding out in all their spots too, he wouldn't stray far from their protection," Ethan answered.

"Is Sokolov's daughter still here?" I asked.

"Yup. Looks like she's real comfy too." He smirked.

"I'll go find her," I announced before turning on my heels and exiting the room.

She wasn't in the main area with the bar and all the pool tables. I took the stairs up, skipping one or two at a time until I got to the top before I realized I had no idea which room she'd be in. I wasn't gonna be barging in on any of these fuckers' privacy. I didn't have a death wish.

Well, I did. But being pulverized by a biker wasn't how I intended to go.

A prospect tumbled out of his room with one of the little club bunnies in tow. He practically jumped when he saw me, distancing himself from her and scratching his head suspiciously. I could use a dumbass right about now.

"Hey kid," I beckoned him over and his eyes jarred open anxiously.

"Uh... What's up?"

"You know where and who everyone is around here?" I asked him and he beamed with pride.

"You know it."

"I'm looking for a Russian, blonde hair, all legs. Where's her room?" I asked.

"I don't think I'm supposed to tell that kind of information to just anyone dude." He scratched the back of his head.

"I'm not just anyone, and that's *my* prisoner." I clutched his shirt in my fist and twisted it pulling him closer to me.

He scoffed.

The fucking kid scoffed in my goddamn face.

"Tell that shit to Ladrón cuz he's already pissed all over her." He freed himself from my grasp, and I wrapped my hand around his arm,

"Where the fuck is the girl?" I pulled my Glock out of my pants and pressed the barrel to his chin.

He was green as fuck.

He trembled, stuttering nonsense about how he didn't mean to offend me or some bullshit.

"I just need to know where the fucking Russian is. Point. Now." My patience was wearing thin and if I didn't come back with her, Ronan would be coming for her instead.

For everyone's sake it was probably better I handled interactions with other humans.

Ronan only had a soft spot for one person, and even his soft spot was full of spikes when it came to Celia Flores.

His finger shook as he raised it up and pointed to a shut door. I shoved him off of me, he stumbled back and fell before scurrying away on all fours and running down the stairs. Whatever, if the kid couldn't handle conflict, he definitely wasn't cut out for a motorcycle club.

I made my way to the door and tapped my knuckles.

"Yes?" she called from inside.

I sighed. I didn't like dealing with this bitch.

Maybe I was holding a grudge but she stabbed my girl with a fucking fork, not to mention the tracker on her arm was the entire reason Papa Sokolov was able to find the high-rise in the first place.

My jaw ticked at the thought, and I pushed the door open.

"Güera." She looked up from her book and scowled when she saw my face.

"I thought I was a free woman now." She had that look on her face like my presence was a bother to her.

I chuckled.

"You're a free woman when we tell you so. Your prison's changed, but not your circumstances. Maybe you give us a little more of what we need and we can consider your crimes paid for, Susana." I gestured my chin towards the hall, and she stood up with a dramatic sigh.

"From one entitled cock-bearer to the next." She clucked her tongue and walked in front of me as if she knew where she was going.

"Maybe it's the company you keep, you ever think about that?" I asked and she stopped in her tracks to look back at me.

"When you're born into this life as a woman, you don't get to choose your company. You go where the man with the most power points you to." She turned forward again and walked down the steps.

"And now that man is telling you to go that way." I pointed to the closed door where Ronan sat with our men.

"You're an irritating one, but you already know that don't you? Irritating men always do." She swung in and out of her accent so often I couldn't figure out if it was an act.

Like she knew it made her sound less innocent.

Innocence could be perceived as weakness.

It made sense.

I didn't change my expression, and I didn't acknowledge her little attempt to disarm me.

I wasn't the same man who entered that basement wondering how my own flesh and blood could stomach to hurt me. I was the man who came out of it.

And at my core, I knew it wasn't a me problem.

But maybe if I'd been stronger I could have saved Celia from all of the pain that was born in that basement.

Maybe the real torture would be living with that knowledge forever.

I opened the door and shoved her in. Ronan was leaning back on what was obviously César's chair, his feet propped up on the table. He was laughing about something with the guys who were still at his side, but the laughter cut short once Susana walked in.

"Bratva Princess," Ronan chided.

"Not anymore." She raised her eyebrows at him, but he just looked at her with disbelief. "You don't believe people can want to change?" she asked.

"I think violent people keep breeding violence," he told her.

"Was your father a violent man, Ronan Zerkos?" She crossed her arms over her chest with interest.

"No. He was a weak man. Cheated on his second wife too and ended up dying of cancer. Got what he deserved."

"Hmm." She sauntered over to him crossing one leg over the other. "So where does your violence breed from then, I wonder?" She leaned her elbows on the table and stuck her ass up too high in the air. She was wearing jean shorts and a tank top with the MC's logo on it. Maybe her goal was to try to seduce Zerkos into leaving her the fuck alone.

"None of your fucking business," he grit through his teeth leaning forward on the desk so that his face was just an inch away from hers. "Where do your people play?"

She slumped into the nearest chair, looking around the room and taking in the rest of the men who sat waiting for information with blank stares on their faces.

"You're signing my death warrant," she said, a bit of anger rising to the surface.

"Heard you were getting real comfy out here in Grimm fuck nowhere," he challenged her back. "Would be a shame if our enemies found out you were hiding here."

"What do you want, you son of a bitch?

"I want to kill my rat, that's it. But if a few Bratvas get in the way, they might have to go as well."

She let out a defeated sigh once she looked around the room.

"If he's under my father's protection you'll find him at Club Moscow, if he's just clutching his coat tails you'll find him with the lower crowd, at Vosk. I can't help you otherwise. I wasn't privy to every safehouse he kept."

Zerkos nodded over to Liam, one of Taylor's henchmen in the tech lab. He wrote down all the information and made his way out of the room to start researching.

"Now, forget me. Haven't we had enough of each other? Unless you mean to fuck me, please, get a hobby Ronan." She chuckled and stood from the seat, getting up without permission.

She was a gutsy bitch and it worked in her favor. Ronan let her leave, and no one seemed to mind.

"You're good with this?" I asked him.

"I think we milked Sokolov's daughter for all we could, let her live her miserable life in peace. If she's happy in the Diablos compound let's wash our hands of this mess and call it a win."

"And Dezmond?"

"Let's go into the city. Tonight." Zerkos rubbed the blond scruff growing on his chin before he pushed up from the chair and left the room.

Another night in the Diablos Locos compound, meant another night drinking to forget we were away from our girl. I would have rather killed a man instead of getting belligerent and coming into my hands to forget the only thing I cared about was south of the border, probably still getting railed by Mateo Kane.

Did she miss me like I missed her?

Doubtful.

All I ever did was say the wrong things, all I ever did was underestimate her.

I still couldn't figure out why she wanted me around. The more I dwelled on it the more I went down a dark spiral of self-loathing. Fuck I needed out of it. I kept bouncing around from desperately wanting to be worthy of her to hating myself because I knew I could never be.

"You good?" Zerkos asked and I stopped in my tracks, realizing I was anxiously pacing back and forth in the small conference room.

"Yeah, I...Uh...I need some air." I nodded at him and pulled my phone out, dialing the number and holding my breath while I waited with a heart full of hope.

The video-call connected on the first ring.

"Hey," she said, all breathy like she was just now finishing up the little scene we'd watched her and Mateo entwined in.

"Hey," I said shakily as I walked out of the farmhouse and sat down on the porch swing.

She wrapped herself up in a blanket and found a chair to cocoon herself in.

"Weird being away from each other, right?" she asked like she knew exactly what I was feeling.

I didn't care what anyone else said.

There was no trauma like shared trauma.

And there was no shared trauma like watching the person you loved go through something you wished you could prevent.

We were the same side of the coin printed on both ends.

Her and I...

We'd always have violent images of each other's pain painted on the back of our eyelids every time we closed our eyes to go to sleep.

Was I grateful?

No, I wasn't fucking grateful.

But had Guillermo turned me into mincemeat any further, I didn't think she'd be looking at me the way she was right now. I was ugly now, but I was, at least, still within the threshold of "ugly enough to feel sorry for."

"Ronan quit the Crows." I wasn't sure why I told her instead of letting him tell her.

I just wanted to talk to her, and I didn't want to deal with the silence. Sometimes I called her and just stared at her face. She was okay with that too. She would just breathe and awkwardly laugh every now and then while waiting for me to say anything at all.

"What?" Her eyebrows furrowed harder than I'd ever seen before.

"I probably should have let him tell you that. I guess that was my way of telling you that I did too."

"Wait, what the fuck are you talking about?"

"I mean, I guess it's not that we quit the Crows, I guess really the Crows are done. We'll be bringing some men back with us." I corrected myself.

"This is crazy, what happened?"

I tried giving her as much clarification as I could, going over the meeting and explaining in detail everything that had happened the last few days while we'd been in Grimm's Reach.

"I never intended for either of you to have to pick between me and the Crows," she said, seeming deflated.

"You didn't. We made choices on our own. This wasn't on you. Okay?"

"Okay," she whispered.

"Morena," I started. "When we come home. I want to do things differently. I want to give you the love you deserve." I forced the words out before I turned into a chickenshit and took them back.

"No," she said, piercing through my heart. "I don't believe in starting over. We're fine building from what we already have. I just wish you could see that too."

"I wish I had your perspective on things," I told her, and she shrugged.

"Doin' anything dangerous tonight?" she asked with a teasing tone.

"On the Diablos compound? Babe you must be out of your mind," I joked, keeping our plans from Dezmond off of a recorded line.

We'd tell her when we got home.

Prison was worse than death for a relationship.

People could say whatever they wanted but at the end of the day, nobody waited. I'd seen plenty of my tío's lose their families in a cell for Los Muertos.

Time was a fickle bitch.

"Be good. Come home in one piece, okay Santito?" She sounded sweet but I knew it was a command.

"Yes, reina." I smirked, hanging up the video chat and sighing out loud.

73

MATEO

"Close your fucking eyes pendejo," she chastised, pushing my back and forcing me to stumble forward.

"I don't like surprises, sunshine," I warned her.

"It's a good one, I promise."

I sighed and closed my eyes, letting her guide me through the villa.

"It better not be a fucking dog. I'm not letting the three of you rope me into taking care of some puppy."

She laughed so abruptly it came out as a snort and I couldn't help but turn towards her to admire how cute she could fucking be.

"A dog? I'm not much of a dog person," she confessed, still finding amusement in it all.

I raised my eyebrow suspiciously at her, unsure if I was buying whatever she was trying to sell me here. And then I took in the room we were standing in. A beautiful white grand piano stood in the center, all its glory on display. Different types of guitars hung on the wall and an assortment of string instruments were propped on their stands.

The cello grabbed my attention. It wasn't my ancient relic but it looked like she did a damn good job of finding something that was as close to it as possible. I could still smell the wood polish on its face, letting me know it was likely something custom made.

"Was I out of line?" she asked, the concern in her voice brought me back to reality, letting me know I had yet to even give her a reaction.

"This is all for me?" I asked, my mouth still agape and my shock clearly evident.

"No, I'm hiring a mariachi band and giving them all the wrong instruments to see how it goes, and I wanted your feedback." She gave me a sarcastic smirk and nudged me on the side with her elbow.

"It's too much," I told her, knowing damn well we'd be using whatever funds were left of the Black Crow Brotherhood to pay for funerals and medical costs. She was in every way, providing for us here.

Her smile deflated.

"I just mean, you didn't have to." I rushed to defend my words, realizing I was hurting her more by not just being grateful like I should have been. "No one's ever given me a gift like this, sunshine."

"I want to give you everything," she said with a hurt look on her face.

"I think it's supposed to be me that gives you everything," I told her.

"Why? Because you're a man and I'm a weak little woman who can't provide for you? Surprise Mateo, I have more money than I'll ever be able to spend in this lifetime, and the next five lifetimes. Let me take care of us." She was all sincerity, even her sharp edges had softened somehow.

It filled me up with a sense of pride that I could get this side of her when no one else could.

I smiled, making her frown. "That's not it at all, Celia," I said, rubbing my hands up and down her bare arms.

She rarely wore sleeves down here, and I was a fan of how easy it was to feel her flesh under mine.

"You think I feel emasculated by the thought of you giving me things?" I scoffed, alarming her with my reaction. "Sunshine, I'd lick the dirt off your feet if it were the only meal you'd allow me to have, and I'd still say thank you. There is absolutely nothing that I or you could do that would make me feel like less of a man because, at the end of the day, I got you. But I'm still allowed to want to give you everything you deserve."

She reached her hand up and cupped my face. "You've already given me everything I deserve."

I shook my head at her.

"We've done nothing but cause you pain. I worry once the shock of everything fades, you'll snap back to reality and catch on to what a huge mistake all of this was. You'll pick Ronan once and for all and tell the rest of us to fuck off." I hadn't meant to blurt it out, I hadn't meant to be so honest, but every time she said shit like that it just felt like a lie.

Waste of space. My mother's words still rang out loudly in my mind.

"I wish you saw yourself as clearly as I see you." She shook her head, moving her hands to my chest where she flattened her palms against me. "You ever wonder if this pain is maybe part of what I deserve as well? I've done a lot of bad things in my life, there's only so many protection candles a bitch can light. Santa Muerte's waiting for me too, you know?"

"Don't fucking say that shit, because I'll fight her to keep you with me," I gritted out, pulling her against me tight.

"You can't fight Death, mi amor. She comes for us all." She caressed her skin against mine, but I gripped her wrist in my hand and kept it from moving.

"Stop it," I told her, not fighting the anger bubbling in my chest.

"Then don't say stupid things about me choosing Ronan." She frowned, but even without her smile she was so fucking stunning I had to remind myself to breathe.

"Can you blame a guy for being insecure? You've known him practically your whole life. And Santos has a fifteen year head start on me. Sometimes I wonder why I'm even around."

"Really?" she asked, sounding surprised. "You're the fucking glue Mateo. You keep us all together. Our family, it wouldn't feel right without you. I wouldn't feel right without you," she told me with a sobering expression on her face.

"And why's that sunshine?" I asked.

"Because you showed me that love doesn't have to be painful." She leaned close and pressed her lips against mine.

I groaned, throwing my head back.

"Don't do this to me. I can't keep calling those fuckers every time I wanna hear you scream just because they decided to leave." I whined and she smiled.

"Technically, you should have gone too but I agreed to keep you."

"Wait..." I pieced together all the fucking clues. "Am I the fucking goldendoodle?" I asked her, and she choked out a laugh.

"Leave me out of this." She pressed her lips against mine once again, but I pulled her back by the shoulders.

"Sunshine," I warned her, and she pulled her lips between her teeth and bit them like she was holding back a smile.

"How about we do something that doesn't involve the others?"

Her hands traveled down to my dick and her small hands gripped firmly around the fabric of my pants. Just the light touch of her fingers forced my cock to awaken under her control.

I groaned again and she lowered down to her knees.

This was shaky territory.

"Celia," I warned as she pulled me from my pants, already hard and precum glistening at the tip of my cock.

She took a breath to prepare herself, but she was trembling at just the proximity. It wasn't right. I picked her up and brought her to my chest before sitting us both down onto the chair in her bedroom, wrapping my arms around her and pulling her into my chest.

She shook silently while I ran my fingers through her hair.

"I'm not broken!" she cried out like she was trying to prove it to herself.

"I never said you were."

"Then why does it feel like I am?" A pitiful noise left the depths of her chest as she poured her soul out into salty droplets over me.

"Because whether or not you want to admit it, he took something from you that you wouldn't have given freely. Regardless of your reason for doing it. Regardless of the fact that it might have been your decision to do it at all."

"It's okay to not be okay, Celia. Perfection isn't expected of you at all times."

"He expected it," she said, a bit of nervousness peeking out from behind the curtain.

She meant her father, I wasn't stupid.

"He's dead now," I reminded her.

A few moments passed before she nodded.

"Thank you," she said, looking up at me and blinking the droplets of tears from her eyelashes.

"I love you, sunshine." I caressed her face.

"It helps when you remind me." She smiled and it stretched up into the scar across her cheek.

I felt so much anger when I looked at it, but I was learning to not blame myself for the things I couldn't prevent. Wallowing in guilt over pain that was dealt to her wasn't fair of me. All she was asking of me was to love her, that I could do.

"I'll keep doing it at every chance I get."

74

RONAN

Dezmond Archer Junior would die tonight. Preferably with my bare hands, but if I had to use a weapon, I'd consider that a solid kill too. There was no way around it, the fates had pulled his cards and they'd announced his end. My brothers had called it, and I had agreed.

There was a part of me that still felt the aching pain of killing someone I considered my own family. Maybe I owed him the decency of a fair fight because of our shared history. Because he was once my brother too. But the stupid fucker's ambition was the very reason we had to bury some of our best men this year.

There was no going back anymore.

The Crows were done but vengeance went further than just a name. We were reaping because he had sowed.

We'd hounded Susana enough to get a few names from her. We paid off some girls she knew to help us get some intel, so we could figure out exactly where we could find Dezmond tonight. It wasn't hard. Just like she said, the fucker was there at Vosk, sitting in a VIP booth with some paid escorts pretending to enjoy his company while drinking some top shelf alcohol that was likely being put on Sokolov's tab.

"Hey sweetheart, go ask your friends to clear the booth out." I slipped some cash into the hand of a nearby girl and nodded over to Dezmond's booth.

She squeezed into the booth and whispered into the closest girl's ear. A game of telephone passed around and soon every girl was looking at each other with wide eyes and scurrying from the table.

Dezmond was too drunk to notice.

Santos shuffled into the booth next to him and Fletcher came in from the other side. I squeezed in, sitting across from the bastard who dared break bread with me while he was plotting to take me down. I pulled my gun out and placed the Glock directly in front of me, the barrel pointed his way but the piece itself was still laying on its side on the table.

He could have reached for it.

I wasn't afraid of him.

"S-shit," he stuttered out, his eyes blinking in an uncoordinated way that let me know he was shitcanned.

"That's the problem about thinking you've got friends in high places isn't it brother? They can't seem to see you from where they're perched."

His fear was savorable, but this place was too full. We needed to get him out of here and we needed to do it without making a scene.

"Zerkos, let's talk this out like men," he slurred, trying to make peace far too late in the game.

"Where's Hughes?" I asked him, wondering if we needed to be on the lookout.

A few of our men were lurking in the corners trying to prevent some sort of surprise or sneak attack.

"Waiting for me to give the signal to report the Diablos Locos compound for some serious illegal activity to the FBI. The raid would go down within the next twenty-four hours, maybe just enough time for you all to scatter the fuck out of here and leave Cove City to the people who really own it." He sneered and I couldn't contain my laughter.

"You think you fucking own Cove City?" I asked, my amusement irritating him further.

"You think *you* do?" he asked, a bitter tone to his voice.

"No, Cove City is a goddess. She can't be tamed by men like us. The sooner you learn that, the better off you'll be, rat."

"I thought you came here to kill me," he snarled.

"*They* would love that." I nodded to my brothers who didn't hide the bloodthirsty look from their faces. "So give me a fucking reason you dirty fucking traitor." I picked the gun up and slid it under the table, switching the safety off.

His eyes widened further than I thought possible.

"Zerkos, you don't wanna do this. We're in public. They'll put you in prison for life." He raised his hands up defensively, his face glistened with sweat as he tried to reason with me by tossing out some legal bullshit that definitely didn't apply to me.

You either lived within the boundaries of the law or you didn't.

I didn't.

He'd somehow forgotten that.

"Then make it easy on me, *brother*." My nostrils flared. "Get the fuck up." I moved the gun under the table, pressing the barrel to his thigh as Santos slid out of the booth.

In a dark alley behind the club we each took turns letting our fists pay back all the pain he'd brought the Crows. Blow after blow of our hands and feet, crunching his bones felt better than I had expected. He didn't fight it, he knew he was a prisoner to the game. He thrashed and fought back even as we stuffed him into the trunk. Then we drove back to the Diablos Locos compound. There was a special entrance we were supposed to use so that the lower tiered members didn't see us dragging someone off to their untimely death.

Best not to have witnesses we couldn't fully trust.

"Zerkos I'm telling you, if there's a single drop of blood stained on my nice oak floors when I get home you're gonna be paying for the remodel from your own pocket. Not my sister's pocket...yours," César declared from the phone as I tried to get instructions on how to get inside his goddamn torture cellar.

This motorcycle compound was a labyrinth and apparently the guy was set on putting up a few more buildings like some sort of fucking commune.

"This seems like a lot of fucking work just to get a prisoner locked up, you need a better system, Villalobos." I'm pretty sure he growled into the phone but then turned to someone near him to bark out an order before returning to the line.

"Why is Ladrón not helping you with this shit?" he asked.

"He's *indisposed*." I cleared my throat, not mentioning the Bratva heir shacking up with one of his officers.

César sighed like he knew his men well enough to not need an explanation.

"I'm gonna need you to leave my wine cellar as you found it, got it?"

"Yeah, yeah." I answered before hanging up the phone and tucking it back into my pockets.

I wasn't dressed for this.

But were you ever dressed for slow and painful murder?

The image of my girl, dirty and covered in blood in that leather dress climbing out of that basement flashed through my mind.

She was always dressed for murder. I wanted to give her my protection but the reality was, my girl looked good dripping in the blood of her enemies, she looked even better when she was the one bleeding them out.

I got the code right on the third try and the room opened up, bright fluorescent lights shone down a concrete wall covered with chains and just next to it was a table full of torture devices. I yanked Dez's ankle dragging him into the room behind me, he groaned, still delirious from the beating he received outside the nightclub from us.

I stretched my fingers out, feeling the burn on the torn skin of my knuckles and smiling and recollecting the satisfying crunching sound of his cheek against my fist.

"Get him hooked up to the wall," I commanded Santos and Fletcher before doubling back with the realization I wasn't anyone's leader anymore.

"Never mind, I got it."

"It's all good boss," Fletcher said, shaking his head like he understood.

The two of them worked quickly, getting Dezmond chained to the wall while he was still wavering back and forth out of consciousness from the multiple head injuries he was now suffering.

"Where's Ethan?" I asked.

"He went with Isaac and Smith to debrief the rest of our men, draw the line in the sand, and figure out who's going where," Fletcher explained.

"I didn't want it to come to this." I scratched the back of my head with a sigh.

"It's a good thing, you'll see that," Santos said, turning towards me. "Our people were already divided, if it was this easy to split off."

"They're split because... they weren't yours to begin with," Dezmond slurred, his head lifting up as he fought his way back to lucidity.

I swung my fist against his face, and it smacked against the concrete wall before ricocheting back down.

"Lights out!" Fletcher whooped.

Santos pulled the smelling salts from his pocket and stuck them in front of his face to wake him back up. Blood was pouring out of his nose violently and there was barely any light left in his eyes.

It wasn't fun when they'd already mentally checked out.

"What's the matter Dez? Is this not how Daddy's plan was supposed to go?" I tilted my chin and hardened my eyes at him waiting for the light of recognition to hit his face.

It didn't.

He was too out of it.

"My father knew you were all unraveling over the Mexican whore—" He didn't get a chance to finish.

I threw my fist again. The impact from the collision of his head against the concrete wall behind him made a deafening sound. Santos rolled his eyes at me and pulled out the smelling salts again to wake the bastard up.

"Good thing we don't need intel from him. You've practically beat him stupid."

I gave him a fraction of a smile. He nodded, and it tore through my heart. I missed our friendship. I spent a lot of time wondering how we'd ever get back to how things were, and it made me wonder if he did too.

She was right, she wasn't supposed to choose. Choosing would have been something she did to us, and this right here, this was the product of my own issues, my insecurities. She loved all three of us... and my problem was that he had loved her back the entire time?

Fuck. Was I the asshole here?

Was it up to me to repair the damage?

We bonded best through violence, maybe this was the closest thing to an olive branch we could get between us.

Dezmond woke up again, moaning a pained sound.

"I'm sorry, you were saying something?" I chuckled, cracking my neck on both sides.

Our captive spit a bloody wad onto the ground.

"He drew up the blueprint for the Crows, they were *his* men first. This should have all been his. It should have been mine," Dezmond yelled, the true source of his rage showing its ugly head and letting us know jealousy was her name.

"Maybe so, and then he opened his mouth about *our* Mexican whore and found himself on the wrong side of my barrel. Then I fucked her with said barrel while he bled out and his corpse went cold." Santos pulled his Glock out of his pants and shoved it under Dez's chin, forcing his head into an uncomfortable position. "Actually, I think it was this one right here."

He pulled the gun back and licked the rim of it before pressing it back onto his flesh.

"Your traitor piece of shit of a father is dead and gone, but my gun still tastes like her."

I laughed, remembering just how unhinged Santos could get when he was the one holding our enemies down.

"Quit playin' with your food Álvarez, if we got all we need from him, let's end this and go home to our woman." I clapped him on the shoulder.

"Yeah, run back south of the border to your little bitch. You think he doesn't know who she is? Why do you think he sold her twice? Why risk killing her when he can just keep selling her and hope someone else will?" He had the audacity to fucking laugh.

Santos smacked his jaw with the butt end of the Glock and his jaw broke, staying lodged on the left side of his face. He wailed, unable to open his mouth to actually speak again.

"Actually, I like him this way," I said, extending my hand for the gun.

I fired one in each kneecap without waiting.

His scream became a feral plea, nonsensical and completely unintelligible.

"I wonder if we can make him scream so hard it'll pop back into place?" Santos asked and Fletcher laughed.

"Y'all are sick motherfuckers."

"I'm not gonna lie, I forgot you were here brother. If this is too much for you..." Santos warned him, but he waved him off, crossing his arms to show he'd be staying put and watching the show till its end. "Let's cut his toes off and mail them to Sokolov," Santos said, turning back to me.

I hadn't seen a grin that big on his face in the last decade.

I wondered if it had something to do with me saying *our* woman.

I nodded my approval and while he stepped over to the table to pick out which tools were the right one for the job, I approached Dezmond Archer Junior. With a quick jab I knocked the end of my gun onto the dislodged side of his jaw, forcing it back in place with a crunch. The feral, animalistic type of scream that came from the depths of his soul tugged at the little bit of love I still had left for the man standing in front of me as I watched the piss drip down his legs.

"What did he promise you? How long had the two of you been working with the Bratvas?" I needed to know, needed to understand how long I'd had rats scurrying under me while feeding them the same food I fed my family at the same goddamn table.

"You better... kill me...I'm not telling you... shit." He struggled to get the words out.

I guess the guy didn't quite grasp the concept of torture. There was nothing threatening about a man that had already been tied up and beaten beyond recognition.

"Did he promise you the Crows? That everything would go back to the way it was before the three of us took over the city your father once thought would be his?"

He didn't answer.

"Oh shit, Santos. I think he promised him more." I laughed, rubbing my hands together and stepping back to let Álvarez get to work.

He snapped the scissor-like pliers open and shut in front of Archer Junior's face. He flinched, trying to keep a hardened face but it was evident that he wasn't brought up to tolerate this life, even if his father had raised him adjacent to it.

"Did he promise you his ugly daughter?" Santos asked with a hushed voice.

His eyes widened, giving him away before he fixed his expression into a pained scowl once more.

"Oof, that's a rough one. You'll need a paper bag to stomach giving it to her after what Celia did to her face." He laughed at our captive, a man we still called brother by habit.

"Not as ugly… as you," he said through labored breaths, reminding Santos that his face was different now too.

I pulled my tactical blade from its sheath in the holster and plunged it straight into his cheek, pulling it out and doing the same to his other side. He shrieked a louder sound than I had ever heard coming from a Prisoner of War. What we were doing to Archer didn't even compare to what we put those fuckers through.

But even though my rage was driving the wheel, in the back of my mind all I could see were the flashes of memories, the last seven years fighting side by side with him and his father. The bridges we built together, the army we raised out of nothing to fight for our cause.

Maybe I owed him a better death.

Santos saw the look in my eyes and exhaled in defeat like he knew I was about to cut the fun short.

I pulled my own Glock out and pressed it to his head.

"Wait, hold on. It's not right." Santos stepped forward before I went in for the final blow.

"What?

"He hurt her too," he said before walking to the table and switching the pliers he was going to use to cut his toes off for some smaller ones. "He owes her too."

I raised my eyebrows at him suspiciously while he squeezed Archer

Junior's jaw until it pried open and he sobbed out from pain, blood dripping out with his drool.

"I just gotta get something real quick."

Archer shook violently while sobbing unintelligible sounds, screeching an awful noise every time Santos yanked a tooth out from his mouth. After collecting a handful, he stuck the bones in his back pocket.

Bloody saliva dripped onto the floor from his mouth, and he mumbled painfully.

"We had some good times didn't we, brother?" Santos gave him a crooked grin, tapping his cheek a few times with the palm of his hand before he stepped back to let me put him out of his misery.

"Here's the bigger secret I want to let you in on before I put you under." I leaned in real close and whispered in his ear, "If you had just waited, you would have had it all. I would have stepped down and given it all to you without any bloodshed. Now our family is divided and at least half of them will die fighting for what they think is right." It was a sad realization, but it was just the way things went.

Blood had been spilled and now it would continue to do so until one side stopped fighting back or died.

That's the way war went.

75

CELIA

I wanted to drive to the airport myself to pick up my guys, but none of my officers would allow it. Here I was, a supposed queen, somehow still fucking being told what to do by men. I hated admitting it but they weren't wrong. It was a matter of security and I couldn't make impulsive and risky decisions now that my tío knew I was readying for war.

The man was brash enough to try to execute a half-cocked attack just to have the element of surprise over me.

It wouldn't matter. What he didn't realize was that he'd already prepared me for this.

I was always expecting him. I had been for the last twelve years. Always looking over my shoulders, paying attention to my surroundings, and memorizing stranger's faces. Who had I seen before, and where.

It was easy to fall into paranoid thinking, but at the end of the day my tío never let me down, he always came for me. It was almost comforting every time it happened.

This would be the last time.

So I caved and let Mateo ride with me to the airport, along with the security detail car that followed behind. All capable and trustworthy soldiers hand-picked by Dominico himself and then vetted extensively by Santos before sending them over to Taylor for probing. She'd dug up more information on each of them than I thought was even possible, from ex-girlfriends to which toys they preferred on the playground in primary school.

Overkill, but apparently necessary.

I opened the door of the car but before I could fully step out I felt a hand on my shoulder.

"Jefa, please get b—"

"Rodrigo, right?" Mateo cut in, peeling one of my guard's fingers off my shoulder. "You seem like a nice guy, but if you ever put your hands on her again it'll be the last time you use them."

Down boy, but he *was* cute when he went into rottweiler mode.

"I-I'm just trying to do my job. I was told to keep her s—"

"Rodrigo, I'm an ex-Navy Seal. I think she's pretty safe with me, don't you?" He spoke with the smooth, calculated tone he got before he went borderline psychotic.

I smirked, some weird primal part of me enjoyed the dick measuring contest Mateo was starting.

My guy however looked uncomfortable and anxious, and I didn't need any rumors about me being hard to work for. Being a woman was a disadvantage on its own.

"Está bien Rodrigo." I waved him off and gave him a look that was enough to tell him to get back to his own car. "Don't scare my men," I told Mateo playfully.

He shut the door behind me before pressing me against it, running his hand up the back of my leg, he let out a throaty growl.

"I liked you in my T-shirts, but I like you even better in these clothes, sunshine," he whispered into my ear, goosebumps raising along the back of my neck as his fingers trailed along the hem of my mid-thigh length pencil skirt.

It was definitely more of Emory's style, but I needed to figure out a way to present myself in public if I was going to be taken seriously. The raggedy band T-shirts and ripped jeans weren't going to cut it anymore.

My papá always donned the finest suits.

I would do the same.

"I said, don't scare my men, Mateo," I repeated myself, giving him my coldest look.

"They don't get to touch you," he warned me.

"I thought you said you liked watching me come?" I challenged, knowing damn well that wasn't what he had meant.

His hands pressed against the car, boxing me in with his arms as he pushed himself closer to me, one foot planted between my legs.

"I'm suddenly finding we may need to reestablish some boundaries, sunshine."

"Oh?" I asked, biting my lip in an attempt to seem seductive knowing it probably looked nothing like I pictured it in my head.

"Yes." He lowered his forehead to mine.

"Name your terms, crazy boy." I batted my eyelashes, looking up at him through them.

"No one else touches you but us."

"And in return, I get?" I teased.

His nostrils flared.

"No one else touches you but us," he repeated as if it was also the answer to my own question.

"Fine. And if I break your rules?" I was having too much fun and since I wasn't allowed to go inside the airport this was the best entertainment I'd be getting.

"Then I'll punish them, cut their fingers off and hang them around their necks. Keep them around as an example so everyone else knows that you are untouchable in every goddamn way." He was speaking so close to my ear that every word pebbled my skin on contact.

"What about me?" I breathed out.

"It's me who'll punish you, flower." His voice came from behind Mateo, who freed me from the cage of his arms at the sound of Ronan's threat.

"Hi," I said with my best sheepish impression.

"Don't 'hi' me when I just heard you say what I think you said." Mateo moved out of the way to let Ronan take his place.

Santos rolled his eyes and walked towards the trunk, throwing all of their bags into it. Ronan gripped my chin between his fingers and pulled my gaze back towards him.

"Care to repeat yourself?" There was no amusement in his expression, but I wanted to poke the bear further, see how wild I could really make him.

"I think not." I shook my head with a smile, knowing that Ronan Zerkos was truly the only man alive who could challenge me like this.

Maybe Santos when he got into that mood.

He scoffed, pulling my chin up higher to give me a kiss.

I moaned into his mouth, missing the way we could wrap around each other so perfectly.

"I'm no longer an injured man. Behave or I'll make you regret it," he threatened before pulling me away from the car and opening the door to the back for me to get in.

Santos grabbed me by the wrist and pulled me into an embrace, stamping a kiss to the side of my face before letting me go. He climbed into the back, and I followed, seeing Mateo already comfortably settled into the passenger seat.

How had I been alone for so long when now I felt so incomplete anytime I was apart from one of them? I'd done so well for myself as a solitary creature, caring for nothing and no one with only a goal to survive until the next day.

That wasn't living, and my tío would pay for wasting so much of my life forcing me to live that way.

"So?" I asked, my eyes meeting Ronan's in the rearview mirror before I looked over to Santos. "Did you deal with... whatever it was you were dealing with?" I asked them, playing along like Santos hadn't already told me the truth.

Their eyes met; Ronan grunted.

I looked back over to Santos who gave me a look that said he was grateful.

"Tell me everything," I insisted.

"The Crows have absolved." Santos spoke and Ronan exhaled loudly.

"Ronan, what the fuck?" I yelled, and he moved a hand from the wheel to scratch the back of his head.

"It's more complicated than what Álvarez is saying," he tried justifying.

"Then explain it better, payaso."

"We stepped down. The crows split in two... maybe three actually," Ronan explained some more without giving me any details.

"Ronan!" I slapped the back of his seat. "What the fuck are you doing?"

"I can't very well lead a criminal organization when I'm here with you, can I?" he asked.

It was a good point, one I hadn't stopped to think about yet which was exactly why he hadn't mentioned it until now, when he had already done it.

"Why didn't you let me in on this? Why wasn't this a decision you thought we could make together, between all of us?" I asked loudly, feeling myself getting angrier the more I thought about him throwing away everything he built for himself because of me.

He fucking laughed.

Laughed.

Mateo pinched the bridge of his nose, and it took everything to not crawl through the middle console to make my point clearer.

"Como?" I asked.

"I'm sorry darling, I just think it's funny that you'd think I'd let you in on a major decision regarding me spending the rest of my life with you, when the last time you had the chance you dropped the ball." His eyes met mine again with a coldness to them. "Completely," he added.

"Fuck." The memory of me leaving a suitcase full of money in our two-bedroom apartment while I drove away with a trunk full of cártel weapons haunted me still.

When you hurt the person you loved the most, you hurt yourself too.

I was plagued with nightmares of Santos' voice calling out to me from the dark telling me that I was going to destroy Ronan. I imagined his reaction for years, how he must have felt and looked when he read my note.

But I never actually asked.

I was afraid of actually knowing just the size of the damage I'd left behind.

"It was the right move, morena." Santos came to his defense, letting me know I was likely going to be fighting this one on my own if I wanted to ride into battle. "Our men were in limbo. Now they are free to choose where to go. Many will follow, soon Crows will be flying south to work for *you*."

"And the ones that don't?" I asked.

"That depends, quite a few have chosen to stay within the comforts of your brother's motorcycle club in Grimm's Reach. They'll make decent prospects out of them. Some are now floating in the abyss, ready to look for revenge over Dezmond Archer Junior," Ronan explained.

"You killed him," Mateo said, not a question so much as he was just confirming it.

"He was in deeper with the Bratvas than we thought," Ronan told him. "Leaving him alive wasn't a possibility. I weighed out all my options."

There was the faintest hint of regret in his tone. Killing someone you thought was family had to be hard, I was lucky to have gone thirty years as a Flores without experiencing it yet.

"That reminds me," Santos said, reaching down to the floorboard and grabbing his backpack. He fumbled around inside before pulling out a velvet pouch with a drawstring. "It's for you." He tossed it my way and I caught it just in time for it to look mildly cool.

I opened the velvet pouch, seeing the yellowish teeth clinking around in the bottom of the bag against each other. I let out a chesty laugh and pulled the strings shut.

"Is this?" I asked and he nodded.

"I pay attention." The smile was so faint on his face, but I could see the best parts of him fighting to come back to the surface.

"How romantic." I kissed his cheek, letting my lips linger against his skin. "I can't believe you brought this on a carry on." I laughed.

"They're not looking for teeth." He shrugged, "It's not illegal to carry them."

"What did we miss down here?" Ronan asked, changing the subject.

"There is a big fundraiser event that we will be sponsoring in El Palacio on Saturday. President Ramírez has demanded my presence. I need all three of you to come with me." I had already told Mateo so he had no input, but Santos and Ronan looked at each other with apprehension.

We'd had plenty of conversations about the politics behind the cártel, that the only way to claim my empire was to rule it from every angle. I needed to solidify my place in our world, make it so the Flores name held power once again.

"All three of us?" Ronan asked, raising an eyebrow up suspiciously.

"Is that a problem?" I crossed my arms, waiting for them to dare deny me.

"I mean you just plan to show up like, 'Hey, I'm running for office, here are my three boyfriends and expect them to elect you?"

I hated when he knew better than I did.

"I haven't figured out the logistics of it all, but I need all three of you there with me. It will make me feel more at ease," I told them.

This fundraiser was a way to reintroduce me to the world, let everyone who mattered know that the Flores Cártel was once again its rightful regime. Of course, only those who really mattered would know me for who I really was, everyone else would see Celia Flores, daughter of the prolific politician Rafael Flores. For all they knew I was coming home after studying abroad to follow in my father's footsteps, first a mayor, then a governor, and eventually a senator just like my papá.

This was my campaign announcement. This was also where the cártel would seal major agreements with the heaviest hitters in the country.

They'd have our protection, our guns, our drugs, we'd have their money. Because I had my family's fortune, the ledger, and the connections, I was able to attain everything my tío was promising, for much, much less.

A bargain anyone would be stupid to pass up.

It was also a trap. The fundraiser was sticky, sweet bait set out to lure my tío into our hands. He'd think we were unprepared, careless, and ready to celebrate. He would surely come for us. But we were more than ready, more than expecting him.

"What are you so nervous about?" Mateo asked with a laugh, like he couldn't believe I was scared of anything.

76

SANTOS

"She's worried they're gonna call her white-washed, gringa, Americana," I told them, she winced at the words I'd been hearing my entire life from the people who called me family.

Having parents who didn't teach you the language of your people, who didn't teach you about heritage or culture, that was a curse in itself. Celia was young when she lost her family. She didn't lose her language but with time she lost that piece of herself that belonged down here.

Now that she was on this side of the border again, her confidence had shattered. She was just as lost here as I was. That wasn't true. She had and she lost, I had never had it at all. And maybe it's true what they said, about better to never have it at all and shit. Because Celia looked like she was in pain, and mentally on the verge of losing what little grip she was holding on to.

She was carrying too much on her shoulders, and she refused to let anyone else bear the brunt of it for her. To take some of her load off.

"They aren't wrong," I told her and she scowled.

We'd finally arrived at the villa, and she was so pissed at me she practically opened the door before the car had come to a full stop. I grabbed her wrist, pulling her to me and slamming her against my chest.

"Let me go," she yelled, beating her other hand against my chest while my brothers got out of the car, confusion written all over their faces.

"What's the matter? Are you mad because I'm lying or are you mad because it's the truth?" I asked her.

"Fuck you! You don't know what it's like." She was crying now, and even though it wasn't my intention to hurt her, I needed her to know she wasn't alone in feeling this way.

"Don't you think I feel it too? Lost out here, because it *should* be home, but it's never been *my* home? Don't you think they feel it as well?" I pointed to my brothers.

"Do you not want to be here?" she asked, her eyebrows furrowing heavily in the middle.

"Now when did I fucking say that, morena?"

"I think what he's trying to say is that it's okay for things to not feel right, to feel out of place here even though it was your home once. We'll make it home eventually, together. We can belong here too," Mateo said.

"He's right. I am afraid of what they'll think of me," she admitted.

"Fuck them," Ronan finally spoke. "It doesn't matter what they think of you. At the end of the day they will still come begging for what you have to offer," he reassured her. "You're enough."

She exhaled and turned on her heels, stepping towards the villa. We followed behind and suddenly she stopped and faced me, sticking her pointer finger in my face, her nostrils flaring hard.

"Call me white-washed again and I'll add your teeth to my collection, querido."

I knew I had crossed a line, but she needed to understand she wasn't alone in these feelings. I'd been in her place my entire life, pushed into a corner by my family because my only parent who spoke spanish failed to teach it to me. The other didn't give a shit if I was connected to my culture and eventually I found myself a grown man, too afraid to learn something new for myself.

"Maybe we should hire a tutor?" I asked my brothers, as we made our way inside the villa.

Mateo agreed and Ronan shrugged like he didn't give a shit either way.

"Whatever you guys think is easier for you," he said, and I frowned.

"What? You're too good to learn the language of the country you're going to be living in?" I asked, not hiding the snark in my tone.

Celia laughed from the front and stopped in her tracks again.

"You mean they don't know?" she asked him.

"Know what?" I demanded.

She laughed harder, a borderline unhinged sort of cackle, and she slapped her hands down onto her thighs in disbelief.

"He fucking speaks spanish." She could barely get it out, she was laughing so hard.

"What?" I asked, not hiding my outrage.

How the fuck I managed to know an asshole for half my goddamn life and not know he spoke an entire other language was beyond me. Ronan shrugged and walked on in front of us like he didn't want to answer any questions. Mateo looked just as stunned as me but not at all pissed off. Celia sobered up from laughing to finally speak again.

"You think he would have survived a minute inside my house if he didn't learn spanish? Take note boys, these are the 'little things' women fall head over heels for." She winked and caught up to Ronan, lacing her fingers into his.

"What the fuck man?" Mateo asked, just as much confusion in his own expression.

"Did you know he spoke spanish?" I asked him.

"Now that I think about it, I remember him saying he had to fight to not get sent down to South America for a mission when we were in the Seals. I just never thought too hard about it, but it makes sense." Mateo scratched his head. "Barely fucking fair if you ask me, he was probably a kid when he learned it."

"He's always gonna be two steps ahead of us when it comes to her," I told him.

"It's not a competition," Mateo reminded me.

"But it could be, and it would be fun to lower him down a few pegs every now and then." I smirked.

He returned it.

"I kind of like how that sounds."

My phone buzzed and I pulled it open, a photo of Celia's tits filled my screen, Ronan's dick squeezed right in between them, the head of his cock just barely grazing her lips.

"How the fuck did they have time already?" Mateo said, astounded, running towards the stairs.

"I fucking told you man, we need to form an alliance." I laughed, following behind him.

We jogged through the villa, sliding on the tile floors until we reached her bedroom door and pushed it open, to find Ronan between her legs, his head buried in her cunt while she whimpered softly.

"I thought you weren't choosing, morena," I teased and her eyes found mine.

"Who said I chose anything? He just undressed me first," she said, moaning just as he ran his tongue up and down her slit.

"Spare me, I haven't been inside her in w—" She didn't let him finish, she pushed his head back down, bucking her hips against his face as she moaned and writhed around from pleasure.

I looked over to see Kane was already undressed.

"Are you coming?" she asked and my dick woke up like it had been personally summoned by her.

Ronan thrusted three fingers in and out of her while his mouth worked her into a frenzy. Her thighs clenched shut, squeezing his head and she cried out, her climax flooding out of her and coating the sheets.

She was fucking beautiful.

She could have anything she wanted.

And she wanted us.

There was nothing that made me worthy but suddenly I didn't care anymore, I was done fighting my own mind. Maybe instead of spending my life worried about what made me good enough for her I would just start working on *becoming* good enough to be hers.

"What do you want from us?" Mateo asked her.

She smirked, her chest heaving up and down as she came down from her orgasm.

"Te quiero," she said, like it was just that easy.

"There's three of us," I reminded her.

"And I want all three of you," she repeated, getting up on her knees.

Mateo climbed onto the bed, and she extended her hand out to me, pulling me close to her while I still stood on the floor. She reached for my belt, and I helped her undo my pants, pulling them down my thighs and letting my cock spring free from the confinement of the fabric.

She bit her lip. More nerves than seduction.

"Morena, you don't have to—"

"You don't get it, I want to. I have to," she told me, her eyes a little too shiny with emotion.

"Why?" I asked.

"Because if I can't, then he won. Then it means he *did* take something from me, and I just... I just can't let that happen."

"I'm sorry," I told her, her eyebrows scrunching in the middle.

"For what?" she asked.

"For not seeing it then, for not realizing *how* you needed me. I'm sorry I let you down. I won't fail you again," I told her, gripping a handful of her hair in my fist and pulling her to my cock.

Zerkos got off the bed and went rummaging through a dresser drawer for something. Her lips parted and I slid inside, feeling her hot mouth accepting me with ease. Her lips wrapped over her teeth, and she moved her head along with the guidance of my hand. Mateo positioned himself underneath her, grabbing her hips and guiding her down to his dick.

Each pump of his cock inside her vibrated from her mouth onto me as she moaned around my shaft. Her back teeth clinked over the metal bars of my Jacob's ladder, sending a jolt of pleasure up my spine and drawing my balls up higher.

Not yet. I told myself, slowing up on her movements and loosening my grip on her hair.

"Does that feel good? Is Mateo all the way inside you?" I asked.

She nodded and mumbled a response with my cock inside her mouth.

She had tears streaming down the side of her face, but she hadn't asked me to stop, and something told me she needed this for her own healing. I squeezed my grip around the hair on the base of her skull once more and pulled her to me, shoving myself as far down her throat as I could.

"Oh fuck." I breathed out just as her tongue swirled around one of the bars in my piercing. "Your mouth is perfect."

The bed dipped from Ronan's weight as he climbed onto it, opening a bottle of lube and squeezing it out onto his cock before letting it drip down to her ass.

"Are you ready for me, Flower?"

77

CELIA

I thought I was ready to answer but it wasn't his fingers inside me that I felt, preparing to open me up so that his cock could slide inside with ease. No, it was the head of his manhood, pushing against the tight barrier of my ass while Mateo made no effort to slow his methodical thrusts into me from below.

"Oh god, you're too much," I dropped Santos from my mouth in order to cry out just as he pressed his way in, bottoming out inside me.

I was so full. It was the kind of sensation that felt so unreal it seemed wrong, feeling both their lengths sliding in and out of me, stretching me to the brim and rubbing against each other through a thin barrier of skin.

"Oh God,"I cried out again just as Santos gripped the back of my hair once again.

"God isn't the one filling up all your holes right now, Morena," he reminded me, pulling my face towards him so that he could use it for his own pleasure. "Should I stop?" he asked just low enough for me to hear, making me realize I'd closed my eyes again.

I shook my head side to side and blinked up at him.

If I stayed looking at them, they kept me grounded. Kept me from glimpsing into the memories I wanted to stay locked tight in the vault inside my head. Because I knew that when I looked up it wasn't the face of a monster that I would see, it was the face of someone who loved me. The face of someone who did whatever he could to keep me safe, and I did the same for him. That's what our scars meant, they meant we loved each other, and that someone else felt threatened by that.

Guillermo didn't deserve my fear, and he didn't deserve an ounce of my memories.

I took a deep breath and shifted my eyes up to him, seeing nothing but love and admiration in the reflection of that hazel stare. He slowed down like he could sense my thoughts and he cupped my face with the palm of his hand.

"Celia?" he asked, furrowing his eyebrows.

"No, please. Don't stop." I shook my head with barely enough time to open my mouth again as he slammed his way in, hitting the back of my throat with every thrust of his hips. They were somehow in sync, each thrust hitting the deepest parts of me like a steady metronome.

So many hands were reaching out, caressing, stroking and rubbing every sensitive part of me, making my head spin from an overload of pleasure.

In and out, in and out. They filled me up, stretching me past what I thought was possible. The first orgasm came from a buildup, my core tightening as it waited in anticipation for the release while my body slow climbed that diving board reaching higher and higher towards bliss, ready to submerge into the water. I couldn't cry. I couldn't scream. Each attempt only muffled by Santos' pierced cock thrusting deeper into my mouth.

"I'm gonna come," he whispered, his eyes staying fixed on mine before he held my head in place, his entire length sheathed down my throat as he emptied his release so deep inside me I couldn't even taste his salt on my tongue. I fought back the urge to gag every time he hit the back of my throat but the sound of me choking on his dick just made him moan louder.

He pulled out of my mouth, his cock slapping Mateo in the forehead, making him scowl. I couldn't hold back my laughter as he shoved Santos away from him, but it was cut short when Ronan yanked on my hair. He pulled me against him, forcing me upright so that my back was pressed to his chest. I dropped my hands to Mateo's sculpted abs, holding myself in place as they both moved in and out of me.

"Oh F—" Ronan cut me off, releasing my hair and wrapping his fingers around my throat.

His thumb stroked up and down the sides gently before he applied pressure. I moaned, closing my eyes to surrender just as fingers slid between my folds and forced a burst of pleasure to cascade all throughout my body. I wasn't sure who they belonged to, and sparks of color were blooming throughout my vision. Just as I was getting to that floaty place my thighs shook and weakened under me, my orgasm coursing through me like a broken power line sparking over wet asphalt.

"Oh fuck yeah, sunshine," Mateo breathed out underneath me, one set of fingers still digging into my hips tightly while the others continued to torment the bundle of nerves full of heat between my thighs. "You're squeezing my cock so good."

Just as he said it, he put all his power into one final thrust, painting my insides with his hot, sticky release. I was breathing heavily, drops of sweat running down the side of my face while Ronan thrusted in and out of my ass slowly and methodically.

"How are you not done yet?" I asked, looking back at him, his hand still positioned around my throat but in a gentle hold.

"Done? I plan on being inside you for so long that our bodies fuse together, and they'll have to medically separate us." I started to laugh but he pulled me off Mateo, the sudden odd feeling of still being full in one hole but not the other always left a confusing need.

"More," I begged just as Ronan pulled me with him, sitting back against the headboard of the bed, spreading my legs apart.

Mateo's cum dripped out of me, coating the base of Ronan's cock while he guided my hips against him slowly. That's when I noticed Santos had been standing a few feet away watching this whole time. He stroked his pierced shaft up and down, his fingers purposefully hitting each bar every time he moved his hand.

He was a God towering over me, and I wanted to lick every scar on his beautiful body. Ronan's hand traveled down, his fingers rubbing me while he taunted my puckered hole with his thick length. I moaned, another sharp bolt of pleasure striking my core while he played in mine and Mateo's cum.

"Come here," I demanded, shifting my eyes back to Santos.

He obeyed silently.

I reached out, my fingers tracing over each fucked up scar from wounds that had been barbarically reopened multiple times. He let out a stuttered breath. Ronan curved his fingers entering me and moving in and out of me. I reached up, clutching Santos' forearms.

"Oh... Oh God," I moaned just as Ronan adjusted us into a more reclined position so that Santos could climb on top.

One fist firmly planted into the mattress while another hand explored my naked body humming in approval as his fingers twirled my nipples between them. Ronan's fingers moved away to make room.

I gasped, feeling him position the tip of his cock at my entrance.

His chest pressed against mine, forcing me harder against Ronan. And then he entered me, each delicious inch of his throbbing erection slid inside me with ease. Each bar of his piercing pushing me closer and closer to another orgasm from the sensation.

"Oh fuck." Ronan groaned. "I can feel your piercings."

"Shit, that's so fucking hot, talk dirty to each other," I whined needily.

Santos chuckled, like he knew the power his mecha-cock had.

"You gonna come from my cock rubbing up against yours Zerkos?" He was challenging him, which made me realize they were in a better place than when they had left.

Something happened while they were gone.

They'd somehow healed.

"Please" I moaned, feeling my overspent body climbing to try for one more orgasm like it hadn't already run a marathon's worth of them.

I reached down, finding my clit still sensitive and swollen but desperate for that friction I craved that I knew would send me right over the edge. I made slow circles, relishing in the feeling of the two of them moving against each other inside me until I could no longer contain it.

My climax burst out of me like a riptide, swallowing up everything in its way as I fought for an opportunity to breathe in between filling my lungs with sea water. Violent and potent, leaving me deaf to all sounds around me momentarily.

"Fuck." Ronan gripped me tight, emptying his release inside of me and pumping me full of his cum as if my orgasm had taken him with me as well.

He moved my hair out of the way and turned my chin to the side, exposing the side of my neck to his mouth. His tongue dragged against my flesh, licking the salty sweat from my skin before he slowly pulled out of me. I shuddered, my body still convulsing in tremors from the powerful aftershocks of the full body orgasm they wrung out of me.

Ronan rolled away and just as I moved to get out from under Santos, he gripped me tight and stood from the bed, keeping me impaled on his steel adorned length. I wrapped my thighs around his waist, feeling him deeper inside of me as he walked me over to my private bathroom.

"I'm not done with you yet, morena," he whispered into my ear, opening the door.

I held his face in my palms while he toyed with the shower controls, and once his eyes found their way back to me, I pressed my lips against his. It was tender, far sweeter than I would have thought possible for two people raised on violence and death. He walked us under the hot stream of water, guiding my hips up and down his shaft in a slow and torturous rhythm.

"I don't think I can come anymore." It felt impossible, there were literally no fucks left inside of me and he was still trying to draw them out somehow.

"Is that a challenge?" He smirked pushing me against the cold tile wall.

I turned my head just in time to see Ronan and Mateo striding into the bathroom, cocky looks on both their faces as they watched Santos thrust into me with a feverish passion.

"Put a timer on, if he takes more than five minutes to get her off I'm stepping in," Ronan threatened and Mateo barked out a laugh.

"Bet I can get her to do it without even using my cock," Mateo responded.

Santos low growl rumbled in my ear, something of frustration coming from him like their back and forth was throwing him off, forcing him to slam into me harder to prove something. My back slid up and down the wall each time he pounded into me, and despite my pessimism I could feel the impossible happening.

My core tightened and I felt it building up inside me again. As if he'd already unlocked the cheat codes to my body, he observed and responded, moving his fingers down to my clit to rub gentle circles, forcing my thighs to clench tighter around him.

"Oh shit!" I gasped, feeling the wave wash me over into nothing but a liquid mess of bones, limp in Santos' hold as I seized from my climax, milking his cock until he had no option but to follow me into oblivion.

The other two stepped into the shower, pulling me off of him while still holding me up, washing my body with care. They followed the same gentle devotion when it came to dressing me, Mateo slipping one of his shirts over my head as if his clothes were the only uniform I was allowed for my sleep.

Waking up every morning to his smell was a comforting feeling. Like no matter how wrong the day could go, at least at night I was surrounded by his love. Ronan carried me to bed and just as he slipped me under the covers, I realized the others were leaving.

"Wait," I said sleepily. "Can we all sleep together?"

They looked to Ronan who only shrugged, crawling into bed on my side. They both followed, settling in on my other side and wrapping themselves around me.

Life was starting to go right.

My heart started beating fast at the thought, because life never went right.

I didn't understand success. I didn't know what it was like to get what I wanted, to have a dream that was coming to fruition. When all you knew was failure, it became a comfortable place to set up permanent residency. Why try to accomplish something when I was so good at just... giving up? The thought alone was terrifying.

Mateo wrapped his arm around my waist and pulled me into his chest like he'd done every night while Santos and Ronan were away.

"I can feel you crying Sunshine," he whispered into my ear. "Was it something we did?"

I shook my head, doing my best to keep my tears silent and undetected. Ronan's snoring let me know I was doing a decent job.

"Pass her here," Santos whispered.

Mateo didn't wait a second, tossing me over his body so that I was positioned between him and Santos.

"What's wrong, Morena?"

I looked between the both of them, the tears streaming down my face as I struggled to verbalize what I was feeling.

"I'm just... I'm just... too happy?" I said, unsure if that was even the emotion I was experiencing because it had been so long since I'd felt anything even remotely close to this before in my life.

"Is that a problem?" Mateo asked.

"Yes. I don't deserve it."

"Yes you do, Celia." Santos' voice was cold, cutting, with a kind of reprimanding tone.

"No. I don't. We're bad people who do bad things. I haven't even begun to scratch the surface of all my sins to come. I don't deserve this. I don't deserve to feel this way." I shook, the silent tears pouring out of me like there was no turning back from this revelation.

"Tough. This is the life you chose. You had plenty of opportunities to leave, now it's time to throw away any guilt, any conscience you've spent the last twelve years growing. You can be a bad person, and still be happy." He wiped the tear collecting at the corner of my eye before it fell.

"Who gets to define what's bad and good anyway?" Mateo asked.

"My body count was double my age before I turned fourteen," I admitted for the first time in my life.

I heard a heavy sigh.

"I get that you're going through some sort of, imposter syndrome bullshit right now. You're looking for any reason to throw in the towel. You're feeling like you don't deserve all the things you've spent your entire life working for, fighting for, and then running away from. But here's the thing Celia, if it's not you, then who? Because I guarantee your uncle will sleep through the night in this very bed after he kills you, and he won't cry a single tear over all the good things he'll get from your death. And *he* most certainly doesn't fucking deserve them." It was Ronan saying everything I needed to hear, letting me know he hadn't been sleeping as hard as I thought.

I inhaled a stuttered breath, filling my lungs up as I repeated his words in my head.

If not me then who?

My fucking traitorous hermana?

She wouldn't have cried over me. She wouldn't mourn me the way I mourned her. She would slit my throat and take everything that was mine. Everything I would have gladly shared with her.

When did I become such a soft fucking pendeja? I turned to my side, facing Santos and letting Mateo snuggle me into him again. Ronan's snoring started up once more and I let the sound of it calm me into a sleepier state, running my fingers over the scars on Santos' chest, reminding myself I would kill her not just for my own revenge, but for his too.

Retribution was coming, and I would find the Celia I buried deep inside me a long time ago to wield it.

That would help me sleep at night.

78

CELIA

The best part about this whole fundraiser gala was that all I had to do was throw money at it. An absolute joy for someone like me who needed minimal interaction with people outside my personal circle.

At the end of the day, I just wanted to tell my people what they needed to do and expect it to get done. It was a fair request to keep myself out of social situations unless they absolutely required it.

The gala demanded it unfortunately, but at least all I needed to do was show up and look hot.

Which I was failing to do.

The Prada box was opened, and the dress was already laid out on the bed for me. Ronan's choice, because I'd still yet to develop a sense of personal style. I really was more of a sweatpants and someone else's T-shirt kinda gal. But this was the event of the year, and it was a big fucking deal.

I painted my lips a dark plum color, opening my lips into an O shape to let the matte shade dry. I was never quite fucking sure if you were supposed to do that or press your lips together to spread the color around.

I was really inept at all this feminine stuff, but it's not like I had someone to teach me. I spent most of my childhood as my father's shadow and when we *were* forced to be apart my mother wasn't discreet in her desire to keep me at a distance.

Her own fucked up way of protecting herself.

I guess I wouldn't want to get close to my kid either if I knew the chances were high that they were going to grow up to kill my husband. I loved my papá, but I was glad he died because, in reality, the odds would have been against us. Historically, time proved cártel seats weren't passed down in peace, they were taken with blood and glory.

The birth control implant in my arm itched from the thought of breeding. The idea alone was laughable. I was thirty years old and probably hadn't even processed a third of my childhood trauma yet. Was I gonna pop some kid out and chain him to that dungeon like my father did to me for the sake of making them a 'better person'? Was I going to force my child into something they likely wouldn't have chosen on their own if they could understand?

No.

I wouldn't be bringing a child into this fucked up world.

I stuck on the sticky strapless bra to my left boob, hooking it onto the right to create the insane illusion of cleavage that I'd never achieve on my own. I wasn't even fully dressed for the night yet and I was already looking forward to taking all this shit off and crawling into a pair of Ronan's boxers and one of Mateo's shirts.

The three of them walked into the room just as I stepped into the dress, pulling it up to my shoulders and giving them my back so one of them could do the clasps. I gasped looking into the mirror just as Santos finished.

"I-I can't wear this," I said, completely horrified at what I was looking at.

The dress was stunning. Black, strapless with a sweetheart neckline and a tight bodice that hugged all the way down to my hips before the fabric dropped loosely to my ankles. It was essentially backless, stopping right above my ass and leaving my back completely exposed.

That was a problem.

Part of my vault of traumas—I needed to keep locked up tight.

"Yes you can," Ronan said, turning my back away from the mirror and forcing me to look at my own face.

"I can't. Find me a jacket if I *have* to stay in this dress," I told Mateo, knowing he wouldn't argue.

"No." I watched Santos step behind me in the reflection of the mirror, my eyes following him as one of his hands ran up the front of my body, while the other trailed softly along the scar on my back.

It looked worse than I thought possible. It didn't heal right. It had reopened so many times in that basement just from the way they had me chained up, hanging by my wrists that it didn't allow for it to scar and fade. No, it was raised up, purple in some places and red in others.

It was a reminder of the women still in that Bratva den, locked in cages and waiting to be sold. I would find a way to go back for them.

"No?" I asked, turning away from him as if he'd never seen the scar before.

He wrapped his hands around my shoulders and turned my back towards the mirror again, this time turning my chin to force me to look in the reflection.

"Fucking look at yourself." He sounded angry, his fingers gripping my chin a little too hard, but it was a welcome kind of pain.

The kind that was supposed to wake you up from a bad dream.

"Don't cover it up. Show them exactly why you're the most feared woman on the planet. Show them why they should be grateful for the opportunity to bow at your feet." He licked his finger and wiped the makeup that covered the scar on my cheek. "There, that's better."

He gave me a soft, sideways smile. It was always sideways now. With the way the scar on his own face pulled at his skin it didn't let it be anything but perfectly crooked. He was right, I couldn't ask him to accept the way he was now if I couldn't give myself the same amount of kindness.

"Fine," I relented before turning back to face him, wrapping my arms around his neck. "You know, she wasn't wrong..." I admitted.

"Who?" he asked, furrowing his eyebrows in confusion.

"My sister..." I said with hesitation, unsure if she was even that to me anymore. "You do look more handsome with that scar." I brushed his curls out of his eyes so I could see it better.

I reached up onto the tips of my toes and pressed a kiss to his eye.

"Te quiero," I whispered.

Mateo cleared his throat, reminding us we weren't alone, and I shrugged, walking back to the bathroom to do one final cloud of hair spray over the curls I knew weren't going to hold all night. No curl could survive the genetics of heavy, pin-straight, Indigenous hair. I was practically Cinderella now, fighting the clock until they'd dissolve back to normal.

El Palacio would be full of civilians at this time, but as the guest of honor it was expected that I would be late. Dominico said it was important to make them wait for me, to make an entrance.

Seemed pompous as hell, but if I recalled correctly that about summed up Rafa.

I'd almost forgotten there was almost no distinction between politician and drug lord in these parts. It wasn't until I was greeted by the military police that I remembered I had paid them to be here.

Funny how that worked.

They kept their faces covered, too afraid of ending up in my ledger.

It was alright, I didn't want men on my side who had too much to lose. I wanted the ones who had already lost it all. There was a distinct difference in the kind of work ethic the two groups put in. The door to the limousine opened up from the outside, a valet waiting with his hand stretched out for me to take. Ronan slapped it out of the way, getting out first and helping me out himself.

"Play nice now, or I'll swap you for the other white boy," I teased.

Mateo and Santos followed behind, a sizable difference to not draw any suspicions but still close enough that anyone who saw knew they were with me. People likely thought they were my own private bodyguards.

Not a wrong assumption either.

"Excuse me? You think they won't be able to tell if your date suddenly goes from blond to black haired?" he asked.

"Not the time for an 'all gringos look the same' joke?" I winked, biting back my laugh.

"You'll pay for that one later, flower. Mark my words," he whispered into my ear as he led me up the steps to El Palacio.

One of the grander buildings in the city.

Photographers' cameras went off nonstop, the constant flash lighting up the dark night sky for us as we walked down the red carpet to the government building. It was beautifully decorated inside. They'd gone all out with my money to make it so. Beautiful black roses covered every banister, and decorative ribbons hung all around made from silk and paper tissue. Bar tables filled the space covered with black silk tablecloths with decorative white lace layered above them, a centerpiece of large candles on each one.

"Señorita Flores." A man tapped my shoulder. "I was instructed to show which way you will make your entrance from." He spoke in spanish, pointing down a tiny side corridor with a set of narrow stairs. "The steps will take you to that balcony there," he showed me exactly where I would be appearing in front of the public for the first time.

I really was Celia Flores again.

I couldn't dig up Cecilia if I tried. That bitch died in Sokolov's trafficking ring.

That was the thing about my enemies, they kept trying to fuck with the dead, but they didn't realize I was the queen of can't fucking kill me. They were going to have to hit me harder than that if they were going to keep me down. Only Santa Muerte knew the day of my death.

I took a deep breath, knowing only one of them would be able to come up there with me.

"Take Santos," Ronan said, as if knowing I wouldn't be able to decide between the three of them.

I nodded, looking over at the balcony again, lined with gold and draped in black and white that wrapped around a spiral banister that led towards the grand staircase. It poured out into the gallery where everyone else waited for me to appear.

It was a bit of a whimsical moment, something I would have been prepared for if our lives had never gone awry. I would have grown up here. I would have likely had my quinceañera here. My papá would have introduced me to the world and made some sort of announcement about me someday following in his footsteps. Letting enemies and allies know.

But that was all ripped away from me.

I would be introducing myself to these people.

These strangers.

Santos gave me his arm and I laced my hand around his bicep, squeezing tight for an extra boost of emotional support. He led the way up the stairs, and I followed behind, the stairs too narrow to allow us to walk side by side. It was a service entrance, something likely built for servers and other employees of El Palacio.

There he was, waiting for me at the top. Presidente Ramírez. I'd been doing my homework for the last few weeks. He was forty years old and in the second year of his term. One of the youngest presidents in my country's history, and his mission was to cut down on street violence and child deaths due to drugs and gangs.

I was more than willing to make nice.

"Señorita Flores, it's so nice to finally put a face to the name I've been hearing so much of." He picked up my hand and pressed his lips to my knuckles.

I could hear Santos' teeth grinding behind me.

"Behave," I whispered, "Likewise Ramírez. I hear you are doing great things for our country."

"Please, call me José Luis."

"Well, José Luis, I was pleasantly surprised by your willingness to work with me and my people. I don't want to jump the gun, but I am hopeful I can make you see the positives in supporting my campaign."

"I am not an ignorant man. I know everything that happens in my country—"

"Your country?" I cut him off.

"Like I said, I am not an ignorant man. I know this country's history. I know you are the prodigal daughter returning. Lazarus coming back from the dead."

My interest piqued.

"And what do you have to say about that?

"Ignacio Flores is a crass man. He has no taste for politics or social decorum. The only game he can play he doesn't play well. His henchmen are unmanned, loose in the streets, feeding drugs to the children and the whores. Anyone who crosses him faces a temper tantrum and risks a bullet to the back of the head." His face twitched like there was a deeper story in there.

"So. The enemy of your enemy is your friend?" I asked him.

"With conditions of course."

"As long as you hold my leash?" I clarified.

He smirked. "You're far more intelligent about the inner workings of our world than I expected from an expatriate, Celia. May I call you Celia?" he asked.

"You may not. I am not an expatriate, and I take offense to that. I was forced out of my home country as a child by a stupid man with dangerous delusions and too many idiots willing to do his bidding." I did my best to reign in my anger, but these days I had no tolerance for ignorant men.

He raised his hands up in defense and chuckled again like I was a kitten with sharp claws he thought too cute to scratch him. I liked them better when they underestimated me. I'd allow him to think he was the one in control, because at the end of the day I was smart enough to know having him on my side was how I'd grow.

I'd force my way into politics with one hand and with the other I'd rule the criminal underworld. His time would run out, mine would not.

I paid attention to all my lessons.

"My apologies, Señorita Flores. It was not my intention to offend. There is much gossip and very little truth when it comes to why the Flores family left México." He put on his charm once again, not seeming to actually be worried about offending me.

"Let's move on, José Luis. I think you'll find me to be a reasonable woman to work with." I cut the drama short, letting him know I wasn't interested in gossip.

He nodded to me and then whistled over a nearby usher.

"We are ready," he told him, motioning for both of us to stand in front of a dark curtain.

The usher disappeared, but minutes later the curtain pulled back, revealing the edge of the balcony and the crowd of people below, waiting on our descent. They clapped politely, the quiet encouragement of upper-class socialites was the same, no matter which side of the border you were on.

There was always someone who thought they were better than everyone else.

Santos remained a few feet behind, giving the illusion of a bodyguard instead of a lover. My papá's lessons always in the back of my mind, directing my every move. A strong woman in politics was one who didn't have a man at her side, but behind her. Once I had established myself, I wouldn't hesitate to introduce my men to the world as mine.

But I had to play the long game, and to do that I had to make sure I was allowed on the board first. A mayor elect with three lovers? That was far too much for Guadalajara. President Ramírez rested his hand on my low back as he walked to my side. I recoiled from the touch as his fingers grazed over my scar.

I could feel Santos' glare burning like a hot laser over my skin, scorching José Luis' hand off my body without even looking back at him. We descended down the staircase, one step at a time, politely smiling and waving to the upper-class drones below us.

The minute I stepped down into the gallery, I became self-conscious. Hundreds of eyes staring at me from all angles. My weaknesses, my flaws, my scars all out on display for them to judge.

Santos' arm was heavy on my shoulder, telling me I could do this.

I *could* do this.

Fuck my scars.

Fuck what they thought. At the end of the day I was the best thing that could happen to them because I was the only one who could put things back to the way they were when my papá was around. And I would do it better than he did.

I was a violent woman, who survived a violent past and had a violent history. Scars were minimal compared to the damage I'd actually done in this world. I wasn't here to make friends. I was here to gain respect, to tell them I was someone to be feared.

I was fucking home and no one else was going to take that away from me ever again.

We spent the next hour walking from table to table, Presidente Ramírez introducing me to his colleagues and supporters, letting them know that if they supported him that they now supported me too.

All he wanted was to keep the kids out of it and reduce deaths in the street. That was such an easy thing to abide by that it felt like I was cheating him out of a good deal. Ignacio had set the bar so low that I was going to be a shining beacon of hope for these fuckers.

I'd have to send him a thank you letter before I deprived him of his guts.

"Señor Presidente." Dominico appeared, nodding to the president before turning to me.

"Dominico, how good to see you. I had heard whispers of your return to politics. It's true what they say then, those who support the Flores family do it for life," he joked, knowing damn well what he was actually saying.

The only way out was death.

Since neither Dominico or I were dead, then he belonged to me.

"Likewise, Ramírez. I'm actually here to show Senorita Flores to the conference room. The rest of her campaign party awaits," he said politely.

Ramírez barked out a laugh. "Like father, like daughter. I remember Rafael was always working, even during parties and social events. I hope you don't inherit all his bad habits. Live a little, eh?" He raised the drink in his hand before taking a sip.

"Claro. Maybe after I win the election I can finally relax." I gave him a smile that was all business before letting Dominico lead the way through the gallery, Santos on my heels barely allowing space between us as he followed. I scanned the room, searching for Mateo and Ronan but by the time I had found them they had already taken note of us and began to walk in our direction.

"Give me a minute in the ladies room, go along without me," I instructed Dominico and veered off towards the sign pointing to the restrooms.

I didn't have to turn my head to see if they were following me. I knew they were.

I opened the door to the bathroom and walked straight to the sink, standing in front of it and taming the stray hairs back down while I took a moment to just...breathe.

79

RONAN

Álvarez drew the short straw and stayed outside the door, guarding the bathroom from any unwanted visitors. She was distracted, fixing her hair in the mirror and touching up her dark lipstick. I looked over to Mateo and gestured to the stalls. Without speaking he moved ahead, opening each door to make sure it was empty inside.

Prowling quietly her way, doing my best to remain unnoticed while she was still in her own world, all her self destructive thoughts clearly weighing down the more reasonable part of her brain. She didn't need to be doubting herself before she walked in there. She needed to show them she knew exactly who she was and who they were in comparison to that.

I moved towards her from behind, slowly wrapping my grip around her throat and urging her head up. She let out a soft exhale, those black eyes devouring me into her abyss with little effort as she gazed up at me, slowly parting her lips in invitation. My free hand roamed upwards, following the curve of her waist until her breast was in my hand and she moaned responsively into my mouth.

"I-I can't." She broke our kiss. "I'm already late as it is."

"Make them wait," I demanded, undoing my belt. "They bow to you, not the other way around, reina." Her skin pebbled up at the use of the nickname.

"In this dress? How am—"

"Stop making excuses, sunshine. Bend her over Zerkos. I want to see your cum drip down her thighs."

I reached down, grabbing the hem of her dress and gathering it in my hands until I'd lifted it up past her hips.

"What if someone walks—"

"Shut up, flower." I let go of her breast and placed my hand between her shoulder blades, with a forceful push I shoved her down, fully bending her over the counter.

She moaned again, this time it echoed through the chambers of the bathroom, bouncing off the tile walls and back to my ears like a siren song straight to my cock. I pressed the hard steel of my length against her, and she turned her head to look back, eyes wide open like she didn't expect me to be ready for her.

I'd been hard all night, a mixture of anger and jealousy every time the fucking president of Mexico ran his hands up and down her back. I'd spent the whole time blowing up Santos' phone asking why he hadn't cut the bastard's fingers off yet, but I already knew my answer.

We had to play fucking nice. I wasn't going to be the man standing in her way. Not after everything we'd been through.

My hands roamed her thighs, giving her ass a big squeeze before I decided to slip my way between them, finding her panties soaked with arousal. I wedged my fingers inside the fabric, pulling it to the side and sliding two fingers between her folds, coating them in her slickness. She whimpered, the side of her face pressed into the marble of the bathroom counter top while she nibbled on her bottom lip.

"Ronan." She called out my name while I continued to toy with her clit, closing her eyes and reaching back to touch me. "We really don't have time," she protested again but only with words.

"It's not up for debate. You may be in charge of that empire out there, flower, but we both know you belong on your knees for us." I gripped her chin and turned her face forward, forcing her to look in the mirror.

I dropped my hand from her face, keeping my gaze locked on her expression in the mirror just as I pressed the head of my cock at the entrance of her pussy. She turned her head to look back again, this time I wrapped her long silky hair around my wrist and with a hard tug I corrected her gaze once more.

Her eyes narrowed with a look full of fire that reminded me of how she stared at me in that high-rise. But it wasn't hatred I saw, and maybe it never had been all along.

"Are you provoking me on purpose?" I tugged harder, forcing her chin to lift higher and a groan made its way out of her chest just as I made my way inside her fully.

"It's so much better when you're angry." She licked her lips, her eyes finding mine in the mirror.

I pulled out slowly, almost all the way before slamming back in at once. Her mouth gaped open, and her eyes shut as she reveled in pleasure.

"Eyes open," I growled in her ear, picking up my pace and thrusting into her feverishly.

Her eyelids flew open at my command. She stared into the mirror, first watching herself with curiosity as she bounced forward with every jolt of my cock, then moving back to me. With one hand on her hip, guiding me in and out of her and the other still wrapped tightly around her hair, she whimpered as she got closer and closer to her release.

"You don't get to come yet," I whispered in her ear, releasing her hair.

Still fully sheathed inside her, I brought her arms behind her, pressing her wrists together at the small of her back.

"You let him touch you as if we weren't watching." Mateo spoke from a few feet away.

Her eyes widened, a smirk playing around the corner of her lips.

"What did I tell you would happen?" I asked her.

She screamed out with my next thrust, this time her gaze moving to Mateo's dark stare.

He hadn't moved at all, leaning against the wall with one foot supporting him and his arms crossed over his chest. Their eyes locked, an intimate moment between them while I continued to pound into her over and over again.

"What did he tell you would happen?" Kane asked her, his voice laced with darkness.

She moaned and writhed against my cock every time I slowed up my movements to torture her further. Her cunt dripped down onto my pants, the wet sounds of us joining together filled the air along with her screams.

"Answer him," I hissed in her ear bringing my hand down to her ass with a hard clap.

A sound erupted from deep inside her chest, confirming just how much she still liked that.

"He said," she cried out with my next thrust, a hand slipping from my grasp that reached between her legs to get herself closer to relief, "he was going to punish me."

"And that means you don't get to come yet." I slapped her hand out from within her dress and she whined, backing into me to feel the full length of my cock deeper inside her.

Mateo let out an unhinged laugh, finally kicking off the wall and walking towards us. He leaned his head to the side, that manic twinkle in his eye I recognized so well.

"Maybe we should stuff her full of our cum, have Santos come in here and do the same before we send her off to her meeting. Then she can think about what she's done while we drip down her legs," Mateo threatened, her eyes jerking to the side to glance at him and she groaned again at the feeling of me pulling her by her wrists to lift her chest higher into the air.

"Fuck," she cried out, getting closer to the edge.

It was a nice threat, but not one we could deliver on. Not when she was already squeezing my cock with a vice grip kind of hold. She'd be coming undone soon enough regardless of whatever I said to try to keep her from it.

"I think she likes the sound of that." I lifted her from the counter so I could see the lust-drunk look on her face in the mirror.

"I thought you were supposed to be in my corner," she reminded him through labored pants just as he reached for his zipper.

He smirked.

"You let him put his hands on you, Sunshine." His voice was low and husky, a dangerous promise hiding behind it.

I moved faster now—in and out—finding myself getting closer to my climax with each pump, my balls drawing up higher as I fought for my release.

"He's the president," she said. "I have to be civil."

Her eyes found mine again in the mirror's reflection. Her erotic sounds echoing repeatedly became the urgent catalyst to my orgasm, forcing my cum to spill out inside her with one final thrust of my hips.

I pulled out slowly, ignoring her desperate pleas as she attempted to push herself back onto my cock.

"He's the president, but you're the queen. I told you this was punishment," I whispered in her ear before pulling her away from the counter and turning her to face me.

"I'm not gonna lie, you're making it damn hard to not want to do that again if this is my punishment."

Mateo yanked her by the hair, pulling her to him with a swift move that had her gasping once her ass slammed against his cock, hard and ready for her.

"Then we'll just have to keep teaching this lesson to you, won't we sunshine?" he asked her.

"Yes!" She cried out, as he entered her.

I had the perfect show watching the mirror, watching him plow into her while he held onto her wrists. It was hotter than I ever thought possible, watching someone else have their way with her. And for some reason all I could think about was why it took me so long to be okay with it.

"Clean me up," I said, turning to face her, her head level with my cock as he kept her folded halfway.

She wet her lips before parting them and swirling her tongue around the purple head of my cock. She lowered her head, taking me further into her mouth and sucking with a vacuum-like force. I removed myself from her mouth, putting my dick back into my pants and ignoring the wet spot before I turned back towards the door to tag my best friend in.

The scowl on his face when I pushed open the bathroom door let me know he understood exactly what was happening inside and was feeling pissed about being left out. I tapped him on the shoulder and gave him a nod to let him know it was his turn, his eyebrows softened, and he pushed his way inside, leaving me to guard the way.

I leaned against the wall, arms crossed at my chest while I listened to my two best friends fuck the only woman I ever loved.

Death really made you see things more clearly.

I understood why Celia had always been so goddamn obsessed with it. Leaving tequila and weed offerings on her altar when we were just kids and telling me to not pay any mind. Almost dying gave you a new perspective on things, nearly losing everyone you cared about in the blink of an eye even more so.

Having Celia at the cost of either of my brothers' lives would have been like drinking a little bit of poison every single day. Not enough to kill you, but just enough to keep you sick and miserable until the end of your time.

A well-to-do looking socialite walked towards the bathroom. I stuck my arm out in front of her and shook my head. Before she could open her mouth to protest, Celia's screams of pleasure leaked out through the cracks in the door. She widened her eyes, giving me a condemning look as if I were the one that was in there right now.

Well, I had been.

She turned her back to me, marching away with an appalled look on her face. Mateo pushed through the door with a satisfied expression that he didn't bother to hide. Santos followed after, and just a minute or two later Celia walked out, lipstick pristine and chin held high. Her dress hugging her curves once again.

"You're not worried about what they may think of you coming out of the bathroom with two men?" I asked her and she laughed.

"Baby, I don't know if you remember, but my papá died in the middle of a senate campaign. No one is batting an eye that I'm not taking a piss by myself." She walked in front of me, and I stayed a few steps behind, happy to play the part of a bodyguard.

It wasn't like I was pretending. I would have easily cut through anyone who tried to get to her. She walked through the gallery and down a wide hallway until large double doors appeared. She took a deep breath, standing straight with her shoulders pulled back.

She was putting up her mental armor and readying for battle.

All I could do was hold her flag.

No, all she *needed* me to do was hold her flag.

And I would hold it till my arms gave out and the colors ran red with the blood of her enemies. I knew she was capable of spilling it all on her own.

80

CELIA

They sat there, waiting for me, filling up each seat at the table in the conference room and leaving the head of the table for me. Men I remembered from my papá's regime, all of them highly opinionated, some clearly bitter over the nepotism in our way of life. None brave enough to actually attempt to try the same though.

Sure, originally I may have earned my title in a less than favorable way, just being born to the right family. But now, none of them could deny that I'd bled my right to call myself queen.

I had already sat down and spoken with most of the men here one on one, for the majority of them, like Luciano Amaro, I already knew we saw eye to eye. Some others hadn't formed an opinion of me yet and we had only been acquainted. A few had already proved to be rooting for my failure, probably thinking that I would be their chance for power.

Men like Fernando Garcia who were just hoping to catch me with my pants down so he could fuck me in the ass and blame it on my not being Mexican enough for his liking. But of course, he couldn't deal with Ignacio himself, so he'd only scrutinize and shame me until it came time for me to do the hard work of ridding the world of my tío.

Then he'd miraculously find the courage to challenge me in hopes of taking everything I'd worked hard to build.

Idiot didn't know I was a servant of death.

You couldn't kill those who worshiped La Muerte. Only she decided when we went.

My time was far from up.

They all stood but Fernando stood once I entered the room. I made sure to let my gaze linger on him as I walked past every other man seated before arriving at my own chair, giving him a dose of my bad side. My father had been gone too long, I would bet good money Fernando here had crossed the line and settled for my tío. Maybe I was just cynical and untrusting.

Great qualities in a leader.

The more I thought about it the less I tolerated him sitting at this very table.

"Good evening Señores—" I switched to spanish.

He interrupted, raising his hand in the air, waving it as if he alone had the authority to stop me from speaking.

"I'm going to cut short the pleasantries, Celia. It's been a long night waiting for you to show your face, why don't we speed things up here so we can all go home?" The fucking audacity of this man made me fight every carnal instinct that screamed at me to throw a knife into his face.

I noticed César in the corner, twirling the sharp point of one on the tip of his finger. He didn't look up; he didn't need to. Both our thoughts were in the same place so when the corner of his lip twitched, I knew our minds were back in the past. The moment he threw that blade in my cousin Carlitos' cheek was the very same moment my tío decided he'd had enough of not being the biggest man in the room.

Too bad for him, even with all the giants now gone, I was still bigger.

"I assure you that just because I'm wearing a dress, it doesn't mean my cock is smaller than yours Fernando. On the contrary, I'm wearing this dress because it is actually so fat it can't be contained by a pair of pants." A few men chuckled quietly to themselves.

He scowled, taking a beat to think up something clever to retaliate, but I was faster.

"Your hostility towards me only proves that I've already succeeded in what I came here to do. Own this country. You're angry that a woman has done in two months what you have failed to do in fifteen years." I stopped and addressed the rest of the room, "What you all failed to do."

There was an awkward beat of silence but it only tasted like the failure of mediocre men. Regardless of how far their loyalty went, there was no denying every man in this room at one point entertained the idea of having the cártel for themselves. None had been brave enough to try to claim it.

"Now, if you are done trying to prove whether or not your dick can hit a g-spot, let's move on to what really matters here. Ignacio needs to die. This week preferably." I gave the deadline wondering which one of my men would prove themselves worthy of being my right hand.

I wasn't hopeful about any yet.

"You're barely Mexican. Why should we have to listen to anything you have to say when you're saying it with a gringa accent?" He said the words with a bitter expression on his face.

I extended my hand out and before I had even blinked there was a pistol in my palm. I didn't bother to check to see who'd placed it there. Only a few voices gasped out loud as I flipped the safety off, nostrils flared at the man who dared insult me.

"Maybe if I hadn't been so busy trying to survive after you all tucked your tails between your legs and went into hiding when Rafa died, I could have dedicated more time to perfecting my spanish."

"So, you're better than Ignacio because Rafael had a hand in you?" He scoffed.

"No, I'm better because I learned who I can be *in spite* of the pitiful men who stood in my way. Get the fuck out of my sight if you want to stay alive." I pointed to the door and Miguel stood up to forcefully escort him out.

"Rafa would have put a bullet in his head," Dominico said from the far end of the table.

"You think I made the wrong call letting him walk out of here?" I asked the men I knew I had no choice but to trust as my council.

"I think it was a kind decision," Luciano answered. "Some men deserve kindness, some do not."

"And Fernando Garcia?" I asked.

"We shall see what he deserves," he said, and I nodded back at him, taking his words as a request to leave and see what Fernando was up to unsupervised.

He stood up and followed him out, back into the gala.

"I have a primo who is acquainted with one of Ignacio's soldiers. I can send him inside with your word, jefa," Miguel answered, sticking to business and moving past the unnecessary drama that had just taken place.

"It's a good idea, better we know where he is than to wait for him to come at us. Even if we are prepared." I nodded my approval. "Get on that. The faster we kill the hijo de la chingada the faster we can focus on the things that matter, the things that make us rich." They all nodded their heads, agreeing that money was the reason for it all.

"Thank you, Miguel," I acknowledged him once again. "Everyone go." I waved the rest of the room off. "We'll continue this once Ignacio is dead." The room cleared out faster than I expected. I sat there in silence, staring at the Rufino Tamayo painting Rafael let me pick out when I was thirteen for this very room in this government building. I didn't realize the momentousness of the occasion then. A child of a crime lord, decorating the walls of a federal building with a painting made by an Indigenous artist. Almost like the statement alone was the art itself. It was too low on the wall, because he thought I should be the one to get to hang it. I was seven years old the first time I spun around in these chairs, and I was fourteen when I first sat through a meeting.

Dominico was the last one out the door, but he turned back to face us before exiting.

"She needs to learn," the old man said, shaking his head.

"She doesn't need to learn shit," Mateo spit out in my defense.

"What do I need to learn?"

"You came here wanting to do something different, but this is a wheel that never stops turning Celia. You wanted to do better than your father, but you can't. If you show these animals a moment of weakness, they will eat you alive. So you better fucking eat them instead. That's the secret to all of this."

"If you knew that, then why did you still come along when I said I'd do it differently?" I asked.

"Because you came in with this brand new attitude, bright eyed and filled with hope. Those intentions mean something, they make you someone worth following. If you leave, someone else *will* take your place, they circle like vultures just waiting for a crack in the foundations."

"Don't I know it." I looked over to Ronan and exhaled heavily, remembering his losses.

"If you ask me, you're the right person for it, Celia. And that's not because of all the work I watched him put into you, but because of something that I think grew inside of you after him," the old man said.

"What if I'm not good at it?" I asked, my voice wavering.

"You could kill all your enemies, baby, and the only person still standing in your way would be you," Ronan said.

It was the kind of realization that sunk itself so deeply into your psyche that you felt it shake you to your core.

"Leave," Santos told Dominico.

I didn't bother waiting to see if he'd completely left the room before I tore my mask off and let my walls down. I hated that anger always manifested itself in tears now, like my body just couldn't process the overload of emotions and the only way to let it out was to cry. I thought I'd built that shell around my heart, that it kept me protected. But it turned out all I did was emotionally constipate myself for years and now it was flooding out like trauma diarrhea.

"Why are you afraid of getting everything you've been fighting for?" Mateo stepped up to me and lifted my chin up, wiping a tear before it dropped.

"I don't know how to accept success."

I clenched my fists around the arms of my chair tightly, biting my lips until I could taste the liquid metal in my mouth. I could feel them, their shadows hovering over me and the heat of their protective shield. Ronan's hand was first on my shoulder, then Mateo's on the other side. Santos kneeled down in front of me, wrapping my hand inside both of his.

"Morena," he whispered.

"What if this was a huge mistake?" I whispered the words I feared the most.

"How could it be? This is your destiny," he said, like he hadn't wanted to escape this kind of life since I first knew him.

"Maybe it wasn't. Maybe it's Caro's. Maybe I'm stealing that chance from her. What if I'm just a fucking fraud?" I covered my face, too ashamed to fall apart in front of the guys I loved so much.

"Is this because of what that idiot said?" Ronan asked, and I nodded my head.

"I just feel like a sham. Like I fooled everyone. Maybe a long time ago this was my destiny, but what if I'm not meant to be here anymore?" I asked, looking up at him, hoping for some answers.

"Then fake it till you make it sunshine." Mateo squeezed my shoulder as he whispered in my ear from the other side.

"What?" I choked out, surprised at his response and he shrugged his shoulders.

"No one knows what they are doing. And if they tell you they do they're fucking lying," Ronan finished Mateo's thought.

"I'm drowning in doubt," I confessed, the tears welling at my eyelids.

"Come back up for air, we can't save you from yourself," Ronan lamented, a sad tone in his voice. "I wish you could see what we see. You're a fucking force to be reckoned with. You've survived hell and you'll survive this too."

"I wish I believed that. I just have this feeling like—"

"Don't even fucking say it." He read my mind, knowing exactly what kind of turmoil was crashing through my mind.

Death.

The end.

I was always thinking about it.

She was my gravity.

The center of my universe.

Everything moved because death allowed it so.

This could only end in death.

This could only end in death.

It was the only way out.

My heart began to race, and I shut my eyes, taking a deep breath in to try to calm myself before the panic set in again.

Not here. Not here.

"What would make you feel better right now?" Mateo's husky voice honeyed its way out in that way only he could sound, letting me know he was ready to cater to any and all of my needs to anchor me back down to reality.

I looked up at him through my eyelashes.

"Do you want to kill him, sunshine?" he asked, no judgment in his tone at all, just a desire to fulfill my need, whatever it be.

I looked between the three of them, mouth slightly agape at the fact they all had the same expression.

"I think so," I said quietly nodding my head.

"Find him. Bring him back here." I heard Santos already on the phone behind me.

Then I heard the deafening boom in the distance and the ground trembled beneath us. We didn't have to guess or speculate what had happened.

We all already knew.

"Find César, there's Diablos on standby. Make sure no one is hurt, and get all the civilians out," I told Mateo. "Find the president, make sure he's safe," I told Ronan.

"Come with me." The last instruction went to Santos, I squeezed my hand around the Glock and the four of us made our way out of the conference room.

Pandemonium had broken out at the gala. Smoke was filling the air fast and people were running through the building, shouting and screaming for each other in a wave of chaos.

He may have been inadequate for all intent and purpose, but my tío had a knack for dramatic murders—I'd give him that.

It would end today though.

Obviously, Fernando had been a distraction, a way to get my tío and his men in the building to fuck this party all to hell and cast a shadow over my name. He didn't understand that I was the shadow, the very thing that loomed over the memory of my family's name. I was annoyed at myself for not seeing that farce for what it was.

Santos walked in front of me, shielding me from anything that might come towards me in the thick wall of smoke.

"I think we need to get out, Morena, there's too much smoke," he yelled over the screams of the crowd rushing towards the doorways to the outside.

Another tremor shook the building, and the rearmost walls began to collapse, bricks cascading into a pile on the ground as Diablos and cártel soldiers worked alongside military police to empty El Palacio and get everyone out safely.

"No. This is our chance. We have to find him," I told him, my eyes tearing up from the insidious fumes overwhelming me.

He didn't argue, pushing through the crowd desperate to get out as we forced ourselves in the opposite direction, deeper into the building.

Two girls in their early twenties were huddled together on the floor, coughing and yelling for help. I pointed them out to Santos and we both rushed over to help.

"You need to get out of here. There's too much smoke, the building is coming down," I shouted in spanish.

"She's pinned under the boulder!" One of the girls responded.

Santos and I both reached for the boulder, finding it too impossibly heavy to move.

"Together," he said, and I nodded. "One, two, three!" We barely lifted it three inches off the ground, but it was just enough for the uninjured girl to pull her friend out from under the rock that had her trapped.

She began wailing, either from the feeling of her foot being free, the pain, or the shock of the entire situation.

Probably all of the above.

"Head towards the exit, find the men in leather," I told them, pointing towards the crowd.

"You think he's still inside?" he asked me, one girl over his shoulder and the other clutched to my arm as we helped them towards the exit.

81

CELIA

"No. He's not here," I told him, stepping into my tío's mindset and realizing what this truly was.

"What?" He looked at me with confusion, putting the injured girl on the ground so she could find her people. "But the bombs—"

"His men, yes. He's not here, he's not this ignorant."

"Then where is he?" Santos asked.

"The Villa." My skin pebbled though I was the one speaking the words. This would end where it started, the very place my tío began his disruption to my life would be the very place it would end.

Cathartic.

That's how it would feel too as I skinned him alive and plucked the teeth from his mouth like feathers from poultry. My papá once said his revenge was so close, he could taste it, smell it in the air.

He died that very week.

All I could taste was blood. All I could smell was blood.

That was enough to tell me that death was on her way.

Santos and I rushed out of the building battling through the chaos of bodies gathered at the front of the collapsing building as it slowly crashed its way to the ground from the weakened foundation.

"Text César, tell him to bring Mateo and Ronan home with him. Tell him to keep ALL of the men outside the villa," I instructed Santos, charging through the crowd while looking for the vehicle we'd arrived in.

"Where are you going? You can't go off alone, Celia." He wasn't wrong, my tío's men along with whatever stray Los Muertos soldiers he'd collected were likely all lurking around here, waiting for us to flood out of the building like mice scurrying from the fire.

"Then keep up with me," I told him, finding an orange Mastretta parked away from the crowd and unblocked by other cars. "Are you driving or am I?" I smirked at him, memories of our youth flashing through my mind.

"Get in," he said, taking his jacket off and wrapping it around his elbow before breaking through the driver's side window.

The alarm went off, but it was already far too loud between the sound of the flames engulfing the historic Palacio, the sirens of the ambulances and firetrucks in the distance arriving, and the screams of innocent people attempting to piece together what had happened. He brushed the broken glass from his seat before unlocking the passenger door for me. Santos reached into the electronics of the car, yanking out a wire that shut off the blaring of the security system before hot-wiring the engine to start.

"It's been a long time since we've done this." He smirked, his hand casually dropping to my thigh and slipping through the slit in the side of my dress.

"We never did it like *this*," I reminded him.

"*You* never did it like this. If you think for one second it wasn't all I thought about during those drives, those runs we made, you're fucking crazy, Morena." His hand rubbed up and down my skin, calming me as I fought to slow down the current of excitement running through my veins.

Cálmate. There was a bigger end game here.

Me and Ignacio.

One of us would die tonight.

I almost didn't care which one.

Closure was kind of like that, like it didn't matter how things ended as long as they did. People seemed to be satisfied as long as they knew the ending. I didn't get the need, why did the book always end just when you got to the part where the main character finally found happiness?

You spent all that time watching them suffer, you cheered them on hoping they could have their happily ever after. When they finally did it was a five-page epilogue with some stereotypical idea of what happiness looked like. A pregnant belly, a picket fence, no threat of death.

Maybe it ended there because they couldn't possibly describe something they didn't understand. Maybe none of them actually knew what it truly meant to be happy. You couldn't write happiness if you didn't experience it for yourself, your readers would surely know it. They'd see past the pretty lies in the words you spelled out and see the sad person beneath it all.

Maybe authors were just truly unhappy people, forcing imaginary creations to undergo the cruel darkness that lived inside their own minds as if the characters weren't simply mirrored shards of themselves.

Certainly cheaper than therapy.

Not that I understood anything of the sort. I was allergic to healing. The thought of being examined under a lens gave me hives.

Or maybe I had just become bitter. Cynical over time, and maybe that was the problem. I'd never been delusional enough to think that I could ever earn myself a happy ending. When I turned thirty, I realized I was really only ten years away from outliving my papá. A rare feat for a Flores. That was what brought me to the Black Crow Brotherhood's door in the first place. I was alive because I was lucky, and I knew that luck would eventually run out.

I might have not been ready to die yet, but we weren't the ones who got to choose that day.

Santos pulled into the villa with a screech as he yanked on the emergency break. He opened his door, but I wrapped my hands around his wrists and pulled him back down to me.

"I want him alive."

He grabbed the back of my neck, closing his mouth around mine and sliding his tongue between my lips. Kissing Santos was like inhaling summer in the middle of the snowy winter, like drinking clear tequila with no chaser.

It was liquid fire.

But it didn't last nearly long enough. He broke free, and the right corner of his lip curled up.

"Then you shouldn't have brought me." He got up, walking around the car and opening my door for me.

"Who said chivalry was dead?" I joked.

He pulled his phone out, scrolling through the texts before shoving it back in his pocket.

"Zerkos and Kane are headed here now, we should wait for them," he said with a wince, like he expected some sort of angry outburst at his logical suggestion.

"We should. But I'm also well aware my uncle will use anything I give a damn about to get to me, and to get what he wants." Both could be one in the same, depending on how you looked at it. "Which is why I need you to stay out here. I don't need distractions and I don't need him to use you against me."

A deep V formed between his eyebrows.

"Fuck no morena, I won't be at the mercy of the unknown again. I won't be helpless," he said with a rising panic as if it was something he had to prove to me.

"You're not at the mercy of the unknown, you're at *my* mercy Santito," I whispered, tapping his cheek with my hand gently. "I need to do this alone, if I'm not out in thirty you can come look for me."

"Screw that. You can't seriously think I'm just gonna let you go in there on your own, to possibly fucking die. You don't know how many men he might have in there, and you don't know what's waiting for you," he screamed.

"I had to watch Guillermo hurt you, over and over again. Every single day I watched him carve you up, I watched him maim you and kill your spirit. I will not risk hurting you again Santos. Whose sins are you paying for at this point?" I asked.

"I'm fucking coming, stop being so goddamn stubborn." He grabbed my wrist, yanking me towards his hard chest with a slam. "We're done making stupid decisions Celia." His nostrils flared out passionately. "We do this together."

I stared at him for a long moment. So many words and emotions silently passing between us. "Let's go," I sighed, releasing the safety on my Glock as we walked towards the side of the villa.

I didn't know how many men he had inside, but we only had so much time before the cavalry arrived. It wasn't that I wanted to do this alone, it was that I *needed* to do it alone. I needed to kill him for the sake of my family, for the things he broke within us... within me. The minute the others arrived it would become a shootout.

I knew exactly where he was, and I knew exactly how to get there without being noticed.

"Are we not going inside?" he whispered.

"Not through the door." I led him through the side of the villa, ducking under the windows and staying closer to the shadows as we snuck around the building.

Once I found the right window, the one just below the veranda door of my papá's second story office, I peeked inside the glass to see if I could see anyone. It was empty.

"Give me a boost to the balcony," I whispered.

He clasped his hands together to hold my foot and lift me up. It was just barely enough to get my arms up onto it. I muscled my way, struggling to get my lower body up on that balcony. Fuck, how much did my legs weigh?

"How am I supposed to get up there?" Santos whispered, too loudly, and I shushed him with a reprimanding stare.

"I'm sorry Santito. I told you I have to do this alone." I gave him one final look before I turned my back to him, ignoring his hissing of my name from below.

"Celia! What the fuck!"

I pulled a bobby pin from my fancy but now disheveled hair and forced it into the lock, jiggling it until I felt the resistance I needed and turning until I heard it click. I opened the door slowly, finding the room still dark and empty. A cloud of disappointment loomed over me. I really thought I'd find him here, waiting for me.

I thought at this point we'd been doing this dance long enough that we moved in sync, a macabre choreography of carnage that only ended with shallow graves. We'd been playing cat and mouse for years and I hadn't noticed I'd become the predator, checking behind the curtains to see if I could strike him first.

Was it all in my head? Was he even here?

My stomach dropped at the thought of him still being at El Palacio, wreaking havoc and promising death to all the men sworn to me. My fears were short-lived. Just then, I heard heavy footsteps and a deep voice barking orders in spanish from outside the door. I ran to my papá's giant oak desk, scurrying underneath just in time to hear the door creak open and see the light shining into the room from out in the hallway.

I smiled to myself, my confidence skyrocketing.

Ignacio never let me down before, why would he start now?

I heard his man anxiously telling him that a car pulled up to the property, but they couldn't find us. I hoped Santos was smart enough to stay undetected, reassuring myself that I'd brought the right man along for the job. Ronan would have broken through the front door with open fire, cutting down my tío's men by the handful until one of them shot him dead.

This was too personal to go down that way.

There was only one person who needed to die. Two who truly deserved it.

But today wasn't *my* day, so one would do.

He kept the light off, slow footsteps tapped on the floor one at a time as he made his way closer to the desk. My heart thundered so hard in my chest I thought surely it would give me away. His feet appeared right in front of me, with a screeching sound he dragged the chair from the desk and plopped down.

Oh, he was making it too easy.

I didn't believe in karma, but it seemed like the bitch was really on my side lately.

A knife to the foot, then a bullet to the head.

No, that would be too quick.

And too loud.

I had to kill him quietly unless I planned to deal with however many men he had trapped in this house with us. I was a ballsy bitch, but the thing about being brave, was also knowing your limits.

I heard the flickering of the lighter letting me know the pompous dickhead actually thought he was going to smoke a cigar while he waited for me to walk into his trap. Like I was that easy to kill. I was feeling sort of fucking offended about the whole thing.

My heart sped up even more and I gripped my knife tighter, the sweat in my palm coating the handle of the blade as I tried to figure out which foot I was going to be stabbing. Then his hand reached into the desk, his fingers wrapping around my throat as he pulled me out and slammed my back against the desk. I couldn't cry out from the pain, he squeezed too tight, his sausage-like fingers crushing my windpipe and putting painful pressure on my eyes.

I sent my arm flying, hoping to stab at him, but my body was too focused on self-preservation. My free hand struggled with his grip around my neck while the other fought to keep the blade in my clutches. He pulled me by the neck, lifting my head off the table just enough to slam it back down with force. I bit back a yell, hoping the noise wouldn't call his men in for reinforcement.

"Maldita," he cursed me. "All this trouble just for a few million dollars," he spat out and I wheezed, slapping and scratching at him while I felt the crushing power of his grip squeezing my arm painfully.

He truly knew nothing if he thought this was over a few million dollars.

It was over *billions*.

It was over everything that was meant to be mine.

I spit, landing right in the middle of his face and painting a disgusted look onto his expression as he fought to decide whether or not he was going to risk giving me a chance to free myself if he cleaned it off.

He pulled me by the throat once more and sent my head flying down twice as hard as before. I cried out in pain, and he squeezed my throat tighter.

"This is over Celia. You will pass the credentials of the dungeons to me, or you will die right here, right now."

I cackled in his hold, the deranged look on my face only provoking him further into a rage-fueled spiral.

"If you kill me, you stay just as fucked, just as poor, and just the same sorry excuse for a jefe that you've been this whole time. So fucking kill me payaso. You don't scare me anymore."

He slapped me across the face, the steel force of his palm cutting into my skin. A pool of liquid metal slid over my taste buds while I mentally accepted my death.

The pressure near my eyes was unbearable as he squeezed even harder, completely disabling me from taking even the smallest sip of air back into my lungs. My vision went fuzzy, specs of colors floated around in my vision.

Maldición.

Was I really going to fucking die like this?

After everything?

"My men will be up here soon, then I'll make them teach you why your father should have never put the stupid idea of a reina del cártel into your naive little mind. I'll let them each take a turn with you, one by one, till you're begging me to kill you sobrina."

"Better not, tío," I rasped, not even sure if he could make out the words as I forced them out of my mouth. He loosened his grip slightly like a dumb, curious bastard, eager for the rest of my sentence. "Maybe I'll fuck them so good they'll drop to their knees for *me* instead."

"Zorra," he spat out venomously, letting go of my throat just to strike my face once again.

I coughed, swallowing a lungful of air.

"Is it not as fun when I weaponize the very thing you all tried to convince yourselves was a weakness?"

He didn't get to answer.

A deafening boom came from somewhere in the house making us both turn our necks as if we'd see what was happening through the closed office door. Santos was creating a distraction, and fuck if it wasn't hot as hell that he could offer me his help without treating me like I was powerless.

"Looks like your men are busy," I taunted, sending my foot up between his legs with as much force as I could muster.

He wheezed from the pain, relaxing his grip around my neck to clutch his manhood defensively as he cursed me in spanish. It was all the time I needed to scamper away, just far enough to give me time to retrieve my gun from the floor under the desk and pull it on him.

"Now tío querido, did you *really* think it was going to be this easy to kill me, or did you come here just to offend me?"

He moved to reach his hand behind him, but I lodged a bullet into the very same shoulder to stop him from pulling out his own gun. He cried out in pain, but the shaking of the villa's foundation let me know his men were far too preoccupied to come to his rescue.

"And here I thought I was going to have to kill you fast and miss out on all the fun. Looks like Carlitos won't be welcoming you to hell just yet." I smirked watching his eyes go wide.

"What did you do to my son?" he seethed, which only furthered new confusion.

"What do you mean what did I do? I killed that pendejo months ago." I laughed plugging another bullet into his other shoulder when he attempted to reach back once again with his uninjured arm. "Vamos tío, I was really hoping to draw this out."

"Sadistic, just like the rest of your family. Your temperament is more suited to *lower* positions, you can't handle what it takes to be jefe," he insulted me through pained grunts.

"President Ramírez seems to think I can, which begs the question... where does that leave you if I'm running the cártel they all recognize as the tried and true version?" I gave him a sinister smirk, stepping closer to him now that he'd dropped to a seat on the ground, arms limp at his side.

"Must be so easy... to fuck your way to the top," he labored out.

I clenched my back teeth together, counting backwards in my head while I silently told myself that future me would regret not killing him slowly. He was antagonizing me on purpose. Pushing me because he knew it was over for him now and all he could do about it was hope I'd deliver it quickly.

I had no such plans to do so.

"I gave him a quick death, because he was a stupid bastard who didn't know any better. But you tío, I'm gonna take my time with you.

I'm going to kill you a little every single day until I tire of playing with you. And when you're dead, I'll use your bones to pick at my teeth after meals, to comb my hair, and to clean under my fingernails. I'll burn everything else you've ever touched. Including Carolina," I promised him.

There was a look on his face that could only be described as utter confusion. Which only let me know one thing, and it was the only thing I needed to know.

My tío was no longer in charge. Someone else was just letting him pretend to play the part.

"How long has she been running the show?" I asked.

He hocked a bloody wad of spit onto the ground by my feet.

"It's going to get really smoky up here soon by the smell of things tío. I'd love to move us somewhere more comfortable but I'm real inclined to leave you here if it might get me answers." I raised the Glock up once more, hoping I wouldn't have to shoot him once again.

There was only so many bullets you could put into a man while still expecting him to stay alive for long-term torture.

"Both of you are just like your mother. Bloodthirsty. Constantly thinking with violence first, assuming the Ortíz name still means anything around these parts and that you can use it to your advantage. You think just because you have both families' blood in your veins it means you deserve this any more than I do?"

"You knew?" I asked him.

"Of course I fucking knew, we all fucking knew. The only person who didn't was you and the sorry excuse for a man that was the Ortíz boy." I barely gave him a chance to finish before putting the next bullet in his knee cap.

It was one thing to spew his shit about me, but César was blameless in all of this.

"What do you know? Who killed Diego Ortíz?" I asked, hoping I'd get any crumbs that could help me unlock all the bullshit secrets our parents buried with them.

"Everyone knows Ortíz killed his own son." He coughed, blood splatter flying everywhere.

"Why would he do that when he needed a successor?"

"He didn't, at least not anymore. He was marrying your mother to be head of the Flores family. Diego was done, he wanted out. No one gets out alive, you know that better than anyone don't you sobrina?"

"Thanks for the reminder, tío." I stepped one foot at a time closer to him until I was standing over him.

I placed the heel of my stiletto over his bleeding kneecap and put my weight into it, ignoring his screaming pleas as well as his cursing and name calling.

There was no bird who could out-sing a serenade by a man on the verge of death.

82

MATEO

There was nothing quite as chaotic as evacuating a building full of people whose language you didn't speak. No wait, there was something that topped that. It was getting a text from Santos saying that Celia was headed to the villa to kill her uncle and that she somehow found a way to ditch him in the process.

He sent a photo of him next to a blown up Mastretta with text underneath saying, 'SOS, probably will get killed by cártel soon' and I practically bulldozed through every civilian in the crowd gathered outside El Palacio in order to find Ronan and rush the fuck out of there to our girl's aid.

It wasn't that I didn't think she was capable of doing it herself. It wasn't that I didn't think she couldn't handle the fight.

It was about how the fuck I was supposed to go on if she somehow needed me and I wasn't there?

Again.

I peeled onto the main road, the tires screeching against the asphalt as the car drifted sideways before entering the grounds of the villa.

A burning sports car was now crashed into the front of the house, blocking the doorway. A portion of the upper level collapsed over it while the flames engulfed Celia's childhood home. Ignacio's men struggled and fought each other to climb out of the building as fast as they could, but each time one of them found their way out Santos would shoot them down.

I hadn't fully parked the car before Ronan jumped out, in full attack mode he pulled two pistols out, firing them off simultaneously towards the incoming lackeys to give Santos a break.

"Where is she?" I roared out over the sound of bullets flying in the fire taking over the mansion.

He pointed to a balcony up in the distance.

"She went up through there," he yelled.

"You let her go by herself?"

"I'm gonna fucking tell her you said that," he thundered at me. "She'll have your balls for saying anyone *lets* her do anything."

"I will actually pay you to keep your fucking mouth shut about that. Help me get up there." I nudged him, both of us leaving Zerkos looking more than capable of handling the mess of men scrambling to get out of the villa just to be shot. The pile of bodies was making it harder for them to crawl out of the blazing embers.

"She was in there." He pointed at the glass door that led to the veranda.

"Give me a boost up," I told him. He didn't hesitate, clasping his fingers together and sending me up with a grunt.

"Hey, what the fuck man? Help me up," he called out from below while I ran into the house.

The smoke was filling every inch of the villa, spreading its thick cloud all around me until I could barely see my hands in front of my face.

"Sunshine," I bellowed out, trying to fan some clarity into my vision but I couldn't avoid the involuntary tears that came from the smoke wafting all around me.

I couldn't see her, but I could hear her labored grunts and the sound of something banging.

"Sunshine!" I screamed again, this time not hiding the panic in my voice when the thought occurred to me that it might be her struggling for her life I was listening to.

I followed the sound into the corner of the room until I was close enough that I could see the scene in front of me. A brutal sight to behold. Celia Flores sitting on her uncle's chest as she bashed the butt of her gun into his face over and over again. Blood splattered over her and poured down his neck.

His face looked fucked, and he wasn't moving, which led me to believe he was dead as hell considering all the blood on the ground, but she didn't let up.

"Sunshine, we gotta get you out of here, there's too much smoke." I grabbed her arm, but she fought me off, yelling a feral screech before sending the gun down against Ignacio's face once more. "Baby, please. Let me get you out of here." I reached for her face and pulled her chin towards me, getting as close as possible as I could so she could see straight into my eyes.

She took a deep stuttered breath, breaking the feral trance she had found herself locked into.

"Get *him* out of here," she said coldly, tilting her head back towards her half-dead uncle before standing up and walking back towards the veranda, where the smoke rolled out easily into the fresh air. I could barely see her anymore, but her voice was still crystal clear when she spoke, despite the roaring of the flames outside the door. "I'm not done playing with him yet."

I didn't bother to check his pulse or give him the dignity of being carried. I dragged the sorry fucker by the leg until I'd made my way out to the balcony once more and then, without any care, I shoved him off of it the same way Guillermo had done to me when Los Muertos attacked the Black Crow high rise.

Maybe Celia had the right idea.

An eye for an eye felt really fucking right.

The Diablos Locos and Celia's men were all pulling into the property just in time to watch the flames engulf the building completely. She was already in Ronan's arms by the time I made it to them, slowed down by dragging Ignacio's corpse along the way.

"What do you want to do with him?" he asked her.

"Have Dominico lock him up in the dungeons, can you ask Emory to keep him alive for now?" He nodded to her before taking Ignacio's leg from me and dragging him over to the group of cártel lackeys who were clearing out the pile of dead bodies out front.

Before I could even ask her how she was doing, Ramírez was already stepping up to her, and in three long strides he was practically touching her again.

"If that is Ignacio Flores you have there, I'm afraid I must ask you to surrender him to the police Señorita Flores. The list of crimes he must pay for is longer than I care to read."

"Then that is *not* Ignacio Flores, and I would appreciate you allowing me to mourn this violent attack I've suffered tonight in my childhood home, José Luis," she scolded him as if he she didn't care what his title was.

"Celi—" he began but I cut him off.

"It's Señorita Flores to you, Señor Presidente. And weren't you just telling me, moments ago, outside El Palacio how you were deeply indebted to Miss Flores for saving your daughter's life?" I reminded him, making Celia's expression soften into a smile while the president's jaw ticked in annoyance.

"I have to turn him in to the authorities. How else am I supposed to convince my followers—your supporters—that he won't be a problem anymore?" he asked her in a hushed voice as if I had no clue what fucking shenanigans they were up to.

"That's your problem to deal with José Luis. Figure it out. I'll double my previous offer towards your budget." His eyes widened at my suggestion. "But Ignacio Flores is mine, this is personal. Es familia," she reminded him.

He gave her a nod and turned back towards the police cars flashing on the far side of the villa's property.

"His daughter?" she whispered at me with a look of disbelief on her face.

"Yeah, look at you. You're practically a superhero," I told her, nudging her ribs with my elbow.

She gave me a smile, and though it was meant to be genuine, the attempted murder on her face really changed the whole vibe. Her smile faded, like she caught my train of thought and didn't like where it was headed.

"Is this... too much for you? Too dark for you?" she asked. "I know with the Crows you were all at least *trying* to do some good where you could. Here... I don't know if there is any good here." She bit her lip, letting me know she was going into that place in her head where she let all her insecurities take over.

"Sunshine, the difference between me and you, is that you hate the darkness and I'm in love with it. It pulls me in, it consumes me.The thing is, Celia, you *are* the darkness, and whether you love yourself or not is irrelevant because I love you enough for the both of us. If I have, for one moment, given you the impression that by your side wasn't the place for me, then forgive me." I brushed my thumb over the dried specks of blood stuck to her skin. "There is nowhere else I want to be."

"Promise?" she asked.

I answered without words, pulling her into my chest and pressing my lips into hers for just a second before remembering there were so many people gathered outside. Zerkos eventually made his way back to her side and Santos joined us as well. One by one her council members left the property after checking in with her and eventually all that was left were the Diablos Locos who had been waiting for instructions.

We stood there, watching the villa burn down until César finally made his way over to say his goodbyes. He'd fulfilled his end of the bargain and earned his freedom, without death.

"Te amo, Princesita," he told her, punching her shoulder softly.

"If I can ever repay the favor, just say the word." She didn't hug him, and he didn't reach for her like I would have expected them to.

Maybe because it would be harder to face the emotions than either of them were prepared for.

"Actually..." César said. "You could tell that stubborn doctor to come back over the border with me."

"What?" She looked at him like she didn't understand.

"That Irish skin, she's gonna burn up down here Princesa. My Médico ended up signing up for a Doctors Without Borders program, so I'm... desperate for a good club doc," he told her, scratching the back of his head nervously.

"Desperate for a good doctor, or desperate for *that* doctor?" I instigated, hoping to force the words out of the man myself.

He gave me a cutting look, but Celia paid no mind.

"If you think I can make Emory O'Connor do anything—" Celia started.

"No, she's just as hard headed as you are. But she's indebted to Zerkos, and she'll go— or stay—where he tells her to."

"I'll see what I can do, Lobito." She reached up on the tips of her toes and placed a kiss to his cheek before he turned around and walked into the mass of leather vests congregated in a circle.

I'd kind of miss the bastard.

And I'd never fucking tell him that.

From the outside looking in, it reminded me of when loving parents dropped their kid off at college and stuck around that first day just to make sure they were settling in okay. Now César would be packing up and heading thousands of miles back to Grimm's Reach, because she had proved she could make it on her own.

"What do you need?" I turned her towards me, wiping a rogue tear that fell from the corner of her eye.

"I need to change out of these clothes, I need a torta like nobody's business, and I need to squeeze the truth out of that ugly pendejo," she said, looking up at me. "In that order."

"And the villa?" Zerkos asked.

"Let it burn, there's another home further south, away from the city. It's smaller, but since The Diablos are gone it'll be just big enough for us all," she explained. "There's another villa adjacent to the property and the Crows can house there."

"Send me the address," Ronan said, casually tossing the keys to Santos.

"Where are you going?" he asked him.

"To get the lady her torta. I'll meet you there." He smirked, and she leaned into him and pressed a kiss to the corner of his lip before turning to Santos and changing her expression into a frown.

"You had to blow up the fucking Mastretta?" she chastised him, flicking her hand in the air to wave him off.

"You ran off like you have no regard for your own safety." He scowled, raising his voice back at her.

Oh. This was going to be an actual argument.

"Because I knew if you went in there, I'd have to worry about whether or not you were going to come out alive too," she yelled back, stepping up to him and getting as much in his face as she could, considering her height.

"So that's how this works? You get to decide whether you live or die while you put us on a shelf to look at us, and keep us safe?"

I spaced myself from them, unsure if this was a "we" thing or a "they" thing. I saw both sides of the argument, and for that reason alone I knew I needed to get the fuck out of here before either of them tried to drag me into their corner.

"At least then I don't have to go through the pain of thinking I'm going to lose any of you all over again. If you're waiting for an apology, it's not going to come from me Santito." She emphasized the nickname like she wasn't happy to be saying it at all.

"Kane, are you not going to say anything?" Santos called out to me, ruining my plans to try to stay Switzerland for this entire thing.

"Uh, well… I mean…" I scratched my head anxiously, "She was handling herself pretty well all on her own. She didn't need me." He didn't like that, scowling deeper at my response. "What? She doesn't need any of us dude."

She laughed, forcing the expression on his face to harden and the scowl on his forehead to deepen.

"Let me remind you of the week she spent in that Bratva cage. Let me remind you she was drugged, starved, and sold *twice*. And maybe you forgot but I had to spend an entire week watching her get mouth raped by my own fucking cousin. When it comes to the four of us, the three of us die before she ever gets hurt, *that* shouldn't be a hard rule to follow." Santos was rarely the type to yell, hardly the kind to verbalize so clearly why he was upset.

He never talked about what happened in that basement. Chalked it all up to it being *her* experience even though he was the one bearing most of the visible scars. She'd been marred by it too, but they were both processing it on such opposite ends of the spectrum that it was easy to forget they went through it together.

Like everything that came her way *made* her who she was, no matter how awful or painful it might have been. While for him it was ripping him apart. He stormed away, heading towards the several options of cars that had been left behind. Her expression had deflated to one full of pain and remorse.

I sighed heavily, dropping my shoulders before pulling her in again to place a kiss on the top of her head.

"Where the fuck are you going?" she asked as I turned away from her.

"I'm gonna see if Zerkos is still around for me to catch a ride with him. You should go with Santos," I told her, knowing damn well I was risking sliding onto her bad side.

Her nostrils flared and she stared up at me through furrowed eyebrows.

"I'm not good at saying the right things. I don't even know how to fix this," she confessed, making me chuckle.

"Sunshine, you're hot as hell and twice as stubborn, but you're right, your communication skills are shit. Get in the car with Santos if you want a ride to your new home," I told her, dropping my tone into that serious one I rarely took with her.

"That's not fair."

"Tough, you wanted three guys, you gotta take care of the fragile little egos that come with them too." I pushed her in the direction he'd walked off to before I ran off to find Ronan, hoping he hadn't left me behind yet.

83

SANTOS

"I'm sorry," she said after five minutes of driving in silence.

"No you're not," I answered.

"You're right, I'm not."

"And you'd probably do it again too, if given the chance," I added, turning my head just in time to get a glimpse of her biting her lip like I really knew her too well for her own good.

"I guess after watching my family go through so much pain, so much violence, I thought I was doing the right thing by prioritizing your safety above everything. The three of you are my family." She shrugged, looking out the window while fidgeting with her nails.

"What do you think would happen to the three of us if he had hurt you? If he had killed you?" I asked.

"What would happen to me if it was the other way around?" She raised her voice.

I sighed.

"Stop trying to leave me all alone in this world," she chastised.

"That's not what I'm trying to do," I gritted out.

"And what would you have done had I taken you up there with me?" she asked.

"I would have k—"

"Killed that motherfucker," she interrupted, nodding like I was just so damn obvious. "You see the problem with that yet?"

"I do," I admitted begrudgingly. "But my wanting to protect you isn't because I don't think you can't protect yourself. It's because you've been doing it for so long. Don't you think it's time to let someone else take a turn?"

"Take a turn?" she asked.

"You've been looking over your shoulder for fifteen years, Morena. Let us watch your back now. Can you do that?" I asked, her shoulders sagging like she was relieved.

"I can try." She breathed out, wrapping her hand over mine and squeezing.

"You can't keep running into the mouth of danger by yourself every time. It drives me fucking insane. Maybe you've forgotten that we do things together, but it's the reason why the three of us are still alive. Okay?"

"Okay." She nodded, her eyes burning straight into mine.

"Thank you." I dropped my hand to her thigh where her fancy dress had been ripped to shreds, exposing her bare leg. There was nothing like feeling her hot skin under my touch. "Did he hurt you?"

"He banged my head up pretty good." She rubbed the back of her head. "But I'll survive."

"Let me see." I told her, but she shook her head.

"You're driving."

"Let me see!" I stepped on the break, forcing the car into a screeching halt.

The smell of burnt rubber filled the car and she rushed to slide her window up, but it was too late.

"You're insane! What are you doing?" She laughed as I pulled her off her seat and folded her over the middle console so that her head was on my lap.

She tried to push off of me, but I grabbed the back of her neck and pinned her down.

"Stay still, I want to make sure you're okay." I ran my fingers through her scalp gently, feeling for anything possibly concerning.

She relaxed her head onto my lap, despite her face being directly on my dick aside from the thin layer of fabric separating us from each other. There were some pretty good bumps and a small scratch that had bled and already dried up around her hair, but considering she wasn't even complaining from the pain, it didn't seem serious.

"See, all fine," she said sarcastically with her mouth plastered onto the crotch of my pants.

"Not all fine," I grumbled, taking my foot off the break and driving on once again.

"Then let me make it better," she said with a honeyed tone to her voice, cupping my dick through my pants and giving it a squeeze.

I could feel her hot breath practically on my cock through the fabric of the designer suit she had me in. She unzipped me, way too fucking slowly, and the anticipation alone engorged my erection further.

"Oh fuck, Morena," I said just as her hand reached inside my pants, the soft skin of her dainty palms squeezing around my shaft and pulling it free.

"Pay attention to the road," she reminded me, each word sending goosebumps down my spine as her exhale tickled the overly sensitive skin.

"Then hurry up and put your mouth on me." I forced her head back down, drawing a yelp from her.

Her lips wrapped around the head of my cock, barely any pressure as she swirled her tongue around, making me nearly forget about the road when she swallowed me down. The heat of her mouth was almost enough to make me come, but the way she moved her tongue around each bar of my piercings was even more intense.

I groaned, a bolt of pleasure running up my spine every time she relaxed and took me all the way down the back of her throat. She picked up speed, her saliva dripping all over my cock while her head bobbed up and down my lap.

How many men would ever get to say they got road head by the baddest cártel queen to ever live?

Her fingers wrapped around the base of my dick. She squeezed and tugged using her own spit as lube while she gagged down my cock with more than audible moans. I released my grip on her hair and trailed my fingers down her back, cupping her ass.

It was sticking up in the air, perfectly taunting me in the reflection of the passenger window. I lifted my hand up and dropped it down with a hard smack. She moaned a deep guttural sound that vibrated from her chest down to my balls.

"Fuck. That mouth." I closed my eyes for a split second, forgetting the road.

She was slobbering more now, one hand gripping my thigh for support with the kind of pressure that would leave a mark. The other hand rolled my balls in her palm, she kneaded them softly, playing with them in her hand while she continued to slide up and down my shaft. I lifted my hand up and struck down once more eliciting a grunt of pleasure from her.

I slid my hand through the rips in the fabric of her dress, letting my fingers roam under the elastic of her underwear. Her back arched further, her ass sticking up higher somehow as she reached for more of my touch. I gave her juicy ass one final squeeze before traveling further down, feeling the slickness pooling between her legs. She was so goddamn wet and it was just from sucking me off.

"Do you want me inside you?" I whispered.

She nodded, mumbling some incoherent bullshit with my cock still in her mouth.

"Fuck," I moaned, closing my eyes again before remembering it was up to me to keep us alive.

I pushed my fingers inside her, a welcome whimper from within her chest greeted me just as I made my way into her tight, drenched cunt. She groaned, the vibrations making my toes curl until I couldn't fight the inevitable any longer.

"I'm gonna come," I warned her, but she didn't let up, using my words as fuel and moving faster, sucking even harder than before like she was going to pull my soul out through my cock.

I'd never fought harder in my life to keep my eyes open, the dark of the night and the weak headlights of the car we'd stolen were proving to be enough of a challenge. Receiving the hottest blowjob known to man definitely turned the game up to hard mode.

I pulled my fingers out from inside her, drawing a disappointed grunt from her before forcing a squeal once I gripped the back of her neck and shoved her as far down my cock as possible. I moved her up and down my length, feeling my core tighten and my balls drawing tighter the closer I got to my release. I took the right turn into the address she'd plugged into the navigation system, peeling hard through the gravel driveway before pulling the emergency break just as I emptied myself down her throat.

She lifted her head up slowly, wiping her lips with the back of her hands before giving me a devilishly sinful look. She then looked past me to my window, and she settled into a proud smirk that spread to her eyes with a dangerous glow.

I turned my head to see Ronan standing next to my window and surely there Kane was on the other side of hers. He opened her door, completely devouring her with his eyes before he opened his mouth to speak.

"Damn sunshine, there's a puddle on the seat," he commented, pulling her by the waist and tossing her over his shoulder.

"I see you've made up," Ronan said with a smirk, extending his hand to me to help me out of the car.

"She said sorry." I grinned back.

"Why do I not believe that?" He laughed.

"She said it in her own way." I followed Mateo into what would now be our new home.

She said it was smaller, and in comparison to the villa it *was,* but for some reason I had been expecting a house.

It wasn't.

It was just a smaller mansion.

She was yelling something at Mateo and pounding her fists on his back.

"What's the problem?" Zerkos asked, catching up to them.

"She's mad because I told her I'd lock her up if she wouldn't take the night off." Kane smirked.

"I need to talk to Ignacio," she shouted.

"He'll be there in the morning, sunshine," he said calmly, taking her further into the house as if their head start had already given him all the time he needed to get accustomed to what would be our new home.

"He's not wrong, beautiful. Give Emory some time to patch him up, get his adrenaline back down so that you can cause him more damage tomorrow," Ronan told her.

Mateo dropped her to her feet in the kitchen, her disappointment was more than evident.

"I've waited so long for this," she told them both, clenching her fists tightly.

"So what's a few more hours?" Zerkos asked her. "Get some rest, go in there with a clear head so you don't make any rash decisions just because you're thirsty for revenge."

"It's not in me to be patient." She crossed her arms over her chest, jaw clenched tight.

"Maybe we can distract you then."

"Unlikely, I'm wound up and there's nothing I want more than to make him pay," she snipped at us, teeth bared like she wasn't taking no for an answer.

"Nothing?" Ronan looked at her questioningly, stepping towards her way too slowly.

She shook her head to confirm. His hand reached up to cup the side of her face, his thumb brushing down her lip before he pulled her to him and locked his lips around hers.

"Then I'll go kill him for you so you can get some adequate rest." He smirked, pulling away from her.

She shoved him playfully. "You're a pain in my ass Ronan."

"And I'll continue to be that till the day one of us dies, flower." He reached over the counter pulling a large paper bag and began distributing the tortas wrapped in aluminum foil to each of us as we gathered around the kitchen for our first meal in our new home.

84

CELIA

I brushed my hand over the black Armani two-piece suit I paired with red bottomed overpriced heels. I couldn't deny how much better expensive clothes felt than my normal jeans and T-shirt attire. "Finally… you show your face," Ignacio groaned from his restraints.

He didn't look nearly as bad as he seemed to be last night, which made me wonder if I should have just killed him instead.

"It was a big night. Had to move into a new house and everything. Who knew the villa could burn down twice?" I mused casually.

"You won't get anything out of me," he spat out.

"Who says I want anything from you? Maybe I'm just going to make you my plaything until your body gives out from the pain. You're a bit expired viejo, I don't think you can take much these days." I walked by the metal table, running my fingers over all the surgical steel tools and torture devices.

"You should have come to me Celia, we could have done this together."

"Together? You mean after you killed my mamá, I should have come to you for help?" I laughed. "That's rich."

"I didn't kill Jamila." He pulled against his restraints angrily.

"That's not even a worthwhile lie. Jamila hated me. If you expected her death to devastate me, you were hurting the wrong sister."

"I didn't kill Jamila!" he screamed again. "Your hermana lost her shit and went out there after I left her with Guillermo. I would have never hurt Jamila on purpose," he gritted out.

I lifted an eyebrow.

Curious.

Maybe I did want something from him.

"Tío. Do you have more secrets for me now?" I tilted my head, pulling up a chair and sitting down casually as I waited.

There was no gossip better than family dirt, it was a Latin American right of passage, after all. If you came from Indigenous ancestors, we were well accustomed to passing stories down as history.

There was always time for gossip.

"I should have been the one to marry her. She was *mine*. We had been together for years when Augustin Ortíz killed his own son and then forced her to marry my brother in an attempt to keep his hand in the business."

"And my mamá just went eagerly? The obedient little pawn she was?" I asked, unsure if I should even bother believing the words coming from his mouth.

"Your mother was as ruthless as you are. You think you're a killer because you're a Flores? Nah Celia, that's the Ortíz blood running through your veins. She orchestrated the whole thing, killed your abuelo execution style in front of your papá's men and told them they followed Rafa now. Made a big show of that ledger full of bought secrets too before she made it disappear from the face of the planet."

"Seems like she wasn't right for a cobarde hijo de la chingada like you then. You make it sound like she was perfect for my papá."

"She *was*. Then he put her fire out, kept her in the background, away from any decisions until she settled for the realization that she'd lost the very thing she'd dirtied her hands for. I would have stoked her flames. We would have controlled this country together." His upper lip twitched angrily.

"But instead, you let my psychotic revenge fueled sister kill her instead. For what? To send a message to me?"

"I told you; I didn't have a hand in it. Your sister is a loose fucking cannon. She makes bad calls up and down, she aligns herself with our enemies because she thinks she'll gain the upper hand. She's robbed me blind and used that money to pay my men to do Bratva bitch work." He spat onto the floor.

"So she *is* getting in with Sokolov?" I asked and his eyes hardened, as if he remembered this wasn't family social time and needed to stick to his promise not tell me anything.

I sighed, grabbing pliers and a rubber block about an inch in size off the table Mateo had left prepped for me. I stepped one foot directly in front of the other until I found myself across from him.

"Abre la boca or I'll pry it open with a hot knife," I promised. He didn't dare to disobey, opening without hesitation just wide enough so that I could stick the rubber block inside his mouth.

I pinched the plyers shut around his back molar, putting one high heeled Louboutin on the wall for leverage. It wasn't as easy to pry a man's tooth out without the adrenaline of survival running through your veins. But he didn't deserve easy, and I relished every pained grunt out of his chest until the tooth finally came loose.

His screams echoed through the dungeon walls.

"I asked if she was getting in with Sokolov." I pulled the rubber block out of his mouth.

"Getting in? She's nice and cozy in their family tree now. She's made arrangements to marry his eldest son." He spat out a wad of blood onto the ground.

"Since when?" I asked, trying to figure out how long my sister may have been responsible for my misfortunes.

"A year now?"

"But she was with Guillermo Álvarez," I said, knowing that what I'd seen between them in that basement was much more than something casual.

"Clever zorra that one. Smart enough to understand just exactly how to use her pussy to get far in this world. She kept Guillermo in line for me, made sure he didn't get too big for his own britches. I guess your papá didn't teach you every lesson you needed."

"Except now it looks like she's the big fish in your pond and she's about to swallow you up tío." I clucked my tongue, "all this blood and war just to hand México over to the Russians?"

He growled with disapproval but we both knew I was right.

Carolina was a garbage truck full of hot trash waiting to unload.

But she was my fucking sister.

Even if she was a pendeja.

"We can stop her together," he labored out.

"I can stop her myself," I told him, shoving the block back inside his mouth, pulling another molar out with a bit more ease this time.

I didn't give him time to mourn his tooth before jamming the pliers back and finding the next addition to my collection. One by one I pulled out his remaining teeth, all aside from the few bits and pieces that were barely hanging on in the front from my previous assault. I was sweating, my hands aching and sore by the time I finished. His head hung from his neck, blood dripping from his open mouth as he moaned and shivered from the pain.

"I gave your papá the gift of an easy death." he mumbled with difficulty.

"I am not my papá. I am the woman both of you helped to create, and you *will* feel the full force of my wrath. I will give you the death you deserve. Nothing more, nothing less."

"Where are you going?" he shouted at me as I turned to leave.

"To beat some sense into my sister."

He laughed like it was an outrageous thought.

"That's not how this ends, sobrina. It ends in blood. It always does."

"I'm better than you. I decide how this ends," I said, turning on my heels.

"You can't leave me here like this Celia," he moaned, and I laughed darkly.

"Tío, that's exactly what I'll be doing. And I'll keep you alive, and I'll come down here and inflict pain on you whenever you cross my mind, until the day I die. Unless you bore me, then maybe I could be persuaded to forget to feed you and put an end to your misery."

He groaned, yanking at his chains and making a loud racket.

I ignored him, placing the pliers back on the table and leaving the torture chamber, striding past each cell until I entered the control center of the dungeons. I gave a smirk and a nod to Taylor Constance and she returned me a beaming smile.

"How are you settling in?" I asked her.

"Well, you pay better than Ronan and considering, regardless of location, I end up between four walls with a computer for a window, I'm finding myself right at home." She laughed.

"Something about having you watching over us makes me feel warm and safe inside," I told her.

"Well, good thing I'm always watching then," she said, raising her eyebrows up suggestively, making me laugh.

"Let me know if you need anything, seriously. I'm grateful you're here. I'm grateful for all that you've done," I told her, implying that I had been made aware that if it weren't for her, Ronan would be dead right now.

"Even death can't separate me from those fuckers, Celia. I'm afraid you're stuck with me." She smiled, assuring me I had no debt to her because her loyalty was to my men.

Which was more than fine with me because their loyalty belonged to me.

"I consider it a privilege, so let me know if I can help you make yourself comfortable here."

"Just point me to a sexy woman who likes cars and I think I'll be just fine around these parts."

"I'll keep my eyes out," I told her, taking that as my cue to stop bothering her and let her continue her work.

She was already tracking down Sokolov for me, but now she was trying to find Carolina too. She really was the best at what she did, and I was thankful every day to have her on my side. My heels clicked over the smooth concrete floor, and I sent a text to Mateo to let him know I'd be heading home from the dungeons.

"You're lighting a candle before we leave?" he asked as I held the match over the wick on the seven-day candle encased in glass.

"Yes, mi vida," I told him, pouring a fresh shot for La Madrina and dropping an unlit cigarette on her altar.

"What if it burns the house down?" The look on Mateo's face was so innocent and cute it made me smile.

"I promise you it won't." I grabbed my packed bag off the bed, but he ripped it from my hand to carry it himself.

"It could happen," he mumbled.

"She wouldn't do that to me." I assured him, knowing Santa Muerte took care of her children.

"Zerkos said the jet is loaded." His tone switched into business mode like it did anytime we talked about cártel related things.

It worked. All of us, doing this together. It somehow made sense, we were moving like a well-oiled machine, and I depended on my guys with my life. On top of that, I'd found myself a solid council who I trusted to call out my bullshit, *respectfully* of course. I was only so tolerable. I was counting all my blessings and I knew they would only keep coming if I let Death loose so she could play.

When you were exposed to darkness so young, it just became something you had to embrace inside yourself. I knew now the only way to not hate myself was to love even the worst parts of myself.

After all, they were the parts that had kept me alive all this time.

85

CELIA

Between Susana's knowledge of her father's day to day life and Taylor's incredible tech-stalker skills it was a piece of cake pinpointing where we were likely to find Sokolov.

Because I'm a spiritual kind of pendeja, I thought it was quite symbolic to pick Friday at midnight, when he was sure to be at the very strip club he'd kept me prisoner in for nearly a week. The very place where he drugged me and sold me like cheap meat at the market. If I was lucky, I'd get to free some girls from that very same fate tonight.

Mateo's hand found mine in the backseat of the car, squeezing it tight and ignoring the nervous sweat as if it didn't bother him at all.

"Hey," he whispered nervously in my ear.

"Hmm?" I answered quietly so that the conversation stayed between the two of us.

"I can't promise to hold back when we go in there." He furrowed his eyebrows in the middle, creating a hard crease.

"His death belongs to me." I growled.

"No Sunshine, his death belongs to all of us. I watched helplessly while you almost died because of the drugs he pumped into your system. He killed my men." He didn't stand down.

"Mateo," I gritted out, hating having to get stern with him.

"How about this," he grinned dangerously, "first one to him gets the kill?" He raised his eyebrows with his proposal, and I tilted my head at an angle while I thought about it.

"No guns?" I asked.

"If that's what the lady wants, that's what the lady gets." He gave me a shameless smirk.

"Fletch and his team will be waiting at the other exits to cause distractions and take down some of their men. We should have plenty of time," Ronan said from the front, making eye contact in the rearview mirror.

"I need you to go down into that basement and free the girls that will be in there," I told him before turning to Santos in the passenger seat. "I need you to check the dressing rooms behind the stage for any girls getting ready to be sold."

"Aye aye, jefa." Santos gave me a two-finger salute.

We parked across the street and just as Ronan was opening his door to get out, I called him back to me.

"Ronan, there was a lion in that basement last time," I warned him.

"What?" he said with a laugh of disbelief.

I was high as hell, but I remembered very vividly what I'd seen. The hot breath on my back and the sharp claws scratching against the smooth concrete floor with an obnoxious sound.

I remembered the bird's warning.

"Just be careful, okay?" I told him.

He turned back fully, reaching for me and pulling me into him despite the middle console standing as a barrier between us. His lips parted against mine, his tongue raking softly against my own for just a brief moment before he withdrew from me, leaving me high and needy for more.

"Focus, morena." Santos growled like he didn't approve of Ronan's distraction.

We got out of the car, the men strapped on their Kevlar vests and double checked all of their weapons. Ronan handed me a vest and I raised an eyebrow at him.

"I don't need that," I reassured him.

"Oh, have you become bulletproof in the last twelve years?" he said with a sarcastic tone.

"I'm not afraid to die," I explained.

His jaw ticked with anger, the scowl forming deep into his forehead.

"Put the fucking vest on, Celia." He pushed it into my chest. "I'm getting real sick of this shit." He dropped it from his hold, forcing me to clutch it fast to keep it from falling on the ground.

I turned to Mateo and gave him a questioning look, hoping he could help me with the angry blonde giant.

"I don't think you realize it, Sunshine, but every time you disregard your life, it feels like you're saying we aren't enough for you to want to do your best to stay," he said with deflated energy, scratching his head and walking ahead of me.

I sighed, turning to see Santos still standing next to me.

"What, you're not going to say something too?" I raised my voice, preparing to snap.

"No. I get it," he said, not bothering to explain himself.

He was gonna make me work for it.

"You get it?" I asked.

"Yeah. You think as long as we're safe it doesn't matter what happens to you. I get it because that's how I feel about you, how I feel about them. I'd give my life a hundred times over to make sure you three have the happy ending you deserve." He started walking away. "But if you take that vest off, I'll be taking mine off too. If you die, I die too," he said without looking back.

Motherfucker.

I slipped on the vest and ran after them, buttoning my coat over the obnoxiously thick Kevlar.

"Espérense pendejos," I shouted. The insult had Ronan stopping in his tracks abruptly forcing me to slam into the concrete wall that was his body.

He turned to face me, a scowl on his face that loosened once he eyed me up and down and appreciated that I'd listened to his demands.

"Thank you," he whispered into my mouth, gripping my jaw with one hand and forcing me on the tips of my toes in order to collect the kiss from him.

"One more thing," I said, forcing a single eyebrow to raise up from him.

He didn't ask, he just waited.

"There was a bird in that basement." His expression became even more confused. "If he's still there. I want him," I told him, not leaving room for discussion.

"Do you want the lion too?" Mateo laughed.

I clucked my tongue in annoyance as I shoved him to the side. The four of us broke up and headed for separate entrances.

"How do you plan to get to Sokolov without drawing attention to yourself?" Mateo asked.

I gave him a knowing tilt of my head without explaining anything.

"Sunshine, I promise you if he sees an inch of your body tonight, he dies by my hands." His expression was serious, fully devoid of humor.

"I guess we shall see." I winked, picking up the pace and walking ahead of him.

I slipped on my coat and nervously patted at it after fastening the buttons, hoping the vest was well hidden underneath. Mateo slipped on his suit jacket and did the same. It was bulky as hell, but these idiots weren't paying enough attention. They didn't know we were coming.

That alone would be their ending.

We paid our cover fee and walked in through the front door, the bouncer unchaining the velvet lined rope after checking our fake IDs matched the names on the list that Taylor had hacked into and gotten us on. I set off the metal detector just as I had expected, but I stuck my boots out, letting the metal buckles clink loudly to justify the alarm. The guard ran the hand paddle over my body, seemingly satisfied when it only sounded after he brought it down to my boot buckles once again and let us go.

The purple velvet covering every inch of the place smelled of stale smoke and none of the hanging neon lights matched. I was overly made up, playing the part of arm candy while Mateo had the ID of some well-to-do billionaire Taylor had conjured up for him and put on the club's VIP list.

The same list all the vile men who came here to purchase women were on. We walked through dark halls together while some less than cheery bikini-clad server led us to the area where the show would be.

Calling it a show made my stomach churn.

Flashes of memories cut through my mind like shards of glass, broken and fragmented from the drugs they'd pumped into my body after days of starving me. I slowed down, palms sweating as I realized what killing Allisher Sokolov would mean to me.

A freedom in a way.

The death of Cecilia.

The death of everything I had pretended to be while running away from who I truly was. The death of an entire world inside of me really, according to Yevtushenko.

We had been sitting at our booth for less than two minutes before a cocktail waitress came by to get our orders. Mateo asked for a soda with lime, she eyed him suspiciously but jotted it down anyway.

"Fortaleza?" I asked, and she nodded her head.

I held up two fingers indicating I wanted a double and she turned away to fetch our drinks. The stage lights flashed on just as she set our glasses in front of us. I reached for the glass, ready to put the straw in my mouth but Mateo covered the top of the glass with his hand, shaking his head at me.

"Not here."

I didn't have to ask why. There were a million reasons, and though I wanted a drink to calm my nerves I also knew I needed to do this with a clear head. Clean, fast, and viciously.

And there was no way I was gonna beat Mateo to him if I was drunk.

"I'm going to the bathroom, text me if things start to seem off," I whispered in his ear, sliding past him on the booth and feeling his hands cup my ass while I slid by.

I ignored his low growl, walking past all the other tables and not taking notice of the disgusting filth who assumed the shape of men, waiting to buy a girl. The cocktail waitress pointed the women's bathroom out to me and thankfully I seemed to be the only one in the building who wasn't already working here.

It was totally empty.

I took off my coat, removing the bullet proof vest and dropping it to the ground.

Sorry boys.

Change of plans.

I unzipped my dress from the side and stepped out of it, folding it neatly and shoving it into a corner with the vest knowing damn well that if *anything* went right tonight, the chances of me making it back here to collect my belongings were slim.

Charged it to the game.

A worthwhile offering in exchange for Sokolov's blood.

I took one last look in the mirror, fluffing up my heavy hair and wiping stray lipstick from the corner of my mouth. I was in that same matching black lingerie that all the girls in this building were wearing, well at least something close enough that no man would be able to tell the difference.

I patted the outside of my boot, feeling for the knife I'd hidden inside. I didn't need a gun for this. I would have to do it from up close. I always knew that I would have to, and in a way, I needed that. Now I just needed to get to the boss man.

I slipped my hand into my bra, feeling for the tiny zip lock bag that contained my secret weapon for tonight. I took a deep breath and sent a silent prayer to Santisima. I walked out of the bathroom, turning back into the hallway and headed towards the stage when a cocktail waitress passed by me with a single drink on her tray.

"Is that for the boss?" I stuck my arm out in front of her and she looked at me with an anxious and hesitant expression.

"He said you were taking too long, asked me to come get it for him myself. Probably better you don't bother him right now unless—"

"No, take it!" She pushed the circular tray towards me, and I nodded, giving a sympathetic smile while she headed back towards the main area with the stage.

I rushed down the hallway, unsure which one of the doors would be Sokolov's but knowing I had a limited amount of time to find him. I pulled the baggy from my tit-pocket and opened it up, pouring the powder into the drink and stirring it with my finger until it dissolved into the vodka clear liquid once again.

Alright. Deep breath, he's just a man. All men can be killed, that's the one thing they all have in common. I picked the door all the way at the end of the hall, knowing it would be easier to go back the way I came if someone caught me.

But fate was good to me now.

After all, the bitch knew she owed me for a lifetime of pain.

He sat in his leather chair behind a desk, as if he were doing the most important work in this ever elite establishment. He was busy on his phone, not bothering to look up as I set the heavy glass in front of him.

"Your drink," I said, turning around and reaching for the door handle.

"You're new," he said, making me question whether it was a statement or if he was waiting for me to confirm.

Was he so well involved in his business that he would know every bar girl walking around here in his cheap underwear he bought by the masses? Would he recognize my face when I turned around? Would he remember me?

"Y-yes," I answered nervously, turning around and smiling through pressed lips.

"All the new girls have to give me a dance. You haven't given me one yet." He licked his lips, staring me up and down as he put his phone on the desk.

Just drink the fucking vodka pendejo.

"W-well, I'm working," I blurted out hoping it would be enough to thwart any suspicion.

"You work for *me*," he reminded me. "What's your name?" he asked.

"Susan." I smiled, remembering his younger daughter's name was similar and watching to see if there was any change in his expression.

Nothing.

"Dance, Susan. Remind me why I keep you well fed and paid." He sat back into the chair, forcing it to recline a bit.

He turned up the volume of the small speaker that sat on the corner of his desk, the same early 2000s soft metal playing out on the main area crackled from it. I swayed my hips from side to side, walking towards him one foot at a time between sensual movements that went along with the beat. I ran my hands through my hair before dropping them down to my chest.

If he were any other man, I'd be riddled with insecurities and shaking from self-consciousness. But he wasn't going to survive to tell the tale of the Latina who couldn't dance well, and the closer I got the more I realized that wasn't what he was thinking at all. He licked his lips in a suggestive way and spun his chair to the side, away from his desk to give me room to climb over him.

I turned around and folded in half, touching my ankles and shaking my ass directly in his face while he made low hums of approval. The song switched to *Aerosmith's* 'Walk This Way' just as he pressed his face to my crack and took a real-time grown man sniff.

I paused, mortified before continuing to move my hips like I wasn't eighteen kinds of uncomfortable. I flinched at the feel of his hands as they gripped my cheeks and squeezed hard just as I came back up.

"You better get used to men touching you sweetheart," he said in his sharp accent. "Otherwise you'll be back on the streets soon," he threatened, letting me know that even the employees in this hellscape were hardly there by choice.

I turned to face him, knowing I was risking him recognizing me by giving him the time to stare, but not once did his eyes move up from my chest even when I climbed onto his lap to straddle him. I took the opportunity to grab his glass from the table, grinding onto his erection to keep him focused on me until I poured it into his mouth.

He moaned, swallowing the drink as I licked up droplets from the corner of his lips hoping it wouldn't be enough to fuck me up on the drug. His hands ran up my sides and he cupped my breasts over my bra, squeezing too hard without care. I fought a wince, biding my time until the heroin kicked into his system.

I had no idea how long it would take, but I trusted Dominico when he said he gave me enough to tame a lion. Sokolov wasn't a lion but I knew his obsession with using the drug meant he not only peddled it himself, he favored it. I knew the drug world well, and I wasn't above it. I knew as the leader of the cártel I would suffer serious losses if I refused to distribute them.

The thing was... drugs weren't the problem.

It was society's response to it. It was the way addiction was handled with either a prison sentence or death. People like Sokolov depended on addicts falling prey to these drugs so that he could keep them in his vicious cycle of imprisonment. I saw the look in the cocktail waitress' eyes when I told her the boss was angry.

Sure there was fear, but the hazy look in her stare told me she wasn't fully here either. I remembered the feeling well. The song switched again to something with a hard beat that I didn't recognize, and the Russian crime lord pulled me closer against him, pushing my hips down into his unimpressively semi-soft erection. My legs dropped from the sides of the chair, so I arched my back, pressing my tits into his face to distract him from my hands reaching into my boot for my knife.

His eyes drooped and he leaned his head back into the chair, but in the same motion it fell down like it was too heavy for him to control. I smirked. *Gracias Dominico.* Maybe it was daddy issues, but in a way, I seemed to find a paternal-type bond through him. One that didn't require lessons in a torture chamber.

I wasn't angry at my papá. He did what he thought was right, and in a way, all his *teachings* helped me to survive, molded me to become who I am today. But I also knew it was my duty to make sure a child was never robbed of their innocence in the way that I was. President Ramírez's request wasn't outrageous, and it was something I intended to do myself once I had been fully established as the *sole* head of the cártel.

I gripped his short blond hair tightly in between my fingers and yanked his head up, his eyes struggling to blink open as I brought my face as close to his as possible.

"Remember me?" I purred into his ear while looking into his eyes and waiting for the acknowledgement to flash through them.

His eyes narrowed as he tried to piece together who I was but either he was too high from the possibly lethal dose of heroin I'd drugged him with, or I'd really just been a blip in his life. I still had nightmares from his cage and the pendejo couldn't even be bothered to remember my face.

"Where is Carolina Flores?" I gritted out, yanking his head hard with one hand while the other fished inside my boot for the knife.

Finally that spark of recognition lit up in his pupils, and just then gunshots rang out outside the door.

86

MATEO

She'd been gone way too long, and rather than believing she somehow might be in trouble, I had a feeling that she'd gone out of her way to find trouble herself. She just couldn't wait, she wanted to see his death and she wanted it by her hands.

As much as I wanted to see the bastard bleed under me I knew it was her right just the same, if not more. I wasn't angry that she wanted it that badly, I was angry that she kept risking her life so carelessly. We all were.

I flipped up my phone and texted Santos;

Celia just went rogue. May need backup.

Rgr.

SANTOS

I casually walked through the main area into a narrow hallway with a lit up bathroom sign. I pushed through the women's bathroom to see if I could find her, ducking low to search for feet but all I could see was a pile of clothes in one corner. I pushed the stall open and sure as shit it was her clothes and her bulletproof vest.

Goddamnit.

Just as I exited the bathroom some big guy walked past me and made his way to the end of the hall, standing post in front of a door. Well, well well, thanks for making it easy for me pal. As I walked closer his face turned with curiosity, like he wasn't sure if I actually had the audacity to square up to a man his size.

I remembered his face. I remembered him in that room when Celia was tied up and drugged after being sold to us.

So I wouldn't feel so bad about killing him to get to her.

"Oh, hey big guy," I cooed out with my hands raised up in the air to the scarred-up, ten-foot tall motherfucker guarding what was surely Sokolov's door. "Remember me?"

He tilted his head and his hand twitched like he was thinking of reaching for his gun. But I was faster, ducking under and swiping my feet below him. He fell to the ground with a hard thud, practically shaking the foundation of the old building. I slammed my heel into his wrist, immobilizing his hand and reaching for his weapon first before tossing it away.

The lady said no guns.

"I'll kill you," he spat out before I felt the weight of his foot against my chest that sent me flying against the wall.

I pushed myself up, watching his eyes slowly shift to the gun several feet away.

No sir.

I barrel rammed into his stomach, punching over and over, each time releasing pained cries from the Bratva lackey. In one quick move he threw me to the ground, the taste of blood filling my mouth and pain shooting through my body from the force of the impact. He stood, a pissed off look on his face that said he considered me annoying at best.

He was too big for us to do this standing.

I knew my odds off the ground with a man this size.

This time I beckoned him, flipping my palms up and making a 'come here' gesture to taunt him. He scowled, and like an angry bull, he charged. But before he could crash into me, I dropped to the floor and swiped my feet over his ankles again, knocking him off balance.

I didn't delay, crawling on top of him and practically tea-bagging the son of a bitch as I laid my fists into his face repeatedly. His fists pummeled into my side, each one a heavy boulder against my body forcing me to spit blood with every hit. I ignored them, gripping his head tightly in my hand and despite his yelling and his savage strikes, I slowly fought against his muscles as I turned his head to the side.

He lifted his top half off the ground, grasping at my arms to stop me but giving me just the space I needed to turn his head by force. It wasn't easy, a man that large had muscles in his neck that were bigger than my wrists. I dug my fingers into his face, fighting against him as he screamed and fought me until I heard the final crack, severing his spinal cord and making him go limp. I let go of his head, struggling to stand up from overexertion and pain. I stumbled towards the wall, resting on it as I caught my breath.

It was the sound of the guns firing behind me that catapulted me back into action, grabbing the gun from the ground and pushing open the door Sokolov's man was guarding. My jaw clenched tight at the scene I'd walked into. Celia's face jerked to the side with shock and eyes went wide at the sight of me. A smile stretched over her face from ear to scar as the man's blood pooled around her hand. It dripped down her arms, her chest, and over her legs.

She was straddled over an older man with silver hair and a tracksuit while wearing nothing but lingerie, one hand gripping his hair tightly while the other held a dagger plunged deep into his mouth from the bottom of his chin.

Allisher Sokolov.

Or it *was* him once.

"You're impossible." I shook my head, closing the door behind me.

"Are you mad at me?" she asked, her expression turning sweet and innocent.

"You're impossible, sunshine," I repeated, pulling her off of him and covering her with my suit jacket. "Seems like the whole gang's inside now, we need to get the fuck out of here," I told her, pulling the knife out from his chin and shoving it into his temple with ease as the blood poured out of his neck.

"Did you make contact with Ronan and Santos?" she asked,

"Who do you think is out there making all that noise?" I pulled the clip out of the dead Russian's gun to check how many bullets were left.

Eight.

I'd have to make do.

"Check him for a weapon," I told her. She nodded, patting Sokolov down and fishing inside the inner breast pocket of his jacket before pulling out a 9mm Luger.

"Stay behind me," I said, putting my arm out in front of her when she tried getting past me to open up the door.

She gave me a look full of sharp knives.

"If you're feeling suicidal, let me know sunshine. I'll take you out myself and do it quick so it's painless. Now get behind me before I knock your ass out and carry you over my shoulder." She looked at me with her mouth gaped open like she couldn't believe I was taking this tone with her, but I was finally starting to understand why Zerkos handled her the way he did.

She was a fucking brat, begging to push every boundary she came across and I wasn't sure if it was because she was aching for a punishment or because she simply didn't know how to live without conflict.

She smirked, gesturing her hand at the door to let me know she'd be a good girl from here on out. A voice message came in from Santos. It was hard to make out with all the noise, but I could hear broken up shouts as he panicked about finding Celia.

"I got her. Regroup outside," I sent back to him.

"I'm cornered. I need help." Santos' voice came in clearer on the next voice message.

"Where are you?" I sent back to him.

"Stuck inside the fucking DJ booth," Santos yelled into his speaker.

I gnawed on my cheek, looking back at Celia.

"Mateo," she warned, knowing exactly where my mind was going. "I swear on all that is—" I interrupted her, pulling her into my body and pressing my lips into hers roughly.

She responded, parting her lips for me and letting my tongue invade its way into her mouth. Her free hand ran up my chest, caressing the side of my cheek and raking through my hair as we deepened our kiss.

"Reina," I whispered into her ear, doing my best to pronounce it the same way I'd heard the others. "Please," I begged, pulling back and looking into her black eyes.

"I can't stay here, not knowing what's happening out there," she yelled, not holding back her emotions. "You can't keep me here, in the dark, with all those guns going off, just waiting for someone to rescue me." Her eyes welled up with tears but not a single one fell.

I knew what she meant when she said in the dark, she didn't mean the quality of the light in Sokolov's office. She was talking about history repeating itself, her traumas. She couldn't handle the idea of being helpless and blind to what was happening out there, while we, her family, might be in danger.

Fuck.

"Fletch, I need cover." I sent the audio message and waited for a response.

"Where you at boss?" he yelled over the background noise.

"Trying to make our way to the DJ booth."

I pulled her close behind me and opened the door to find Russians, cártel grunts, and stray Crows alike dead on the ground. Men hiding behind bodies and open doors shooting towards this end of the hallway. We couldn't go back the way we came.

"Run to that door on my count." I pointed to the door across the hall from us, it was only five or six feet away, but a bullet didn't care about that kind of distance.

It was still far enough to die getting there.

"One... Two... THREE!" I pushed her towards the door, barreling myself in front of her and hitting an incoming Bratva soldier dead smack in the chest with a bullet just as she pushed open the door to reveal the back-stage area.

It was a complete clusterfuck out there—bodies lying on toppled tables, blood and booze dripping from every surface of the place. Any civilians were likely nice and dead at this point, not that there was much to feel guilty about.

Every fucker inside this place was here to buy a woman.

We gave our men one rule only.

Don't shoot the girls.

I pushed Celia against a corner, sheltering her from any Bratva asshole in the audience. That's when I noticed the three dancers huddled in the opposite end, using the blind spots in the stage to their advantage for cover. I put my index finger over my lips to signal them to stay quiet, and they nodded fearfully, crouching down further.

I could only hope that they had no reason to fear for their lives. Sokolov's men would have had no need to injure or kill any of the women who were working here, and our men weren't set out for that kind of mission. As long as they avoided a stray bullet, they could make it out of this.

Right now, I needed to focus on getting my best friend and keeping the woman we loved alive.

87

RONAN

They were supposed to be waiting outside, waiting for a signal or some word from us that it was time to go inside and wreak havoc on Sokolov's little slice of hell when I got the text from Kane that Celia had snuck off and was now missing.

"Let me find this stupid fucking bird, or she'll never let me live it down," I whispered into the phone, unsure if I was heading in the right direction in this pitch-black basement.

There was a dripping of a faucet somewhere in the distance, loud and constant enough that in the two minutes I'd been down here it was already driving me to the edge of madness. If anything was alive down here, it was certainly insane from it.

"I'm not waiting anymore Zerkos, I'm going in." Santos clicked off the line and I sent a voice message to Fletcher and Ethan to let them know it was time.

I pulled my Glock out, just in case, and delved further into the dark abyss of the basement, kicking the bodies of the Bratva grunts who'd seen me breaking in through the window.

"Dirty slut," a kid's voice called out, couldn't have been more than ten years old.

My fury ripped through me, and I pounded my heels through the space, no longer afraid of who I'd find down here because I knew I'd rip through them in order to free the child that had found themselves stuck in Sokolov's grasp.

I pulled my phone out to shine the flashlight, trying to find the source of the voice and only seeing empty kennels stacked one on top of the other. If they weren't down here, then they likely were already up there, being sold off.

"Lion!" the kid yelled from behind me, but just as I spun to find the voice my light shined a mere foot away from the gigantic jungle cat asleep in the corner.

There was a heavy chain joined to the wall and it connected to a metal collar on its neck. In a matter of seconds my emotions ranged from pure unadulterated fear for my life like I'd never felt before, to feeling like the luckiest bastards alive.

That leash was all the friend I needed in this world right now.

I took a few steps back, my shoulders hitting against something and causing a loud rattling and wings flapping behind me. I sent my arm back just as I turned to see what I'd stumbled into, knocking what seemed to be a small bird cage off a table. My reflexes were faster than my own brain, catching it before it had a chance to fall and injure the parrot inside but not quick enough to stop it from having a full-on, aviary-style freak out.

There was no greater piss-your-pants type of moment like feeling the hot breath of a giant feline on your back. To hear the low growl of an animal you know you'd likely never be able to defend yourself against just seconds away from you. I jerked forward, diving onto the ground with the bird cage glued to my chest as the Lion rose to his hind feet, paws stretched up into the air while its leash kept it from coming any further.

Fucking Christ.

I was getting too lucky. Which meant it was going to run out soon. I rolled out from underneath him before he had a chance to drop his paws onto me and scrambled backwards. I shouldn't have been shocked, she warned me about the goddamn lion, but for some reason it seemed too outrageous to believe. Guns went off upstairs and I knew my time was being cut short. I could only hope Santos had been able to successfully free the girls that had been kept in these now empty cages before bullets began to fly up there.

"Slut!" The bird parroted out, relaxing me at the realization that the voice didn't belong to a child.

Was I more angry that I'd been sent on a mission to rescue a foul mouthed bird, or that said bird was now impeding me from heading straight into the fire myself? I backed up as much as possible from the roaring cat, getting away from the lead of his chain so I could finally turn my back to him and run. I took the basement stairs three at a time, pushing the door open with my shoulders to total chaos.

Our men had completely overrun the place from every entrance and exit, bullets flying through open air as Sokolov's grunts shot at us from every angle. I slipped back through the basement door, dropping the bird's cage on the ground.

"Alright little dude, I'll have to come back for you."

"Cocksucker!" the little shit cawed out like it understood me.

I pulled a second pistol from its holster and readied myself, opening the door and shooting first at the Bratvas standing just a few feet away from me. Soon as they dropped to the ground Ethan came charging towards me with a grin on his face like I'd just saved his life.

"There's a fucking bird on the other side of this door. Get it out of here," I told him.

"Are you fucking serious right now?" His eyebrows creased in the middle of his forehead.

"Deadly. That bird is fucking family to her." I gave him a flat stare before I turned and headed past the hallway, following the sounds of yelling and bullets flying.

Sokolov's men used the corpses of their patrons as shields while their fingers stayed glued to the triggers on their automatic rifles. I slid behind the bar, both guns ready to fire, but there was only one small waitress, covered in blood hidden among the bodies.

"Stay hidden okay?" I told her and she nodded her head. "It'll be over soon."

I peeked my head up above the bar to scan the room. There were five Bratva's shooting into the booth, too many of them for me to see who may be trapped in that corner. A bullet whizzed past my head just a hair away from my ear and I sank to the ground once more. Then I heard her scream.

Guns readied at the top of the bar before I raised my head up to see out again. I cleared a path for them, Mateo at her front and Fletcher on her six as they ran towards the DJ booth. I shot at the men surrounding it, taking two down so that Mateo could slip inside for protection.

I needed to make my way there. I hopped over the bar one bullet flying straight into a Bratva grunt's head, as I dropped my head just in time to avoid one to the brain myself. Celia shot three times, one bullet missing but the last two hitting the remainder of the men surrounding the DJ booth.

From another door, four more men ran out, their semi-automatics burning through the room at rapid speed. Fletcher was giving her cover and shooting at Sokolov's men hiding behind toppled cocktail tables as they ran towards the DJ booth to Mateo. The bullet hit Fletcher dead center in the forehead, his body falling limp in front of her. She didn't scream but her eyes went blank, wide and full of a terror I hadn't seen in her before.

She'd killed plenty of people before.

She'd been a child killing other children. She murdered innocents. She took the life of her own family. But she'd yet to see a good man die. One that had pledged to protect her, one that had fought for her and now alongside her.

I charged, dropping my body over hers as fast as I could, shielding her from the incoming rain of bullets as I laid on the ground on top of her.

"Are you hit?" I asked, crawling behind the DJ booth and pulling her into me.

She had that vacant look still on her face like she wasn't fully registering the chaos all around us.

"Baby, I need you present for this." I gave her cheek a hard tap and she blinked at me in shock.

"Fletcher—"

"Is dead," I confirmed. "We can mourn him later, we have to get the fuck out of here," I said it to her but it was meant for me.

I'd lost plenty of brothers in the middle of action. The battlefield wasn't the place for grieving unless you were prepared to drop into the grave as well.

"Okay," she whispered, shaking her head.

"If you're in the building, get the fuck out." Santos said into his phone, advising our men to head out.

"Sokolov?" I asked.

"He's dead," Mateo confirmed.

"Pluto?" she asked me with worry.

"Ethan got him out," I assured her, watching her shoulders relax.

"Any captives?" She asked.

"Four were tied up backstage. They're already loaded into the van," Santos answered.

"Let's roll the fuck out of here then." I reloaded my clips, tossing a gun to Mateo.

"Wait," she yelled, her eyes wide with a look I didn't recognize from her.

Worry.

"I love you. All of you pendejos."

I raked my fingers through her hair, a soft smile pulling at just one side of my face. She looked between the three of us, no response needed on our part. She knew how we felt. She knew how hard the three of us loved and fought to keep her.

She was saying she loved us in case she died.

We wouldn't return the sentiment because we knew she *wouldn't*.

I remembered the candle she'd lit, and I pulled her chin towards my face.

"You're protected, remember?"

She smiled and nodded, some of the weight seeming to lift off her shoulders.

"Ok, take cover," I warned them, Mateo and Santos dropping their bodies over her despite her clueless protests.

My brothers and I were so in sync I didn't have to let them in on the full scope of the plan, they knew me well enough to read the signs and react accordingly. I pulled the grenade from my belt, pulling the pin and tossing it over the booth towards Sokolov's men surrounding us.

They yelled but the blast soon overpowered any other sounds in the room. The high pitch sizzling in my ear muffled any chance of communication between us. I grabbed a smoke bomb next and pulled it, tossing it over and letting the smoke fill the room to give us the cover we'd need to get the fuck out.

Cries of pain amplified throughout the room and bullets flew aimlessly through the smoke. Santos and Mateo surrounded Celia, the four of us moving together in a tight huddle towards the exit. A sharp pain hit me in the chest, sending me stumbling backwards and dropping to my ass.

"Ronan!" Celia cried, but I waved her off.

"Get her out of here, it was my vest," I wheezed, taking a second to catch my breath on the ground.

"Mudak!" I heard in the distance.

They dragged her out screaming, reaching for me. But I would only be moments behind. Bullets were still whizzing by, and the smoke was burning my eyes.

The bullet cut the air behind me, nearly hitting me from behind. I checked my six and ran for it, stepping over the dead bodies to get to the neon EXIT sign. Footsteps charged towards me, but I couldn't bother to turn around to see who was coming, my eyes watered heavily from the smoke, I wouldn't see them until it was too late.

It wasn't easy for a man my size to be tackled to the ground. So when it happened, it took me a few moments to register what was happening. Those were all the seconds he needed to throw his fist into my face not once, but three times.

I pressed the barrel of my Glock into his gut and pulled the trigger repeatedly, plugging six shots straight into his stomach. Blood pooled out of his mouth, and I rolled him off of me to let him die in peace. I sprinted to the exit, pushing the door open, hurting but relieved to have gotten out in one piece.

The fresh air invaded my lungs with no warning, a sharp gasp filled my chest as I took a moment to get my bearings back before looking around. Emergency vehicles surrounded the building, cop cars, and flashing lights of every sort gathered outside. Celia sat on the edge of an ambulance with a blanket wrapped around her while a paramedic looked her over, Mateo and Santos on each of her sides.

Her eyes lit up when she saw me but the scowls on my brothers' faces told me we had much bigger problems. I scanned around, seeing a few other women being looked over by other EMTs and some giving statements to federal agents.

Then I saw Ethan, walking towards me while wearing a vest that read FBI on it.

I saw red.

"You fucking rat," I charged towards him, fist high in the air but my brothers got to me first, holding me back from dishing out what he deserved.

"In our fucking house!?" Santos yelled from behind me, his fury just as strong.

He raised his hands up defensively, looking back and waving off the concerned agents who were watching. I fought against Mateo and Santos' hold on me, knowing damn well they were keeping me from a prison sentence by containing my rage.

"Ronan stop," Celia yelled, jumping off the ambulance and standing between both of us with her hands on each of our chests.

"Looks like I lost *two* brothers in there." I gritted out, nostrils flaring widely.

"Zerkos you're still my brother. Fletcher was still my brother," he said angrily like he had any right.

"You don't get to say his fucking name." Mateo added.

I pointed at the building like he would magically appear in its stead. "Fletcher would have ripped you apart if he knew you were a fucking pig."

"The whole time?" Mateo asked innocently.

Ethan didn't answer, he just gave him a look like he'd regret hearing the words themselves.

"We'd been trying to nail down Sokolov for five years before the word spread about the Black Crow Brotherhood. It was a long game to play undercover but I knew you could get me him. I would have preferred alive, but I'm not angry about one less asshole in the world," he said like we'd done him a favor.

He was all business now, showing his true fucking colors. Reminding me why the only good cop was a dead one.

"You fucking—" I lifted my fist up again but Santos held me back, Celia still keeping herself between us.

"You came to México," she said, a frown in her expression that told me she didn't trust him just the same as me.

"I knew it was just a matter of time before we ended up in Sokolov's steps, thanks for not making me wait too long." He smirked. He fucking had the nerve to smirk.

"And now?" she asked him.

"Now I think it's time you find your way back down to the other side of the border, Miss *Gomez.*" He emphasized her old alias before looking back at the rest of us. "All of you. My boss isn't looking to arrest any Crows for this, but if the investigation gets messy, he won't be there to back you up. Which means I won't be able to either, brothers," he said like it upset him.

He'd completely crushed my reality in a matter of seconds.

"You're not my fucking brother." I shoved past him, crossing my fingers no other boy in blue would be harassing me while I tried to make my way to the car.

"I know right now you don't want to hear this," Mateo said behind me just as I reached to open the back door, knowing damn well I was too angry to get behind the wheel right now. "But if he hadn't... betrayed us," he considered his words carefully, "we would probably be looking at federal prison right now."

"You're right. I don't want to hear this," I confirmed, scowling at the site of the white parrot in my seat.

"Cocksucker!" he chirped, tugging at the final fiber of my patience as I shut myself into the car like an angry child.

I was always the person being lied to.

Every goddamn fucking time.

At what point would I learn and stop trusting the people around me?

88

CELIA

Wounded wasn't even close to the right word.

Ronan was hurting badly from the sudden loss of two friends he considered family. Despite my men's justifiable anger, I lingered back in an attempt to get more information from Ethan, but didn't find out too much that wasn't already obvious.

He was a nepotism baby, both his parents were in the bureau which meant by the time he was a senior in high school, he knew he'd already been accepted into training and was making his way through the ranks. He'd been obsessed with human trafficking issues since he was young and decided to make it his life's mission to save those who couldn't save themselves.

Despite my feelings towards bootlickers and those who wore the boots themselves, he wasn't a bad guy. But that didn't mean he deserved Ronan or any of the guys forgiveness, even if he had given us a legal pass. It didn't seem like he was seeking it either, that badge was the blade that cut the threads of their bond, and now there was no room left to heal the damage.

He'd go his way and we would go ours.

I sat next to Ronan in the back, opening up the cage and letting my foul-mouthed little friend climb up my arm and perch onto my shoulder. He buried himself into the nook of my neck, using my hair for warmth and comfort.

"Whore!" he shouted ten minutes into the drive, breaking the uncomfortable silence in the car and forcing a laugh from Mateo.

We all laughed, unable to hold back and pretend like the bird wasn't able to lighten the mood.

"I'm so sorry," I told them all, shaking my head, unsure which thing exactly I was most sorry for.

Maybe if I'd kept that vest on, Fletcher would still be alive, maybe if I hadn't gone looking for Sokolov by myself none of this would have happened.

"Everything that was supposed to happen did. Fletcher didn't deserve to die, but I can promise you he would have rather it been him than any other innocent person in that room. You included," Mateo spoke.

"I'm not innocent," I reminded him, but he just cleared his throat like he didn't want to get into it.

I didn't either.

They'd just suffered a monumental loss, the last thing I needed to be doing was throwing a pity party for myself over guilt.

There were very few things in this life I allowed to permeate my conscience.

Leaving Ronan was one of those things.

The deaths under my name could not be.

That was a lesson I learned long ago to ensure my own survival.

We stayed a few extra days in Cove City. It was all the time we needed to bury Fletcher and allow his family and the Crows to mourn him before we all headed back south. My sister was nowhere to be found and after a few days of paranoia and constant checking behind my shoulders, I finally concluded that she went into hiding for self-preservation.

We were doomed to repeat my papà's fate.

Chasing each other until one of us had finally drawn our last breath.

An exhausting concept I had already long tired of.

Once we'd returned back to México my phone blew up with missed messages from Ramírez, dozens of texts and phone calls telling me it was not wise to leave the country this close to election season.

He needed to be reminded that he was working for me, not the other way around. But I was too exhausted, too burned out on death and violence to be anything but apathetic to the entire situation.

Our hacienda was waiting for us, not many lights turned on despite the fact Chiyo and a few other family-related Crows were living there as well. My heart dropped at the thought of having to explain to her what happened. Why Fletcher wasn't with us and why he wouldn't be coming home.

We didn't even share a language.

Like my thoughts alone were powerful enough to summon her, she came running through the doors at the sound of our car pulling into the property. She waited at the entrance with hands clasped and one by one we stepped out of the vehicle.

She ran to us, as if she'd been expecting him to come out of the car as well, slowing down to a stop with a confused look on her face once she saw there were only the four of us. She looked past as if maybe there would be another car following us, as there often was. My men had gone home to tend to their wounds, the Black Crows that remained would be arriving from Cove City within the next few days.

Ronan looked away, Santos looked down, Mateo stuck his hands in his pocket. She turned to me as if she was waiting for me to confirm what she feared.

I shook my head, unsure of what else I could do or say.

Chiyo dropped to her knees, a heavy sob blowing out into the wind.

It wasn't fair, their love hadn't gotten a real chance before it had been crushed to nothing but dust.

But maybe we weren't all supposed to get a chance.

I looked at my guys, realizing I had not only gotten a second, but a third and fourth chance as well.

It definitely wasn't fucking fair.

The men walked towards the house, brushing past her with awkward glances and no words of comfort.

They had none for themselves, how would they conjure them for her?

I stopped in front of her, standing silently while she continued to cry, her tears falling down her cheeks and wetting the soil beneath her.

"Where am I supposed to go?" she asked.

It was the first time I'd heard her voice.

"You don't have to go anywhere. But if you decide to leave, wherever you go, I'll help find a place for you there." I assured her.

"I'm starting to think, there's no place for me in this world." She lamented in perfect English, letting me know my original belief about her being the smartest person in the room wasn't wrong.

She played them all.

But regardless of wits, ferocity, or strength, there was one human flaw that forced every human to crumble in pain, to split into shards of themselves.

Grief.

Loss.

La muerte.

I'd long forgotten that pain. When I laid in the hospital bed with a bullet in my shoulder at the age of fifteen and mourned my entire family, I had begged Santa Muerte to cast her protection over me like a comforting blanket, not to prevent me from dying but to prevent me from feeling what death inevitably did to all of us.

It took.

It robbed us, not only of the people we loved but of the parts inside us they helped to create.

I saw how badly she was hurting, even if it no longer resonated within me.

"I'm sorry. He was a good man, and I would have preferred if it would have been me instead." It was all the comfort I had to give her.

It was the truth.

Handling my own pain was enough of a chore, I couldn't find that place inside myself to sit down with her and cry for the life that was lost. Trying to find words of comfort was nearing an impossible task, and I wasn't sure if it was because I'd been molded to be this way or if it was the human condition itself.

"Take as much time as you need, my home is yours Chiyo," I told her, walking towards the entrance and leaving her to mourn privately, unsure if that was even what she really needed.

"Señorita, you have a guest in the piano room," my maid let me know as soon as I stepped through the door.

I sighed, thanking her and mentally preparing myself for whatever bullshit Ramírez would throw my way. I wasn't in the mood to deal with him, but it looked like he was going to make that my problem anyway. I understood the importance of keeping a powerful man in my pocket, my papá had taught me that lesson well. But it was clear José Luis thought I was his tool, not the other way around.

I wanted to say it was a credit to my work ethic, my influence, my power.

But I knew the reality.

The pussy between my legs made him think I was someone he could use and manipulate to his desire. He was about to learn that my pussy was still the biggest cock in the room, despite what he thought he knew.

I sent a text through our group chat, letting the men know I'd be in a meeting and not to interfere before I left my phone on the bookshelf by the door. I glanced over at Santisima's altar, the protection candle had burned all the way down to the bottom of the wick, all the wax gone and the glass stained a dark black color. I pushed my way into the room, but it wasn't Presidente Ramírez waiting for me.

"I thought I'd make this easy on you. Bring the fight to you, woman to woman and all," she said as I walked into the room.

"You think you'll be able to kill me and my men will just let you walk out of here scot-free? You think once you've murdered the mayor elect of Guadalajara, you'll just be able to take my place in everything I had a hand in?" I raised an eyebrow and she cackled loudly.

"Carajo, no. But it *is* impressive how fast you've taken over down here. He really did teach you everything, hmm?" she asked, the envy turning her eyes a bright green color. "Regardless, I have no intention of doing any of that anymore."

"Then why are you here?" I asked, growing tired of her incomplete thoughts.

"Think of this as your final test hermana. We all know you can't be reina if there is someone left to challenge the throne."

"So what? You came here to die?" I laughed out, crossing my arms over my chest.

"Bueno, no. You're going to kill *yourself*," she said matter of factly.

"And why would I do that, Carolina?"

"Because my big sister would never kill me, she'd kill herself first before she ever hurt me. And she'd make sure that whatever happened, that I'd be okay in the end, since she failed me so deeply before." There was so much hatred and delusion in her eyes that for a moment I almost considered her words.

"While all of that is true, you're not my sister anymore. How long have you been watching me suffer from a distance? How long have you been putting obstacles in my path? How long have you been sharpening the knife our tío wanted to use to kill me?" I raised my voice, stepping towards her slowly.

She smiled something sinister, like my reaction was everything she'd been hoping for.

"You give him too much credit. He was weak like papá, he wanted to leave you in peace to die in America, old and disconnected from cultura. The credit goes to me. Who the fuck do you think put you in that Bratva cage to begin with? The moment I saw you outside that bar in Cove City I sent your photo to Guillermo to set the pieces in motion. He signed your death warrant and put the timer on his own primo. Between that and my future sister in law giving Dezy Junior all the intel to feed back to Sokolov, I knew we just had to wait for the right opportunity before they left you all alone and defenseless.

"You've been after me all this time?" I asked. "Why?"

"You think Ignacio gave a fuck? He wanted you alive so that he could force you to open up the dungeons and he'd let you go free. He underestimated you the entire time, he underestimated me too. That's why it was so easy to take it all from him. He should have known better. A Flores won't ever stop fighting for what's theirs."

"That's where you're wrong." I shook my head. "I would have gladly let you have it all. I would have walked away for you before you tried your best to take everything I care about from me."

"The pinche gringos and little Álvarez? Please Celia, I was doing you a favor. It's easier to choose one when you don't have to."

"I'm not choosing, they're all *mine*," I declared, grinding my teeth together.

"Regardless, you wouldn't have walked away. It's not in our nature."

I thought about it.

I wanted to argue, to tell her that I was better than them. Better than her.

But I wasn't.

I wanted this. It was mine.

If I let her live, we were doomed to play out the same scene until one of us finally killed the other, repeating our family's curse.

I would break it now, save us both the pain of a miserable lifetime.

Correct my papá's mistake.

I would kill my sister.

Because for the first time in my life, I had something to live for.

89

CELIA

"So then, how did you expect this would all go down? You were always the one with the flair for dramatics hermanita." I gave her a side-eyed look. "You can't really think my men won't come looking for me in anything short of a few minutes."

"It's actually *them* we're waiting on." She smiled from ear to ear.

"What did you do?" My heart dropped. "How did you get in here?"

"There's always a hole in the security, Celia. You should always expect that if you have enemies alive, there is someone close to you, working with them." She wasn't fucking wrong, and I wasn't sure if I was angry that she was giving *me* lessons, or if it was because I'd been so naive to not suspect otherwise.

And I already knew which pathetic pendejo it was that had betrayed me.

Fernando Garcia.

He'd involved himself in our business just long enough to get what he needed to feed it back to my sister.

"How many of my men did you kill?" I asked, wondering how many lives I'd have to push down and bury beneath the reach of my conscience.

"Just your security here. Kept your little maid alive if she promised to bring you inside without suspicion and lead your boys up to their rooms without a fuss. Looks like she gets to live after all." She walked towards the wet bar and unscrewed the cap to the tequila and poured two shots.

"Why are you here? Did your fiancé not tell you that his daddy is dead yet?" I hardened my eyes, waiting for the change in her expression.

She schooled it well, but she didn't hide the way she momentarily froze. As if all her thoughts had bombarded her at once with all the possibilities. If Allisher Sokolov was dead, then his son would be the new Bratva king.

"Good. Then he'll be twice as pleased when I come home wearing your crown." She narrowed her gaze my way, downing her shot and wiping the stray drops spilled from the corner of her lips.

"Or maybe he won't need a wanna-be cártel bitch if he's got his own." I suggested, throwing her off.

I thought this would be hard. That her death would be another scar in my psyche that would never heal. That I'd carry the pain of this my entire life. But when I looked at her, I saw nothing but the sum of my pain over the last fifteen years. How differently this would have ended had she stayed at my side instead of coming at me from behind

I truly believed Death always had a plan. Maybe I'd been made to mourn Caro all those years so that when the time came for her to die by my own hands, My heart would already be calloused over. The wound; already healed before the knife could cut me down.

"Why did you kill Mamá?" I finally bothered to ask.

"Because in the end, she favored you most," she said bitterly.

"Ha! Jamila had no love for me, you're delusional. You were her favorite."

"Then why did she refuse to tell me where our fortune was? Why did she hide that key from me when I went begging her for it? Why did she choose to die over letting me be reina?"

She wasn't my little sister anymore.

She wasn't anything to me anymore.

"To keep you safe you fucking idiota."

We were taught that family was everything. That no one from the outside would love you and be there for you like your blood. But here I had created a family with three men who I'd give my life for over and over again. And there stood my sister, asking me to bleed myself open for her.

She poured herself another shot and finally picked the other glass up in offering to me.

Fuck it.

I grabbed the glass and downed it knowing my sister wasn't smart enough to use poison against me or drug me like the men who held her leash.

And if she was, then I guess I deserved to die for being stupid enough to trust her.

"Ronan," she chirped, her eyes lighting up, making me turn around to see him with a purpling eye and his wrists bound tightly.

The gun pressed to the back of his head was held by a bald man. I could only assume he was working for the Russians. There was one more Bratva on his other side, because clearly it would take two men to outmatch Ronan Zerkos. His green eyes were raging with anger, and just as he opened his mouth to speak the Bratva grunt bashed the butt of his gun to the back of Ronan's head. He dropped down to the ground unconscious with a hard thud.

I screamed, but before I could run to him Carolina had a gun cocked and the sound of the safety coming off forced a chill up my spine.

"Tie her up, Adrik." She nudged her chin at me and the same grunt who'd knocked Ronan out pulled my arms in front of me with little to no effort despite my best attempt to fight against him.

He pulled a zip tie from his pocket, closing it around my wrists too tight before walking over to Ronan and doing the same to him.

"You're going to sit right here hermanita. We're going to play a little game," she said, using her gun to gesture to the Victorian style red, velvet couch with two matching chairs across from it.

"What the fuck are you talking about?" I sat down, doing my best to hide the creeping panic that came with the thought of how many men might be hiding in my home right at this moment.

"You said you didn't have to choose between them. Let's up the stakes shall we?"

Mateo and Santos came in next, both looking worse for wear than Ronan had, not a shocker considering their size compared to his. Three grunts surrounded them, all with guns pointed at their backs as they pushed them further into the room. That's when I realized one thing was not like the others.

Among her 'soldiers' was Fernando Garcia.

Traitor to the Flores Cártel.

Mateo's eyes registered Ronan before looking my way, the worry etched deeply into his expression.

"Celia." Santos rushed to me, but a shot rang out, the bullet hitting a framed piece of art causing the glass to shatter and spray onto the floor.

I screamed, trying to get up once more but Carolina pressed the gun harder against my temple.

"Everyone sit," Carolina commanded, eyeing Santos with a hateful stare. "Away from *her*," she clarified.

They both took a seat on opposite chairs from me, Ronan was still on the ground knocked out next to us.

"Wake him up." She gestured to her Bratva lackeys.

Which begged the question, where were her cártel men?

Loyalty must have been hard to buy these days. I didn't need to blackmail for it, I had earned it.

"Where are your men?" I asked with a smirk.

"These *are* my men," she gritted out.

I laughed, forcing her upper lip to curl up.

"Fine, then where are Ignacio's men?" I clarified.

"Dead."

I didn't press any further.

I didn't need to.

They were dead because she killed them. Because they refused to bow to her and her deranged plans of washing away everything the cártel was by merging it with Bratva bullshit. We didn't deal in the sale of flesh, and we never would. There were many fucked up things I was willing to be blind to for the sake of money and power.

Human trafficking was not one of those things.

They slapped Ronan's face a few times until he finally woke up, roaring, and readying himself for a fight before the gun in front of his face reminded him of our situation. We were outmatched, and worse yet we were outgunned.

"Glad you could join us, Ronan," Carolina said in a cheery voice. "You were always like a brother to me, you know?" She sighed. "Way more than that pendejo César."

Ronan's jaw hardened, the muscle bulging as his brain slowly pieced together what was going on.

"What's your plan?" he asked.

"Well," she drew out the word. "My big sister is going to pick one of you to die, before I kill her."

"Why?" I asked.

"Because you don't get to have everything you want if I didn't. And let's face it, neither of these assholes fucking deserve it either." She pointed her gun at all three of my men.

"And if she doesn't?" Ronan squinted like the pain of the hit to the head was catching up to him.

"Then I'll make her watch me kill *all* of you, before I kill her." She placed her index finger over her lip like she was thinking. "In fact," her eyes widened, "I *will* kill you all." She laughed loudly, clapping her hands together. "Why leave witnesses? We just upped the stakes again hermanita. Now we're choosing who you get to watch die, while the others die after watching me kill you."

I turned my head to the side, my eyes burning straight into Fernando Garcia's hateful stare. He thought he was clever, that he'd fall to his knees for my sister and somehow steal it all out from underneath her.

Lackeys with too much ambition always thought they could rule. They didn't understand the game, they didn't know the logistics, and they certainly weren't blood thirsty enough for it. At least Carolina had the taste for it, even if she was shit at the admin portions of the job.

"Hurry up, or I'll choose for you." She demanded.

"Choose me, flower," Ronan said softly, "There isn't a world for me if you aren't in it and I can't watch any of you die."

I shook my head, tears pooling at my eyelids as I refused to make the decision.

"It's me, morena. Say it," Santos demanded but I hung my head down, looking away from all of them. "Don't make me go through this again."

"I can't," I refused, crying as my entire world crashed around me and I realized there was no one left to save us, there was no one who would care.

Fletcher was dead and gone, César had gone back to his motorcycle club, and we... we had been bested, just a foolish and rookie move was enough to be the blade in our guillotine.

"How romantic," she said sarcastically. "You have two minutes." Her voice dropped to an icy tone as she stepped back and sat on the piano bench, noisily clanking the keys without an ounce of skill in her bones.

When the worst thing that could ever happen to you finally happened, the whole world slowed down. You played every action, every thought or movement you had leading up to it, wondering if at any point there was any chance of it going any other way. If you could blame something other than yourself for leading down this path of no return.

"Caro! Stop! Let them go," I cried, raising my head shamefully.

If there had ever been any doubt in my mind that I needed to kill her, if there had been any shred of love left inside of me for her, it had rotted and festered right before me. But that didn't matter, because she was going to be the one getting the last laugh.

I'd already gone through the pain of losing Ronan... twice.

A third time would kill me.

But for once I didn't have it in me to be a selfish bitch. He'd suffered my loss too many times as it was, and he didn't deserve to watch me die. If that was the only gift I could give him in this life, it would have to suffice.

"Have you made your choice hermanita? Or shall I choose for you?" She spun her pistol towards Mateo, his big brown eyes full of fear.

I nodded slowly.

Every second up to this moment was still replaying in my head.

What could I have done differently?

What could I have changed?

Even if I had gone inside with them together, none of us had weapons on us after our flight.

Hindsight was more than twenty-twenty here.

I had cost us our lives.

"Wait," I shouted just as I heard the click of the safety.

"It's okay sunshine," Mateo attempted to calm me while Ronan shouted, telling her to point the gun to him instead. "I love you fuckers."

Santos' hazel eyes had a blank fog rolling over them, something I recognized from our time in his primo's basement. He'd given up. He didn't care if he was the first or the last to go because he knew this was how our story would end. I think somehow, we all did. Our protection had run out, and in the end people who dealt in death were almost always next to die.

"Ronan!" I screamed. "I choose Ronan," I sobbed, closing my eyes so I wouldn't have to meet his.

"I love you, flower."

"I'm sorry, baby, I can't let you watch me die. I love you," I explained hoping that he'd be able to somehow forgive me in his last seconds of life as if it would matter at all.

We would all meet again in hell.

I was sure of it.

Me and the demons who found themselves at the end of my leash willingly.

Just as we had figured it all out, it would be over.

I guess only good people got happy endings.

What had I ever done to deserve something more than exactly this?

"Wow, I was not expecting that one, I'm not gonna lie. Really thought she loved you more than that Ronan." Carolina chuckled, the blast of the gun ringing out was almost as loud as the scream that barreled out of my lungs.

But it wasn't his body that dropped down to the ground, it was the bald Russian. The shock and surprise of Taylor Constance charging into the room with her pistol burning hot had us all freezing in the moment out of disbelief. Her distraction was enough to throw my sister off and give me the chance I needed to overtake her.

I elbowed her in the side, using my bound wrists to knock the gun from her hand.

"Por que consigues todo?" she spat out, yanking my hair and ripping it from the scalp.

I screamed from the pain, sending my bound fists down to her face simultaneously.

Gunshots rang out all around us, but I couldn't focus on anything but Carolina, knowing if I took my eyes off for even a split second she would use that as a chance to kill me. Taylor said she was always watching, and though there was a part of me that wanted to question the breach in my privacy, I couldn't help feeling anything but grateful for this window of opportunity she had given us.

"Because I'm better," I hissed out, bashing my forehead into her nose as I pressed both my hands down into her throat, earning a forced choking sound from her. "Stronger," I panted, cutting off her breath. "And I want it more."

She scratched at my arms but the weight of my body sitting on her chest was too much for her to push me off. My fists moved on their own, repeatedly coming down her face with all the force my arms could muster. Her screams of pain muted in my ears and my vision lost focus as my muscles repeated the action my brain no longer connected to.

Her bones crunched under my hands and eventually the burning sharp pain radiating through my extremities dulled. The bullets died, or maybe they just ran out. The room went quiet. Nothing but the sounds of my fists still hammering into her face. I felt hands on my arms, pulling me back and lifting me off of her.

I screeched a feral sound, panting heavily through my rage.

"Your hands, morena," was the only thing Santos could manage to say.

I looked down at them, bloody, cut up with shards of bones from my sister's face sticking out of them. Wrists still bound, my middle fingers broken and bent into awkward shapes. I didn't bother to look at her face to see the damage, I knew she was long past dead. I opened my mouth and the involuntary wail of a broken woman echoed out of my lungs.

Santos was there to catch me as I fell into him, his hands no longer zip tied and able to hold me to his chest as I mourned my little sister for the second time.

"Call an ambulance," Mateo said with worry in his voice.

Ronan was already on his phone and the way he paced back and forth let me know everything was not okay.

Then I saw Taylor, on the ground, eyes wide and blood pooling at her mouth. Mateo hovering over her with his shirt pressed into a wad against her stomach.

"Taylor!" I rushed to her side, unable to touch her without feeling a burning pain against every part of my hands.

Santos cut my restraints before lifting her head up under his lap.

"I told you, that I'd do anything for these fuckers." She choked on her own blood with a smile, her eyes fluttering closed.

"Taylor, keep your eyes open," I commanded her.

We'd lost too many innocent people already.

They'd lost too many of their friends.

I was not worth these deaths.

Santa Muerte please.

Why them and not me?

"You can't shroud me from pain if you keep taking everyone from me!" I screamed, my tears falling over her face and my yells not registering any reaction from her.

As if La Madrina heard my plea, the sounds of the ambulance drew closer and closer to our home.

"We have to get her into the main area," Ronan instructed, reminding us of the dead putos in the room that were going to be drawing more attention to the situation than we needed.

"Call Dominico, have him reach out to Ramírez to clear this mess." My voice sounded hoarse though I couldn't remember screaming. Santos nodded as Mateo and Ronan lifted Taylor off the ground and carried her out of the piano room.

The paramedics rushed in, loading her into the gurney while trying to explain to Mateo in a language he didn't speak that he'd have to meet them at the hospital separately. He didn't take their no for an answer, climbing in anyway and disappearing with the sounds of the sirens.

I stayed sitting there on the floor, paralyzed and numb as I thought about the last half of the year. Was this who I had been meant to become all along? Had there been another path set out for me that kept begging me to stay the course, but I just refused to follow it? Or was my destiny always meant to be one filled with carnage and death?

I was built for it.

I knew I was.

I shook off the imposter syndrome crawling up my spine once again and reminded myself that I'd made every promise against my enemies come true.

"Raa Cocksucker!" Pluto's voice jarred me out of my thoughts, making me involuntarily laugh as I looked up to find Ronan holding his cage.

"Hola Amigo." The tears rolled down my face and he turned his little head to the side as if he was trying to recognize my pain as something he understood.

"Hola Puto!" he cawed, forcing my tears to stream down faster with my laughs.

"I didn't know you spoke spanish."

Ronan sat, placing the cage on the ground and bringing me into his lap. The bird alluded to conversation every now and then, mostly letting us down each time it turned into repetitive insults. He plucked the sharp bones sticking out of my hands one by one, the burning sting a welcome pain. We sat there together for an hour before his phone rang. He lifted me up to reach for his cell in his pocket.

"Where are you?" he asked as soon as he answered.

"Okay, go without us. We'll meet there soon, ask Kane if he needs any clothes."

I waited anxiously for him to disconnect the call and give me all the information.

"Santos made contact with Ramírez, he'll make sure there are no questions from the paramedics. Dominico is sending a crew to clean the bodies up while we're gone." He lifted me up to my feet, my legs barely able to hold me. Instead of letting me get my bearings he lifted me up into his arms, carrying me out of the room and taking me up the stairs.

"Where are we going?" I asked.

"Taylor's in surgery," He told me, some of the weight of the universe lifting off my shoulders.

"She's not dead?" The tears began again, I no longer fought to wipe them or prevent them from falling.

I think I had finally learned that crying didn't make me weak.

It made me someone who felt pain.

"Looks like she's gonna make it." He carried me through my bedroom and sat me on top of the closed toilet lid once we reached the bathroom. "We can go to the hospital after I get you cleaned up. Get your hands checked out. The mayor elect can't show up to the hospital covered in blood."

He walked to the shower, turning it on and adjusting the faucets to a warm temperature before helping me to stand. He pulled each item of clothing off of me with complete and total care, being careful to not hurt my hands any more than they'd already been damaged.

"I love you," I whispered into the air, unsure if it was even loud enough for him to hear.

He looked up at me from a kneeled position as he undid the buckles on my shoes and helped me out of them. I had a million ideas of what might have been coursing through his head right at this moment.

Nothing said I love you quite like being the first one picked to die.

"You're my entire world. It was the right choice," he reassured me, the sobs pouring out of my soul with a ferocity I'd never experienced before, making me unsure if I'd ever be able to stop myself from crying again.

He helped me into the warm stream of water, washing me gently and avoiding doing anything but letting the water carefully roll off my skin to avoid any more pain. My hands throbbed, but it was the kind of ache you could ignore. The kind that reminded you that you finished that very thing you sought out to do.

I'd won.

It was all mine.

Even if it had cost me just as much.

90

CELIA

"And you're sure she can be trusted with... my secrets?" I asked my dearest friend through the phone awkwardly pinned between my cheek and my shoulder.

"Dr. Hernandez is very well recommended for her professionalism and her discretion in your circles. I've sent all her information to Dominico *and* Taylor, if they didn't find any reason to be suspicious, then neither should you, Celia," Emory said in a condescending tone..

"I've just never really done this before. Not like this, not with the intent of bearing it all," I explained anxiously.

"And that's why it's never worked for you before. Real communication requires work, consistency, honesty. Things we all know you don't excel in. If you can't give her the bare minimum, then don't bother wasting her time," she snapped at me as if she knew I was starting to chicken out.

"Ouch amiga," I said with a laugh.

"It's a waste of *your* time too, if you can't respect her time, at least respect your own. You will never heal if you don't sort through your damage. It's not up to them to fix it for you."

She meant my guys.

She wasn't wrong, I couldn't lay the burden of all my problems, my fears, my traumas on them. Sure, they could be there for me, but it wasn't up to them to always have to clean up my messes.

It had been a week since Carolina had died and I hadn't slept more than three hours total. It wasn't that I couldn't sleep, it was that I was afraid to. Afraid to close my eyes and deal with the aftermath of every horrible thing I'd done to claim the throne I could finally sit on.

"How's Grimm's Reach?" I asked, the sarcasm in my tone too clear.

"I don't want to talk about it, don't change the subject," Emory snipped at me.

"Fine," I said. "Besos." I hung up without another word, knowing she would be mad for about thirteen seconds before she got over it and found something else to irritate her instead.

With some struggle, I used my wrists and the few uninjured fingers to put my phone in my purse, standing at the door as if I hadn't just had an entire conversation in front of this person's house, trying to decide whether or not I would be going in at all. I knocked with my elbow, my hands still badly injured, wrapped in gauze and splinted.

"Cecilia Gomez?" The elderly brunette opened the door to her modest home.

I nodded, appreciating that Emory was thoughtful enough to not give the name that was associated with my political career. Dr. Hernandez wasn't a stupid woman, she would have had to have been living in an alternate dimension to have missed my face plastered around the news with the upcoming election.

The fact she was opting to stick with the alias let me know Emory might have been right about whether or not the doctor was trustworthy. She led me through her home until we reached double wooden doors that opened into a beautiful office. A rich mahogany desk sat in front of a backdrop of bookshelves, nothing but psychology textbooks displayed on the shelves.

She gestured to the sofa and took a seat on the opposing chair. I followed suit, sitting down as well.

"Thank you for clearing your schedule for me on such short notice," I told her.

"I understand you've had a family tragedy recently. Is that where you'd like to start?" she asked, getting down to business without asking a single word about me.

I fidgeted with my hands nervously on my lap.

"Actually, I'm not sure. I've never really done this before, I'm not sure where to start..." I told her truthfully.

"Here's the thing Cecilia, in order for me to help you out of the grave you've dug for yourself, I need to understand just how deep you've dug it.

That's the only way therapy can work." she said, as if she somehow knew everything that was going through my head without knowing anything at all. "Start with what hurts the most."

I nodded my head, letting out a deep exhale before opening my mouth.

"I spend a lot of time wondering what would have happened if my father had a son..."

EPILOGUE

TWO MONTHS LATER

"Congratulations to the newest mayor of our beautiful city," Ramírez announced in the town square in front of El Palacio. "Celia Flores has my vote of confidence not because of the legacy her father left behind, his footprint stamped into the sand of our city's history, but because of her passion to do the right thing for our people, for my home town. I can't wait to see what she does in the upcoming years." He raised a glass of champagne into the air as he talked me down from the podium.

I had just delivered my acceptance speech, thanking all those who campaigned for me and the citizens who supported my infiltration into politics. They didn't know Celia Flores wasn't just their mayor, but the jefa of the biggest crime organization in central America.

Not knowing would keep them safe.

Coming to terms with the fact that there were no good guys or villains was something I had to do as a child in order to sleep at night. There were just people, some who did worse things than others. Some of us enjoyed doing bad things, and some of us did it under a justifiable premise that it was for a better cause.

I wasn't ready to define where I fit into that mold and there was likely a good chance I'd never need to.

Dominico and Luiciano waited for me on either side of the steps as I descended from the stage, joining the crowd to listen to the rest of President Ramírez's speech. He had big plans, which required big money, and that's where his vote of confidence started and ended with me.

But I'd already proven to him that I was a woman of my word, spreading the message loudly that any child found being used under my name would result in lethal consequences to the perpetrators. With the dungeons reopened there was no need for deaths in the streets anymore, we handled our business quietly and in private.

I'd made fast changes and lucky for me, I hardly had to lift a finger to do it.

"They are waiting for you inside for photos, let's make this quick eh reina? We have that amnesty meeting with the new Bratva leader later today," Dominico reminded me.

It was just a video call, but it was necessary to be punctual, to be civil. Allisher Sokolov's eldest son, Viktor had taken over after his father's untimely death. There was no hiding the cártel's involvement, especially when I sent my sister's head and his men's desecrated corpses back to his door as a message.

He was fresh on the throne, just as I was. We both understood the nature of the game and his father's death benefited more than it hurt him. The sting of my sister's loss and knowledge that the cártel couldn't become something under his control and manipulation likely didn't feel great either, but now he was free to marry whatever unfortunate soul would capture his attention.

If anything I'd done him a favor.

But still, we had to make nice. Forgive, not forget, but let el pasado ser el pasado.

Set up rules and establish boundaries.

The border would be one, to start. Some shithead racist had been elected and it looked like we had gotten the hell out of the United States just in time to watch the fireworks from the good seats.

The military police nodded towards my men, an amusing show of respect, considering they still covered their faces in fear for what my soldiers would do if their identities were discovered. Ramírez and I had an understanding, as long as they stayed out of my way, I had no reason to get in theirs.

Politics were boring, I knew well why my papá dreaded his civil duties. I was much more inclined to the blood and gore side of the business. Reporters and photographers took my photo, all of them calling to me at once and not giving me the opportunity to focus on a single camera at a time.

Flashes filling my eyes and a sense of victory and accomplishment washed over me at the realization that I'd done everything that I'd set out to.

Not bad por una muerta.

Hell, I'd even been resurrected from the dead.

Luciano and Dominico stayed by my side, reminding me of every single photo of my papá that existed documented in history. His men were always at his side too, ready to take a bullet for him.

And it wasn't just the two of them, they all believed in what I stood for, in doing things differently. In ruling with respect.

I'd long burned the ledger as a show of good faith, erasing every trace of blackmail and debt each name had acquired and given them the option to stay rich and by my side or go retire with my blessing.

I didn't lose a single soldier that day.

But I had one left to let go of.

Santos was tired of war, tired of gang life, tired of violence. Which was good, because he couldn't afford another scar on his body anyway. We'd moved out to a secluded place so that he could spend his days relaxing in the sun like the goddamn perfect househusband he'd become. I knew he was done with all the death the minute his knife sliced through Guillermo's throat.

So I promised myself I'd never let him take another life in my name again.

I had to let go of all my chefs because he'd decided cooking was solely his responsibility. He settled into a life of comfort easily and nothing made me happier than to see it. He deserved this freedom.

Ronan was the head of my security team now, because god forbid he let my safety be under someone else's control. I preferred it that way, it kept him close to me in my everyday life and I was glad to always have him within range.

Mateo easily fit into the dungeons, preferring to keep a place in my cártel and getting his hands dirty where it counted. He was a fast learner, and Dominico was teaching him everything he'd need to learn so that the old man could retire rich and in peace.

I pulled my phone out to check on Ignacio through the surveillance feed, wondering if the day would ever come where he'd give up and die so that I could stop dragging this on. In some ways I kept him alive for me, to punish him anytime grief took over me for the things that I was forced to do because of the path he put me on. Some days I kept him alive because I was a monster who enjoyed hurting him.

Some days I kept him alive because I was tired of killing my own blood.

"Are you ever gonna put that poor old man out of his misery, flower?" he asked, not hiding the amusement from his face as I pocketed my cell phone once again.

"Kill him? He's family, Ronan." I laughed, walking past him.

"Your idea of family has a really wide range, sunshine," Mateo added. "Exhibit A, the fucking bird."

"Don't bring Pluto into this." I shook my head, waiting for him to open the door to the Escalade for me. "He's my goodest boy," I chirped.

"You know, it wouldn't hurt to talk me up half as much as you do that parrot," Mateo complained, getting into the car behind me and shutting the door.

Ronan chuckled from the front, Santos was already waiting for us all in the passenger seat. I straddled Mateo and ran my hands through his hair.

"Mi vida, I didn't know you wanted to be my goodest boy." I smiled, pressing my lips gently to his as Ronan pulled away.

"Sunshine, I want to be your everything, whatever you'll let me be I'll be it for you. Quiero ser tu todo." He blinked slowly with a smile forming over his face.

"Now, now, you know what I said about using Spanish against me," I whispered into his ears as his fingers traveled up my side.

"How can I resist when I know how wet it gets you?" He peeled my suit jacket off, sliding his hands underneath the thin satin material of my tank top, his touch just light enough to send a chill up my spine.

"Mmm," Escaped my throat.

"No fucking way, you start that shit now, while I'm driving, and I *will* pull over," Ronan said from the driver's seat.

"Then you're going to have to pull over because I'm not stopping," Mateo taunted from beneath me, his hand cupping my breast and his tongue raking against my neck.

I gasped as he lifted my top up and placed his mouth over my nipple, his tongue swirling wildly across the hardened bead.

I cried out, my sounds forcing a growl from Ronan's throat from his frustration.

He veered off the road going into the desert.

"What are you doing?" I shouted.

"Taking a shortcut," Ronan gritted out like he was angry we were starting without him.

It wasn't my fault somebody needed to drive.

I gasped at the feel of Mateo ripping my suit skirt at the side, making room for me to properly spread my legs and sit into a deep straddle over his engorged erection.

"Mmm," I moaned as he kissed up my neck, his fingers gripping my back and pulling me somehow even closer to me.

His hands traveled lower, giving my ass a hard squeeze before his fingers slipped through my thighs, coating themselves in the slick arousal forming between my legs.

"Fuck." I tipped my head back while he toyed with my clit.

His hands gripped at the fabric of my torn skirt and with one more tug he ripped it completely up the side, pulling it off of me and freeing me from the little barrier it provided.

"Let's see if I can make you come before we get home." He smirked, pulling his monster cock out of his pants and slapping my pussy with his thick length.

He lifted me, hovering me a few inches above his lap as he positioned himself in the center of the backseat before spinning me and facing me forward.

"I want them to have a good show," He whispered in my ear just as I made eye contact with Santos through the mirror in his visor.

His smirk was almost unnoticeable.

"Take her shirt off," Ronan instructed.

"Watch the road," Santos chastised.

"I can do both," he countered.

Mateo didn't fight it, lifting the silk top up and pulling it off my shoulders before tossing it down to the floorboard. I was completely naked now, exposed and legs spread wide over his lap, his thick throbbing cock waiting to find its way inside of me. His hands caressed me, moving all over me as he reveled in bringing me to the point of begging.

I wasn't past it when it came to them.

I would only ever beg again for them.

"Please," I whined desperately as his fingers rubbed up and down against my clit.

He lifted me up again, this time positioning the thick head of his cock right at my entrance, no warning or declaration before penetrating me with the full length of his steel.

"Oh fuck!" I gasped.

"Do you think he can make you come before we get home, Flower?" Ronan teased, pressing the button on the smartscreen display of the car to show the GPS estimated time of arrival at less than six minutes.

I shook my head, knowing it would only increase the challenge and fuel Mateo to prove me wrong even though I knew damn well it would likely not take him more than four. He pulled out of me, emptying me, and leaving me with an aching need.

"Drop your knees to the floorboard," he commanded, bending me over the middle console so that I was smack dab between Santos and Ronan.

He pulled my arms out from behind me, placing my ankles in each hand before I felt his palm press against my low back, urging me to tilt my tailbone up towards him.

His hand moved to the back of my head, pushing me down further into the middle console so that my breasts were smashed up against it. I moved my cheek to the side. I was turned to see Santos, eyes full of lust and desire like he was wishing he'd picked the back seat himself instead.

His nostrils flared and he adjusted himself with the next thrust of Mateos cock slamming deep inside of me.

I cried out, biting my lip as each thrust of his hips hit deep inside, bringing me closer and closer to unraveling.

Santos moved my hair out of my face, tucking it behind my ear while his eyes stayed glued to my face, like my expression was the best thing he'd seen yet.

"How good does his cock feel, morena?"

"So good. So good," I mumbled, the discomfort of my position somehow making it easier to lose myself to the pleasure.

Ronan chuckled, the engine roaring louder letting me know he'd stepped heavily onto the accelerator.

"Half a mile," Santos announced, his taunting forcing Mateo to pull all the way out before sending his full length deep inside of me all at once. His fingers found the bundle of nerves between my legs, giving me just enough of the friction I craved to let go.

Three more full thrusts and the build up inside me finally crashed, my orgasm pulling me under, forcing me to let go of my ankles and cry my release in Santos' direction while Mateo kept my head pressed down and thrusted into me repeatedly.

He didn't come, but he tucked himself into his pants regardless.

Ronan peeled into the driveway, the car drifting slightly from the use of the emergency break at such a high speed before we came to a full stop. Ronan jumped out of the driver's seat and dashed in front of us, barking spanish orders at anyone who might have been hanging around out in the open as he yelled at them to go into their rooms.

I screamed as Mateo tossed me over his shoulder, naked, ass bare and facing the sun. I lifted my head off his back to see Santos following close behind, his eyes narrowed as he focused on me with a predatory gaze.

I moaned hard with the feeling of a hard hand against my backside as we crossed the threshold, not having to be told that it came from Ronan before seeing the satisfactory smile plastered across his face.

Mateo carried me past the living area and out into the courtyard, dropping me onto a long leather bench. The three of them loomed over me without moving, they were lethal, mine. We were always together now, always the four of us. Santos was the first to drop his pants to the floor, his pierced cock standing tall and threatening me with pleasure.

"You know, we *can* take turns right?" I laughed, but their expressions remained hard.

"But you scream so much louder when it's the three of us ruining that greedy cunt of yours." Ronan's words were so filthy they alone had the power to start the fire inside me up again.

"Make room." Santos closed in on me, sitting behind me and practically pulling me onto his lap with my ass over his cock while his hands traveled down my thighs.

He spread my knees apart, running his fingers up and down my slit. I dropped my head back to his shoulder, a moan falling through my lips as his touch sparked pleasure all the way through my body. Ronan turned around, walking through the courtyard and back indoors.

"Where are you going?" Mateo shouted to him.

"I'll be back."

I switched my focus to the way Santos' hands moved up and down my body, caressing me, moving over the sensitive parts of my thighs before he'd slip a finger or two inside me briefly. Always teasing, never fully committing, and driving me wild with want.

"Oh fuck, morena. You're drenched." He lifted his fingers up to show me the proof, shoving them in my mouth to lick clean.

I swirled my tongue around them, before he pulled them from my mouth with a loud popping sound.

"Fuck me, please," I begged through my whispers.

Mateo chuckled, stepping closer to the edge of the bench, where my cunt dripped down over the leather fabric. I was sensitive everywhere, aching to be touched and for the next release when he lowered his head between my legs and slipped his tongue inside me.

I gasped, my fingernails gripping tight around Santos' forearms.

They lifted my hips up into the air, Mateo's mouth staying locked around my clit even as Santos impaled me onto his thick shaft. I shuddered at him filling me up, each bar of his Jacob's ladder rubbing up against me in the most delicious way.

He thrusted into me, each time a wild spark of pleasure surging through me, threatening to bring me closer to ruin as pleasure spread throughout my body. Tremors took over me as I convulsed from pleasure around Santos' cock.

Mateo's head lifted up from between my legs just as Ronan reappeared, taking his shirt off and reaching into his pocket and pulling out a clear bottle.

"Are you ready for me to fuck your ass, reina?" Santos whispered in my ear.

"No," Ronan answered for me, dropping his pants down and stepping out of them before he coated his cock in lube.

He threw it in our direction, barely giving Santos the heads up he needed to catch it.

"You don't want me to—" Santos started.

"I want to feel those bars against my cock while we're both inside her," Ronan explained with a smirk.

"Wait, what?" I finally understood what he was suggesting, worrying about what state they wanted to leave my poor pussy in.

Rest In Peace.

"You can handle it. You can handle anything, can't you?" He taunted me as Santos' fingers locked tighter around my hips.

He layed back on the bench, bringing me down with him so that my back was pressed to his chest. Ronan climbed over us, his hard abs against me and sandwiching me between the two of them.

"Oh fuck, you're dripping, flower." Ronan exhaled into my ear.

Santos pulled out of me just enough to allow for Ronan to push the tip of his cock inside me, both of them in the same hole was way too much. Way too intense, and he wasn't even fully in yet.

"Oh shit. Oh fuck!" I cried, Mateo laughing from the side with his manhood in his hands, stroking up and down and making me lick my lips with desire.

He walked towards me like he could read my thoughts. Each step closer Ronan pushed himself deeper inside me, coating himself in my arousal and filling me up. I reached out, wrapping my hand over Mateo's cock and earning the sound of his pleasure.

He groaned, his fingers pinching my nipples and squeezing my breasts with a gentle touch. Santos and Ronan moved slowly at first, until they'd both found their way fully inside me, bottoming out and wrecking me with a fullness that was near maddening.

And then they moved on their own terms, uncoordinated and out of sync in a purposeful way so that Ronan would feel every single one of Santos' piercings against his cock as well. He dropped his head to my shoulder, biting down like it was nearly too much for him too.

I felt my climax building inside me again, every thrust of their hips taking me deeper into an altered state where I could feel myself losing the ability to feel anything but bliss. It erupted all around me, taking Santos with me as he held me tight against his body and emptied his release into me.

Santos pulled out of me, and Ronan lifted off of us so he could roll out from under me. Ronan laid down on the bench and I crawled over him, sitting on his erection once more and grinding down on him. I felt Mateo's hot hand pressing onto my spine, urging me to lean forward as he settled in behind me. I opened my eyes to find Santos' cock, still covered in cum right in front of my face, almost dripping onto Ronan's forehead.

I opened my mouth to take him in just as Mateo squeezed the bottle of lube over my ass and let it slide down my crack. I hollowed my cheeks, relaxing my throat as Mateo thrusted his fingers into me from behind. First one, then two and eventually three fingers filled my ass and moved at a slow and delicious pace.

I cried out again as Ronan began to move once more, all three of them finding a new rhythm together, filling all of my holes and forcing me to fall apart again, making me come until I was nothing but an empty bag of bones being handled by them.

That was the easiest part about this. How effortless it was to be in control of my world and still drop to my knees for them because I wanted to be cared for. Because they could make me feel like I didn't have to worry about only being strong.

I was theirs.

There was so much power in relinquishing everything to them.

And I always would.

Santos pumped his release down my throat just as Mateo emptied himself inside me. Ronan proved once again that his stamina had no end once the other two stepped back. He flipped me on my stomach over the bench, holding nothing back, he moved with the ferocity of a soldier as his fingers tormented the most sensitive bits between my thighs.

We cried together as he forced one final orgasm from me, sweaty and panting from exertion and bliss. They carried me up to our room, washed me and dropped me onto the silk sheets of the bed. Ronan draped a blanket over me before sliding in next to me.

"I just need a fifteen hour nap, then we can go again." I mumbled out sleepily as the other two cuddled in around me.

"What is all this?" Santos said with marvel in his voice as my hands came off his eyes and his tia and primos shouted surprise.

"It's your... retirement party. *Officially,*" I clarified.

Though he had easily slipped into a life of comfort and peace we had never actually discussed him leaving the life. Mateo, Ronan and I all knew he had long been done. He'd killed too many people for Guillermo, and he'd seen too many innocent lives snuffed out to keep going.

So had I.

But some of us were built differently. All I wanted for Santos was happiness and if I could provide it to him by taking the guns out of his hands and replacing it with a Michelada instead, then I was happy to do it. I had plenty of good soldiers. I had the best of bodyguards. My man deserved for war to be over.

He deserved a way out that didn't involve a shallow grave.

And more than that he deserved the community and village that his family thrived on. He deserved to have them here. With Guillermo's untimely death and the family losing the financial means Los Muertos had provided them, I took it upon myself to move the Álvarez familia across the border.

There were no tears shed at the mention of her son's death, and I was sure in some way, she knew that I had been responsible. But Santos' tia thanked me regardless and within days they had made their way south and settled in like she had never left. After all she'd been a girl too when she first left. It was funny how the motherland always welcomed you back with open arms, no matter how long you'd been away.

I'd been so afraid of her judgment, of what others would think of me, and sure, there were certainly some along the way who felt I was less than for not having grown up here. But at the end of the day, my connection to my country was in my blood, it was in my eyes, and it was in my skin.

And even if I'd lost all those things, it would still be mine because Latinidad was in my soul. It was something no one could take from me, though they wanted to try. It was something you lost because you either gave it away, you let it die inside you, or because they'd stolen it from you. But the beautiful thing about it, was that it was a lot like a fire, all you needed were a few small embers to stoke it back to life.

We stayed up too late, dancing around the fire, drinking strong drinks before giving up on the night. Or rather, the now early morning. Some of Santos' primos passed out on the floor of whatever rooms they could find to avoid trying to find their way home drunk despite Mateo's offer to drive them.

"What a sunrise," Taylor said from her wheelchair as we made our way back inside the house.

"Glad to share it with you." I smiled at her, Ronan squeezed her shoulder from her other side, and with a slight gesture of his head he silently asked to push her in.

She nodded, and we followed the rest of the way into the guest room she'd been making residence in. Didn't feel right to keep her any further away from us. It was probably not going to be as temporary as we all tried to make it out to be. She *was* family. Because family was more than blood, more than who you slept with, more than who you created. It was the people who were there for you unconditionally.

The ones who cheered you on, who made you believe you were worthy of love and happiness.

"When are you gonna stop milking it and get out of that chair? I was shot *twice* and was walking a week later," Ronan teased her.

"Look my ugly friend, I have absolutely *nothing* to prove. I'm gonna relax and heal on my own." She elbowed him off her chair and I chuckled.

"I think I keep you around because no one puts him in his place like you do," I told her.

"What can I say, I have a way with the assholes. Goodnight Celia."

"Buenas noches amiga." I shut her bedroom door and followed Ronan back through the hallway to find Santos and Mateo sleeping on the couch together.

Their legs entwined and Santos' head resting on Mateo's chest.

"Take a picture, this is adorable," I whispered to Ronan, knowing damn well my phone had died at least three tequila shots ago.

"Should we wake them up?" he asked, and I shook my head.

"Nah." I pointed to the other couch. "They look so comfy." Ronan walked over to the other sofa, laying down and gesturing me towards him.

I sank into his hold, melting in his embrace and smelling the lingering scent of the bonfire in his clothes.

"Te quiero," I told him.

"Te quiero mucho, mi amor," he responded. "Is this everything you wanted?"

"And more. Is this enough for you?" I asked, lifting my head up from his chest.

"Enough? You're everything." He squeezed me tighter.

"You think it's enough for them?"

"They wouldn't be here if it wasn't, flower." He kissed the top of my head, his fingers raking gently through my hair, coaxing me into a peaceful sleep.

It was enough. Because we were together.

We were enough.

GLOSSARY

Adios – goodbye
Blanca - white (a nickname)
Cállate, zorra - shut up, slut
Cantil - pit viper
Chinga tu madre - used like "go fuck yourself"
Cobarde- coward
Despiertate - wake up
Entiendes - understand
En el infierno - in hell
El pasado ser el pasado - the past stay in the
Gigante - giant
Hermanito/a - brother
Hijo de la chingada - son of a bitch/whore
La madrina - The godmother (a name for Santa Muerte)
Lobito - little wolf
Maldita - cursed
Médico - doctor
Monstrua - monster
Morena – nickname/term of affection for Brunettes/Brown women
Papá - father
Para una Muerta - For a dead woman
Payaso - clown

Pendejo - idiot/asshole
Por favor - please
Por que consigues todo? - why do you get everything?
Primo/a - cousin
Princesa/ita - princess/little princess
Puta madre – serves as "mother fucker"
Que chingados - what the fuck
Que perro asco - that's fucking disgusting
Quiero ser tu todo - I want to be your everything
Rayos - used in the way "Crap" is
Reina - Queen
Salud - health/cheers
Sicario - hitman
Sobrina - niece
Solo los que son fuerte aguantan - Only the strong endure
Te quiero - I love you
Tía/o – aunt/uncle
Todo se fue a la verga - everything went to shit
Vete al diablo - go to the devil (go to hell)
Yo sabía - I knew it

ABOUT THE AUTHOR

Santana Knox is a Latina author, a South American immigrant, a mother, wife, devotee of Santa Muerte and creative who yearned for Latin presence and representation. Santana got tired of letting the voices in her head drive her crazy, and decided to write down the stories they were begging to tell instead. A lover of the unusual, and a hopeless romantic when it comes to toxic villains, Santana's books should always be taken with a grain of salt, specifically the kind that keeps demons away.

BOOKS BY SANTANA

Heartless Heathens:

A why-choose, Gothic Romance stand alone

Rink Rash:

A Rivals to lovers sports romance

Darkling, Beloved:

No Way Out: Horror Romance

No Way Back: A Horror Romance

Lit Fic:

Crossed Over: A coming out story

Novellas:

The Guy Sure Looks Like Plant Food To Me

Dreams of truth: A Dark Romantasy

ACKNOWLEDGMENTS

My husband, for pushing me to do the damn thing even on nights where I'd painted our heroine into a corner I didn't think she'd find a way out of.

To every person who has stood by me. To the immigrants and the immigrant children who were forced to adapt to survive.

To Siany for all the help with making sure the language was right and that Mexican culture was well represented in this series.

To all of the sensitivity readers that worked on this project and helped shape mine and Celia's story.

I'm eternally grateful.

To every reader who has taken a chance on me since...

I write for you.

www.ingramcontent.com/pod-product-compliance
Lightning Source LLC
Chambersburg PA
CBHW060819310726
48980CB00002B/341

9798992379839